HEALING WINGS

HEIDI M. GRANT

ISBN 978-1-64300-315-3 (Paperback)
ISBN 978-1-64300-316-0 (Digital)

Covenant Books, Inc.
11661 Hwy 707
Murrells Inlet, SC 29576
www.covenantbooks.com

Note from the Author

I present this as a warning to parents and guardians. This is not a children's book. The contents of this book deal with a subject that can be quite graphic in nature. I have attempted to present this story in such a way as to allow the broadest audience access to it, while still being faithful to the subject matter.

PROLOGUE

SEARCHING

Narden

Four years. We'd searched for four years. Every lead was a dead end. Every hope shattered of finding Lady Ari'an, the youngest daughter of the House of Nori'en.

"The House of Nori'en stands in the middle of the country of Faruq, both politically and geographically. Because of its location in the grasslands of the country, it can't generate enough variety to rank high, but to reach the rest of the country, all of the variety from the other houses must pass through its borders. The rulers are Lord Cristeros and Lady Hin'merien," I told my oldest brother, Renard, as we passed over the mountains.

Lady Ari'an was their youngest daughter. If she was still alive, she'd be eighteen now. I'd been patrolling over Torion Castle the day before she disappeared. If I'd just waited another day, watched over the family while they were touring the countryside, she never would have vanished.

"Almost all," Renard corrected. "The House of Almudina has its own trade routes and avoid using contractions. They do not sound formal enough."

"I'll remember that next time I sit down to tea," I snapped back, turning a backflip as I watched a mountain pass underneath us.

From above, Renard shook his head, but didn't comment. He had to fly higher than I did, because . . . well . . . he was brown. He had to be far enough from the ground to look like a bird. I'm mostly blue. I mean, the tips on my scales are this gold color, but that doesn't show up from a distance. Adenern, my other older brother, had the same colors as me, but the gold was his boots, nose, and tip of his tail, which made him a bit more noticeable on patrols, but not by much.

"Tell me about the House of Almudina," Renard continued.

I sighed. For once, I'd like to just fly somewhere without having to recite the history of the world.

"Well?" my brother asked.

I wanted to torch something, but managed to reply, "The House of Almudina is the ruling house of Faruq. They are geographically located under the House of Suvora to the south and to the east of the House of Nori'en. They have their own trade routes to most of the houses and to the countries to the east. The ruler is King Viskhard, who also rules all of Faruq."

"You could sound at least slightly interested," Renard told me.

"Then I'd be lying, and it's morally wrong to lie." I smirked at him.

He rolled his eyes. "Narden, you have to learn this. You know that."

"Faruq exports wheat from the grasslands, fish oils from the coasts, and wool from the mountains. We trade with Verd to the north primarily, but some to the east. Everybody thinks some stone god or another is going to help them, if they say the right thing and don't mess up some ritual. The House of Suvora thinks it's the greatest thing in the world, and we're stuck at the bottom of the trash heap," I snapped. "What else do you want to know?"

It was his turn to sigh. "Where do we fit in?"

"I just told you! The House of Rem'maren is the bottom of the heap. We take whatever anyone else has left over"—I grinned sarcastically — "and we're happy for whatever we get. Oh"—I switched into my previous monotone— "ruled by Lord Grath and Lady Margree, associated with the dragons, and worships one god without images, commonly thought that we're too poor to make any."

Renard blinked at me in exasperation. "No, Maren. Where does Maren fit?"

"Oh." I'd lost a little bit of my steam, being wrong does that sometimes. "We . . . we . . ."

"We are independent . . .," Renard began.

"Because no one wanted the mountain wilderness between Faruq and Verd until we showed up, and now they want our hides," I continued for him.

He looked rather displeased. Maybe that wasn't exactly what he was going to say.

"One last question." He sighed. "Tell me about Verd."

"That's not a questi—" I started, but he didn't look like he wanted me to finish that comment. "Verd, the country to the north of Faruq, exports stone, big stone, little stone, soft stone, hard stone . . . and dragon relics," I growled that last part. "They don't have houses the way we do . . . or rather how Faruq does, but the priests do divvy up their country to favored nobles. The ruling class is the priests who choose a new puppet king every few years. They worship several of the same gods that Faruq does, but include sex in most of their rituals."

Renard smiled wryly. "Would you like to practice some maneuvers the rest of the way?"

"Now that's a question!" I grinned, going into a barrel roll.

I glanced down at my reflection as we spun over a mountain lake. The horns on my head looked . . . shaggy. It was a youth thing, all of us between about twelve and twenty-six looked like that. We could break them off, but that usually looked dumb . . . particularly if everyone knew we'd broken a horn running into a wall, or a tree, or the side of a mountain, or the ground . . . Learning to fly had its drawbacks. I was past that stage now. Mighty One be praised. Now, I could soar.

I barely noticed Renard blend into the sky. We could all do that, but it took a lot of effort. He was going to come at me from somewhere. Watch the clouds for movement. Watch the birds nearby to see if they're disturbed. I glanced over the trees to make sure no one was down their trying to shoot us, and there's the ripple! Pity, I hadn't noticed it sooner, because the blow to my side stung. I tried to snag his tail.

"You look like you are trying to hold on to a fish," Renard told me. "Tighten it up."

I sighed.

The last half of the journey into Verd's territory didn't take nearly as long, but I was sore when we got there. I'd gotten a few licks in, but Renard was six years older. He'd been out of training two years now, so he looked well-groomed, horns all even, no patchy places in his scales, and he could do what he wanted. Well, sort of. He still patrolled, and he was the eldest, so he had to accompany our father Tragh to the counsel meetings, and he had quite a territory to look after . . . maybe I was better off even with the politic lessons.

We found our brother Adenern waiting for us with Lord Grath.

Adenern looked, surprisingly, excited.

When we were close enough to hear, he yelled, "We found the horse!"

"What?" I asked.

"The horse she was riding during the survey, when they all went to—" he started.

I interrupted, "I know what a survey is."

The last thing I wanted was another political lesson on nobles touring their countries each year to check on things.

"Are you certain it's the same horse?" I asked.

He nodded enthusiastically. "Lord Grath thought you would want to help him question the fellow who stole it."

"Where is he?" I asked, scanning the forest below.

Adenern dove. I took a moment to make sure nothing was about to attack us and then followed. Renard circled above watching.

CHAPTER 1

THE TEMPLE

Ari'an
Four Years Earlier

My family went out that spring to survey the countryside, and that was the first year I was allowed to go as well. My sister, Pher'am, went when she was twelve, but my father and mother made me wait two years longer than she had. I'd asked why a few times but only received the vague answers of "We will tell you when you are older" and "It is safer for you to wait a little while longer." It was probably because of my hair, Pher'am's was this perfect golden color that practically glowed in the sun. Mine glowed too, but then everyone noticed the red in it. It wasn't proper to have red hair. Really, it wasn't even red . . . no one would even notice if the sun went behind a cloud.

I'd begged and pleaded to come though, and they finally let me this year. I was so excited!

Pher'am sat straight on her horse looking only ahead. I straightened, trying to stay still. This was my first time out of the castle on horseback. Whenever I traveled before, I was always in a carriage, but the spring countryside survey was always done on horseback.

At the town of Nor'quitarn, a little milling town because of its place on the river, I dropped behind a bit to look at the vendors by the road. This town was the closest to our border with the House of Suvora, and after Suvora was the kingdom of Verd.

The vendors here had far more varieties of goods than the other towns because they were so close to the other House. I never knew chickens came in that many sizes. The ones served at the castle were always huge. The pots and pans were little. The fish, someone pushed one onto my leg trying to sell it, were still moving. Booths of all sizes and colors lined the street. The wings on the cats at one booth ranged from reddish to a dark blue when the light hit them just right. One kitten was entirely purple, and another was brilliant green.

My mother was talking to Pher'am about something, and my father and the magistrate were discussing what the harvest might turn out to be like. No one noticed me, and when I looked up, they had turned a corner.

I hurried my horse along but didn't see them down any of the streets. Backtracking, I turned another corner to see if I could find them from that road. I didn't see them. Again, I turned around, but couldn't find the road I'd come from. The houses were too close together. I couldn't see where I was. All the shutters were closed. I was getting worried. If I didn't find them soon, they'd never let me travel with them like this again.

I stopped to ask a man on a corner if he knew in which direction the nobles' survey would be going.

"Wha' would a nickin like you's want with the nobles' survey?" he asked, with an odd look on his face.

"I'm . . . I am the daughter of Lord Cristeros and Lady Hin'merien, and I must find them." I tried to sound authoritative through my nervousness.

"Sure you's are, pretty," he sneered.

I kicked my horse to move on, but he snatched the bridle.

"Let go!" I snapped, "Before I have you arrested."

"Arrested, pretty nickin?" He laughed. "How could you's have anyone arrested? What temple did you run from?" he continued. "If you's nice to me, I might not takes you's back."

I didn't like the way he was talking. "Unhand my horse now!" I glared at him.

He grinned showing a missing tooth. "Not till you's show me what you's can do."

His hand touched my leg and moved up toward my knee. I kicked him in the face and tried to wrench the reins from his fingers. He wouldn't let go. He glared at me, wrapped his fingers around my arm, and ripped me from the saddle. I slapped him across the face only for him to hit me full force back. I doubled over as he slammed his fist into my stomach. Trying to call for help, I realized that I couldn't breathe right. I tried to glance around to find someone who would help me, but no one was looking at us.

He kicked my feet out from under me. As I fell to the ground, I heard him laugh. "Pretty nickin has spirit."

Then my world went dark.

I don't know how long it was before I woke. The bumping road hit my head against the side of a cart. I moaned in pain.

"Oh, the pretty nickin's 'wake now," I heard that awful voice say.

I looked up. My horse was tied to the back of the rough wagon.

"Returnin' you's will fetch me a pretty price, nickin," the voice continued, "and you's horse will pay too."

I didn't recognize the road. There wasn't a town in sight, only trees and trees. The road behind disappeared in those trees and ahead were more trees.

"Where are you taking me!" I yelled.

"Oh, you's should know, nickin." He laughed, his eyes had a bloodshot look now. "You's and me are going back home." .

This wasn't the way back to the Torion Castle. I knew that much. The mountains were farther away back home.

"My's trip wasn't as good as I's hoped, but bringin' you's back will fetch a nice price to pay me back for this bad trip," he continued.

I didn't know where he was taking me, but I knew I had to get away. I tried to jump from the open wagon but realized too late that he had my wrist tied to the side. The rope went tight, cutting into my wrist. My head smashed into the side of the cart as my legs dragged along the road. I managed to keep my legs out of the wheel, and finally got them under me. At that moment, he urged his mule to a trot. I screamed for him to stop, but he just laughed. I tried to pull myself back in, but I couldn't while I was running. Suddenly, the wagon stopped. I tumbled forward only to have my arm stop me. I screamed in pain. My head was wrenched up, and that man was looking into my face. His breath was foul and his clothes not much better. Why had I ever asked him for directions?

"You's should know better than that, nickin," he sneered.

Then he backhanded me and hefted me back into the empty wagon. I cried out in pain again. He jumped up after me, laughing. With more rope, he tied my hands behind my back, still secured to the side of the wagon.

I stayed in that position for three more days. He threw some food at me occasionally, and then laughed when I couldn't eat it. I finally was able to resituate so my face could reach the floor. He laughed all the more and urged the mule to a trot again, so my face would bounce against the baseboards.

At night, he'd stop and tie my feet to my hands. I couldn't sleep, because of the painful position. In the mornings he'd set a bowl of water in front of me and climb into the driver's bench. If I wasn't able to drink it fast enough, my face would land in the bowl. I'd sputter as the water went everywhere, and then try to quickly sit up, so my face didn't hit the bottom again.

We crossed the mountain pass and finally came to a walled village. A huge temple stood in the middle of the town. The man stopped before we entered the gates of the temple. He came back and roughly mopped up my face, my hair was raggedly tangled down my back by now.

"I's don't want you looking too bad when I's take you's back," he explained.

We entered the town, and he drove the cart straight for the temple that towered over the other buildings. He pulled up at the elaborate gates set into walls just as elaborate and called in Verdian that he had an escaped nickin for them. Someone opened the gates for him, and the wagon bounced in. The walls were as decorated inside as out, and the courtyard held statues of different gods and goddesses. The center held one statue of a god larger than the rest, around the base were carved women. I wasn't certain if they were supposed to be groveling or kissing his toes.

When the wagon came to a stop, I heard someone ask, still in Verdian, "What have you brought us?"

"I's found her when I's was trading my wares," he explained. "I's knew she was you's from her hair."

I heard footsteps come to the side of the cart.

"Oh my," the voice said.

I looked up and saw a well-dressed man. From the close crop of his dark hair, I knew he was a priest. Finally, someone in authority.

"I'm Ari'an," I heard a voice crackle. Was that me? "Of the house of Nori'en, and I demand to be released at once." I started coughing.

"Hmmm," the priest answered looking me over, "what have you brought us indeed?" Turning to the man, he said, "She is not one of ours."

"What!" he bellowed. "I's dragged her all the way back here just for you's to try to weasel out of paying me's my's dues! I's won't stand for that."

"If you will kindly let me finish," the priest interrupted calmly, "I was saying that she is not one of ours, but we would be willing to buy her from you."

"That's better," the man muttered.

"She is not worth as much as a returned nickin," the priest continued.

"You's had best pay me's proper!" the man exclaimed.

"Her hair is not a straight red, which means she is a mix breed, and well, she is obviously not even broken. We will have to do more work on her, but I think we can come to some sort of agreement."

Then the haggling began. What was going on? I wasn't a piece of meat or a horse to be bought and sold. What were they doing? I tried to say something again but started coughing immediately.

When they were done, the priest untied me from the wagon and led me into the temple. The building loomed almost as tall as the sky. There were windows high above, but none below. The stones in the walls were each carved with a design. I didn't understand the pictures, but there were lots of women at the feet of not as many men.

The priest took me to a room and untied my hands. A hard bed with metal rings at the corners stood in the middle, and a little table sat to the side of it. In one corner, there was a large hook in the ceiling.

The priest picked up a pitcher and poured a glass of water and handed it to me.

"Be careful not to drink too fast," he warned as I gulped down the water.

"I am the daughter of Lord—" I began again, but he laid his fingers on my lips.

"Shhh," he said, "do not speak."

The door opened behind him, and two men came in. One was another priest, while the other was a red-haired man wearing nothing but a cloth around his waist with his hands tied behind him. The priest led him by a rope around his neck. The tied man looked greedily at me.

"What's going on here?" I asked, startled.

The first priest's hand whirled around and smashed across my face.

"Do not," he said forcefully with narrow eyes, "speak."

The other priest had untied the man's hands, and he started toward me.

"Break her," the first priest ordered as the two priests walked out of the room.

The door locked behind them. I screamed, but no one heard, or no one cared. I learned then what a nickin was.

My dress was in tatters when the two returned. I cowered in a corner when I heard them walk in. No one should see me like this, I thought, as I hid my face. The man they had brought lay sleeping on the bed. He'd done his work. The second priest quickly tied the man's hands, woke him, and led him from the room.

"Get up," the first one ordered, kicking me in the side. I didn't move, so he kicked harder. I cried out in pain, and he hit me across the head. With tears streaking down my face, I slowly stood, trying to hold my dress together.

Roughly, he grabbed my arm and threw me to the bed. I closed my eyes and sobbed. His hand grabbed my face and wrenched it around.

"Stop making those awful noises," he snarled.

"I am the daughter of—" I started through a sob.

He backhanded me again and glared, "I told you to stop talking. No one cares who you thought you were. You could not possibly be the daughter of anyone important."

I stared into his eyes, terribly frightened, and then I remembered my mark. Everyone in the house of Nori'en had a mark on the back of their necks. The ink master placed it there two years after we were born. I pulled my hair around and jerked my head out of his hand.

"Look," I said as triumphantly as I could through the tears.

"What have we here?" he said placing his hand on my neck. Then he grabbed my hair and jerked me to my feet. "You are sadly mistaken, nickin, if you are pretending to have something back there." He quickly pulled a knife from his belt and sliced through my hair. I collapsed to the floor as he threw my hair down on top of me. "You stop pretending here," he sneered. "You always belonged here, remember? No imaginary mark will ever change that."

The other priest reentered the room, and the first bellowed, "Clean this thing up," and stormed out.

"Put this on," the new priest ordered, throwing what was hardly any cloth in front of me.

What was left of my dress covered more than that would.

"No," I said and glared into his eyes.

He yanked me to my feet and thrust me against a wall. "Do not speak," he whispered into my ear as he tore what was left of my dress off my body.

I screamed and tried to turn around, grasping for my dress.

A rope tightened around my arm, and he threw me to the bed.

"You should have done what I told you to," he sneered as he adeptly tied my arm to one of the corners of the bed.

I kicked at him, but grabbing my leg, he had it roped to the other end of the bed before I knew it.

"Let me go!" I screamed.

His hand flew to hit my face. I tried to block with my free hand, but he just as quickly secured it to another corner. Then he hit me.

"You are certainly making cleaning you up easier." He laughed, as I tried to kick with my only free limb.

Now, I was tied to the four corners of the bed. I pulled against the ropes, but they only bit into my wrists and ankles.

The cleaner he used burned my skin as he ripped off the scabs that had formed on my legs and my face. I cried out in pain, only to have him rub the spot harder.

"How did a pretty nickin like you manage not to be broken before?" he asked, wiping between my legs.

"I'm not a nickin," I cried, closing my eyes.

The blow struck a raw spot on my cheek.

I gasped in pain as he snapped, "Do not speak."

Then he left the room.

I heard their voices behind the door as they walked away, "What if someone comes looking for her?" the second asked.

"Who would look for a noble in a place like this?" The other laughed then added, "And whoever heard of a noble with red hair?"

Their voices faded, and then there wasn't a sound except my own crying.

I don't know how long I lay tied like that. The room had no windows, just three oil lamps burning close to the ceiling. I cried for a little while, but the tears running over the sore spot on my face made my cheek burn even more. I screamed at the top of my lungs, but no one came. The ropes bit into my wrists and ankles. I tried to move, but that only made them hurt more. I don't know how, perhaps it was because of sheer exhaustion, but I finally fell asleep.

My dreams took me back home. *My mother walked with me through the gardens explaining which god or goddess each one honored. My father danced with me again at the farewell banquet for Dreanen, who along with his brother Danren had fostered with us. Pher'am, Danren, and I jumped our horses over the practice course in the stable yard. The stars came out, and my mother leaned over me to kiss me good-night. "Wake up, nickin," she said.*

16

The pain raced through my head like a dog after a rabbit. My eyes flew open, and I starred into the priest's face again.

"Having good dreams," he sneered.

As I realized that I couldn't feel my hands or my feet, I looked around to see where they were. I was still tied to the bed, and they'd brought the red-haired man back. A new priest held him this time, while the second one held what looked something like a bridle with a spiked bit in his hands.

"No!" I screamed. "You can't do thi—" As adeptly as he'd tied the ropes on my arms, the second priest rammed the bit into my mouth and secured it around my head. My tongue raked across the spikes as I tried to finish my sentence. I felt the blood drip down my throat.

The first leaned close to my face. "Now, nickin, you *will* learn to be silent."

The new priest released the man's hands when the first nodded to him. I tried to scream as he lunged toward me, but that sent the bit into the sides of my mouth. I moaned in pain and raked the cruel piece across the roof of my mouth. Another spike rammed into my tongue as a sob broke from me. If I held my mouth still, nothing touched, but the blood running down my throat choked me. I tried my hardest to keep from coughing, but I couldn't always stop myself. I let the tears fall; the pain on my cheek was nothing compared to the searing in my mouth.

The third finally took the man from the room while the second yanked the bridle from my face and quickly released my limbs.

I rolled over and coughed blood onto the floor, soaking the bits of my cut hair that were left there. I couldn't do anything but lie there because my hands and feet wouldn't lift me. It scared me that I could see them, but all feeling was gone. If I tried to move, they just flopped.

The second yanked me to a sitting position. I stifled a yell, expecting a barb to rip into my mouth again.

"Very good, nickin." The first laughed cruelly. "I was not sure you would learn so fast."

The second held a glass to my lips. "Hold this in your mouth, but do not swallow."

The liquid seared the inside of my mouth. I quickly spit it back out just as the second grabbed my jaw and stared me in the eye. His grip intensified the pain, and I tried to pull lose only to have him clench tighter.

"Hold it," he ordered with narrow eyes, "until I tell you to spit it out."

Again the burning liquid entered my mouth, and I pinched my eyes closed, trying to bear the pain. The tears ran down my cheeks and dripped onto my bare legs.

"Spit it out," he finally ordered, and I obeyed willingly.

"Eat hardy." The first laughed as they walked out.

A bowl lay on the floor near the door; in it were some chunks of meat that didn't look cooked through, on top of a chunk of bread, and some vegetables.

I was hungry, but I felt sick too, and my mouth burned intensely. I stared at the food for a while, turned quickly, and threw up by the bed. My hands and feet felt like a thousand fire-seared needles were jabbing into them. I curled up on the bed and cried, trying to keep my mouth from moving as much as possible.

So I learned. I learned to never make a sound no matter how horrible the pain was. I learned to scream and sob alone in my room without a noise being heard. I learned to obey quickly if I didn't want to be hit or beat with a whip. I learned to breed and how to tell if I'd kindled. I learned to miscarry without the priests finding out. I learned to be sold to please the men who came for the temple's "services." I learned to forget everything I once thought was real. I learned . . . I learned . . .

I didn't know how long I'd been there. The lamps never went out in my room. I never felt rested when the priests came to teach me something new, take me to a customer, or breed me. The food was brought only when they thought I deserved it.

CHAPTER 2

RESCUE

It felt like I hadn't slept at all, when they brought me to line up with some of the other girls again. This was done in a large room. It had carvings in the walls and even some plants growing from pots.

This was strange, not the lineup itself, but my presence in it. Customers came wanting a certain look to their nickins sometimes. Most of the time they wanted a certain performance and didn't care about the look, but it wasn't uncommon for one to want a look. What was strange about this was that I hadn't kindled. The priests only sold my services when I had.

The first time I was part of a lineup, I'd tried to call out to the man looking at the girls, but my throat was too dry for the sound to come out as anything more than a whisper. The priests hadn't given me anything to drink for . . . I don't know how long, and one of them was right behind me to drag me from the line. They whipped me for that, tied me on my back to the bed, and brought in one of the men to breed me.

One of the priests whispered into my ear before they left, "Never try that again."

The pain searing into my back made even the bite of the ropes seem like nothing. I arched my back when I was alone to lessen the pain, but I couldn't hold that position forever. Every time I had to lie back to rest my arms and legs, the searing made me silently scream.

The line was no different this time, the customer walked up and down looking at us. He'd stop every once in a while and lift heads to look at faces. He came to me and did the same. I looked past his ear. I knew better than to meet his gaze. I'd be whipped for a stunt like that. He had brown hair, clipped to his ears, and a well-groomed beard. I'd never seen him here before. Why did he look familiar?

I heard him gasp slightly.

"She is—" He cleared his throat. "She will do."

One of the priests grabbed my arm and began hauling me off while another one led the customer off to take care of payment. "Remember, the room must have a window, or I will not—" He choked a little, and another priest ran to get a drink.

A window? *How did I know what a window was?* I thought as the priest led me down a hallway. Opening a door, he shoved me onto the bed, quickly retrieving a chain from the leg of the elaborately carved piece and fastening the clasp to my ankle.

"Enjoy yourself," he sneered then left the room.

There *was* a window, and I could see daylight and clouds through it. I stood up and took a few steps toward it. The chain went tight while I was still ten steps away. I couldn't get any closer. The customer's rooms were always so big. I could have stood at the window if I was still in my room. I fought back the tears and the wisps of memory that flowed through my mind.

I didn't hear the door open, but I did feel the pain as the butt of a small whip slammed into my skull. I collapsed to the floor biting my lip until it bled to keep from crying out. I clasped my hands together so I wouldn't rub my head.

"Was that necessary?" the customer snapped, rage in his voice.

The priest took on a light soothing tone, "She should be focusing on you and your needs."

I looked out of the corner of my eye to see the priest hand the whip to the customer. "You may need this yourself." He laughed. "She has gotten overly excited about things that do not concern her in the past, so you may have to be a bit rough with her. It can be more fun that way though."

"That will be all." The customer seemed to try to keep his voice even, but it still shook with a bit of anger.

The door closed, and I jumped as I heard the whip hit the floor. I knew I should get up, but I was dizzy from the blow to my head. I hated everything about this, but if I could make it to the bed, I wouldn't have the bruises from this man taking me on the floor. I tried to get my feet under me, but my legs wouldn't work right.

"Easy there," I heard the man's voice speaking quietly by my ear.

I stayed still while he moved his hand along the back of my neck. I knew not to move while he was touching me. That was so the customers could feel my body first, but that never lasted long. If I moved, he would hit me with the whip. I heard him let his breath out as if he'd been holding it as he brushed my hair from my neck.

I felt him lean forward a bit, I braced myself to be shoved to the floor or turned and slammed onto my back.

"I am so sorry, my lady," he finally whispered, standing.

Why did his voice sound familiar? I turned my head slightly, as he quickly walked to the window. He drew his sword and flashed it into the sunlight for a moment. I turned my head slightly and saw the whip lying on the floor. Was he going to hit me with the sword instead?

He trotted back to me and lifted me to my feet. "Lady Ari'an, we are going to get you out of here." The name sounded vaguely familiar.

I hazily looked into his face and swayed backward. He looked like someone from a distant memory.

"I need you to stay calm?"

Of course I would stay calm, they would whip me if I got excited.

I closed my eyes. I could see a dance hall from one of my old dreams. *Dreanen and I were dancing, but he didn't have to count for me anymore. His father came up behind him and tapped him out. Dreanen bowed to me, I curtsied, his father bowed to me, and I curtsied again. "Good evening, Lady Ari'an," he said as we began to dance.* The voice and face were the same as this man's were.

Something crashed in front of me, and I opened my eyes. Blue scales with gold tips filled my blurry vision. I stepped back, but tripped over the chain, falling to the floor. The fall jarred my head making it throb again.

"Help me get this chain loose" was the last thing I heard the man say before the world went black.

My brothers and I circled above the temple watching for the signal. I prayed it wouldn't come from here. The Lady Ari'an should never be in a place like this. I flapped my wings and glided on the air currents. My brother Adenern circled near me while Renard was quite a bit higher.

I saw the flash as Adenern yelled, "There it is!" I dove for the flash locating the window it came from as Renard and Adenern lit the courtyard with their flames.

I grabbed the windowsill and ripped out part of the wall. I quickly landed in the room barely stopping before I hit the girl standing near a bed at the far side. That couldn't be her, could it?

"Help me get this chain loose," Lord Grath called from a leg of the bed. The girl collapsed, but he caught her before she hit the floor. I ripped the leg off the bed with my claws, and turned so he could climb into the saddle. My tail made quick work of the rest of the wall, and we sailed out. I lit the ground below, including a stable, as I left. Renard and Adenern kept up their assault for a while longer, but joined us within the watch as we flew toward the mountains of Maren.

"Is that her?" was the first question Adenern asked when he caught up.

"I am afraid so," Lord Grath yelled from the saddle, the wind still making it hard to hear.

I could see when I glanced back that he had leaned her against his chest with her head resting on his shoulder. The bed piece lay across her lap so it wouldn't pull down on her leg as I flew.

"How did you recognize her?" Adenern asked, matching my speed so he could talk to the lord.

"She was the only one with hair long enough to cover the mark on her neck, and her face looks a bit like Pher'am's," he called back.

"May I go back with Renard and kill every last one of them for doing this to her?" he called angrily from my side.

I felt the same way, but I had to take them to a safe place first.

"No!" was the firm reply.

"What!" I bellowed. *"WHY NOT?"*

"King Viskhard does not need a war with Verd right now," he answered.

"I am not talking about going to war, sir," Adenern replied, quite a bit more calmly than I would have. "I just want to destroy a little temple."

"That 'little' temple is the pride of Verd. Destroying it would be an act of war," Renard called from my other side.

"As it is, His Highness will have to send an official apology about not being able to keep his dragons in check," the lord yelled.

"Apology!" I choked out the word. "We have to apologize for rescuing a noble?"

"I hate politics," Adenern muttered.

We flew on for five more hours until we reached my cave in Maren, a place set high into one of the mountains. Generations of comings and goings had worn the edges of the mountain below our caves smooth. We could fall for several leagues before hitting anything. That was good because when we first learned to fly, we usually did fall for a few leagues.

All our entrances around the top of the mountain were quite roomy, so there wasn't any problem landing, even though I really wasn't good at that yet. At least I didn't hit the wall this time. I would slide along the smooth surface when I did, but I specifically landed in the middle, or tried to, this time.

There was guest room with a bed, a wardrobe, and a washstand in one of the side caves for when I had a human visitor. Farther back was the entrance to the room of pools that the whole family shared. That entrance was more elaborate with semiprecious stones set into it. They would sparkle in the right light. Not that evening dusk was the right light though.

HEIDI M. GRANT

Lord Grath put the lady in the guest room, pulling a cover over
her. He worked for a while filing the chain before he was able to take
it off her leg.

He threw the thing onto the cave floor as he came out of the
room. I immediately torched it imagining that it was the whole horrible temple that I sent up in flames. The wood from the bed burned
nicely, but the metal chain and clasp just melted into defiant shapes.

Renard flew back in hauling a tree with him, glanced at what I
was doing, and chuckled. I glared at him, but he just shrugged and
said, "I would have done the same thing. It just looks amusing."
The metal did kind of look like a two-headed snake with antlers
and one leg.

Leaving the deformed serpent, I started to help Renard and
Adenern tear the tree into firewood.

"Can you three be quiet about that?" Lord Grath called as he sat
down a safe distance from our chopping spree.

All three of us stopped and looked at him as if he had that metal
serpent's head sprouting from his neck.

"I do not want her to wake up to what sounds like a house falling on top of her."

It made sense, but how on Arnbjorg were we supposed to quietly
turn a tree into firewood? We ended up just ripping off the branches
and leaving the trunk lying near the cave entrance. Renard and I
tossed most of the branches aside while Lord Grath arranged some
in the central fire pit. When he finished, Adenern set the pile ablaze.

"We will have to leave her here tonight," began Lord Grath
when we gathered around the fire. "Renard, you can go back to the
border and continue your patrols. Do you still have Adenern's saddle
here?" he asked me. I nodded and went to fetch it as he continued,
"You will have to take me to Caer Corisan tonight, otherwise they
might send out a search to look for us. We certainly do not need to
worry them." He glanced toward the side cave where Lady Ari'an
slept. "You will bring me back in the morning with some appropriate
clothes for her." He looked up at me as I returned with the saddle
dragging along over my tail. "If she wakes up before I return, try to

24

stay out of sight. She does not need to be scared by you on top of everything else she has been through."

"Why do you think she hasn't woke up yet?" Adenern asked.

"Has not," the lord corrected. "They hit her across the head with the butt of a whip before I signaled for you."

"Why?" I asked wondering what she could have done to deserve that.

"She was looking at the window."

"*What!*"

Three people hushed me at the same time.

"How could they do that to her?" Adenern asked looking toward her room.

Lord Grath didn't answer. He seemed to be trying to keep his own temper restrained.

"For the same reason you would hit a horse with a crop if it was doing something you did not want it to," Renard answered for him.

"There's a difference between a horse and a person," I snapped.

He met my eyes. "She was not a person to them, just a piece of property to use for whatever they wanted."

"That doesn't make it right," I snapped keeping my voice down.

"No, it does not," Lord Grath said rising, forced calm in his voice, "but it is terrifying what you can get away with when you define someone as a nonperson."

He took the saddle from my tail with a grunt and then helped Adenern into it. After my brother lay down, he was able to mount. "I will see you in the morning," he called as they flew away into the approaching darkness.

Renard yawned and, nodding to me, "I'll leave after some sleep," and retired to his own caverns.

I glanced around my cave and realized I was hungry. Lady Ari'an would probably be hungry when she awoke, so I set off.

I snagged a nice bull elk. Being autumn, I tried to hunt females, because antlers disagreed with me. In the spring, I went after bulls so the cows could raise their young.

Returning, I threw some more wood on the fire while I burned the hair off the elk. I tore the meat into pieces and tossed them by the fire. Because I wasn't incredibly coordinated, I had to rescue a leg and thigh from the flames. I've never been fond of raw meat, though I knew some dragons that were. If I tried to cook it myself, I ended up with scorched raw meat, which wasn't much better, so I'd learned to just let it roast by the fire.

CHAPTER 3

WAKING UP

The first priest stood over me with that wicked grin on his face. "I would not worry," he said. "We will take good care of your little wretch." I could hear the baby crying in the background.

I sat up drenched in sweat and gasping for air. I looked around trying to find the priests. They were always there when I woke up. Why couldn't I see right? It was so dark. My mind cleared a little. Why was it dark at all? I bit my lip to keep from whimpering. What were they going to do to me now?

I could feel something soft under my hands. It was fur, soft animal fur. I began to see further in the darkness. The fur was an entire blanket. I caught my breath and looked around, peering as best as I could into all the corners of the room. No one was there that I could see. I quickly buried my hands in the fur and drew the blanket up to my face. I couldn't hold the tears back anymore. I sobbed without making a sound into the blanket. I didn't understand what was going on. They'd only given me fur once as a garment, but once they discovered that I liked stroking the hair, they'd torn it off me. Fur reminded me of something then, but I couldn't quite remember what anymore. The fur blanket made me feel warm. I was always too hot or cold. They had never given me a blanket before.

What sounded like a six-horse carriage crashing through a building brought my attention back. They were back, and they were going to beat me for having the blanket. I caught my breath as I realized the door was open, but no one was there. I hadn't noticed at first, but there was a bit of light coming through the opening. A sliver of silver seemed to be slowly growing from the floor. I bit my lip to keep from calling out in surprise.

The growing sliver was the moon rising in the sky. I could see stars too, and in front of them, the distant shape of trees. I let out a silent whimper as a cool breeze blew past and lifted my hair. It was fresh air that smelled crisp and new, not the stagnate air from my room. I noticed that the door opened into a larger area where the trees and sky filled the air.

I swung my legs off the bed and began to walk toward the opening, leaving the blanket on the bed. The scene drew me. I could feel myself trembling, but I wanted to be closer to the sky, the trees, the stars.

I heard movement from the room. I glanced up to see Lady Ari'an walking toward the cave entrance. I quickly camouflaged with the stone near me, a trait I had only recently learned. I certainly didn't want her to see me and then run screaming off the edge of the cliff.

She kept walking toward the entrance.

Then she walked out the entrance. So much for not scaring her off the cliff. I raced to the entrance and leapt off, two wingbeats quickly carrying me down to where I could catch her.

I wanted to be closer to the trees, so I walked toward them. They were so far away. I didn't think I would reach them. I wasn't watching where I was going and stepped off a cliff. The drop was straight down, fresh air raced past me, the ground screamed toward me, and then pain stabbed into my side.

I stifled a sob. I should have known they would have me tied to something. Now they would drag me back to my room. I'd stumble on a rock, but they'd keep pulling. I'd fall, the stone floor would scrap my face, but they wouldn't stop. I tried to hold back the tears. They hated it when they saw me cry.

I rose back through the air. Whatever bound me dropped me back on the floor, and I again heard what sounded like a horse carriage hitting a building.

I stayed right where I lay. They wouldn't want me to get up without permission.

She lay where I'd dropped her. I prayed that I hadn't hurt her too much. I knew that I'd cut her with my claws when I'd grabbed her. She was tense when I'd snagged her from the sky, but then she'd gone limp, and now she didn't move. Had she passed out from the fall? Her side was bleeding, but thankfully not very much. Had I dropped her too hard? I couldn't lay her down gently. I was a dragon! I just didn't have the coordination for it.

She just lay there, limp and motionless. I could see all her ribs. Over those bones, whip scars spread across her back, some still healing. I took a deep breath, shoving back the urge to go to that temple right then and rip apart every stone, board, and priest I found.

I just waited. They would hit me with something soon. Someone had probably left to get an appropriate device. It would be terribly gruesome for doing something as horrible as walking outside.

"Please," I heard a shaky voice say, "are you all right?"

It was a new voice, but he couldn't be talking to me. I heard something heavy fall in front of me.

Maybe they wanted me to put it on. *Once, I'd had to put on a harness with blades on the front. Then they'd tied my hands behind my head. It was to teach me not to roll onto my stomach when they brought breeders in. The man they brought hit the harness several times, making it cut my chest. The priests just laughed.*

"Maybe next time," one had sneered as he pulled the harness off me, "you won't try to roll away." I never did again.

I looked at the thing without moving my head. It was a chunk of meat, a cooked chunk of meat.

"Please," the voice came again, "are you hungry?"

29

What were they trying to do? This was a reward. They rarely gave me meat, and never fully cooked like this piece. It didn't make sense. Maybe they were trying to make me go insane. I started shaking. I didn't want to go insane. I couldn't hold back the tears any longer. I felt something large quickly move past me.

I had to do something to make her stop shaking. I raced to her room and grabbed the blanket. Maybe she was just cold. She certainly didn't have enough clothes on to keep her warm. I hurried back out with the blanket in my teeth. She was sitting up now rocking back and forth. The shaking hadn't stopped, but now, her body convulsed with sobs, eerily silent sobs. I hurried over. She threw her head back and screamed. The noise should have deafened me or at least made my ears ring for a week, but no sound came.

I heard something coming toward me; I couldn't take it any longer. I screamed at the top of my lungs, but knew better than to let a sound escape. Whatever was coming stopped. There was a whoosh sound as something else fell to the floor. I turned to it immediately. I would face this threat directly. The blanket lay on the floor near me. I reached for it instinctively, and then drew back. They wouldn't want me to take the blanket.

"It's yours," the voice stammered a few steps behind the blanket, "you can have it."

I saw something glitter past the blanket. I focused on that. It had to be a knife or sword that they'd cut my hands with if I took the blanket. The firelight behind me danced on the glimmering object. It didn't look like any blade I'd ever seen before. It moved, rippling in the light. They were scales, blue scales with gold edges. I let my eyes travel along down the legs to the tail and around the back to the head, a head whose eyes were looking straight at me. It was a dragon. I gasped. Someone, I couldn't remember who, had once told me that dragons protected people.

"It's all right," the voice came from the dragon, "you're safe here." He was talking to me.

She gasped, but still no sound came. Had I suddenly gone deaf? A branch snapped on the fire. I glanced at it as it shot off a shower of sparks. I'd heard that. Had they cut out her tongue? I felt fury race through me again. I looked back at the girl. She was standing, staring at me. She took a step toward me. I circled away, not wanting to scare her anymore.

He glanced away from me at the fire, and I lurched to my feet. It was a dragon. I took a step forward. He moved away toward the fire. I was too vile for a dragon to help me. I ran toward the room. My foot caught the blanket. I broke the fall with my hands. The fur was soft against my face. I just lay there.

Oh no, what had I done! I crept toward her praying she hadn't hurt herself. "Please," I asked again, "are you all right?"

She looked up at me. I'd come too close. I was two steps from her face. I froze, hoping she wouldn't scream again.

He was so near I could feel his breath on my face. I could look into his eyes. They were the same shade of blue as his scales. I reached out, he stopped breathing. My hand touched his nose. He was real.

I glanced down at her hand, but my eyes crossed. I quickly closed them, but before I could open them, something covered my snout up to my eyes. I jerked my head up. It didn't let go. I opened my eyes expecting to see the blanket, but it was her. Lady Ari'an had wrapped her arms around my snout and was hanging on. I felt her gasp, but again no sound came. As gently as I could, I lowered my head to the ground until first her feet, then her knees touched the floor. She didn't let go. Her grip was strong considering how badly she was shaking.

"If you're trying to suffocate me, you're doing a bad job," I tried to say, but her arms were wrapped around my jaw too. I sighed and rested my head on the floor. Still she held on.

I couldn't let him go. If I did, he'd go away, and they'd come back. The priests hated dragons. They wouldn't even let a customer have me unless he left his shield with a dragon insignia outside.

Help me, please, I begged him silently.

I hoped I wouldn't have to sneeze anytime soon. I knew that both Dreanen and Danren had bragged about dragons to her, but I still didn't expect this. It was nice not to have a person run screaming when she saw me though. I laughed at that. She loosened her grip a bit.

"Would you mind releasing my face?" I mumbled.

He said something that sounded like "oud ou ein re es eg ma fac."

I let go, stood, and stepped back slightly.

"Thank you," the dragon stated, swiveling his jaw and raising his head.

I didn't want him to leave me, so I stepped toward him, again. He cocked an eyebrow, if a dragon had eyebrows, and looked at me.

I figured that I should introduce myself, but how should I do that? I bobbed my head in the best bowing attempt I could manage and said, "Good evening, my lady, I am Narden, and it is a pleasure to meet you."

I saw her lips quiver, her eyes glazed, and she sank to the floor pulling her knees up to her face shaking again.

"My lady," someone singsonged.
I looked up to have the back of his hand slam into my face.
"You are no lady," the second priest snapped. "No lady would ever find herself in a place like this. No lady has red hair either."
I rubbed the back of my neck. I couldn't feel the mark back there. I never could. He grabbed my hand, bending my fingers backward. I bit my lip to keep from calling out. I felt the blood trickle down my chin. Finally, he let go. I cradled my hand fighting back the tears.
"Don't ever let me catch you doing that again." He hit me again.
"My lady," a voice called. I must not respond. They would hurt me.
"Lady Ari'an!" the voice was frantic. "Please, stop!"
"Please," it whispered near my ear.

What had I done wrong? She wouldn't stop shaking. Rolling onto her side, she continued to clutch her knees to her face and shake.

I didn't know what to do. I went for the blanket again. I knew she wasn't cold, but I could move the blanket. Maybe somehow it would help. Lord Grath had brought it from her castle, because we'd been told she liked fur. It was a gift for her fourteenth birthday, but that was four years ago. I wished they would have brought a blanket that she recognized, but this was the best I had.

I dropped the blanket over her. It landed fur side down, missing her shoulders, but settling just below them.

I felt the fur touch the skin on my side. I grasped it in my hand before I realized it. I froze. They wouldn't want me to do that. I couldn't get my fingers to let go. I opened my eyes to look at the cover, willing my fingers to release it, but they wouldn't respond. It was so soft. I saw the scales past the edge of the blanket. My other hand reached for those. I crept closer wrapping my arm around them.

I pulled the blanket over my shoulders and rested my head on the leg. The scales weren't slimy, but they were hard and cool.

Well, at least she'd stopped shaking. I lay down with a sigh, leaving my leg out for her to hang on to. She rubbed her face across my toes.

"Careful," I warned, "I have sharp claws."

She buried her face in the blanket. Her breathing slowly steadied.

"Lady Ari'an?" There was no response.

Well, I guess it was all right for her to sleep there. I could stay awake just fine. I'd actually stayed awake for a week once without any problems . . . except I slept for three days afterward. One night wouldn't be hard.

I was hungry though. I glanced at the dying fire. If I angled my tail just right . . . Yes! I could roll some of the meat over to me. I toasted off some of the dirt, but couldn't get it all. I never could. The elk wasn't too bad, just a little gritty at times.

I watched the constellations slide by while the second moon rose.

I thought about flying over Torion Castle where I used to see Ari'an ride in the stable yard. *I'd seen her leave on the nobles' survey of their lands. I wished again that I hadn't left. If I'd stayed watching them, maybe this never would have happened. I had been due back at the border by the next morning. I hadn't wanted to be late again, so I had left.*

We didn't find out she was missing for three months. I didn't see her when I passed over Torion Castle, but I wasn't there all the time. I thought I was just not there when she was outside.

We'd finally found her horse last year. Actually, Adenern saw it. There was a huge celebration on her twelfth birthday when she received the horse, a beautiful five-year-old dapple-gray. Her pony's age had begun to show, and she needed a new mount. Adenern and I were both circling for that event. We took a special interest in the noble family of Nori'en. Watching the two girls grow up was fun, especially milestones like that. We laughed about funny things the girls did all the way back home.

34

We weren't laughing when we finally found the horse. Lord Grath was able to find out from the peasant who owned the mare where he bought her and who from.

We traced back through seven different sales till we finally found the man whose story didn't quite make sense. He'd said that he had raised the mare from a foal. It took some persuading for him to tell us the truth. I helped with that.

That information took us to the great temple in Verd. We didn't even know if she was still there or if they would even have her as a "possibility" for his lordship, disguised as a merchant, to choose from. The Mighty One was with us, and that part was actually pretty simple.

I glanced at the girl, as she silently whimpered in her sleep. I didn't want to imagine what they had done to her while she was there. The place shouldn't even exist. Such places were outlawed in this kingdom at least five hundred years ago. But the neighboring kingdom of Verd was powerful, and their king was not willing to change such "minor" things that pleased his people and kept the priests wealthy.

Even though we'd gotten her out, how many other girls were there who would never escape? Lord Grath had looked through at least fifty in five groups before he'd found Ari'an.

Politics dictated that we should have left her there longer while we worked out a diplomatic compromise. I hated politics. At least Lord Grath had not made us wait for the Verdian ambassador to tell us, probably in six months or more, that they would never keep a noble in any of those temples. Lord Grath probably realized that Adenern and I would have attacked the place ourselves to find her.

The sun finally rose. I couldn't feel my toes on that foot, but that wasn't too bad. At least I knew why they were asleep.

A shape passed across the rising sun then circled back. Adenern landed with Lord Grath on his back.

CHAPTER 4

FIGHTING MEMORIES

I dreamed in snips and short pieces that didn't connect. That was better, because I wouldn't wake up wanting to scream. What did wake me was the sound of the carriage wreck again. I sat up. Another dragon stood near the entrance of the cave. Most of his scales were also blue, but without the gold edges. Instead his wings were gold, along with the end of his tail and the tip of his nose. The scales on his legs were also gold halfway up his forearm in the front and to the first joint on his back legs.

I rose, quickly moving around until I could hide behind Narden. The new dragon laughed. "I see you managed not to scare her too much." He lay down on the floor so a man could slide out of the saddle on his back.

It was the customer from the temple. The one who'd barely touched me. I hid my face in the scales before me. Had he come to finish what he couldn't yesterday?

"Lady Ari'an," he called. The name made me shudder. I fought back the memory. "I brought you some new clothes."

I peeked around the dragon's neck. He held a large bundle in his hands. When he saw me look, he held it out toward me. It was a trick. I knew better than to wear that much even though I wanted to. The priests would certainly do something nasty to me.

"Lady Ari'an." As he spoke, I ducked my head again. "If you could change quickly, we can be on our way. I would like to have you home by the end of the week."

"This is your home," he snapped. I shook my head crying. I looked away. "This has always been your home," he sneered wrenching my head up so hard my neck screamed in pain. He forced me to look at him. "You shouldn't pretend the way you do," he leered, "it is not good for you."

I forced myself to keep from shaking my head. I didn't want to go back. My hands clenched as I bit my lip fighting the tears.

"Oww!" I called, "Hey, I'm a bit sore there."

I quickly turned my head to look at the lady. She'd clenched down on my wing, and it hurt, especially since I'd been lucky enough to get nailed by a spear right there when a group tried to raid our border a week ago. Her eyes stared vacantly past me. She was shaking again, and she'd bit down hard enough on her lip to make it bleed.

"Not again." I sighed.

"What is wrong?" Lord Grath asked, moving around my front legs. His eyes widened when he saw. "What did you do to her?"

I glared at him. "I didn't do anything to her," I snapped.

She focused on him and silently whimpered.

I saw the man step toward me. He'd certainly take me this time. I whimpered, closing my eyes. I needed to do something, but I couldn't remember what. I tried to lift my leg to take a step, but my leg didn't work right. I fell.

"Eeyee," I called as she collapsed to the floor. She'd ripped off some of the skin from my wing as she fell.

Lord Grath hurried to her, but just as he reached her, she looked up at him. The sheer terror in her eyes made him step back. She was a hundred times more afraid of him than she was of me.

He continued to walk back baffled.

"Maybe," I suggested, "it would be best to leave her here for a little while."

Lord Grath shook his head. "You know I cannot return for her for at least four weeks if I do not take her with me today," he stated turning to look at me.

"Maybe that's not—" my brother started. He had stepped around to see what was going on.

"Is not," the lord corrected.

"Maybe that is not," he continued, making a face, "such a bad idea."

I stifled a laugh.

Lord Grath glanced over at him. The face was long gone by then.

"She probably does not remember much from before she was taken, considering what they likely did to her, so staying here would give her a chance to adjust to being around people again."

Lord Grath wasn't convinced. "How would staying here help?"

"Well," my brother started, he had the I-have-a-great-argument look on his face, "surprisingly, she does not seem to be scared of Narden, but rather of you. That being the case, Narden, and perhaps I as well, could show her what it is like to be an equal with people. We could fly her over different towns, even take her to see Torion Castle, but still allow her not to have to interact with other humans. When she is ready, we could take her to Caer Corisan to meet some of the people there, and then when she is completely ready, you could take her home to her family."

Lord Grath sighed. "That is a wonderful idea, except for one thing."

"Oh?"

"What am I supposed to tell her parents?"

"Oh."

"They don't know we have her yet," Adenern inserted. "Maybe you could just not tell them for a while longer."

He glared at him. "Their own searchers proclaimed her dead two years ago. I will not lead them to believe that our own search is turning up more dead ends, not after the horse."

"You could at least let her stay for the four weeks," I picked up. He glared at me.

"It is a valid argument."

"Fine," he relented, "but if I find that you are just using the lady to cope with each other, I will not be happy with you."

"Hey," I put in as he went to remount Adenern, "maybe with a lady around, we won't fight as much."

He narrowed his eyes at me as I grinned.

The smile quickly faded as I turned back to the quivering girl at my feet. I sighed. I wasn't an expert on how to cope with situations like this. I snagged the blanket in my teeth again and dropped it over her. This time it managed to cover her top half, but left her legs sticking out. I sighed again. I hated being that uncoordinated. She responded though. She slowly sat up, letting the blanket fall. Her fingers wrapped around the edge before it slipped away entirely.

The man still looked familiar, but it didn't take me as long to remember why. He was Dreanen and Danren's father, but none of them existed. Did they? I heard the man step back. The dragon was saying something, but my mind wouldn't clear enough to understand the words.

Their father rarely came to visit. Their mother came every other month, but their father might come every fourth.

"He works with the dragons a lot," Danren explained once.

"We have a treaty with them," Dreanen interrupted. Danren glared at him, but he ignored it. "The gist of it is that most of the men of Remmaren have to spend half of their time with the dragons, and in return, the dragons help protect the borders."

"Why?" was that my voice? I sounded so young.

"Yes, my lord," Danren prodded, "why do we have to spend so much time there?"

Dreanen flushed momentarily. Then Pher'am walked in.

"Dreanen, would you care to help me oversee the table setting for tonight's dinner?" she asked.

"Of course," Dreanen jumped up.

Pher'am looked quite surprised for a moment. "Really? I mean, please come with me then, my lord." She curtsied then led the way to the dining room.

Danren and I waited until they turned the corner at the door and then burst out laughing. Dreanen always did have trouble admitting he didn't know something.

I held my breath. The girl had the distant look on her face that usually accompanied her violent shaking, but this time she didn't even shudder. The corners of her mouth begin to twitch. I gasped, was she really going to smile? The sound caused her to glance at me. The look vanished along with all traces of a smile.

Blue and gold scales filled my vision again. I started, searching frantically for something, but I wasn't sure what.

"Easy there," I heard a voice say. I turned my head, focusing on large blue eyes directly in front of me. Quickly, I glanced away. It was the dragon. Narden is what he'd called himself. I lightly placed my hand on his nose. He was still real.

"That's better," he continued as I looked past his head. "You are hungry by now, aren't you?"

I couldn't answer that. I wasn't allowed to. I ducked my head, closing my eyes. After a moment, I looked up again. I was so hungry. I really was.

"I'll take that as a yes," he said. Then he smiled, which was quite odd to see. Unlike a human smile that shows the front teeth first and then edges back as the smile grows, his started by showing his back teeth first and then crept toward the front of his mouth.

He turned before the grin exposed his front teeth. "Come on over here then." He almost sounded like he wanted to laugh.

"Now, I've been told by many people, both human and dragon, that my cooking leaves much to be desired, so I'd like to apologize right now."

He began pawing through the ashes left from last night's fire. I started to walk toward him, the blanket dragging behind me. Glancing down at it, I realized it was far too expensive to drag through the dirt. I vaguely recalled a woman's voice lecturing me about never soiling expensive things, but the thought of eating even badly cooked food drove the memory away.

I wrapped the blanket around me, glancing quickly around to make sure no one but the dragon saw. If anyone found out I had myself covered this much, they would certainly take the whip with the glass tips to me. The thought almost made me drop the blanket completely, but it was so soft, and I began to smell the meat.

The dragon offered me a chunk stuck to one of his front claws. I just stared at it. It looked like a hip from a large animal, and it really was cooked, even burned on one side.

She didn't take the piece I offered her at first. "It's not that bad," I tried to reassure her. I hoped that by mentioning my bad cooking I hadn't convinced her not to eat. What do people expect from a dragon anyway? Nice china and some parsley as garnish? I sighed just as she reached for the chunk letting the blanket slip to the ground.

She stared at the piece as she sank down on top of the blanket. "If you dust off the ashes, it'll be a bit better," I suggested just as she tore into it.

I took a step back shocked. She didn't even swallow before taking another bite. Wolves didn't even eat that ferociously. She finished the chunk quicker than even I would have, broke the bone and began sucking out the marrow. Then she choked. I nearly panicked. If she had something lodged in her throat, I wouldn't be able to do anything about it. She coughed up the piece of bone quickly, spit it out, and continued breaking the bone.

"There's more here," I told her fishing another piece from the ashes. I didn't want her to lodge another bone fragment. She looked up with a bone still in her mouth. She just stared at the chunk.

I couldn't believe it. He offered me more. I almost felt full from the meat I'd just eaten, and he would let me have more. I felt my lip quiver. I closed my eyes trying desperately to fight back the tears.

"It's all right," he coaxed, "you can have it."

I couldn't fight it anymore. I buried my head in my hands and let the tears come. I wasn't scared this time. I was just overwhelmed, and I didn't understand. I had distant memories of having enough to eat, but I didn't know if they were real.

Finally, I got control of myself again. I looked up at the dragon to find that he looked worried. I almost broke down again. I reached for the piece he still held out to me. I ate slowly this time. The full feeling I thought was only a dream came before I even finished all of it.

"Are you thirsty?" the dragon asked.

I looked up at him again, hoping that he could see that I was. He laughed again.

"I'm sorry," he managed. "I should have offered you a drink sooner, but I didn't think of it. I know I should have, but I don't remember everything I should most of the time, and you had me worried so often that I completely forgot."

He was funny.

I stopped talking. The faint hint of a smile disappeared again. Was I just imagining it?

"I can't actually bring you a drink," I started to explain. "I don't have the ability to set a bucket down without dumping it." I turned to go to the back of the cave where the springs were, but found she didn't follow.

"Are you coming?" I asked turning to look at her.

She rose shakily and started to walk toward me. I continued on.

He turned a corner, and I hurried to catch up. What I saw took my breath away. Through what might be considered a doorway, a huge cavern opened up to reveal pools of varying sizes scattered throughout.

"This way, my lady," the dragon said. "The ones there would burn your tongue."

I followed him in a daze. Distantly I could remember pools like these, but under the open sky. The light in this cavern sprinkled in from holes in the ceiling, danced back off the water, and sparkled off the walls. Across the myriad of pools, I could see other openings in the walls. They were similar to the one I'd walked through. I tried to ignore them, trying not to imagine that the priests were watching me from the dark.

"Here you are," the dragon stopped beside a clear pool near the far side. I stepped up to it. I could see the bottom of the pool a few steps below. It wasn't dirty like what the priests brought me. I knelt beside it shakily. My hands trembled as I dipped them in the crystal water. The water chilled my hands. I drew them back without holding any water. I'd seen dirt wash off my hands to mar the beautiful surface. That was wrong. I shouldn't drink from such a place. I would make it unfit for anyone else.

"It's all right," the dragon said next to me. I looked at him fighting back the tears. "See," he said sticking his nose in and taking a long drink, "it is just fine."

The dirt from his nose swirled for a few moments then settled to the bottom. Slowly I cupped my hands into the water, the coolness felt so nice against my skin. I drew my fingers to my mouth and drank. Closing my eyes, I drew my hands up again and again.

I opened my eyes to watch the water settle. Light came from behind me. Glancing around, I saw that Narden had lit some torches set into the walls. I turned back to the water and saw the torches reflected in the slightly rippling surface. Then I noticed another image.

As the water stilled, I saw the reflection of a young woman looking back. Tired eyes that appeared almost dead stared at me. The dirt-encrusted face leaned toward me. A faint trace of wood scraps crossed her left cheek. She wore a slightly extended breast band with thin straps over her shoulders. A brand on her right upper arm identified her as one of the nickins from the temple. A scar from a whip laced over the same shoulder. I knew that scar.

A new priest came in with the usual two. The new one carried a whip.

"You did something you were not supposed to," the first priest said. "You deliberately fell on the stairs," he cooed in a mockingly soft tone. "You are trying to lose that wretched thing inside of you." A grin crossed his face. "If that is what you would like, we can help you with that."

A hook was set into the ceiling. It had always been there. I had not known what it was for before this. The second priest had me lashed to it, before I knew what was happening. The whip whistled, the stroke crossing my back with a snap. I bit my tongue so hard it bled to keep from screaming. The blows continued. I lost my footing, but my knees couldn't reach the floor. I tried to put my feet back under me, but they wouldn't work. The rope bit into my wrists as another whiplash bit into my skin. The tip of the whip curled around my shoulder, cutting across the bone.

"You idiot!" I heard the first priest yell. He tore me around to look. "Tend her at once," he ordered. The second cut my arms loose. I collapsed to the floor. "If that does not heal," the first bellowed, "we will not be able to use her for the higher customers." I saw him turn to the other priest and tear the whip from his hands. "Get out!" He snapped the whip across the floor. The man tore from the room.

The reflection's eyes widened with mine as I realized who the wretched girl staring back at me was.

CHAPTER 5

CLEAN

I was getting a bit more of a drink from the pool next to hers when she fell over backward and frantically scuttled away from the water. She bumped into the end of my tail and clambered over it. Then she peeked, shaking, over my scales.

"What is it?" I asked glancing into the pool.

I expected to find a salamander or one of those annoying winged frogs, but there was nothing in the water. I glanced at where the spring entered and exited farther up, but there was nothing there either. The only thing in the water was my own reflection.

"Whatever it was, it's long gone now," I reassured her, but she still quivered.

"Would you like to clean up a bit?" I asked, trying to distract her from staring at the pool.

She glanced up at me, then back at the pool.

"If you would come over here," I said coaxing her away from the water.

Her feet quickly followed, but her eyes continued to dart from me back to the pool. On the other side from where we'd entered, I motioned to a curtained-off area. She stared at it, frozen in her steps.

"It's all right," I reassured. "It's a bathing area for humans when they're here. Not that a lot of humans come here often"—I didn't want her to think someone would barge in on her—"but it's here when someone needs it."

She took a few steps forward and began to reach out her hand. She stopped, glancing back at me.

"Go ahead," I urged.

Slowly, she raised her hand, drawing back the curtain. She gasped silently. The motion still unnerved me. Not for the first time, I wondered if those vile men had managed to cut out her voice somehow. I'd originally thought they'd cut out her tongue, but I'd noticed she still had that when she scarfed the elk earlier. I closed my eyes, fighting down the urge to go to the temple and tear every stone apart, burying every last one of them in the rubble.

"I'm sorry, I am out of soap right now, but you are more than welcome to rinse off at least," I managed to say that without sounding like I was going to kill something and turned to go. I heard the curtain fall. Walking from the cavern, I thought that a warm bath would do her good. Then I heard feet behind me.

I turned, cocking my head to the side. "Don't you want to be clean?" I asked puzzled.

More than anything, I wanted to be clean again. I knew water wouldn't wash my filth away though. I didn't want to be alone either. If the dragon left, they might come back. The dragon might help me . . . if I was with him, but if I wasn't . . . I fought the images of the vengeance they might take if they found me.

"All right." He looked concerned, but tried to hide it. I stared at my feet. "Would you like to look outside?" he asked.

I looked up at him then glanced at the opening of the cave. Daylight shone through the opening revealing trees climbing up mountains that I hadn't seen the night before. I looked back at the dragon hoping he would let me go closer.

He laughed lightly. "Hold on while I blow the torches out."

He walked back into the cavern with the pools. I followed next to his tail. He glanced back looking concerned again. Then he sat back on his haunches and flapped his wings forward. I had expected him to go around and blow the torches out like candles, but in the wind from his wings, the flames flickered and went out just as well.

He turned. "Come on then."

We walked back to the front of his cave. I could feel my eyes growing wider and wider as we approached. The view was gorgeous. The trees wrapped around the mountains like the wings of a bird on a nest, while the mountains themselves spread out like the bird in flight. I took another step forward.

"Careful," the dragon said next to me, "I don't want to dive after you again like I did last night."

I touched my side where he'd clawed me when I fell. It had scabbed over and wasn't even as deep as some of the whiplashes I'd had before. I glanced down at my side and saw the cliff go straight down. I froze. The cliff went straight down for leagues before reaching the top of the tallest trees.

"Get back!" the dragon yelled, but my feet wouldn't move.

His tail came around throwing me back. I looked up as I landed to see him turn and block part of the entrance.

I didn't know Adenern was coming back, and I didn't see him in time. I had been watching Lady Ari'an's eyes and mouth open wider and wider as she took it all in. I glanced up to see his final approach. The sun was over the mountain, so the entrance was engulfed in shadow. She didn't move when I yelled, so I pushed her back with my tail.

I braced myself against the blow. Adenern saw me too late, tried to turn, and plowed into my side. I rolled backward with him on top of me. We'd crush her if I didn't do something. I caught the rocky ground with my claws, throwing both Adenern and myself into the air. He landed first, scattering ashes, unburned logs, and what was left of the elk in his wake. Luckily for me, he broke my fall, not happily though, I might add.

"Are you trying to kill me?" he snapped clambering to his feet. He glared at me showing some teeth.

"Are you trying to kill her?" I glared back.

He glanced at Lady Ari'an, who looked scratched but at least not smashed.

"What was she doing there?" he returned to giving me a nasty look.

"Looking outside." I tried to calm my voice down, but didn't manage all too well.

"Couldn't she look outside farther from the entrance?"

"Couldn't you look where you were landing?"

"Well, you shouldn't live on the side of the mountain that shadows soonest!"

"Would you like to trade with me then?"

"Of course not!" He backed off. "You're the one who has to house people when they're here. I'll be doing enough of that later on."

Lifting my eyebrows, "Careful there," I warned. Glancing at Lady Ari'an, I froze. That hint of a smile was back.

I landed on my back knocking the wind out of my body. Gasping for air, I saw the other dragon collide with Narden. The sound of the six-horse carriage hitting another six-horse carriage filled the cave. They tumbled toward me. Covering my eyes I waited to be crushed, unable to breathe or move. Air rushed by me, and the two carriages collided with a house behind me.

I heard the argument, while trying to breathe. They reminded me of some others I vaguely remembered.

"Can't you watch where you're going?" Danren snapped.

"I wouldn't have to if you didn't get in my way!" Dreanen shot back. He could argue impeccably when he was calm, but if he was mad, he left logic in the dust.

I heard myself laugh at the two older boys piled on the floor. I had chased Dreanen who wouldn't give my soft toy horse back. He'd turned the corner and collided with Danren. I quickly retrieved my horse before he snatched it again.

Adenern saw me freeze and quickly looked at the girl. "Is something wrong?" he asked sounding much less angry.

"Shhh!" I hissed.

I wanted to see her smile. With the way she screamed and cried without making any sound, a simple smile would seem normal. Like something that she should do.

"Is she all right?" my brother asked moving next to me.

The faint hint disappeared again as she focused on the movement. I sighed. Her eyes widened as she took in my brother.

I glared at him. "Can't you be quiet when you're asked?"

"Why?" he glared back.

"Oh, never mind." I started for the middle of the cave to retrieve the rest of last night's supper.

"You could have at least asked her to change her clothes while I was gone." He followed me, glancing at the girl who slowly stood. "That outfit is anything but appropriate."

"I'm sorry, I was busy with other things." I rummaged through the remains of the fire and looked around the scattered logs for any leftover pieces.

"Like what?"

"It took a while to calm her down after Lord Grath scared her out of her wits, and then I gave her something to eat. I showed her where to get a drink after that."

"And you couldn't point out the bath?" he interrupted.

I'd noticed that Lady Ari'an had been trying to creep along the wall to go by Adenern without him seeing. He'd glanced at her when he made that statement. She froze staring at him.

"I did show her the bath, but she wasn't interested."

"Why wouldn't she be interested? She's filthy."

"Do you mind?" I snapped. "You're being extremely rude!"

He closed his eyes. "I'm sorry," he managed. "I'm still upset at this entire situation. She never should have had this happen to her in the first place." He opened his eyes. "I just wanted to come back and find her looking like she used to, not like this still." He motioned at the girl against the wall. Slowly he put his foot down. "What's wrong with her?"

"Not again." I sighed. "Find her blanket," I ordered.

He didn't move.

"Now!"

49

She'd started shaking again.

"She's filthy," the first priest ordered, "clean her up."

He wrenched my face around. "But do you know that you will never be anything but filthy?" he sneered.

I fought the tears. "You are a filthy little nickin, and that is all you will ever be."

The new dragon was right. I was filthy. I'd never be clean. I felt the tears come as my vision blurred.

The new dragon dropped something soft on me. I gripped the blanket and slid to the floor.

He backed away. I couldn't keep the sobs away any longer.

"What's wrong?" I heard him ask.

"I don't know." Narden sounded cranky.

"Well, why don't you ask?"

"She doesn't talk. I'm not sure if she even can."

"Excuse me?" the new dragon was enraged. "If I ever see one of those people again, I'm going to tear off their arms."

"I'll help," Narden growled.

I looked up at them. I hadn't heard everything, but I hoped they weren't talking about me. If they did tear my arms off, I wouldn't have that horrible brand on my arm anymore. Somehow, I didn't think they were talking about me though.

"Easy there," Narden cooed as I looked at him. "It's all right. You're safe here."

I looked over at the new dragon. "Don't worry," he continued, "that's just my brother, Adenern. He won't hurt you."

I traced the lines on the new dragon with my eyes. He was slightly bigger than Narden, but had the same blue to his scales. His face was wider as well, but the slope to his nose was the same. He still had the saddle on, but instead of holding a person, it was covered with sacks.

Narden followed where I looked. "You're still saddled," he told the other dragon, surprised.

The new dragon, Adenern, seemed to glare at Narden quite often. "I hadn't noticed."

"Well, aren't we the cranky one today?"

"Well, you haven't been up for two weeks."

Hearing a bickering argument like those were so odd, but vaguely familiar. The priests never argued. They always knew exactly what to do, or at least did whatever the first priest said.

"Why don't you go to sleep then?"

"I have a saddle on, or have you forgotten?"

"Why do you have it on anyway? You could have just carried that stuff."

"Lord Grath wanted it here and thought that Lady Ari'an would be able to take it off."

They both looked at me. "I'm not sure that's a possibility." Narden sighed.

I studied the saddle. Two straps wrapped around his shoulders like a pack. He wouldn't be able to get it off without damaging it, possibly beyond repair. I knew what it was like to be in something I couldn't sleep in and also couldn't take off. I knew far too well what that was like.

"I can at least offer you a little something to eat," Narden said retrieving the last of the meat from its scattered locations around the cave.

"That'd be nice," the other dragon replied flopping down. He made an annoyed sound and resituated so the saddle and its contents didn't jab him in the side. He ended up positioned like a cat about to pounce. He even swished his tail a bit like one. I almost smiled at the resemblance.

I didn't want him to be uncomfortable. It wasn't fair to him. The buckles weren't complicated. I'd figured out how to undo some of the contraptions the priests put me into. Getting them back on before they found out was usually harder. I slowly crept forward, hoping he wouldn't notice. I just had to get the saddle off. I wouldn't have to put it back on. The dragon wouldn't be able to do either by himself though.

I caught the movement out of the corner of my eye as I tossed the last couple of chunks of elk to Adenern. Glancing at what Lady Ari'an was doing, I gasped and whispered, "Don't move."

He didn't listen and jumped to his feet. The saddle lurched to the side, one strap dangling. Lady Ari'an jumped back, tripped over the uneven ground, and fell. Scuttling away, she regained her feet and quickly hid behind me.

"Why don't you ever listen?" I sighed.

"I thought you said she wouldn't take it off." The saddle hung precariously to the side.

"I didn't think she would." I turned my neck and looked at her, a partial smile on my face. "You're just full of surprises, aren't you?"

She blushed, just barely. I gasped.

"What is it?" Adenern started toward me, "Is she hurt?"

"No." She kept beside me, but crept away from the sound of Adenern moving. "Do you mind?" I turned back to him. "You're scaring her."

"Why is it that I scare her, but she's perfectly fine with you?" At least he backed away as he asked.

"I have no idea." I sighed. "And why are you asking me, you're the one who knows everything."

He glared at me yet again.

I smirked back.

"Do you think you could convince her to get this the rest of the way off?" He motioned at the saddle with his head.

"I don't know," I answered, turning my head back to Lady Ari'an.

Narden looked directly at me. I couldn't meet his eyes. I shifted my gaze between his face and my grimy hands as he spoke.

"Would you be willing to take his saddle the rest of the way off?" he asked softly.

I glanced closer to his eyes momentarily, then glanced over at the other dragon. He was watching me. I shied out of his view.

"Please?" Narden asked, "I know he'd appreciate it."

I peeked back over his tail. "Please," the new dragon asked just as softly.

I backed up until I bumped into Narden's nose. Spinning around, I put my hand between his nostrils to balance myself.

"What if he doesn't watch while you're getting it off?" he suggested.

I looked close to his gaze again, hoping he'd know that I thought I could.

"Will you look away, Adenern?" Narden still watched me.

I heard the other dragon sigh and shift his weight. Peeking at him once more, I saw that he was looking out the front of the cave. Glancing nervously at Narden, I began to creep across the gap. I stopped halfway there and looked back. Part of me wanted to just run back and hide, but he wouldn't be able to get out of the saddle without my help. I wanted to help, so I forced my legs to keep walking.

Reaching his side, I had to lean under him a bit because of the lopsided saddle. I pushed the strap through the loop and pulled, but it didn't come undone like the other one had. I put my hand on the dragon's side and felt him hold his breath. Biting my lip, I pulled harder; the buckle released. I jumped back to get out of the way of the saddle, but it fell on me anyway. My legs were stuck underneath, I pushed at it frantically, but it wouldn't move.

I was trapped. They'd tied my legs down at the hips earlier. When they undid the ropes, I couldn't feel my legs. I saw them, but they were completely numb. I was in a pit, where they'd brought me after I'd kicked at the second priest again. A large bag was lowered onto my legs. I glanced up at the priests standing over my head outside of the pit.

"You can come out as soon as you get that off," one of them said.

I pushed at the bag, but it was far too heavy for me to move with just my arms.

"I would hurry if I were you, nickin."

Water began to pour over my head. The pit began to fill. I shoved at the bag, trying to get my legs to respond. The water came to my waist, but the bag didn't even shift as the water began to cover it. The water was up to my neck.

"Learn, nickin, that you do not do anything without our permission."
*The pit filled too fast. I couldn't get the weight off. I tipped my head
back for a last gasp as water covered my head.* The weight came off.

I opened my eyes as I heard something crash against the wall. I
wasn't in a pit. I closed my eyes again and screamed.

Adenern had hit the saddle off her as soon as he saw her start
to shake. She opened her eyes and looked around terrified. Then
she threw her head back and let out that eerily silent bloodcurdling
scream. I felt my scales shiver. Adenern stepped closer.

"Lady Ari'an," he cried out frantically. He glanced at me then
stared at the girl. "Mighty One have mercy," he breathed, staring at her.

I moved next to him as she focused on his face. The terror
slowly left her face as she gasped for air. Softly she reached out her
hand touching his nose. In the blink of an eye, she wrapped her arms
around his snout just like she had mine; and just like me, his head
shot up. He crossed his eyes trying to look at her then looked at me
for help.

"Put your head down," I ordered trying not to sound panicky.

Thankfully, he did. She was sobbing silently again, but had
stopped shaking at least.

He looked at me again. "'Ut am i su'ose t' ou?"

"I'm not sure," I answered.

"Ut?"

"Just wait," I told him. "I'm sure she'll let go eventually."

Adenern didn't look like he was all too pleased with that suggestion, but I wasn't about to try to pry her off. He did sigh and rest his
head on the floor though.

"Hey, look on the bright side," I chimed in, "at least she's not
scared of you anymore."

Adenern was half asleep by the time she let go, but she did let
go of his nose sooner than she had mine. Before he drifted off he
mumbled something about the bags being for the lady.

She just stared at my brother when she let go of his nose. If she
could look anything besides scared, hungry, or dazed, she seemed

almost surprised that dragons slept . . . and snored. At least, Adenern did. I hadn't been told that I did yet.

"Lady Ari'an," I interrupted her thoughts. She looked up at me frightened then shuddered and stared at her feet.

"Look over there." She glanced up at me briefly then glanced where I motioned. I put my head near her and said softly, "They're presents for you. Why don't you go open them?"

Presents? I didn't get presents. I didn't get anything except an occasional change of clothes and some food if I was good. I looked at the dragon. He'd just called me a lady again. I knew he shouldn't use any title to call me. In fact, if any of them found out he called me anything but a nickin, I'd be in trouble. The dragon seemed to want to call me by this strangely familiar name though, and I couldn't tell him not to. The priests weren't here, so maybe I wouldn't be in trouble. I glanced around, wondering if they were hiding somewhere, counting up the things I did wrong. They wouldn't work with a dragon though, would they?

I heard something fall in front of me with the sound of broken ceramic.

I glanced at the saddle that lay in front of me now, and then at the dragon who grimaced.

"We probably broke something when we fell," he explained. "I'm sorry."

He . . . apologized to . . . me. I fought back the tears. Whenever he spoke to me, I recalled, he always spoke like I wasn't just the trash the priests referred to me as. Why did he think so highly of me? Wasn't I just something to be used, like a bed, and when I got too old, they'd throw me away?

"Please, open them?" he asked close to my face.

Looking up, I touched his nose with my hand. Whatever the reason, I was worth something to him. He actually cared about me. I felt my lip quiver and quickly bit it to make it stop. If he wanted me to open those bags, that's what I would do. He deserved to have me do whatever he wanted.

I slowly reached for one of the bags. All of them were secured to the sides of the saddle, but that was simple enough work. I knew how to untie almost any knot by now. I could even retie most knots with just one hand.

The first bag was full of broken dishes. The designs were beautiful though. A little more than a watch ago these had been a gold-rimmed set with hand-painted flowers. It was so amazing to hold such pretty things, even if they were in pieces.

She handled each broken piece as if it was the finest porcelain in the kingdom. Fingering the designs, she sorted each of the larger pieces into separate piles of what type of dishes they once were. The smaller pieces she set in another pile and left the chips in the bag. The care she took for each piece surprised me. These were the common dishes of Caer Corisan. Some of the fortress workers painted them as a hobby. Many of the dishes there were worth far more than these simple ones.

The next bags once contained apples, but they now had a more applesauce consistency. The nuts in the next sack were better off, but the nutcracker wouldn't be usable again. Next was a bag of bags, each one contained some dried food. She whimpered when she saw the bag of dried fruit. Once that had been her favorite treat, but with the way her lip trembled, I wasn't sure if she wanted them or not.

"You can have some if you'd like to," I tried to reassure her.

She looked up at me momentarily, and then stared back at her hands. She never looked me in the eye for very long, but at least she acknowledged that I was talking to her. Gently she fingered some of the dried fruit and then popped a piece in her mouth. Closing her eyes as she chewed, I saw a couple of tears streak down her face. Quickly she put the bag aside. The next sack had sheets and blankets for the bed. Another fur blanket was in there, which she held for a long time. She pulled the last thing out slowly. It was a soft stuffed toy. She let out another silent gasp and clutched the toy to her chest, burying her face in its fur.

The last bag had soap wrapped in some towels in it. At the bottom were several dresses. Setting the soap to one side, she pulled one out, looked at it for an instant, and then threw it. Scrabbling to my other side, she began to shake again. I sighed. We'd been doing so well.

They brought two outfits in. One was a nice dress that had lace at the cuffs and hem, the other was a breast band with shoulder straps and a skirt that would barely come down past my hips.

"Hurry and get dressed," the second priest said curtly and left.

I quickly put on the dress. It was nice to have a full dress on again. The priest came back with two others. "Wrong choice," he sneered.

They tied me to the chain hanging from the ceiling and cut the dress to ribbons on me, ripping open my back as well as the dress when they came to that section.

Untying me, the second priest threw another full-sized dress on the bed. "Hurry and get dressed," he said again and left.

I put on the other outfit. They didn't rip it off when they came back next time.

I was beginning to have a routine for dealing with this. I grabbed the first blanket, dropped it on her, and put my head close to hers. Of course, the blanket now covered her face.

"It's all right," I said softly. "You're safe here."

Eventually she did calm down and stopped shaking. I sighed. This was going to be much harder than I originally thought.

CHAPTER 6

LIVING WITH
DRAGONS

She wouldn't let me out of her sight for over a week. Adenern slept that week in the middle of my cave. Occasionally, he would roll over, snore, or mumble something about naming the bath pit. He'd always been a bit odd when he slept. Anyway, I noticed that Lady Ari'an didn't eat unless I suggested it.

Of course, I didn't eat until Renard stopped by with an elk. The young lady took to him quicker than she had Adenern, but then again, Renard didn't try to crush her as his introduction. He talked to her about Caer Corisan, her family, and a bit about how Verd responded to her rescue. They called it a raid by those uncontrollable beasts, though, and said we'd killed thirteen people, which I knew wasn't true. He was a lot more patient with the lady than I thought he would be.

It's not that Renard's not patient. He's just formal most of the time, which can turn into impatience when he's talking to me. She had several shaking episodes while he talked. It was taking her less and less time to recover from them, which was nice. I still hated that she became that scared at all, especially at something as harmless as talking.

Renard caught a couple of elk for us. One had antlers though, which would look nice as a dagger hilt, but as dinner, they're not so much fun. He caught a bear two days later and even brought a nice fat cow from Caer Corisan after that. They kept flocks of sheep and

58

herds of cattle for us to have once in a while. Normally, we only eat those late in winter, but they let him take one for the rescued lady.

I was finally able to convince Lady Ari'an to take a bath. She'd washed off her arms, legs, and face in the pools, but didn't seem to want to be left alone. I think she just complied because I kept bringing it up.

She was gone for quite a while, hopefully enjoying a nice warm soak. The alone time allowed me to clean out the cave a bit and harass the sleeping Adenern, one of my favorite pastimes. When he'd wake up, I'd tease him about the silly things he said. It would usually end in my being thrown out of the cave or chased around the cavern of pools until I'd dive into the deep one and hightail it out the waterfall. I never seemed to win those fights, but I couldn't help getting into them. What else were younger brothers for?

He was telling me not to stick flying mice in his ears when Lady Ari'an walked in. She was still in that horrible outfit, but she did look substantially cleaner.

I walked into the cave still a bit wet. I didn't have anything to change into, so I just put on my old clothes. I'd washed them out in the bathing pool. The pool had actually been carved complete with steps leading down and a place to sit or lay in the steaming water. Warm water was so nice. The priests only cleaned me in cold or boiling water. The only warm water they gave me was to drink.

I could almost see the bath at Torion Castle when I closed my eyes. Remembering things from before my time at the temple was hard. I'd been taught that all of those things were fake, but both Narden and Renard told me that those places, people, and memories were real.

When I walked into the cave, Narden was poking Adenern in the ear with his tail. He must have heard me coming because he turned to look at me. If it is possible for a dragon to look sheepish, he certainly did. Flipping his tail to his other side as though he hadn't been doing anything out of the ordinary, he walked toward me.

"Don't you feel better now that all that dirt's off?" he asked.

I almost smiled and ducked my head. I did feel a lot better.

"Now wouldn't you feel even better if you changed into one of those nice dresses Adenern brought for you?" he continued.

I looked up at him startled, then glanced at the sack of clothes. I felt the tears come to my eyes. I wanted to wear something else, but I couldn't. I shook my head slightly and froze. Hearing Narden gasp, I closed my eyes. I wasn't supposed to answer questions even with a headshake. I fought the feeling of a blow smashing across my face.

"That was amazing," I heard Narden whisper.

Surprised, I stared at his nose.

"I wasn't sure you remembered how to do that!" he sounded so excited.

I almost met his eyes again. He wanted me to respond? I looked away. No one ever actually wanted me to respond to questions. The priests would ask quite a few, just to make sure I didn't answer. Narden was happy that I responded. I didn't understand.

"If I ask you 'yes or no' questions, would you shake your head or nod to answer me?" he sounded so thrilled.

I glanced closer to his eyes, closed mine while biting my lip, and nodded once. I fought the tears knowing that if they ever found out, I would be in so much trouble.

I opened my eyes to see Narden let out a whoop and spin in a circle. Then he flopped down in front of me. I put my hand on his nose, trying to calm my breathing. No one would hurt me here on purpose. Narden had told me that several times. He would then apologize again for scratching me when he caught me, and for Adenern almost crushing me.

I was so excited. She would actually answer me! It was like having a baby say "da" for the first time, not that I knew anything about babies talking, but I'd heard about the excitement. I didn't know what to ask her first.

I finally decided to ask her the question I'd just asked, "Will you, please, put one of those nice dresses on?"

She stared at her hand on my nose and shook her head slightly.

"Why not?" I realized after I'd asked that wasn't a "yes or no" question. "I mean, do you not like them?"

I glanced over at the bag. The dress I'd pulled out was beautiful. I shook my head again.

He seemed at a loss for a moment, then asked, "Did they do something to you so you don't want to wear one of those?"

He seemed to be forcing his voice to be calm. It took me a moment of studying my fingernails and the scales around my hand. Finally, I nodded.

Narden growled. I looked up at him and stepped back. His voice still had that forced calm to it, but he wasn't as successful this time.

"I promise you," he started, voice quivering with anger, "I will die before I let them do anything like that to you again."

I looked up into his eyes, so surprised by his statement that I actually held his gaze for a moment. I was trash to be used and thrown out when I wasn't usable anymore, but for some reason that I couldn't comprehend, Narden thought I was important. I sat down and buried my head in my knees. I couldn't hold the tears back anymore. Sobs raked through my body, as I felt the blanket fall over me again.

Another week went by before I could convince her to stop sleeping on my leg and sleep in the guestroom instead. She'd slept there for five days before it happened. I was dreaming about visiting Rem'maren. The major fortress Caer Dathen shone in the summer sunlight. Lady Margree came out to greet me without screaming. She opened her mouth to say something when I did hear a scream.

I woke with a start, the sound still echoing through the cave. Lady Ari'an shot out of her room like an arrow from a bow. She raced to me clambering up my arm and onto my back.

I tossed and turned when I went to bed that night. A horrible scratching sound kept coming from the walls. I'd almost drifted off when I felt tiny claws run over my foot. I sat up staring at the beady eyes shining back at me from my feet.

I'd actually managed to kick the first priest. I felt so proud of myself, because they left right away. When they came back, my pride quickly vanished. The second priest tied me to the bed even though I struggled to get away. Then the first one smeared what looked like honey mixed with nuts on my legs.

"I hope you like rats," he said looking at me with those cruel eyes.

The second priest stepped out of the room momentarily, returning with a cage of rats the size of my hand.

"Think twice," the first priest said as he opened the cage, "before kicking me again."

After they left, the rats slowly crept out of the cage. At first I was happy to see any other creature, but then they started eating the honey-and-nut mixture. They bit my leg. I tried to kick them off, but my legs were tied to the corners of the bed again. That deterred them for only a moment. Soon they were back digging into my leg with both their teeth and their claws. I screamed, and they scurried away for a moment. Then they came back. The blood began to run off my leg. They didn't come off when I kicked anymore, and screaming didn't faze them either. My blood mixed with the honey on my legs.

I moved my feet away from the beady eyes. The eyes scurried off the bed to the wall. Following them I saw several other eyes watching me. I screamed as loud as I could, rolling from the bed and racing from the room. I saw Narden looking at me. As quickly as I could, I climbed up his leg onto his back. He looked at me then at the room. I saw a small brown body scurry out of the room.

"A mouse?" I was shocked that she'd screamed, but to find that the first sound from her mouth was because of a little rodent like that was a bit much.

I looked at the quivering girl on my back. "You never used to be scared of mice," I reminded her. "You used to rescue them from the castle cats, remember?"

She buried her head in my scales and whimpered. The sound actually came from her shaking body.

It took me a moment to overcome my surprise. "Did the mouse touch you?"

I felt her nod more than I saw it.

"Where did it touch you?"

She pointed at her leg with trembling hands.

"You know," I said trying to lighten her mood, "if you had something covering your leg, say one of those nice dresses over there, a mouse couldn't touch it."

She looked at the bag of clothes piled by the wall, then slid off my back. Hurrying over to them, she picked up the dress on top and pulled it over her head. Then she began pulling the rest of the contents of the bag out. Nearing the bottom, she came across a pair of stockings and pulled them over her feet. She straightened shakily.

I just let my jaw hang. I was far too surprised to say anything.

I would do anything to keep from being touched by one of those things again. The suggestion of putting on one of the dresses made sense. If I had one on, I could have my legs covered, and the mouse couldn't touch them. The dress came to my ankles. They would still be able to get to my feet. Frantically, I searched though the bag looking for something to protect my feet. Near the bottom, there were several pairs of socks along with some undergarments. I pulled out one of the pairs of socks and quickly pulled them over my feet.

Turning back to the dragon, I saw his mouth hanging open. Glancing around I knew I heard more of those horrible little feet beginning to surround me. I hurried back over to him. Sitting between his front legs, I pulled the skirt around my legs, pulled my hands into my sleeves, and buried my head in my knees. Maybe if all my skin was covered they wouldn't bite me.

I looked around occasionally trying to locate the rats. I could hear Narden above me cooing, "Easy there. You're safe here."

I knew I started shaking whenever I thought I heard their claws, and he didn't like it when I shook. Burying my head back in my knees, I tried to calm down again and again.

Slowly she would stop shaking only to throw her head back, frantically look around, and start shaking again. I did my best to reassure her, but I don't know how much it helped. Ever so slowly, the shaking fits came further and further apart. If nothing else, I was certainly learning patience from this experience. Finally, her head stayed down and her breathing evened.

I watched bats and owls fly past the entrance with the occasional winged deer. I typically left those alone unless I was feeling like a real challenge. Since flying is one of my major advantages, when my prey can fly too, it takes a lot more work to catch. They were beautiful creatures though. Slowly the sun rose blinding me if I ever mistakenly looked directly into it. One speck seemed to be moving closer, but I couldn't look directly at it without seeing spots.

Eventually the speck grew to the size of a bird, then a horse, and now the dragon landed lightly at the entrance. He took a quick glance at the girl curled in front of me, and cocked an eyebrow.

CHAPTER 7

REMEMBERING
THE TRUTH

"Adenern said she was sleeping by herself," the voice wasn't loud, but it still jarred me awake.

Glancing around I tried to identify the voice. It sounded familiar, but not quite right. Renard was standing in the doorway blocking out the sunrise. I wondered why his landing hadn't awakened me. It wasn't as loud as Adenern's or Narden's, but his landings did sound like a light chariot hitting a tree.

"She was," Narden answered glancing at me. He flashed me a reassuring smile, as I turned to study my fingers. "But we had a run-in with a mouse last night."

"A mouse?" My head shot up, I caught my breath, and tensed. The voice wasn't Renard's.

"Well, I think it was a mouse," Narden replied.

I slowly stood and began to creep behind him.

"I didn't actually see what sent her screaming from the room. I saw a mouse run out later, but she might have just had a bad dream," Narden continued.

"Did not," corrected the new dragon as he glanced at me. I froze. He cocked an eyebrow at Narden.

I knew that was a hint as Narden picked up the introductions. "Forgive me, my lady," he began, "Lady Ari'an, this is my father, Tragh, son of Terigen, successor to the line of Gary. Sir, this is the

Lady Ari'an, daughter of Lord Cristeros and Lady Hin'merien of the House of Nori'en."

I felt sick and glanced around expecting a blow. That was never to be said. No one knew that. I used to repeat that name to myself when the priests weren't there. I would whisper it under my breath just to know that I could still speak and that I did have a name, but I stopped that long ago. The lady whom Narden named didn't exist. I'd made her up, the priests told me time and again. I felt myself quiver, knowing that soon this dream would have to end. It couldn't go on, and when I woke, they would beat me for sleeping so long, or mumbling in my sleep, or for something else I'd forgotten that I'd even done.

Fur fell on my head again, and my knees gave out under me. I gripped the blanket around me, trying again to sort out what was real and what wasn't.

I sighed knowing that I'd set her off yet again. The blanket seemed to help sometimes, but I'd seen her shake for watches occasionally glancing around with terror on her face. If I hadn't been so concerned about her at those times, I probably would have taken off to destroy the first Verd settlement I found.

"This happens often," my father said behind me.

It was a statement, not a question, but I nodded anyway. "It's like a window fell out of a tower, and all the panes are shattered on the ground. I can't put them together, no matter how hard I try. I can't even find all of the tiny shards, and if I could, I wouldn't know where to even start." My voice cracked, and I stopped to take some deep breaths to regain some control.

"You are doing the best you can, and she has improved a little bit." I turned back to my father.

He had a saddle on his back with more bags tied to it. I heard a slight clink as he walked into the cave a bit farther and lay on the floor. His eyes didn't leave the girl huddled on the floor.

"Lord Grath," he began, "sent word to Lord Cristeros and Lady Hin'merien."

"What?" I snapped swinging around to face him.

Out of the corner of my eye, I saw Lady Ari'an's head shoot up, and she glanced around terrified. I quickly turned back to her and said as softly as I could, "It's all right, I just got a little excited. You don't need to worry. You're safe here, remember."

She glanced toward my eyes and then stared just below them. Her shaking slowly stopped, and she placed her hand on my nose. She glanced at my eyes again, and then dropped her head and hand to her chest.

"You seem to calm her down quicker." I turned to glare at the voice behind me.

I forced my voice to stay low, but refused to fight away the undercurrent of anger. "How could he?"

I hadn't expected him to meet my gaze so firmly, but I refused to back down.

"The letter will take at least two weeks to reach them, and with the weather turning, it may take longer." His voice matched my volume, but was much calmer. "The return trip will take just as long. He promised you three weeks, you will have at least four."

I let out an exasperated sigh, but couldn't argue with that logic. The last thing I wanted to think about was sending her away, especially in this condition.

I felt the hands lightly touch my side, and out of the corner of my eye, I saw her peek around my side at this new dragon to enter her world.

Giving my father one last glare to assure him that I still didn't like the situation, I turned to Lady Ari'an. "Would you like to take his saddle off for him? I think he has some more presents for you."

She took a step back, her eyes flitting nervously from me to him for a moment.

I backed out of the new dragon's sight. Something about him had made Narden angry, and I wasn't sure yet if I should have anything to do with him.

"I would greatly appreciate your assistance, my lady," the new dragon said.

"You don't have to if you don't want to," Narden began.

"*Do not*," the other dragon called.

Narden rolled his eyes and let out an exasperated sigh. He reminded me of someone else who people often corrected, but I couldn't pin down the memory.

The new dragon continued, "Both he and myself would greatly appreciate the service."

I felt my lips almost turn up at the sudden formality in his speech.

I glanced back up at him then crept to where I could look around at the new dragon. He caught my eye, and I ducked behind Narden, hiding my face in his scales.

"Please," Narden said near my ear.

I looked toward his eyes for a moment, then closed mine again. I swallowed hard and peeked to look at the other dragon again. He was discretely admiring the walls. If I could remember how to laugh, I might have. I glanced over my shoulder to make sure no one else was watching and quickly pointed at the new dragon then back at Narden. I dropped my hand to my side and glanced away, hoping that nothing would hit me again.

Narden gasped above me, and I cringed expecting a blow.

"Is everything all right?" the other dragon had glanced over.

Narden stammered something that I didn't quite make out, and then returned to gaping at me. I looked up at him once in a while, but then glanced around the room. Someone would catch me. They always did . . . except recently. Maybe nothing would hit me here.

I couldn't tell exactly what she was saying when she pointed to my father and then back at me, but she had pointed. Before the incident with the mouse the previous night, she'd not pointed. Now she was repeating the gesture. Maybe I could get her to continue to do that. Maybe, if she remembered how, I could get her to write something someday. My spirit soared higher than my wings could have ever taken me. She was trying to communicate with more than just a head shake.

With a start, I realized that I hadn't answered her. What had she meant? I wasn't sure, but I had to take a shot at answering her first question.

"He's safe," I started.

"He is," my father interrupted me.

She looked like she might almost smile again as I rolled my eyes and started again, "He is safe." I glanced behind me. "He *is* my father." I lowered my head to in front of Lady Ari'an and whispered, "He *is* picking on me, because my brothers happen not to be here at the moment."

My father cleared his throat behind me. She almost smiled again. She nodded ever so faintly then peeked around my leg. For several moments she watched my father and looked across the floor, probably deciding how best to get over to this new dragon. Slowly she began to walk over to his side. Glancing back at me occasionally, I encouraged her with a nod of my head and reassured her, "It is all right. He won't hurt you."

I had learned how to remove these saddles without dropping them on myself. I'd put Narden's saddle on and taken it back off numerous times. The bags clinked as I set the saddle on the floor. The new dragon ruffled his scales, which seemed to be something that all dragons did when their saddles were taken off. He mentioned needing to meet with someone and left.

"He's—he is not being rude, he is just quite a bit busier than we younger dragons are," Narden explained as the shape faded back into the distance.

I glanced at the new bags attached to the saddle, then over at Narden.

"Why don't you open them?" He grinned. "I would like to see what is in them, wouldn't you?"

I untied the bags from the saddle and then opened them. There were only three this time. The first contained dishes. The same beautiful paintings covered each one. They were each different, but done in a style that matched each other. Some of the plates had flowers, trees, forests, skies, or animals. The last plate was different, done on a silver plate instead of the brown pottery. It bore the most complicated design of a blue dragon in the center gliding down to a castle fortress. I traced the flags flying from the castle. They were the colors of Rem'maren. A forest lay behind, blending into mountains and a starry sky.

I heard Narden move behind me and let out a low one-note whistle. It had taken me a while to get used to a dragon whistling, but he often seemed to whistle or hum, occasionally singing a line or two of a song.

"Armel did that one. He's one of the counsel and the leader of Caer Corisan. He's an exceptional craftsman. He also does all of the carving for Caer Dathen." Bending his head closer, he added, "Set it down over there, and I'll show you something."

Obediently I placed the plate on the ground away from the other dishes. I stepped back just before Narden let a short burst of flame loose on the plate. Had he lost his mind? Certainly, that would ruin the beautiful painting.

"Come and see," he exclaimed excitedly still staring at the plate.

Slowly, I stepped forward trying not to shake. He had just ruined the most beautiful plate I had ever seen, and now he wanted me to come look at its charred remains.

I peeked at the plate closing my eyes after the first glance. Quickly, I looked again. In place of the dragon and the castle stood a mountain with a waterfall cascading from a cave three quarters of the way up. The mountain fell straight down with dragon heads, bodies, or tails coming and going from numerous other caves, none of which were lower than halfway up. The bottom of the mountain turned to forest while the top turned to a daylight sky with three dragons circling.

"Now this is the mark of his true work," Narden said near my ear, followed by what sounded like a hiccup, but much deeper.

A small cloud of smoke leapt from his mouth and engulfed the plate. I gasped as the smoke dissipated and revealed the crest of Rem'maren, a green and silver dragon on a brilliant blue background.

Narden laughed as the crest changed back into the original fortress. I loved that sound. At first the fact that a dragon laughed surprised me. These were creatures hated and feared by most people. They could travel few places where people would not either run screaming in fear or try to shoot them down to chop up their bodies as trophies. They lived in fear for their lives every day. Perhaps today a knight would scale their mountain and kill them as they slept, but they slept peacefully.

They laughed as though the world was not against them. If they could laugh, perhaps I could too. Inside I laughed, because a plate could change, because one hidden picture that I feared had ruined the first was even more beautiful, and because a dragon could still laugh. Perhaps, my hope had not died yet.

Lady Ari'an was far from the best of company, but it was nice to have someone there. Her presence also gave me a break from my studies. My father insisted that I still practice several formations, and my landings. Adenern or Renard came by sometimes to practice with me, but mostly it was just my lady and I.

She was always attentive, and did anything I asked. After a time, I began to wonder if she did what I asked just because she wanted to please me. She lived on the edge of fear. Hundreds of tiny things would send her into those terrible shakes. Each tiny step she made toward the girl she once was terrified her. Constantly, she looked over her shoulder to see if anyone watched. Many times she screamed in noiseless terror at some foe that I couldn't see. If I could have, I would have destroyed every fear, every memory, every invisible enemy for her, but this was a battle I could not fight. I stood by her as best I could, praying that these horrors would soon never haunt her again.

The four weeks passed too quickly. Still she would not speak, and she did not voice a scream again. Rarely, she would gasp at some new thing I did or something that someone brought. Renard and

Adenern brought such things often simply to see how she would respond. The keepers of Caer Corisan sent gifts to the imprisoned lady. Captive not to the dragons who cared for her daily, those at Caer Corisan at least knew better than that, but rather by the terrors ripping through her own mind.

Lord Grath arrived to read the response from Lord Cristeros and Lady Hin'merien to us. It certainly surprised all of us including Lord Grath. He had waited to read the letter to us all in Lady Ari'an's presence. Breaking the seal, he began to read:

> *To my Lord Grath, son of Regiten, lord of Rem'maren, master of the dragons of Maren; from the Lord Cristeros, the fourth of that name, son of Cristeros of the third, and the Lady Hin'merien, daughter of Trin'geren, lord and lady of the House of Nori'en. Greetings to you.*

I have to admit, I was half asleep by the end of that.

> *Life and peace to you for the deliverance of our beloved daughter from the lands of the north. We are exceedingly grateful for her rescue by your creatures and your calm control over the beasts.*

Two indignant snorts greeted that remark, to which Lord Grath glared at Adenern and myself.

> *We wish for the complete return of our daughter to our home, which we indeed believed was beyond all hope. If her condition is as extreme as you mentioned, however, we will consent to her remaining with your beasts, if they are indeed helping her recover her mind and are not holding her against her will. To determine her condition, I, Lord Cristeros, will*

be visiting your fortress of Caer Corisan, within the week and wish prompt visitation with our daughter whether there or at the dwelling of your beasts.

Thank you again for the deliverance of our daughter and may the gods and goddesses smile warmly upon you for all of your years to come.

A stunned silence greeted the ending of the letter. Finally, Adenern broke the stillness with the obvious, "Well, this is certainly unexpected."

"I'm not supposed to host lords here!" I exclaimed.

Lord Grath raised an eyebrow.

"I mean real lords." That wasn't the right thing to say either.

Thankfully, Adenern burst out laughing drawing the stare away from me.

"You never know who is going to come visiting these days," Renard added, sounding less surprised than I knew he was.

"What if he decides to kill me!" I suddenly realized that I was going to have a fully trained knight of a greater house in my cave.

"He is not going to kill you," Lord Grath turned back to me.

"We won't let him." Adenern laughed.

"Will not," corrected the lord, "but you will not be here."

"WHAT!" both of us bellowed.

"It would look like we were holding Lady Ari'an hostage if too many are here," Renard spoke. "Also, we do not want to overwhelm him since he is only coming to see his daughter and determine her condition."

"That's easy for you to say," I snapped at my diplomatically correct brother. "You're not the one who's going to die if he decides he doesn't like you."

"How is he going to get here, if Renard and I don't bring you and him?" Adenern asked Lord Grath.

The question gave me hope, until the answer came, "You know that Caer Corisan has winged horses in their stables."

"I'm going to die," I muttered.

"You are not going to die," Lord Grath glared at me.

"He already thinks I'm a beast that's keeping his daughter against her will," I retorted. "What's going to keep him from trying to rescue her from my evil clutches!"

"He did not say you were holding his daughter captive." He was beginning to get angry, but I was a little more concerned about my own skin at the moment.

"He did call us beasts," Adenern put in.

Lord Grath took a deep breath before saying with only a slight quiver to his voice, "If you want, I will voice your concerns to him and insist on his swearing no harm to you on this visit."

"Oh," Adenern put in, "so *next* time he can kill him."

The glare turned on him. "Why are you two so hard to reason with?"

Adenern looked at me with a twinkle in his eye, and I knew exactly how to answer. "We get it from our mother," we said at the same time.

Even Renard laughed as Lord Grath threw his hands up in disgust.

"I will personally make sure that he does not kill you," he finally answered. He still sounded angry, but there was a hint of amusement in his voice. "Since he plans to arrive within a week, he is already traveling, so do not try to convince me to delay him."

I was about to respond when I noticed Lady Ari'an over Lord Grath's shoulder. She looked extremely lost in the doorway to her room. "Is something wrong, my lady?" I asked, moving away from the fire toward her.

The other two dragons and the lord turned to make sure she was all right. She turned her head toward my voice, but her eyes didn't focus. She glanced at Lord Grath for a moment then at her hands. She flicked a pointed finger at him that most people would have missed.

"Would you like for Lord Grath to come over here?" I asked, beginning a well-known game to try to find out what she wanted.

The shake of her head answered.

"Would you like his help with something?"

Another shake.

I sighed, knowing that this could take a while.

I searched for another question as Lady Ari'an slowly flattened her hands into a sheet and held them slightly in front of her.

"The letter?" I started, a smile creeping across my face. She hadn't done anything but point, nod, or shake her head before. "Would you like to see the letter?"

I glowed as she nodded.

"Lord Grath will have to bring it over," I told her. If I tried, the thing would be in tatters when it arrived, a condition which is not particularly good for letters.

She ducked her head for a moment, then slowly nodded. The progress was slow, but she was a bit more comfortable with Lord Grath now. She wouldn't come near to him, but she didn't hide in terror anymore. I'd told her many times that he wasn't going to hurt her, but four years of men doing nothing but hurting her battled against my word.

Lord Grath walked over slowly and held the letter out to her. Moments passed as I watched her gather her courage and reach for the letter. Once it was in her hand, Lord Grath backed a few steps away, turned, and walked back to the fire.

She watched him sit and begin talking to the other two dragons. Slowly she brought the letter close enough to her to be able to read in the flickering light. She stared at the paper for a long time then folded it to complete the broken seal. The three at the fire turned suddenly toward her when they heard her gasp.

This seal couldn't exist. They'd told me it didn't exist. This was the standard of the House of Nori'en, a winged horse and a winged lion harnessed to a messenger's chariot. We were the crossroads of the realm. All the other domains bordered ours, so all messages went through our land. We knew how to travel faster than any other domain, except of course for the dragons of Maren, but were they even a part of the realm?

No, I wasn't a part of this. Even if the House of Nori'en existed, I didn't have their mark. I'd thought I did for a long time, but I didn't, or did I? I couldn't see the back of my neck where the mark was placed. Slowly I moved my hand to the back of my neck, rubbing the spot where the mark should have been.

"It is the same signet," the voice came across the room.

I glanced up to see Lord Grath staring at me.

"Your mark is the same as the signet of the House of Nori'en." I couldn't keep my eyes on him as he looked directly at me. "I can show you if you would like."

Quickly I glanced almost directly at him again, my eyes wide. How was that possible? I stared at him in disbelief.

"If you will bring me the mirror you have, I can show you." How could I look at the back of my neck with just one mirror?

Rising slowly I crept into my room without turning my back on the man. The mirror had been wrapped in the clothes of the first shipment. It was the only breakable thing that survived for the most part. It was a hand mirror with the handle and frame made out of mother of pearl. I loved just looking at the colors even though the frame had broken off at the top. The mirror had cracked down the middle and had a chip out of the top as well. I ran my hand over the beautiful colors that flickered in the dim light. It was still lovely even though it was broken.

I walked back into the room still staring at the mirror. When I looked up, I backed against the wall in fear. The only person in the room was the lord. The dragons were gone. I started breathing hard. He would certainly hurt me now for not letting him have me before.

I felt my hands begin to shake as he said, "This way, my lady." Then he bowed and walked into the room of pools.

If I didn't follow him, I'd be safe. The dragons would come back soon. Wouldn't they? Why had they left at all? What had I done wrong to make them all desert me? I felt the tears in my eyes.

Then I heard Narden's voice from the room of pools, "That should be enough for her to see by."

Were all the dragons in there? I took a few deep breaths and crept toward the doorway. Kneeling down, I peeked around the corner to see all three dragons approaching the lord from different parts of the room. Torchlight danced on the walls sparkling off the many pools. I fought back the tears of relief. They hadn't abandoned me. They'd never abandon me. I rose and crept into the room.

"If you step up to this one," Lord Grath said looking at me from near the middle of the many pools.

I glanced at Narden, who smiled and whispered, "It's all right."

I would have to walk toward this man, away from the dragons. I didn't want to, but if he hadn't harmed me when we were alone, I reasoned to myself, why would he now when there were three dragons watching?

I placed one foot in front of the other until I was ten steps away. He stepped back from the pool and away from me, leaving me plenty of room to reach the pool without coming close to him. I watched this carefully. He wasn't going to ever hurt me, I finally realized. For a moment I met his eyes, but couldn't hold mine there. He didn't think I was trash. He never had.

"If you will move the hair from the back of your neck and hold the mirror behind your head, you will be able to see your mark in the mirror's reflection in the pool," he instructed.

I stared at the back of the mirror for a moment. I knew this trick. Why hadn't I thought of it before? Pher'am and I had used this technique to see the back of our heads after the maids fixed our hair for special occasions. That was only if Pher'am was real and not just someone I made up like the priests had told me. If I did indeed have the mark of the House of Nori'en on the back of my neck, maybe Pher'am was real as well.

Pulling my hair away from the back of my neck, I positioned the mirror behind my head. Taking a deep breath, I looked into the pool.

I hated the face that stared back at me. Her eyes still had that tired and dead look to them. Her skin and hair were clean this time, and the green dress she wore did look nice. It hung from her like a sack though. She was far too thin and her cheeks sunk in. They weren't quite as hollow as last time. I could see all the sinews in her neck, and the scar. Perhaps one day her body would fill out again. Maybe then her face wouldn't be so thin.

With all of the good food the dragons brought me here, I wouldn't be able to see all her bones when I changed clothes soon. Some day those eyes might laugh, but that scar. The scar would be there for the rest of her life. Whenever someone looked at her, they would know that something wasn't right. The rope-burn scars on her wrists and ankles would give it away too.

I stared at the wrist holding the mirror for a long time. That scar was deep. The wound still hurt sometimes if I bumped my hand on something, but it had stopped sporadically bleeding two weeks ago. The wound in my side where Narden clawed me was almost well too. Narden told me often that I would be well soon, but I didn't believe him. My scars ran too deep.

Slowly my vision moved from my wrist to the mirror reflected in the pool. Finally, I focused on the back of my neck, and collapsed to my knees. I started shaking violently. I couldn't stop. I heard one of the dragons race from the room with the others following. Lord Grath knelt where he was and gently tried to calm me with his voice. I couldn't understand the words. My mind was racing too fast.

They'd lied. They'd all lied. I wasn't one of them. I was never supposed to be there. I was a noble of the House of Nori'en. I had the mark.

Anger and terror battled with relief inside of me. I felt something soft fall on my back, brushing my face. I clutched at the blanket pulling it up to my eyes. I managed to set the mirror down without breaking it any further. Behind me, I heard the man say something and then walk from the room. Tears blurred my vision, but I saw a blue shape come in front of me. I couldn't focus to see his eyes, but I put my hand on his nose.

The sobs escaped from her like a dam breaking. I quivered from the howls. I waved Renard, Adenern, and Lord Grath away with my tail when they raced back into the room. Slowly they backed out again. Throwing her head back she wailed at the top of her lungs.

I didn't say anything. Four years of walls were beginning to crumble in her mind. "Mighty One, have mercy," I whispered and continued praying for her silently.

It seemed like watches before she stopped sobbing only to replace the sobs with gasping. Painfully slowly, she began to breathe normally and the tears stopped. Finally she wiped her face on her sleeve and looked at me.

"Thank you," she mouthed, and her eyes focused on her hands.

My own eyes widened, and my jaw hung open like a hole in the roof.

CHAPTER 8

A LORD'S CALL

I sat alone in the entrance to my cave the day Lord Cristeros would arrive. Lady Ari'an was bathing in the other room. Occasionally, I could hear a splash from the pools. I was dreading the lords' arrival. If Lord Cristeros did try to attack me, what was I supposed to do? Roasting Lady Ari'an's father in front of her eyes wasn't an option. With my coordination, even trying to just knock him off balance with my tail so Lord Grath could disarm him would probably end in some serious bruises, if not broken bones. If I tried to defend myself, it would probably be seen as an act of aggression. Renard was the expert on social graces. It certainly was not my area, not that I really had one anyway.

I let out yet another sigh and glanced around. I could see Lady Ari'an peeking around the doorframe. I smiled at her and told her that the visitors hadn't arrived yet.

She walked up behind me and cautiously peered over my tail through the entrance. My nervousness wasn't helping her. I knew that. We both needed something to take our minds off the impending meeting.

"Would you like to go for a ride?" I asked and laughed at her wide-eyed response.

I'd taken her for rides before, but she always looked at me as though I'd lost my head when I asked. She didn't even wait to nod but turned and raced to get my saddle.

One of the things I vaguely remembered from before the temple was wanting to ride a flying horse. I was sure that riding a dragon had to be quite a bit different, but it was still a wonderful experience. The first time did make me a bit queasy, but I'd gotten used to it.

When I returned with the heavy saddle in my arms, Narden was behind me. Lifting the saddle was hard for me, but he couldn't help because he couldn't angle it just right to get the equipment on his back.

He lay down on the cave floor. With a swing that threw me against his side, I landed the saddle on his neck. I scrambled up his leg and pulled the saddle onto his back. Sliding back down, I grabbed a girth. I had all of them pulled tight in a moment, and Narden shook, ruffling his scales. He always did that just after being saddled.

Once more I climbed his leg and settled into the saddle. The stirrups were longer for a dragon's saddle than a horse's, because people didn't have to put as much pressure on the sides. A simple nudge would do when someone wanted the dragon to change directions. That was only a suggestion anyway, because the dragon certainly didn't have to obey the person. There were also no reigns, but there was a ring on the saddle to hold on to if someone needed more balance, as well as some straps to keep people from falling off.

I clutched the ring as Narden ran to the entrance and leapt out. The drop before his wings lifted us always scared me, but not enough to refuse the next ride he offered.

I wanted to throw my arms out and laugh, but I couldn't bring myself either to let go of the ring or make such a deliberate sound.

Narden had told me some of the leg commands, and I asked him to dive with a tap of my toes to his shoulders. He glanced back to make sure I'd used the right command, and I nodded. I saw him laugh as he pulled his wings in and shot down nose first. I asked him to pull out of it with a tap of my heels to his flank. I knew he would have plummeted longer, but I just wasn't brave enough yet. I asked him to spiral upward, and he laughed as we left the trees far below. He'd told me how to ask for a loop, and even though I wanted to see how it felt to be upside down in midair, I wasn't brave enough yet for that either.

Circling back toward the mountain and Narden's cave, I threw my head back and laughed silently. He'd never seen me do that yet, but sometimes I just felt too happy not to. Normally, I would slip into my room or the room of pools and hide next to the door, but he couldn't quite see me on his back either. I wished I could stay up there and never have to think about anything but circling and diving. Thoughts of the temple still haunted me, and often tortured me in my dreams, but up in the air with nothing to remind me, I almost felt free.

Sometimes, I would close my eyes and see a young girl jumping over ponds in a faraway garden where nothing ever truly went wrong. Things happened to that little girl that she thought were the end of the world, but they were minor setbacks that lasted no more than a day. Sometimes, up here, I could almost be that little girl again.

I don't know how long we stayed up there, but all too soon Narden headed back to the cave. I braced myself for the carriage crash. When he landed the first time that I went flying with him, the impact would have thrown me out of the saddle if it weren't for the straps holding me. This time, I lurched forward at the impact and landed hard and slightly lopsided in the saddle. I could certainly understand why Lord Grath insisted that Narden work on his landings.

The last pass over the mountain revealed two small dots in the distance. I knew what they were and that Lady Ari'an had not seen them. As she slid from the saddle, I glanced back at her. Her eyes were shining, and her cheeks were red from the air rushing past. She almost looked like she would smile at any moment. This would be a good time for Lord Cristeros to come.

Glancing out the cave entrance, I saw the horses and their riders clearly now. Lord Cristeros looked like he might be airsick. I fought a grin and turned to wander into the room of pools. Glancing at Lady Ari'an, I saw that she was focused on the approaching riders as well. Her expression was far less amused than I knew mine was. Although her cheeks were still flushed from the ride, the rest of her face was deathly pale.

"We talked about this visit, remember?" I told her softly.

Turning her head, her eyes focused on my nose. "Your father is coming to see how you are. He's not going to hurt you."

She followed me into the room of pools, and we both waited in the shadows of the doorway as the two men and their horses landed.

Lord Cristeros dismounted first and leaned on the saddle for a moment. Lord Grath dismounted looking far less green. He'd told me several times that riding a winged horse was far easier than riding a dragon, so I didn't expect him to look sick. Maybe it was better for them to come on the horses instead of dragons after all.

As Lord Grath secured the horses, I felt Lady Ari'an's hand on my side and turned to look at her. A shocked look spread across her face as she stared at the two men.

"It's all right," I whispered. "He's your father."

I knew this man standing next to Lord Grath. I glanced at Narden as he whispered to me. He was right. That was my father! He'd told me for several days now that this man was coming to visit me, but I hadn't believed it could be my father.

A rush of memories flooded me as I closed my eyes. I didn't know this man from the temple. I'd never seen him there. This man . . . I'd danced with this man. Sometimes, I would place my feet on his, and he would dance for both of us. That was so long ago. It was as though someone else's life played through my mind. This man had never hurt me like the priests, breeders, or customers had. I felt tears in my eyes and fought to hold them back.

"Lady Ari'an," I heard the now familiar voice of Lord Grath call, "there is someone here to see you."

I looked at Narden. What if this man who knew the girl I once was, didn't believe I was the same person? I didn't believe it at times. How could I expect him to? I shook my head at Narden.

"It's all right," he said the familiar words. "He won't hurt you." There was a pause, then he added, "Please, go see him."

How could he ask me to do that? I wanted to run away from the door and hide in a dark corner where no one could find me, but Narden had asked. He'd asked me to go meet this man that I once knew.

Closing my eyes, I forcefully commanded my feet to walk out of the door, and nearly fell over when they obeyed. After taking a few steps, I curtsied and opened my eyes in the light of the entrance.

The man looked horrified. I knew I shouldn't have come out. I wasn't who he thought I would be. I wasn't the girl he was looking for. She had disappeared years ago, and I didn't believe she would ever come back.

"Ari'an," I heard his voice crack with the name.

The voice was the same as I remembered it. He took a step toward me, and I cringed. I didn't want him to come any closer, but my years at the temple had taught me not to back away from a man. I still did sometimes, but I wasn't supposed to. I wished Narden was out here. Then, I could've hid from this man behind him, but now, I was alone.

I raised my head and opened my eyes, Lord Grath held my father's arm, keeping him from coming any closer.

"Ari'an," the man's voice was a bit stronger now, "do you know who I am?"

I stared at my hands and slowly nodded just once. I hoped he wouldn't hit me for answering.

"You know I'm your father?" I heard him take a step forward.

I cringed slightly, but managed to nod again.

I heard movement behind this man and glanced up to see Lord Grath untying a bundle from one of the horses.

The new man followed my gaze as Lord Grath walked back to him. The man took the bundle from him and turned back to face me.

"I brought you a present," he said and took another step toward me.

I wanted to run, but I knew I shouldn't. The bag twitched, and I stepped backward. Certainly, he wouldn't bring rats, would he?

"It's all right," Narden's voice came from past the doorway.

The man froze and looked into the darkness. The slight look of fear that passed over his face surprised me. I'd thought men weren't afraid of anything. The priests and customers at the temple certainly weren't. They'd laughed at my fear as though it was a joke. It took the man a moment to compose himself and look back at me.

Lord Grath walked up slowly to stand behind him. "He will not harm you," he said. I wasn't sure if he said it to me or to this man.

That made me feel the tiniest bit better. If this man was afraid of Narden, maybe I didn't have to be afraid of him. The thought was comforting, but it didn't take my fear away completely.

Slowly, he pulled his eyes away from the darkened doorway and looked back at me. Occasionally, he glanced back into the shadows as he began slowly walking toward me. I had to hold my ground. I had to keep from shaking. I wanted to scream, but somehow I concentrated on just breathing instead.

He stopped ten steps away. I could see the embroidery on his shirt. I'd never seen that shirt before, but I recognized it as a visiting shirt. It was a fancier one used to visit other nobility. His wife probably stitched the design on it. It too bore the seal of the House of Nori'en, only in far more colors than the wax seal of the letter. The lion was in gold while the horse was white. The harnesses were in blue while the chariot shone silver. All were against the burgundy background of the shirt. His cloak was blue while the breaches were beige. It was a traveling outfit except for the shirt. Why had he worn that shirt while traveling?

"It is the seal of our house," the voice startled me out of my thoughts.

I met the man's eyes by accident. They begged for recognition from me. I looked away and nodded with my eyes closed.

"Your mother suggested that I wear it to meet you," the man continued. "She thought it might help you remember."

Opening my eyes, I focused on the design again. Vaguely, I recalled a woman teaching me those stitches. At one time, I could have made a shirt like that. A sound from the bundle in the man's hand returned my attention there. That hadn't sounded like rats.

"Would you like to see what I brought you?" his voice was gentle, reminding me of Narden.

I continued to stare at the bag and nodded.

He took a step toward me, and I began to back away toward the room of pools. He took another step and began to open the bag. What if this was a trick? The thought ran through my mind. What if there was something horrible in that bag? Lord Grath was too far away to stop whatever was in the bag. What if he was only pretending to have a present for me, but really he was going to grab me when he came closer?

Narden couldn't do anything if the man already had me. He would take me back. I turned to race back into the darkness. I heard footsteps behind me. A hand wrapped around my arm.

"Ari'an," his voice was near my ear.

I turned for a moment to face the man. I'd started to shake. I screamed. My knees wouldn't hold me. His grip didn't lessen, but the floor came closer. My knees collided with the rocks. I tried to pull my arm away. It wouldn't come.

"Ari'an," the voice was just as close, but not as harsh.

"Let her go!" I'd never heard Narden sound like that before.

The man wasn't looking at me anymore. He was staring over my shoulder. He looked as terrified as I felt.

Slowly, I turned my head. That wasn't Narden, was it? That dragon looked at least twice the size of Narden, and he had blue with gold-tipped spikes all over his body.

"Let her go," the dragon growled. It was Narden's voice, but he was livid. He was far past the temper he showed to his brothers, father, or Lord Grath.

I felt the hand release my arm. I felt the man stand and step back. Then I heard the ring of a sword being drawn. I glanced over my shoulder to see the man looking a bit bolder facing off with Narden.

"Lord Cristeros," I heard Lord Grath say from a distance, "I do not believe you want to duel him." He sounded like the calmest one of the group.

The contrast between his voice and Narden's almost made me laugh hysterically.

"Put your sword away, and he will stand down," Lord Grath continued.

"Not until I have rescued my daughter from this monster," Lord Cristeros said with venom in his voice.

"MONSTER!" Narden bellowed, and I saw smoke rise from his nostrils.

"Monsters," he growled, "are men who lock others in chains just because they are different and can't help it."

"Monsters locked your daughter up and used her for four years," his snarl shook the walls menacingly.

"What is it that you call yourself," the man sneered back, "since you are keeping her against her will?"

"I am not keeping her against her will!" The shout loosened rocks from the walls, which skidded down and piled on the floor.

"Lord Cristeros"—Lord Grath had stepped forward to stand just behind the man—"perhaps you should ask Lady Ari'an herself if she is a captive here."

There was a long pause, but the two never broke eye contact. "Ari'an," the man said, "this beast is keeping you here as his prisoner, correct?"

I shook my head, still in the crumpled heap on the floor. Narden keep me against my will? He'd impale himself first.

"She is too terrified of you even to answer," the man's voice was nasty.

"You idiot," Narden snarled, "Lord Grath told you she hasn't spoken since she's been here."

"Then how is she supposed to answer?" the man snarled back.

Before Narden could growl something back, Lord Grath interrupted. "She has answered you"—the man's eyes flicked toward him for a moment but did not stay—"the same way she answered about remembering you or wanting the present." He continued, "She either shakes her head or nods."

"I'm not taking my eyes off this beast so he can tear off my head," the man snapped.

"Then you are at a standstill," Lord Grath said with a calmness that impressed me. "He is not going to let you take her against her will, and you are obviously not going to trust me enough to ask Lady Ari'an yourself."

"What does trusting you have to do with this beast imprisoning my daughter?" the man snapped.

Lord Grath began in that eerily calm voice, "I have staked my life with these *beasts*, as you call them, countless times and have never been disappointed in them. I trust them entirely and would not have brought her here if I had the faintest notion that they might keep her here against her will."

"May the gods curse you if you are lying to me," the man muttered at Lord Grath and then asked me again, "Is this beast keeping you here against your will?"

He looked over at me. I shook my head. He didn't look like he believed me.

"Would you like to come home with me to your mother?" he asked glancing at Narden out of the corner of his eye.

The question took me by surprise. I stared past his ear at Lord Grath for a moment then shook my head. I couldn't go back. I didn't belong among those people. I was filthy, and I couldn't wash it off. They would never accept me. I jumped to my feet as the man stepped toward me again.

"You cannot mean that," he said sounding hurt.

"Leave her alone," rumbled the dragon, and the man's eyes immediately returned to his.

I backed toward Narden.

"Enough," Lord Grath said still calmly, but forcefully. "You have your answers, Lord Cristeros. Now, if you would like to talk to her anymore, you need to respect her wishes."

Slowly he lowered the sword till the point rested against the floor. I crept around Narden till I couldn't see either man anymore. Narden brought his head around to look at me.

"Are you all right?" he asked in the soft tones I was used to.

I nodded and rested my hand on his nose. He opened his mouth to say something, I heard Lord Grath yell from the other side, and Narden bellowed in pain. Both his tail and his head whipped around. I saw the man's sword fly across the cave from the impact of Narden's tail. The blade sank half its length into the wall near the ceiling.

"You son of a leech!" Narden bellowed drawing a breath.

The man again looked terrified, but that didn't matter to me. Blood was running from a huge gash in Narden's leg.

"Narden!" Lord Grath yelled stepping between him and his target. "He's unarmed."

"AND I WASN'T LOOKING!" flames escaped toward the ceiling as he bellowed.

"ENOUGH!" Lord Grath yelled.

Narden studied him for a moment staring over his shoulder at the man behind him.

"Where is your honor, my lord?" Narden spit out as he took a step back and lowered his head.

"It is time to leave, Lord Cristeros," Lord Grath said turning toward the shaken man. "Perhaps, if the two of you are calmer, you may return to visit your daughter tomorrow."

The man backed toward his horse and glanced up at his sword.

"That will be returned to you," Lord Grath said evenly without looking up, "only if Narden sees fit."

The two mounted the horses. Lord Grath turned toward the exit while the man chose to back his horse without taking his eyes off Narden. He finally turned, and both horses jumped out of the entrance and soared into the sky.

CHAPTER 9

PATCHING A DRAGON

Narden watched for a moment then turned and began limping toward the room of pools leaving a trail of blood behind him.

At the entrance he turned to me and said, "My lady, I'm going to need your help for a little while." He sighed looking at me. "After that, I will fully understand if you want to scream or cry or shake, but please, try to focus for a little while."

The spikes on his body were beginning to lie back down, and I realized that they were scales and that he had another layer of scales underneath.

I looked at his face and nodded weakly.

"There is a box on a shelf to the right of the door to your room. It has a knife and scraper and some other things in it," he said shifting his weight off his hurt leg. "Will you bring it?"

He turned before I could nod my reply and continued into the room of pools. I hurried to my room, giving the sack that was left on the floor from that man a wide berth.

I'd seen the box before, but never opened it. I knew better than to touch things that weren't mine. I hurried back into the room of pools with it.

Several of the torches were lit illuminating the pools. Narden lay with his leg in one of the coldest pools. Adenern stood next to him. How had he gotten here without me noticing? I stared at him frozen to the spot.

"Well, you could have helped," I heard Narden snap as he glanced up at me.

"You seemed to have it completely under control," Adenern said. "Plus if Father found out I was here and not on patrol, half of his hair would turn white."

Narden's head snapped back around at him as Adenern looked up at me, appearing slightly startled.

"Anyway"—he smiled—"if you're sure you can handle everything, I have to get back. Renard's covering for me, but I don't want to push my luck with Lord Grath heading back to Caer Corisan."

He turned and walked to the other side of the room, disappearing into one of a dozen other openings into the room. "Good day to you, my lady." He turned back and bobbed his head at me before disappearing.

I stared at the darkened cavern he'd walked into until Narden passed in front of me limping toward one of the hotter pools.

He glanced back at me then at where Adenern had left.

"I'll take you to see his cave sometime. I'm just waiting for him to get it cleaned up a bit. I was so glad to find out that I didn't have to share a cave with him when we moved in." He smiled though his voice was tense with pain. "He is such a slob."

I should have guessed that there were more dragons living through those openings, but I'd never seen any others enter or exit them before. I followed Narden glancing over at the opening wondering if anyone else would walk in or if anyone was watching.

Narden lay down next to one of the hottest pools and looked directly at me. Accidentally, I looked into his eyes for a moment. They still looked angry, but were calming. I quickly looked down at the box in my hands.

"My lady," he began, "I'm going to ask you to do something that you're not going to like, but I need you to trust me."

I stiffened a bit and felt a chill run through my body. I looked up at his nose.

"I've never told you this before, but dragons have three layers of scales," he continued.

I could feel him studying my reaction.

"The outside layer, the third set, can be stood up as an intimidation tactic, sort of like a cat puffing up its fur. You saw me do that out there." He nodded his head toward his cave. "That set also doesn't have any feeling like your hair or nails. Do you understand?"

I nodded. It made sense.

"That layer is used for bandaging cuts, but I can't do that part by myself. I need you to cut off a section to put on my leg." He paused.

I took a step back horrified. He wanted me to cut him? I'd hurt him. I wouldn't! I felt the tears in my eyes. I felt his breath, and I looked up. For the second time in only a few moments, I looked into his eyes. They weren't angry anymore. He was in pain, but he was being patient. I shook my head and looked away.

"Ari"—he gasped cringing slightly as he shook his leg a bit—"I need you to do this for me. You won't hurt me, if you do what I say."

I shook my head again.

"I might bleed to death if you don't help me," he said, with a twinge of pain in his voice.

I studied his nose for a moment.

"Please?"

Slowly, I nodded.

I heard the smile in his voice. "All right then"—he lay down on the side without the injured leg—"if you will just open up that box."

I opened it to find three different knives. The blades were at odd angles. There was also two scrapers, one with a wide blade, and the other a narrow one, along with a large ball of twine. I took a deep breath setting the box on the ground with a shudder.

"You'll need the big knife first, and if you would work on my shoulder, please, I would appreciate it," he said watching me.

I looked at him, puzzled.

He glanced around, probably to see if anyone was watching. "My sides are a bit ticklish," he whispered.

Had I not held a knife in my hands about to cut open someone I truly cared about, I might have laughed at the thought of a dragon being ticklish.

"Now, that's a good enough spot," he said lightly.

I lay the knife up against the scales on his shoulder, my hand trembling.

"You're going to cut down perpendicular to the way the scales grow, all right?" he said softly.

I nodded and began to pull the blade down.

"You'll need to press harder than that."

I pressed a tiny bit harder.

"A bit more."

I leaned my weight against the knife and heard a popping sound. I froze. I was going to kill him.

"That's perfect, now just saw down a little, but try not to go any deeper."

I nodded, forcing my hand not to shake as I cut down.

"Very nice. You can stop there. Now, if you will just turn the knife so you can run the blade parallel to the scales. I'll tell you when to stop."

This cut was much longer than the first, and I felt Narden cringe at one point, but I wasn't sure if it was because of his leg or me.

"All right," he said.

I glanced up to see him smiling at me.

"You're doing great, now just make the same length of cut above the first one."

Obediently, I continued cutting across his shoulder. I stopped when the cut was the same length as the last one.

"We're almost done. Grab the little scraper and put it where you made the first cut. Very good. Now just pry up those scales a bit. Perfect. Now grab the big one, and do the same thing working your way around."

This was better than using the knife until I got stuck.

"You didn't cut quite deep enough there, so grab one of the smaller knives and just slice through that piece of scale."

I did as he said, hating using another knife on him. I pried off the rest of the scales without incident.

"Nicely done. You could be a physician at Caer Corisan, though you probably wouldn't want to be. They don't get a lot of respect from most people. Now if you will just put that over the slice on my leg there. Perfect. Now tie it down with a bit of that twine at both ends. Wonderful!"

Narden lifted his injured leg, shook it, cringed slightly, and then plunged it into the boiling pool. I gasped stumbling backward. Was he trying to burn himself now? He pulled his leg out after a moment and cut the two pieces of twine with his claws.

"Don't worry," he said glancing at me and my horror-stricken face, "I have to seal it so it doesn't fall off. I doubt you want to do that again anytime soon." He laughed. "Also, I don't burn as easily as you do." He winked and started limping toward his cave.

I glanced at the other openings around the room and quickly followed him.

CHAPTER 10

A FATHER'S GIFTS

Well, that had gone about as well as I'd expected. No one was dead, but I had a nasty injury. I tried to keep myself from thinking nasty things about Lady Ari'an's father. It wouldn't help her if I didn't like him, and it certainly wouldn't make Lord Grath happy.

When we'd walked back into my cave, I settled near the entrance and rolled onto my back. Watching the birds and occasional mouse, deer, horse, or rabbit fly by from this angle was always amusing. I glanced at Lady Ari'an, who was watching me with an odd look on her face.

"I'm keeping my leg elevated," I explained as the sack that Lord Cristeros had brought made a noise.

Both of us turned to look at it. The sack moved slightly and fell over. Lady Ari'an backed away from the wriggling bag.

"Why don't you open it and see what he brought you?" I suggested, if for no other reason than I wanted to know what live animal was in there.

Lady Ari'an responded by looking at me as though I had spontaneously sprouted another head. Obviously, her curiosity wasn't as strong as mine was.

"I'm sure whatever he brought isn't going to hurt you," I tried to reassure her.

She backed farther away from the bag.

"Oh, come on," I snapped, "I don't want whatever's in there to suffocate or starve. How would that look?" I screwed up my face. "That monster wouldn't even let her open the present I brought her after we left. I told you I should have taken her from his clutches then," I mocked in my best Lord Cristeros voice.

Lady Ari'an looked surprised and slightly taken aback, but she started toward the sack. Each time it moved or made a sound, she took a step back and looked at me. I was pretending not to watch. I didn't want to snap at her again, and with the temper I was in, that was becoming more and more of a possibility.

Eventually, she reached the bag and slowly pulled the drawstring, jumping back as she did. The bag twitched, and a paw reached out to snatch at the drawstring. Lady Ari'an gasped, and I rolled over slightly for a better view. She knelt down on the floor and watched the sack. It continued to twitch and make sounds. The drawstring swung back out, and a moment later a calico kitten flew out of the bag to pounce on it. Lady Ari'an let out another gasp and scuffled to the still twitching sack.

She ran her hand along the kitten's back, and the kitten rolled over to bat at her fingers. She giggled, and I caught my breath. Out of the sack rolled two more kittens locked in a wrestling match. One was black with a white tuft on his neck, and the other was a brown tabby with white socks, nose, chin, and beard. Lady Ari'an giggled again at that, and I continued to hold my breath.

Standing, she raced to her bedroom and returned with a hair ribbon. The kittens each dove at it, occasionally, wrestling each other for it. She let out another gasp as the black kitten spread its wings and launched himself at the middle of the ribbon. Not an experienced flier, he missed and landed on the tabby and white that jumped up, shuffled backward, and tried to be intimidating by arching its back and hissing. Being slightly bigger than Lady Ari'an's hand, the stance was less than effective, but rather humorous.

She laughed. I thought I was going to fall out of the cave. She really laughed. The kittens tackled each other on the floor and pounced on the ribbon. Lady Ari'an ran over to me and met my eyes for a moment. The smile on her face vanished as she looked away. After a moment, she tugged on my wing and pointed to the kittens.

"They are silly kittens, aren't they?" I laughed.

I saw the corners of her mouth tip up in a smile, and she nodded.

"Your father brought you a good gift," I said, partly just to hear myself say something nice about him.

Lady Ari'an froze, the smile disappearing from her face. She looked up at me with a puzzled expression. She glanced at my leg and then back at the kittens.

"Don't worry," I said standing up and skirting around the kittens, who all arched their backs and hissed. I stifled a snicker. A kitten trying to scare off a dragon was a funny sight to me.

"He has the common misconceptions about dragons." I forced myself to laugh. "Most people go through their lives thinking we're heartless, mindless, brutal monsters who will eat you as soon as look at you." I forced myself to sound far less sarcastic than I wanted to.

I glanced back at Lady Ari'an standing with her back to the darkening sky. Some of the light played in her red gold hair. She glanced at the kittens, who had managed to tangle themselves up in the hair ribbon. She smiled slightly. *She's turning into a beautiful young lady*, I thought as I wandered back to start a fire.

Lord Grath and Lord Cristeros returned the next day. I have to admit that this visit went somewhat better. Lady Ari'an sat at the back of the cave leaning against my side with the three kittens asleep on her lap. She had been dozing off and on for a while. She simply refused to disturb the kittens when they fell asleep.

The two lords landed, and Lord Cristeros looked quite a bit less airsick this time. I felt Lady Ari'an tense next to me, but she didn't scream, bolt, or start shaking. She watched him through fear widened eyes as he approached. He came quite a bit closer than Lord Grath ever had, and I could feel Lady Ari'an's muscles becoming tighter with each step. What seemed to help her, though, was the fact that Lord Cristeros kept on glancing nervously at me every couple of steps. I had half a mind to yell something, just to see what he would do.

He was well within my burn-to-a-crisp range when he stopped. I noticed that he hadn't replaced his sword, which I felt was a show of trust on his part, so I resisted blowing smoke to spook him.

Crouching down to be level with Lady Ari'an, he softly said, "Hello again."

Lady Ari'an glanced up and then shifted her eyes away.

"I realize that I scared you yesterday," he continued, glancing at me, "and I would like to apologize."

I cocked an eyebrow.

"I was under the wrong impression regarding your state of mind, and I thought you would not mind my touching you seeing that I am you father," he continued. To his credit, he kept his eyes on her face even though she didn't look up at him.

"Do you understand?" he asked when she didn't respond.

She nodded slightly.

"Would you mind if I came closer?" he asked with a half laugh.

She closed her eyes and nodded her head ever so slightly.

"You do not want me to come closer?" he sounded surprised and slightly hurt.

With her eyes still closed, she bobbed her head a tiny bit again.

Straightening back up, he said, "I see." Then he glanced at me with a slight glare.

I glared back and bristled a bit, but he had already turned and was walking back to the horse where there was an odd-shaped parcel tied to the saddle. Lord Grath shook his head slightly at me and mouthed, "Do not."

I felt Lady Ari'an shift slightly, and I glanced over to find her looking at me. When my scales raised, I must have jabbed her in the back.

"Sorry," I mouthed. I took a deep breath, settling my scales as Lord Cristeros turned to face us again.

"I am pleased that you like the kittens I brought," he said taking a few steps.

She looked up to about the man's knees then back down at her lap. The kittens had begun to stir, and one was rolling across Lady Ari'an's lap playing with the buttons on her dress.

"I brought you another gift today," he continued, coming to a stop where he had knelt before.

I could almost feel the effort it took for her to look at what the man held, but when she did, she immediately caught her breath. He held a ya'tar, a twenty-stringed instrument held against the shoulder and strummed. I had occasionally seen Lady Ari'an practicing this very instrument in the gardens when I would fly over Torion Castle. I wondered what Lord Cristeros would have said if he'd known how often I flew over his home. I smiled slightly at the thought.

Lady Ari'an rose to her feet, the kittens tumbling to the floor, and took a step forward. Then she seemed to realize what she was doing. With a start, she stepped backward and bumped into me.

"You can take it if you'd like," I told her reassuringly.

"Must she receive permission from you to accept gifts from her own father?" Lord Cristeros said darkly.

"What?" I turned my head to glare at the lord.

Lord Grath tactfully stepped between the two of us. Lady Ari'an shifted fearfully. Lord Grath was less than seven steps from her, but at least his back was to her.

"I believe you may have misunderstood Narden," he began calmly. "He often encourages Lady Ari'an to help her overcome her fears in new situations," he explained.

Apparently, Lord Cristeros accepted that explanation, because when Lord Grath stepped away, his attention returned to Lady Ari'an. He did frequently throw me dark looks. I felt like blowing smoke at him just to see his reaction, but I knew Lord Grath would not be amused. I switched my tail irritably, for which Lord Grath added his own dark looks.

"What if I leave your ya'tar right here and you can take it after I back away?" Lord Cristeros suggested. He gently set the instrument on the floor and stepped back.

Lady Ari'an continued to watch him intently as he reached Lord Grath.

I knew this man, or I had known him once. He had a kind manner then. He spoke to me at every meal even when I wasn't supposed to answer. He often took over some of my lessons. He was the person who started teaching me the differences between riding a pony and a horse.

"Her horse would fetch a better price than that," the nasty man with the wagon had mumbled as he stalked back to his wagon at the temple. I'd barely heard him as the priests led me into the temple.

But that had never happened, had it? I'd always been at the temple. I'd imagined another life that I didn't deserve, they'd told me. They beat me until I believed it, but then how could this man from that fake life be standing here? How could I recognize an instrument that I'd never played sitting on the cave floor? Why did my fingers itch to brush the strings? Where were the songs running through my mind coming from, and why did I know what strings to play?

Narden didn't like this man, but he did tolerate him. The man didn't seem to like Narden either. Was one of them lying? I couldn't bring myself to believe that Narden would lie to me. He cared too much to lie to me, but that left this man as a liar. That didn't seem right to me either.

From that other life, I could vaguely remember hearing this man speak about the horrible beasts that the lords of Rem'maren tamed. Had he meant Narden? Indeed he was a dragon, but a horrible beast? That certainly didn't describe him.

"You can take it, if you would like," Narden's voice interrupted my thoughts.

I was still staring at the man. How long had I been standing there? I glanced at the ya'tar on the floor. I did want to pick it up, brush the strings, and maybe even play one of the songs racing through my mind. Would the man attack me if I moved away from Narden? The dragon was safe, but was this man?

"It's all right," Narden reassured me.

I wanted to believe him, but the man kept glaring at Narden anytime the dragon spoke. I glanced at the doorway to the room of pools, a plan forming in my mind. Slowly I took a step toward the instrument, never taking my eyes off this strange yet all too familiar man. He didn't move, but stopped glaring at Narden and looked hopefully at me. I paused. Would he be able to catch me? I glanced at the instrument again. It didn't appear to have any type of twine attached to it. Carefully watching for any change in the man's posture, I approached.

As quickly as I could, I snatched up the ya'tar, turned, and raced for the room of pools. I heard a yell behind me, then running footsteps. I could hide in there. It was dark, but I knew where everything was. This man did not. Narden would realize he was after me to hurt me. I'd be safe soon, and I would have my instrument. I turned right when I entered the room and raced into the darkness. Within twenty steps, I ran into a wall. I fell back stunned. There hadn't been a wall there before.

I stared at this new wall and saw a dim flash of gold move.

"Easy there," the wall spoke in a familiar voice.

I heard the running steps behind me. The man swore upon entering the room and not seeing me.

"Quick," Adenern whispered pushing me slightly sideways with his tail, "lie down against the wall."

I hurried to the wall making more noise than I should have. The footsteps started toward me. I lay against the wall on my stomach. I could see the man's silhouette against the doorway. Lord Grath stood behind him, but the view was blotted out. I felt Adenern lie next to me and lean against the wall above me. Then, as I touched his scales, I felt them grow rough.

"Narden," Lord Grath said in a muffled voice, "will you light some of the torches so we can see, please."

I heard the muffled sound of the dragon entering the room and a blast of fire. The man swore again and seemed to turn. A slight bit of light entered from under what looked to be a solid wall in front of me.

I glanced around at the gray rock, had Adenern moved a stone over me instead of himself? The rock felt warm though. I looked through the slit to see Narden glaring at the man who now had his back to me.

"If you don't want more light," he said with a quiver of anger in his voice, "you can certainly look for her in the dark."

"You scared her away, beast," the man's anger was far more pronounced.

"WHAT!" Narden roared, the sound bouncing off the walls as he ruffled his scales.

The man took a step back and laid his hand on his empty sword hilt.

Lord Grath stepped between them and looked pointedly at the man. "I believe Lady Ari'an would just like a few moments alone, my lord."

He shifted his pointed gaze upward to the rock I was under. I froze, terrified. I didn't want to give myself away.

"If you will accompany me into the entrance, she will most likely join us soon," Lord Grath continued.

"Will that stay here with my daughter?" the man asked vehemently.

"Narden will join us as well," Lord Grath said evenly.

"I am not leaving my back exposed to that beast," the man said; I could hear the glare in his voice.

"I could say the same thing," Narden spat back, but didn't say anything else when Lord Grath turned his face to him.

"You can come after him, if you wish," Lord Grath returned his gaze to the man.

"He would ambush me as I came out," the man said with an even tone of contempt.

"What? Unlike you—" Narden began, but Lord Grath cut him off with another look. He took a deep breath and continued to glare at the man.

"You will just have to trust him, my lord," Lord Grath said. His patience amazed me.

The man stood silently for a moment. "I suppose if it wanted to kill me, it would have by now."

Narden rolled his eyes and ruffled his scales again.

With even steps, the man made his way out of the room. He didn't stop watching Narden till he turned out the doorway. Narden rose to follow, but Lord Grath raised his hand, and the dragon lay back on the floor. Both watched the rock I was under. I wasn't surprised because I was certain that they knew this massive boulder hadn't been there before. Finally Lord Grath turned and exited the room. Narden held back a moment and grinned at the rock. Then, he left as well.

I felt the rock move and glanced up. I gasped as I watched the rock turn from a gray-and-black stone to blue-and-gold scales. The rough feel under my hand smoothed as I watched the change. Adenern chuckled lightly, took a few steps away, and shook his scales. Turning to me and grinning, he lay down.

"Father's going to kill me"—he laughed quietly, glancing over his shoulder at the door—"but that was fun."

Turning back he must have noticed the shocked look etched onto my face.

Moving his head closer, he whispered, "Don't tell anyone we can do that. It's one of the things that can save our skins in nasty situations." He grinned again and added with a shrug, "I have heard of other types of lizards being able to take on the colors of objects around them, but the texture thing is something no one's been able to explain yet." He looked lazily around the room. "The change isn't hard, but holding so still gives me nasty muscle cramps." He shook his scales again and returned to looking at me. "What do you have there?"

I looked down at my hands. My knuckles had turned white from clutching the instrument so hard. I relaxed my grip and held it out to him.

He whistled lightly, his eyes widening. "Is that your ya'tar? Did your father bring it?"

I wasn't sure how to answer. I guessed it was mine, since it had been given to me, but was that man my father? Sometimes I thought he was, but at other times I couldn't believe it. I glanced around confused.

"Can you still play it?" Adenern asked excitedly. "I haven't heard any real music since my last trip to Caer Corisan."

I looked down at the instrument. Still play? Had I ever played it at all? I passed my fingers over the strings gently. It was slightly out of tune. I sat down to tune it, turning the knobs and plucking the strings lightly as though I knew what to do. Memories flashed through my head, from when the orchestra master taught me long ago.

Was it even I that he'd taught? For a moment I could see the room I'd learned in. The carpet was a deep red that muffled the steps of the people who entered. Most of the castle didn't have carpet, but the orchestra master insisted on having it in that room. That way our focus, supposedly, remained on him and not the people entering the room. That man out there, my father, often came to listen to me play.

CHAPTER 11

TRUCE

The strings were tuned now. I could hear muffled voices from the other room. They sounded calmer, but not by much. I strummed at the strings aimlessly.

"Do you remember any songs?" Adenern asked, sounding like a child asking for a new toy.

I faintly recalled a song I'd learned.

It was the most complicated song I'd learned so far. The orchestra master had insisted I learn it, as had my mother and father. It was for the sending-away feast for Danren. I'd practiced for so long. I didn't want to disappoint anyone, especially not my parents. I also didn't want Dreanen to tease me about my bad playing. Dreanen didn't return with his father though.

The night came with all of the extra pomp given to such events. I felt as hot and stifled in my new dress as the stuffed birds that were to be served. Before the feast, the three children were to perform their pieces. Pher'am went first with her pipe. I'd always teased her that she played the tem'na because the orchestra master knew how much wind she had. Her song was far grander than mine was. Next Danren played. He made a few simple mistakes. He winked at me before sitting down. He'd made those mistakes on purpose to make me feel better. It had worked. I played my song flawlessly.

Someone used an oath nearby. It sounded like my father. Had I done something wrong? I focused on my hands and the instrument.

The rocky floor beneath me wasn't where I was supposed to be. I looked to the right at the pools ten steps away. I wasn't in the banquet hall. I was in the room of pools.

I heard a sound in front of me, but before I could turn my head to look, Adenern cut into my thoughts, "That was a beautiful song."

I turned my head and focused on him. I felt the edges of my mouth curl up. I heard Narden draw a quick breath and hold it from the doorway.

"Would you like to play another one?" Adenern asked.

I didn't know any other complex ones like that, but I knew a few easier ones that could sound complicated. I started to play one of those. I glanced up at Adenern, who was smiling with his eyes closed. I heard a sound in front of me again. I turned my head to look, expecting to see Narden. The instrument made a horrible noise as my hands clenched in fear.

I saw Lady Ari'an freeze with that look of absolute terror on her face. Soon she would start that violent shaking. I wanted to try to calm her, but her father was in my way. I couldn't get close enough to her to draw her focus. Maybe if I got her blanket quickly . . . but I didn't want to leave her alone with Lord Cristeros. He didn't understand that she was terrified of him.

I stood frozen in place watching as the scene in front of me continued.

"That was beautiful, Ari'an," Lord Cristeros said, his voice stuttering a bit. He seemed to be confused by her terror.

When he glanced over at Adenern, my brother gave him a toothy grin. I think that unnerved him a bit. Lady Ari'an stumbled backward, barely gaining her feet before he looked back at her. Again she froze. The lord took a step toward her, and she began to shake.

If I could only hide behind Adenern again. I had to get to his other side. Maybe if I could get over his tail, I'd be safe. I took a step backward, but the man took two toward me. I turned to run, but he grabbed my arm. I turned to look at the man's hand. He was too strong for me. I couldn't get away. He'd take me back. He'd hurt me. I'd be punished soon. I tore my eyes from his hand. I focused on Narden behind him.

Help me, please, I screamed inside. *Don't let him take me. If I go back, they'll do everything they can think of short of killing me. They might even do that when they were through. I'd broken too many rules.*

My legs weren't holding me up anymore. The man grabbed under my arm with his other hand. He was holding me up. He'd drag me away soon.

"Ari'an," was it that man's voice, or did I hear one of the priests mocking me?

"Ari'an, of the House of Nori'en," the second sneered, slamming me into a wall, "there is no such person. You are only insane just like every other nickin."

Choking out the name had made my mouth bleed again. I tried to fall to the floor, coughing out blood, but he held me up. I tried to push him away, but one of his hands clamped around my throat. I tried to scream, but he tightened his grip. I couldn't breathe.

"You are a slave to Verd, just like every other red-haired abomination," he hissed at me. "You have never been anything but a filthy nickin. You are useful only to please your betters, and when you cannot do that anymore, you will be of no more use than a burned house. You will be cleared away to make room for something that can be used. Be thankful that the great Verd has use for such beasts as you. If he did not, you would be left to die like an injured rat."

He released me, and I sank to the floor gasping for air and choking on the blood in my mouth.

"Nobility," he sneered, "never has red hair. The gods would not allow it."

He turned and left the room. I watched the door for a long time. Finally, when I thought he wouldn't come back in, I threw my head back and screamed. It was the first of many screams like that. I screamed at the top of my lungs, but if I made a sound, he might come back in. I forced myself not to let even the sound of the air racing from my lungs escape from my mouth.

I raced back with her blanket as quickly as I could. Entering the room of pools, I saw her throw her head back in one of those silent screams. Lord Grath had pulled Lord Cristeros away from her. His face turned from horror to anger as I rushed past, but at that moment, I didn't care if he stuck a sword right through me. Adenern was trying to talk to her, telling her that it was all right and that she was safe here, but she obviously couldn't hear him.

I dropped the blanket over her, as I heard Lord Cristeros say, "This is what they did to her."

I whirled around ready to give him a piece of my mind, and if it came down to it, a costly piece of my hide as well.

His enraged voice continued, "Verd will pay dearly for this outrage."

Empty air was the only thing that came out of my gaping mouth. I turned back to the terrified girl at my feet and muttered at the same time as Adenern, "I'll help you with that."

I was about to begin reassuring Lady Ari'an when I heard Adenern chuckle next to me. I looked over at him aghast. He was fighting a smile and motioned toward the two lords with his head. I glanced at them and stifled my own laugh. I had never seen anyone look so utterly shocked as Lord Cristeros did at that moment.

Turning back to Lady Ari'an, I noticed her eyes had finally lost the glazed look they had whenever she shook. I moved my head down close to hers, and she rested her hand on my nose.

"You're safe here," I told her. "It's all right."

In two days, Lord Cristeros returned again. Lady Ari'an refused to see him. She hid in the room of pools the entire time. I did see her peek around the corner a couple of times, but she would not come out. I thought my visitor would not be happy, to say the least, when I told him that he wouldn't be able to see her. I assumed he would want to have another carving match with my side. Instead, he looked at the room of pools and told me he understood. I was surprised that Lord Grath didn't have to scrape my jaw off the floor.

I was just recovering from that shock when he asked me if I would assist him in bringing some furniture from Caer Corisan. He could have knocked me over with a leaf at that point. Finally,

I managed to tell him that I didn't feel comfortable leaving Lady Ari'an alone and that Adenern would probably be better suited for the task.

As they sat around my fire, he continued to talk to me, asking about my family, how my injury was healing, and if Lady Ari'an had always been so terrified of people since her rescue. He was shocked when I told him that she'd actually been far worst and had improved quite a bit. I explained about her pointing at things now and even doing hand motions occasionally. I told him about her laughing at his kittens, and he smiled. Lady Ari'an had smiled like that once.

The lord asked if she'd spoken at all, and looked angry when I told him that she hadn't. I tensed a bit expecting an outburst about monstrous beasts scaring her so witless she couldn't even find her tongue, but the statement didn't come.

"Do you think they might have cut out her tongue?" was what he asked instead.

"No," I answered. "I've seen it when she yawns, and she screamed once."

"She screamed?" he sounded surprised.

I glanced at Lord Grath. "Didn't you tell him?"

He cocked an eyebrow at me, and I rolled my eyes. Then I explained about the mice that night. "Since then, I haven't heard anything but gasps from her, even when we've surprised her with something," I finished.

Turning slightly, he asked Lord Grath, "Was that the reason you suggested I bring the kittens?"

Lord Grath nodded. "I thought it would help if you presented the solution to one of the fears of your daughter."

He glanced at the room of pools, and I saw Lady Ari'an duck her head back around the corner. "How cold do these caves become in the winter?" he asked returning his gaze to me.

The question took me back for a moment. "Not very," I began. "We close up most of the gaps including the entrance there," I explained. "We have a back way out that we use then. The room of pools heats everything exceptionally well." I chuckled lightly to myself.

"Those who are fool enough to come here in winter rarely survive the snow, and those that do are in no condition to challenge our hides."

"This is as impregnable as a fortress then," he said with a tone of awe in his voice.

"And a far cry less drafty and leaky," I added.

"Then she will be safe here until spring," he stated.

Before I could voice my surprise, he turned to Lord Grath and asked, "Did the dragons and the lords of Rem'maren build this place then? The doorframes are carpentry beyond any skill I have ever seen."

"No," Lord Grath answered, "these places were built by those who know far more than any of us who walk or fly this world today." He looked at the doorframe of the room of pools. "They brought the dragons here as protectors and established for them a sanctuary where the protectors would themselves be protected."

"The ancients who did the great works in times past built these?" Lord Cristeros looked around in wonder.

"No," Lord Grath answered, "those who built these places and Caer Corisan were not immortal or gods. They were men and, I am told, even women who could bleed and die like all others. Wanderers, they called themselves. People with a mandate from the One."

"I am not convinced that mere men could build such places as these," Lord Cristeros replied skeptically.

"I would agree that such people are far from mere, but they were indeed flesh and blood like you or I." He sounded almost ready to laugh. "I have heard that if the dragons ever are in need of their protection again, they can be called to return."

"I am not certain I would wish for such great men to return," Lord Cristeros said looking around the cave.

"If the time came when this world was threatened beyond the dragons' ability to defend," Lord Grath said standing, "I would want nothing less. It is time we were leaving, my lord."

"Of course." He turned to me and bowed. "It was a pleasure to speak with you, sir. I hope that we can have many more such discussions."

I remembered enough manners to hold my mouth closed and bob my head.

"If you would see that Lady Ari'an receives this," he said as he turned and walked to his saddle bags, "I would be most appreciative." He walked back and set a medium-size embroidered satchel in front of me. "It is a gift from her mother and sister."

"Of course, my lord," I managed, still a bit surprised by the entire conversation. "Wait, my lord," I quickly called as I rose on my hind legs.

Pulling the sword out, took more effort than I imagined, but it came after a moment. Setting it down, I sent it skidding toward Lord Cristeros. He picked it up carefully, and then thanked me.

I watched them fly away and felt a hand on my side. I turned to Lady Ari'an and laughed out loud. I heard Adenern laughing from the room of pools.

"That went surprisingly well," I told her. "Shall we see what your mother and sister sent you?"

She opened the satchel to find an assortment of embroidery threads and cloths carefully arranged by colors. There was even a set of diagrams of different stitches on a parchment that made absolutely no sense to me. Lady Ari'an seemed quite pleased with it though.

Over the rest of the week, Lord Cristeros and Adenern brought a table, chairs, a fur rug, and several winter sets of clothes. I was quite surprised at how quickly the lord had changed from wanting to take chunks out of my hide to actually addressing me by name and even laughing at some of my jokes. I could tell that Lady Ari'an noticed the change and seemed a bit more at ease with her father, though she still became nervous if he came too close.

He said his farewells at the end of the week and told Lady Ari'an that he would not be able to return again until spring because of the snows, if then. She seemed torn by the statement, almost as though she wanted him to visit again sooner but was afraid that he would at the same time. I watched him fly off and laughed.

"He's finally getting the hang of riding a flying horse," I told Lady Ari'an.

The corners of her mouth turned up a bit, and she ducked her head.

"You don't ever need to hide that pretty smile of yours," I said as I turned away from the evening shadows and jumped toward the back of the cave.

I was in an exceptionally good mood. "Hey"—I spun around to face her—"I want to go swimming."

I wasn't sure if I'd wanted that man, my father, to leave. Since he had started to get along with Narden, I had not been quite so afraid of him. Perhaps it was best though. Now, I wouldn't have to pretend not to be afraid when he stepped close to me.

Narden was in such a great mood as he bounded like a new foal to the back of his cave. I almost laughed out loud at him. I expected him to ask if I'd like to go for a ride. The idea of a dragon swimming took me completely by surprise.

"Would you like to come?" he asked, his eyes sparkling.

I looked away. Long ago, I often swam with Pher'am, Dreanen, and Danren. There was a pool in one of the castle gardens dedicated to the god of the sea that was large enough for everyone. The man who'd just left sometimes came to join us, as had my mother on occasion. I'd loved to swim then. One of the new outfits the man had brought was for swimming. The sleeves were short though, and the legs and skirt would only reach to my knees. Now that I was wearing dresses again, I didn't want to expose my legs and arms. The scars were too deep in those places.

"Please?" Narden asked, spinning in a circle like an excited puppy. "I'll make it fun for you, I promise."

I stifled another laugh and nodded.

I hurried into my room to find the outfit and change. The whole thing was a wonderful shade of blue that reminded me of some of the ponds in the castle gardens. The shirt tied to the pants keeping everything from slipping out of place in the water. The pant legs tied just above the knees to keep them secure as well. I wrapped my blanket around my shoulders and hurried out.

Narden wasn't in the main part of the cave, and light was shining from the room of pools. As I approached, I heard an occasional splash. I laughed silently at the thought of a dragon swimming, and entered the room.

He had about every tenth torch lit all the way around the room. I could see the entrances to the other caves and wondered again who might be behind them. Narden was nowhere to be seen. For the first time, I noticed that only five of the caves could actually be entered. As I walked toward the deepest pool, I noticed that the others were blocked off with boulders or seemed to end after two steps with a flat wall of stone.

Perhaps this was only where Narden's family lived. I could tell which one was Adenern's because he'd left through that one only a few days before. Perhaps, the fifth cave belonged to Tragh's wife, I thought excitedly. Maybe I would be able to meet a female dragon soon. Why would she live separate from Tragh though? I wondered that as I looked down into the deep pool in the center of the room.

Under the water, I saw Narden glide by and spin with his wings fully extended. How deep was this pool? There was a shallow part at the other side where I could wade in, so I began to walk around. I watched the dragon do a backflip and dive out of sight. I searched for him as I approached the shallow end. I couldn't see him anymore. I folded the blanket and set it a safe distance from the water where it wouldn't get wet. I studied the water again and noticed my reflection.

The girl that stared back at me still did not seem healthy, but there was a smile on her face that made her eyes not seem so dead. The smile quickly faded as I caught sight of the mark on her arm. How could I have forgotten? I was branded. I was a nickin used for service in a temple of Verd, the mark screamed. That brand had been burned into my skin soon after I'd arrived.

I heard an explosion of water behind me, and quickly covered the brand with my hand. No one could see it. I had to get away to hide that mark. I turned to see Narden land with an explosion of gravel nearby. He shook the water out of his scales and turned to grin at me. The grin vanished when he saw me though. He must have realized I was branded.

He took a step forward, and I backed into the water.

"Lady Ari'an," he sounded concerned, "is something wrong?"

He took another step, and I backed up more.

"Did I scare you?" he asked, sounding slightly frightened himself.

I shook my head and looked away fighting the tears. I rubbed my arm knowing that I couldn't make the brand disappear, but hoping it would anyway.

"That's a lie," he sounded angry.

My head shot up, and I stared at him for a moment. Was he calling me a liar? I hadn't lied to him.

"That brand is a lie," he growled.

I gasped. How had he known I was upset about that? He came a few steps closer and lowered his head to look into my face. I met his eyes for a moment and then studied his nose. His nostrils flared a bit as he spoke.

"They were wrong to brand you as though you were a piece of livestock," he began, his voice cracking a bit with rage. "You, Lady Ari'an of the House of Nori'en, are a person who is far more valuable than any animal. You are priceless because the One has valued you above all other things that he created. Don't ever forget that, Lady Ari'an."

I met his eyes for a moment.

"That brand is a lie."

I looked away. How many times had they told me I was worthless? I was cursed by the gods. They had beaten that into me time and time again. How could Narden stand there and tell me otherwise? Who was this One that could remove the gods' curse? Why would I be of any value to him? I looked at Narden's nose again and took a deep breath.

I didn't know this One, but I did know Narden. He had not lied to me yet. Why would he begin to now? I lifted the edges of my mouth in a slight smile.

"If you would like," his voice was calmer now, "you could tie a handkerchief or scarf around that so you don't have to look at it while you're swimming."

I ran back to my room and found a blue scarf. That lying brand would not stop me tonight. I was going to swim with a dragon and enjoy it.

CHAPTER 12

THROUGH THE WINTER

The autumn days grew steadily colder. One morning, I awoke to a rumbling sound coming from the entrance cave. Cautiously, I peeked out from my bedroom. A solid wall of rock was slowly descending from the ceiling of the entrance. I watched as it connected with the floor making the entrance disappear entirely. Slowly I walked toward the new wall. If I hadn't known that there had been an entrance, I would never have known that this wall was new.

I carefully put my hand on it, expecting it to feel different than the other walls, but it didn't. It was completely indistinguishable. When I'd overheard that they sealed the entrances, I'd thought that they would have to move boulders themselves. This was amazing.

Narden wasn't in the entrance room, but I heard his voice echoing from the room of pools. He was singing again. Occasionally, he would sing when I wasn't around. I often awoke to the sound. He had a nice tenor voice, but I rarely recognized the songs. Sometimes he would even be singing in a different language.

Today, however, I knew the song. I'd heard both Dreanen and Danren singing it on occasion. It had something to do with their god and how he rescued all the slaves from a kingdom once. I'd always liked the tune, and the idea of a god who would rescue slaves had always appealed to me. Slaves could make no fancy sacrifices or build great gardens to buy a god's favor, but this god favored them anyway.

I listened as Narden sang of wonders performed for these slaves, wonders that humbled even the great gods of the kingdom they were in. Suddenly, the song struck me in a way I had never thought of before. This was a god greater than other gods, but he was a god who favored the helpless.

This was a god of slaves, a god who rescued those who were beaten, those who had scars from whips and ropes. This god rescued the branded from their tortured lives. I slid to the floor with my back to the new wall.

These thoughts frightened me, but in a way far different from the terror I knew at the temple. What service would such a god require? Slaves could not offer gold or gems. They could not build costly temples to offer elaborate sacrifices. Did this god demand human lives? I had heard of gods who did. There was a war god in a southern land that demanded two babies not yet weaned for every fifty enemies slain. I couldn't remember what the rest of the song said. I thought it told what this god demanded, but I wasn't certain.

Narden wandered in from the room of pools. He saw me sitting against the new wall and stopped singing.

"Lady Ari'an," he started toward me sounding slightly worried, "are you all right?"

I shook my head. I wanted to hear the rest of the song.

"Is something wrong?" his voice had a tone of panic. "Did your hand get caught in the entrance?"

I lifted my hands to show him and shook my head. How could I make him understand that I only wanted to hear the song?

I felt tears start in my eyes. What did such a god demand? Certainly, such a powerful god would demand an enormous payment, but what could slaves have to bargain with?

Narden was looking into my face now, close enough for me to reach out to touch his nose.

"I can open the entrance if you want," he said. I knew he was searching for why I was upset.

I shook my head, fighting to make a sound in my throat. "Please," I whispered. I heard him catch his breath. For a moment I looked into his wide eyes. "Sing."

Slowly, he let the air escape from his lungs. The breeze ruffled my hair and always smelled like burnt wood.

"My lady"—he almost laughed—"I would sing for the rest of my life if that's what you wanted. What would you like to hear first? Do you want me to sing what I was or start something new?"

He watched me for a moment, then laughed again. "I'm sorry," he began. "Would you like me to sing something new? I know a fun song about snails and flying frogs."

I shook my head.

"Do you want to hear what I was singing then?" He seemed almost puzzled.

I nodded.

"All right." He took a few steps back and cleared his throat. "Do you want me to start over?"

I shook my head. I wanted to hear the end.

"You want me to start where I left off then?"

I nodded.

He thought for a moment, probably remembering his place, and then started into the new verse.

I closed my eyes. The song continued telling about how the god guided this people through battles and wastelands. The god conquered great armies for them. He provided food and water in vast deserts. The slaves started to worship one of the old gods of the kingdom they'd been freed from. The god disciplined them, but never completely cast them aside.

Loyalty. This god wanted absolute loyalty, but that could be given to a god who could defeat any other god.

The song told of times when these freed slaves were blessed for helping others who were weak.

This god rewarded mercy.

Narden sang of kings who came from the future generations of those slaves. Many of these kings turned away from this god. They took bribes to buy favorable judgments. These kings were punished, and sometimes their entire families were wiped out.

Justice. He required justice.

The song ended with a list. Loyalty, mercy, justice, and . . . love. Love? Was it possible to love a god? Gods were things to buy blessings from or be appeased when angry. How could such things be loved? The other things seemed too simple.

Narden asked if I wanted to hear another song. I shook my head. I wanted to think.

The list was indeed simple, but far from easy, I realized. A complicated ritual sacrifice could be performed in a day. A feast might last a week, but loyalty would have to be given every day. Mercy would need to be offered even when someone didn't want to. Justice had to be done even when the price was high. These were costly things, but such a cost even a slave could afford.

A god who redeemed slaves puzzled me. A god whose sacrifices weren't offered in goods that could be bought or sold in a market, but in the way that people lived their everyday lives. What kind of god was this?

I wished I could ask Narden to explain, but I'd fought to speak earlier and my voice would not come again.

The dragon moved his head close to mine again. "Are you all right, my lady?"

I met his eyes for a moment and nodded. I was confused, but not in a way that I didn't know where I was or who to believe. I also realized that I was hungry. With my hand on Narden's nose, I got to my feet. I pushed the puzzling thoughts of this unusual god from my mind. Perhaps I would be able to learn something else about him later, but right now I wanted something to eat.

She'd spoken. I wanted to dance or fly around the cave, but I had neither the skill nor the coordination for either. Fighting to remain calm, I tried to find out what she wanted me to sing.

I was slightly concerned about the confused look on her face as I sang. She didn't move for a long time, staring into space. I wasn't certain if I should interrupt her thoughts or not.

The song she'd picked certainly wasn't the most fun or entertaining. It was a song I knew well though, which was probably why I'd been voicing it without much thought as I was setting the entrances to close in the five open caves.

Lady Ari'an rose to her feet slowly and glanced at my nose. Then she walked toward the cabinet that Lord Cristeros had brought to store food and dishes in. I watched her, wondering what had passed through her thoughts.

As she set a plate on the counter and began setting different selections of food on it, I wandered toward the back of the cave to toss a few more logs on the fire. This was always an interesting game of hit or miss. Once I'd managed to send burning logs flying across the cave, but that was years ago when I'd first moved in. I was much better now, but did occasionally send a log rolling somewhere it shouldn't go.

By the next day, I was trying to find the accounts from the song in the only book currently in my possession. I knew I should read it more often, but reading it was even more difficult than tossing logs on the fire.

An odd thump woke me the next morning. I glanced around sleepily. Where had the sound come from? I heard Narden let out a frustrated sigh from the entrance cave followed by another thump.

I dressed quickly and peered around the thick curtain dividing my room from the main cave. My father had brought this on one of his last visits. I'd actually preferred having the doorway open. A large section of one of the corners of the room couldn't be seen from the entrance cave, so I could change there without anyone seeing. I was adjusting to the curtain though. The curtain couldn't be locked or barred like a door might be. I could still come or go as I pleased. I couldn't see into the entrance cave anymore though, and the light from the fire could only be seen around the edges.

I stared at Narden for a long time. He let out another annoyed sound then flipped an enormous book that lay in front of him closed with his tail, picked it up in his mouth, and then dropped it on its bound edge. The book fell open, but from the look on Narden's face as he glanced at the pages, it wasn't open where he wanted it to be.

Quietly, I walked over to the where the dragon now had the book returned to his mouth. He glanced up at me and jumped slightly. He started to say something, realized he couldn't be understood with the book in his mouth, and dropped it. It fell open to one of the first or the last few pages. He glared at the book for a moment then looked up at me.

"I didn't mean to wake you, my lady," he said apologetically.

I glanced from his nose to the book on the floor in front of him.

"Trying to find something in here like that is like trying to move a sand dune with a beggar's cart," he said with an annoyed laugh.

Walking over, I picked up the enormous volume. As large as this book was, it was extremely plain. The cover was made of thick leather and the pages were an even type of thin material. I opened the book and nearly dropped it in surprise. The writing inside wasn't by hand. I'd heard of books like this, but had never seen one. These types of books were made far away in places where things wrote words faster than a person ever could. The words weren't ornamented as the books I'd seen before were. These were written in a plain hand, if I could call it that. How could someone find anything in a book like this even if they had hands that could easily turn the pages? The pages all looked the same.

"I hate asking this, but would you be willing to flip the pages for me?" he asked, looking somewhat defeated.

I glanced at his nose then stared at the book. Slowly, I nodded. Maybe Narden knew something about finding things in this book that I didn't.

He flopped down on the floor next to me, and I sat down leaning against his side. I flipped the pages as he directed. I passed a couple of titles written larger and in the middle that stood out from the rest of the writing. They seemed to be names of some type, but they were names I'd never heard of before. After quite a bit of flipping, Narden found what he was looking for and just read for a while. I studied the two pages, wondering how he'd figured out that this was what he was looking for. There were no markings that distinguished this from the other pages. There were no pictures intertwined with the words showing what the story was about. The pages were plain, painfully plain.

After studying the pages for a little while, I started to read. It was easy enough to read even though it seemed to be written in an old dialect. Absently I skimmed over the words, before I realized that this was part of the song Narden had sung for me yesterday. This was the story of the god freeing the slaves. I read intently now. The song had simplified the account drastically. It hadn't been a simple thing this god did. In a few short lines the song told of a story that took up quite a lot of pages in this book.

Narden stood and stretched after a time then ruffled the scales on his back. I looked up, realizing that I was stiff as well.

"You can keep reading if you like," the dragon reassured me. "If you'd like, you can take it somewhere more comfortable than this hard floor."

I closed the book and stood stiffly. There were furnishings in my room that the dragons had brought, but I didn't want to go in there. Instead, I walked to the writing stand with a cushioned chair that set against the back wall now. I took the book there setting it on the stand and sat down. At that moment, a small cry escaped me as I realized my mistake.

I turned quickly from wandering into the room of pools when I heard Lady Ari'an's distressed squeak. Hurrying over to her, I looked over her shoulder. One of her hands lay on the book while the other covered her mouth.

"Did you drop in on your hand?" I asked wondering why she looked so upset.

She shook her head, and I could make out the gleam of tears in her eyes.

"What is it then?" I certainly didn't want her to cry.

I'd never be able to find the story again. It was lost, buried in this book of undecorated pages. I had wanted to read more of it, but why had I shut the book? When Narden hurried over, I felt both foolish and hopeful. He asked me about dropping the book on my hand, and I shook my head. I fought the tears as I glanced at his nose. How could I tell him what was wrong?

I took a shaky breath. I wasn't supposed to talk. They'd beat me if they knew. They'd come up with some new vile way to punish me for breaking that, the most important, rule. They weren't here though. They'd beat me for wearing the clothes I did, for answering with a nod or shake of my head, or for being with a dragon. What could they add to all of that? They couldn't touch me here, not with Narden and Adenern protecting me.

"It's gone," I managed to whisper.

Narden stared at me with a look of surprise for a moment, then glanced around with a puzzled expression.

"What's gone?" he asked.

I fought to form the words, "The story."

He gave me a blank look. "The story you were reading?"

I nodded.

"It's still in the book you're holding, my lady," he said sounding confused.

I knew quite well that it was in the book. "I can't find it," I whispered.

"What?"

"There're no pictures."

"Oh!" Narden laughed. "I should have known. That caused me a problem at first too."

He flopped down next to the writing desk and looked over the back of my chair at the book.

"Open it up," he instructed.

We soon had the story located, and Narden explained that he found a specific story in the book by remembering what stories it was around and what area of the book it was generally in. The story I was reading was near to the front and began after another story about a slave.

I continued to read long after Narden wandered off again. He returned a while later and asked if I was hungry. His scales dripped water as I looked at him and saw the dismembered carcass of a buck cooking near the fire. I was indeed hungry.

Stretching, I rose and went to the cupboard that housed the provisions and dishes I used. My father had brought it as well. I pulled out a plate and some dried vegetables, and then went to the fire to sit.

The winter flew by with Lady Ari'an there. I wasn't nearly as bored as I had been the past few winters. The deep snow secured the borders far better than the dragons could, which freed us up to spend more time at home. My father and Lord Grath both insisted that I start taking patrols again. It was easier to learn defensive moves and attacks when there wasn't someone actually trying to kill us.

I hated leaving Lady Ari'an, but she was rarely by herself. When I wasn't there, my father, Renard, or Adenern were there. The only time she was actually alone was when one of us left for a short hunting trip. Those became rarer as the winter continued, and we brought more meat back from Caer Corisan when we returned from our patrols.

Lady Ari'an noticed the lighting coming from the walls within the first few weeks of winter. No one quite knew how it worked, and I explained that to her. The inside of the caves, except in the room of pools, mirrored the light outside somewhat. As the day progressed, the caves became brighter; and in the evening, the light would mellow. The light would continue, however, until everyone turned in for the night and then dim but never entirely go out. People didn't always notice it during the spring, summer, and autumn when the entrances were open. This was just one more thing the Wanderers had left.

On clear days, Lady Ari'an would bundle into several layers of clothes, including her fur-lined cloak, and we would open the entrance and take short flights. I brought snowshoes from Caer Corisan after one of my border patrols so we could take short walks through the mountain snows. The winter seemed to pass far too quickly. It did not seem like four months passed between Lord Grath's last visit before I closed the entrance and his return in the spring.

On one of our walks, Lady Ari'an discovered the first green sprouts poking through the snow. Soon after that, she told me of the gardens at Torion Castle and how she always watched for the first signs of green. At that point, she asked me to call her by her childhood nickname Ari.

There was still a slight chill in the air at night when Lord Grath returned. A month had passed since Ari's last shaking fit and two weeks longer since she'd woken up screaming in the night. She still had nightmares several times each week, but thankfully they weren't affecting her as badly anymore.

That day, I saw Adenern's silhouette approaching as the sun began to set. Why he was approaching my entrance puzzled me until I noticed he had a passenger. With a start, I realized that Ari could leave at any time now. Over a week ago, I'd noticed fresh supplies arriving at Caer Corisan by mule trains. During the winter months, the fortress was as snow locked as the mountains the dragons lived in, and only we were able to bring in supplies. If Lord Grath could make it here, Ari could make it to the fortress and then to her home. I'd probably never see her here again, and possibly nowhere else either. I doubted I'd be welcome at Torion Castle even if Lord Cristeros was friendly toward me. Ari more than likely would never visit Caer Corisan after she returned home, or if she did, it would be rare indeed.

I backed away from the entrance, stunned by those thoughts. They'd been present in the back of my mind, I realized, but I'd never dwelt on them. Now, I couldn't push them off until spring. Spring was here, and I would soon lose my companion.

"M-my lady," I stammered. "We have company."

I looked up from the writing desk surprised. Narden hadn't called me "my lady" for almost a month. If a dragon could look pale, he certainly did. I watched as he took a deep breath and shook his scales. Something had unnerved him. Glancing out the entrance, I saw the approaching dragon. I caught my breath as I made out the figure of a rider in the dimming light.

The blue and gold reflecting in the last of the sunlight gave away that the dragon was Adenern. Some distant memory, from my life before the temple, told me that I needed to set out refreshment for the approaching guest.

"Are you all right?" I asked Narden as I pulled my table toward the fire.

He turned his head to look at me with a bit of a dazed look in his eyes.

I heard Ari ask me something, but didn't quite comprehend the question, buried as I was in my own thoughts. I turned to look at her and saw the worried look on her face. I didn't need to make her nervous before Lord Grath even arrived. This would be the first time she would interact with another human in four months. I needed to avoid scaring her into her old habits, even if I was upset that she would be leaving, possibly as soon as tomorrow.

"What was that?" I asked focusing on her.

Looking at my nose, she met my gaze more often now, but only for short periods. "Are you all right?" she repeated.

I laughed at the irony of the question. I asked her that less frequently now, but to have it turned on me was amusing.

"I'm fine," I told her, "I was just thinking."

I turned to stare at the approaching figures again, Ari was clanking something behind me, but the sound was distant as my thoughts wandered away. The place would be painfully lonely without her here. Maybe I'd at least be able to fly by Torion Castle on the days I wasn't on patrols. That was more dangerous now than it had been when Ari was abducted. The situation with Verd was tense. Several dragon hunters had been spotted on the trails before winter closed in. They pushed into the mainlands as well, which was safer for them, but not for us. In the mountains, there were far more places to hide than in the hills and flatlands of the rest of the country.

Help was close at hand in the mountains as well. Taking on one dragon was a difficult matter to begin with, but take on one whose brothers came to help him, and that dragon hunter didn't stand a chance. A lone dragon was rare outside of these mountains, but help was also rare. My father would probably not allow me to leave for months if not a couple years. I was behind in my training because of my visitor. I would pay for it now. I let out a sigh, and silence filled the cave.

I looked up at Narden when I heard the sigh escape his body. He was just lying there, staring out the entrance at the approaching figures. He'd been sunning himself in that spot, but the sunbeam had moved to the right. Normally, he would slowly roll along with it, sunning his back, sides, and chest as he went along. Narden just lay on his side now forlornly looking out the entrance.

I'd just been going through motions that I distantly remembered. Enjoying the memories of my mother telling me what should always be set out for visitors of a lord status. I didn't have everything in my little cupboard. We would have to go without the roasted rice and fruit-stuffed pig. I had liked the wings on those delicious meats the best.

I knew my mother would never have allowed me to set such things out myself. I had been a lady, and ladies oversaw such things. They never did such menial tasks themselves. I had no servants here though. The maids I'd had back then would have all run screaming out of the entrance the moment they saw Narden.

The memories had made me smile, but as I watched Narden, I felt the smile fade. I didn't like the look on his face. Something had upset him about the approaching visitors. I began to feel on edge. Setting the spice sprinkler on the table, I noticed my hands were starting to shake. I swallowed hard. Maybe I was overreacting. I needed to know what was wrong.

Narden stared at me blankly for a moment when I asked again.

Finally, he shook his scales and answered, "Nothing is wrong, my lady."

That was the second time he'd called me that in less than a quarter of a watch. Something had to be wrong. Was he lying to me?

CHAPTER 13

FEARING HOME

I saw immediately that I'd upset Ari. Forcefully, I pushed my sad thoughts to the back of my mind. For now, I needed to reassure Ari, and that was far more important than feeling sorry for myself.

I might as well break the bad news to her myself. She'd probably take it better from me than she would from Lord Grath, who she hadn't seen in four months.

"Ari," I began forcing my voice over the lump in my throat. "I have some good news for you." I forced a smile too.

The skeptical look on Ari's face told me clearly that she was not buying it. I shook my scales again to clear my head.

"You'll be going home soon," I managed. "I know that your family will be thrilled to see you."

I watched Ari's eyes widen as she looked past me out the entrance at the approaching figures. She took a step back as the color left her face.

Go home? What was home? I had vague memories of Torion Castle, but was that home? I knew that's where Narden meant.

A vivid memory gripped my mind of the temple. I felt a quiver run through my body as I fought to throw the thought away.

I heard the first priest laugh as he dragged me to my feet by my hair. "This is your home now," he sneered throwing me at the stone platform that was my bed.

I gasped at the memory of the sharp pain in my side. I saw Narden standing there. I could even hear the concern in his voice, but I couldn't understand the words. I fought to stay on my feet as I turned and walked slowly into the room of pools.

I heard the sound of Narden stretching into my room. His back was just a little too tall to fit in fully, and it always scrapped on the top of the door. I would find a scale or two outside my room when I returned. If I hadn't been fighting so hard to keep the memory from sending me into a fit of shakes, I would have laughed, as Narden trotted through the doorway with my fur blanket dangling from his mouth. He looked almost like a puppy with a favorite toy.

Pulling off one of my shoes and the stocking as well, I plunged my foot into the coldest pool in the room. The shock forced every other thought out of my mind. I learned to do that almost two months ago. It was then that I was finally able to keep some sort of awareness of where I truly was. Occasionally, the memories won, and I wasn't able to stay focused. Narden always looked scared and angry when I came out of those, not that I wasn't shaken as well. They were much fewer now, for which I was thankful.

Yanking my foot back, I looked up at the worried dragon. He mumbled the familiar question through the blanket.

I didn't need to understand the words to answer, "Yes, I'm all right."

I took the blanket from him and rubbed my face in the fur. I trotted over to the bath area to retrieve a towel to dry my leg. As I picked up the cloth, I heard the familiar sound of a carriage crash in the entrance room.

Glancing at Narden, I saw that he was a bit pale as he walked into the other room. I still didn't like that he looked so nervous. He'd never been nervous around Adenern before.

I peeked around the corner to see Lord Grath dismounting. It amazed me that he could look so unruffled after landing with one of the younger dragons. I always felt like my stomach would never return from where it had been imbedded in my skull after one of those landings. Narden had thankfully improved, but whenever I rode Adenern, I felt like my insides had been thrown out of my body and then shoved back into all the wrong places.

I didn't want to leave the room of pools just yet though. Narden's reaction had me worried about what I should expect. He'd said the phrase "When Lord Grath returns" casually several times during the winter. Why was he acting so oddly now that Lord Grath had returned?

I stayed in the shadows of the doorway as Lord Grath greeted Narden. Turning, he glanced around the cave.

"Where is my lady?" he asked looking back at Narden.

Narden took a deep breath. "She had a slight episode as you were coming."

Lord Grath glanced at my room and then stepped toward it. "Lady Ari'an, will you join us, please?"

I almost laughed, knowing that Lord Grath spoke to an empty room.

"If you give her a little time," Narden said, "I am almost certain that she will join us soon."

The lord turned around with a last look over his shoulder. "I have matters to discuss with her before I leave."

I couldn't help blurting out, "You're taking her away."

I noted the surprise on Lord Grath's face. My tone had been harsh, but I was far from pleased with the situation.

"You are," he corrected.

I turned in a circle and lay down cocking an eyebrow at the lord. I wasn't in a mood to have my grammar corrected at the moment.

"You have known since the agreement that she could stay through the winter months then she would return home in the spring," he answered evenly.

I swallowed hard. "So you're here to bundle her off, without so much as a day's notice."

The raised eyebrow told me he didn't appreciate my tone, but I really didn't care.

"I am here to discuss the situation with Lady Ari'an," Lord Grath continued; later his calm tone would impress me, but right now my own calm had fled.

"*Discuss*," I sneered. "Which means you're going to *tell* her that she's going home and to pack her things, if she's even allowed to take them with her!"

"Her family has waited almost five years for her return, and they are quite anxious to see her safely there," was the even answer. I knew him well enough to see the anger rising in his eyes even though his voice didn't betray it.

"And she has no choice in the matter," I shot back. "If she doesn't feel ready for traveling halfway across the country to be entirely surrounded by humans whom she hasn't seen in almost five years, as you pointed out." I lowered my voice to a menacing growl, "She'll probably be in hysterics for another year at least, if she ever gets over the shock at all."

I watched Lord Grath's eyes narrow as he came into his correcting fatherly look. "This is not about Lady Ari'an."

"IT'S NOT!" I bellowed. I matched his glare and snarled, "Then who is it about?"

"You."

Had I been standing up, I would have fallen over. How did he know that was part of the reason I was upset? After seeing Ari almost go into another fit of shakes, I was greatly concerned about the shock she would experience if she did return suddenly to an only-human environment. I'd had no intentions of mentioning that I didn't want her to leave, but Lord Grath had seen right through that.

I didn't like being cornered and blurted, "That's beside the point."

"Oh," Lord Grath said in that maddeningly even tone, "you are not concerned about not seeing her again?"

I glared.

Adenern stepped between us. "I'm sure Narden would like to be able to see Lady Ari'an again, but he has brought up some good points."

I didn't hear the rest of the conversation. I hadn't thought much about leaving even though Narden had mentioned it once in a while. He'd always said it as a passing thought as if it were a long way off. I ripped off my shoe and stocking again plunging my foot back into the pool. I needed to think clearly, and there were too many possibilities. What if something happened on the trip back? I couldn't ride one of the dragons all the way back to Torion Castle. What if I was ambushed? The company could be attacked that was escorting me. What if the ambush took me back to Verd?

The water helped me think slower, but I couldn't shake the thoughts. What if I did make it back to Torion Castle and panicked? Narden wouldn't be there. I couldn't run into this room and dunk my foot to regain the little bit of control the chill gave me.

I looked around frantically. I had to hide, but where? I glanced over the entrances into Tragh's, Renard's, and Adenern's caves. My eyes fell on the last opening. I'd never been in that one. They wouldn't think to look for me there.

I hurried toward it, taking the paths between the pools instead of going around. I slipped twice expecting the splash to bring all three from Narden's cave instantly, but each time, no one came through the doorway. I couldn't hear their voices from this far away, so I couldn't tell if they had even heard the noise. I rushed into the dark entrance feeling my way along the wall. I wanted to pray for an opening to hide in somewhere, but I couldn't think of which god to pray to. The ones I knew at Torion Castle had not answered me when I was at the temple in Verd. Certainly they would not answer me here. The god that Narden's book spoke of might do something, but what would I owe such a great god if I asked him for anything, even such a small thing as a place to hide.

I touched a curve of the wall. I turned with it and realized I was brushing along scales. Immediately, I froze. I'd never seen a dragon enter or exit this cave. I'd never been told that a dragon even lived in here. I caught my breath and fought over the lump in my throat.

"Hello," I called. "Is someone here?"

What if the dragon was dead?

"Young lady," a voice in the darkness answered, "I would turn on the lights, but I am certain you would scream, so shall we continue this conversation in the dark?"

I swallowed hard. "I won't scream, sir. I've been staying with Narden, so I'm used to dragons."

The voice chuckled lightly. "If that's what you want," the accent was so strange, then he said a word I didn't recognize, and the walls in the cave began to glow softly, slowly increasing in intensity.

I gasped at the walls. I'd noticed that the walls in Narden's and the other dragons' caves glowed, but I didn't know the light could be turned on and off. How was that even possible?

The cave was the same size as Narden's, complete with the little side room. There was a pool where the entrance would be in Narden's cave, but no entrance to the outside, just solid wall.

Turning to the new dragon, I would have gasped again, but my lungs were already full from the surprise from the lights. This dragon was terribly different from any of the others I had seen. His scales were a mixture of a beige skin color and a silver gray with no apparent pattern. One of his wings was in tatters along his back while the other looked like it was too small to ever have let him fly. As he turned his head to face me, I saw that the two horns on his head looked as though they grew in wrong. One seemed to be in the proper place on his forehead but was too small, the other was the proper size but was too far to the left of his head. I glanced at the floor to gather my nerves only to find that his toes were too short on his back feet and too long on the front. I took a step back, closing my eyes.

"You've impressed me, young lady," the dragon said evenly. "Are you planning on screaming soon, or should I stop waiting?"

I forced myself to open my eyes, to look at his face, realizing that it would be rude to talk to him with my eyes shut. I glanced at his eyes briefly, only to find that it wouldn't have mattered if I had kept my own eyes closed. The dragon was blind.

"What happened to you, sir?" I blurted out. Realizing as the words left my mouth that I had been rude after all by asking such a question.

"You are indeed a brave girl." The dragon chuckled. His grin spread from the front of his mouth to the back. I took another step back. I had grown used to the other dragons smiling from the back of their mouths forward. I felt like running away from the apparition, but my legs wouldn't respond.

"I volunteered for an experiment that never should have taken place," he said with a slight tone of sorrow in his voice, "and my prodigy and I are paying the price, but I'm afraid that's as much as I will tell you about that."

The answer didn't make any sense to me, but I wasn't about to try to find out more. Actually, I wanted to make as polite of an exit as I could.

"Now," the dragon continued, "what brings you into my home?"

Suddenly, my recent thoughts flooded back to me. I still needed to hide, but would this dragon be willing to help me? Should I even ask?

"Sir," I began, trying to think of what to say.

"You can drop the formality, miss," the dragon said shifting slightly. "I was named Gary, but that is an odd name here. If you like, you can call me by it." He lowered his head toward me. "And who are you?"

I stared at him for a long time, who am I? I was someone once. Was I someone now?

"Once," I said feeling the quiver in my voice, "I was Lady Ari'an of the House of Nori'en."

"You're not anymore?" the dragon asked quizzically cocking an eyebrow at me.

"I'm—" My voice broke. I took a shaky breath. I glanced back at the room of pools. I'd had that name beaten out of me for too long. I was fighting back yet another memory of the whip slashing open my back. I couldn't go back out there until Lord Grath left, and he certainly would still be there now.

As I turned back, I again saw the large pool reflecting the cave lights back from its surface. I took a few steps toward it asking quickly, "Is that cold?"

The dragon turned his head toward my footsteps. "Is what cold?"

Of course he wouldn't know what I was talking about. I fought tears. "Your pool." My voice sounded too shaky. I'd lose this battle soon.

"It can be," the dragon sounded puzzled. I couldn't blame him.

"Please." I fell to my knees next to the pool. The water was warm. I felt my hands begin to shake in the water. No one was here to help me. The shaking began to travel up my arms.

I began to hear the first priest's voice, "The filth does not learn quickly, does it?" I saw him sneer. "Beat it till it cannot move."

Distantly, I heard a word I didn't understand. The sudden shock of the frigid water threw me away from the pool. I stared up into Gary's nose.

"Are you all right?" he asked facing the pool.

I laughed at the familiar question. The face turned down toward me.

"You must be the girl staying with Narden," he said, seemingly looking at me with his vacant glassy eyes.

"Yes, sir," I said.

"Just Gary, Lady," he said as he turned slightly and swung his tail in front of him a few steps.

His tail was too long as well, but he seemed to be using it to help him determine where he was going. It was an interesting procedure. His tail curved above his hip and shoulder to slope about four handsbreadths of his tail in front of him. This part swung just barely over the floor scratching the spikes on the end over the ground. The spikes weren't right either, but that did not surprise me now. They stuck out at odd angles and varying lengths for about the last two handsbreadths of his tail.

Reaching the wall, he turned back toward the pool and lay down. "Now, Lady," he continued turning his head back toward me, "what brings you to my home?"

"I'd—" My voice shook. I took a breath and glanced over my shoulder. "I'd rather not say."

Looking back at him I saw that he had an eyebrow cocked. In a strange way, he reminded me of Narden for a moment.

"Well, miss," he said with a harder tone to his voice than I had heard before, "seeing that you barged into my home without either announcing yourself or being invited, I would say that I have a right to know why you are in here."

I swallowed hard. For a moment I considered running from the cave, but that wouldn't help. This dragon lived here too. If I ran somewhere else, not only would I have the two dragons in Narden's cave looking for me, but also this dragon. I already knew that I had nowhere to hide outside of here.

"I'm hiding, sir," I caught myself and added, "Gary."

"Hiding from whom?" he asked evenly.

I didn't want to say anymore but finally added, "From Lord Grath, Sir Gary."

"Just Gary"—he tilted his head to the side—"and why are you hiding from Lord Grath?"

Glancing over my shoulder, I could hear voices in the room of pools. They were faint, but I took a step away from the entrance. I realized that they would see the light coming from this cave. They would find me soon. There was nowhere else I could go.

"He'll take me away," I blurted. I could tell that my voice had a frantic pitch now. "They'll find me and take me back to the temple if I leave."

I glanced around frantically. "I'll panic, or start shaking, and I won't be able to stop."

I had to find somewhere to go. "They'll think I'm insane."

There was a small cave opening into this one just behind the dragon. "They'll lock me up."

I trotted toward the little cave, fighting the sobs that threatened to reveal where I was. The tail shot in front of me. I froze. "Please," my voice broke.

I heard the dragon sigh. "Just don't move anything." The tail lifted from my path, and I hurried into the room. The little room was lit only by the light coming from the larger cave. The near corner couldn't be seen from the outside. I curled into that corner, making myself as small as I possibly could.

I heard steps approaching the cave. One pair was human, the others were dragon. I felt myself beginning to shake. Biting my lip, I fought as hard as I could to keep control.

"Greetings, my lord," I heard Lord Grath call from outside the cave.

I heard the gray dragon sigh heavily. "What, Grath?" he almost growled.

I heard the human footsteps enter the cave. "Good day to you, your grace."

"Drop the formality, Grath," the gray dragon answered. "What is going on here?"

"Have you seen Lady Ari'an?" Lord Grath asked.

There was a silence that made me certain that they could hear my heart beat.

"I haven't seen anyone in a very long time," the dragon answered flatly.

"My apologies, my lord," Lord Grath began, but the light growl cut him off. I heard him sigh and then say, "Lady Ari'an seems to have run off, and we have not been able to find her."

There was a moment of silence, and then the dragon said, "Are you sending her to an insane asylum?"

"A insauni . . . your pardon?" Lord Grath sounded so surprised that he'd lost much of the formality in his voice.

"Hmmm," the gray dragon shifted his weight and lay down in front of the small cave opening where I was hiding. "Do you think she's crazy?"

"Pardon?" Lord Grath asked again, still sounding surprised, all formality gone now. "She is not crazy."

"Hmmm, so you're not sending her to a temple for the insane?"

"What?" he stammered this one.

"You don't seem to communicate your intentions very well."

"Your pardon?"

I heard Adenern's chuckle a bit farther away. "Gary, you have accomplished something that I've spent most of my life trying to do."

I stopped myself before laughing. I could almost picture the glare Lord Grath would be giving the dragon at this point.

Adenern didn't seem to notice though. "Gary, she's in here, isn't she?"

The dragon didn't say anything.

"Did she say why she came in here?" I heard Narden ask.

They knew I was here. The dragon Gary must have nodded. He was still lying in front of the entrance, but what good was that? I was trapped . . . I'd never get out . . .

I was controlling my temper with quite a bit of effort, but I was close to toasting everything in sight. I kept my voice even as I asked, "May I speak with her, please?"

Gary cocked an eyebrow at me and then said, "Don't touch anything."

He stood up and moved away from the doorway he was blocking. Quietly I slipped in and glanced around. I felt the rocks tear into my feet as I clenched the hard ground in my claws. I knew this would happen. Ari was huddled in the nearest corner shaking.

"Adenern!" I yelled, "Get her blanket!" I heard him race from the room as I crouched in front of the lady.

"Ari," I whispered, knowing that if I spoke any louder I would sound as irate as I felt. "Ari, can you hear me?" She didn't respond.

"The only way you will ever get out of here is if you are bought or dead, nickin. No one will ever buy you. You are worth less than what we paid for your sorry body. You will die here. You are trapped like the stupid

animal you are. You will never get out," they told me as they beat me. The laugh ran through my bones.

I'd wedged the plate into the door when they'd left before. I'd slipped out of the door, but I didn't know the route to get out of the building. There was nowhere to hide, the halls were the same gray stone that ran without closets or crevices. There were doors, but they were all locked. They found me. They dragged me back to my cell by my ankles.

"Ari," the voice was distant, and I couldn't make out the rest of the words. I opened my eyes. A glint of gold sparked in the darkness.

"Ari," the voice said again. "Can you hear me?"

Her eyes were open, but didn't seem to see the room or me in front of her. "Ari, focus on me, please."

Her head turned up toward me. I watched her eyes clear slightly. She was still quivering, but not shaking violently like she had been. I needed to get her out of here quickly before something else happened.

"Ari, would you like to go for a quick flight around the mountain?" I asked trying to sound calm.

She glanced at my nose and then shrunk into the corner.

"I won't take you away," I told her. "You're not going back to the temple ever."

She looked up at me for a moment and then glanced toward the door where I could hear Lord Grath and Gary discussing Ari's sanity in the other room. I kept from growling with a lot of effort. Ari was certainly not insane. Terrified of people, I would agree, but that didn't constitute insanity.

Adenern's head poked in at that point dangling the blanket. If I hadn't been so mad, I might have laughed. I glanced at Ari. "Do I look that silly when I'm carrying that?"

She barely glanced up, then closed her eyes again and huddled into the wall. Adenern glared at me and mumbled something.

"Ari, we need to leave, please." I was fairly certain that if I could just get her away from here for a little while, she would calm down.

Slowly she stood and stepped toward the entrance. Lord Grath looked over at that moment, and she immediately sank back into the corner.

I turned and lay down in front of her. "Please, Ari."

Narden was asking me something. He wanted me to walk out of this room into Gary's cave. Lord Grath would take me away if I came near him, but Narden wouldn't let him . . . would he? I could still hear the priests yelling in my head. I wanted to leave, but I couldn't walk through that room.

"Ari, you can ride if you like." I glanced up at the dragon and slowly pulled myself back to my feet.

She climbed onto my back and took the blanket from Adenern. I felt her lay flat and pull the blanket over her head. I walked through the doorway and through the cave. Lord Grath asked if he could speak with Ari. I narrowed my eyes at him and felt the growl run through my chest. "No."

The flight we took around the mountain went well enough. I saw Adenern and Lord Grath leave through Adenern's entrance as I circled around the third time. This setback didn't fly away with them though.

Ari didn't say another word to anyone for almost two weeks, and then only to answer a question that couldn't be answered by a nod or shake of her head. She didn't eat for two days. It was five days before she would even nod to answer questions again. Three nights in a row she woke up screaming. She kept near walls and jumped at every sound for a month. I lost count of how many times she had a shaking episode.

Tragh came during the second week, and I refused to let him talk to Ari about what had happened with Lord Grath. She would hardly respond to me about anything and looked absolutely terrified whenever I mentioned Lord Grath even as a passing comment. She barely glanced at Tragh whenever he was around and wouldn't answer him, Adenern, or Renard.

CHAPTER 14

PREPARING TO STAY

Surprisingly it was Renard who managed to get her to laugh again two months later.

I was dozing in the back of the entrance cave with Ari leaning against me and two kittens on my back when he crashed into the cave.

I'd been watching Renard approach for several moments. He was flying a bit erratically as he came. At first, I'd wondered if he was hurt, but the patterns looked wrong for trying to escape an attack or if he'd been injured. I stood up while watching him approach.

He came barreling into the cave landing with a crash that made Adenern's landing sound like a leaf landing in the moss. Narden jumped to his feet his scales spiking in all directions. He skidded to a stop an handsbreadth away from me.

"WHAT ARE YOU DOING?" Narden bellowed behind me.

"I am profoundly sorry, my lady"—Renard gasped—"but he was so excited to see you that he was giving me all the wrong signals."

I caught my breath and backed into Narden, which hurt considering I backed into scales the size of my hand.

"WHAT?" Narden snapped behind me.

"You may want to have a firm talking to him about that, and you may want to give him some lessons on proper dragon-riding etiquette." The grin didn't seem to match what he was saying. "Why don't you sneak around and help him down."

I must have looked absolutely horrified, because he added with a huge grin, "Don't worry. I know you will like him."

I had seen that he was wearing a saddle as he approached, but there hadn't been anyone that I could make out in it. I stood frozen for a moment while Narden growled, "What are you trying to do?"

"Just trust me on this," Renard said with a wink.

Leaning around to look at the saddle, I saw a short fuzzy leg tied to the saddle. I glanced up at Renard slightly confused. He just stood there grinning. Stepping around to his side, I saw the largest winged-deer–shaped soft toy I had ever seen tied flat to the saddle.

I was ready to kill my older brother when he crashed into the cave, and then those lines about flying badly because a toy was tied into his saddle almost made me rip off his horns right then and there. But then Ari smiled. She hadn't smiled since the incident. Pulling the stuffed toy that was as tall as she was from the saddle, she threw her head back and laughed.

Renard's grin got even bigger as he threw his head back and laughed with her.

Things got better after that. She had that toy with her often and smiled every time she looked at it. She started talking more after that as well.

With as frightened and jumpy as she still was and how much she acted like a child at times, her nineteenth birthday almost took me by surprise when it arrived the next month. Almost.

I left the morning before to get everything from Caer Corisan that I could possibly carry for the celebration. Adenern and Renard arrived within a few watches of me. We stayed there that night. I had been terribly nervous about leaving Ari without anyone there with her for that many hours, but Gary had started spending time outside of his cave again. For some reason that was far beyond me, he and Ari had become friends. I'd noticed Ari would wander over to his cave with my book once a day. I could hear her soft voice reading to the old dragon across the room of pools sometimes. Gary wasn't the type of person I would normally spend a lot of time with. Sadly to say, I thought he looked creepy, and he could do things to the caves that I just couldn't understand. Ari had taken to him though, so she didn't seem at all put out when I asked her if she would be all right spending the evening with Gary.

The people at Caer Corisan loaded the three of us up in the morning with all the presents that had come from her family, Lord Grath's family, and the people of the fortress. They'd taken to calling her their lady in the mountains, which tickled me considering they had never once met her. I also realized at that point that Danren had forgotten to send anything for her. That made me feel rather stupid.

We took off in the late morning when every last bundle was finally settled into place where they wouldn't poke, pinch, or hinder our flight. Not that about three hundred pounds of stuff each wasn't enough to hinder anyone's flight. Tragh had arrived about a watch before. He would be flying surveillance because of our loads. The last thing we needed was one of us getting ourselves killed on Ari's birthday.

We arrived early in the afternoon. Normally, the flight would have taken a few watches or less, but the extra weight slowed us up considerably. When we arrived, Ari was still over with Gary. Tragh went over to fetch her, as the rest of us collapsed onto the floor of the cave. Gently of course, we didn't want to break anything.

Ari followed the older dragon in looking somewhat nervous. When she saw the three of us panting on the floor, I didn't blame her for immediately asking if everything was all right.

Renard was the only one with enough wind to laugh, which made Adenern and I both glare at him. He didn't seem to notice at all though.

"You cannot possibly mean that you do not actually know what today is," he said with mock disbelief.

I heard the swish of Adenern's tail as he thumped Renard in the chest. "Of course she doesn't remember, it's not like she was *born* today or anything!"

I wasn't going to participate in all this nonsense, so I hauled myself to my feet and the best I can describe it is that I waddled over to Ari.

"Pay no attention to them," I whispered.

"What are all the bundles for?" she whispered back.

"They're for you." I smiled. "We thought we'd bring you a little something for your birthday."

She took a step back and bumped into Tragh. "It's my birthday?"

"Four days past the third new moon in spring," I told her.

She looked a bit taken back for a moment. "Father gave me a horse last time," she said, looking up with a slightly glazed look in her eyes.

"Yes," I said, "the pretty gray one."

She looked somewhat surprised at me. "How did you know that?"

"I patrolled that area back then," I told her glancing up at Tragh, who had an eyebrow cocked and then smiled slightly.

Ari took a moment before looking over at Renard and Adenern. "It's all for me?" she finally asked.

"Yes it is." I grinned. "There are a lot of people who care about you."

She looked absolutely shocked by that comment. I watched her turn to stare at me, then at the packs strapped to my saddle, and finally at Renard and Adenern.

"You may want to work on Renard's stuff first." I leaned down to tell her. "He has all the food."

She still stared at them looking shocked for a moment, then she slowly walked over to Renard.

"I would work on that blue one first, if it were my birthday," Renard hinted.

Ari looked at him for a moment then reached for the tie. Then I watched as she almost dropped the bundle.

I'd pulled the tie partially lose before grabbing the bulging package. It was warm! I nearly dropped the thing, but caught it before it hit the floor. If this was another animal, I certainly didn't want to drop it. Slowly, I lowered the bundle to the floor where I heard it clank. I glanced up at the dragons, who all seemed to have stupid grins on their faces.

Cautiously, I opened the bundle to find several more cloth-wrapped bundles, all of which were warm. I glanced up at Renard who had the oddest smile I'd ever seen on his face. I pulled out the largest bundle and unwrapped it. Inside was a pot with a glass lid containing a vegetable soup. I hadn't eaten anything that was this well prepared since before the temple. I nearly dropped the container, my hands were shaking so much. Instead, I quickly set it down.

I heard Renard burst out laughing. I glanced up at him, quite shocked. He leaned his face close to mine and whispered, "Now, you see why I was carrying that."

"Hey!" Narden called from across the room. "I've gotten much better!"

"I have become . . ." I heard Tragh say.

I laughed. Narden had become much better at landing. I was fairly certain that he could rival Renard now, but it was always entertaining to watch the brothers bicker for a little while. They never stayed at it long, and usually ended up laughing at the end.

I pulled the next lumpy bundle out to find a loaf of berry bread that was also still warm. Each bundle in that package had some tasty treat in it that I hadn't had in years. Two other bundles had food in them as well, one of which contained chilled cream and frosted chocolates.

Most of what Renard had were cooking things such as a little oven that could be set over a small fire to bake things, many different dry goods to bake with, measuring bowls, and several cooking scrolls, including many with very basic instructions. Adenern explained that one of the cooks at Caer Corisan was "absolutely mortified that the Lady was confined to eating scorched meat and raw vegetables."

Scorched meat was better than raw half-rotten meat, and fresh vegetables were far better than wilted as well. I didn't mention that though. The dragons were having such a good time telling me different stories about the gifts.

I didn't mention that I didn't know how to cook either. That wasn't something any of the teachers ever worked with us on at Torion

Castle. "A lady needs to know what the finished product should be, not the details of how to make that product," I remembered my mother telling me once. That was such a long time ago though. Obviously, the woman at Caer Corisan did not feel the same way.

There were presents from my family, the dragons, and most of Lord Grath's family including him and his wife. I was a bit nervous opening their gifts, because of the incident with him. Also, Lady Margree absolutely hated the dragons from what I understood. They sent several wonderful tapestries that didn't seem to hint either at my leaving or Lady Margree's dislike.

Dreanen and his older brother Drenar sent a beautiful tea set that Narden actually carried. I wondered why Danren hadn't sent anything, but Narden mentioned that he was very busy right now in his training and may have sent his present a bit late.

The dragons had apparently worked with some of the carpenters at Caer Corisan to make a bed, dresser, stand and mirror with a chair that had scenes from their history carved into them.

Adenern brought bedding, table linens, and wall hangings. I noticed that he didn't have a single thing that was fragile tied onto his saddle. I didn't mention that, but I did feel proud of Narden that he was trusted to carry such breakable things even though he was younger. The cave was completely covered in packaging and presents by the time I was done opening everything. There were several soft animal toys, a bed covering with the House of Nori'en crest stitched on and another one with the Dragon Lords for the House of Rem'maren.

CHAPTER 15

DRAGON MAPS

The afternoon turned to evening as I picked up the spare packaging and sorted the new treasures.

I heard the sound of a dragon diving into one of the pools and glanced up to find that Tragh was the only one left in the entrance cave. He was watching me while he lay against the back of the cave. He smiled when I looked up and waved for me to come over.

I picked up a couple of pieces of discarded packaging on my way.

"Have a seat, my lady," he said, pulling my desk chair over with his tail. I sat somewhat puzzled.

"I meant to talk to you sooner about something, but there have been far too many things to manage lately."

I felt a bit nervous, wondering what this would be about. I had the sinking feeling it was about taking me back to Nori'en.

"I have something to show you," he said, motioning to a leather-wrapped tube hanging from his neck.

I took it gingerly and heard a grating on the floor behind me. Glancing over my shoulder, I saw Tragh's tail pulling over my desk. The desk came to a stop in front of me. Setting the tube on the desk I pulled out the cork and withdrew a large rolled parchment. As I unrolled the sheet, I saw that it was a map of Faruq. I'd seen a map of this land before, but never paid much attention to it. This one had no lines dividing the different houses' lands.

"My lady," Tragh began, "we are here." He tapped his tail on the mountain range running near the edge of the drawn land. I blinked, maybe I hadn't noticed it before, but there was a mountain drawn into the range that had two dragons flying around it. The blank parchment continued for about two hand's spans from where the drawing stopped to the edge of the sheet.

"Do you know what is here?" he asked tapping the blank area. I shook my head. How could anyone tell where anything was on this map?

"This is Verd." At that word, a line crossed the map along the border of what must have been Maren. Colors flowed out of the blank space tracing out the mountains, forests, and plains.

I gasped and pushed back from the desk a bit. The space filled in to less than a hand's span from the edge of the parchment. Slowly, I leaned over the sheet and cautiously brushed my hand over the page. It felt normal enough to me.

"How did it . . .?" I began to ask, and then swallowed hard.

Tragh chuckled behind me. "If you would like a detailed explanation, ask . . . Gary." It took him a moment to get the name out. Tragh never did seem to approve of informal addresses, but Gary was his elder and would be called what he wanted to be called.

"From what I understand, there is something within the parchment that will draw or erase the parts of the map you request," he said.

I touched the map again. It felt like any other parchment I'd handled before.

Looking over the new lines on the map, I realized that the border of Verd was within leagues of the mountain where Narden lived. I leaned back with a start.

"The temple you were at is here." He tapped a point a few leagues inside the border. "It's the closest temple like that to Faruq's border, which is here." Another tap, and the line extended and traced around Maren and into more of the blank part of the map.

"This is the land of the House of Suvora," he said as the colors filled in for that area. "It is the only border that Faruq actually shares with Verd."

The colors came to a stop when the border of the House of Suvora connected. "We are fairly certain that you were taken through that land, but not along one of the more heavily used trade routes."

"The House of Nori'en is here." The map began to fill in again, starting from the border of the House of Suvora's land.

"The sea is to the north and the House of Maren is south with the Chayyim River as the border there." The map continued to color, filling in the river into more of the blank area after finishing with the two Houses' borders.

"That is as far as we need to consider for now," Tragh said above my head.

Once more I brushed my hand on the sheet, everything felt just like it had before. "Maren borders Verd," I managed.

"Yes, my lady, which is the matter I would speak to you of," he replied.

"You . . . you said that only Suvora bordered Verd," I whispered.

"My lady"—he chuckled—"the House of Maren is not actually a part of Faruq. The dragons share an alliance with the House of Rem'Maren and, by that alliance, a truce with Faruq."

I stared at him and then the map for several moments. The dragons ruled their own land? It was an odd thought to believe. I had always understood that the dragons were the servants of Rem'Maren. I wondered what else I didn't know.

"Lady Ari'an," Tragh continued while I trailed my thoughts, "the reason we would like for you to return to Torion Castle is because we live far too close to Verd's border for you to be completely safe here. Dragon slayers travel into these mountains whenever the weather permits."

I looked back at the hand span between where I was now and Verd's border. I could understand his concern. Seeing the border, that close to where I was and within another hand span of the temple where four years of my life were stolen made me shudder.

"Sir," I started, gathering my thoughts, "were is Nor'quitarn?"

Glancing up at him, I saw that he had an eyebrow cocked at me. "Here," he answered, tapping a spot half a hand span from the House of Suvora's border inside Nori'en's land.

Half a hand to Suvora border and then almost three hands to Verd's.

"Where is Torion Castle?" I asked.

He indicated a place a hand's breadth into Nori'en and another hand's breadth from Suvora's border.

"Why didn't he take me through here?" I asked indicating a pass between the borders of Nori'en, Rem'Maren, and Maren. I could tell that it would have been shorter to go that way. I was the first thing he sold back in Verd, so a shorter trip to get rid of me would make sense, especially with the trouble I caused him.

I heard Tragh shift behind me. "We guard that pass," he answered. "He wouldn't have made it to Verd with you if he had come that way."

I took a deep breath. "Sir," I started, "I was not safe here." I set my finger on Nor'quitarn. "Why would I be safe here?" I set my thumb on Torion Castle, marking the distance between my fingers.

I took a deep breath when he didn't say anything. "Also, if I would have been safe here"—I indicated the pass between Maren and Verd—"why am I not safe here?" I set my thumb on the mountain with the dragons circling it.

I was frightened by the thought that I was within less than a day's travel from the temple, but what scared me more was not having the dragons around to protect me. I had seen the extent that Narden and Adenern would go to in order to keep me from even being scared.

Narden had often stayed up all night after I had a nightmare in case I woke up again, which I often would. Both he and Adenern had protected me when my father had frightened me. I had no doubt that Narden would have injured my father if he had tried to force me to do anything at all. Adenern had hidden me when my father followed me into the room of pools.

I knew now that my father was not going to harm me, but at that point, I was scared of any human. I was scared even when Lord Grath came near me. Narden and Adenern understood that. If there was ever a real threat to me, I had no doubt that they would risk their lives to keep me safe. Hadn't they already done that when they rescued me from that temple? Didn't that make this the safest place for me?

I hadn't heard anything from Tragh and turned my head slowly to look at him. He had a smile that it looked like he was trying to fight off.

Finally, he threw his head back and laughed. "You will do well," he finally managed.

Narden wandered into the room at that point looking somewhat surprised by the dignified Tragh's mirth. "What is going on?" he asked walking over.

Tragh took a deep breath. "We are discussing Lady Ari'an's travel plans."

I glanced at the map on Ari's desk. I'd known that this would come up again. I swallowed hard. At least this time, we would have more notice. I was also glad that Tragh brought it up. I knew I couldn't have managed the discussion without telling Ari all the reasons she should refuse to leave. Aside from her safety, I didn't want her to leave because I was used to having her here. Life was more fun with her around. I held my tongue and managed, "Let me know if you need anything, my lady."

I walked back into the room of pools. I walked as far from my cave as I could. I didn't need to listen to their conversation. That would only upset me. I would find out from Tragh or Lord Grath when she would be leaving. What was the point of bringing all the presents we had today if she was leaving soon? I flopped into a far corner and stirred the water of a near pool with my claws.

It took a bit before Adenern noticed me. He wandered over and asked what was wrong. I explained. By the time I finished, Renard had joined us as well.

"She won't leave until winter at the earliest," he said.

"What?" I asked.

He explained.

I watched Narden walk away. He called me "my lady" only when he was upset about something. I could imagine that my leaving would upset him, but at that moment, I wasn't planning on leaving at all. As far as I was concerned, someone would have to drag me screaming from this place, and I could imagine that Narden would certainly not allow that.

"My lady," Tragh started, he had a graver tone to his voice than he had earlier. I turned back to him, watching his nose or eyebrows as was my custom. I didn't look people in the eye. I had a hard enough time looking at their faces. Meeting their gaze still scared me. I didn't even look Narden in the eye very often. "It is not only your safety that concerns me," he said evenly.

That statement startled me.

"Also," he continued, "this is not the safest place for you in Maren."

I turned back to the map, looking over the mountain range.

"Lord Grath and Lord Cristeros have come to the agreement that you can stay here until winter begins," he continued.

"Sir," I gathered what little courage I had, "I don't like having my life decided for me." I cringed thinking how my life had been decided for me during the four years before. Even suggesting that I should have some say about what happened to me scared me, but the thought of leaving scared me more.

"Which is why I am discussing this with you now," he said evenly.

"Should one of them speak to me about this then?" I asked wondering why they would have sent Tragh.

"Lord Grath tried to," I heard him lie down next to me.

"When?" I asked not remembering that conversation.

"The day you met Gary," he answered.

"Oh." I didn't want to dwell on that day too much. It was a bad day. "He wasn't going to take me away right then?"

"No, but things often do not work out the way people plan," Tragh said evenly, lowering his head to meet my gaze, which was focused on his neck at that point.

I looked away, skirting my eyes across his claws to the side wall to the desk.

"Lady Ari'an," he said sternly.

I closed my eyes for a moment then slowly met his gaze. I bit my lip and shuddered.

"Have I hurt you?" the question shocked me.

I shook my head, ducking my gaze to the floor.

He cleared his throat, I looked back up and shuddered again.

"Have I ever yelled at you or treated you in any way that is not equal to your station as a Lady of the realm of Faruq?"

I shook my head again, wanting desperately to look away.

"Understand this," he said moving his head closer to me. "You look down to no one. You are and always have been a Lady of the House of Nori'en. Even if you were not a noble, you are still a person, making you equal to any other person anywhere."

I closed my eyes for a moment, fighting desperately to keep from shaking.

"Lady Ari'an," his voice was softer now. I opened my eyes and ducked them to the floor before forcing my gaze back to his, "what happened to you was terrible. It was wrong, but it was not your fault. Do not let that determine how you live the rest of your life. You have every right to walk down any street anywhere on Arnbjorg with your head up. Do you understand?"

I did, sort of. Four years of beatings screamed in my mind against everything he'd just said. I wanted to believe him. I wanted to know that I wasn't worth less than the dirt on the floor, but I couldn't believe it yet. I felt my hands shaking.

"I understand, sir," I heard my voice break, swallowed hard, and ducked my head, "but I don't think I believe it," I whispered.

"At least you are honest," he said softly. "Belief can change. We will work on that."

I turned back to the map, not wanting to "work on that" at that moment. I fought to keep my vision clear, but several tears did fall on the map. I wiped them off quickly and was surprised to find that the colors on the map did not smear. Again, I wondered about this parchment in front of me. Focusing on that took my mind away from the previous discussion.

Tragh was quiet for a long while. He was, probably, waiting for me to calm down. "My lady," he finally said, "we need to continue discussing your eventual move from here."

I nodded, not looking at him.

He didn't say anything for a moment, then continued, "Your safety is not the only concern involving your stay here."

He paused for a response from me, but I continued to stare at the map.

"Gary is the oldest dragon," he continued. "He is also one of the first who came to Maren."

I was surprised by that and glanced at Tragh. I'd heard that the dragons had been here for at least seven generations.

"He is over seven hundred years old now," Tragh continued, "and a prize target for anyone wanting to carve a reputation out of one of our hides. As you can probably tell, he is not able to defend himself as well as he once could."

I wouldn't want to see Gary in a fight. I'd seen him move fast, but he couldn't fly, and he certainly couldn't hold his own in any type of combat.

"No one could come up here, could they?" I asked. Knowing that Gary's cave didn't have a direct entrance from outside and that the other four dragon's entrances went straight down for at least a league or more depending on whose entrance it was.

"You would be amazed at what people can do when they put their minds to it," Tragh answered sounding a bit sad. He looked at me for a moment and then continued, "Add that prize to returning a runaway to that temple in Verd, and the risk might be appealing enough for someone to attempt."

I'd never thought I might be less safe here because of the dragons before. I glanced around, expecting someone to appear in the entrance at that instance.

"My lady." I turned to Tragh as he spoke, "Will you take a deep breath for me?"

I inhaled and held my breath for a moment, then exhaled as Tragh continued, "You are as safe here now as you were many moments ago."

That was true, but moments ago I hadn't know that I wasn't safe here. What if . . .

Tragh cut into my thoughts, "I told you all of this so that you would understand why we would like for you eventually to move to a new location."

I needed to calm down. I wanted to be part of this decision, didn't I? I wanted to hold some sway over what happened in my life, didn't I? I sat on my hands, forcing them to stop shaking. I knew that wasn't "appropriate behavior for a lady," but at that moment, it was far more appropriate than going into a shaking fit or screaming.

"Lady Ari'an," Tragh's voice had a deep compassionate tone to it, "please, understand that we never would have brought you here if you were not safe here."

I stared at the map grappling with every thought that screamed for attention within me.

"We had originally thought you would be here a day at most." I heard him laugh lightly. I glanced at him surprised.

"It is not a common request from a noble to come live in a cave in the mountains with a group of large lizards. Especially, since most noble ladies see a dragon and scream." There was an odd twinkle in his eyes.

I could understand his point; looking around I couldn't think of anywhere that I would rather be, but I could certainly understand why most people would not want to be here. There were no servants to delegate work to. There were no fancy carpets or silverware, no tables to ensure were set properly to match the colors of the visiting dignitary. I didn't mind. I liked the calm here. There were no people to please of any type.

He continued, "When you did stay longer, we thought you would want to leave with your father."

"Then I stayed through winter," I continued watching Tragh smile.

"When Lord Grath came last time, he intended to speak to you about all of this," he continued, coming to our current point.

"Gary is the authority here." He cocked an eyebrow when I glanced up with a surprised look on my face. "I and a couple of the second and third generation handle most of the minor details, but he has the final authorization on everything if he chooses."

I had not once thought that Gary was important in this hierarchy. I had also thought that Tragh was the final authority, but now there were two others equal to him. Another thought came to me that I hadn't considered before.

"How old are you?" I glanced up and quickly added, "Sir."

He cocked his eyebrow at me again. "I do not usually disclose that information."

I felt my face go red; of course that was rude of me to even ask.

The dragon leaned toward me a bit and said, "Just between you and me, I am sixty-eight."

"Wha . . .?" I caught myself before uttering my surprise. My face must have betrayed me though.

Tragh cocked an eyebrow at me again and said, in a completely serious tone, "Do I look younger than that?"

"N-no," I stammered looking at my fingers, "it's just . . . I thought . . ." I glanced up expecting an offended look on his face. He was smiling and had a twinkle in his eyes that I knew from Narden and Adenern. He was teasing me.

I stared at his nose for a while trying to think clearly. "Sir," I finally managed, I stopped before asking, "Why are you so young?" which I knew would sound inaccurate at least. If he were human, sixty-eight would be an elder, but if dragons lived to be five hundred . . . He was waiting for me to finish my statement. "Why, sir, are you one of the lower lords if . . ." What was I digging myself into?

I heard Tragh laugh. "I am the eldest in Gary's line, which automatically places me in a position of authority." He paused for a moment. "If something happened to me, the position would fall to Renard."

I thought about that for a moment. "Why isn't there anyone else?"

I noticed that Tragh looked a bit saddened by the question. *You are prying into matters that do not concern you,* I heard a woman's voice say in my head. I vaguely remembered my mother telling me that when I asked her about some of the discussions that my father was having with the Lord of Sparins.

"I'm sorry to pry, sir," I said looking at my hands. "This is none of my concern."

"This is your concern, and it does tie into what we are discussing," Tragh responded immediately with a sharp tone to his voice.

I glanced up surprised. He had the impassioned look about him that Narden often had when he was defending me in an argument. "You are a lady of the realm, and as such, matters that affect your realm concern you," he continued. "Most noble ladies would not consider it a concern to them and will ignore important matters when they do not see any direct effect to their fashion." There was an undertone of a growl in his voice. "I expect better from you."

I had never met many ladies of the realm. My parents had not taken me to other Houses. I often thought now that they shouldn't have taken me anywhere at all no matter how I pleaded. They could have told me of the dangers if they did take me places. I wasn't sure how well I would have listened, or if I would have believed them, but at least I would have known.

"Gary's line," Tragh continued, "is the line of leadership, in the same way that Lord Grath will transfer his title as Lord of the House of Rem'Maren to Lord Drenar, Mighty One willing. As such, his line is the one that must respond to threats when no one else can or will." I glanced up when I heard him let out a heavy sigh. "His line is also the first to be betrayed."

"His line is short," I said softly, remembering the phrase from a conversation I'd overheard between my parents when speaking of one of the other Houses' family trees.

"Very," Tragh said.

"So I shouldn't be here," I said, unable to keep the quiver from my voice.

"You are welcome here," Tragh answered immediately. "I am not demanding that you leave."

I glanced up at him forcing myself to meet his gaze.

He smiled. "Was that hard?"

I looked at his nose and nodded slightly.

"It will become easier with practice," he replied with a saddened tone to his voice. A moment passed, and he continued, "You have a right to know what decisions are made and why, especially when they involve you. Do you understand why we would like to move you to Caer Corisan at the end of autumn before winter sets in?"

"It's dangerous to have me here," I whispered fighting back tears.

"Lady Ari'an," Tragh said evenly.

I realized after a moment of silence that he wanted me to meet his gaze. I felt the shudder run down my back. I would win this battle that my memory fought with my body. I pulled my eyes along his nose until I looked into his eyes.

"Stay there," he said softly. "You have nothing to fear from me."

I bit into my lip and fought the urge to tremble or lower my gaze.

"You are welcome here," he continued, "you will always be welcome here. If you need to stay here into next winter or longer, you are welcome here." He watched me for a moment. "Do you understand?"

I nodded and returned my gaze to the end of his nose.

"Lady Ari'an," he said again, and I pulled my gaze back to meet his, "You are a lady of the realm, and as such, you cannot spend the rest of your life here. Do you understand?"

I nodded again.

"Lady . . ."

I met his gaze, and he cocked an eyebrow. I felt myself smile slightly; even though his scales were brown, not blue, I could see the resemblance between him and Adenern and Narden when he did that.

"Caer Corisan is the next step to moving you back into the society you should be a part of." He paused for a moment, and I nodded, immediately meeting his eyes again.

"Do you believe you can move there before winter comes again?" he asked.

I didn't answer for a moment, then said, "I don't know."

"Will you plan to?"

"I can try, sir."

"I will not bring this to your attention until summer, all right?" he told me.

I nodded and focused on his nose again. "Please, sir, would you send notice when Lord Grath is coming . . . or anyone like him?" I managed to ask.

"I will do my best, but I cannot always guarantee such things," he said with a slight smile. "I am proud of you, my lady."

I met his eyes from surprise.

"You have come far, and you will do well as a lady of the realm."

True to his word, Tragh did not mention my moving to Caer Corisan again throughout the rest of that spring and into summer. The dragons were gone more often and for longer periods of time during those days. Adenern came back once with a gash across his shoulder.

CHAPTER 16

POLITICS

Verd was not happy with Faruq when spring came, to say the least. After the accusations that they took a noble and used her as a temple prostitute were denied, Verd started raiding the House of Suvora's lands. Without Ari testifying to a gathering of both Verdian and Faruqen officials, King Viskhard would not declare a situation of tension much less war itself. That put the borders in a state of flux. The king would not deploy the army to assist in case Verd thought it was an act of war, so the borders were left to seek help wherever they could find it.

Since we had brought on the situation by rescuing Lady Ari'an, Maren was one of those who assisted. The Houses of Nori'en and Rem'Maren also sent aid, being directly involved in the situation as well.

The quaint little villages of Suvora were not happy about having dragons flying over their homes. We were blamed for several fires that Verd set in the barley fields. I was becoming quite agitated by early summer. The villages started launching things at us whenever we patrolled. At first it was just rotten vegetables, but when a cart of broken glass was catapulted at Adenern, I was within an hands-breadth of burning down the entire town.

Adenern needed to get back to Caer Corisan immediately to have the wounds treated. That was the only thing that kept me from torching something there.

Rem'Maren sent troops to each village to keep incidents like that from happening. That helped us, but now they were mad that they had to house the soldiers. It didn't seem to matter that we caught or chased out raiders from that area every day. I suggested we let them deal with the raiders themselves at one point.

"How many children would you have lost to Verd because you were not there?" my father asked in response. "How many with red hair would you have sent to the temple we rescued Lady Ari'an from?"

I knew he was right, but the politics of the situation made me want to burn down someone's farm.

Shortly after that, Adenern and I started patrolling Maren's border. That kept fruit from flying at us, but since the raiders coming into Maren's border knew they would face dragons only, they brought the equipment to deal with a dragon. Having things flung at us was less common now, but when attacks happened, they were far more dangerous. Maren was mountainous though, so that worked in our favor. We could come over a mountain unexpectedly. The dragon slayers had to go around. They could hide in the forests, but so could we, and we were better at it.

Adenern faced down three dragon slayers and a knight early on. He came away with a gash the length of my leg across his shoulder. The dragon slayers and the knight didn't come away at all.

Ari patched up that wound on him. I found out later that the physician at Caer Corisan said he couldn't have done better. That was my lady.

She also hung each of the tapestries from her birthday around the entrance cave. When we landed, we saw Maren's hung from the ceiling about twenty steps from the entrance. About ten steps behind that to the left was the House of Rem'Maren's attached to the wall. Next to Ari's room hung the House of Nori'en's tapestry.

The other pieces of furniture that we'd brought were organized into sections near the back of the cave. There were the two cabinets with the dishes sitting in the back left corner with the table and chairs about five steps out from that corner.

Ari embroidered the cloth on the table herself. The picture was a duplicate of the landscape from the map that Tragh had shown to her. She only stitched in the landscape of Suvora, Maren, and Nori'en, none of the towns or borders. She added the Houses of Sparins and Darya, which were to the south of Maren and west of Nori'en.

The linens over the two cabinets were both birthday presents by Pher'am. Those were reproductions of two of the gardens at Torion Castle.

Her mother, Lady Hin'merien, sent one of a waterfall, which graced the shelf of books standing in the corner across from the two cabinets. The linen ran down the side, following the line of the waterfall. It was all very pretty. Ari impressed me arranging it all like that.

Her desk stood in front of the bookshelf with its pen stand of quills and different inks.

The floor had five deep carpets that Adenern brought as gifts from Lord Cristeros. They looked worse for the wear that a dragon puts on such things. Ari would wash them off every once in a while, and they would look almost new, if you didn't notice the snags and cuts in them, of course.

She received notice the week after Adenern's run in with the dragon slayers and knight that Lord Grath would come the next day.

I watched her receive the news from Tragh with a bit of apprehension. "He will be discussing with you a trip to Caer Corisan," he told her.

I watched with surprise as she met his eyes and said, "Yes, sir." She'd come far over the year she'd been here.

That afternoon I helped her wash the rugs and tapestries. She dusted the cabinets and all the dishes along with her bookshelf and the books on it. I told her I thought sweeping a rock floor was silly, but she did that too. It did actually look better when she was done, but I didn't admit that to her.

Tragh left early that afternoon after I insisted. If she was doing all this work to get ready for Lord Grath's visit, I wanted him at least not to know what all had been done.

The next morning after a night to dry, everything was rehung or placed. She pulled the best dishes from the cabinets and made sure that all the silver matched. (Living with dragons has a tendency to leave metal objects bent or melted.) She polished every piece they would use. She also managed to cook an impressive meal on her little stove, which was quite an accomplishment considering the thing had to sit over an open fire to cook anything.

She lost the sleeve on one of her dresses to that stove that morning. While checking on three loaves of bread, the lace on the cuff apparently became too hot and started on fire. She noticed immediately and simply tore the whole sleeve off and threw it into the flames. After looking over her arm and finding no burns, she went right back to that stove and kept working.

I wasn't sure if she did all this as a proper reception for the Lord of a House, or if she kept busy to distract herself from the visit that was coming. I didn't ask her.

I helped her when requested to, but mostly left her to her own activities. She didn't need me to tell her what to do or not do, and I needed the time to get used to the idea that she wouldn't be here soon. Caer Corisan wasn't far, but with as little time as I spent at home lately, I didn't have much faith in spending a lot of time at the fortress after Ari moved there. I wondered yet again what she would take with her when she left. I didn't talk to her about her trip. She had been doing so well lately, I didn't want to be the one to send her into another relapse.

After Tragh told me that Lord Grath would be coming the next day, I buried myself in memories of my mother preparing Torion Castle for dignitaries who visited.

I started just to give myself something to do. With Narden, Adenern, and Renard gone so often now, I was bored sometimes. Also, Adenern was hurt, and keeping busy kept my mind from drifting to why. I knew in the back of my mind that they were in these fights because of rescuing me. I understood that I wasn't the only cause, but I was the main cause.

Verd and Faruq never had good relations. I had memories of my father discussing such things long before I was taken. I did know that I was the catalyst this time. All the discussions I remember overhearing involved Verd looking for or using some little thing or another to start trouble.

Also, I was nervous about seeing Lord Grath again. The last time he had been here was the day I'd met Gary. I prayed to the god I read about from Narden's book that I wouldn't have a shaking episode while he was here. I knew that the gods that my parents served would not answer me if I didn't have something to barter with. Narden's god answered slaves, so he might answer me. He might not require a heavy repayment for such a small matter. I had very little I could offer a god. I did not have a room I could dedicate to him. I didn't even own the room I slept in. I had no place to dedicate a garden to a goddess. I had no animals that could be sacrificed. Hopefully, Narden's god wouldn't request such things.

One thing led to another as I straightened up the entrance cave. As I got ready to clean the rugs, I realized that the tapestries would look dingy with the clean rugs, so I washed those too. Narden helped a bit with that. I washed things in one of the medium pools that was fairly hot, and occasionally I couldn't get things back out. The heat didn't seem to bother him, so he would fish things out for me.

As part of my birthday, the dragons brought several long drying rods from Caer Corisan. One of the cooks saw all the things that were sent from my family and had the sense to send things to help clean with. The rods sat on two crossbars creating three points where I could hang things.

She'd also included dusting cloths and several brooms. I used almost everything that day. I felt better having something to do that was productive.

Otherwise I had nothing to do here but bring up memories of the temple, waiting for the next meal, the next breeder, the next lash, the next priest to undo a shackle. If I kept busy, the silence wouldn't bring up such memories.

A small part of me was looking forward to moving to Caer Corisan. I was still nervous about how to interact with other humans, but certainly there would be more things for me to do there. I didn't mind working. I didn't want to be a lady who just sat around criticizing or embroidering all the time. I hoped the people at Caer Corisan wouldn't treat me like that.

I waited to do the less noticeable things until the morning that Lord Grath was to come. *I remembered my mother once saying, "If you are expecting something unpleasant, do not merely wait for it to happen. You may have to work to resolve the problem, but if it is something unavoidable, do not push it aside. If you cannot resolve it quickly, stay occupied so that it does not worry you to exhaustion while you have to wait."*

That morning, I worked on dusting off the dishes in the cabinet. I only used a couple of plates or cups, but the cabinet had enough to serve several people. Lord Grath would probably not see more than the dishes I had set on the table already.

I hoped he wouldn't mind the meal. I'd put it together as best I could. That thought made me pause, I had not seen him eat here before, but he had never been offended when one of the dragons brought in a deer or cow, skinned it, and cooked it. I had noticed that a dragon's cooking had about two varieties, either not cooked or burnt. I wondered if that was why one of the first things the dragons brought almost a year ago had been food that was already cooked or didn't need to be cooked. I also wondered if that was the reason that Lord Grath didn't eat here.

CHAPTER 17

HOSTING A LORD

Narden noticed when Renard approached in the distance. I looked out the entrance. They were still a long way off. Five more cups and then I would check again, I told myself. I wiped off those cups, each with a flower design etched in silver. The matching saucers lay in a pile on the front ledge.

Glancing over my shoulder, I saw that they were not quite close enough for me to approach the entrance to meet them yet. I set the saucers on their edges on the ledge and placed the cups in front of them to add a bit of color to the cabinet. I noticed that even though I felt nervous, my hands weren't quivering even a little. Maybe Narden's god did answer prayers.

With a deep breath, I turned and walked halfway across the entrance cave. I stopped and closed my eyes as I saw Renard land.

I heard Lord Grath dismount and the customary shaking scales after he unbuckled the saddle and pulled it from Renard's back.

"You have done marvelous work here, my lady." It was Renard who spoke first.

I opened my eyes and looked at him. Realizing that the words I'd opened my mouth to say hadn't made it out of my throat, I swallowed hard and tried again. "Thank you, sir."

I glanced at Lord Grath and was surprised by the awed look on his face. I watched as his head turned to take in the whole cave. Finally, his eyes came to rest on me.

I took a breath and curtsied. "Welcome, my lord," I managed.

I straightened and, with a great effort, pulled my eyes to meet his. I took a step back and glanced around. He was beaming. I'd not seen someone look that proud since my father danced with me at the harvest feast when I was twelve. I'd managed not to miss a single step that evening.

He bowed and asked, "Would you mind if we spoke privately, my lady?"

I hadn't expected that. I had thought that Narden would be here like he usually was when Lord Grath visited. I glanced over at him. He looked somewhat upset by the question also.

Tragh's words came back to me from when he requested that I meet his gaze. Lord Grath had done nothing to me that I shouldn't trust him. He'd never hurt me. He'd helped rescue me. I had no reason not to trust him. The thought of being alone with him still scared me. I bit my lip and took a deep breath through my nose. "That would be fine, sir," I answered.

Narden looked shocked, but I would explain later. He and Renard walked into the room of pools. I saw Narden look back at me from the door. "It's all right," I mouthed to him, and then he was gone.

I turned back to Lord Grath and again didn't manage to force the words out of my throat that I wanted to say. I needed to do this. I swallowed hard again and managed, "Would you like something to eat, my lord?"

He smiled and offered his arm. "Will you join me, my lady?"

I couldn't breathe. I hadn't expected this. I did of course have two places set at the table, but I had thought the closest I would have to come was the distance between my place at the table and his. What was I to do? I couldn't think of a dignified way to turn down his offer of escort. I fought hard, forcing my foot forward. Then took the next step, and the next. I put my hand on his arm and closed my eyes.

I felt him take a step forward and moved with him. I took two steps, three, five, ten, and fifteen. Then I heard a scrapping on the floor. I jumped and pulled my hand off his arm, opening my eyes.

It took me a moment to realize that all Lord Grath had done was pull the chair out for me and was now offering me the seat. I sat lightly and felt him push in the chair to the table. I watched his feet walk around to his chair, pause while he pulled it out, and then disappear under the table.

I followed the edge of the table till my eyes found his hands resting on the edge. Then I made it to his shoulders but couldn't get any farther.

"This looks wonderful," he said as I saw his arm move to motion at the table.

I needed to get this not being able to get words out on the first try under control soon. Finally, I managed, "Thank you."

"Would you mind if I blessed the food?" The question didn't surprise me anymore. Tragh, Renard, Adenern, Narden, and even Gary blessed their food. It was an odd tradition, thanking a god for something that you caught and prepared (well, burnt in the dragons' cases) yourself. I had not heard a human do this before, but the same god was patron to the House of Rem' Maren. I shook my head.

I looked him full in the face when he started. The words weren't any that I knew. They also didn't have the same tone to them that Gary's language had. I found months ago that the words Gary spoke to change the pool temperature and bring the lights on were from a language that he spoke when he was young. Occasionally, he would say something in that language. I knew a few phrases now because of that, but this was entirely different.

Lord Grath smiled at me when he was done. I forced myself to hold my eyes there. I wanted to run as fast as I could from the table, not because the words sounded bad, nor because Lord Grath was someone I should be afraid of. I didn't want to look him in the face like that. What if he reached across the table and hit me? Any of the priests would have, but he wasn't one of them. I forced myself to believe he wouldn't, and realized he was waiting for me to answer something he'd just said.

"I-I'm sorry." I glanced at the table and grimaced. I'd lost that battle after all. "I didn't hear what you said," I finished.

"That is from a language that was already ancient when Gary was young," he repeated.

I looked up at him again. Was it possible for something to be older than Gary? I was glad that question didn't make it out of my mouth. What was I thinking? Arnbjorg existed before Gary ever came here. Tragh told me that. Rem'Maren was the youngest house and started at the same time the dragons came. All the other houses were older than Gary as well.

"I have something for you, if you would like it," he continued.

He pulled a large book from the pack he'd carried over to the table with him. He offered it to me across the table. I stared at the book for a long time. If I took it, I'd have to almost touch his hand. He could grab me then. He hadn't done anything to hurt me yet. If he was going to hurt me, he would have when we walked over, or had he been waiting until the dragons would be off their guard? He could have been lulling me into trusting him only to betray me now. What if I couldn't scream if he tried to grab me? Sounds hadn't been coming out of my throat very well.

My mind raced through all the things he might do. Somehow it came to rest on one event. If he was going to hurt me, he had all the opportunity he needed when I was still at the temple. I wouldn't have screamed there. No one would have cared what he did to me.

Slowly, I reached across the table and took the heavy book. He didn't do anything except let go of it.

I set the book on the corner of the table and opened it. Much like Narden's book, this one had no pictures. It did, however, have numbers in one corner of the pages that increased every two pages. That was an interesting way to keep track of where you were in a book. What struck me the most was that on one page there was writing. I had opened to a story that I knew from Narden's book. On the other page, there was nothing but ornate lines. Little lines with swooshes, longer lines with tails, most of the lines looked like whoever drew them had tried to make fancy little boxes but left off some of the sides.

Lord Grath's voice sounded beside me. I jumped, looking up in fright. He was standing at the corner of the table looking down at the book. I hadn't heard him stand up. I hadn't understood what he'd said, but it sounded similar to the accent he'd used to bless the food. I looked back down at the book and found his hand tracing along a line of the little boxes. He continued to talk in that odd language, and I realized he was reading the boxes.

"You're reading it backward!" I told him as I watched his hand trace from the right side of the page to the left. Of course it sounded wrong.

He laughed. It was a nice sound, but having him do anything that close frightened me a lot. "It seems like that, but this is a language that is written from the sword hand to the knife."

"Why?" my curiosity beat my fear.

"That is a question that I do not know the answer to, but it is often asked." Then he continued, "There is a stipulation to accepting this gift."

After too long of a pause, I realized he was waiting for me to look at him.

I certainly didn't want to. I could just close the book and push it away. I didn't need to accept this book when I couldn't read half of it. I could continue to read Narden's book for these stories. Maybe there was a copy at Caer Corisan so I could still read the book when I went there. I didn't need my own copy.

Tragh would be disappointed though. He would tell me that I was Lord Grath's equal. In fact the House of Nori'en was older, so in a technical sense, I outranked him even though I was the youngest and a daughter of my house. I put my hand on the book and closed it. I didn't want to disappoint Tragh. I could look a dragon in the eye, a leader of Maren nonetheless. How many people could do that? Why should I fail looking at a mere human?

I fought hard and looked up. I saw him smile. Then he put his hand on my shoulder. I didn't think I could breathe any faster, but somehow I'd just managed to. He could do anything he wanted to from here. There was no way I could stop him. Somehow I managed not to look away.

"To keep this," he said, "you must learn to read it all. There are all together three other languages in this book. To keep it, you must learn to read them."

He didn't let go. He was waiting for my answer. Why couldn't he wait for my answer at the other end of the table? Why couldn't he at least take his hand off my shoulder?

"Yes, sir," I finally managed to whisper.

His smile grew, he let go of my shoulder, and walked back to his seat.

My breath came out in a puff, and I felt every muscle in my body noticeably relax. I stared at my plate and then closed my eyes. I needed to breathe, just breathe. That was all I wanted to do at that moment.

To his credit, Lord Grath said nothing. I didn't know if he was watching me. In fact, I didn't care. He wasn't standing over me. He wasn't touching me. I could concentrate on nothing at all. I didn't have to be afraid.

I heard a slight thud on the table and then a heavier one a moment later. I lifted my eyes to the edge of my plate and noticed that my water glass was now full. That was thoughtful of him. I reached for the glass and was surprised again that my hand was not quivering in the least. I owed Narden's god more than I thought I would.

I drank the whole cup before setting it back down. I saw Lord Grath's hand pick it up again and heard the swish from the tablecloth as he lifted the water pitcher and the sound of the water flowing into the glass this time. He set the glass back down in front of my plate.

"Thank you, sir," I managed in slightly more than a whisper.

"You are welcome, my lady." His voice was soft. It had a tone to it that reminded me of when Narden told me that it was all right. I wanted to cry.

"You haven't eaten anything, sir." It was the only thing I could think of to distract myself.

"Neither have you," he answered with that same soft tone.

I began to reach for the bread, but realized that would only move uneaten bread from the serving platter to my plate. I still wouldn't eat it.

"I'm not very hungry, sir," I answered pulling my hand back from the plate.

"I can understand that," he replied. "Would you mind if I ate some of this? I am interested to find out how a lady of the realm's cooking tastes."

I looked up at his elbows in horror. What had I done? In trying to set out a proper reception for him, I'd done something that ladies of the realm never did. They weren't supposed to cook.

"I-I-I . . ." I swallowed hard and tried again, "I'm sorry, sir, I didn't mean . . ." I stopped again, "It's not proper."

"Hang proper!" he said.

My head snapped up instantly, and I looked him full in the face. He had an irked look on his face that faded into a smile.

He leaned forward slightly and semiwhispered, "Do not tell them that I said that," and tilted his head slightly toward the room of pools.

I laughed. I stopped almost immediately locking my gaze back on my plate, but I couldn't stop smiling. I looked up after a moment and said, "But, sir, you are always correcting Narden and Adenern when they say . . ." I trailed off realizing that I'd met his eyes without thinking about it.

He happened to be chewing on a piece of bread that he swallowed before answering, "That is a matter of grammar and etiquette."

"Both of them are in Gary's line," he continued. "They will eventually have positions of authority. They will meet men and dragons who will not consider a word they say if they do not say it with the correct phrase. It will be hard enough for them to make themselves heard because they are dragons. It will be that much harder if their speech sounds even remotely uncouth."

"That is why Tragh corrects them also?"

He nodded.

"M-ma-ma . . ." I started. I closed my eyes and mentally shook myself. I did not need to sound like a goat on top of everything else. "May I ask you something about Gary's line, sir?"

"Of course, my lady." He ladled some soup into his bowl.

"His line is short," I paused trying to word the next part.

A moment later, I heard, "That is not quite a question."

"I know," I replied, "I just . . . I did not want to ask Tragh or Gary because I thought it might upset them." Realizing I was playing with the edge of the tablecloth, I moved my hands to the top of the table.

I glanced up at Lord Grath who had a slightly concerned look on his face. "You are welcome here, my lady," I could hear Tragh say the same words months ago in my memory.

"No, sir, that's not what I wanted to know." I then added, "I'll go to Caer Corisan in the fall. I-I-I should be able to handle that, but . . ." I trailed off again.

"I am proud of you, my lady," I heard him say. "If I had a daughter, I would want one with your courage."

"What?" I met his gaze by accident again.

He set his spoon down and met my gaze directly. I certainly couldn't look away now.

"You, my lady, have managed in a year's time to change from a terrified girl to a lady of the realm," he began.

I wanted to interrupt, but my throat refused to let any sound out.

"You live with dragons, a feat, I would like to tell you, most men in this realm could never accomplish."

I still couldn't get anything out of my mouth.

"You also prepared a delicious meal and cleaned a dragon's cave"—he smiled—"which I have never before heard of a lady of the realm doing, even when there is no one else for them to order to do the task."

Still nothing.

"You have volunteered to make a transition that will not only be uncomfortable, but frightening for you. Finally, you managed to deal graciously with several moments today that I know frightened you terribly, and I have not seen you so much as quiver even once."

"My lord!" That came out much louder than I had intended.

He tilted his head to the side and folded his hands on the table.

"I would hardly consider myself a lady of the realm at this point in time," I began. "I have no idea what the proper linen is for hosting a lord from any of the houses. I cannot tell the difference between maroon and burgundy though I know that if the Lord of the House of Sparins even sees burgundy in any of the . . ." I couldn't think of the word and waved at the tapestries and rugs around the cave.

"Trappings," Lord Grath volunteered.

"Trappings," I continued, "he will storm out of the castle and not trade with your house for at least a year."

I took a short breath and continued, "Dragons are by no means hard to live with. They don't ask you to sit up straight or curtsy to the proper level when they enter a room or whatever other thing you can think of that makes you feel like a doll on display." I lowered my voice a bit and studied the water pitcher. "They'll also protect you."

"I cook"—I brought my eyes back up to his chin, his beard looked a bit unkempt—"because I don't want to eat raw or burnt meat all the time, and if I didn't clean these things, no one would. I've been terrified most of this time, and the only reason I didn't absolutely panic is because . . ."

I studied my spoon that I'd been playing with, realized I was playing with the spoon, and snapped it down on the table. "It's because Tragh would be disappointed. I'm going to Caer Corisan because it's the right thing to do, and I'm not shaking right now . . . because I asked your god to keep me from shaking while you were here."

Lord Grath didn't respond for a long moment. I finally ventured to look up at him again. He was beaming.

"Do you realize what you just told me, my lady?" he asked.

I wasn't getting words out again.

"You have told me today that you are willing to learn," he said as he pointed to the book on the corner of the table, "so I have no doubt that you will figure out the proper color schemes for a reception for Lord Astucieux, if you ever have to hold one for him."

"You have told me that you are not only not afraid of dragons but that you also see them as people who are to be treated as such."

"You, my lady, are willing to do what you need to, even when it is something that would be considered below your station because it needs to be done, and you will do what is right even when it is not what you would like to do."

"If there were traits that I could choose for a lady of the realm, you have them. You, my lady, may not be the most sophisticated woman at the king's court, but you are loyal. You are willing to see people as they are and not as they appear to be. You are willing to put others before yourself. You . . ." He waited.

Slowly I lifted my eyes to his.

"Will do well as a lady of the realm."

I focused on my plate again. I wasn't sure if I should cry, laugh, or just wave off what he'd said. I certainly didn't see myself the way he did. I felt like a terrified child pretending to be a noblewoman. I wanted to run into the room of pools and hide behind Narden for the next few watches. I wanted to bury my head in my blanket and look at nothing at all until I could make the memories in my head dim.

During this whole encounter, I had heard seven different priests scream at me for looking at them. I'd fought the urge to cringe when four distinctly different beatings came to mind. The only thing that held me in place was that I didn't want to disappoint Tragh.

I wasn't sure how long I had been lost in my thoughts. I heard the light clink of dishes against each other. I jumped when I saw Lord Grath's hand pick up the plate in front of me. I watched his other hand pick up the bowl, saucer, and the silverware in turn, and set them on top of the plate. He moved the cup of water closer to the corner of the table and picked up the book also.

I watched him open the bottom cupboard door and pull out my dish tub. He placed the dishes in it and placed it back in the cupboard. He opened the top cupboard, and I jumped to my feet.

"I-I-I," I stopped and took a breath. I really needed to be able to say things on the first try. "I can do that, sir."

He turned and smiled at me. "I know you can. You seemed to be preoccupied though."

I took a step toward him and stopped when his smile broadened.

"If you would put this where you would like it kept and bring over the map that Tragh left with you," he continued, "I would appreciate it."

He held out the book to me again. I'd done this just moments before. I could do this again. I swallowed hard and stepped toward him. I took the book, turned, and walked over to my desk . . . and nothing happened. I remembered turning my back many times at the temple so my back would catch a blow instead of my face.

I set the book on my desk and watched him pick up my cup again and whisk the tablecloth off. He set the cup back on the table and folded the cloth. Back at the cupboard, he opened the cabinet that I keep linens in and set the tablecloth on the bottom shelf. It struck me as odd that he knew where all these things were supposed to go.

CHAPTER 18

LEARNING A MAP

Remembering that I was supposed to find the map, I pulled it from the bottom row on my bookshelf and walked back over to the table. I pulled the map from its case and spread it across the table. There wasn't a single mark on the map. I hadn't been able make it work since Tragh left. The map went blank after a watch, and I couldn't remember where the places were.

Lord Grath came over to the table, standing across from me, and placed his hand on the corner of the map. He just stood there for a moment, and I wondered if he didn't know where things were on that map also.

He lifted his hand off the map, and I saw a small compass star where his hand had been. He looked up when he heard me gasp. He looked slightly puzzled for a moment, then closed his eyes, and I saw his face look slightly annoyed.

"I apologize, my lady," he started, "Tragh did not show you how to use this map."

It wasn't a question, but I shook my head slightly. He still looked slightly annoyed.

"It wasn't his fault, sir," I told him. I certainly didn't want him to be upset with Tragh. "It was already started when he showed it to me, and it's not as though he could put his hand on a corner of the map."

He looked up at me and chuckled. "You have a plate that Armel made. Will you bring it here for a moment?"

What did that have to do with anything? I walked to the corner of the table and stepped away into the space between the table and the cupboard. Two steps and I was on Lord Grath's side of the table. Three more steps and my back was to him. I opened the right side of the cupboard and brought out a soft white cloth. I unwrapped the plate inside and carried both back to the table.

"Narden can make this change," he said reaching for the plate. I nodded handing the plate to him.

He traced his finger along the front edge of the plate and held it up to me. I took a step back. The plate had the dragon's mountain on it. He traced his finger along the back edge, and the picture changed to the crest of the House of Rem'Maren.

I took the plate from him and stared at it. Gingerly, I traced the front edge and nearly dropped the plate when it changed. I had thought it only worked for the dragons. When Lord Grath changed it, I thought of course it would work for him, he was a dragon lord.

"Will it work for everyone?" I asked still staring at the plate.

"No." I glanced up at him, and he had a smile on his face. "Just like this"—he motioned at the map—"it will only work for people who know how to use it. The plate will eventually turn back to a painting of Caer Corisan, but if you trace the center ridge on the back, it will change immediately."

I tipped the plate and traced the ridge he said, and true to his word, the plate changed to the original painting of Caer Corisan.

Still staring at the plate, I heard him say, "When we are finished, I will show you how to turn off the map as well."

Once more I traced the front edge of the plate making the mountain reappear.

"Is there a way to make a different picture stay?" I asked.

"Turn the center ridge on the back until you feel it click."

I tipped the plate over and gripped the center ridge. I had noticed that this ridge was deeper than most plates, but had thought it was just part of the design. The ridge did indeed turn, and I felt the click. I turned the plate back over and saw that the mountain was still there. Tracing the front edge again brought up the painting of Caer Corisan.

"How does it do that?" I breathed. I was a bit nervous that if I spoke too loudly, the plate would shatter in my hands.

"Armel explained that to me once," Lord Grath began, "but I must admit, I did not understand most of what he said."

I looked up at him. It struck me as odd that Lord Grath didn't understand something. "When you go to Caer Corisan, you may ask him yourself if you wish."

"Now, my lady," I looked up at him as he spoke, "all four corners have a compass point. Leave your hand on a corner for a little while, and it will appear."

I set the plate on the table next to where the parchment ended and placed my hand on the corner nearest to me. I frowned at the map when nothing appeared. Pressing my hand harder against the sheet, I left it in place longer. When I lifted my hand again, the compass point was aimed at my edge of the table. I noticed that there was a dragon gripping the compass point in his claws with his wings spread behind him. The dragon was a gold color with what looked like gray and green flecks on his scales.

The sheet moved as Lord Grath turned it so that north faced toward him. The compass at his corner had a blue dragon who seemed to be sleeping wrapped around the compass point.

"Do you remember where we are?" Lord Grath asked.

I stared at the blank sheet for a while and then shook my head. "I think Verd is over there"—I pointed toward the northwest corner of the map—"but is Maren directly under it or off this way, and the House of Suvora is under Verd?"

"You are right." He tapped the map where I thought Verd was, and the sheet began to color in.

"Maren is the buffer between most of Faruq and Verd." He tapped the map where Maren was, and the colors continued to spread into that area of the map.

The areas looked familiar now. "The House of Suvora is here then?" I touched the map where Maren stopped and jumped back when the detail began there also.

"Rem'Maren is here." He touched south of Maren, and the detail started to fill in there as well.

I stepped toward the map again and leaned over it. I studied the border between Maren and Rem'Maren for a moment and then touched a mountain on the border of the pass. "And this is where Caer Corisan is?" I held stead this time when the details of Caer Corisan filled in.

"Very good." I glanced up and noticed he was smiling again. "Now, do you remember where we are?"

I studied the mountain range that ran through Maren. "Here?" I finally asked pointing to a mountain along the line.

"Very close," he answered. "That is actually where Raleigh's line is." He touched the mountain that I'd pointed at, and I saw a red dragon etch onto it. He was sitting on the top of the mountain blowing fire into the air.

"Gary's line lives here." He touched a mountain closer to the river, and I saw the two dragons etch on to the map flying around the mountain.

"Otto's line lives here." He tapped a place several peaks to the north of Gary's mountain. The gold dragon from my compass point appeared on that mountain. "And Indigo's line is here." The map etched in the sleeping blue dragon wrapped around a mountain to the southwest.

I put my hand on the corner of the map opposite the corner with the sleeping dragon. After a moment, I took my hand away, and a compass point with the two dragons from Gary's mountain remained, flying around the compass point this time.

The map shifted, and I glanced up to see that Lord Grath had the fourth corner compass drawn in and had lifted the map to show it to me. There was the red dragon blowing fire into the air. The point of that compass was the dragon's flame.

"Why are they the same?" I asked staring from the corners to the mountains on the map.

"They are the likenesses of the original dragons who came here from what I understand," he answered.

I glanced at the different mountains again. "But I thought Gary was one of those original dragons." None of these looked anything like him.

Lord Grath flipped the map over to the blank side and said "Gary," tapping a section of the parchment. A gold-and-blue dragon colored near the center of the parchment. The problems that I had noticed on Gary matched on this dragon, except Gary was beige and silver . . . and blind. This dragon had clear blue eyes and had a blue body as well.

"What happened?" I asked and realized that was a rude question. I looked down at my feet. "I'm sorry, I shouldn't have asked that."

"Lady Ari'an." I didn't look up. There was a long pause, and then I heard a slight sigh. I glanced at his hands. "My lady," he continued, "I am going to tell you of several people who you may ask anything you want. They will not consider your questions rude or inappropriate."

He paused again. "Do you understand?"

I nodded but still didn't want to look up.

"Lady Ari'an."

I pulled my gaze off his hands, up his arms, to his shoulders. I closed my eyes for a moment then met his gaze. He held up a finger between his eyes. "Stay here."

I swallowed hard.

"You may ask anything you want of myself or my sons. You may also ask Tragh or his sons. Tragh, Renard, and myself along with Drenar will probably know more than Adenern, Narden, or my youngest sons, but you are welcome to ask any of us."

He looked directly at me for a moment, and I swallowed hard. "Do you understand?"

I nodded.

A crooked smiled spread on his face, and he said, "I would warn you to be careful about what you ask Gary. He can be . . ."

"Cranky?" I filled in remembering several times that Gary had been less than friendly.

"I was aiming for a slightly nicer way of saying that, but that is the idea."

I glanced back down at the picture.

"Gary," Lord Grath continued, "has done what most people do after a while. He has gotten older."

"He lost his sight while trying to rescue his son, Diggory." Lord Grath tapped the parchment to the upper right of Gary's picture. The picture of the other blue dragon filled in. The picture looked like a clean depiction of Gary.

"He did not get there in time though," Lord Grath said softly.

"But he had other children, didn't he?" I couldn't imagine losing a child and my sight on the same day.

"No." He tapped the parchment to the left. "His two grandsons were ambushed about ten years later with the help of Yacob from Otto's line."

The gold dragon colored in.

"From what I understand, he did not want to take orders from Aedelred or Adelwin and felt that he was better suited to leadership."

"What happened to him?" I asked looking over the pictures.

"The counsel found out, and he was condemned for the murders."

He set his hand to the lower left and continued, "Since, the three children of Aedelred and Adelwin were between five and eleven years old at that time, the other leadership positions fell to Raleigh's line."

The red dragon appeared on the parchment.

"Raleigh's eldest died about a century and a half later, and Matej from Indigo's line took his place." He tapped the right corner nearest me, and the sleeping blue dragon traced onto the map.

"The fourth position comes and goes depending on if Gary has a living descendant who is old enough to hold that position."

"Tragh," I said softly. Then I looked over each of the pictures. Each one looked far different from the next except for Gary and his son. It wasn't only the colors that varied. Indigo's blue was much darker than Gary's. The red dragon was broader and looked, if a dragon could, short. The gold one, Otto, was thin and long reminding me of a vine.

"Why isn't there a leader from Otto's line?" I asked.

"Otto," Lord Grath began, and I looked over at the gold dragon, "decided that since his son killed Gary's only son, his line would never have a leader of Maren."

"Is he still alive?" I asked. For the first time I realized that there might be hundreds of dragons, and I had only met five.

"No," he answered, "he died about ten years ago."

I took a step back from the table and looked Lord Grath full in the face from surprise. "Only ten years ago?" I was alive when this ancient dragon died.

"He is the only dragon I know of who has actually died of old age," he replied.

I realized I was staring and ducked my gaze to the edge of the table.

He turned the parchment over and began, "Now, my lady, returning to your move to Caer Corisan."

The map was still on that side of the parchment. I swallowed hard. I knew I needed to do this, but I didn't want to.

"Would you consider visiting Caer Corisan within the next two weeks?" he asked.

I stared at him as I felt a wave of fear run through me. I had thought I wouldn't need to go there for at least another month, maybe even two or three.

"I am not asking that you stay there at that point. I am only asking you to go there, spend part of a day there, and then come back here," he continued.

I looked down at the map and tried to organize my thoughts, two weeks, but I wouldn't have to stay. "How long would you want me to stay that day?" I asked a bit louder than a whisper.

"How ever long you choose," he answered evenly.

"Would Narden be there?" I asked. I didn't want to go without him. I might panic, and I wanted Narden to be there to help me calm down.

"I can arrange that," he answered.

I'd nearly driven myself and Renard out of our minds the day Lord Grath came and spoke with Ari. Every moment that went by I was certain that I would hear her scream or that Lord Grath would run through the doorway to tell me to come quickly to help. After we left my entrance cave and walked to the other side of the room of pools, I turned around to go back to the doorway. Renard told me that it would be rude and disgraceful to listen to them talk from the doorway, but I really didn't care about being rude or dignified at that time.

As I hurried back over, he said, "I will stop you if you do that."

I turned and looked at him. Renard didn't make threats very often. A threat like that from Adenern, I would have laughed off, but this was unusual for Renard. He was lying next to a pool aimlessly watching his tail swirl in it. Then he looked up at me and cocked an eyebrow.

"But . . ." I began, pausing as I collected my thoughts.

"Not the best way to begin a sentence," he said returning his gaze to his tail.

"Thanks," I snapped.

He looked back up with his head leaning to the side, but didn't say anything else.

"I will not let her get hurt again," I growled.

"Will Lord Grath hurt her?" his reply was even.

"Of course not!" I threw back at him.

"Then you do not have anything to worry about."

"She might get scared or something." My voice was lower now.

"You do realize that you are not going to always be there when she is scared." That even tone was aggravating.

"Of course I do." I knew it, but I didn't want to believe it.

"You're not going to always be there, Narden," he told me. "Grant her this time when she is safe, and it will not be as hard the next time."

He had a point, but I still didn't like it. I did stay away from that doorway the entire time that Lord Grath spoke with her. It wasn't easy. At least ten times I made it halfway across the room where I could catch a word or two of the conversation before I realized that

Renard had stopped whatever he was doing and was watching me. Slowly, I would turn around and walk back to a place where I couldn't hear anything from the entrance cave anymore.

From there, I would pace around the pools or along the wall. After a while, I would again catch a word or phrase and stop, straining to hear more. Renard would shift, I would realize he was watching me again, and I moved away until I couldn't hear anything. That day I realized that the temperature did not have anything to do with the color of a pool, that Gary would get really mad if you walked past his doorway more than fifty times in a watch, that Adenern had closed his outside entrance already, and that Renard had the patience that most people just wish for. I was fairly certain that he was going to throw something at me, tackle me, or something, but he just stayed where he was. I think he may have even fallen asleep once.

I tried my luck when I noticed his eyes were closed for a while and headed toward my doorway. I wasn't going to listen long, just check to make sure Ari was all right. I was three quarters of the way across the room and could understand most of the sentences when I heard Renard clear his throat behind me. I froze and turned to where he had been. He wasn't there. I heard a claw tapping on the rocks to my left. Looking that way, I saw him standing across that pool from me.

"How'd you do that?" I had been listening to every sound in that cave and had not heard him move one scale.

"Walk with me, and I will tell you." He turned and started back toward the other side of the room.

I turned slowly to follow. From the snips of conversation I'd heard, Ari did seem to be all right.

"Do you know who you remind me of?" He glanced over his shoulder.

I wasn't all too thrilled with being compared to anyone at that moment and snapped back, "No." I watched the torchlight play off the ponds as we walked.

He just chuckled. "You remind me of me when Hana had our first child."

My head shot up, and I glanced quickly around. "Should you be talking about that?" I hissed at him.

He shrugged and looked slightly saddened for a moment. "My wife died three years ago, Narden. I don't think it's that big of a deal if I mention her once in a while."

She'd died bearing their second child. Renard hadn't been there because he was on patrol at that time. I'd never asked him about it.

We'd reached the other side of the room now, and Renard settled back into his spot next to the pool he had been at before.

"Be glad that Lord Grath will not take as long as a baby." He chuckled. "Did you know that she was in labor for six watches? I was certain that it was at least twenty."

"Hasn't it been six watches?" I asked glancing back at my doorway.

"No," he said with a hint of a laugh, "it hasn't even been one yet."

With a sigh, I returned to my pacing. What could they possibly be talking about for this long? Had Ari had an episode, and I didn't know about it? How had Renard gotten to the other side of the room without me even noticing? I turned back toward him. It looked like he was dozing again.

"Renard," I whispered.

Opening his eyes, he lifted his head and looked at me.

"How did you do that?" and I motioned toward the other side of the room of pools.

A smile spread across his face. "Oh, that?" He said evenly, "That was simple. I put one foot in front of the other."

"What?" I snapped. "That was more than just walking."

"Oh," he said as if something just dawned to him. "You want to know how I was *able* to come up beside you without you noticing."

I glared at him and began pacing back toward him.

"That was actually simple too," he added and then paused.

"Won't you share?" I asked when he didn't say anything for a moment.

"Practice."

"What?" I snapped.

"A lot of practice."

I flopped down next to him with a sigh. "So it's basically like flying."

"More like landing," he answered.

I, actually, managed to snicker at that. I knew quite well how complicated landing could be. Flying was something that we had to learn quickly. Jumping out of a cave leagues above the ground, we had a few moments before we wouldn't have to learn anything ever again. Landing took much longer. Learning to land hurt.

My first try landing, I missed my cave entrance and smashed into the side of the mountain. Thankfully, my father and Renard were there to make sure I didn't keep sliding down the side of the cliff. It took two days before I could move my head without the room spinning. Five days after that, I managed to land in my cave but scraped two layers of scales off my left side.

"Hopefully, not as painful," I added.

"No," he answered, "just time-consuming."

"And where do you get all this time from?" I teased. I knew that Renard was almost as busy as Lord Grath and Tragh.

"That is still not the best way to begin a sentence."

I stood up and did a mock bow. "Yes, my lord."

He gave me a crooked smile and laughed. "I take it where I can find it," he replied, then added, "like right now."

"You don't seem to be practicing anything," I told him.

He gave me that crooked smile again. "I must be doing rather well then."

"All right, I'll bite," he'd made me curious, "what are you practicing?"

"Please, don't." He laughed. "I don't need to explain any more scars."

I slapped him with my tail.

He looked overly aghast. "What? Do you know how hard it is to explain to a three-year-old why I have teeth marks on my arm?"

"You know quite well that I wasn't going to actually bite you." I laughed.

He cocked an eyebrow at me, giving me a shifty look. "I can never quite tell between you and Adenern."

"Well," I replied, "I can never quite tell with Adenern either, so what are you practicing?"

"Watching."

"Watching what?"

"It is not particularly important what I am watching," he said evenly returning to swirling his tail in the pond, "it is how I am watching that matters."

"All right, so *how* are you watching things?" Sometimes I wondered who was more annoying between my two brothers.

"Discreetly."

"Do you realize that one-word answers are a bit rude?" I might as well turn his arguments on him.

"Yes." He gave me that crooked smile again.

"Thanks."

He looked back over at his tail again. "Do you realize that Lord Grath is walking toward us?"

"What?" My head snapped up. There he was, in fact, walking across the room of pools!

I glanced down at Renard. "Discreetly, huh?"

"Yes." He was still watching or at least pretending to watch his tail swirl the water in the pool.

CHAPTER 19

CAER CORISAN

Now, I was flying toward Caer Corisan with Ari for her first visit. She had been extremely quiet the last couple of days but had reassured me that she did indeed want to visit the fortress. I knew it was a good idea. She needed to grow accustomed to the place since she would spend the winter there. I came up with many excuses why she shouldn't go, but they all boiled down to I didn't want her to leave. It was so nice to have her around. *This was the right thing to do though,* I reasoned again.

I was far too consumed with my own thoughts, especially flying across Maren with such precious cargo. I glanced around slightly. We were over halfway to the fortress I judged from the landscape. A sparkle caught my eye as I glanced through the trees. I blinked and heard Adenern holler, "Look out!"

Swinging hard to the right, I felt a pain clip the edge of my left wing and seer through my left side. One of the saddle straps came lose, slapping the buckle into the fresh wound. The saddle slid to the right, but held. Ari, to her credit, didn't scream, pull on the saddle, or give me mixed signals. She did lean to the left when the saddle stopped sliding.

I heard angry shouts from the ground as I caught a wind current upward. I felt my wing tear a bit as I flapped to gain altitude.

I'd have to glide to make sure I stayed in the air. That would take me longer to get to Caer Corisan, but if I rushed, my wing might tear all the way through. Neither I nor Ari would be going anywhere then. I could feel blood running back along my side, but there wasn't much I could do about that at the moment.

More shouts erupted as Adenern attacked the people on the ground. His first day back in the air, and he was already in a scramble. This was supposed to be an easy assignment, I thought wistfully, and realized it might have been if I'd payed attention like I was supposed to.

I prayed that Adenern would be safe. He didn't need another injury this soon after recovering from his last one. Then again, this was life in a country that was at war in everything but name.

I prayed that the saddle wouldn't give during the rest of the way to Caer Corisan.

I heard Ari yell over the wind, "You should land!"

I shook my head and felt pain run along my neck from the movement. The ballistic arrow must have hit a muscle along my side. That meant the wound was deep. It took me a moment before I could get enough wind to call an answer back to her.

"I wouldn't be able to get airborne again!" Landing was probably going to rip through my wing. If it didn't, taking off from the ground would.

She didn't say anything else for the rest of the trip. The quiet was somewhat unnerving, nothing to concentrate on but the wind and the blood running along my side and off my back leg.

Finally, Caer Corisan came into view. Never before did I think that fortress built directly into the top of a mountain looked so inviting. Normally, it looked intimidating. Assaulting it without help from dragons would be nearly impossible. The walls were an average man's height thick, and they rose directly from the cliffside of the mountain.

I felt Ari shift a bit in the saddle when she saw the fortress. I took a wingbeat to gain the top of the wall and felt the saddle shift again while the tear in my wing expanded.

I didn't top the wall properly and pushed off it with my front legs. I felt the saddle shift for the last time and then the sickening feeling of another strap breaking. The weight fell off, and I dove after Ari and the saddle.

Wrapping my claws around her arm, I spread my wings. The updraft caught. Angling toward the carts of grain against the north wall, I felt my wing tear through. I dropped Ari over one of the carts praying she wouldn't break every bone in her body from the fall and dove hard to the left. She certainly wouldn't live if I landed on top of her.

Pain shot through my left side from the harsh movement, and my vision blurred. I knew the ground was approaching fast. I braced my feet for the impact. I still couldn't see. Hitting a wall, I felt the stone ripping my left side open further. I heard a horse scream, felt the ground slam into my right side, and then black.

I jumped when I realized there was smoke rising from the fortress. Had Verd taken Caer Corisan? I heard the strap creak and realized that I shouldn't have moved. Narden didn't seem to be concerned about the smoke, but maybe he hadn't noticed.

He nearly hit the wall, but managed to jump over. The impact threw me to the back of the saddle, and I heard the strap creak, then snap. The saddle lunged to the right, taking me with it. I closed my eyes gripping the saddle. Not that it would do any good, I was going to die. Pain ripped into my arm, and I jerked upward. Something popped in my shoulder. The pain took my breath away as I looked up. Narden had my arm. I watched in horror as the slit in his wing ripped from the back edge halfway to the front. Then, he let go.

I hit something. It wasn't ground. I opened my eyes to see grain piling in on top of me. Taking a deep breath, I held it. I wasn't going to live through a fall like that and be drowned in a harvest. I forced my feet toward what I thought was down and scraped my knees against wood. The grain had closed in around me now. I fought through the weight to get my feet under me. I couldn't move my right arm. Suddenly, I was sliding. Light came back, and I gasped. Someone pulled me to my feet. Everything hurt.

Slowly, I opened my eyes. Someone was standing in front of me. Behind him, I could see Narden lying on the ground about thirty steps away. He wasn't moving. I took a step toward him and cringed as pain shot through my arm. When I opened my eyes, I caught a glint of silver as someone pulled out a knife near Narden.

"NO!" I screamed, and began to run toward him.

I felt someone grab me from behind, pulling me off my feet. Whoever it was said something. The voice sounded familiar, but I couldn't place it. I slammed my elbow into his chest. His grip loosened a fraction but still held. I kicked back. The person with the knife had reached Narden.

"NO!" I screamed again. "They'll kill him!"

"LADY ARI'AN!" the man who held me yelled, "He has three layers of scales!"

I kicked again before realizing what he'd said. Then I recognized the knife the man had near Narden. It was just like one of the knives that were in the kit at Narden's cave. I glanced around quickly. The fortress wasn't on fire. The smoke I'd seen came from a forge near the eastern wall. There was a cart full of grain dumped next to me and the chaos from Narden's fall, but the fortress hadn't been attacked.

I felt my feet touch the ground, and the man let go. I nearly fell. Whoever that was caught my left arm before I hit the ground. He yelled someone's name. Why did his voice sound so familiar, but it wasn't quite right. I heard someone run up.

"Find a fur blanket, and see if the physician can be spared."

How did he know about the blanket?

"It is her arm," he continued.

I turned to look at whoever this was. I was quivering now and beginning to shake hard. He was looking away from me, but still had his hand on my arm. At first, I thought it was Lord Grath, and the voice did sound somewhat like his, but it wasn't. This man's beard was cut wrong, and his build was slightly thinner. He looked younger too, but not much younger. Did Lord Grath have a brother? I took a step back and managed to keep my knees from buckling.

He looked over quickly and let go of my arm.

"You are going to be all right, my lady." It wasn't a question. It was a statement of fact. He had a tone that sounded too much like Lord Grath's.

My ears were ringing. Every part of my body hurt, and my right shoulder screamed of it. This was too much. I vaguely heard the servant run up and felt the blanket wrap around my shoulders. I gripped the edge with my left hand. This wasn't my blanket. The fur on this one was black and half the length, but it was still soft. I felt my knees giving out again, and felt whoever this stranger was grab my left arm again. Then he put his other hand on my back. I kept my feet somehow.

He barked another order about a chair, a drink, and some water, and I heard the feet run off again. I looked around slightly. I couldn't focus on most of the activity. People were running everywhere. Then I saw Narden. He still hadn't moved. Now there were two pools of blood spreading out from his side and wing. There would only be one in a few moments when they flowed together.

"He's going to die," I whispered.

"Lady Ari'an"—I looked at the man who looked like Lord Grath—"he is not going to die." It wasn't a reassurance. It was a statement of fact. How could he know?

Something pressed against my knees, and I felt them give again. This time he didn't keep me standing, but he did keep me from falling. He lowered me onto the chair. It was nice to have something under me. My knees felt like water.

Something touched my left hand. I jerked. A cup rested against it, and some of the liquid splashed on the man's hand.

"You need to drink this. It will help you calm down," he said.

I touched the glass with my hand, but my hand was shaking too much to grip it. He moved the cup to my lips, and I pulled back. I didn't like being forced to drink things. The priests at the temple poisoned me that way. They'd laughed for what seemed like days and then finally gave me the antidote when I was too weak to fight anymore.

"My lady, please." I looked at him, then looked at the cup. I shook my head. I wouldn't take that from someone I didn't know, not willingly at least.

He looked concerned, but he didn't force me. He set the cup on the ground and picked up a bowl of water. He dipped a towel into it and moved his hand toward my face. Again, I jerked away.

"Lady Ari'an," he had a calm tone to his voice. Everyone was running around, Narden was bleeding to death in the corner, and he sounded calm. How could he be calm?

"Your head is bleeding," he continued.

The statement was so odd that I just stared at his ear for a moment. I'd not looked him full in the face yet. Suddenly, what he said sunk in, and I pulled my left hand out of the blanket and put it to my head. A warm sticky substance ran onto my fingers. Pulling my hand away, I saw it was blood.

I looked around frantically. I wanted someone I knew to tell me what was going on. I couldn't remember hitting my head on anything, but my arm hurt so much that everything else felt like a minor bump. I didn't know what to do. I wanted someone I knew to tell me . . . anything.

"Lady Ari'an," the voice cut through my thoughts. "Stay with me," he said. I'd leaned forward, and his hand was on my shoulder keeping me from falling out of the chair.

The towel touched my head, and I cringed. "Easy," I heard him say, "I will not make it any worse."

He took the towel away and then wiped a cloth over the cut with an ointment on it. I gasped as my head burned for a moment. The pungent smell of the ointment brought tears to my eyes. I heard someone running toward me and jumped again. Slowly, I focused on a figure approaching from Narden's direction. Past him I could see that Narden's side injury was entirely patched now and the split in his wing was halfway sewn up. Maybe he would be all right.

"Let's have a look at that arm," the new figure said.

I looked up to find a man dressed in nice peasant's clothes covered in blood. I shied away from him.

"Easy, my lady," Lord Grath's look-alike said in front of me. I focused on his coat buttons. "This is Galen. He is going to fix your arm."

I felt the physician pick up my arm, and I gasped from the pain. He felt along the length of my arm.

He told the other man, "It's dislocated. It's not broken though."

"First good news today," he replied.

I felt something touch my lips again, and I jerked away. The physician held a bottle to my mouth. The contents smelled foul.

"Drink this so I can set your arm," he ordered.

I turned my head away.

"Tip her head back," the physician ordered.

I looked around frantically and tried to stand up. My legs weren't working.

"No," I heard the other man say, evenly but with a tone of authority.

I looked up at his face. He was focused on the physician, who seemed quite surprised.

"I won't set her arm without some sort of painkiller," the physician told him.

"You have done it before," was the even reply.

"In battlefield situations, where there wasn't any other option," he fired back.

"Pretend." If I hadn't been terrified, hurting, and confused, I might have laughed.

"You're asking me to set a lady of the realm's arm while she's conscious and without anything to numb the pain." He sounded like he was talking to a child.

"No"—Lord Grath's look-alike had an expression on his face that I wouldn't have crossed—"I am telling you. She is not going to drink anything against her will."

"She's in shock!"

The look he gave the physician could have burned a dragon.

"Fine, but you are taking the blame." He pulled a short wooden rod from his pocket and held it to my mouth. "Bite this," he ordered.

I saw the other man take the rod from his hand and kneel in front of me. I'd been looking at the rod and ended up looking him full in the face.

"Lady Ari'an," he began in a soft voice. The tone was so different from what he had just used on the physician that I held my gaze on his face. "You need to bite on this so you do not bite off your tongue when he sets your arm."

I didn't want anything in my mouth, but I understood what he was saying. He hadn't forced me to do anything else that I didn't want to do. I nodded and reached for the rod. I realized that my hand was shaking too much for me to hold it and clinched my nails into my palm. He lifted the rod to my mouth, and I held it in my teeth. Closing my eyes I fought memories of the bridle the priests used on me at the temple.

Pain shot through my arm, and I bit the rod harder than I thought possible. I couldn't see anything but white for a moment, and then my vision turned to spots of color and slowly came back to the unknown man in front of me. He had his hand on my left shoulder holding me in the chair again. I leaned away from his hand against the back of the chair. He reached up and took the rod out of my mouth.

"I'm all right," I whispered.

He laughed. I stared at him in amazement. He stopped quickly, but was still smiling. "My lady, you have an odd definition of all right—if being attacked while riding a dragon, falling at least twenty steps, nearly drowning in a wagon of grain, dislocating your shoulder, and having Narden pass out from his injuries, is all right."

I laughed because I didn't want to cry. I felt something touch my head and jumped. The physician was putting a sling over my head. He'd already bandaged the gashes on my arm where Narden caught me. The physician still looked miffed, but it was an impressed type of miffed, as if he was trying to look mad to cover up the impressed look.

"My lady," the look-alike continued, "I would like for you to move inside. I would prefer if you did not have a heat stroke with everything else you went through today."

I glanced over at Narden. I didn't want to leave him out here. At least here I could look over and see him. If I went inside the fortress somewhere, what would happen?

Several people were setting up a canopy over Narden. Finally I took a moment to look at what must be the courtyard of Caer Corisan.

People weren't running around anymore. Several people were shoveling the grain from the wagon I had landed in into a different cart. Others were throwing buckets of water over the blood in the dirt, washing it into the drainage lines and out of the fortress. How could life just go on like that?

There was the forge on the eastern wall and some little craft shanties. Farther on there were what looked like stables, at least three of them. Why would they need that many horses?

"My lady"—I turned back to the stranger in front of me—"we can go right there if you would like." I followed his pointing hand to a large window. "You could see everything in the courtyard from there."

Once more I glanced around. I would be able to still see Narden from there. I nodded slowly. I demanded that my legs work, and they did this time. I leaned on the chair for a moment with my good arm, while he picked up the blanket, and then we walked into the building.

The cool air inside surprised me, and I swayed for a moment. I felt him take my arm and support my back with his other hand. I stood looking around the inside. We were in a large room, decorated for a dignitary's arrival. I wondered who was coming. I felt him let go of my arm and motion toward a hallway to my right. I looked at it for a moment, and then took a step forward.

The hall was wide enough that at least ten people could walk side by side here. I would later find that all the hallways on the first level were that wide to allow the dragons to move through them easily. The doorways were also larger than normal, I noticed, as I walked through one on my right. It was a nice room, but everything in it was stone. There was a stone couch along each wall, with little stone tables at each of the ends.

The stranger left me just inside of the doorway and walked over to a wall that had a stone handle sticking out of it. He pulled it open to reveal several wooden shelves of cushions and pillows.

He took several out and arranged them on the stone couch that looked out of the window. He motioned me over, and I sat down. The cushions were soft, but it was obvious that they were on stone. On another day I might have laughed at the thought of trying to make a stone couch comfortable.

"My lady"—he was handing the fur blanket to me—"would you mind if I left you for a short while? I would like to find out what condition Narden is in."

"That's fine," I whispered.

I pulled my eyes to his face when his feet didn't move for a long moment. He looked skeptical.

I looked back at his feet. Those used to be nice shoes I realized. They had blood and dirt all over them now.

"It's all right," I said slightly louder. "I'd like to know how he is too."

"Would you like anything to eat or something to drink?" he asked after he took a step away.

I looked up at his coat. It too was nice, but had blood and dirt on it as well.

"Just water, please," I managed to whisper.

"I will come back in a little while," and then I heard those once nice shoes walk away.

I was alone. I looked out of the window and saw him start across the courtyard. He had a hurried walk that didn't quite make it to a run.

I glanced around the room. My vision blurred, and I felt a sob hit my throat. I didn't let the sound out, but I couldn't stop the tears now that they'd started. I pulled the blanket to my face and cried. I don't know how long I cried. I wanted to scream. I wanted to run back to Narden's cave, but I couldn't. I was here in a room, in a fortress I couldn't leave, surrounded by strangers.

I fought against every memory that came. I didn't win against some of them. I felt my head throb from blows that I received a year ago. I felt a whip stroke cross my back. I threw my head back and screamed without letting a sound escape.

I heard something shatter. It was the sound of pottery breaking. They'd tie the pottery shards to the ends of that whip. I didn't want to see. I buried my head in my hands. They would pull me to my feet soon. They'd hang my tied hands on the hook from the ceiling. Then the lashes would start.

I heard a voice that didn't fit at the temple. I couldn't remember where I knew the voice from. I felt something touch my hands. I couldn't fight them. They'd beat me harder if I did. I felt my hands leave my face. I heard that voice again . . . louder this time.

"Lady Ari'an!"

I jumped, opened my eyes, and looked him full in the face. It wasn't one of the priests. It was the man who looked like Lord Grath. I glanced around the room. I wasn't at the temple. There was a broken water pitcher near the door. A servant was mopping the spill up with a towel. A pottery cup with a large chip out of it was rolling across the floor.

"I'm sorry," I whispered.

"Lady Ari'an," he answered softly, "you have no need to apologize. It has been a hard day for you."

I sniffed and wiped my eyes on my sleeve. I felt something soft on my face and jumped a little. The stranger held out a handkerchief. I took it lightly and held it for a moment before wiping my eyes again. Hearing him stand up and move away, I glanced up. I didn't want to be left alone again. He moved to the closet in the wall and pulled a few more cushions out. Walking back over, he set them next to me on the stone coach and then sat down.

I watched my hands play with the handkerchief and felt him reach around my back. I jumped and looked around slightly to find I was leaning against his shoulder.

"Easy," he said softly, "you're safe now. No one is going to hurt you here."

I believed him. I'm not sure why, but I did, and I felt myself relax a tiny bit.

CHAPTER 20

A NIGHT AT THE FORTRESS

The next moment that I remembered, I heard a familiar voice say, "You know she's going to panic when she wakes up."

"Shhh," I heard someone hiss over me.

"What?" It was Adenern. "It's true."

"There is no need for you to wake her to prove it." That voice was familiar too.

I shifted a little, felt my head throb, and started to pull my hand up to my head. I ended up brushing someone's knee. I sat up immediately and felt my head scream in protest. The room spun for a moment. I couldn't remember where I was. I took a gasp of air and realized I couldn't move my right arm. Looking down, I tried hard to remember why my arm would be in a sling. Then everything came back to me. I jumped to my feet. My head screamed at me again, and my legs gave way. Someone caught me before I fell.

"Easy," I heard that voice say as he lowered me back onto the couch.

I put my hand to my head and just sat for a moment while the room stopped spinning.

"That went better than I thought it would," I heard Adenern say. He had a light tone that didn't seem to fit with my screaming head and immobile arm.

I raised my head slowly when it stopped pounding. Adenern was sprawled against the far wall. He had a few smaller scale patches on him but didn't seem to be very beat-up. That was a relief. I hadn't had time to worry about him, but it was nice to know he was all right.

Glancing out of the window, I realized that it was dusk. I couldn't make out Narden's shape through the growing darkness. It almost looked like he wasn't there. I stood up slowly. My head didn't complain as much this time. Walking over to the window, I peered into the darkness. With a start, I realized that Narden was indeed not there.

I felt someone move next to me, and I jumped, making my head swim.

"Easy." That seemed to be something he said frequently. "Narden woke up about a watch ago and moved into the injury stables."

I followed his pointing hand to a building across the courtyard. There was torchlight coming from the windows. I wondered why they'd put an injured dragon in a stable. Wouldn't that upset the horses? Maybe they were well-trained horses.

"Would you like to go see him?" he asked.

I nodded, and saw the room spin for a moment.

"I would like for Galen to look at where you hit your head," he sounded concerned.

I nodded slightly and started across the room. I turned left at the doorway.

As I started down the hall toward the large entrance room, I heard Adenern call, "He's not in the best of spirits and seems to be a bit deaf right now, so watch you head. He might bite it off."

I turned quickly wondering what he meant and immediately felt dizzy. Lord Grath's look-alike followed me, looking concerned as I leaned against the wall for a moment.

"Are you all right?" I heard him ask next to me.

I almost told him I was, then remembered his response earlier today, and laughed lightly. Glancing up, I realized he had a confused and slightly more concerned look on his face. That only made me laugh harder.

Finally I managed, "If you think that being attacked while riding a dragon, falling at least twenty steps, dislocating my arm, and having a head wound that I can't remember where it came from is all right, then you have a strange definition of *all right*."

He threw his head back and laughed with me. When he caught his breath, he told me, "I can tell you about the head wound at least. You hit the side of the wagon when you fell out."

I thought about that. I could vaguely remember that, but the panic of nearly drowning and trying to get my feet under me covered most of the memory.

I was feeling a bit steadier on my feet as we continued down the hallway and across the courtyard.

I'd demanded to know where Ari was when I woke up only to have Galen give me a look that would have instantly boiled water.

"You can wait," he said with a forced even tone to his voice.

"Is she all right?" I pried.

"You can wait." He was holding some fingers up in front of me.

"Three," I snapped and then followed his hand from right to left with my eyes.

"I'm disappointed to see that they didn't sever your temper along with your skin." His tone was losing its calm.

"I learned from the best," I retorted.

He looked straight at me for a moment and said, "Move into the stable." Then he turned around and walked across the courtyard mumbling about the disrespect of younger generations toward physicians and something about never happening when he was that age.

I growled, flinching when the vibration rattled the wound on my side.

"Jair," I called as I saw him walking by. He was one of the young servants here; he was here for up to a year before going into training for twelve to fourteen years.

"Where's Lady Ari'an?" I asked.

I must have startled him because he just stared at me blankly for a moment.

"Well?" I snapped.

He stammered something incoherent and hurried off. I caught myself before letting out an aggravated sigh. There was a cart of grain dumped nearby that I didn't need to catch on fire. Why someone dumped the thing was beyond me. Grain was not an easy thing to clean up as the three people shoveling it into another cart could testify. It was also an awfully flammable thing to leave lying around with dragons coming and going as often as they did here.

Pulling myself to my feet, I realized that putting weight on my right front leg was going to leave me back in the dirt. I began to shake my scales and cringed again. I hobbled into the stable and flopped into the first available stall.

The place was set up like a horse stable, except we didn't get locked into the stalls. We got to *choose* to stay there. Like now when I should be finding Ari, but couldn't limp quickly enough to search for her. I let out an exasperated breath and scorched the wall a bit. The walls were stone, so it wouldn't do any damage. There were enough smoke and fire marks in here that one more wouldn't matter anyway. Blowing fire could get one in trouble in here though, because the half walls dividing the stalls wouldn't block a good blast or a badly aimed one. When you suddenly toasted someone's back, wings, or horns, they could get really mad.

Adenern sometimes did it for fun when he was stuck in here. He'd see if he could blast the very back wall from one of the front stalls. With twenty-five stalls between him and that wall, he hadn't yet, but he had gotten into a number of scuffles for his troubles. I blew out another irritated breath.

I ignored the red dragon in the stall across from me. He didn't seem injured, but was quite skittish. He was curled into the back of his stall, with his eyes staring at me.

Jair hurried back in, glanced around, and trotted up to me. "Sir," he began, "her ladyship is fine and is with my lord, but . . ." he seemed to be searching for a way to tell me bad news.

I pictured Ari missing an arm or with half of her face ripped open from the fall.

"What is it?" I growled.

The red dragon jumped and looked around as if expecting someone to stab him.

"She's . . ." Jair trailed off for a moment.

I growled again.

"She's asleep, sir."

"She's unconscious?" I envisioned her never waking up or not being able to remember anything if she did. Forgetting the temple wouldn't necessarily be bad, but I didn't want her to forget me.

"N-n-no, sir," he stammered, "she fell asleep on my lord."

"What?" That didn't make any sense. I couldn't picture Ari falling asleep in a strange place like this, much less on someone.

He mumbled something that I didn't quite catch again. I was getting very tired of this. "Go get his lordship," I growled.

"Y-y-yes, sir," Jair stammered, bowed a couple of times, and ran out.

I made a note to myself never to ask him about anything again. Jair always seemed to get exceptionally nervous when talking to me, my brothers, my father, Lord Grath, Lord Cristeros; as I thought about it, I realized that he didn't really do all too well talking to anyone with any semblance of authority. I sighed and stared at the wall for far too long.

Finally, I heard footsteps again. I looked up only to find Jair coming back, looking somewhat frightened. Again, I pictured Ari lying unconscious somewhere, probably almost dead.

He bowed, and I nearly toasted his hair in my impatience. "My l-l-lor, sir, I . . . She . . ."

"WELL?" I bellowed at him. The red dragon across the way nearly jumped out of his scales.

Jair's eyes widened, and he finally managed, "He said he can't come."

"WHAT?" I noticed the red dragon cower into the back of his stall. I nearly yelled at him to stop that, but caught myself. Smoke was coming out of my mouth every time I opened it, and I realized my scales were spiked, at least where the layer wasn't missing or patching my side.

"H-he . . . he . . ."

"Don't start that again!"

"He said he wouldn't disturb her ladyship." He was trembling.

"WHAT?"

"H-h-he . . . H-h-he . . . He said you were to stay here and that h-he would bring the lady when she w-w-woke up." I watched him cower after finishing that statement.

I kept quiet for a short while before growling, "Get out."

I have seen very few people run that fast even to get away from a dragon.

I slammed my tail against the stall wall. I didn't notice the pain at that point but would notice the ache the next day. I began to pace and nearly fell over when my right leg didn't support my weight. I hobbled the length of the stable and back.

I couldn't ignore a direct order from him. That would be like disobeying a command from Renard. He was in charge when Lord Grath wasn't present. I would give him a piece of my mind when he did come. If he wasn't concerned enough to tell me something other than "she's asleep," then she was probably just asleep . . . unless . . . What if he'd said that so I wouldn't worry? What if Ari was almost dead and no one knew how to tell me? What if . . .

I hobbled toward the entrance again. Stopping near the door, I looked back. I shouldn't disobey a direct order from him, but what if Ari was dying?

I glanced back at the stalls. The red dragon was watching me with wide eyes. I turned back and nearly ran into Adenern.

"What are you doing here?" I snapped.

He looked surprised for a moment then grinned. "I'm so happy to know that you are so thrilled to see me still alive," he bemoaned in an exaggerated tone.

"Leave off it," I snapped. "I am glad to see that you're alive and"—I glanced over him quickly then took a better look. He barely had a scratch on him—"and unharmed, but I'm more concerned about Ari right now."

"Oh, she's fine." He pushed past me, and I cringed when he raked across my side.

"What?" I turned to follow him.

"I heard you've been saying that a lot lately." He nodded to the red dragon who backed away.

"WHAT?"

"Galen mentioned it when I saw him. Said you were in a bad mood too." He looked at the stall I'd been in. "That's impressive, did you do that?"

"What?" I glanced at the stall and noticed that there was an indentation in the stone that looked like my tail.

"Oh, never mind." He flopped into the stall next to the red dragon, who didn't seem all too thrilled. "I thought you might have been worried about me." He sniffed and mimicked wiping a tear from his eye. "But I guess you have more important things to be concerned about."

"Lay off," I snapped.

"You are in a nasty mood." He stretched and scrapped his claws across the floor. Somehow that red dragon managed to shrink even further into the corner of his stall.

"I'm worried about Ari," I growled.

"I told you she's fine." He rolled onto his side and started picking at the plaster between the stones.

"And how do you know?" I'd lost my patience quite a while ago.

He rolled onto his back and started flicking bits of the plaster he'd pulled out into the air. "I just saw her."

"What?"

He cocked an eyebrow at me and started flicking plaster bits at me. "Are your ears attached to you shoulder?"

"WHAT?"

"Well, you don't seem to be hearing all too well right now. The only reason your ears would have been damaged is if they were attached to your shoulder where you got sliced." He was still flicking plaster bits.

"Stop that," I growled.

He rolled over and stared at me for a moment. Then he got up and started walking toward the entrance.

"Where are you going?" I demanded.

"To watch Ari sleep," he called back. "You are in much too foul of a mood to stay around." He glanced over his shoulder and called to the red dragon, "You may want to wander somewhere else for a while. I don't think he's going to be very pleasant company."

"WHAT?"

"I gathered that already," he called back and disappeared through the door.

I hurried—well, hobbled as quickly as I could to the entrance. Adenern was disappearing into the mounting darkness as he crossed the courtyard. He was blowing smoke rings into the air. Not having mastered the skill yet, he blew a few puffs of fire once or twice. Someone called that they didn't need a fire on top of everything else that had happened that day. He laughed.

Once again I was stuck. I knew I should stay where I was because I was injured, and hobbling around the fortress could easily break open my wing or my side. I really wanted to make sure that Ari was all right. It didn't make sense to me that she would fall asleep, but I supposed it was possible. It had been several watches since we'd arrived. She did get really tired when she was stressed, and I could think of few things that would stress her more than being left alone with complete strangers.

I wondered if she'd had an episode. She probably had . . . and I hadn't been there to help her. I slapped my tail on the stone floor and cringed at the pain this time. I remembered what Renard told me about not being able to always be there for her, but this was different.

I was supposed to introduce her to people here, spend a few watches, and then head back with her. I had not been there for her because I hadn't been paying attention while we were bringing her here. I hadn't noticed the launcher until I was nearly skewered. If Adenern hadn't been there, I probably would have been . . . and Ari would be dead right now . . . or worse, headed back to that temple.

I scorched the wall for a moment and then hobbled back to the stall. I glanced over my shoulder at the entrance and noticed my stitched wing. It was split more than halfway across. I growled at it and flopped into the stall. I would be stuck here until that healed, and Ari would have to go back with someone else, probably Adenern all because I hadn't been paying attention. I promised myself that any time there was even the faintest possibility that Ari could be hurt, I would never be caught off guard again.

At least she wasn't dead. She might be hurt though. Adenern hadn't mentioned that she was hurt, but all he'd said was that she was all right and asleep. How could she sleep at a time like this? I stood up to go to the entrance again, but decided not to. Nothing would change if I went there. I turned around and flopped back down, cringing when I hit my side.

Closing my eyes, I growled. This never should have happened. I pulled myself to my feet deciding to go to the entrance after all and almost stepped on her.

Narden stared at me for a moment with his mouth hanging open. I glanced around, wondering if I should say something. I hadn't noticed the red dragon in the area across from Narden when I'd walked in. The areas looked almost like horse stalls but much larger and without doors. They also had stone walls instead of wooden ones, reaching about to my shoulders. Open air continued to the ceiling about ten steps above the divisions.

The red dragon didn't look hurt but seemed to be quite frightened. I wondered what could possibly scare a dragon. I felt sorry for him though. I knew all too well what it was like to be frightened.

"Are you all right?" I heard Narden ask.

I fought hard to keep from laughing too much.

"What are you laughing at?" he sounded almost frantic.

"Sir," I began, "if you think being attacked while riding a dragon, falling twenty steps, nearly drowning in a wagon of grain, dislocating my arm, and hitting my head on that same wagon, all while in the company of complete strangers is all right, you have a strange definition of *all right*," I managed.

"What?" he stammered and quickly added, "You nearly drowned? What happened to your arm? How did you hit your head?"

I heard something thump on the floor behind me and noticed that Lord Grath's look-alike had brought up a chair. It too was stone. I wondered for a moment when I sat down if every piece of furniture in this place was made of stone. I thanked him and looked back at Narden, who was now glaring at him. He handed me the blanket, and I pulled it over my shoulders.

"What happened?" Narden snarled. He wasn't addressing me, but the tone made me stare at him.

The man didn't answer the dragon right away, only looked at him with a very calm face. I was impressed. It was not an easy task to keep eye contact with a dragon, much less to do so calmly with an angry dragon.

Eventually, he began, "You were attacked at . . ."

"I know that," Narden snapped.

"All right, you arrived here," he continued.

"I never would have imagined that." Sarcasm dripped from his words.

I was impressed that the man still kept the calm tone to his voice. "When the saddle broke, you saved my lady, but dislocated her shoulder."

Narden stared at me with a horrified look on his face.

"You dropped Lady Ari'an in a wagon of grain and passed out," he continued.

"We managed to retrieve my lady from the wagon, but she hit her head on the side on the way out."

"Now, if you will excuse me"—he bowed first to me then to Narden—"I would like to find Galen."

He turned, nodded to the red dragon who had moved a couple of steps closer, and walked out.

I watched him leave then leaned toward Narden. "Who was that?" I whispered.

"What?" He looked at me blankly.

I remembered what Adenern had said about Narden being deaf, but I'd thought he was joking. How could he have lost his hearing?

I sat down hard. I'd dislocated Ari's arm. I knew that I'd scratched her badly when she fell, but dislocating her arm . . . She said something that I didn't quite catch.

"What?" I asked looking up at her. A frightened look came over her face, and I quickly looked around to figure out what had startled her.

There wasn't anything in her line of vision but me. "What is it?" I asked quickly. Maybe she'd seen a mouse.

"Can you hear me?" she asked.

"What?" What type of a question was that?

She looked even more horrified. "You've gone deaf," she said just above a whisper.

"What?" I was certainly not deaf.

"I thought he was just joking. I didn't think he was serious. How . . ." She glanced around with a frantic look on her face.

"What?" Who had she been talking to? What was she talking about?

She jumped out of the chair and swayed for a moment.

"Are you all right?" I didn't like the way the color was completely missing from her face.

Shaking her head, she looked frantic and hurried from the stable.

For once I couldn't keep up with her. I hobbled to the entrance, but she was already halfway across the courtyard. She called to one of the servants who hurried over to her.

"Do you know where . . ." I started to ask the youth who ran over when I called for help, and realized I still didn't know the man's name. "Do you know where he is?" I managed.

"Where who is?" the boy asked.

"The . . ." I felt my hands start to shake. Who was he? I didn't know how to find him. I didn't know his name. "Th-the lord who was helping me."

"Lord Drenar?" the servant asked.

"I-I-I don't know." My legs stopped supporting my weight, and I fell. I felt the gravel bite my hand as I reached out to catch myself.

"I'll go get him," the servant called as he ran off.

"Mighty One, have mercy," I breathed.

She'd collapsed. I turned around, remembering that Drenar'd brought a blanket. I put my weight on my right leg and smashed into the stone floor. I felt my side rip open, but didn't care at the moment. I pulled myself back to my feet. I wouldn't be quick enough to get the blanket across the courtyard. She would be beyond panicked by the time I got there.

"You!" I yelled at the red dragon who had looked over his stall when I fell. He looked far too scared, but I didn't particularly care how he was feeling at that moment.

"Take that blanket to Lady Ari'an," I ordered.

"M-m-me?" he stammered weakly.

"NOW!" I bellowed at him.

I don't think I've seen a dragon move that fast before. Had I been less concerned about Ari, I would have been impressed. He bolted past me with the blanket and was to her in half a heartbeat. I saw that Drenar was already there, kneeling next to her. I took a moment to steady myself. Then I started across the courtyard.

It was only a moment or two before I heard footsteps running toward me. I looked up and saw him coming. He skidded to a stop and knelt in front of me.

"What happened?" he asked. It was the first time I'd heard him sound even a little panicked.

"He can't hear me." I sobbed.

"Thank you," he said.

I glanced up because of the odd answer. He was taking a blanket from the red dragon. He draped it over my shoulders, and I clutched the corner.

"Now"—he was looking directly at me now, I studied his knees—"who can't hear you?"

"Narden." A sob caught in my throat with the name.

"What?" I heard Narden ask behind me.

I buried my face in the blanket and cried.

"Hold on," Drenar told me and pulled Ari's hands away from her face. If I'd had hands of my own, I would have choked him for touching her.

"Why do you think he cannot hear you?" he asked her.

"Who can't hear her?"

"Hold on," the tone was gruffer than usual.

"He won't answer me when I ask him things." She was still crying.

"You," I called to the retreating red dragon.

He turned and stammered again, "M-m-me?"

"Of course you," I yelled at him. "Find someone to bring her some water."

"Y-your p-pardon?" he stammered back.

"now!" I watched him look around frantically and then run toward the first person he saw.

"Narden, can you hear me?" Drenar asked as I turned back.

"What?" Why did he think I couldn't hear him?

"Can you hear me?" he said a little slower.

"Of course, but what does that have to do with . . ." I began, but he held up his hand.

"My lady"—he turned to Ari—"how did you find out that he was deaf?"

"What?" Why in the world would she think I was deaf?

"Stop," he told me.

I growled.

"Adenern, said it when we left him." She sobbed.

"Someone called," Adenern was walking out of the entrance hall.

"you!" I bellowed at him.

"What?" he yelled back.

"You told her I'm deaf!" I almost lunged at him, but the pain as I spread my wing and ripped out the stitches stopped me.

"What?" He laughed. "I never . . ." He paused for a moment. "I was joking." He turned to Drenar. "She thinks he's really deaf?"

"I'm going to rip off your tail," I growled.

"Stop." There was a hand directly in front of my face. "Calm down right now." It wasn't a suggestion.

"It was a joke, because you've been so snippy lately and 'what?' was the only thing you were yelling," Adenern answered looking concerned. "I didn't think she would take it seriously."

I forced my scales to flatten and took a deep breath. I heard footsteps approaching and swung around to see who it was. I cringed from the movement and noticed that my side was bleeding again along with the tear in my wing.

Galen was walking up with a pottery cup in his hand. He looked far from pleased. Past him I saw the red dragon slink into the stables.

"You"—he pointed directly at me—"should be resting, not running around this courtyard and . . ." His eyes narrowed as he saw my side and let out an exasperated sigh.

"Here," he snapped, thrusting the cup at Drenar, a bit of water sloshing out in the process. He pulled a knife kit from the bag at his side and started working on patching my side. Then he moved to restitching my wing.

I heard Ari say something, but I didn't quite catch the words. Looking toward her, I saw her shakily holding the mug and looking at me.

Drenar glanced over at me and smiled. "Yes, he can hear just fine. He had a hard day though."

I nearly growled something at him, but Ari laughed. I could only imagine how frightening her time here had been, and she laughed. I sat down hard. Galen called out something about my bleeding and needing to hold still, but I didn't really care. Ari was all right. She was even laughing, and I hadn't been there. I knew I should be proud that she had managed so well without me . . . but it hurt. She didn't need me, at least not as much as I thought she did.

When Ari stopped laughing, Drenar began, "I am fairly certain that you will not be leaving tonight. Would you like to have your own room, or would you rather stay with Narden?"

"Narden," I heard Galen snap, "needs his rest."

"I rested quite enough today, thank you very much," I snapped back, turning my head to look at him.

"What part of 'hold still' did you not understand?" he growled, and then muttered something about liking it better when I was unconscious.

"Would it be all right if I stayed with him?" I heard Ari ask.

Galen growled something again, but I missed it, probably another statement about holding still.

"I will have a cot brought to the stables," Drenar replied.

"Are you all right?" I asked leaning my head down toward Ari.

She laughed lightly for a moment. "It's been a rough day," she answered. "I will be though."

A metal bar was thrust in front of my face. "Light this," Galen ordered. I glanced at him somewhat annoyed, but he wasn't looking at me. "You may want to move," he told Ari.

She looked confused for a moment then slowly stood and walked to my other side watching the physician over my neck.

I looked back at the bar. There weren't many of these left. From what I had heard, most of them broke a long time ago. Galen and a few other healers still had one. This bar was for sealing the scales used for bandaging wounds. It heated quickly and would hold the heat for a while, a surprising feat for a metal bar. The handle was a rubberlike substance, but it wouldn't melt. They were one more thing left by the Wanderers from what I understood.

Galen hadn't told Adenern to move. He was listening to Drenar tell a boy what needed to be brought to the injury stable. I grinned slightly and scorched the bar. Adenern jumped five steps in the air. When he landed, he gave me a scathing look.

"I'm sorry," I said innocently batting my eyes, "I must have gone blind as well as deaf."

He sneered at me, then threw his head back and laughed. "Did you hear that, Ari?" he called. "He admits it. He is deaf." Turning, he ambled toward the kitchen area of the fortress.

I glanced around at Ari to make sure she hadn't taken him seriously this time. She seemed to be trying to fight smiling.

"Hey," I yelled as something burned into my leg. I whirled my head around to glare at Galen. The glowing red bar waved in front of my nose.

"Hold still," he growled through clinched teeth.

I watched Narden hobble back across the courtyard. I blamed myself that he was hurt at all. Both Narden and Adenern blended in with the sky, but I must have stood out against it dreadfully in my black cloak. It was fair that I was hurt, but Narden was hurt because I hadn't thought to wear something that would camouflage.

His mood seemed to have gotten better, but I hoped he'd forgive me for nearly getting him killed.

After Narden settled into the stable and the servant brought a cot for me, Lord Drenar bowed and left. He was Lord Grath's eldest. I knew that much after catching his name from the servant in the courtyard, but I'd never met him before.

He was at training when Dreanen and Danren came to foster in my father's house. Dreanen and Danren took after their mother, but Drenar . . . he looked just like Lord Grath with only a few differences. Maybe it was because Drenar had a different mother. Lady Megara died before I was born; maybe if I'd met her, I would see more of her in Drenar.

Narden went to sleep almost immediately once he reached the stable, contrary to what he'd said earlier about not being tired. I was soon asleep on my cot in the next stall.

CHAPTER 21

MISUNDERSTANDING

"Good morning, sunshine," Majorlaine called far too loudly. She was a woman with the personality of a rose. It was lovely until she was crossed, and then, watch out for those thorns.

She sounded like she was in a particularly good mood today. I wondered, momentarily, if lighting her dress on fire would make her not quite so chipper. Shifting slightly, I stopped wondering about anything as I fought the urge to yell. Everything hurt! I should have suspected that I would wake up to this since I did fall from the sky yesterday, but it still took me by surprise.

I woke with a start when I heard a moan run through my dreams. It sounded like someone was hurt. I forced my eyes open and stared at a stone ceiling above me. I rolled stiffly out of my cot and forced myself not to gasp from the pain that ran through my body. I'd rather be sore than dead, but this was awful! I pulled myself to my feet and cringed. My head didn't hurt anymore, but the pain seemed to have traveled through the rest of my body. I glanced over the short stone wall and realized that Narden was talking to someone. I ducked, not recognizing the woman he spoke to.

Slowly and carefully, I turned my head expecting my hide to be purple and black instead of blue and gold. I wasn't so fortunate. I never had seen a dragon bruise, but I hurt so much that I expected I'd be the first.

"Hungry, feller?" she called cheerfully.

I turned my head slowly again, hoping that the bees doing jumping jacks in my head would stop soon. Majorlaine wasn't actually talking to me, which irked me slightly. She was talking to the red dragon across the hall.

"Here you are." She pulled a boiled roast from her wagon and laid it in front of him.

"Thanks," he whispered as she turned to me.

"Now," she told me with her hands on her hips.

I had the incredible urge to toast the pony pulling the food cart when he tilted his head to the side and the harness caught the morning light just right to blind me. Ponies were usually pretty gamy, but this was a plump pony that resembled Majorlaine in more ways than just the weight and frizzy gray hair.

People didn't cross that pony either once they knew him. He was a sweet animal as long as people were nice to him. He also had the innate ability to determine people's personalities. I once heard Lord Grath tell her that he was going to take Kip, her pony, on his next diplomatic mission so Kip could tell him who was being truthful. Majorlaine refused and didn't speak to his lordship for a week for even suggesting such a thing.

I moved my head too fast to get my eyes out of the light and nearly fell over when the movement sent shots of pain running through my neck.

"Kip," she chided the pony, "be more careful with that harness." After backing up the cart into a shadow, she patted his nose. "I know you're not used to it being so clean, not that it mattered." She glared at me under her bushy gray eyebrows. "You didn't even get to meet her ladyship."

"WHAT?" I yelled at her. I heard a very soft giggle from the stall to my right.

Majorlaine, whose hearing wasn't what it used to be, or so I'd been told, didn't seem to notice. Instead, she shook her finger in my face. "We had all been looking forward to meeting her, but then you had to run into trouble. You young'ins couldn't stay out of trouble if you tried." She retrieved a bucket from the back of the wagon. "Drink this," she ordered putting it under my nose.

I looked at the murky concoction with skepticism. It didn't smell nearly as bad as some of the other things she made. Her cure for an upset stomach smelled so bad, that we never were sick again just so we didn't have to drink the stuff.

I took another cautious sniff and cocked my eyebrows at her. "This is liquor?" I told her.

"I see that fall didn't knock all of your wits out," she told me, as she fished another chunk of boiled meat out of the wagon. "Of course it's liquor, can you think of a better way to dull pain?"

"And I'll have a headache that would kill a knight's horse when it wears off."

What was she thinking? Galen would skewer her with one of his dragon splints if he found her giving me this as a painkiller.

"From that little bit?" She shook her head at me. Only to a dragon could someone call a bucket full of alcohol a "little bit."

She shrugged, "Your choice," and she pulled the bucket away replacing it with the roast. Rummaging in the cart a moment longer, she pulled a pouch from the back corner and dumped the contents over the roast.

I stared at the meat in horror. "What was that?"

"Painkiller." She gave me that annoying "you should have taken the first offer" smile of hers.

"Galen won't . . ." I began.

She interrupted, "Galen won't anything. He left this morning and left that"—she motioned at the green powder covering the roast—"for you."

"Lovely," I stated sarcastically, at least the roast was small. The powder smelled like a burnt skunk. I thought I might wait until Majorlaine left and then either see if the powder would burn off or shake most of it off.

I glanced up when I heard the clink of the harness as the pony shifted. Majorlaine stood there with her hands on her hips, watching me. "Well, go on," she said.

I stared at her in horror. She wasn't going to leave until I ate that thing!

I looked at the roast again and took a deep breath. I downed it in one swallow, but some of that noxious powder stuck to the roof of my mouth making me gag. Majorlaine laughed. If I hadn't been coughing at that moment, I might have considered lighting her shoes.

"Now that wasn't so bad." She patted my nose when I stopped coughing.

I glared at her.

"When Adenern had to take that last time he was here, he . . ." her voice trailed off. "Land's sake, what are you doing in here?"

I turned my head too quickly and caught my breath with the pain, fighting the dizzy sensation that made me want to lie down and go back to sleep.

"You're not supposed to be here," Majorlaine's voice was picking up a sharp edge. "How did you get into the fortress?"

I backed up hard against the wall of the stall. I cringed from the pain that shot through my back.

"You shouldn't be in here," the woman continued, rounding the divider. "What were you doing sleeping in here?" she snapped.

She grabbed my arm, pulling me forward by the sling. I gasped as pain shot through my shoulder.

"That's nothing compared to what you're going to feel when Armel gets through with you," she snapped pulling me out of the stall, "unless you start talking right now. What are you mute?"

"Let her go." I saw some of the lose stones in the wall shake with the growl.

"Narden," the woman snapped, "stay out of this. She probably got in with the tailors."

"I said," the rumble was deeper now, "let her go."

She glanced over at him and must have noticed that all the scales that hadn't been damaged were spiking because her grip on my arm loosened.

It took her only a moment to recover though. "Now, see here." She wagged her finger in the dragon's face. "I don't know what she's told you, but she's obviously lying. You should know better."

I watched his eyes narrow as smoke began trickling from his nostrils. He turned his head suddenly and encompassed the little wagon in flames. The pony looked somewhat frightened as the wood began to burn.

Immediately, the woman released my arm. I saw the red dragon streak from behind the cart and race from the stable. The woman hurried toward the pony and began expertly unbuckling the harness.

"You!" she yelled as she worked.

I knew I couldn't do anything directly to her without harming Ari, but I would not let Majorlaine drag her from the building like a criminal. I could also see that she was hurting Ari. If she was going to hurt Ari, I would see to it that she paid. I heard the pony shift impatiently next to me and knew what I could do.

Ignoring the pain that shot through my neck, I whirled my head around and flamed that wagon. As I suspected, she released Ari to tend to her pony.

"Behind me, quick," I called to Ari. She darted behind me and then leaned against my scales. I could feel her beginning to shake.

"You!" Majorlaine yelled and then stated something in el'brenika. I barely knew the language, having learned bits from Gary, my father, and Renard, so it took me a moment to translate it. When I had, I was ready to kill her and her pony.

"Call her that again," I snarled, "and I will roast that fat pony alive."

She retorted something that I didn't quite catch, which was probably to her benefit. If anything could be positive in this situation, she was at least insulting Ari in a language that Ari didn't understand.

I caught something about no good and was about ready to make good on my threat when Drenar raced in. I glanced up briefly when I heard his feet hit the stone floor. It appeared that he had just woken up. His shirt was mostly buttoned, but not tucked in, and he wasn't wearing shoes.

The pony was detached from the cart now, and Majorlaine dragged him toward Drenar while the little wagon continued to burn. It wouldn't catch anything else on fire in here. Having dragons in mind, the designers of Caer Corisan had made almost everything out of stone. The ceiling had very good ventilation, so the smoke would travel out without letting rain in.

I turned my attention to Ari while Drenar dealt with Majorlaine. Ari was quivering a little bit but not nearly as badly as I had expected.

"It'll be all right, Ari," I told her softly. She looked up at me, and I watched her take a deep breath. I forced myself to calm down as well. "Lord Drenar will get it all sorted out. It's just a misunderstanding," I said, hoping she wouldn't think everyone at Caer Corisan would treat her like that.

I caught the words *spy* and *thief* in el'brenika as Majorlaine hurried past me. I heard bare feet following her.

"She stole this from Armel himself. This is his best fur blanket. The only thing he has to keep him warm on winter nights, and she stole it from him." From the corner of my eye, I saw her thrust the blanket under Drenar's nose.

He took it from her and said evenly, "She did not steal this from Armel." Then he called my name.

I turned my head slowly, fighting both the urge to roast Majorlaine and the pain in my neck. She was normally a nice woman, but she jumped to the worst possible conclusions all the time.

"You can't tell me he *gave* it to her." She had a frantic pitch to her voice.

"Will you hand this to my l—" Drenar began, but Majorlaine cut him off.

"You can't give that . . ." She snatched at the blanket, but I had it and tossed it to Ari before the woman could grab it. She shrieked that phrase again at the top of her lungs.

Snarling, I spiked my scales. I noticed Drenar turned deathly pale and was silent for a moment. He said something to me that took me a moment to translate. It was something along the lines of, "She doesn't understand el'brenika, does she?"

I fought for the words, not wanting Ari to know what we were talking about. "You better pray she doesn't," I growled at Majorlaine.

She'd been dumbstruck by our response, but regained her voice quickly. Her face turning red, she growled back, "Well, I can say it so she does understand. She's nothing but a spying, thieving . . ."

Drenar grabbed her arm and pulled her forcefully toward the entrance. It was a good thing he did because she wasn't going to make it to the next phrase in front of me.

As Drenar spoke close to her ear, I watched her suddenly freeze. Then she glanced back at me. Her face was as white as Drenar's had been moments before.

I knew very little of the language that they were speaking. The woman seemed to switch back and forth between it and common with an ease that I admired. Whatever she'd said, though, made Narden want to kill her. I was glad I didn't know the words, because I was having a hard enough time not going into a shaking fit as it was. I forced myself not to imagine what she could be saying.

Glancing down at my dress, I realized that I must look like a vagabond. The fall and tumbling out of the wagon had torn part of the skirt. I could see that the riding breeches underneath were scraped up as well, but not nearly as badly. One of my sleeves was split exposing the scar around my wrist. There was blood on my shoulder, probably from the scrape on my head. The blood on my blouse was from Narden's shoulder that the wind drove back on me as we flew here.

Narden turned away, and a moment later, I saw something falling toward me. Quickly covering my head with my good arm to block the impact, I cringed from the movement as my sore body yelled in pain. The black fur blanket settled over my head. I relaxed, pulling it around my shoulders.

Hearing Narden say something in el'brenika, I glanced up. He didn't speak that language very often, and his accent was horrible compared to the other people I'd heard speak it.

I heard the woman start to say something, accusing me of being a spy and a thief. Next I heard footsteps hurrying off, which stopped after a moment.

"You don't mean that's . . ." her voice trailed off. I peered cautiously over Narden's back to see her leaning against the wall for support. "But she looks like . . ."

"She fell off a dragon, yesterday?" Narden snapped sarcastically.

"You didn't offer her a bath?" She seemed to be regaining her composure, at least the color was coming back to her face.

"We were busy," Narden growled. "It was on my list of things to offer her today right after breakfast."

"She hasn't eaten yet." The woman seemed horrified.

"No." He was still mad, and the questions seemed somewhat odd even to me, especially for someone who'd just called me a spying thief. "People don't often eat while they're sleeping."

"She slept in here," the scandalized tone in her voice made me laugh slightly. It made me think of what my mother must have sounded like when my father gave the news to her that I'd be staying with dragons for a year.

Narden turned back to me, letting Lord Drenar answer that question. I noticed him cringe as he turned his head toward me.

Over his back, I heard the woman demand, "Certainly, you could have found a more suitable place for her to sleep than in a *stable*."

I didn't catch Lord Drenar's answer, but I could guess it from her response of, "What do you mean she *wanted* to sleep here?"

"Are you all right?" Narden asked.

I smiled slightly and nodded. "It was a misunderstanding," I told him.

He let out a derisive snort. "As if anyone here shouldn't recognize you."

I carefully glanced down at my clothes and laughed. There was nothing but silence above me.

Looking back up at his nose, I asked, "Have you seen me lately?" He looked stunned by the question as I continued, "I look like I fell from a dragon yesterday and never took a bath afterward. My own mother wouldn't recognize me."

He continued to stare at me for a moment then laughed with me.

I watched her for a moment wondering about that statement. I wasn't sure her own mother would recognize her anyway. She was much different now than she had been when she was fourteen. Her hair was far redder than it had been five years ago even though it still looked more gold than red.

She was thinner than she used to be when she was young, as well. I wondered if her cheeks would ever fill out again, and I knew, as few people did, that her ribs still showed. Her clothes didn't hang off her the way they had, but they were still too loose for the current fashion.

She didn't have the same confident air that she used to have. Now she looked frightened more often than not, and she didn't laugh unless she actually felt like it. I could remember times when I saw her laugh just to laugh when she was young. I laughed with her now, because she might stop if I didn't join in. I liked hearing her laugh.

I heard the bare feet start walking toward my stall again. Carefully, I turned my head to look at Drenar.

"How is she?" he asked softly.

I would have glanced at Ari, but I didn't want to move my head more than I had to. I was feeling dizzy as it was. "Better than I thought she would be," I answered.

Out of the corner of my eye, I saw her look over my neck at Drenar.

"Lady Ari'an," he addressed her directly, "do you feel able to accompany me to breakfast?"

She didn't say anything, but she must have nodded after a moment because he bowed, and she stepped around my tail. She drew back slightly when he offered his arm, and he immediately retracted it, motioning toward the entrance with his other arm. She started down the hall, and Drenar walked along with her.

As she took a step forward, I felt my stomach wrench hard. I almost felt sick, but I didn't think it was from that nasty medicine I'd just eaten.

Ari was entering a world where I couldn't follow. In that world of humans, fancy clothes, and elaborate dinners, I couldn't protect her. I felt like I was having part of myself torn out and thrown to crows. She'd come back, I was sure, but I wouldn't be there when she was scared. I couldn't protect her out there.

To my surprise, she stopped at the stall Majorlaine had pulled her pony into. I saw her mouth open. She'd get the words she wanted to say out in a moment. I expected her to tell the woman that she should be flogged for calling her a spy and thief.

I was completely shocked when Ari finally said, "He has a very pretty harness." Then she hurried out the entrance.

Walking across the courtyard with Lord Drenar, I glanced around a little, but I noticed that the people who saw me stopped to stare as I walked past. I bit my lip. I knew I looked horrible. I should have asked for a change of clothes last night but hadn't thought about it. I should have asked for something to wash with too, but I hadn't thought of that either. I must have looked like something a dog had pulled from the trash. I almost laughed when I wondered if the phrase "something the dragon dropped" would be in common use.

Lord Drenar brought me to the room with the stone couch again. Excusing himself, he left. Someone had returned the cushions to the cabinet, so I walked over to the little doors and pulled one open. Lifting a velvet pillow from a shelf, I ran my hand over the soft fabric.

I thought about what I remembered of the fabric. I didn't want to start thinking about something that might scare me, and this seemed like a safe thought. I remembered my mother telling me to change out of my favorite dress when I was a small child because velvet was a winter fabric, and it was summer. She'd found a silk dress for me. Silk was a sheer fabric that stayed cool. It wasn't soft the way velvet was.

I hoped the dried dragon's blood and my own blood hadn't rubbed onto the beautiful black fur blanket that was still in the stable. Who had the woman said it belonged to? I hoped he wouldn't be upset if it was stained. I wondered if anyone had asked him if I could use it. Lords and ladies typically didn't ask servants for permission to use their things, but that didn't seem right to me.

What did I know about being a lady? I knew more about being a . . . I forced the thought from my mind and walked toward the window. I saw Majorlaine walk out of the dragon stable leading the little gray pony. I realized Narden had completely destroyed the little wagon. I understood why he'd torched it, but I wondered if he would apologize. Narden didn't strike me as the kind of person who apologized when he felt that he'd been wronged—or in this case, I'd been wronged. I wondered if she'd be able to replace the cart.

CHAPTER 22

THE CARPENTER

There was a thump behind me, and then something scraped on the floor. I turned around half expecting Adenern to have crept in and to see him rearranging the furniture. Instead, I found one of the servants positioning a wooden table in the room. I jumped when I saw him.

"I apologize, mistress," he said bowing to me, "I didn't mean to surprise you."

His dialect was from a southeastern house, sort of. I wondered how he ended up working this far north and west. He was shorter than me, but not by much, which was surprising. Servants had a tendency to be much shorter than lords and ladies, or at least I'd been told that. I remembered someone saying something about their not eating as well and having to do harder labor. I tried to recall who. I thought it was my father, but I couldn't remember for sure.

I glanced at him as he came back in with a wooden chair. He had brown eyes and nearly brown hair that seemed to be trying desperately to be gold but not quite making it. He was older than Lord Grath, but I couldn't tell by how much.

"Lord Drenar will be back in a little bit," he told me when he noticed I was watching him. He laughed lightly. "He had to go get properly dressed. Having to run to the stables so Narden didn't scorch, Majorlaine, didn't leave him time to put his shoes on."

227

"I didn't mean to cause trouble," I said softly, watching my hand fidget in front of me.

He laughed outright, I looked straight at him not meaning to meet his gaze but doing so by mistake. I had to stay there, because it wouldn't be proper to look away. The fact that he held his own gaze to mine surprised me. Servants normally wouldn't do that, or at least they didn't at Torion Castle. It felt like he was studying me.

He laughed, and finally looked back at the chair he was positioning next to the table. I let my breath out hard without making a sound. Looking down at my feet, I took a few silent ragged breaths.

"Majorlaine probably deserved it." He was still chuckling. "She can be set in her ways, but she's stuck around."

"Do people not stay here?" I asked hoping if I kept him talking he wouldn't notice my hands shaking.

"Not all people," he continued, walking over to the cabinet to retrieve a cushion for the chair. "The men will come and go and come back, but women don't stay long here if they come at all."

I looked up startled by that. "Why . . ." I stopped. I wanted to know why women didn't stay here, but it might not be wise to ask him. Was there something wrong that I didn't know about? What did the men do to the women here? I glanced out the window and noticed that there was only the one woman, Majorlaine, in the courtyard but probably twenty or more men.

"Don't be scared, mistress," he said, and I glanced at him slightly. "No one here's going to hurt you." I accidentally met his gaze again, it looked terribly sad. "This"—he waved his hand at the walls—"is Caer Corisan. More dragons come here in one day than most people would see in a lifetime even in Rem'Maren." He shook his head slightly. "After scaring their children into being good by threatening that they'll turn into dragons if they're not, what woman would want to come here or have a daughter come here to work?"

He walked to the door and picked up the other chair standing there. "Even the people in the villages near here think their daughters would end up burned or eaten." The sigh he let out tore at my heart.

"Armel," I heard Lord Drenar laugh from the door, "are you talking Lady Ari'an's ear off?"

It was such an odd thing for him to say that I felt my jaw drop. He was leaning on the doorframe with a huge grin on his face. I glanced at the older man wondering how he would respond. The name *Armel* sounded familiar, but I couldn't quite place where I knew it from.

"I am surprised," he continued, "that you would be setting up the breakfast furniture, even though you wanted to meet"—he smiled at me—"my lady last night."

The man, Armel, walked straight up to Lord Drenar and began waving his finger in the lord's face. "You want to know why I'm here?"

The lord didn't move from leaning on the doorframe. He didn't say anything either.

"I caught Ishmerai dragging these across the courtyard." He motioned at the table and chairs. "*These!*" he reemphasized. I glanced at the table, there didn't seem to be anything fancy about it to me. The wood wasn't even coated.

"I nearly skinned him right there," he continued, "then he tells me they are for the lady here, and I knew I'd never see them again if I didn't bring them myself." He shook his finger in Lord Drenar's face again. "Now, you promise me that"—he seemed to search for a word for a moment that wouldn't come to him—"that Adenern isn't going to come in here and scorch the things. I can just see him testing them to see if they'll burn."

Lord Drenar was still smiling when he said, "Adenern left this morning to show Hafiz where Narden was attacked."

"All the better," he said walking back over to the table and lovingly running his hand over the wood. "Narden's not going to head in here and torch it either." He gave the lord a slight glare.

"I doubt Narden will be going many places with as sore as he looked," Lord Drenar answered.

"He managed to torch Majorlaine's wagon," Armel replied sharply.

"Majorlaine's wagon ends up burning at least once a month," he laughed in reply, moving into the room so a huge man could come in with a tablecloth draped over his arm, a tray with a water pitcher and two short but stout cups.

He began to spread the tablecloth, but Armel snatched it off. Shaking the linen in his face he snapped, "What are you doing? First you *drag* this masterpiece across the courtyard and then you try to cover it with *this?*"

The black-haired servant seemed as surprised as I was. The tablecloth had a beautiful embroidered design of the mountains around the edge. The table was the plainest wood I'd ever seen.

"I didn't want it to get scratched," the servant stated.

"Scratched!" The man shook the tablecloth viciously. "You *drag* it across the courtyard and then worry about it being *scratched* by some *dishes?*"

"I'm sorry," the servant managed, turning his pale-blue eyes to meet Armel's gaze.

He yanked the tray from the servant's hands and then smiled broadly. "Well, good, at least you'll admit when you're wrong." He tossed the tablecloth back at the man adding, "Now, scram before I find something else to complain about."

The servant looked bemused and just stood there for a moment holding the bunched-up tablecloth.

"Well?" Armel began tapping his foot.

"Sorry," the servant managed to say and hurried from the room.

I glanced at Lord Drenar, after watching the exchange, and found that he was trying to keep from laughing. He said something to the servant as the man hurried past that seemed to amuse him even more.

"Armel," the lord began, watching the older man deftly place the cups and pitcher on the table, "you know quite well that table wouldn't be scratched even by dragging it across the courtyard. It fell, if I have the story right, off Adelwin's back, and no one found it all that winter and half of the spring, and it did not have a single mark on it from the whole ordeal. As for Adenern trying burn it, he has tried that before and never managed to."

"Well," the man huffed, "there's a first time for everything. Speaking of which"—he turned suddenly to me and bowed. I watched as the tray rolled up his left arm, across his shoulders, and came to rest on his right palm—"would you care to have a seat."

Before I realized what had happened, I was seated at the table. I put my right hand on the table to steady myself from the sudden movement. The man had taken my arm, took me the two steps to the chair, and I was seated before I could take a breath. I heard water pouring and looked up to find him next to the table with the pitcher and my water cup back in his hands. Setting that in front of me he picked up the other cup, poured it, and had the pitcher back on the table before I could have said two words.

"Now"—the tray rolled around his hand and came to rest between his fingers—"what would you like to eat this fine morning? I know that Majorlaine served roasts to the dragons, but if you would like something more traditional, I know that the cooks can serve eggs in the shape of a swan."

I stared at the table blankly, trying to imagine swan-shaped eggs and failing completely.

"Armel," Lord Drenar interrupted my thoughts, as he walked over to the table, "would you excuse us for a moment?"

"But I haven't even gotten her breakfast yet." The tone was surprised, and I noticed that his accent came out more when he was startled.

"If you would have a variety brought, but not a lot of the individual items, please," the lord replied evenly. The man looked momentarily distraught but then straightened, bowed to me again, and hurried from the room.

Lord Drenar watched the doorway for a moment then shook his head. He still had a slight smile on his face though. "My lady," he turned to me and lowered his voice, "I had not realized that your presence here would be considered this much of an event."

Sitting in the chair across the table, he tapped his fingers on the wood for a moment and watched the door. "I started to see it when I arrived two days ago and noticed that the staff had doubled in size." He rubbed his forehead with the hand that had been tapping the table.

"Mintxo,"—he glanced at me—"the head cook for the human population here, has probably fixed a breakfast for you that with what is left over will feed the expanded staff for the rest of the day. That's only breakfast, which he's been preparing since Majorlaine ran across the courtyard to tell him you, had not in fact left with Adenern, and in actuality, were still here and needed breakfast, which was"—he glanced out the window—"all of a quarter of a watch ago. The eggs in the shape of a life-size swan will be one of the minor things he's fixed for the meal."

He took a breath and continued, "'Disappointed' will not begin to describe him when he finds out you are eating here"—he motioned at the little room—"which means that no less than thirty-seven people, who I can individually name, will ask you to eat lunch in the banquet hall, which I am certain no fewer than fifty people are decorating for breakfast right now."

"Armel, at least, had the foresight to realize that you would not be eating in the hall, intercepted Ishmerai, who I sent to get a small table, and had him start to bring this one, knowing full well that he would demand to bring it himself when Ishmerai did not carry it exactly as he would." The lord returned his head to his hand and sat silently for a moment.

Lifting his head back up he looked me full in the face, the sudden movement caught me by surprise, and I found that I was meeting his gaze. I felt my muscles stiffen, and my fingers tighten around the edge of the table.

To my surprise, he immediately looked away. "I'm sorry," he said, "I did not mean to do that."

I relaxed only slightly, realizing that somehow he knew that I didn't like to meet a person's gaze. I didn't know how he knew though.

He took a deep breath and looked past the left side of my head. "My lady," he began in a calm tone, which made me realize that his previous statements had all been in a faintly annoyed one, "I would prefer not to send you off without a meal or in your present attire, but if you would like to leave now"—he thought for a moment—"I can send for Renard and have him here shortly."

"If you would like to eat and wash," he continued, "Adenern may return by then. He could take you back, if you would prefer that."

I heard birds outside of the window in the silence that followed. I thought about the options he'd given and the one he hadn't said while I stared at the table. I could leave now. Even though I hadn't seen Renard, he was somewhere nearby and could be here quickly. I would like to eat and clean up, but to ride Adenern back . . . I moaned inwardly at the thought of taking off and landing with him. I already ached, if he took me anywhere, I'd want to die at the end of the ride. I could stay . . . If I left, I glanced out the window again, I would have to leave Narden here.

"I'd prefer not to travel with Adenern," I told Lord Drenar.

"Would you like me to send for Renard to take you back now?" he asked.

I shook my head. "I'd like to eat something first, sir." I glanced back at him and noticed the brief puzzled look that crossed his face turn to a smile.

"Of course"—he laughed lightly—"I can also have Renard come after you have eaten. Would you like to bathe before he comes also?"

I thought about that offer for a moment and asked, "Is he nearby then?"

"Yes, my lady," he answered.

I licked my lips and studied my fingers. "Will he be near here all day, or will he be going somewhere else?"

He didn't answer right away, so I glanced up. His brow was furrowed, and he was studying me intently. I felt the blood drain from my face, and my hand tightened around the edge of the table again.

He immediately looked to the side and apologized. I again felt my stomach drop to my feet because this man, who I'd just met, knew enough about me that he would apologize for making me uncomfortable.

"I could, in theory," he continued, "send for him at any time. I would have to give him the order myself because he is at a sensitive post right now." He paused for a moment then continued in a nonchalant tone, "Why do you ask?"

As he spoke, my eyes wandered over the fine grain of the plain table, to the cupboard, to the stone coach, and out the window. I could see the stable where Narden was from where I sat and noticed that the red dragon was cautiously looking out the door. I saw him quickly duck back inside as a cart rolled by. I wondered what had happened to him that he was so skittish. He seemed to be afraid of things that none of the other dragons I'd met had even flinched at. Not that I had met many dragons.

I looked back at my hand on the table, I took a breath and forced my eyes to travel from my hands to Lord Drenar's face. He was studying his fingernails or at least pretending to. He stopped after a moment, and I saw his gaze travel across the table to my hand. I had it just lying on the table and refused to let it look nervous. At that point his eyes went to the corner of the table and traveled up the wall next to the window till they were even with my own. I saw that slightly puzzled look cross his face again. A slight tilt of his head brought his eyes even with mine. The whole event took less than two breaths.

I swallowed hard, I would say what I wanted to looking at him, or I would not say it at all. I opened my mouth and realized my voice was stuck in my throat again. On the second try, I had it. "I would like to stay."

Lord Drenar began to say something, but an excited shout from the hall interrupted him. I nearly sprang from my chair at the sound, making my shoulder and back scream in pain. I vaguely remember the lord excusing himself, as footsteps ran down the hall accompanied by a voice yelling something that I couldn't make out. My vision had gone a bit blurry from the pain, and my hearing was off as well as I bit my lip to keep from gasping.

Slowly, things began to come into focus again. I noticed that the Armel fellow was back.

"Are you all right?" he asked when I looked at him.

I glanced away and forced words through my throat, "I'm very sore."

I heard the other chair move on the floor. "I can imagine why. I saw you fall yesterday." His accent faded as his voice lost the concerned edge and settled into a conversational tone.

I thought hard trying to distract myself from the yell in the hall and the pain in my back. If I didn't focus on something else, I would fall into a memory from the temple. I felt one hovering at the corner of my mind waiting for me to lose enough control for it to take over.

"It's a nice table," I said the first thing that came to mind that connected to the man in the chair across from me.

"This?" I saw his hand wave across the wood. "Are you joking, my lady?"

"Wha . . ." I started wondering what was wrong with this man. He'd just yelled at a servant for putting a tablecloth on it.

I glanced at the table and then past the man's head to catch a glimpse at his face. He had a twinkle in his eyes and a smile that he was trying not to show. He was baiting me, but for what reason?

I thought about demanding he tell me what was going on, but that would spoil whatever he was planning. He was sitting far enough away from me that I could easily scream if he tried anything. I could hear Lord Drenar talking to someone a little ways down the hallway, but I couldn't understand the words. He would notice if I screamed.

I decided that I would play whatever game this man was up to, for now. I glanced over the table and ran my hand over it lightly.

"Well, sir," I began, seeing Armel tilt his head out of the corner of my eye, "from what you said earlier, it is an old table, but it does not show much wear, and the wood itself seems new."

"Oh?" he asked nonchalantly.

"Also," I continued, "if what Lord Drenar said was true, it is hard to damage to the extent that a dragon cannot burn it."

"Do you have a reason to doubt him?" The question caught me off guard, as he leaned forward on the table.

"Well . . ." I began then caught sight of his face again, he still had that half grin. I tilted my head and replied, "He has not given me any reason to doubt him as of yet, but I did only meet him"—I glanced out the window—"less than a day ago."

"What do you make of him so far?" the question followed quickly.

"He is," I paused for a moment searching for the words I wanted, "not like any of the other house lord heirs I have met."

"How so?"

"He's . . ." I searched for some description that would fit, "human."

"Really?" He glanced at the doorway where the sound of Lord Drenar's voice drifted from. "Are most of the heirs you meet not human?"

"They look like they should be, but . . ." Should I really be talking to this man about things like this? I followed his gaze to the doorway and finished, "They seem more like statues that no one should touch."

"You will find that the House of Rem'Maren is more than it appears," he said in a tone that reminded me of a sleight of hand artist finishing a trick.

I glanced at him as he leaned back and folded his hands behind his head. My gaze was just enough off his face that I noticed the change in the table. The wood was turning black starting at the two corners nearest him and spreading across the grain.

"What did you do?" I moved away from the table, horrified. I would admit the table was plain, but the wood grain had been magnificent.

The man didn't respond as the black covered the table and spread down the legs. I blinked at the table wondering if the discoloration would stop at the table or continue across the floor. I noticed that close to me the table seemed to be changing again. The black lightened first to dark green and continued to a middle shade. Then it took on a brushlike quality. The change stopped about half an handsbreadth from the table edge. At the top of the green, in the center of the table, the black began fading to a deep brown and spreading back up the table.

Suddenly, I remembered why Armel's name sounded familiar. The plate I had that changed from Rem'maren's crest to Caer Corisan's crest and then to Gary's mountain was made by this man.

Meanwhile, the table had stopped turning brown and was branching into green again but quite a different shade of green. I realized it was a tree growing from a grass field. The remaining black faded to a radiant blue. The upper left corner continued to fade to a brilliant white taking the shape of a cloud.

I looked over the table to see if anything else would change and found two words writing into the field in the form of a vine twining in the grass. The script was one I couldn't read. The vine continued up the tree sketching two more words into the trunk of the tree. The next words I recognized as a name as the vine twined along the first branch of the tree. It continued to cross the tree adding names as it went. As it neared the top of the tree, I began to recognize the names. I saw Mattan, who was Lord Grath's grandfather. Seraiah was his father, and then I expected his name, but instead Gwaredd scripted in followed by Grath. Lord Grath's brother . . . Gwaredd . . . I finally remembered hearing about him. The man died during his training from what I understood. Lord Grath's three sons came next: Drenar, with Dreanen and Danren following after a space. The names of Lord Drenar's two sons followed.

The vine stopped growing at that point, but flowers began to appear beginning at the top along the vine followed by an additional vine sketching in the names of women. I recognized the name of Lord Drenar's daughter Batel, followed by his deceased wife's name, Hana. Lord Grath's younger two sons were not married as of yet.

Beside Lord Grath's name, two women's names appeared. His second wife's name, Margree, traced in first with a vine twining around Dreanen's and Danren's names. His first wife, Megara, who'd died shortly after Lord Drenar's birth, scripted in next, followed by Lord Grath's mother.

I gingerly brushed my fingers over Lord Grath's two wives' names. They were sisters, but from what I understood, they were very different. Lady Margree would have nothing to do with the dragons. They were a part of her life that she ignored as completely as possible. Her sister, Megara, had incorporated the dragons into her life as the Lady of Rem' Maren. From what I had heard, she had not only learned to ride the dragons but had planned to visit Caer Corisan, something that hadn't been done by a lady since three generations before.

I wondered if a lady from another house had ever visited the fortress before. It was little wonder that the servants here would make such an event of my visit. I remembered the banners in the entrance hall and wondered what else had been decorated. I could picture every corner in the fortress being cleaned out even though I was only supposed to be here for a few watches and could never possibly see every corner of the place anyway.

The table beneath my hand felt the same as it had before it turned black. I could still feel the grain of the wood even though the picture betrayed nothing of the texture.

"Did you make this?" I asked the man softly, when I noticed that the final name had sketched into the picture.

It was in the same script as the first name and was linked to it. The woman's name next to the trunk was in common, which surprised me since the man's name was in the strange script.

Armel replied in Gary's language. I understood the astonished tone, but didn't know the words.

My puzzled expression must have tipped him off that I didn't understand because he immediately added, "Sorry, mistress."

"This"—he motioned at the table—"is a masterpiece. I could make nothing so grand."

"You made the plate I have. It's beautiful." By mistake I looked directly at him, but he was brushing his hand over the table lovingly and wasn't looking at me. I took a moment to study his face, noting the laugh lines at his eyes and the lines from his smile by his mouth. His forehead bore wrinkles as well. Overall, his face looked weathered. I wondered how old he was.

"A trinket." He waved his hand at me brushing away my reply. "This"—he spread his hands at the table—"this is far beyond my skill. When I finish a piece, it is complete. This is designed to be added to. I cannot match this, and"—he rapped his knuckles on the table, causing me to jump—"this is wood." He paused and then added emphasis to the word, "Wood!"

He turned quickly on me and asked out of the air, "Would you like it?"

"What?" The word came out before I could stop it.

"Would you like it?" he repeated.

"Armel," I heard Lord Drenar say sharply from the doorway.

His voice startled me, and I looked up at him. I had no idea how long he had been there. A young servant stood behind him with his mouth hanging open.

"It is my table, and I can do what I want with it." Armel's tone had a sharp edge to it.

Lord Drenar looked like he was about to reply, but I held my hand up to him as he had to Narden the night before.

"It is a magnificent table, sir," I told Armel, and I saw him begin to beam. "It is worthy to be displayed in the grandest hall in Faruq"—I looked straight at him—"but I cannot accept it." I continued before anyone could interrupt me, tracing my hand along the edge of the table. "I feel that it belongs here at Caer Corisan, and I will not be here long. This is a treasure of the House of Rem'Maren, and it should stay with them."

I thought Armel would look disappointed or even offended, so I glanced at Lord Drenar first to gain some confidence. I saw a look of relief leaving his face as he glanced down at his hands. The table was an antique. Understandably, he wouldn't want it to leave their house. It puzzled me slightly that Armel would have the authority to give something like this away, but I didn't know exactly what relation he was to the house either. The table probably belonged to him as a gift for some service he rendered to the house.

I managed to pan my gaze past Armel's face, and to my absolute surprise, he was still beaming! I saw him bow, and my gaze snapped back to him. It was a formal bow that matched any I had seen done by the royals of Faruq. Who was this that he could do such a thing seamlessly?

"You will do well, my lady," he said without a hint of accent. Straightening, he continued, "Will you be taking breakfast in the hall then?"

CHAPTER 23

THE COURAGE
TO STAY

The thought that I should curtsy, and the debate of how formally I should, flew from my head at his question. I had thought about eating in the hall, but I was nervous about dealing with that many people. I glanced down at my hands and saw the rips in my dress exposing my riding breeches underneath. I was a complete disaster. I certainly couldn't meet people like this. The woman, Majorlaine, had mistaken me for a thief!

"I can have Ishmerai draw a bath in your rooms, if you wish, and Faber will have a dress that will fit you well enough until he can put together another one for you," he continued.

How in the world did this man know my objections before I even said them?

"Armel," Lord Drenar began with a sharp edge to his voice, "Lady Ari'an can take breakfast wherever she wishes."

"Yes, my lord." He didn't look away from me. "Where would you like to breakfast then?"

I glanced at the table as I debated my answer. I wanted to show these people my appreciation for all of the effort they put into my visit, but would I be able to handle meeting as many as would come, if I ate in the dining hall? I traced the trunk of the tree with my fingers. I couldn't use the argument that I wasn't presentable because I could bathe and change my clothes as Armel had offered. Ultimately,

240

the table helped me make my decision. This wasn't a piece that should be used to serve a meal on. This was a piece that could possibly date back to when Rem'Maren became a house in Faruq, over seven hundred years ago.

"I'll," my voice almost failed me, and I swallowed to make it work, "I'll eat in the hall if you please."

Armel bowed again and left the room saying that he would call for someone to show me to my rooms.

"You don't have to do this." Lord Drenar turned to me immediately. He had a deeply concerned look. "Armel should never have pressured you."

I thought about that for a moment and then looked directly at him. "My lord, this is what I should do." I glanced at the doorway for a moment. "What did he mean by *my* rooms?"

"When Majorlaine and Xander heard that you were going to be staying here when winter set in, they began setting up a place for you to spend your time." he shook his head. "Xander will go into convulsions when he finds that you are going to use those rooms now." He looked like he was trying very hard to hide his frustration as he turned to me again. "If at any point you want to leave, let me know." He studied me for a moment being careful not to look me full in the face. "You really do not have to do this."

I met his gaze and managed to even smile a little bit. "I know, sir, it is my choice."

I could stay or leave when I chose to. No one was forcing me to do either. I knew that the servants here wanted me to stay, and that Lord Drenar could have Renard here in a very short time if need be, but I could choose either way. I rubbed my wrist feeling the indent where the rope scars were. No one would keep me here against my will.

A short deathly pale man appeared in the doorway. He bowed to Lord Drenar first then to me.

He tumbled out some words in an accent I didn't recognize. I thought it had something to do with my rooms, but I couldn't quite follow the statement.

"She just needs somewhere to clean up," Lord Drenar answered the man. "Do you have a better place for her to go?"

The man looked hopeful for a moment, then a look of total defeat came over him.

"No," he answered, "'there's nowhere better.'"

Lord Drenar turned to me and asked, "Would you like for Xander to show you to your rooms?" He paused for a moment, and probably noticed I turned a bit pale.

I didn't really want to start wandering through the fortress, following people I didn't know.

"I could go with you."

"I'd prefer that, sir," I answered softly.

He bowed and told Xander to lead the way. The poor man looked like he was going to his execution as he turned to the right and proceeded down the hall. A turn to the left and another to the right brought us to a long staircase. Watching my feet to make sure my legs made each step, I climbed my way to the top.

At the top of the stairs, I stopped, taking in the sudden change. The floor had a thick carpet of deep blue, and there were rolls of golden fabric draped along the wall. Tassels matching the carpet held the fabric to the ceiling. The doors were all made of rich wood, and each had a dragon carved into it etched in silver. Between the doors, elaborate tapestries hung depicting mountainous landscapes.

The short man stopped in front of the first set of double doors on the right.

I slowly put my foot on the floor and felt it sink into the carpet. Carefully, I walked the short distance to the door, worried that if I breathed too heavily the decorations might all disintegrate.

Bowing, the man opened the double doors. I carefully walked past him into an enormous room. I heard him straighten after Lord Drenar walked past him, and he said what sounded like "I'm sorry" and "It's not finished yet."

I glanced around the room while we waited for the man to unlock the door and come back. In the corner, there was an upturned couch with the carpet for the floor rolled up leaning against it. There was a curtain swaying in the wind of the open balcony, but the other curtain was lying in a pile on a chair that had six different fabrics draped over it. A desk in another corner was missing a leg while the matching chair that supported the piece where the limb should have been was missing its back.

Xander hurried past me and pulled opened a door to the left. "You can wash here, and see it swings in and out."

He pushed the door, and I took a step back in surprise when it didn't stop at the frame but continued past.

He caught the door and continued talking, "And see"—he flipped a little handle on the inside of the door, and a metal piece swung out of the side of the door—"it will bolt on the inside but not the out."

I must have looked extremely confused because flipping the little handle back, the man darted into the room, pulled the door shut, and I heard the dull click of him turning the small handle again. There was no keyhole on this side of the door. Then he began rattling the door from his side.

"How is that possible?" I stared at the door. Even the doors at the temple locked with keys. I could look out the keyholes, but all I ever saw was a wall.

"Armel and Xander worked on it for the last three months," Lord Drenar told me.

The door swung open again, and Xander walked out.

"See?" he asked.

I nodded to the question.

"And see." He motioned me into the room.

I took a cautious step forward and looked in. To my surprise the already full bathing area was set into the floor instead of sitting on it. The man darted into the room again and motioned to two wooden boxes set into the wall. One was a reddish hue while the other was a bright blue.

"And see, you can push the red one to warm the water and the blue one to let it cool," he told me.

I felt the blood drain from my face at the thought of someone bringing water in to adjust the temperature while I was bathing.

"There is actually a fire underneath the basin," he continued, "so no one has to enter, but it will take a bit longer to change the heat than if the water was brought to you directly."

I glanced at him surprised. It was a bit frightening that these people, who I had never met, knew so much about what I would want. It was simple little things that most people wouldn't think of, a door that would lock from the inside but not the out, a tub that would heat the water so I didn't need to have someone bring water. How would they know these things?

I heard footsteps behind me and jumped at the sound. Lord Drenar steadied me as I turned. Another man had entered carrying a bin in front of him. This man was much taller than Xander, but still quite round. His hair was light blond, almost to the point of being white.

He bowed to me and the lord, which was quite a feat considering the size of the bin he carried. Setting the bin down, he looked me over. I felt myself blush and clutched my hands together to keep them from shaking. I still had dragon's blood caked in my hair and to my clothes. My sleeves were torn along with part of my skirt. If I turned my hand wrong, the scar on my wrist would show.

"Would you like a full skirt?" the man asked, "or not so full?"

I glanced up slightly as he drew two skirts from the bin. One was a full skirt in light blue with floral lacework covering the whole thing, while the other, about half as full, was a deep red with beadwork. Both were beautiful, but seemed far too elaborate.

"Do you," I started and then realized it might not be my place to ask for something else.

I glanced at Lord Drenar who was looking slightly perplexed at the middle-aged man.

"Do you have anything simpler?" I managed.

Glancing back at the lord, I noticed the perplexed look disappear from his face and a slight smile replace it.

The man looked me over again and then dove back into the bin. He draped a couple of pieces of fabric over the side of the bin while he looked.

"Would this be more suited to my lady's taste?" In his hands he held a full dress done in purple velvet. It was a dark shade and didn't look like it had any buttons. The cuffs, the neck, and the hem were all done in a black fur. A sash, also in the purple velvet, ran from the sides of the waist. The neck was high, and the sleeves were long. The skirt would reach to the floor and cover my ankles.

"It is beautiful, sir," I told him, and I watched a smile spread across his face.

"Also"—he walked past me and put the dress on a counter in the washroom—"if you would"—he stopped in front of me on his way back and held out a spool of twine with bits of parchment pinned in the center—"take your measurements while you are here, I would like to have your clothes fitting better soon."

I took the twine gingerly, nervous that he was only two steps from me.

"The sheet will explain what I need," he told me. Turning, he pushed the bits of fabric hanging over the side back into the bin, picked it up, and walked from the room.

"If you need anything"—Xander motioned at a cord hanging near the double doors as he followed the tailor out—"just ring."

Lord Drenar hurried to catch the door before it swung shut.

"If you need anything," he told me. He glanced at the cord for a moment. "Also, if you would ring when you are finished, I will escort you to the dining hall."

With that he walked out the door, closing it behind him. I was left alone in a room I'd never seen until moments before. I looked around slowly, a curtained doorway resided to the left of the washroom with a matching doorway across the room. That one had a closed door instead of a curtain. A slight breeze blew through the curtain that half covered the balcony.

I felt my nerves getting the better of me and hurried over to the enormous fireplace across from the washroom. The fire crackled as I pulled the poker from the rack hanging on the mantle. I turned and swung the poker, making sure that I could handle it easily. Hopefully, I would only need to stall anyone who might still be in here for a moment, while I screamed.

At least a quarter of my mind told me I was being excessively fearful, but I wasn't listening. I would look in every corner of these rooms before locking myself in a small room, in a strange place, to take a bath.

Since the closed door was the closest, I decided to start there. Slowly, I pulled the door open moving behind it and looking through the crack between the hinges. I couldn't see anyone, but the room was a mess. I nearly laughed. It looked like this was the place where someone had thrown in everything that wasn't finished that could possibly fit. Stepping around the door cautiously, I took a better look inside.

It was about half the size of the main room with a large window in the wall that matched the blowing curtains in the main area. The window was half covered by a chair piled too high with curtain linens. Half of a far more elaborate desk than the one outside was on its side pushed into one corner.

The next corner had another couch in pieces piled on itself. Four rolls of carpet large enough to cover the main area were folded in half and resting against yet another couch on the back wall. That couch was in one piece except the legs were wedged into the right corner of the couch.

What was possibly the framework for a bed was jammed between the side of the couch and the next wall. What would be the mattress if it had any filling was draped over a lumpy mass next to the frame. A chair to match the one on the other side of the room was next to the mass along with far too many bed linens. Only one of the arms was missing from that chair.

The last corner had an enormous amount of curtain rods in it. Leaning against the wall closest to me was what looked like the door from the curtained room across the main area.

The middle of the room was covered in boxes and crates of every type of fabric or trinket I could think of.

Turning to leave, I glanced at the covered shape again. It was large enough to be a person. I felt my stomach drop to my feet and ran from the room. I was halfway to the bell cord when I stopped. What if it wasn't a person? What if someone came all the way here to pull the cover off something in a room that they would probably be embarrassed that I went into? The room was storing things so it would be the perfect place to hide, but would someone hide in there by merely draping a cover over themselves? What if it turned out to be nothing? I took a step back toward the room. What if it turned out to be someone?

I froze staring at the gaping doorway. Who would lie in wait for me here? One of the servants, perhaps, who just wanted to catch a glimpse of the visiting lady and ran in here to hide when he saw us coming. Or had someone else snuck in here? Did someone smuggle themselves in? Had someone from Verd, an assassin, heard that I was coming? Would they go to the trouble of getting into this fortress? It would be difficult, but could someone do it?

I glanced at the cord again. Walking to the door, I turned the handle and pushed it open just a hair. Gently I picked up the end of the cord and wrapped it around the handle until it was almost taut. If I ran from the room, the bell would ring as I left. Finally, I turned back to the room of broken pieces.

Firmly gripping the poker in my hands, I forced my feet to take one step after another. I came to the door and peered in. Had the mass moved?

I took a silent deep breath, I would succeed on the first try or not at all. "I, Lady Ari'an of the House of Nori'en, guest of Lord Drenar of the House of Rem'Maren, demand that you reveal yourself."

Did I see the cover move slightly . . . or was it the wind . . . or just my imagination?

"If you do not show yourself, you will be punished." I took a step toward the mass, then another. I'd warned them. Pulling the poker back, I swung it with all the force I could manage.

THUNK! The poker sounded against the mass. The form didn't move, but the blow knocked the mattress cover loose. It slid to the floor revealing the half-finished carving of two dragons. I squinted at the thing, recognizing it as a replica of the image of Gary and his son that I'd seen on the back of the map.

My knees stopped holding me. As I dropped to the floor, the poker clattered on the stones beside me. I sobbed and laughed until I could do nothing but draw one breath after another. I could feel my arms and legs shaking. There was nothing I could do to stop them but wait. I drew one breath after another until I could pull myself to my feet. I stumbled out of the room, collapsing again on the carpet outside.

The breeze helped me regain a measure of calm. More carefully, I stood up. I made my way into the washroom and poured a glass of water from the pitcher sitting on one of the counters. I left the glass on the counter since it took both my hands to steady the pitcher enough to get anything in the glass. I almost dropped the pitcher off the counter trying to set it down. I laughed nervously at the thought of how many broken dishes I would cause in this place.

The cup took both of my hands and all of my concentration as well. Even with the added effort, I spilled half of the water down my front. A few more moments and many ragged breaths later, I pulled myself back out to the main room. I walked carefully to the curtain waving in the breeze. There remained still two more places I had to check before my mind would rest enough so I could wash.

I leaned against the wall next to the curtain and steadied myself. Slowly I drew the curtain aside to see an empty balcony overlooking the courtyard. A green dragon with brown and golden patches circled to land. Another one, brown with lighter strips, took off from one of the walls. The mountains rose behind the walls stretching as far as I could see. It was a beautiful sight of greens turning to blues turning to purples that did much to calm my nerves.

A few more breaths, and I walked slowly to the curtain-covered doorway on the other side of the room. Again, I pulled a curtain back slowly and peered inside.

"Mighty One be praised," I whispered, repeating a statement I'd heard from Narden and his brothers.

The room had only two pieces of furniture, the first a cabinet of drawers pushed against the wall, the second a canopied bed, designed without legs, that rested on the floor.

Leaning against the doorframe, I took a few breaths then made my way to the entrance doors. Carefully, I unwound the cord from the handle and pulled the door shut. A key stood in the lock on the other door. Turning it, I heard the lock click.

Taking the key with me, I returned to the washroom and heard the lock click in the door as I turned the small handle. I threw my weight against the door with what was left of my strength. It didn't open. Dragging my feet to the pool, I tested the water with my hand.

Sinking against the wall, I pushed the small red box into the wall. Distantly, I heard a bell ring. Sliding down the wall to sit on the floor, I waited for the water to warm, forcing myself to think of anything but other times when I had been terrified.

I took up pacing, well, hobbling from the front of the stable to the back and then to the front again. On my second trip back to the entrance, I noticed that the red dragon had slipped out while my back was turned.

He was silent as well as quick. I wondered if he had learned to fly yet. He was still quite young. He would have just arrived here. It was little wonder that he was as skittish and frightened as he was.

Stopping short, I realized I'd just thought of that dragon as young, as if I was ancient! I started laughing. I was twenty-four years old. Gary was past seven centuries. I'd just called someone who was just over thirteen years young.

After that short reprieve, I continued my pacing. I wanted to know that Ari was all right. It was bad enough when I was out patrolling somewhere and she was at my cave. She was even safer here than there, but here she was among humans.

I'd noticed how many more people there were around than usual when the fourth stableboy came in to change the water troughs within the same watch. Two of Galen's assistants came to check my patches, and I had never before seen both of them at the fortress at the same time. Then Besnik, a dragon that resembled a calico-colored cat, showed up. He worked with Galen as well, mostly doing the attaching work for the scale patches. He had the precision to be able to torch a horse harness off the back of a horse without even singeing the horse.

About half a watch after Ari left, I heard one of the kitchen hands running across the courtyard. I glanced around to see him race past with more buckets than he would be able to carry when they were full. Someone asked him what his hurry was, but the boy didn't manage a very coherent answer. I managed to hobble to the entrance by the time he returned, spilling more water than was staying in the buckets.

"What is all this about?" I asked someone standing nearby who was watching with a bemused look. If there had been a fire somewhere, I knew that he wouldn't just be standing there, so I could at least rule out that possibility.

The answer he gave me, I couldn't believe. "What?"

The man glanced up at me, I couldn't quite remember his name at that moment, but I knew he was one of the blacksmiths. "Apparently, the lady is staying for a while. He"—nodding his head toward the boy—"is hauling water for her to bathe before she takes breakfast at the grand dining hall."

That was what I had heard the first time, but I still didn't believe it. Even here, stories grew fairly quickly. I hobbled toward the boy who was setting down the buckets to try to grip them better.

My shadow crossed one of the buckets while I was still several yards away. The lad immediately looked up, stood, and then bowed. The effect of which was that the one bucket he still had in his hands dumped what was left of its contents on him.

"Where are you taking all this?" I asked him.

"I'm . . . I'm . . . I'm drawing water for the lady's bath," he stumbled over the answer. The boy was about ten, so he only recently started to work here. "I'm . . . I'm . . . I'm . . . taking it to her bath."

Imagine that, drawing water for someone's bath to take to their bath. I swallowed the sarcastic reply and worded my next question, "Why?"

"Because she's dirty, sir." I saw the boy's face take on a look of shock when he realized what he'd said. "I didn't mean . . . She's not . . . I mean she's . . . She wanted a bath before breakfast, sir, honest."

"Where is she eating breakfast?"

"In the grand hall," the boy said quickly.

"How do you know that?"

"Armel told me."

Armel was walking back to his workshop with the table I'd seen him carrying earlier, so I hobbled into his path.

"Where did you hear that Lady Ari'an is eating in the grand hall?" I asked him.

He looked straight up at me. "Why I'm fine. Thank you for asking, and yes, it is nice weather we're having."

I sighed holding back a growl. "Why did you tell him"—I pointed my tail at the boy trying to balance the buckets—"that Lady Ari'an is eating breakfast in the grand hall?"

"Because she is." He would have crossed his arms over his chest had he not been carrying the table, but he did give me his what-an-obvious-question look.

It took more effort to not growl at him this time. "How do you know that?"

"She said so." The look was turning into the why-are-you-asking-me-dumb-questions look, but I didn't particularly care.

"Did you hear her say that?" I snapped.

"Why yes, I did. Lord . . ."

"WHAT?" That couldn't be right.

He didn't even pause. "Drenar tried to talk her out of it, but she insisted."

"WHAT?" I caught sight of Lord Drenar walking out of the entrance hall and started hobbling over to him.

"I hope you have a fine day also," I heard Armel call behind me.

I started toward the entrance hall, pausing every few steps to catch my breath and manage the pain that shot through my side at each step. I didn't care that Galen would give me a piece of his mind when he found out.

I saw him stop to rub his head. Hearing me coming, he looked up. "What are you doing out of—" he began, but I cut him off.

"Why is Lady Ari'an eating breakfast in the grand hall?" I hissed at him.

I saw two servants and a green-and-gold dragon suddenly come around three separate corners to listen.

"I had hoped to keep that under wraps." He glared at me.

"It's true?" I sat down hard and cringed as the pain shot through my shoulder.

"You shouldn't be here," he started again.

"Who talked her into it?" I snapped ignoring his statement.

He thought about that for far too long. "No one," he finally answered. "It was her decision."

"WHAT?" I heard something rattle in the hall as the sound echoed.

I saw Drenar lose his patience at that moment, a rare sight, but not one I particularly cared for. I heard his teeth grind and watched blood flush his face. "She is eating in the grand hall," he growled, "because she wants to." He then walked past me with his fists clinched.

"Wh . . . where is she now?" I finally managed.

"Taking a bath! Now, go back to the stables!" he yelled over his shoulder.

I knew he would calm down soon, but I also knew it took a lot to make him mad. I could lose my temper at the drop of a pin, but Drenar could keep his head in almost any situation. I realized then that he was upset about Ari dining in the grand hall as well.

There was nothing I could do here. I couldn't talk to Ari while she was bathing. I didn't understand what could have possibly come over her to decide to eat in the grand hall.

Turning slowly, I made my way back to the entrance. The stable looked farther away than it ever had before. I wanted to curl up in one of the nearby rooms and rest, but I wouldn't try Drenar's patience anymore. One step at a time with more stops than I wanted to count, I made my way back to the stable.

I curled up just inside the entrance, barely out of the way. I couldn't focus on anything but the throbbing in my shoulder, and I could feel blood trickling down my side again.

CHAPTER 24

MEETING EVERYONE

Time passed. Galen came in at some point. He gave me a lecture, I'm certain, while patching my shoulder for the third time, but I wasn't listening. He gave me something to swallow that I didn't argue with. Besnik came shortly after to help me to a stall. Leaning heavily on him, I hobbled farther into the stable.

He said something after I curled into one of the corners, but I still wasn't listening.

"Narden!" I turned my head slightly to look at him. "Sir, what did Galen give you that you're this—"

"Will you leave me alone, please," I interrupted him.

"I thought you might want to know," he said as he started to leave, but I didn't pay much attention to the rest of the sentence.

Suddenly, I realized he'd said something about Ari. I stood up fast, too fast, and yelled in pain. Besnik was back at the stall in an instant.

"Are you all right, sir?" he asked.

"I'm fine," I hissed through the pain.

He gave me a skeptical look and started to say something about fetching Galen, but I interrupted him.

"You said something about Lady Ari'an."

I saw him grin. "You would've been proud of her, sir, she met every one of the humans here while she was at breakfast."

"What?" Certainly the people here would have more sense than to all try to meet her at once.

"I heard Majorlaine's teeth almost fell out when the lady asked her to join her." He laughed. "She even told Lord Drenar that if he needed to rest, he could go lie down. I can just imagine how some of them reacted to that."

"Where did you hear all this?" I asked wondering what wall he fell off to believe that.

"Armel told me," he sounded slightly incredulous, "he should know since he was there for all four watches."

"Four watches?" I stared at him.

"It would've taken her that long to eat everything Mintxo whipped up anyway. I heard she spoke to each of the boys too." His grin turned proud. "Tam won't forget that. He was really upset when he found out about . . . you know." Besnik turned to go. "I'm off to the main stables. She's coming to meet all the dragons, and I'd like to at least see her before I head back out to patrol."

I watched him leave. Ari had met people, humans, for four watches? That couldn't be right. I wanted to go find someone to get the right story, but the last time, it hadn't turned out well, and now, the walls kept spinning every time I blinked.

Lying back down, I heard running footsteps outside. I fought to keep my eyes open and realized Galen must have given me some sort of sleeping drug.

I took a deep breath while I looked at the full-length mirror back in my rooms. One of the boys had been overly excited to tell me what must have been his favorite story. He'd accidentally knocked a glass of wine on my lap. At least, it had been white wine.

This dress was a deep-purple velvet in about the same style as the other one. Instead of fur at the collar and cuffs, it had lace. I fingered the lace wondering how they'd managed to make it soft and still stand up. It was thick, as well, with several overlapping designs.

I took another deep breath and smoothed the dress again even though there wasn't a single wrinkle in the fabric. This should be easier. After all, I was meeting the dragons now.

I'd nearly lost my nerve so many times over the last few watches. Several of the masons had grabbed my hand and shook it. Armel had told me after prying my hand out of the first one's grip that it was an old custom that some of them still held when meeting people. At that piece of information, I almost told Lord Drenar that I wanted to leave.

He looked like he was going to throw up, though, so I decided not to bother him. I became used to it after the tenth person. They all let my hand go after shaking it . . . and telling me that they were so thrilled to meet me . . . and that they hoped I would enjoy my stay . . . and what it was they did at the fortress.

Armel told me that they didn't expect me to remember all the information about their occupations or even their names. I tried hard to remember a lot of them though. Several of them had the same name, which would make it easier if I could just remember which ones they were. It was something that helped take my mind off having my hand grabbed so many times.

I took one more deep breath and laughed at the memory of the egg swan. I had no idea how Mintxo, who I'd made quite happy by complementing the meal, had managed to get those fluffed eggs in that shape.

I walked out of the room with the bed and over to the bell cord. One more deep breath, and I pulled the cord.

I stepped out of the room to wait in the hall. I studied the closest tapestry and noticed that something seemed to be missing from the picture. I took a step back in order to see it better. It was a mountain scene like the rest of the tapestries. I noticed that some of the spires of Caer Corisan could be seen behind one of the mountains.

Glancing at one of the other tapestries, I realized what was missing. There were no dragons in this one. The sky held only clouds. I squinted at the piece, wondering if it could be from a time before the dragons came to Arnbjorg. I gingerly ran my fingers over the fabric.

Somewhere I had heard that Caer Corisan was built when the dragons came, so the piece couldn't be from before then. Could it?

I heard footsteps on the stairs and then Armel's voice came to me, "My lady has found our hidden treasure."

Turning, I asked, "Does this one change?"

"Change?" he repeated then smiled, "No, what you see is what there is."

I turned to look at it again. "Why are there no dragons on it?"

"Aren't there?" he asked coming to stand at the other end of the tapestry.

I glanced at him, wondering how he could possibly not have noticed. He was tracing his finger over the linen. His finger moved in a specific pattern and then repeated the movement. I glanced over the piece again expecting it to change. It didn't.

"No, there ar—" I began, and then realized the pattern he was tracing was already part of the tapestry. It was a shape that at first looked like it was part of a fir tree. I squinted at it, realizing that it was a dragon of the same blue green as the pine curled around the base of the tree. The dragon's scales were spiked matching the trees branches, but he didn't seem to be angry. He actually seemed to be sleeping.

Armel's hand moved to a nearby outcropping of brown-gray stone. I gasped as I saw this dragon had his wings out stretched but matched the outline of the surrounding stone perfectly.

I quickly glanced over the tapestry again, but didn't see any others. I squinted, looking more slowly. There in the river was an outline. I began to trace it and found that dragon was looking directly at me.

"I've been told that there are five hundred dragons on here, but I've only found a hundred twenty-seven," Armel told me.

I stared at him blankly. How could there possibly be five hundred dragons on here? I spotted another outline as I looked back at the tapestry.

"You didn't make this then?" I asked.

"Me?" he laughed. "Weave? No, this was done by one of Faber's ancestors. He told me once that he'd found more than three hundred on here."

Footsteps sounded on the stairs again. I turned to find Lord Drenar coming up. He looked better than he had during the meal. He glanced at Armel, and I saw his brows furrow ever so slightly.

"I thought I'd keep the lady company while she waited for you to escort her to meet the flock," Armel told him evenly.

"He was showing me the hidden dragons," I added. I didn't want him to be in trouble for being there.

"Anyway," he continued, bowing to me then the lord, "I have work to do." With that he moved past Lord Drenar and walked down the stairs. He had a bounce to his step that seemed out of place for a man his age.

"Are you all right?" Lord Drenar asked.

I glanced at him noticing he still looked a bit pale. "I am fine. Are you?"

A slightly confused look passed over his face for a fleeting moment. "This visit has not gone as was planned."

I smiled, that was all too true. I didn't know how many people I would have met yesterday if Narden hadn't been attacked, but I wouldn't have my arm dislocated, and Narden would probably have been with me the whole time.

"Is he all right?" I asked.

"I asked Galen to give him something to put him to sleep since he seems to panic every time he hears any type of rumor about what you are doing." He rubbed his head then smiled.

"I should go see him." I studied my nails.

"He may not be awake, but we can certainly try," he answered.

"If you'd rather, I could have Armel take me to see him and the other dragons," I offered realizing that Lord Drenar must be exhausted from dealing with everything. He'd managed the crowd during breakfast, making certain that I only met a few people at a time.

"No, if Narden saw you walking around without me, he would probably burn whoever you were with." He smiled slightly.

"He is a bit protective," I told him.

He laughed slightly. "A bit is not how I would describe him." He offered his arm. "Shall we away?"

I swallowed and lightly put my hand on his arm.

Narden was asleep when we came in. He looked worse than he had in the morning. His side had been patched yet again, and he was pale. Before meeting Tragh's children, I never would have believed that a dragon could look pale.

I considered staying there, but so many wanted to meet me for some reason I couldn't grasp. There were no other dragons in this stable though. I put my hand on Narden's nose and wished him a sound sleep. Briefly, I wondered if his god answered such prayers.

The next stable was packed. I walked in, and a head peered out of every stall in there. I immediately took a step back, bumping into Lord Drenar.

"I thought you said there usually weren't many dragons in here during the day," I whispered.

"There usually aren't," he said sounding slightly irritated. "We will meet them outside," he said more loudly, and we walked back out the door.

I heard several of the dragons shuffle inside. I sat down on some crates and put my face in my hands.

I heard someone yell something inside the stable as Lord Drenar apologized to me. The movement stopped inside the stable.

"You do not have to do this," he told me.

I laughed. "It's not that. Dragons I can cope with as long as they don't scorch me or something like that. It was just a lot." I took a breath. "I didn't expect there to be that many."

"There shouldn't be that many," Lord Drenar said as he looked back at the stable with a deep scowl on his face.

"I've dealt with some of that," a voice said over my head.

"What are you doing here?" Lord Drenar asked, sounding surprised and slightly irritated again.

"They listen better to me when I'm actually here," the voice replied.

A golden-brown dragon stood above me. He was stockier than any of Tragh's family and slightly shorter as well. The golden hue in the brown scales was unnoticeable at times, but when the light caught them right, the gold gleamed. Realizing that I had been staring at the sunlight playing off his back, I quickly began to study my fingers.

"My lady," Lord Drenar was saying, "this is Mael. He and Armel run the fortress."

"You mean," I started, "this is not yours?"

Lord Drenar looked surprised for an instant and then smiled. "No, Caer Corisan is not part of my inheritance. The fortress has not had a lord directly over it for over two hundred years."

"Two hundred fifty-three to be precise, my lady," the dragon told me with an elaborate bow. I had never seen a dragon bow before. He managed the motion as flawlessly as if it was something he had learned as a child.

"The fortress is part of Maren then?" I asked watching this new dragon.

"Not quite," he answered, smiling. "It's in between."

"Normally," Lord Drenar said, "both leaders are not here at the same time."

"Anyway," the dragon continued, "I was just shoeing those who had more pressing duties out the back when you walked up." He looked back at me. "If you would like, I will finish up and then you can greet the rest."

I felt my eyes widen. "You mean some of them are supposed to be patrolling the borders right now?"

He laughed as he turned back toward the entrance. "Nothing quite that important."

Lord Drenar pulled another crate in front of me and sat down. "Are you all right?"

I glanced up at him. He reminded me at that moment of string pasta that had been stretched too far. "I may be doing better than you right now."

A look of surprise crossed his face and actually stayed. "I . . . This was not what I had planned." He glanced at the stable. "And I thought they would have more sense than that."

I heard Mael bellow something in el'brenika, and a sudden rush of movement followed from inside the stables.

Suddenly, I realized that the stable shouldn't have a back door. The building was flush against the outer fortress wall. With the flurry of movement from the inside, I stood quickly and took a step back bracing myself for a flock of dragons to race past me. I cringed at the dull rumble that echoed from the stable and closed my eyes. No dragons came.

Opening my eyes, I glanced around. There wasn't a dragon in the courtyard. Hearing wingbeats above me I looked toward the sky. What must have been a hundred dragons of all colors were scattering in every direction. There were a couple collisions and quite a bit of yelling, but the sky quickly cleared.

I leaned forward and looked into the stable. The back wall was entirely gone now presenting a breathtaking view of the surrounding mountains.

Lord Drenar stepped around me and studied the stable as well. I was certain that he was looking at the dragons, not the view though.

"It looks as though Mael left as well," he said then looked at me. "Do you still wish to proceed?"

I smiled at the question. "Yes," I told him and stepped into the stable.

I wanted to see the inside more fully and certainly couldn't do that if I met the dragons in the courtyard. The place was very similar to the injury stable that Narden was in, but held far more stalls. There were a few flammable items, like a wooden pushcart and some buckets scattered around as well. I supposed a healthy dragon was more careful with what he caught on fire than a hurt one. The stalls stopped at the open wall that the dragons in the air left through.

There were more dragons than I could remember from those first introductions. There were reds, greens, golds, blacks, browns, silvers, whites, and blues of every shade I could think of. There were dragons with strips, or spots. Some faded from one color to another, while others just suddenly shifted. Others had boots or splotches. I met each one and remembered only about ten of the names.

I took a moment to admire the view while Lord Drenar spoke with one of the last dragons about the attack yesterday. While I looked over the mountains, I made the mistake of looking down. The drop made the entrance to Narden's cave look like a baby step. Far below a thread of a river twined away from the side of the mountain. Stumbling backward, I ran into one of the stalls.

"Are you hurt?" an unfamiliar voice quavered.

I glanced up to find the red dragon that had been in the stable with Narden watching me cautiously from the last stall. I had thought all these stalls were empty since all the other dragons seemed to get as close to the front of the stable as possible. Here he was though.

"No," I told him, "I just didn't expect the view to go that far down."

His eyes darted about looking everywhere but directly at me. In contrast to the deep red of his scales, his eyes were a bright green. Something about the way he was acting seemed familiar. Why was he so scared?

"Are you all right?" I asked taking a step toward him.

"W-wh-what?" he asked looking directly past my head.

"Are you hurt?" I put my hand out to touch his nose, and he jumped back hitting the wall.

What had happened to him? "You're safe here," I told him. For the first time, he looked directly at me. I forced myself to keep meeting his gaze. His eyes darted away, looking to where Lord Drenar was.

He brought his gaze back to me but kept glancing back at the lord. "Can I ask you something?" he blurted out in a whisper.

"Of course," I told him.

He looked around frantically again. He seemed to start to say something but didn't manage to get any words out. With a start that I managed not to show, I realized that he was acting like me.

"You were in Verd?" the question threw me so off guard that I took a step backward.

I wasn't sure I wanted to talk about that, but why would this dragon ask?

"Yes, I was," I managed to answer.

"B-but you're from Nori'en," he stammered.

I held my head up and looked directly at the young dragon. "I am Lady Ari'an, daughter of Cristeros and Hin'merien of the House of Nori'en."

"H-h-how did you end up in Verd?"

Of all the things that this dragon would want to know about, why would it be this? I swallowed hard. "I was taken."

"Y-y-you were at one of the temples?"

"Y-yes," I picked up a stammer of my own, "I was."

"If"—he glanced at Lord Drenar again, who remained in conversation with the other dragon—"if I d-don't do well enough here, will they sell me there?"

"W-wh-what?" Why would he think that someone would sell him to Verd, of all places? "No," I told him firmly, "no one is sold from this place."

"Is everything all right here?" Lord Drenar asked walking up behind me.

The red dragon shrank back into the corner and began shifting his gaze around frantically again.

"I'm all right," I told him. I wasn't sure about the red dragon though.

Lord Drenar turned to leave, and I walked with him, glancing over my shoulder at the scared creature. When we were at least five yards from the stable's entrance, I stopped. It took Lord Drenar a moment to realize I was no longer walking with him. He turned and quickly took the few steps back to me.

"Are you all right?" he asked looking concerned.

"That red dragon," I began, glancing around to see if anyone was nearby, several people quickly looked back at what they were doing, a couple boys kept staring, but there was no one within hearing distance if I kept my voice down, "what happened to him?"

The lord didn't answer me right away, as if trying to word the reply, "He was about to be killed when we found him."

I stared at him for a moment. "Where did you find him?"

He looked around momentarily, ran his thumb over his fingers, and took a deep breath. "Einheim is from Verd."

I was stunned for a moment.

"Verd hates dragons," I finally managed. "How could he possibly be from there?"

"He was hidden by a good woman there"—the subject seemed almost painful to him—"but he never should have been there at all."

A thought struck me that frightened me. "Are you sure he's not a spy."

What if Verd had somehow bribed him?

Lord Drenar looked shocked for a moment. "Lady Ari'an," he said slowly, "Einheim is twelve years old. I am certain he is not a spy."

Twelve years old, to a human he would be a child preparing to become a man; as a dragon, wouldn't he only be a baby.

"He's scared," I told Lord Drenar.

"I know," he answered, looking back at the stables.

"He needs somewhere quiet," I told him.

"That is why he was in the recovery stable originally, he must have moved to the main one after Narden . . ." his voice trailed off.

I looked around the courtyard for another stable. I saw the horse stable, but that wouldn't do. There weren't any other dragon stables.

I could understand why he wouldn't want to be around Narden, with as badly as his temper flared last night. I had a pretty good idea about how he would have reacted earlier that morning when he found out what I was doing. I should have told him myself, but everything happened so fast.

I nodded at Armel as he came walking up. "Could he stay in a room?" I asked Lord Drenar.

"That is unusual," he told me.

"Could who stay in a room?" Armel asked.

"Einheim moved from the recovery stable into the main one," Lord Drenar told him.

"I didn't see him in there," Armel replied looking puzzled.

"He was in the far back," the lord replied.

"You want him to stay in a room?" Armel turned to me.

"He needs some place quiet," I told him. "He's . . . he's scared, and that stable"—I motioned toward the one I'd just left—"is anything but quiet, and Narden is probably a bit . . ." I searched for the word, "temperamental at this point in time."

263

"You have a gift for understatement," Armel said looking at the stable intensely. "He would have to be on the ground floor. Otherwise, he might catch something on fire by accident."

"You are considering this?" Lord Drenar sounded so surprised that I took a moment to watch him.

"Of course"—Armel cocked his head to one side—"it is her ladyship that's asking after all."

I caught a slight movement out of the corner of my eye and glanced at the . . . they'd called it the recovery stable. I saw a hint of blue move in the inner shadows.

"Excuse me," I told the two men and began hurrying toward the entrance.

I'd slept on my tail, so it decided to wake up much slower than the rest of me. I glanced around at the stable walls taking a moment to remember why I was in this stable at Caer Corisan. I heard voices say something about being scared outside. I recognized Ari's voice among them.

Lunging to my feet, I felt pain shoot through my shoulder. Oh yes, that was why I was here. I took a moment to let the pain subside and started toward the entrance. My balance was too far off, and my head still felt like it was asleep. Falling against the nearest wall, I waited for the pain to stop again.

I heard footsteps enter the doorway then begin to run toward me. "I'm all right"—I gasped at the feet—"how's Lady Ari'an?"

I looked up slowly when the feet didn't answer immediately. The light from the doorway silhouetted the hem of a purple dress. The figure was far too thin to be Majorlaine. I brought my eyes to a pair of small hands reaching for my head.

"Ari?" I asked, looking her full in the face. For a moment, I forgot how much I hurt. The light was shining off her hair, highlighting the red, her face seemed to have more color than I had ever seen in the caves. Part of her hair was pulled back into two braids that exposed her ears while the rest fell over her shoulders. A flower was stuck into one of the braids.

She'd said something that I hadn't understood. "What?"

"You're not all right," she told me. "Should I go find Galen?"

I let my legs slowly slide me to the floor. The sharp pain was subsiding from my shoulder, just in time for my tail to remind me that it was waking up. "No," I gasped, "don't go," I took a breath, "please."

"Are you bleeding again?" She hurried to my hurt side and ran her hand along the seam of the patch.

I laughed. She was safe, she wasn't scared, she was here, and she looked absolutely beautiful.

She hurried back around. "Did you hit your head?" she asked sounding deeply concerned.

"No," I laughed then took a deep breath. "I'm really glad you're here."

I felt one of her hands touch the side of my nose and move toward my horns. I glanced up looking into her eyes by accident. They were glistening.

"Are you all right?" I asked preparing to get to my feet.

She set her face against mine. "I'm fine." She laughed, wrapping her arms around my neck.

I closed my eyes. She was all right.

CHAPTER 25

RECOVERING

Narden recovered one day at a time. I spent the next day with him to make sure that he stayed calm. Armel stationed Hafiz and Ishmerai to keep other dragons or humans out respectively. Both were incredibly intimidating in physical stature.

I'd met Ishmerai at the almost breakfast I'd not had on Armel's table. He was only slightly taller than I was, but his arms were three times the size of mine while his legs were three times the size of his arms. I would never have looked at his face if it hadn't been for his eyes. His complexion was dark from long watches in the sun as a mason. His hair was nearly black, but his eyes . . . his eyes were blue. They too showed the time in the sun, only they had faded to almost white.

Hafiz, Ishmerai's counterpart among the dragons, had almost an identically striking appearance. He was the opposite build of Einheim entirely. Where Einheim was long and as thin as a new tree branch, Hafiz was squat and as wide as a hundred-year-old tree trunk. On top of that, he was almost black on one side and the same hue of white blue as Ishmerai's eyes on the other. When I'd met him in the stable, his dark side had been facing me. He turned to look at me when Lord Drenar introduced him, and I took several steps back from the contrast. The color changed straight along his spine. Half of his face was dark, the other the faint blue. His eyes matched the light blue.

I'd managed to say some type of greeting to him, and he'd smiled.

"Brace yourself, my lady," he'd told me. "I'd hate for you to be shocked later."

With that statement he reared and spread his wings, widening his frame five times. The underside of each wing was the opposite color making the contrast even more striking. He spiked his scales, and I saw that they were at least an handsbreadth and a half longer than Narden's.

He was the type of dragon that gave children nightmares, I realized.

I was nervous having the combination of those two keeping intrusions from the recovery stable. I couldn't quite shake the feeling that they could kill Narden, take me, and no one would be able to stop them. Ishmerai alone might even be able to manage it.

I heard them joking throughout the day with people who passed by or each other though. They also were planning a major construction project in a place called Elea. I asked Narden where that was at one point and found out that it was the closest village in Rem'Maren to the House of Nori'en's border.

He slept most of the day, while I read or worked on my needlework that Adenern brought from the caves. The group that went with him to find the ambush stopped there when they had finished scouting.

Day followed day, and Narden began to recover. After a week, Narden could put weight on his injured shoulder again. After a week and a half, Galen told him to start getting more exercise. We started walking around the courtyard. Galen said that Narden would need to rest often. He shouldn't have worried about it.

I couldn't go very far without someone coming up to me. It might be one of the boys coming with flowers or some little trinket to give to me. I had more dragon figurines done in every substance than I thought imaginable after only a few days. The flowers I wore in my hair until Faber brought some new dresses for me.

The new dresses had buttonhole slits lining the cuffs and hem where I could weave the flower stems in. Of course that meant that

I ended up with more flowers each day, but it cut down on the figurines.

When Narden was up to walking up and down stairs, we started walking along the top of the wall. On the first walk we took there, I realized what had been missing from the courtyard.

As we walked along the north side of the fortress wall, above where the main stable was located, I noticed a road twining around the nearest mountain. The road abruptly stopped at a little guard station that matched the stonework of the fortress. The gap was at least a league away, which wouldn't be too far to hike if it wasn't for the cliff that dropped practically straight down to the river below. I glanced around the fortress walls quickly looking for a road that led into the fortress. There wasn't one. The road across the chasm was the only road that led to the fortress, or rather led close to the fortress. The fortress itself had no gate whatsoever.

The canyon started at the northwest corner and continued around all of the north wall and into at least half of the east wall. The eastern edge of the fortress continued into the mountain itself, and the southern side was entirely underground. The southwest corner of the fortress wall came out of the mountain while the mountain itself sloped sharply up to the summit along the western side.

If I hadn't known better, I would have guessed that the mountain had been designed to fit the fortress instead of the fortress fitting the mountain. I'd heard that there were caverns and halls under Caer Corisan that led into the mountain itself, but I never ventured down there during my visit.

As Narden improved, I became used to the eccentricities of Caer Corisan. Majorlaine's cart would end up on fire every other week at least, sometimes sooner. Everything on the ground floor was made of stone while above the ground level things looked more like a typical military fortress. There were weapons rooms, sleeping rooms, storage rooms, and the wing where my room was which was reserved for nobility. Most of the rooms in that area had more dust than a drought-ridden field. The lords of Rem'Maren didn't usually stay more than a day at the fortress, and when they spent the night, they housed near Armel, on the main floor.

Most of my things were brought from Narden's cave over the next week and a half. Then the snows came. Narden was still unable to fly when the first frost hit, but he was walking without much of a limp. His wing was taking longer to heal because he seemed to rip the stitches out every other day.

I realized that he had a very protective temper when it came to me, so I tried to keep him as calm as possible. I had a few episodes when someone surprised me badly, or I had just been around too many people for too long.

After two weeks, I stopped sleeping in the stall next to Narden and moved to the rooms that were set up for me. That way, he wouldn't panic every time I spooked a bit.

A week after that, I wrapped up my leg in the blankets while I slept. I think that is what triggered the nightmares. I woke up not able to feel my foot and started shaking. I crawled off the bed into the corner waiting for one of the priests to come, but no one came. Eventually, the sun rose lighting the dark room through the window.

That was a bad day.

Ari chose to stay at Caer Corisan while I recovered. I hadn't expected her to. Certainly, after everything that had happened, she would go back to the caves, but she stayed. She had a few episodes while she was there. I helped her through some of them, but she made it through the rest and still stayed.

I was probably overly protective considering how many times Galen had to patch me back up after I got mad at someone. I didn't want her hurt by anything ever again, but I knew that was impossible. Day by day, she became more self-reliant. Something happened a week after she started sleeping in the nobles' quarters, but she didn't talk about it. I could tell something was off for at least a week because she was suddenly skittish about everything. I expected her to start sleeping in the recovery stable again, but she stayed in her quarters.

Everyone kept telling me that it was a long winter that year. Supposedly the snows came early and stayed late, but the time was far too short for me. Come spring her things were packed and began to be shipped back to Torion Castle.

I still did border patrols once my wing was better, but I came back to Caer Corisan when I wasn't needed instead of returning to my caverns. I probably should have started staying at the caves more as winter dragged on. Ari's leaving might not have been so hard then.

Narden seemed to fall into a depression as winter dragged on. Someone suggested that it was the weather and the long winter, but I had a feeling that he wasn't thrilled with the idea that I would be leaving when the roads cleared.

I received a few letters from home that I shared with him. When the last one came, I ran to the stables to read it to him. Adenern was visiting with him when I came in.

Adenern had been trying to cheer me up with news that Faruq was finally moving toward declaring war on Verd, while I, as he phrased it, "moped in the stable."

Then again, they'd been moving toward declaring war on Verd for over a year. I would have told him that, but Ari came hurrying in at that point.

It was great to see her looking that excited. She greeted us both, and then pulled a folded piece of paper from one of the pockets in her dress. Faber had a knack for putting pockets in any outfit without making them obvious. It was an odd talent but helpful.

"My parents sent me a letter," she told us, "would you like me to read it to you?"

"Of course," Adenern told her flopping down in the middle of the aisle. I smiled then hit Adenern with my tail. "Oh, sorry," I told him, "I just did not expect someone to be lying in the middle of a walkway."

He ruffled his scales at me but didn't get up. Ari, meanwhile, had sat down on one of the nearby benches built into the wall. She was glancing around and said, "It is empty in here today."

"It's not dinnertime yet"—Adenern yawned glancing at the empty stalls—"the place will start filling up in about a watch."

She smiled, and then began unfolding her letter. I listened half-heartedly as she read about harvest amounts and trade deals. Then I heard the phrase, "Be certain you tell none of this to the young Lord Dreanen if you see him."

I saw Adenern sit up at the statement, so I hit him hard with my tail. He cringed and scowled at me.

"Maybe you shouldn't share this if it's supposed to be kept a secret," I told Ari.

She glanced up, looking concerned. "You won't tell him, will you?"

"No, I won't, but," I started to shrug toward Adenern, but she interrupted.

"And it's such exciting news!" she exclaimed, her eyes traveling to the letter, "he's going to be married."

Never again would I see Adenern that pale. I stood up and took a few steps forward as she continued, "He's to marry Pher'am on the second new moon after harvest next year."

"Y-your sister," Adenern stammered.

"Yes." She looked up at me since I had walked into her line of sight, blocking Adenern from view. "It's so exciting."

"I thought Pher'am was engaged to Lord Bashkim of Almudina," I said quickly.

"She was, but he died of a fever two years ago," she answered frowning as her eyes continued to scan the letter.

"Rem'Maren couldn't afford Pher'am's bride price," I objected, knowing full well that the nobility of Rem'Maren married second cousins twice removed of the ruling nobility. Rem'Maren didn't have the standing to warrant a ruling marriage, and they also didn't have the wealth to buy one.

"Apparently"—Ari smiled at me—"you helped out with that."

"What?" I felt my jaw drop as I stared at her.

She laughed as she looked back at the letter. "Apparently," she repeated, "the rescue of a certain lady of the house warranted a reward and covered most of the bride price."

She grinned at me. "So Rem'Maren only had to pay five hundred cattle, and Elea on the border is going to Nori'en."

"So where's the wedding going to be?" I heard Adenern call from behind me.

I turned to glare at him again. From the corner of my eye I saw Ari lean to the side to look at him. "You won't tell Dreanen, will you? It would ruin the ceremony."

He smiled. "No, I won't tell him." He grinned at me. "It's a silly superstition anyway."

She frowned at the letter thinking about that statement. "But you still won't tell him?"

"Of course not." He laughed. "I would never tell him such a thing."

I was going to kill him. He would die as soon as we were alone.

Ari smiled back down at the letter. "Since Elea is part of the arrangement, the ceremony is going to be held there."

I heard the evening bells begin tolling to mark the watch. "Oh, I am supposed to meet with Lord Grath soon," Ari exclaimed jumping up from the bench.

Folding the letter, she pushed it back into her pocket.

"I'll walk with you," Adenern volunteered pulling himself up from the floor. "Master Sunshine here is just too cheerful for me today."

"Are you all right?" she asked me, looking concerned.

"I'm fine," I told her, "and that is wonderful news."

"I wish you could be there," she said studying her fingers, "but that probably wouldn't work out."

"No"—I tried to smile at her—"probably not."

"*Is* he all right?" I asked Adenern as we walked across the courtyard.

"Oh, he's just depressed that you will be leaving soon," he told me, "and I think I may have upset him about something or another."

"He seemed to think that you might tell Dreanen," I told him knowing full well that he often didn't take things seriously.

272

"No, I won't tell him," he told me again. "It's a silly superstition anyway."

I frowned at my hands. He'd said that before, but I'd heard often while growing up that the gods would curse those who knew when they were to be married or who they would be married to. I had once asked who I was to marry, but my father had told me very sternly that I was not to know because then I would have no children, and the land I would rule would turn to a desolate waste. I never asked again, and I knew better than to tell Pher'am when I found out she was to marry Lord Bashkim.

The dragons, at least Gary's family, and the lords of the House of Rem'Maren believed there was but one god. They believed that one god did punish and could curse, but he also rewarded and forgave. I shook my head at the thought of a god who forgave. All the other gods I knew of would curse the person, their family, and even their descendants after them for generations upon generations.

It made sense that Adenern would not believe that the gods would curse Dreanen for knowing who he was to marry, but would the one god they believed in curse him? I could not remember anything like that in the book. I even remembered stories where the betrothed knew each other from the book.

"My lady," I heard Lord Grath's greeting, "you look perplexed."

I looked up at him and smiled.

"I hope Adenern is not disturbing you," he continued.

"Oh, no, sir," I told him, "we were just chatting."

I saw him wave Adenern off as I took the arm he offered me. The dragon yawned, stretched, and then jumped up to the ramparts.

"One would never believe he hates cats," I told Lord Grath as we walked toward the dining hall, "he certainly acts like one."

He pulled out my chair at the table and, after I was seated, took the seat across from me.

"You received a letter today?" he asked.

I pulled the letter out and opened it again. "Did you hear the news?" I asked and then realized who I was asking and felt my cheeks color.

He smiled and laughed. "Yes, I heard the news before you did."

"I'm sorry," I apologized, "that wasn't the right thing to ask."

"It is fine, my lady," he said, "I was hoping to tell you myself."

One of the young servants, Tam I believe his name was, came out of the kitchen to pour the wine. When he left, Lord Grath continued, "Adenern and Dreanen are close, so if you would avoid telling Adenern as well, I would appreci . . ."

I felt the blood drain from my face as he looked at me.

He smiled slightly. "I see you have already told him."

"I didn't know," I began, "I didn't mean to . . . he promised me he wouldn't tell . . . I've ruined everything . . ."

"My lady," he interrupted my panic, "you have ruined nothing. Adenern will not tell him since he promised he would not."

"Are you certain?" I asked swallowing hard.

"Yes, Adenern will not tell him."

So I discovered one more thing that made me realize that I was in a culture that I didn't really know. I was a guest just visiting for a few months. I never knew who knew what or whom, or even what should or shouldn't be done.

For example, I saw Majorlaine yell at Armel because one of the dragons singed her pony's tail. I never would have dreamed of saying some of the things she did to the ruler of a fortress like this. Armel just laughed and asked her to see if she could manage not to breathe fire in the same situation.

I saw Galen hurry out of the stable with his hat on fire dunk his head in the nearest bucket of water, then calmly stand up, and walk back into the stable. Buckets of water were everywhere. A huge pool at least three times the size of the room of pools at Narden's cave lay under the mountain inside the fortress. I was told a glacier filled it from the mountainside itself. There were pipes that moved the water everywhere.

One day I came back to my rooms to find the carpet flooded. Armel was placing some pipes to run water directly into my washroom. It wasn't going too well, apparently. I slept in a different room that night.

I watched billows of dust fly from the wall that afternoon and evening as people raced to clean the room I would sleep in. I offered to help, but they wouldn't hear of such a thing from a visiting noble. I saw Majorlaine, though, coming down the stairs with a pile of dingy linens that looked as though they would disintegrate if someone breathed on them wrong. Then again, in this place any linen could disintegrate if someone breathed on it wrong.

Majorlaine never seemed to mind if I asked to help her prepare the dragons' meals. If someone caught me there though, I was immediately, but very politely, ushered away with the statement, "Guests should not be working in the kitchen."

It wasn't like any normal kitchen though. Practically everything was bigger. The oven was at least three times the size of a normal oven. The pot that sat on top of it was huge, and to reach the rim and stir it, Majorlaine had to stand on a two-sided ladder that had five steps. The stone table in the center of the kitchen was the size of a noble's bed. It had legs on the four corners and a center brace as well. It was big enough to butcher two bull elks on at the same time. The utensils were as long as my arm most of the time. Thankfully, the knives were all of a normal size. There was an intimidating ax hanging on the wall though. That was used to quickly cut up the whole animals that came in. It was more about quantity here than finesse. The quicker the animals could be cooked, the more dragons could rest for a bit at the fortress instead of hunting for themselves.

I developed a routine after a while. I would wake up early and hurry to help Majorlaine until someone found me there. Then I would wander over to visit Narden or his brothers if they were present. I'd also visit with the other dragons until their breakfast came. Then I would pick up Einheim's meal from the cart and take it to him.

I could relate to that poor dragon since I had been trapped in Verd as well. He liked to ask questions about my life. I eventually told him the details of how I was taken to Verd, but I avoided any discussion about what had happened at the temple.

He enjoyed stories about Narden and his brothers' antics. I was also teaching him how to read, working out of the book Lord Grath had given me for my birthday. I would eat my breakfast with him if Narden, his brothers, Lord Grath, or Lord Drenar weren't around.

My next stop was to visit Armel. He seemed to know something about any subject from carving to world history. I would share the history accounts with Einheim the next day.

Then I went to the library to work on translating some of the other pages in the book and reading some other books or scrolls. Frodi was the expert on the library, so if I had any questions or couldn't find something, I spoke to him.

That room was at the back of the fortress just before the halls into the mountain started. The books and scrolls were stacked on shelves and in nooks from two handsbreadth above the floor, to discourage mice, to six times my height where the ceiling sat on top of the last set of shelves. All the shelves were stone, with a stone staircase to each level and a metal ladder that slid in a track along each level. Wooden shelves had been added in the middle of the room, housing the newer additions to the library. Newer, though, could mean as long ago as two hundred and fifty years, since that was when they began adding the wooden shelves. Those did not reach past the second level.

After lunch I would sometimes go back to the library or would practice on my ya'tar. I would also take a walk along the parapets if the weather wasn't too bad in the afternoon. I even embroidered some of the dresses Faber had made. Some of them just seemed to be missing details, and I found out that as good as Faber was as a tailor, he didn't embroider.

On clear days I would watch the sunset from a room that opened up to the western sky, the colors were spectacular as the light danced over the mountains. Sometimes someone would join me. Narden would be there whenever he could. Renard would come sometimes. Adenern wasn't much of a sunset personality. Occasionally, Einheim crept out of his room to watch, but he had to cross the courtyard or walk through most of the ground floor to get there. He started coming more often as the winter crawled on. I caught him a couple of times watching the sunrise in the northeast, which was closer to his room.

The people at the fortress had a variety of games that they filled the evenings with. I was certain that someone would end up dead from some of the rough things the younger men and dragons played. I played some of the other, less violent, games played on boards, some I knew, and some I learned.

I would tell Einheim about some of the games when I visited with him in the mornings and eventually convinced him to come to watch. He even ended up playing some of the dragon-oriented ones and turned out to be very skilled at any game that required speed.

The days came and went, and one day I found myself climbing into Narden's saddle for what I was certain would be the last time. We flew with Adenern and Renard. Lord Grath met me with a bodyguard and carriage to take me to Elea where my family would meet us.

Before this, my father and Lord Grath came to discuss the travel arrangements with me when the roads finally began to thaw. I had to run into the fortress to laugh when I saw my father awkwardly riding Adenern. I would discover later that he had actually volunteered to ride a dragon to Caer Corisan instead of one of the winged horses. He stayed a few days, and I gave him some pointers on how to ride a dragon. He was doing better when they left but still looked like an amateur.

The smiles from those thoughts quickly faded as we neared the way place. Had it not been for the circumstances, I would have been thrilled to see the hidden location. It was just a stand of trees with a couple of small buildings to house a few humans. Apparently, there were any number of these way places throughout Rem'Maren. These were places where the dragons could pick up or drop off humans without causing a stir in the towns.

As I said my goodbyes to the dragons, I fought back tears. I demanded promise after promise that they make sure to tell Tragh and Gary that I would miss them as well.

Then I was on my way to Elea, the border town that would transfer hands when Pher'am married. I watched the dragons' take-off as the carriage rolled away and was surprised that they did not turn back toward Caer Corisan. Instead, I watched them rise until the only one I could identify was Renard, and he looked like a bird against the blue sky. They followed the carriage from the way place to Elea. The next morning, when we set out for Torion Castle, I again saw the familiar birds. I wondered where they spent the night. Certainly, they did not fly all night circling the keeps or castles where we stayed. Occasionally, I would catch sight of Narden or Adenern when they flew beneath a cloud, but I could not tell who was who.

I believe other dragons would occasionally join them, because I would sometimes see other dark shapes flying with them, but it may have been birds. I did finally see Renard turn toward Rem'Maren when we reached Torion Castle. The day was clear, so I found myself wishing that there had been many many clouds. Then I might have seen Narden and Adenern make the turn as well. I wasn't able to watch until he disappeared, because too many people hustled me out of the carriage and into the castle.

CHAPTER 26

A SISTER'S WEDDING

This was supposed to be home. I didn't feel like I'd come home though.

The castle hadn't changed. The stonework had always been decorative, for show rather than for protection. This wall was dedicated to this god and had a mural etched into it. That wall was dedicated to a different god. The tapestries had changed some and yet not.

My father escorted me to my new room. Everything was so elaborate. The canopy over the bed, the dressing table, the chairs, the washbasin and stand, even the chamber pot was decorated. It all made me long for the simplicity of a dirt floor in a cave or the tapestries displayed at Caer Corisan. The tapestries here were to keep some god or some visitor appeased.

When I asked about my old room, I found that it had been dedicated and was rarely to be disturbed. I wanted my old room, but it might have held the same familiar but distant feeling that the whole castle did. I could remember growing up here, but I wasn't that girl anymore. Everyone either expected me to be her or expected me to break like a porcelain doll.

I found that I was guarded at Torion Castle as though, if I were left alone, I would disappear again. It was very unnerving to look up to find someone, whether a soldier or a servant, pretending not to watch. I never could walk the gardens alone during the day and began the habit of sneaking from my room at night just to be by myself.

I continued the studies I had left six years before. I was far behind where I should be. My parents asked me to work on my dancing only once though.

I was working on the steps by myself since Pher'am worked with the dance master and my father was elsewhere. The dance master surprised me by taking my arms to lift them to the proper position, and I panicked.

My legs wouldn't support my weight. Falling to the floor, the shaking started. I fought hard to make it stop, but I couldn't for a long time. I wanted one of the fur blankets I was used to at Caer Corisan or Narden's cave. I wanted to hear him tell me that it was all right, that I was safe. Even one person to calmly tell me that nothing would hurt me would have helped, but all I heard were people panicking around me. They didn't know what to do. They didn't know what I needed. They avoided ever having to deal with the situation again, so I never continued my dancing lessons.

I was now almost to my twenty-first year and so far behind in my other studies that I wondered if I would ever learn everything. At least, thanks to Armel, I was not behind in history.

When the history and diplomacy master discovered how much I knew, he told me that I knew more than I needed to. Instead I studied diplomacy and politics until I was ready to burn all the procedures books and scrolls the man had.

I wondered if Pher'am knew something as harvest approached, but I didn't mention anything. I didn't want her to guess, because of something I said. Then the thought struck me, was there an arrangement for me to marry?

I shuddered at the thought. Weddings were normally such an exciting time, but what would my husband be like? What would he expect? What would he know about . . . my time in Verd. Certainly, there would have been an arrangement before I was taken, but would it hold now? They'd declared me dead, when I was not found in three years. Wouldn't that have annulled any arrangement?

When my father returned from a trip to Elea, I found myself in his rooms fighting a quiver. I could keep my body from shivering, mostly, except for my hands. Those I hid behind my back as I waited for him to finish the document he was writing.

He smiled up at me and motioned toward a chair. I sat down gripping my hands in my lap. He put the quill down next to the ink-well, adding one more spot to what might have been a plain handkerchief at some point in the distant past.

"What may I assist you with, Ari'an?" he asked me.

"Sir," I began fighting the quaver out of my voice, "I know that I am not supposed to be informed about my own betrothal."

I had rehearsed every line I intended to say so many times over the last two weeks that I could have said them in my sleep.

I saw his brow furl slightly, but I continued anyway forcing any hint of a shiver out of my voice. "I would like to know, though, if I am betrothed to someone."

He glanced down at the sheet he had been writing on, and then looked back up at me. "No, my dear, you are not betrothed."

I felt my nerves calm immediately. I had prepared myself for the worst possible answer and had not received it.

"You were betrothed, before the . . . incident," he continued, "to Lord Perparim of the House of Darya." He sighed. "They pressed for a release from the agreement after the first year you were gone."

He rose to his feet to look out the window, then looked back at me. "The only way to absolve the agreement without losing face on either side was to declare your death."

I'd seen my grave. It was in the garden that held the other memorials. Such things were hard to remove considering the work it took to place them. They planned to remove it when the ground thawed the next spring.

"The family has a new arrangement for Lord Perparim now, so we cannot request that our original agreement be reinstated," he told me.

"Of course, sir," I told him and smiled, "that is all I wanted to know."

I turned and walked from the study. I hurried through the halls to my room as fast as I could.

In the safety of my room, I collapsed against the wall, sliding to the floor. I wasn't betrothed. I wouldn't be married to someone who would hurt me. Lord Perparim came from a good family, but I had met him only once. Unlike Rem'Maren, the House of Darya was a high house, even having ties to the royal family. Lord Perparim would not inherit the house, but he might end up with a castle and a couple of small villages at the edges of the land. I wondered what the man would have been like, but at least I did not need to worry about it.

Soon it was time for Pher'am's wedding. My mother was so frantic about the event that it was nice that it occurred on schedule.

Elea was a trading town, since it was on the border of two houses. Our arrival in ornate carriages and white horses had people lining the wide main street. There were people hanging out of windows and off balconies. The shorter buildings had people crowded on the thatched roofs. I hoped no one would fall through. The taller buildings had wooden shingles or were flat roofed to allow business to continue on the very top levels. Most of the taller buildings were in the center of town and constructed of stone. Those were the ones that the town relied on for trade. The smaller buildings were on the edges, homes and workshops that hadn't reached a level of prominence yet. On the very outskirts of town there were some dilapidated little houses that never would have any level of prominence. Some of them were even still inhabited.

On the far edge of town stood the villa constructed for this event. It would probably be used for festivals and things later, maybe even a wealthy merchant would live there, but right now the building was just for Pher'am and Dreanen's wedding. It was built to look like a set of feasting tables. The three sides emphasized the landscaping in the center. There was a fountain, bushes, and flowers, all of which looked like they'd just been uprooted from where they had been and plopped down in this orderly display.

I saw Dreanen briefly but did not get the chance to speak with him. He had grown up well. He didn't have as broad of shoulders as his father or Lord Drenar. He had a beard though, cut short and a long mustache.

Pher'am looked beautiful. The dress was a pale blue detailed with lavender flowers that traveled around the dress in a vine pattern, and even threaded into the lace at the sleeves and hem. She wore the traditional headpiece veiled in lace with every shade of hair woven along the edge cascading down her back to her knees. The veil covered her face while the hair disguised her actual hair color.

My immediate family and a few cousins, aunts, and uncles witnessed her vows before the Lady Parda, who presided over the marriage ceremonies for the women from ruling houses. Dreanen would be taking similar vows on the other side of this wedding chamber. They would meet for the first time in over a decade in this chamber. I couldn't help but catch on to the excitement, even though I was a bit nervous about how Dreanen would treat my sister.

If he was like Lord Drenar, I wouldn't be worried, but I'd heard that he was quite different. I heard he was eccentric, whatever that meant, depending on who said it. I'd heard he was unreliable. What I heard always came from a servant who heard from a servant whose cousin heard from . . . and so on, so perhaps it was the information that was unreliable, but it still made me nervous.

Dreanen and Pher'am took part in the week of celebrating that followed the ceremony. I spoke to Dreanen briefly one evening, as I hovered near the curtains of a balcony in the ballroom. I didn't like being around this many people, but the crisp nighttime air helped me to keep calm. I saw him walking toward me, and had several thoughts simultaneously that fought for my attention.

The proper and polite thing to do would be to go to meet him, but that would entail walking through or past at least thirty people in groups or as individuals. My feet and legs entirely refused to do that.

The next thought was to flee as quickly as possible either along the wall or out to the balcony. Was it this balcony or the next one that had the staircase leading into the courtyard? I couldn't remember. If I went out onto the balcony, and it was the wrong one, I'd be trapped. If I went to the other balcony and it was the wrong one, I'd still be trapped. Why was I trying to run away from him anyway? Not that I actually had the option of getting away. Staring down at my feet, I realized they were still frozen.

"Good evening, my lady," I heard someone say in front of me.

I looked up quickly to figure out which stranger was talking to me. Dreanen was rising from a bow.

I couldn't convince my tongue to greet him, but finally managed to say the thought that was repeating in my head, "You sound different."

To his credit he didn't look offended but chuckled instead. "People have a tendency to do that when they get older."

He glanced over the crowd in the ballroom as he continued, "I've been meaning to talk to you since I found out you were here."

"Oh," was the only word I managed.

I had thought of a congratulatory statement as he spoke, but it didn't make it out.

"Several mutual friends wanted me to send you their greetings, if I saw you. A few sent letters as well." He reached inside his coat and produced three envelopes bound together with twine.

"Adenern said that I—" he began, but my tongue loosened enough to interrupt him.

"He didn't tell you, did he?" I blurted out.

He seemed slightly confused, as he held the letters out to me. "Oh, tell me about this." He motioned to the crowd. "No, he didn't tell me."

I finally managed to take the letters from him.

"Had I seen him more often," the young lord continued, "he may have gloated and teased me about knowing something that I didn't, but I don't see him frequently."

"Oh." I must have looked confused, because he looked at me with an inquisitive gleam in his eyes.

"Lord Grath, your father"—that was a dumb thing to say, of course he knew that Lord Grath was his father, I studied my hands— "h-he told me that the two of you were close."

I glanced up to see him smile and look back over the crowd again. "Oh, we are, but the dragons are busy right now, and you can probably imagine the trouble we would cause."

Something caught his eye across the room, and he lifted his glass in acknowledgment. I followed his gaze and saw that Pher'am was discreetly motioning to him. I wondered how long she had been doing that. She seemed to be waiting with a group of people.

"If you will excuse me, my lady"—he bowed to me—"duty calls."

I hadn't congratulated him, I realized, as I watched him thread across the room. He was stopped at least eight times by well wishers. He seemed to be taking everything in stride. Pher'am thrived on social events, so it did not strike me as odd that she was enjoying herself. I had heard that sometimes the weeklong celebration was too much for brides or grooms. I could imagine how trying it would be, especially since they'd just found they were going to be married. It was nice that Dreanen was enjoying himself too.

I had never been at a wedding before. I would have attended one for a cousin when I was fifteen, but before that, I was still considered a child, and children did not attend these. I had looked forward to that first wedding and even had planned out what I wanted the dress to look like for each night of the celebration.

Those plans were nothing like what I wore now. The sleeves would have been shorter, perhaps ending at the elbow instead of covering the heels of my hands in the lace cuffs. The neck would have been down, not too low, but the collars on all my dresses came up my neck now, some even to my chin. I would have danced too. I would have danced with my father and possibly with the groom.

I jumped when I felt a cool glass touch my hand. Quickly looking up, I found Lord Grath holding out a glass to me.

"It is customary to at least lift a glass during a toast," he told me looking toward the front of the room.

I glanced toward Pher'am and Dreanen and noticed that there was indeed a lord, whom I didn't recognize, toasting the couple. I couldn't hear what he was saying, but I took the glass and raised it.

When the speaker finished, I started to raise the glass to my mouth, but found I couldn't move it. Glancing down, I discovered that Lord Grath's hand rested on the top of the glass.

"Drink sparingly," he told me raising his glass again, "this will last a while."

I looked back toward the couple and found that another relative was making his speech. The speeches did last a while. I dutifully raised my glass and occasionally took a swallow. I noticed several guests, who drained their glasses on each toast, could barely stand by the end of the speeches. I saw one collapse on the floor while two of his drunk companions tried to help him up. That endeavor managed merely to overturn two chairs and a table.

I heard Lord Grath's clothes rustle next to me. Bowing to me, he offered his arm. "Would you care to take a brief stroll with an old man for the sake of days gone by?"

I felt my cheeks grow warm, as I glanced at my feet.

"You cannot be that old," I told him.

"Perhaps not compared to some such as Gary or Mael," he quipped back at me.

It was nice to see him in such a good mood. I placed my hand lightly on his arm. We strolled onto the balcony and down the stairs, which were indeed on this balcony, not the one farther along.

"I noticed that Dreanen delivered the letters he had to you," he told me, as he nodded to the people we passed.

"Yes," I answered. "He said Adenern insisted he bring them in case he saw me."

"Adenern can be very persistent when he wishes to be." Lord Grath chuckled.

"I would never have thought that about him," I replied. "He always struck me as easy to get along with."

"He does not often make trouble unless he believes it will be entertaining," he told me.

We walked in silence for a few moments while I thought about everything that had happened since I had last taken a stroll with this lord. Eventually, my thoughts came back to the wedding. I worked up my courage to ask the question at the back of my mind.

"S-sir," I began, feeling the slight quiver in my voice, I paused for a moment.

Lord Grath stopped walking and looked directly at me. I fought hard to keep his gaze, but I would realize later, not as hard as I used to.

"Yes, my lady," he answered.

"What is Dreanen like?" I asked, quickly adding, "I mean, I haven't seen him since he was twelve, and I would like to know that Pher'am will be taken care of."

"He is much calmer than he was at twelve," he told me. "He decided several years ago that he would not become ruffled by things." Lord Grath smiled. "That means he does not always take things as seriously as he should, but I have a feeling that Pher'am will help him with that. If what I have heard of your sister and her tendency toward order is correct."

"I doubt you have heard most of it," I told the lord as we continued on.

He chuckled. "My middle son is as easy to get along with as Adenern and pretends to be just as unconcerned, so your sister will have her work cut out for her."

"So he is nice?" I asked, wanting to clarify.

He stopped again and looked at me intently. "Your sister is safe, my lady. He will never harm her."

I felt the blood drain from my face, wondering how he could have guessed that was my concern. I had tried not to be obvious.

"Oh," he said, and I looked up, "look where we have found ourselves."

I glanced around wondering what was so special about a horse stable. It was at one end of the large building, opening in the back to a corral for the horses.

"Would you care to see the carriage which Armel crafted for the couple?" he asked.

While glancing around, I noticed a figure walking toward us. The figure was shadowed, which made him menacing in my mind. I quickly looked up at Lord Grath then back at the figure. I saw Lord Grath follow my gaze.

"You are astute, my lady," he told me, waving at the figure.

I squinted into the darkness and took a step back, bumping into the stable door.

"I saw you walking and thought I would stop by for a chat," a familiar accent told me from the darkness.

I felt the air leave my lungs as I realized I had been holding my breath.

"Armel"—I laughed as my nerves calmed—"what are you doing here?"

"Why," he pretended to be indignant, "I was part of the entourage accompanying his wedded lordship."

"How many came with you?" I asked, glancing at the sky.

"Enough," he told me. "Oh, and you won't find any up there tonight with all those clouds."

I had hoped to spot one of the dragons who might have accompanied them. Perhaps Narden was there or his brothers. Maybe Einheim had learned to fly by now, but the sky was too overcast. Armel was right.

"So have you come all this way to see my handiwork?" he asked.

"Of course, Armel, I traveled all the way from Torion Castle just to see your wedding gift to the happy couple," I teased.

"I knew it," he quipped back, as Lord Grath opened the door to the stable.

Armel lit the lamps as the lord guided me to the magnificent carriage. The emblem of the House of Rem'Maren was engraved on both sides, surrounding the matching doors. As I ran my hand over the sides, I noticed that the wheels were engraved with a dragon chasing his tail while his wings spread out as the spokes. I walked toward the front of the carriage to find the reins were designed as the mountain range. The carriage was built for a team of six. The crossbars for the horses returned to the dragon design. The beam down the middle was the dragon's body, while both his front and back legs branched out to form the beams in front of the horses. The dragon was breathing fire, which billowed into the front beam.

"How long did it take him to do this?" I asked Lord Grath, remembering that I saw parts for the carriage in Armel's workshop while I was at Caer Corisan.

"He has working on it off and on for ten years," Lord Grath answered behind me.

"The arrangement was only finalized this year, though," I stated, puzzled. "How did he know?"

"Armel," laughed Lord Grath, "does not need the details to know that a gift will be needed."

I glanced around wondering if the horses to draw the magnificent carriage would be winged, but they were missing entirely. All the stalls that lined the wall were empty.

"Sir," I began startled by the realization, "where are all the horses?"

"I believe," Lord Grath answered, "Faber and Ishmerai moved them to the other stable."

"Why? W-wh-what's wrong with this one?" I didn't like it when things weren't as I expected them to be.

"Nothing is wrong with this stable," he told me, "the hayloft merely had larger doors."

I glanced up at the hayloft where Armel was stepping away from the open doors while swinging a lantern.

Suddenly, a shape the size of a warhorse blocked all light from outside. I gasped as the shape glided past the loft and landed on the far end of the stable.

"He begged so often, that I finally told him if it could be arranged, he could visit with you," I heard Lord Grath say, but I was already running toward the dragon who's gold-tipped blue scales glittered in the light from the lanterns.

I didn't notice when the other two men left the stable. I threw my arms around Narden's neck when I reached him and felt the cool scales on my face. Stepping back, I found him grinning.

"How have you been?" I asked. "What have you been doing since I left? Are you still patrolling the border, or are you working somewhere else? How is your father, and Renard and Adenern, and Gary of course, and Einheim, and—"

He was laughing. He'd controlled it for a little while, but now he was laughing outright. I laughed with him. When he calmed down, he began to answer my questions.

I had pushed aside how much I missed her so that I could just get through the days. I couldn't control myself when I saw her, though, and just started laughing. I knew I couldn't visit with her for very long, in case someone decided to check on the stables. I knew Lord Grath and Armel would hold them off, but how long that would last was debatable.

"I'm fine," I told her, "I haven't had any major problems since you left, so I don't have any new scars. I'm actually working more inland again."

I didn't want to tell her that I was part of a circuit that went from Torion Castle to Caer Corisan now. People often became quite jumpy when they discovered that we traveled that far from our territory. I knew Ari wouldn't, but the fewer people who knew, the safer we were.

"The family's doing fine," I continued, "and everyone sends their greetings."

We talked about people we knew, antics Adenern had recently done, who recently torched Majorlaine's cart, and what projects Armel was working on.

I asked what she was doing and received an earful about how far behind she was in most of her studies. I also discovered that she would more than likely never dance again.

On my few excursions over Torion Castle, before she was taken, I remembered her practicing in the gardens. I had wondered if she would start again; apparently she would not. She was also not learning anything about plants, since that was low on the list of lady-like studies. She spoke very sadly of that. I knew she loved watching plants grow and would have enjoyed that study immensely.

All too soon I saw Armel duck into the stable and waved to me. I quickly said goodbye to Ari, who fought valiantly to keep from tearing up. She gave me one last hug around my nose and walked to join Armel as I jumped back up to the hayloft and ducked out the doors.

I gathered from Armel that a group had come to admire the carriage, and to his credit, he actually looked distraught by the situation. I told him it was all right and quickly excused myself from the crowd that entered. I returned to my rooms earlier than usual that night. I had thought that I would never see Narden again. As excited as I was to see him, it hurt to see him leave once more. I wished, yet again, that the dragons could visit Torion Castle, but I knew that nowhere else would be quite like Caer Corisan. Even some of the villages near Caer Corisan were wary of the dragons.

I didn't see Lord Grath much the rest of the week. In fact, I didn't see Pher'am much either, and my parents only at the banquets. I actually felt quite lonely for once. At Narden's caves I was sometimes left alone, but I knew a friend would come back within a few days. At Caer Corisan, I was the center of attention and everyone made an opportunity to talk to me. At Torion Castle, I was too busy to really notice, but here, amidst all these festivities, I was alone. I didn't join in the dances, I didn't make toasts, and I didn't visit with many people.

Actually, I began to notice that quite a few people avoided me too. It took several days to realize that it was happening and why. I had ducked into a curtained room to avoid meeting up with Lord Perparim. I did not know whether he was aware that I had once been betrothed to him. I decided to save him the trouble of an awkward meeting and just avoid him. I stayed in the cool room for a while, watching the people walking among the gardens below.

I caught snips of conversations as they walked by the doorway behind me, not paying attention to them until, "Did you hear that the young Nori'en lady returned."

Suddenly, I was listening.

"I heard she ran away to be a priestess in Verd," one voice said.

"That is not what I heard, but that would not surprise me considering her hair. You can never trust people with red hair," the second voice replied. "I once was swindled out of a perfectly good horse by a redhead," he continued.

The voices faded down the hall, and I found myself sitting in the room, wondering what else people thought of me. What other things did they say, when no one else was supposed to be listening? There was no possible way I could have been a priestess of Verd, because my hair was . . . I pulled a strand around to look at it. My hair barely had any red in it! The only time it was noticeable was when the light hit it just right. Supposedly, the red came from my grandfather, but he was bald by the time he was sixteen . . . or did he just shave his head?

I caught other bits and pieces of conversations like that as the week progressed. Some said that I'd been taken, others that I ran away, and one that I had chased a peasant lover, been captured by pirates, and sailed halfway around the world until a dragon stormed the ship and carried me off intending to eat me. The subject changed before I found out why the dragon did not eat me. That one actually made me laugh, considering I had never seen the ocean and knew quite well that dragons did not eat humans.

The last two days of the celebration, I didn't leave my room much. I couldn't hear people as they passed by the thick door, which they rarely did anyway. I couldn't hear the people in the garden because the walking paths were far enough away. I wondered if this was how the dragons felt most of the time.

The servants finally came to pack my things and seemed surprised to find me in the room. I wondered what stories they would start to explain that.

CHAPTER 27

CATCHING UP

Three days later we were back at Torion Castle, and I found myself busy remembering how not to insult the second son of the Lord of Suvora about his questionable heritage when discussing pork, which stitch made a ripple effect for water scenes on handkerchiefs, and why never to place a fork in a soup bowl.

That winter flew by, and I found one day that I had missed spring entirely, because summer was half over. That was the day I discovered that we were to attend another celebration at Elea on the second moon past harvest for Dreanen and Pher'am's one-year celebration. With everything else, now I had fittings for new dresses. I had learned to appreciate how Faber did fittings. If he intended to make me a new dress, he left a ball of string on the table by the door with a selection of fabrics, laces, or furs. I knew what measurements were needed from watching him tailor countless outfits whether for me or someone else.

After seeing the castle tailors' work, I became amazed at how quickly and accurately Faber managed things, whether a stableboy's shirt or a dress for me. He had once told me that if the measurements were accurate, everything else came together.

The castle tailors never seemed to get the measurements right though, so I ended up at countless fittings for countless dresses only to hear, "However did you manage that," directed at one of the understudies by the head tailor. "We will have to begin all over."

I hated those words.

Those words meant yet another round of measurements, followed by two more sets of measurements within the week, and then at least four fittings before hearing yet again, "However did you manage that? We will have to begin all over."

I didn't panic when people touched me anymore, but I hated the endless amount of poking and pinching that these tailors did to measure me. I wanted to request that someone call Faber to make the dresses, but he would be too busy to leave Caer Corisan. The tailors here would probably never let him do anything, since he worked on stableboys' clothes.

One day, after a particularly nerve-racking fitting, I hurried off to a part of the castle where I believed no one would find me. I was late for a handwriting lesson, but my hands refused to stop shaking. I wouldn't have been able to hold a quill anyway, so I went to my old rooms.

Few things had changed in those rooms since riding with my family for that spring tour years ago. The rooms were kept up, dusted, sheets changed, and the like, but the objects were rarely disturbed. I sat down at the little vanity stand and realized I had grown since I was fourteen. I thought about the last time I had used the hairbrush that sat moldering on the stand. I had been so excited that day. I didn't become that excited anymore. New experiences were more apt to frighten me than to excite me.

I looked over the other objects on the vanity. A variety of combs and brushes, and a few old powder containers sat around on the ledges. I avoided opening any of those, since they would probably have an odor that I refused to discover.

I opened some of the drawers to view the contents. I found an old doll in one that I remembered playing with but didn't remember putting in that drawer. Perhaps she was moved there when someone came in to clean or reminisce. Underneath the doll, I found the old letters I had received from Dreanen and Danren after they'd left. I picked them up and smiled.

The top one, I noticed, had never been opened. Breaking the Rem'maren seal on the back, I found that the letter was from Danren.

The letter spoke of the weather, especially the cold winter in the mountains that year. It mentioned training with some of the dragons but didn't mention names. I wondered how often he met up with Tragh's family. I had not seen any of the trainees older than twelve or thirteen while at Caer Corisan, but there were many places in the mountain range that the dragons and humans used besides the fortress.

I hadn't heard from Danren since the rescue, but then again, the only thing I had heard from Dreanen before the wedding was that he sent me a birthday present while I was with Narden. I couldn't quite remember which one was from him though.

Danren

I returned to Caer Corisan on an evening in the late summer of my twenty-fourth year. I had expected things to look larger and was actually surprised by how normal everything appeared. Adenern's landing had nearly jarred all the teeth out of my skull, but he hadn't managed to throw me. I had a strong inkling that was indeed his intention, since he seemed slightly disappointed when I dismounted normally.

Walking into the main entrance, I realized that my right leg was entirely asleep, and I had achieved a slight limp because of it.

"Danren, my son, how was your journey?" my father asked when he met me at the entrance.

I grimaced remembering how often Adenern had tried to drop me out of the saddle with rolls, loops, sudden stops, and any other thing he could think of. Had it not meant a long sudden drop, I would have pulled out my sword and stabbed him.

"He has a tendency to be . . . annoying," I answered glancing back at the dragon while a stableboy pulled the saddle off in the courtyard. He had an obnoxious grin on his face as he watched me.

Lord Grath smiled at the remark as we walked toward one of the side rooms. We discussed my return celebration, which would occur at Elea in two months, along with the things I needed to practice between now and then. After a good dinner, I retired to the rooms assigned to me.

Pulling out my sword, I looked it over, and then began to polish it. I parried an imaginary foe around the room for a little while and then wandered into the sleeping quarters. I flopped down on the bed and immediately stood up when I began to sink. Thinking it was some sort of trick that Dreanen arranged, I looked the bed over thoroughly only to find that was indeed how the mattress was supposed to be.

I slept at least half of the night through because of sheer exhaustion and then woke with a terrible neck ache from lying wrong on the mattress. After lighting a lantern, I began wandering around the quiet fortress halls. Examining things I hadn't noticed before or reexamining those I had, I waited for my neck to stop hurting.

I wandered through the quiet kitchens of both the dragons and humans. I wandered through the grand hall, noting the year's worth of dust that covered everything. I avoided the walls or guards' stations, lest I have to explain why I was awake at this watch. I walked past the visitors' stairway and then stopped to look up the dark expanse.

Shrugging I walked up the stairs, knowing there wouldn't be anyone there. I paused at Lady Ari'an's old quarters surprised to find one of the doors was off its hinges and leaning against the opposite wall. I looked into the room and found that work was going on inside again. I wasn't entirely sure why, since no one used this area, but there was free time here often enough, and the people liked to keep busy. A new door was lying in front of her old sleeping room, waiting to be finished and hung. A couple of rugs lay in the corners also.

With a start, I realized that I had not written the lady since her return from Verd. I had stopped writing her when she disappeared, but it hadn't crossed my mind to start again when she returned. I thumped my head against the wall in disgust. Why I hadn't thought of it, I wasn't sure. Certainly, I should have, but things were so busy what with the war that did not actually exist and, well, everything else, but I should have sent her at least a courtesy note.

I hurried back to my quarters, putting my lantern out and ducking into a side room when I saw Ishmerai out patrolling the hallways.

Adenern was here, and he was all too well known for pulling pranks. Some of the younger dragons had caught on to his habits as well, which was the reason for the new hallway sweeps in the night. The pranks were innocent enough, such as pulling all the cushions out of a closet and either tossing them around the room or hiding them somewhere else. I hoped they wouldn't get any worse than that, but I had no way of knowing for sure.

Back at my room, I sat down to write Lady Ari'an a courteous note, and realized I had no idea what to say to her. I awoke in the morning to find that I had drifted off at the desk, knocked over my inkwell, and managed to stain not only my sleeve but half of my face as well. A lot of scrubbing and a new shirt later, I had managed to remove the ink from my face. The rest of the day, however, everyone who spoke to me asked if I was upset about something, because my face was such a bright shade of red.

CHAPTER 28

THE SHOCK OF
A LIFETIME

My study masters were not happy that I had not caught up when the time came to leave for Pher'am and Dreanen's celebration. I had disappointed them, but I honestly worked as hard as I could. I hadn't found time to walk through the gardens once during the summer or the fall. Each day I was so exhausted I never had trouble sleeping. The maids came and packed my trunks for the trip without my even realizing it until the day they were loaded onto the wagon that would transport them to Elea.

The next day I was back in a carriage heading there myself. Finally, it was quiet, and I realized all the things I hadn't found time to do. I had wanted to send letters to my friends at Caer Corisan, especially Tragh and his family. I hadn't even managed to send a general note to everyone there. I had wanted to make a tapestry for Narden's cave since the ones that had been there were brought to Torion Castle with me.

Eventually, I noticed how beautiful the autumn countryside looked as I watched it pass. I considered thanking the harvest gods and goddesses for the beauty, but found that I thanked Narden's god instead. I still had a bias against the gods and goddesses I'd known as a child. Narden's god actually seemed to care, and I didn't have to barter with him. I didn't know what would happen if I drew attention to the fact that I didn't sacrifice to the other ones.

Three days later I found myself at Elea, where a general panic had fallen over all the attending servants. My mother was yelling at a group at the far side of the villa's courtyard. I couldn't quite make out the words, but from the broken trunk nearby, I guessed it had to do with that. She saw me as I approached and waved the servants off, who all quickly disappeared.

Pulling out a fan, she told me, "This is a complete disaster." Motioning at the broken trunk, she continued, "Your gowns are completely ruined."

"Certainly, I have enough gowns in the other trunks," I told her laying my hand on her arm and looking at all the other trunks still on the cart.

The look on her face was of utter shock. "These were the important ones."

"Maybe I could wear something that belongs to Pher'am," I offered. "She should have some gowns from last year's celebration that would fit me. One of the tailors could adjust it a little if needed . . ." I stopped when I realized that her face had changed to a look of absolute horror.

"Maybe a tailor could make me something new," I was running out of suggestions.

"What tailor could possibly manage that even within a week?" My father walked up as my mother dissolved into tears.

I watched them walk away, not knowing whether I should follow or not. I had never seen my mother that upset before. I looked at the broken trunk again. There was mud splattered all over it, and the latch and hinges were broken off.

Hearing footsteps behind me, I turned to find Lord Drenar, Dreanen, and Pher'am approaching. I felt a smile cross my face as I hurried to greet them.

After some customary greetings, Lord Drenar asked what had happened to the wagon. I explained about the broken trunk.

"It probably fell off the wagon at some point," I told them. "My mother, Lady Hin'merien, is very upset about it." I wasn't sure what to make of her reaction, so I guessed, "She must have been quite attached to them." I looked up from the trunk. "Are you all right, Pher'am."

My sister smiled through her white face. "Yes, of course . . . I just felt the baby."

"Faber is coming, isn't he?" Dreanen asked his brother.

"Yes, he should be here in two days." Lord Drenar was watching his brother keenly.

"Could he come sooner?" Dreanen asked. "I know he managed to make Mother a dress for His Majesty's coronation in a week when the tailors at Ryuu had nearly duplicated the dress Lady Aedelflaed wore the first night."

Lord Drenar thought hard about the question for a moment. "I believe he could." He turned and waved to a stable hand. "I will send Einheim for him," he told us as he walked toward a stableboy.

"Einheim is here?" I asked Dreanen excitedly. "Is Narden as well?"

"Well, Einheim will not be here long"—he motioned toward Lord Drenar, who was accompanying the boy to the stable—"but I am afraid Narden will not be able to make it this year."

"Who is Narden?" Pher'am asked.

I fought not to sound too disappointed. "A good friend from Caer Corisan."

"Shall we continue our conversation inside?" Dreanen asked, taking his wife's arm and setting it on his.

"You should see your rooms," Pher'am told me, looking as though Dreanen had just reminded her. "You must be exhausted." She motioned to someone behind me. "Please, take Lady Ari'an to her chambers so she can rest," she told the servant who walked up.

The maid curtsied and then motioned toward one of the multiple entrances. I followed her through a few turns and a set of stairs, and then found myself in the guest rooms set up for me.

After the maid left, I looked over the rooms. There was a locked door on the east side of the room that made me nervous. The closets were all empty. The bed in the side room was on a similar base as the one at Caer Corisan so that no one could hide underneath it. The decorations were lavish, far fancier than last year's, but then Pher'am was managing the gathering this year, and she loved to be lavish. Fabric looped along the walls just below the ceiling while tapestries hung from the ceiling. They weren't as detailed as the ones at Caer Corisan, but many of them did have dragons worked into the design. There was a little dressing table with a chair across from the locked door, and a full sitting table in the center with lounging chairs surrounding it. A couch rested along the wall with the locked door, looking for all the world like it was meant to blend into the tapestry above it.

I wandered out to the balcony that stood on the west. I watched the sun as it set, the first sunset I had actually watched for a year. In the pastures in that direction, I saw a shape take to the skies. I smiled at the thought that it might be Einheim. He finally had learned to fly. The shape was out of sight to the north before my eyes, after staring at the setting sun, could focus on it.

The next morning, a knock on my door disturbed me from enjoying the sunrise. I hurried over to open it and found Faber standing there holding a ball of twine. I smiled and held out my hand for the string.

The man laughed and then bowed to me. "Now, my lady, I have two days to make you a dress that will make all who see it completely amazed, so I do need this back right quick," he told me as he handed me a pair of snips.

"You only have two days?" I asked in surprise, "Can you do that?"

"It will be a challenge, but a challenge that I look forward to," he told me with a broad grin.

"If you can wait," I told him, "I can have this to you in a moment."

He bowed. "Of course, my lady."

I shut the door and hurried to the sleeping chamber. Closing that door behind me and locking it, I quickly took my measurements.

"Is there anything I can do to help?" I asked Faber as I handed the cut twine and the remaining ball back to him.

"As a matter of fact," he replied looking over the lengths, "I would like for you to look over some fabrics if you have time, after breakfast of course."

"Where are you working?"

After giving me directions from both my rooms and the dining rooms, he bowed and left.

Although the next couple of days were busy, it was a nice type of busy. Unlike the hectic panicked approach that the study masters took, Faber actually seemed calm. He laughed and joked about things, he told me stories of things that had happened at Caer Corisan since I had left, and he kept up a steady pace working on the dress the entire time.

Contrary to the dire predictions of my mother and Pher'am, the dress was indeed complete in two days, and more importantly, they could not find a flaw in it. I heard later that my father offered Faber a position at Torion Castle with a hefty incentive, but Faber turned him down saying he was too old to live in such a lively place. I felt so proud that Faber had accomplished the feat. Especially since he was from Caer Corisan. The fortress was considered the heel of all Faruq, because of its close association with the dragons.

I missed most of the celebrations of the last two days since I wanted to help Faber as much as possible. No one objected, even though the only thing I ever did for him was try on a piece.

I stood admiring the dress in the full mirror in my room just then. It was done in lavender silk with nearly transparent lilac fabric covering the skirt. The sleeves ruffled to the wrists where they were secured by matching thin chains. The cuffs, after being secured around my wrists, ruffled back out over my hands.

We had tried wider cuff holders, but I nearly panicked when I felt the thick metal band clasp around my wrist. Faber had removed the piece instantly and called for a glass of water. In a moment, I found a scrap of fur draped over one hand and the cool glass in the other.

From the wrists dangled two thin chains braided together—one in gold, the other in silver. These ruffled with the fabric to the cuffs, rimmed the cuffs, and then returned to the rings. To match the cuffs, two other thin braided chains hemmed the neck, while a thicker one hemmed the base. There was also a braided chain around the waist that looped in and out and connected to a beautiful jeweled emblem of the House of Nori'en. The dress was done in two pieces, and the chains also clasped the top and the skirt together.

I had told Faruq that he would have to start working on a dress for Pher'am so that I didn't look better than she did. He had laughed and told me that she would just have to make do for the day.

A knock on the door brought me back from reminiscing. I hurried over and opened it to find Dreanen standing outside.

"My lord," I told him, "I was not expecting you." It was the only thing that came to mind.

He glanced up and down the hall. "I've been trying to catch you for the last two days." He looked directly at me and seemed to start to say something but only managed, "Is that the dress?" His eyes widened in astonishment.

I smiled and took a step back, turning in a circle as Faruq had me do often to view the total effect. He stepping into the room and closed the door behind him glancing over his shoulder. Swiftly, he walked over to the balcony and looked down.

Turning back, he glanced around the room. "Are you alone?"

"What?" I was starting to be frightened. I took a step back toward the door and reached for the handle.

He had already looked into my bedroom. "No one else is here?"

I shook my head tightening my grip on the handle.

He grabbed the chair that sat in front of the little dressing table and carried it over.

He set it a few steps from me. "You'll want to sit down for this."

I turned the handle and began to open the door. Before I could even put my foot out, he had pushed the door shut and was holding it there.

"I realize I'm scaring you, and I normally wouldn't do this," he told me as I stepped away, "but we're running out of time." I could feel my hands shaking and my arms were beginning to as well. "I know you have no reason to trust me, but I need to tell you something."

My knees weren't holding my weight, and I sank into the chair he'd brought over. "Please, don't hurt me," I whispered.

"Ari, that's the furthest thing from my mind right now," he said.

I was losing it. I was shaking all over now. He'd said something. What had he said . . . It was . . . It was . . . "You're getting married."

My head snapped up as soon as the words sunk in. "W-wh-what?" I stammered. My mind started working a little. "I can't get married. I'm not betrothed." The statement had shocked me out of shaking except for my hands, which hadn't received the message apparently.

"Who told you that?" he asked looking around then hurrying past me.

"M-my father." I heard water pouring a ways behind me.

"When?" the voice was coming back.

"Last year." I felt a glass pressed into my hand. I brought it to my mouth to take a drink. "Before your and Pher'am's wedding."

"Well, this was worked out only about six months ago, so he wasn't lying," he told me. "Do you want a blanket?"

"What?" the question seemed misplaced.

"I know there's a fur blanket in here," he told me. "Do you want it?"

"Yes, please," I told him. One of the dragons probably told him that I liked fur.

"Anyway," he continued as he hurried back into the bedroom and returned with the short fur spotted blanket that had been on the bed, "I know the man you're marrying." He wrapped the blanket around my shoulders and moved several steps in front of me. "And I need you to trust me on this. He's less likely to hurt you than I am, and you can put a dragon's weight in gold on that." He turned at the sound of footsteps in the hall outside. "Please," his tone was pleading, "just go through with the ceremony."

There was a knock on the door. "Can you stand?" he whispered.

I nodded and got to my feet. "Can I take this?" He pointed at the blanket.

I handed it to him, and he picked up the chair and hurried across the room. Placing the chair back in front of the stand, he tossed the blanket into the bedroom. The knock came again.

"I'll be there in a moment," I called as I hurried to follow him. "Who am I marrying?" I asked as he hurried back out to the balcony.

He turned to look at me with a grin on his face. "Now, that would spoil the surprise." He looked down and pulled out a grappling hook with a knotted rope attached to it. "And I promised I wouldn't tell you who." He hooked the railing and threw the rope over. "Toss this to me when I get down." He glanced at me for a response. "You look surprised," he told me as he hopped over the banister, "contrary to popular opinion, I do occasionally plan things out." He began to climb down.

"You knew you were going to do this?" I asked.

He laughed from a few steps below. "I had hoped not, but it was a possibility."

I tossed the hook to him when he'd reached the ground and tried to gather my nerves. With a start, I realized that the entire courtyard was deserted. The only person there was Dreanen, who was whistling merrily while strolling toward the entrance beneath the balcony. I heard the clank of the hook on stone, and assumed he had dropped it somewhere.

I heard the door handle rattle behind me and a voice call to me again. I had managed to stop shaking and hoped my voice wouldn't quaver and give me away. I turned the lock and pulled the door handle open to find at least a dozen of my women relatives waiting outside my door.

I glanced at them and turned to my mother. "What is going on?" All those women standing there had completely distracted me from Dreanen's antics.

"Oh, it is simply so exciting," cooed one of my cousins that I couldn't exactly remember who she was related to, but I thought her name was Flutura.

"My darling," my mother began after giving a sharp look to the young woman, "we have some very important news for you."

Suddenly, I realized why the courtyard was empty. Dreanen had said I was getting married. He had neglected to mention that I was getting married today. I stumbled back into the room and collapsed onto the couch.

"You may have some notion as to why we are here," my mother continued as a few of the other women whispered behind her. I caught something about a dreadful shade of white and something else about fainting, but didn't quite catch the rest.

"Today"—she sat down on the couch beside me—"you are to join a new house."

I had passed out from pain and blood loss at the temple, but this was the first time I had felt like passing out so I wouldn't have to cope with things. After Dreanen had told me, I had thought I would at least have a day or more to get used to the thought, but now, I knew why he had been in such a hurry. The grappling hook even made some sense.

I jumped back to the present, when I felt someone touch my head.

"Be still, darling," a second cousin told me who I realized was working on my hair, "that pin came quite close when you startled like that."

I heard someone else comment that if I would simply not chew upon my nails, they would be quite lovely. I guessed that came from the lady who was filing my nails. Someone else noted how beautiful my eyes were as she began mixing powders on the little stand by the couch.

I glanced around for a familiar face. I couldn't find my mother or Pher'am in the sea of women crowded around me. I heard some-one compliment how lovely the dress was.

"I'm getting married, today," I finally managed to whisper.

"You are being joined, yes," I heard a voice say next to me and glanced over to find my mother's sister, Lady Je'hona of Almudina, I believed. She resided at the king's palace as a lady-in-waiting to one of his daughters, I vaguely recalled.

As quickly as all these women started working, they finished. I'd been hurried over to the full-length mirror, turned around three times, pronounced perfect, and left there. As I watched the women politely pile out of my room, I finally noticed Pher'am holding my arm and my mother seeing the herd out.

"How are you feeling?" Pher'am asked.

"I . . ." What had she asked?

"You will be fine," she said in a reassuring voice. "I was stunned when I first found out as well."

My mother returned and guided me toward the locked door at the side of the room. I realized I had not found out what was behind that door. Mother turned a key in the lock, opened the door, and ushered me through.

Now, I found myself in a room crowded with men and women. I had a vague recollection of this same group at Pher'am's wedding, but the setting had been different, hadn't it? There were just too many people. I caught sight of some of the ones from just moments ago in my room. They packed in behind me like . . . like . . . sheep getting in out of the rain. I almost laughed at the thought of all these people "baaing." If I laughed, I might start crying, and if I did that . . . I might not stop . . . especially here with all these sheep . . . or people.

"Kneel, my lady," I heard a voice say in front of me and glanced up to find Lady Parda, the dispenser of vows there.

What was I doing here? I vaguely heard her saying something to the crowd about vows and keeping oaths.

"Now, to you, Lady Ari'an of the House of Nori'en, today you join a new house." I looked up from studying the pillow under my knees and tried to focus on the speaker.

I was getting married today. The thought ran through my mind again, and I felt decidedly like throwing up. I knew that if it wasn't for the lavender veil, everyone would be able to see that I was as white as a clean sheep. There were those sheep again. I looked at the veil fabric and realized that it matched my dress. Had Faber known that this was happening today? Was one of the ruined dresses what I was supposed to wear today? Had the vower just asked me a question?

"Y-ye-yes?" I stammered.

The woman smiled and continued on with the speech. What had she said before that? What was the question? What had I just agreed to? Why couldn't I focus? She presented another question.

It had worked last time. "Yes."

What had the question been? I had no concept of what the original question was, but this one was trying to come to my mind. It had gods near the end. What had that been? I worked hard to remember that one question and agreed to at least four others while I tried to recall it.

"Do you, Lady Ari'an of the House of Nori'en," that was how the question had started I was certain. All the other questions seemed to start that way.

"Swear to uphold, honor and . . . and . . ." What had the next word been? I agreed to something else. "Follow." The word had been *follow.* "The gods" had been next.

"There is one god," I recalled Adenern saying. I remembered Narden and Renard saying that as well. Hadn't Tragh even said it once? I vaguely remembered the statement in a child's voice also. I felt the vower's hands under my elbows, and I rose back to my feet. I heard several people nearby talking excitedly and many shoes walking along the floor.

I felt a band clasp around my upper arm. "Of the House of . . ." What house had it been? I knew the houses. Why couldn't I remember what house she had said?

I glanced around and realized the room was empty. Why was the room empty? I walked to a nearby couch. There was a matching one on the other side of the room. Where the pillow I'd knelt on and the arch were, where the vower had stood just a moment ago. Why was the room empty?

I sat down hard on the sofa . . . because I was married. I glanced at the door I'd come from then the double doors at the end of the room where everyone had exited. With a sinking feeling, I pulled my eyes to the door across from the one I had entered through. That was the door. It matched the one, I didn't fully remember stepping through, but I knew I had. He would come through that door. For a fleeting moment, I considered pulling one of the many sofas in front of the door. What good would that do, though? He would still come.

I heard a faint knock. Which door had it come from? I glanced at the double doors and, from the corner of my eye, saw the dreaded door begin to open.

I never agreed with these types of wedding ceremonies, once I was old enough to understand what was going on. It was annoying to find out moments before the ceremony that I was getting married and then still not know who I was now married to until I walked into the lady's own room of vows. I just couldn't understand the superstitions behind all the pomp either. Supposedly, one god would do something nasty if the parties knew when they were getting married, another would do something if they knew who they were marrying, and so on. I held my tongue through the ordeal, since I knew that my father had agreed only because the other family insisted.

When the vower was done, I had no idea what his name was, he motioned to the door to my right. I walked over to it. What was I supposed to do with the door? Should I knock or just open it? I decided to do both, and walked into the next room that looked startlingly like the one I had just come from . . . without all of the people.

The young lady was sitting on a coach across the room. How was I supposed to address her? Did she have a certain title? Would she be offended if I asked? I decided to shoot an arrow at a bat, and plunged in.

"Excuse me, my lady?" I started and realized I had not yet worked out what I was going to say after that. "I hope you are doing well." I should have thought of something better.

The poor young lady's hands were shaking even though she had them gripped tightly in her lap. She wasn't looking at me either. From the tilt of her head, she was looking at her trembling hands.

I didn't want to frighten her more. It was possible that she was shaking from being excited, but I decided to be safe. I sat down slowly on the couch that matched her own, but was on my side of the room.

"I promise you, my lady, that I will not hurt you. I will not even touch you without your leave." I paused, she didn't respond. "I mean unless of course you tried to jump off a balcony or something like that." She had looked up, and I didn't quite know how to continue. "You know, something that would risk your safety or the like, I mean I wouldn't want to see you hurt simply because . . ."

"Danren?" the veiled woman asked from across the room.

I wanted to look at the man, but I couldn't pull my eyes from my hands. They were rebelling and refused to stop shaking even when I gripped them tightly. The man started talking, but I didn't quite hear what he said. At least it was only one man, I tried to reassure myself. Certainly, he would not be around all the time. I'd have some quiet, wouldn't I?

The man's voice was drawing me out of my thoughts, which I really didn't want to leave. I didn't want to think about the man sitting across the room from me, but something in his voice was familiar. The voice was far too familiar, like I'd just heard it . . . but not quite.

I risked looking up at him and almost jumped, it was Dreanen . . . but no. It couldn't be Dreanen. I'd just seen him, and his hair was shorter, and his beard was cut differently. Who could possibly look that much like Dreanen, but not be him? The man looked at me briefly then studied his own hands. He seemed to be fumbling for something to say. He'd just said he wouldn't hurt me or touch me, but was clarifying what not touching me entailed. I would have laughed, if I hadn't been so frightened. Then I realized who it was. It was Dreanen's younger brother, Danren.

I knew that voice, but certainly, they wouldn't have done that. No one would be that cruel, especially the way these weddings were set up. My father never would have agreed to something like that, certainly.

"I do apologize, my lady," I began, "you appear to know me, but I am afraid that I am at a loss as to who you are."

I watched the lady move the veil from her face as she spoke, "Y-y-you probably do not remember me, but we played together as children when you and your brother fostered with my family."

I choked on the name, but finally managed to get the childhood nickname out, "Ari?"

The corners of her mouth turned up ever so slightly then disappeared as she bit her lip.

"If you will excuse me." I pulled myself to my feet and walked out of the room as calmly as I could manage.

CHAPTER 29

A SON'S QUESTIONS

He left. He just left. I didn't understand what that was supposed to mean. Was he coming back? He had clinched his hands into fists as he stood and then hurried from the room through the double doors. I felt like throwing up, but wasn't sure if I would be sick from relief or anxiety. That was why Dreanen had asked me to trust him, because I was marrying his brother. Could Danren be trusted though?

I stayed sitting in that one place for what seemed like watches, then I rose and paced, and finally decided to return to my room. I realized how much all of the pins in my head were hurting me, and I wanted to at least take out the extra bits of hair and the veil. Danren knew who I was, so what was the point of keeping the disguise on?

Would he knock before coming into my rooms or just enter? I wanted to change out of the dress as well. The beautiful thing was soaked from sweat, but could I change quickly enough? There was a door to my bedroom. Wouldn't I hear the main door open from in there?

Closing the door, I glanced down the hall wondering where I would find my father. To my surprise, I found Dreanen leaning against the wall outside the doors to the room where I had taken my vows.

"He's waiting for you in his rooms," my brother told me polishing his nails on his shirt.

"Who?" I was not in a mood to guess.

"Why father, of course," he answered looking up at me, "that's who you're looking for, right? Or did you want Lord Cristeros?"

I started past him heading toward the man responsible for this.

"I thought you would talk to her longer than a moment," Dreanen told me as I passed him.

I stopped to glare at him. "I did talk to her longer than a *moment.*"

"Not much longer." How could he possibly laugh like that at a time like this? "You do have a lot to catch up on."

I felt distinctly like punching him, but refrained enough to make it to the end of the hall and turn the corner. Then I slammed my fist into the wall. I would find bruises on my knuckles tomorrow, but felt very little of the pain at that moment.

I made it to the door to my father's rooms without meeting anyone else. I marched in without knocking, not trusting my ability to not put a nasty dent in the door. The doors were thin board things that wouldn't keep a mouse out much less a man who put any effort into getting in. The whole place was like that, but since it was just being used for fancy events like this, why would it matter that it would all collapse in a bad wind!

My father looked up from his desk when the door slammed against the wall. This room barely held the desk and the two chairs on either side. Had the chair on my side of the desk been a hand's breadth closer to the door, it would have flown when I stormed in.

"*What were you thinking?*" I yelled at him.

He did not seemed at all fazed, but simply motioned to the chair across from him. "Have a seat, Danren." In fact he was aggravatingly calm, which meant he was expecting this. "You are probably wondering why . . ."

"*Why?*" I shot back, interrupting him, "*WHY?* There shouldn't even be a *why!*" I was in a rut and was not about to be stopped. "She shouldn't be married to me!"

"Would you have her married to someone else?" the question came as I took a breath.

"She shouldn't be married at all!" I snapped back.

"That was not an option," he replied evenly.

"Why would that not be an option?" I stormed.

"So we return to why." He again looked up from the papers he had been sorting on the desk.

"Fine." I gritted my teeth. "Why?"

"Lord Cristeros approached me last spring," he began in that dreadfully calm tone, "and informed me that he heard a rumor that Lord Astucieux would come in the fall to make an offer . . ."

"A rumor," I told him sarcastically.

"He was able to verify the rumor and the offer," my father continued.

"Certainly, they would never have married her to Lord Astucieux even if the rumor was accurate. He has *five* wives already, and I can tell you the only reason he would be interested in Lady Ari'an," I snapped at him, knowing full well what Lord Cristeros's response would have been.

"Lord Astucieux was planning to make an offer which they could not refuse," he replied.

"What was he going to offer, a seat of the court?" I snapped.

"That and more." My father paused for my next interruption, but I did not have one.

A seat of the court could only be granted by the king himself or by someone who the king had bestowed the honor on. For Lord Astucieux to have such a thing to offer would mean that he had a very powerful influence on the crown itself. An alliance like that would have elevated the House of Nori'en to the foot of the throne.

"How did they refuse?" I stumbled over the question.

"They did not," he answered. "The offer was never made. They could not have simply refused the offer, anyway, so Lord Cristeros approached me last spring."

"You said that already." Now I was severely puzzled.

"Yes," he continued, "and informed me of the rumor and what he had learned of its authenticity. He then informed me that if I made any offer for his youngest daughter, he would accept it right then. He had the document with him for the arrangement and the scribe who had written it to fill in whatever gaps were left."

I simply stared at the man. "A-any offer?"

"It came down to two flocks of sheep, a herd of cattle, the village north of here, and you," he finished.

There were only fifty animals at most in a flock or herd. "That's only one hundred and fifty animals, and that village was practically theirs with Lady Pher'am's arrangement. Their entire livelihood is based off of Elea."

"And you," he repeated.

"What on Arnbjorg is so special about me?" This made no sense at all.

"You will treat Lady Ari'an with all the dignity, respect, and honor that she deserves," he told me.

"So would Drenar," I replied immediately.

"Drenar," he told me, "has already inherited, and I have my doubts that the responsibilities of his wife would suit Lady Ari'an."

Drenar was a public figure within Rem'maren's borders and outside of them as well. I could not easily picture Lady Ari'an traveling from one function to the next with the ease that would be required. I stood to leave, feeling somewhat foggy. I understood, but what was I supposed to say to the young lady I had left in that room? How could I possibly explain all this to her?

"Did you wish to know what you are inheriting?"

I took a step toward the door before I fully comprehended the question.

Returning to the desk, I realized that one of the Wanderer maps was spread on the table. "It would probably be important for me to know that," I told him.

He traced along the river. "You will have from the River Frid to the beginning of Kohinoor Pass."

It was a small area, only about five villages and no . . . "Where is Lady Ari'an going to live?" I asked frowning at the map, "I will not have her staying in a hut while some place is built."

"Your inheritance includes Caer Corisan," he told me.

I stared at the map again, Caer Corisan was indeed within that section of land, but . . . "Caer Corisan is not yours to gift."

"No, it is Armel's wedding gift to you and Lady Ari'an," he replied evenly.

I took that in for a moment. "You mean I can tell her?"

He looked up from the map at me. "That you have inherited Caer Corisan? Of course, you may tell her that."

"No," I knew that, "about training and everything else."

"The counsel is still discussing that," he answered evenly.

"So she . . ." I was fumbling for an argument and waved my hand at the ceiling. "What if . . ." I couldn't quite find the right words, clinched my fist, and returned the hand to my side.

"You have a vow to keep," he told me in that same even voice.

One day, when I was far less confused or angry or whatever else I was, I would ask him how he managed to stay so infuriatingly calm.

I found my answer and looked directly at him. "Then I vow this to you now. I will protect her to my utmost ability. She will never return to Verd. If it ever comes to her safety and her knowledge, I will not sacrifice her safety."

With that I left the room and too soon found myself outside of the room where Lady Ari'an took her vows. How on Arnbjorg had they ever managed to convince her to take wedding vows? More pressing, though, was how was I supposed to explain all this to her? What should I tell her?

I had changed my dress, paced my room, jumped at every sound either outside of the doors or in the courtyard beneath my balcony, and finally sat down to work on a scarf, which I had started to embroider three weeks ago. I soon found that I had rammed the needle into my finger at least four times and was both bleeding through the scarf and dripping on the chair.

I threw the piece down and hurried to the washbasin. After pouring water over my finger, I grabbed the nearest towel and wrapped my hand. I could not think of a worse moment for the knock to come on my door.

I spun around and stared at the large door to my room. I fumbled the towel and caught at it as it fell. My elbow caught the water jug on the stand and pitched it to the floor. The shattered pieces danced around the stand and across the wood floor. I found myself on my knees trying to pick up the pieces as I heard a door open.

I stared at the door only to find it still shut. What was going on? Was I going insane?

"Lady Ari'an," I heard that voice from inside the room and glanced toward the sound. He'd come through the other door, the one to the room of vows.

"Are you all right?" the question was too familiar.

I felt the pieces fall from my quivering hands. A sob stuck in my throat, and I threw my head back.

I had hoped never to see her do that. It was one of those screams without a sound. She was shaking violently, and I watched her sob for a moment without making a sound. Hurrying toward the balcony, I saw Drenar laughing in the courtyard below. He glanced up at that moment, and I motioned for him to hurry.

The message received, I turned to look at Ari'an again. She had her face buried in her hands, but I could still see the silent sobs shaking her frame. Glancing into her sleeping quarters, I saw a fur blanket thrown on the bed. I hurried to snatch it and heard a knock on the door.

I ran across the room and threw open the door, Drenar hurried in. "What happened?" he asked taking the blanket from my hand.

"I don't know," I told him watching as he threw the blanket around her shoulders.

"Did you touch her?" He glanced over his shoulder.

"Of course, I didn't touch her," I snapped, taking a few steps toward them.

"What did you do then?" he asked.

"I asked if she was all right." What did he think I'd done?

"Before that?" He was looking back at Ari'an.

"I knocked on the door," I snapped at him.

"You weren't in here?" His voice sounded shocked.

"Of course, I wasn't in here!" I yelled at him, "I was trying to . . ."

Ari'an was staring past me with a look of absolute terror on her face.

I collapsed onto the couch. I had caused this. I did not know how, but this was my fault. What had I done? What had I done?

I heard footsteps coming toward me and cringed. The steps passed me, and then they paused and began to come back. They paused again then curved off. *The steps passed me again, and I heard the door open. I couldn't stop shaking, and my sobs were out of control.*

Steps came again, this time they came directly to me. I pulled my head from my hands and looked at the shoes. I felt something cover my shoulders and gripped it when it touched my hand. It was the fur blanket from my room at Elea. *What was it doing here?*

Someone yelled something from a ways off. I didn't understand the words, but remembered hearing, "She's not fit for a dog. I could find a better nickin at Raab than this thing."

I heard a soft voice near me that didn't fit. It was a voice I knew, and it was saying a name I knew.

"Look at me," I heard it say.

I pulled my head from my hands with the effort it would have taken to lift a wagon full of harvest wheat and found that I was just barely looking over the tips of my fingers.

"Lady Ari'an"—I looked at the man in front of me—"no one will hurt you here."

What was he doing here? He didn't fit here. He asked something but turned his head to do it. I didn't catch the question. I heard someone yell behind him. That would be one of the priests. He would have a whip or a club. I would feel it soon. I looked past Lord Drenar's head to see which priest it was.

It wasn't a priest. I saw the man's face turn deathly white and watched him crumple onto the couch. What was going on? I fought to remember why I was here on a wood floor in a room that looked familiar but not by much. Why were my knees soaking wet? I looked down at the floor to find I was kneeling in a puddle of water strewn with broken bits of pottery.

I had knocked the water pitcher off the washstand. I looked up at Lord Drenar again. He had been saying something.

I remembered hearing, "You're safe," at one point and "no one will hurt you," at another. He now asked, "Are you all right?"

I nodded. I could replay every event of that day, from waking up to knocking the pitcher off the stand. "It's been a hard day," I told him.

He chuckled. "I can imagine. Danren," he called over his shoulder, "would you find a glass of water somewhere?"

I heard the man on the couch walk from the room, and the door closed behind him. Lord Drenar helped me to my feet and walked me over to the couch where Danren had been. I sat down and took the handkerchief that he offered.

"How are you feeling?" he asked.

I choked on a sob and told him about the day. It had started out so well, Faber had finished the dress, I had tried it on to admire it, and then found out I was going to be married today.

He told me that Danren had an excellent character and that he would never hurt me. I remembered Danren saying that he would not touch me without my permission, but wondered if that would last. I didn't ask though because at that moment a light knock sounded on the door.

Lord Drenar called for the person to come in. I glanced up to find that Danren was walking toward us. He held the glass out to me, but I couldn't take it. My hands refused to move. On top of that, after seeing the glass, I had looked down at his shoes and couldn't manage to look any higher than that.

"Is she all right?" I asked Drenar as I walked over.

"She will be," he told me. "Do you just need to calm down?" he asked Lady Ari'an.

She nodded, but she wouldn't look at me. I couldn't blame her, though. I couldn't imagine what was going through her mind. She was probably terrified about what I would do to her. I made up my mind right there that I would indeed never touch her. I would give her no reason within my power to control to be afraid of me.

I offered the glass to her, but she didn't take it. Drenar took it from my hand and pressed it into hers. She took a few swallows and then just held the glass, staring at the water inside.

"We can leave for Caer Corisan whenever you would like," I said, trying to think of something to say. She didn't respond. "Will you tell her that?" I asked Drenar, who nodded.

I was no use in that room, so I left. Leaning my head against the wall, after the door closed, I wondered what I was going to do. This certainly had not gone well. In truth, I did not believe it could have possibly gone worse.

CHAPTER 30

TRAVELING BACK

The man left, and the door had clicked shut behind him before I fully comprehended what he had said.

"Leave for Caer Corisan?" I stared blankly at Lord Drenar.

He chuckled, which was such a nice sound to hear after all the shocks that day.

"Armel is handing Caer Corisan over to Danren," he told me. "You will be living there."

That was the first piece of good news I had heard that day. Unless I included the dress being finished, but since that had turned out to be my wedding dress, I wasn't certain if that was actually favorable anymore.

"He did not receive an inheritance from Lord Grath?" I asked wondering why Armel would hand over Caer Corisan. He wasn't old enough to retire yet, was he? He certainly didn't seem that old. Where would he go? I couldn't remember that he ever mentioned having family elsewhere.

"He inherited five or six villages in the area as well, depending on how Llinos fares through the winter," Lord Drenar answered.

"I couldn't leave now." I sighed.

I wanted to be as far from this place as I possibly could be, but it was late afternoon now. Only late afternoon, it seemed like it had been days.

"I will find out," he told me. "Will you be all right if I leave?"

I nodded. Certainly, I wouldn't be able to leave now. Certainly, it was too late to begin the trip, but I wanted to hope.

I watched Lord Drenar leave and heard muffled voices in the hall, followed by a faint knock on the door.

"Come in," I called thinking that Lord Drenar must have found a servant in the hall, sent the message, and came back.

I glanced up as the door opened, to find that it wasn't Lord Drenar at all but rather Danren.

I never did get used to that look of shocked terror that appeared on her face whenever she saw me.

"You should tell her," Drenar had said to me. Agreeing with him had been a bad decision on my part.

I realized again that I had not yet worked out what I was supposed to call her. Lady Ari'an was the catch-all title, but was I supposed to use it now since she was my wife? The last time I had called her that, she had gone into a fit. This had been a bad decision.

"My lady," I finally managed, and watched her take a ragged breath. "We can leave for Caer Corisan tonight, if you would like that." I paused, but she didn't say anything. "Einheim is nearby, as well as Jair, who is almost as fast." Still no response. "We would arrive tomorrow, if we fly straight there, but the nights have been warm lately." I knew I was rambling, but I couldn't stand the silence.

"We," he had said. Of course, it would be we. I fought the tears. It would always be we now. What would he do? I had to fight the images that rose before my eyes, and I latched onto something he had said, a name that I knew.

"Einheim is that fast?" I asked. It would be amazing to be at Caer Corisan in half the night.

"H-he is, yes," Danren stammered a little on the answer.

She had said something. I felt so relieved. I had wondered if she would ever say anything to me.

"He is actually faster, but he would have to stay with Jair." I laughed.

It was a nervous laugh that sounded somewhat forced. It was nothing like Lord Drenar's kind chuckle.

"He can beat Jair?" I needed to keep talking so I didn't panic again. I was, in fact, surprised by that information since Einheim would have only started flying a year and a half ago.

She had glanced up at me when she asked that, and I thought for a fleeting moment that things might become a little better, but then she wrung her hands and glanced nervously around her feet.

"Yes, he is. He came in first at the spring races this year in speed," I told her, just trying to keep her talking. "He has a hard time with landings though, so if you would rather ride Jair, he will not jar you."

I knew Jair, but I had a special bond with Einheim. "No," I fought the quaver in my voice, "Einheim is fine."

"All right," he told me. "Do you have anything to pack, or would you like to leave immediately?"

What would I pack? All that I had here were fancy ballroom dresses. I didn't even have anything that would be suitable to travel in, especially not on a dragon.

"I can . . ." I began and caught myself. It took all my willpower to say it, "*We* can leave whenever you are ready, sir."

I fought the choked sensation in my throat. I knew I couldn't send her alone, but I knew that the last person she wanted anywhere near her was me.

I turned to leave and heard her rise. Glancing behind me, I saw her reach out her hand as if asking me to stop, clinch her fist, and then the hand dropped back to her side, defeated.

"Yes, my lady, what is it?" I asked as softly as I could.

She still looked startled by the question and glanced around. After a moment, she managed to stammer, "D-do you know a dragon named Narden?"

I had to smile at the question. "Yes," I told her, "I actually know Narden quite well."

I had decided not to ask, when he turned back and inquired what I wanted. I had decided that I would ask someone when I arrived at Caer Corisan, but now I had to ask him. Danren seemed patient enough, but I would have rather had this conversation with someone else.

"D-do," I needed to stop stammering, "you know if h-he," why couldn't I keep my voice from doing that? "is at Caer Corisan?"

I avoided looking at him. I couldn't afford to lose my focus again, and remembering that this man was now my husband was hard on my nerves. I could pretend that I was talking to almost anyone if I didn't look at him.

"No," he began, "he will not be there right now." There was a pause for a few moments. "But he should be there within a week or two."

A whole week, perhaps two . . . Narden would make sure that I wasn't hurt, but . . . what would happen in that time? Would it be better to stay here? I glanced out the balcony toward the crowd that had gathered in the courtyard below.

The door closed, and I jumped. I glanced around and found that I was alone.

I knew the people at Caer Corisan or at least any who were there a year and a half ago. I didn't *know* most of the people in the courtyard below. I could recognize most of them from Pher'am's wedding last year, but I felt like a stranger here. Who would care what happened to me here? I wondered if my own parents would care anymore. Why would they agree to marry me off? Why would Lord Grath agree to such an arrangement?

"I know the man you're marrying," I heard Dreanen tell me, *"and I need you to trust me on this. He's less likely to hurt you than I am, and you can put a dragon's weight in gold on that."*

Could I trust either of them? I sat down and fumbled for a handkerchief as I began to cry trying to figure out why I was even here. It must be more honorable to be the wife of the youngest son of a low house than an . . . an unmarried whore in a center house. Perhaps that was what my family thought of me. It was better to pawn me off on Rem'Maren than to have me shadowing their house.

Rem'Maren would accept, of course. A marriage of one of their sons to . . . to me would increase their standing. They now had two marriages to a center house. I wondered what the bride price had been, but fought off those ideas. I didn't want to imagine what Lord Grath had been swindled out of for someone her own family didn't want.

Why was I married to Danren instead of Lord Drenar though? Certainly, a marriage, even if I was the second wife, to the heir would have decreased the bride price some. I couldn't think of a good reason I was married to Danren.

I wasn't sure whether I should feel sorry for him, since he was now married to the likes of me . . . or scared of him. What must he have thought about the fit I went into earlier? The man must think me entirely insane. What would he do to me?

I'd known Danren over a decade ago. A lot happens to a person in a decade. I could attest to that, though, I doubted anything nearly as drastic had happened to Danren. I knew how different Dreanen was from the perpetually annoyed child who everyone found fault with. Now, he was an easygoing adult who would use a grappling hook to exit my rooms. Had Danren changed that drastically as well?

I had finally managed to control my tears and went to the wash-basin. Then I remembered that I had shattered the pitcher on the floor, the pool of water was still there along with the pottery shards. I began to towel up the water. At that point, I realized my dress was still wet. I couldn't travel in this. The days were still warm, but the autumn nights were brisk. I knew how cold flying could be during the day, so I started toward my sleeping room.

A light knock sounded on the door, I glanced at the wet dress. What should I do? Should I open the door or just call for the person to come in? Would it be Danren or someone else? Watching the handle turn, I realized the answer.

I wasn't certain whether I should just walk through the door after knocking like I had been, or wait for an answer. No answer came, so I began to open the door slowly.

Ari'an stood across the room looking pale. "We're ready," I told her.

I needed to change, but I didn't want to tell him that. I stood there trying to think of something to say for several moments.

"Did you still want to go to Caer Corisan now?" he asked.

I nodded. "I need . . ." I searched frantically for some excuse to gain a few more moments alone. "I need to find my cloak." That was a good reason, or at least the best reason I could think of.

I turned, but starting toward the sleeping room, I heard, "I brought you one."

The horrified look she gave me chilled my blood. "Faber made it," I explained, "it's . . . it's fur lined, and he told me that it was the warmest one he had."

I walked over to the couch and draped it over the arm and stepped away. Maybe she just didn't want to take it from me. I could certainly understand that.

It was a beautiful cloak done in dark-blue velvet with a black fur lining. It even had a hood and sleeves. He set a hand muff on top of the garment. Why had he thought of that too? Maybe the cloak would be warm enough.

Forcing my feet to take the next step, I walked over to the couch and pulled on the cloak.

I was putting the muff on one hand, as he asked, "Is there anything else you need?"

This was my chance, but I didn't want to tell him that I needed to change my dress. What would he do if I did?

"No," I said looking at the muff.

"Dreanen showed me a way to the stables that does not cross the courtyard," he told me.

She didn't respond. "I thought you might want to avoid all the people celebrating in the courtyard."

She slowly nodded. "If you will then, my lady." I bowed to her.

I would have to walk past him out the door. Then he would be behind me. What would he do then? What was I *thinking*? If he was going to do something, he had the perfect opportunity right now. We were in a room alone, with enough noise coming from the courtyard that very little that I did would be heard, short of throwing myself screaming from the balcony itself. On top of all that, he was in fact married to me, so who could fault anything he did to me?

I hurried as quickly as I could into the hallway then stopped. I didn't know which way to go to the stable. I tensed when I heard him walk behind me. He would offer me his arm, because that would be the polite thing to do. I couldn't refuse because that would be like slapping him in the face.

She didn't move for a moment, and then walked quickly enough past me that some might have said she ran. This was certainly not going well. Drenar had the ability to calm anyone, and it was probably a good thing that he was the diplomat, but right now I would have given anything for that ability.

I straightened and began to follow her through the doorway. With a start, I realized that I was supposed to offer her my arm. That would be the proper thing to do in normal situations like this, but this was far from normal.

I could offer her my arm and hope she refused. There was no one around, and I certainly wouldn't tell anyone. What if she accepted and then had another fit? I wouldn't risk that. I decided simply to be thought inconsiderate and walked past her.

I had just sealed myself to my fate when he walked past me. It took me a moment to realize that he'd said, "This way, my lady."

I kept a few steps behind him as he took several turns through the halls. On occasion, we passed a window where I could measure our progress around the courtyard.

There was a carriage with four horses, as well as four other saddled horses waiting. Drenar opened the door to the carriage as we approached. I stepped in expecting Danren to follow, but instead the door closed behind me.

I glanced out the little carriage window and saw Danren take the reins of one of the horses. I didn't recognize one of the party, but the man who drove the carriage that brought me from Caer Corisan was driving this one. Drenar took another horse, and I saw Ishmerai from Caer Corisan take the last.

The carriage made its way through what was left of the courtyard amidst cheering shouts. The progress was slow until we passed through the gates, then all the horses started into a canter. I rubbed my head where I struck the back of the carriage at the gait change. It was within the short part of a watch when we reached a way station.

The place was surrounded by trees, but as I stepped from the carriage, I realized there were no dragons. The riders dismissed the coachman, and then spread out, searching the trees for a few moments. Then each lit a torch, waved it above their heads twice and then extinguished them. I heard the horses move restlessly that Danren was holding, and then the sound of wingbeats.

A shape bloated out the stars overhead, and then moved to my right. The sound of tree branches breaking was followed by the thud of a heavy object colliding with the ground.

"Are you all right?" Ishmerai called from the shadows.

I heard the sound of scales shaking, then a soft response that he was fine. I smiled at the voice, realizing that it was Einheim. Another shape blotted what was left of the moonlight and landed far more softly.

"Is it just the two?" I asked Ishmerai as he walked up.

"Oh, no," he told me, "Hafiz and Bikendi will be flying surveillance as well."

I glanced up to try to find their shapes circling overhead, but I couldn't see them. Ishmerai and the other man pulled dragon saddles down from the carriage roof. We were mounted and off within a few moments. Barely into the flight, I shifted to readjust after the rough takeoff. Glancing over my shoulder, I saw Ishmerai and another dragon rise from the trees. They began circling the two saddled dragons in opposite directions.

Soon, I found myself huddled over in the saddle fighting the cold that wouldn't go away. I usually enjoyed dragon flights, but the bite of the wind seeped through the cloak into my wet dress. The moments took forever, and each wingbeat seemed like watches.

CHAPTER 31

BACK AT CAER CORISAN

I jumped when Einheim made a sharp turn and realized that we were finally above Caer Corisan. The walls slipped passed, and we glided toward the courtyard. I tried to grip the saddle, but my fingers didn't want to obey. I pulled my clinched fists open and held on as best as I could through the cold pain in my hands.

The landing nearly threw me from the saddle, but my feet were caught in the stirrups. I fumbled out of the stirrups and slid from the saddle. My legs didn't want to take my weight. I felt my knees giving out beneath me. If it wasn't for that, I would have jumped when someone came up in front of me and threw their arms around me.

I heard Majorlaine exclaim about how good it was to see me, and I leaned heavily on her shoulder.

"Why, you're soaked to the bone!" she exclaimed.

That wasn't true. Only my skirt had been wet, and it was only damp now.

"Why didn't you have the sense not to fly through a storm?" She wasn't talking to me.

I heard Einheim stammer something about it not raining.

I whispered that I had spilled some water before we left.

"Left where, child?" she exclaimed, "certainly not before leaving Elea!" She didn't give me time to answer. "You must be frozen to the bone."

She began shuffling me toward the entrance, and I soon found myself in my old room. She had a lovely fire going within moments, and I found myself seated in front of it wrapped in a thick blanket.

"Now, you hurry and change from those wet things," she told me, "and I will fetch you up a hot drink and have a word with *his lordship*."

I heard her mutter something about people's incompetence in letting others travel in such a condition, as the door closed behind her.

I sat just enjoying the warmth on my face for a little while. I was so tired, but I managed to stumble to my feet and walk into my old sleeping chambers. There was a door on the room now, and Majorlaine had lit a fire there as well. I saw the old wardrobe in the corner and opened it, expecting to find my old dresses covered in dust. Instead, I found only a handful of dresses, but all of them were new. A soft brown velvet one looked warm, so I managed to change into it.

Pulling the blanket back around me, I walked out to the large fireplace. I curled into the chair and felt the warmth sink into my skin.

I had just discovered that someone had thought that it was a brilliant idea to set up my sleeping arrangements in what used to be the storage room attached to Ari'an's old rooms. That explained why they had been doing work in there. For some reason, I couldn't seem to convince anyone that it wasn't a good idea. I kept on hearing that my arguments didn't make sense, because I was, when everything was said, married to her.

At that point, Majorlaine burst through the door, stormed up to me, and began waving her hands in my face.

"How dare you," she snarled, "drag that poor girl all the way from Elea, sopping wet!"

"Wha . . .?" I started to ask, but Majorlaine was not going to be interrupted.

"If she catches her death, you will be the only one blamed," she continued.

I glanced around only to realize that everyone else had fled the room.

"You should know better than to do something so stupid," she finished, turned around, and stormed back out of the room.

I listened to the door slam echoing around the room for a few moments. Slumping into the nearest chair, I wondered how everything seemed to have gone so horribly wrong.

I started awake when the door opened. Looking up, I found Majorlaine walking in with a mug.

"This will warm you right up," she told me, "and don't you worry about Danren pulling a stunt like that again."

"Pardon?" I asked, but she just continued on.

"Imagine, not letting you change with your dress all wet." She sighed collapsing into the other chair that lounged in front of the fire.

"I didn't tell him," I tried to explain.

"Well, why ever not?" She sat up and leaned toward me. "He hasn't hurt you, has he? If he has . . ." She glared at the door and shook her fist at it.

Hurt me? I kept on expecting him to. I kept on expecting him to do something, but the fact was, "No, he hasn't even touched me."

She looked almost as shocked then again said, "Well, why ever not?" She glared at the door again. "You're the prettiest lady I've seen in a long time, and he knows better than to believe any of those stories about you."

"Stories about . . ." but I was interrupted.

"Don't you worry one mite about those." She waved her hand dismissing my interruption. "All that matters is the truth anyway."

She looked back at me. "And don't you worry about him either. He looked so exhausted when I saw him that, I'll be surprised if he doesn't just collapse into bed." She waved her hand at the storage room.

I looked over at it. Certainly, he wouldn't be . . .

"But here I am, keeping you awake after such an exciting day." She stood and took the empty mug from me. "You just go on to bed and don't worry about a thing."

I stared at the door long after it had closed behind her. Slowly, I pulled myself to my feet and walked to the storage room. I forced my hand to grip the handle and pull the door open.

My knees gave out. It had been converted into another sleeping chamber. I gripped my hands to keep them from shaking, but it didn't help much. Whose idea had this been? Had Danren suggested it? I hadn't known about the wedding, but had he? I knew that Dreanen thought the secrecy around the ceremonies was a silly superstition just like the dragons did, but had he told Danren?

At that moment, a light knock sounded on the door. I jumped to my feet in surprise and raced for my own sleeping room. I shut the door behind me and fumbled around the handle. I prayed that there would be a lock on the door, but all I could find was the handle. I crumpled to the floor, crying as I heard the door to the main room open.

I heard footsteps in the room outside, a silence as they stopped, and then they grew louder. I crawled away from the door. There was certainly nothing that would stop him now. I saw shadows creep under the door and dance mockingly in the firelight. The footsteps stopped. I would find later that my fingernails cut the palms of my hands from clinching my fists so hard. The silence dragged on. Why didn't he just throw the door open?

The footsteps started again. How much closer could they come? With a start I realized they were fading away. Then they stopped again.

I needed to talk to Ari'an. I wanted to explain to her what was going on, why she was even here, and everything else that had happened. I made my way slowly up to her room, trying to think of what I would say. I started dozens of conversations in my head, and each one sounded just ludicrous.

"Lady Ari'an," I thought to begin, "I wanted to explain . . ." Should I be less formal? "Let you know why you are married to me." Oh yes, *that* sounded grand. "You were going to be married to Lord Astucieux." No, starting like that certainly wouldn't do! "It would be worse if you weren't married to me . . ." That was horrible! "Lord

Cristeros and Lady Hin'merien made an arrangement with my father and mother . . ." as if that wasn't obvious!

I decided to start over. "My honorable lady . . ." Was that too formal? It would show that I had a high regard for her . . . wouldn't it? "I hope you are comfortable . . ." Of course she wasn't comfortable! She was probably scared out of her wits!

I found that I was now at the door, and I hadn't even figure out how to say the first sentence. I should have brought something for her. I could have found some flowers, or perhaps she was hungry. I probably shouldn't put this off though. I could start by asking if she was hungry . . .

There was no answer to my knock. Had she heard it? Should I just walk in? Did she know yet that I was supposed to be staying in what used to be a storage room?

I opened the door a hand's breadth and called out, "Lady Ari'an?"

No answer . . . I pushed the door open a little and looked inside. There was no one in the main room. The fireplace was crackling away, and I saw what used to be the storage room door standing open. Ari'an's sleeping room was closed though.

I walked into the main room debating what to do. I stopped near the fire and warmed my hands for a moment. I really wanted to explain things to Ari'an, but I certainly was not going to barge into her sleeping room. I could just knock and wait for an answer.

Heading over to the room, I noticed some of the work that had been put into preparing the room. The carpet was similar if not the same as it had been, but the curtains to the balcony were more elaborate now. There were sculptures on either side next to the curtains, as well as a couple on either side of the fireplace.

I raised my hand to knock on her door and then realized that she might be asleep. It had been a hard day, and it was late, so she could have fallen asleep. I didn't want to disturb her if that was the case, and even if I just knocked lightly, I might still wake her.

Turning, I walked back to the fire and collapsed into one of the chairs. I supposed things could wait until tomorrow.

I started awake later and noticed the fire had died back. I hadn't realized that I was so tired. Stumbling to my feet, I made my way to the old storage room. I would sleep there tonight, because with as groggy as I was, I was liable to fall down the stairs if I tried to make it to another room. Tomorrow, I would argue about moving.

I huddled in a corner watching the door. I didn't want to move. Any noise could tip him off. He might come back. I must have dozed a little, but the night dragged into day. I rose stiffly to my feet and stretched. Creeping my way to the door, I opened it slowly.

Glancing across the dark main room I realized that Danren's door was open. I jumped and noticed movement by the fireplace. He was sitting in the chair with its back to me. I saw his head rise, and he stumbled to his feet. I pulled the door to and watched through the crack as he walked. He seemed either drunk or exceptionally tired, as he stumbled into the other room and closed the door.

I snatched a dress from my wardrobe, changed, and hurried from the room. I found Majorlaine down in the dragon kitchen, whipping up breakfast for whoever was around.

She heard me come in and started to smile then frowned deeply when she looked at me. "My word, child, you look like you hardly slept at all." Her eyebrows came together for a moment. "He shouldn't have kept you awake all night, even if you two had a lot to catch up on."

I stared at her for a moment then said, "I just didn't sleep well. He didn't do anything that should have kept me awake."

"Well"—she went back to flipping large steaks on the top of the stove—"you just have a seat and rest those tired bones." She laughed. "You look like I feel in the morning most days."

She chatted at me for a while. I don't remember most of what she said until she shook my shoulder.

"My word, child, you shouldn't sleep on a table as nicked up as this one." She turned my face toward her. "Well, at least you didn't get any marks on your cheek." She pushed the side door open and pulled the little wagon that she had been piling with food through. "You just stay right there, and we'll have a nice chat over breakfast when I come back," she told me when I stood to follow her.

I sat back down at the table and fiddled with the large dirty spoons and forks that were left there.

"Lady Ari'an," a voice sounded behind me.

Jumping up, I dropped the fork on the floor, which clattered over to Ekaitz's feet.

"Lord Danren has been searching everywhere for you," he told me. Ekaitz was one of the kitchen attendants who worked with Mintxo.

Stooping he picked up the fork and plunked it into the bin he was carrying. He would gather all of Majorlaine's used dishes so they could all be washed together with the human breakfast dishes.

"Mintxo fixed such a nice breakfast for the two of you," he continued, "but it's all cold now." He said the last with a saddened frown on his face.

"I-I-I," why was I stammering, "I am certain that anything that Mintxo and anyone who helped him makes will taste wonderful either hot or cold." I paused, working up to my question, "Is Lord Danren waiting too?"

"Oh, no," he told me as he left with the dishes, "he ate and has been looking for you ever since." As I hurried after him, he continued, "Actually, I think he was looking for you before too, but Mintxo found him and demanded he come to breakfast. I suppose we should have checked with Majorlaine for you, but we did look through all the stables, even the horse ones." He paused for a moment. "I don't know if anyone told you, but Narden's not here right now . . . actually, none of Gary's family is."

"I knew about Narden," I told him.

I had hoped that one of the others, even Adenern, would be here, but I supposed they probably hadn't known that I would be coming. They might have thought that I would stay at least a few days at Elea. Maybe they would come soon.

He pointed me off to the dining hall as we passed. "Breakfast is all set up for you in there." He began to walk away then added, "Oh, and I'll let Lord Danren know where you're at."

"You don't have to," I told him quickly. I really didn't want to meet up with Danren anywhere.

"Oh, it's no trouble," he replied. "You just leave it to me."

I sighed heavily. Glancing at the table in the hall, I felt my stomach growl. I was hungry. I hadn't eaten anything since breakfast yesterday. I hurried in and picked up the plate waiting for me at the one long table occupying the center of the room. Maybe, if I was quick enough, I would be gone before Ekaitz found Danren.

I spooned a couple of eggs onto my plate and a scope of vegetables. I picked up a biscuit and stuffed it into my mouth. Looking around while I chewed, I found that the hall was set up less formally than when I visited the first time. It was still dressed for a celebration, but there weren't quite as many banners and only two tables, this one with food on it, and another that held the settings for two people to eat.

Ekaitz nearly ran me over with a tub of dishes as I walked into the side entrance near the kitchen.

"Hey!" he said as if he was surprised to see me but looking for me nonetheless, "I found your wife."

I must have looked puzzled. As things like this continued to happen, I wondered why people expected that I was used to being married after one day.

"You know"—he shuffled the tub to lean on his leg—"she's so tall." He held up his hand to about my chin. "Blond hair with bits of red."

"You found Ari'an?" I blurted out, realizing that was of course who my wife was.

"Well, there isn't another lady here who looks like that." He shifted the tub back to both his hands.

"Where is she?" I was trying very hard to keep my temper today, but things like this weren't making it easy.

"She's over in the hall getting breakfast," he told me, as someone yelled for him from the kitchen.

I headed toward *the* hall, which was the local way for calling the grand hall. For some reason, I didn't really expect her to be there, since I had been told by multiple people when I asked if they'd seen her, "Well, isn't she" or "Wouldn't she be" or something else that pointed to a location that when I arrived I was told she'd not been there and to try a different place.

When I walked into the hall, and she was there, I stopped short. The first couple of times I had run off somewhere expecting her to be there, I had started to work out what I was going to say to her. Nothing ever sounded quite right, but I would at least attempt to work out something. After the fifth or sixth place, I stopped doing that.

Now, I had actually found her and couldn't think of a single thing to say for a moment. "Lady Ari'an," I finally managed, "I have been searching everywhere for you."

She turned suddenly, and I felt as though I had been run through with a saber. She looked absolutely horrified to see me there.

"I-I've been hoping to talk to you," I tried to explain. Why on Arnbjorg did she have to look at me as though I was going to throw her off the nearest wall?

"Lord Danren," I heard someone call behind me, "you are harder to find than Galen when Cumas is here."

I turned to find Armel hurrying toward me.

"Hold on a moment," I told him as he started to say something.

Turning back to the table, she was gone. There were easily seven exits she could have taken.

Sighing heavily, I turned back to Armel. "Yes, what can I help you with?"

I began to choke on the biscuit when I heard Danren behind me. I spun around fighting the urge to cough bits of bread over everything.

He said something that I didn't catch. Then he turned toward someone coming up behind him. I ran. I flew down the nearest hallway, around a corner, and into a room, where I did proceed to cough biscuit over the table in the center.

Why had I fled like that? Certainly, he wouldn't do anything to me in the grand hall, especially with all the servants coming and going to clear the table.

The only reason I could come up with was that the man terrified me. He hadn't given me a single reason to be scared of him. I knew that, but that didn't change my feelings. I didn't want to talk to him. I didn't even want to see him. What was I going to do when night fell, and I needed to go to sleep? I pushed that thought from my mind and realized that I had left my plate on the table in the grand hall.

I was still hungry, but I didn't want to run into Danren again. He was looking for me, but had he seen which door that I left through? I could loop around and come back through the opposite side. He wouldn't be expecting that.

I stood up and slowly edged toward the doorway. Peeking out, I saw that no one was in that hallway. Turning right instead of left, I walked up to the next corner. There was a servant hanging sheets outside the windows to dry but no one else. I made my way down that hall and cautiously around another corner. This was near the laundry areas, and there were servants hurrying around with bundles of clothes. Several of them greeted me, and I did my best to sound cordial, but probably failed miserably. Two more corners, and I was back at the empty grand hall. Danren wasn't there, nor was there a single servant. In fact, there wasn't a dish left in the place. Even the tables were gone.

I sat down on a bench in the hallway, wondering what to do now. I was still hungry, and food would still be available in the kitchen, but there were a lot of people there. Certainly, one of them would run off to tell Danren where I was.

An idea presented itself, so I rose to my feet and made my way to the dragon's kitchen to find Majorlaine. She was back working on lunch when I walked in.

Turning she told me, "Welcome back, my lady."

"Majorlaine," I began, "I went to the grand hall to eat breakfast."

"I figured as much," she told me as she stirred an enormous pot over a fire. "Did you enjoy yourself? Mintxo has been planning that meal for weeks."

I felt so terrible about not having any of it now but continued on, "Actually, I missed it."

"What?" She spun around spilling chunks around the room from the spoon she held.

"I didn't want to disturb everyone in the kitchen, so I just came back here," I told her.

"Well, I'm a cow's hoof if you think I'm going to stand here and let you go till midday without eating a thing!" she exclaimed and stormed out of the room.

The plan worked. Majorlaine would come back with enough for me to eat for a week. She would probably give the kitchen staff a hard time and not speak with Mintxo for two days, because he let me go hungry, but she would have found something else to not speak to him about for that long with or without my help.

In due time, she came back looking ruffled and set a heaping plate of food in front of me. As I ate she continued working.

When I finished the, she turned back to me. "I bet you would like a nice hot bath."

I thought about it for a moment. It would be nice, but what if Danren was in the rooms? I stood up and walked over to the door outside. Certainly, he wouldn't do anything if Majorlaine was with me, but couldn't he order her away? I glanced out into the courtyard and around the walls, solving my problem. Danren was looking over the north wall with Armel. The washroom had a lock on the door. At least I hoped it still had the same lock, so I would be fine.

"That would be wonderful," I told Majorlaine, and hurried across the room toward the inside entrance.

"Well, let me come with you and show you what Armel did to the basin," she said as she followed me out.

I soon found that the washroom still had the same lock, and Armel had finally managed to work out a pipe system that brought hot and cold water directly into the tub. After locking both the main room doors and washroom, I played with the knobs for a while before getting the temperature to where I wanted it.

Armel wanted to go over some things, so I decided that I could look for Ari'an just as well following him around as I could going from place to place on bird chases by myself. I found out quite a bit about what Armel wanted me to take over right away and what he would still do, but I did not find Ari'an.

Things continued like this for about a week. I'd run into her occasionally, but for one reason or another, she would duck away before I could talk to her. I thought about writing her a letter but decided that would be far too odd. Eventually, I stopped looking for her. She didn't want to talk to me, and I didn't fault her for that. Maybe in a month or two she would come around, and I could explain things to her then.

When I did see her picking up some lunch about two weeks after the wedding, I quickly told her that I would be away for a while, but that Narden should be able to stop by soon. For a brief moment, the terrified look left her face, and she looked almost happy.

CHAPTER 32

THE ROUTINE

Danren walked away before I managed to ask how long Narden would be visiting. I could find out from someone else. I had developed a routine by now that was similar to my old one. I woke up before Danren did and hurried off to help Majorlaine in the mornings. Unlike my visit before, no one shooed me off when I helped at various tasks. I decided it was because I was actually living here now, instead of just visiting for an extended period of time.

Narden actually arrived the next day. I was so happy to see him that I completely forgot about dodging Danren. I realized that I'd forgotten when I walked into my rooms that evening and the fire was roaring in the hearth. One of the chairs in front of the fire was tilted, so I couldn't see the occupant. I edged around it silently and found it empty. I was nervous all through the night, but I discovered later that Danren had left that morning.

It was nice to see Ari laugh and smile again. With everything that had happened to her recently, I wasn't sure how exactly she was doing. She didn't mention being married or anything at all about Danren, so I left the subject alone. We caught up on everything else that had happened since though. She talked about all the lessons she'd had to go through back at Torion Castle. I told her about some

341

of the calmer scrapes I'd been in. She had enough to worry about without me adding any near-death encounters to it.

The border situation was worse than it had been before, but winter would soon be here, and things would calm down at least while the roads and passes were locked up with snow.

I found out on that visit that not only did Armel want to step back from running Caer Corisan, but Mael wanted to as well. A greater shock was that he wanted me to take over. I could understand Armel passing things on to Danren, but Mael was over three centuries old, and I hadn't even topped three decades yet. He hadn't assumed any responsibilities about running the place until he was at least one hundred and fifty! He assured me that he'd still be around to help me out, but that he wanted to leave it in my hands eventually. That didn't make me feel much better.

From what I gathered, Danren and Narden would work on three-week stints. One would be here for three weeks and then the other would take over for the next three weeks. The only good part about all this was that I would at least be able to see Narden for a time each month.

I almost ran into Danren the evening after Narden left. I was coming around a corner and heard footsteps in front of me. Glancing up from the dishes I was taking to the human kitchen for Ekaitz, I found the last person I had expected to see. Later, I would admit one of the last people I ever wanted to see.

He was studying a rolled-up scroll in his hand, and occasionally tapping it on the palm of his other hand. He glanced up when I stopped, looking almost as shocked to see me there as I was to see him.

It wasn't as though I had forgotten she was here. I just hadn't expected to see her. I needed to think of something to say . . . "I hope you are well, my lady." That sounded dumb.

She didn't say anything.

"I hope you have a nice evening." I was going to find myself on the other side of the world if I dug this hole much deeper.

I decided to just pass her, since Armel was waiting for me. I nodded as I walked by and noticed she took a step away from me as she cringed. Things hadn't improved any since I'd left.

Things continued not improving as winter came and went. When she didn't know I was near, I noticed Ari'an humming or singing lightly as the days became longer again. Whenever I was near, though, she looked terrified.

Vaguely, I remembered how much she liked the gardens back at Torion Castle as a child. I wondered if she would like one here.

I broached the subject with Armel a few days later to find out if it might be at all feasible. I knew the courtyard was far too small here to do something like that, but something might work out nearby, perhaps in the valley or on the other side of the mountain.

To my surprise, Armel informed me that there used to be an elaborate garden in part of the concealed fortress. Much like the dragon caves, it had the ability to seal off or open along the cliff face. Viewing the enormous area, I realized that it would be a lot of work to clean out all the dead foliage, dust, and the old broken furniture. There was no possibility I would be able to clear everything out in ten years, especially with all the other things I was supposed to be doing. I would have given up on the idea, if Einheim hadn't walked in at that moment.

Apparently, Armel had mentioned the garden idea to a few people, and Einheim had worked up the courage to find out if he could help with the effort. I set him to work throwing everything that was broken in a pile. Since he was here healing up from a hole in his wing, he might as well keep busy. He'd been patrolling the border between Suvora and Verd, when one of the villages hired dragon slayers, from Verd none the less. Suvora'd requested the patrols, and now this!

We had henceforth stopped patrolling the area, and Lord Grath was working on a settlement. We would get something out of it, but there were at least ten dragons laid up now because of the incidents.

Throughout the next week, the dragons or servants with free moments came up to me to ask about the project and volunteer time. To my surprise, Ari'an never found out as the project was worked on for the next year. I'm certain she suspected something was going on, but what exactly it was did not cross her path. Apparently, keeping secrets was one of the things the people of Caer Corisan specialized in.

A short winter followed a long summer that year, and spring came too soon for the garden to be completely ready. I had wanted to present it to her for her birthday, but it wasn't ready by then either. I asked Faber to design a nice dress for her instead, and Armel threw in a pretty bracelet. I found later that she thanked the two of them warmly. She told me thank-you as well, but it lacked any enthusiasm.

She had stopped cringing or looking terrified every time I spoke to her by then, but there was an air of dislike about her whenever I was around. I couldn't really blame her for that. It wasn't as if the whole situation was my ideal either.

I realized that the garden was complete just before autumn descended upon the mountains. I was finally satisfied with everything. There was enough open space for Ari'an to design and work with, but enough of an established setting to give it a nice growing feel.

There was a ground cover of clover since it wouldn't need to be cut like grass, interspersed with other short flowers. I had helped Armel design and install the little pond in the center complete with a small rocky waterfall. The stream from that circled the garden to water it, and then disappeared back into the fortress wall.

We had debated having the stream run out of the opening, but had decided that was more of a liability than we wanted. There was no reason to give someone on the outside the idea that there was an entrance here when it was closed up. If the stream didn't work right and flooded the place when the entrance was closed, we'd possibly have as big of a mess as when we started.

The problem was that when I realized that the garden was done, it was on an evening that I was supposed to leave. I could present the garden to her right then, but the sun was setting; and by the time I found Ari'an and got her back down here . . . well, it looked better in sunlight. We hadn't installed torches because gardens were mostly for daytime.

I could wait until I was back, but hadn't the garden been waiting long enough? I decided on a compromise. I wouldn't present it to her, but I could have Narden do it. He had helped with the place as well, and she would take it better from him than me anyway.

I found myself humming and singing a few verses of a song I knew as I made my way up through the fortress. Hafiz would be waiting to take me off, and I didn't want to keep him waiting too long.

As I passed by one of the corridors leading into the concealed part of the fortress, I heard part of a song that Narden used to sing for me coming from the darkness. Had he come early? Every once in a while, he would surprise me. I hurried to drop off the fabric that Hafiz had brought for Faber, and then ran back to where I'd heard the song. It had been faint before, but was much stronger now. I hurried through the passages following the sound as it became closer.

In one more turn, I would find him. I even knew this song, so I could join in when I discovered him. Maybe he had even started singing as a game to get me to find him. I could think of so many things to talk to him about.

I stopped suddenly as I rounded the corner and found Danren barely two steps away from me. I hadn't expected him, and Narden was nowhere in sight. The singing stopped suddenly as well.

Ari'an came around the corner. Had I not been paying attention, I would have run right into her. I stopped, wondering why she was in such a hurry. I noticed the shocked look on her face. I couldn't have missed it unless I was completely blind.

"Is something wrong?" I asked, hoping that Hramn, one of the new dragons, hadn't caught the horse stable on fire again. We'd had to replace five horses and a milk cow last time.

"Where's Narden?" she asked. What an odd question. Certainly, someone had told her that he wouldn't be here until tomorrow.

"He is not here yet."

"Yes, he is." She was looking past me.

I didn't often speak with Danren. Actually, I avoided meeting up with him at all out of sheer habit. I didn't like being in this situation. I no longer thought that he was going to try anything. He had plenty of opportunities long before this. The truth was he didn't even seem to like me. He might even resent me.

Of course, Narden was here even if he said the dragon wasn't, I had heard him singing.

"He is coming in the morning," the man told me.

"No, he is here now." I was a little irritated. "I heard him singing."

He laughed. How could he dare to laugh?

I had never thought of this, but I chuckled slightly at the idea. "No," I told her, "you heard me singing."

"Excuse me?" She had stopped looking completely terrified when I spoke to her at least six months ago, but this mortified look that she gave me now was almost as bad.

"How dare you," she said.

I stepped back in surprise.

He had no right to sing that song! It was a nice song about joy and beauty. The song talked specifically about the gardens of the hereafter that Gary's line believed in. He shouldn't ever sing such a song. I knew quite well that he wasn't happy being here, and even if he did believe in the same god, how dare he sing!

"My lady." How dare he look sad! "You will not hear me sing again, unless you so request." He walked past me looking upset.

CHAPTER 33

THE CHOICE OF
A LIFETIME

I arrived in the morning, feeling refreshed from the sleep I'd had that night. I only slept well about half of the time anymore.

Ari was waiting for me in the courtyard and began telling me about all the little things that had happened at Caer Corisan while I was away. I knew most of the events, including that Majorlaine had gone through four carts in the last two weeks because of Hramn's inability to speak without spitting fire. Everyone had their problems adjusting to young adulthood as a dragon.

We chatted about basic things for a while, before I was able to edge in Danren's surprise.

"There are some other exciting things happening in the fortress, I've heard," I started off.

"Pardon?" she asked looking blankly at me. I could tell she was trying to think of what could possibly have happened that she hadn't mentioned already.

"Yes," I smiled. "I heard that Danren has been working on a project for some time."

"Oh." The tone she used brushed off the importance of anything Danren did. "I don't actually talk to him much."

"Well, that's probably a good thing in this case only, since it's a surprise for you," I told her.

I honestly didn't like the way she treated Danren, but I couldn't blame her for it considering everything. Typically, I avoided talking to her about anything that referenced him, but this was something special. I couldn't exactly avoid mentioning him in this situation.

She looked at me skeptically, but I continued on, "Would you like to see it?"

She smiled obligingly and nodded.

I led her down to near the garden and then asked her if she would mind riding the rest of the way with her eyes closed. Again, she obliged me with a smile and nodded.

I walked into the garden and almost to the center before I stopped. Asking her to open her eyes, I heard the gasp. She remained motionless for a few moments, then slid to the ground. Slowly, she walked toward the pond in the center.

She took everything in for a while then turned. "Why didn't I know this was here?"

"It was a surprise," I told her enjoying the emotions of wonder and joy that played over her face.

"But it's always been here," she continued.

"No," I told her, "it was Danren's idea to put it together for you."

"It couldn't have been Danren's idea," she told me. "You must have thought of it."

I didn't like where this was going. "No," I told her again, "it was Danren's idea."

"But you did most of the work." She was trying to find someone else to blame, so to speak.

"A lot of people worked on it," I told her.

She nodded as if she'd hit upon the solution.

"Danren did a lot." I wasn't convincing her. Maybe it would have been better if he *had* presented the garden.

I knew better than to believe that this had been Danren's idea. He probably heard someone mention that I would like a garden and told them to start working on it for him. I could see almost everyone else who was a regular at Caer Corisan working on it. There were still a few people who resented having a lady from any house at the fortress. I had seen a few of them before, but I was much better acquainted with them now. I could not even begin to imagine that Danren had much to do with this other than trying to take the credit.

I would need to thank him anyway, though, since Narden continued insisting that he'd actually had something to do with this. I had three weeks to think of a nice polite thank-you that still portrayed that I knew he hadn't done any work.

I enjoyed the garden immensely. After I thought about it for a while, and especially after winter came and the garden was closed up to keep out the cold, I remembered seeing the room on my previous visit. The place had just been used for storage and was never opened up that I could recall. This had been the place that broken things were left until someone found the time to work on them.

I occasionally came across the new storage areas where things were left. It wasn't hard to find them, because now I spent more time down there than I had before. From what I understood, the tunnels went on for leagues with rooms as big as houses branching off from them. Most of the tunnels were blocked off because they were unused. No one wanted some new trainee to be lost and never found down there.

I planned through the winter what I would add to the growth come spring. Through the long winter days, Einheim often helped me haul in stones to set around the pond. The stones grew a variety of moss over their surfaces rather quickly. Mintxo enjoyed the mushrooms that grew there that winter. Since the stream was from one of the warmer springs and there wasn't a good way of lighting the huge room without opening the entrance, there were plenty of them. Mushrooms were far from my favorite growing things, but it was nice to have something growing through the winter.

Adenern brought Lord Drenar for a visit that winter. Narden joined the group after a couple of days, and we had a wonderful time playing games in front of a hearth fire on the ground level. We sang as well from the plethora of songs that both Gary's and Lord Grath's families knew.

One day during his visit, Lord Drenar asked me how I was coming along at learning to read the book Lord Grath had given me. I told him that I was doing quite well at it. Narden knew the languages reasonably well, but Armel excelled at them. Both had helped me quite a bit. There was occasionally a verb tense that I failed at, or I would miss a word and the statements wouldn't make sense, but overall I was succeeding at it.

It was much more interesting than learning the proper spoon placement for a lord of the fourth rank. Spoon placement was never taken into much consideration here, which I was so grateful for.

Lord Drenar asked me to bring the book down to the hall where we had dined, and I willingly obliged him. I read some from where I was currently working, and he complimented me on my accent. I told him that I was even picking up some el'brenika since living here.

He smiled then asked, "So what do you think of this god of ours?"

I thought about that for a while. "He is different, sir." Then I continued, "He is nothing like the gods I grew up with."

"In a good or bad way?" he asked.

"Oh, a good way," I answered quickly. This god was far better than any of the gods I had known as a child.

"So which of the gods do you serve then?" he continued.

I was startled by that question. "Why the House of Rem'maren's of course."

"Why is that?" he asked.

"It . . ." I started then paused, "it was part of my agreement when I joined this house."

"Is that the only reason then?" He was in a questioning mood this particular evening.

"What other reason would there be?"

I participated in the ceremonies back at Torion Castle when I returned there. It was proper to honor the gods of those you resided with.

"Did you ever consider that a god might want a loyalty that reached beyond the house borders?" The question made me think.

"Well, I would suppose that they might, but their jurisdiction ends with house lines," I answered, "doesn't it?"

He pulled the book over to him and began flipping through the pages. He began to show me where the book called any god but its own nothing more than stone images, charlatans, and worse of all, agents of an evil one.

Also, he flipped to pages that spoke of an allegiance to this god up to death. Such an allegiance was given to kings, I had thought, but not gods. He showed me places where this god defeated other gods in their own territory. I remembered the stories I had read, but had never considered their implications.

He asked me what I thought, and to my surprise, I believed the book. I knew how fickle other gods could be and how little help they actually were.

The next question was whether I would like to align with the god of the book permanently or continue on with whatever gods I happened to be near.

I thought about the implications of such a thing. Not all the people at Caer Corisan believed in the god of the book. Several thought he was a fraud, but what did I believe? Such a question had never crossed my mind before. I had been taught to believe whatever was the closest. What would happen if I was ever cast from the House of Rem'Maren for whatever reason? Should I switch to new gods then or stay with this one?

I pulled my gaze up and looked Lord Drenar directly in the eyes. "I would like to follow this god no matter where I am."

He smiled and told me that I should tell the Mighty One then, not just him, and so I swore my allegiance to the one god in heaven and renounced all others.

CHAPTER 34

TRAGEDY

Spring came again, later than the year before, but it did indeed come again. There finally came a period of consistent enough weather that we opened up the garden. I was surprised to find several flowers already budding. Many people—including Majorlaine, Einheim, and Armel—worked that spring to help me put in several new plants and pounds of seeds. I could not find three of my favorite flowers from childhood though. The garden was warm enough because of the stream to support several types of flowers that didn't normally grow in the mountains. Most of them, we found, but those three were too far south to come by easily.

I had actually forgotten about my birthday approaching in the excitement of getting the garden up and running, so to my surprise, I found a beautiful silk bundle sitting on the table in the main room one day. A letter was attached to it with a velvet ribbon. The envelope had Danren's seal on it and read "To Lady Ari'an of the House of Rem'Maren."

Inside the envelope was a short note wishing me a nice birthday. I opened the bundle slowly wondering what Danren had suckered someone into doing for me in his name this time. As the silk fell away, I gasped. The bundle contained a basket lined with flowers from my garden, but inside the basket were three pots. Each contained the flowers that I had not been able to find, and all of them were in bloom.

Narden must have told him that I wanted these. Certainly, he wouldn't have cared on his own. Certainly, he sent someone else to find them as well. I would thank Narden, and I wished I knew who hunted them down. Maybe I would hear that from someone. I would thank Danren also, of course, if I ran into him anytime soon.

I didn't see him very often now, and Narden was busy as well when he was here. Border raids had nearly doubled that year. Verd was upset that Nori'en still refused to trade, and Suvora was finally feeling the threat. Maren had lost four dragons and five of Rem'maren's soldiers that patrolled just in the last month.

The next month there were three dragons down and two more soldiers that I had known. There were a total of ten that fell that month, but I hadn't been familiar with the other five. Thankfully, the dragons were good at getting out of scrapes alive, but that meant that the injuries mounted week after week.

At one point just before fall, there were over seventy-five dragons with a range of injuries. Some were merely in for scratches or wing holes, others hung on to life by a thread. Three more were lost in the recovery stable a week before the first snow, while their soldiers died from injuries elsewhere.

Renard took an extra patrol over the mountains, and Adenern returned to the Suvora border for an additional week. Narden and Danren even took some patrols, but not many since Armel and Mael did not want them injured. Their patrols ranged inland instead of on the borders to add an extra measure of caution. They were less likely to be attacked by marauders from Verd inland, but just as likely to have an attack mounted from a village they passed over.

Then the blow came. Renard had been missing for a week as well as Lord Drenar who was with him. Then Hafiz found Renard's body. A search was put together for Lord Drenar until Lord Grath came and identified that one of the mangled bodies that was found with Renard was that of Lord Drenar. The body was burned and the ashes taken back to Lady Margree.

I walked in a haze for days. No, he couldn't possibly be dead, and certainly not Renard as well. Renard would glide over the wall any day and would laugh that any of us thought him dead. He would tell us that he had to take Lord Drenar back to Ryuu because of some diplomatic emergency that had come up, and we would all laugh together over how absurd it was to think that either of them were dead.

What was worse was the way Danren was acting. He was walking through a fog as well, just like everyone else at Caer Corisan was, but I felt that he had no right to grieve like the rest of us. Yes, Lord Drenar was his brother, but he had rarely seen him as a child. Perhaps they had grown closer together while Danren was training, but he still had no right.

There were too many things to be done when we found out about Renard's death that I needed to finish. Otherwise, I would have swapped places with Narden much sooner. Ari'an was devastated by the news, especially since Drenar died as well. I would see her occasionally, and she was always cordial in her greetings. She had never forgotten to thank me for the gifts I gave her, but there was no feeling in the thanks.

She no longer looked at me as if I was going to kill her or worse, but the way she looked at me now was just as painful. It was a look that had progressed from the original look of terror to annoyance and was currently at despise. That combined with the many dragons healing from injuries and the deaths of Drenar and Renard . . . something was going to give if I couldn't get Narden here soon. The injured would stay the same, and it wouldn't bring either one back, but at least Ari'an liked Narden. Perhaps she would begin to heal if he was here.

A week after Lord Drenar's and Renard's deaths, I walked outside carrying something. I think I was carrying old curtains to Majorlaine, who would make more bandages from them, but I had walked outside with them instead of just walking through the hall. Majorlaine wasn't even in the direction I was going. I found myself doing this often that last week. When I concentrated, I could remember where I was going and how to get there, but if I didn't, I would find that I had carried my breakfast dishes to the top of the wall instead of the kitchen.

A dragon shadow blotted out the sun, so I glanced up to see who it was. To my surprise it was Narden. He was not due here for another week and a half. I had wanted him to come sooner, but knew that would only happen if Danren sent for him, which I thought was beyond all possibilities.

I dropped the curtains in my excitement, but then stopped. Was he injured? Was that why he was here early? I saw him shake his scales and turn to Armel, who came out to meet him. He didn't seem to be injured.

What if he was here to bring more bad news? What if Adenern had died as well, or Tragh, or even Gary? At least Narden was alive though. I could go on as long as he was still alive—but to lose anyone else—.

He spoke to Armel for a few moments then turned. Seeing me, he smiled slightly, but it was a pained smile. He made his way over as I gathered up the curtains that I had dropped in the dirt.

I had hoped to surprise Ari, but she was in the courtyard when I arrived. At least, it had been a little bit of a surprise for her, but I had planned it differently. She was carrying the old curtains from one of the meeting rooms near the hall to Majorlaine, but that didn't explain why she was in the courtyard. Perhaps someone had told her that I was coming early.

I walked with her to make her delivery in silence. She seemed content just that I was there, which was a marked improvement from how she had been. She went with me as I ran around doing every-thing needed to keep Caer Corisan from collapsing into a heap of rubble. Armel was just as busy, and I wondered how he had managed when he was the only one running the place. Danren and I tried to meet with him or Mael a few times each week to make sure we weren't all performing the same tasks. We had a system that usually worked well, and thankfully, now was one of the times that it was working. That freed up the evenings, at least, for just spending time with Ari.

One evening, I had been reading to her from the book, helping her pronounce through a section, when she blurted out, "Why did he have to die?"

I had wondered that myself. I knew the technical details such as he was in an area that had a band of dragon slayers. The lance had gone through Renard's wing and brought him straight down. After that it was a matter of numbers. From the scene, we could tell that he had killed every one of the attackers, but he lost too much in the fight. He managed to drag himself almost a league away, but no farther. I shuddered at the thought of what would have happened if he had lost. Little bits of his scales sold as miracle remedies, horns and claws used as trophies, but I shook off the thoughts. It hadn't gone that way, at least.

The cold answer was that he had just been in the wrong place, but I knew that was not the question that Ari was asking. She wanted to know why he'd had to die, and I didn't know the answer to that. I didn't know why good people died and the ones who caused so much harm just continued on and on, so I didn't answer.

"Why did it have to be him?" Her voice cracked as the tears came.

As bad as it was to lose anyone, I understood where she was coming from. Why indeed could it not have been someone else?

"Why couldn't it have been Danren?"

I froze at the statement and felt my blood run cold.

"W-what?" I finally managed to stammer out.

Ari turned to face me, and she had a dark look that made me hold my breath.

"Danren should be dead, not Lord Drenar," she snapped. "If Danren had died, they would have married me to Drenar, and he at least was friendly to me."

"What?" I could feel my temper heating my blood back up.

"Danren hates me," she told me, the tone of her voice matching the look in her eyes.

"He does not." This wasn't going to continue.

"He never wanted to marry me," she told me. "He gets other people to give me gifts in his name."

No more. "That's not true." I felt the growl through my teeth.

Ari stopped and looked shocked.

"You've sold him short, Ari," I told her. My scales had spiked slightly, and I was having a hard time controlling my voice, but this would stop now.

I knew Narden had a temper, but never before had I seen it directed at me.

"He has never hurt you." His voice was a low growl. "He has never even touched you."

"That's because he hates me," I managed as I looked at my feet.

"Look at me," he snapped, and I pulled my eyes up. "No, *that* is because he promised you the day you were married that he would never touch you without your permission."

I didn't like that she was looking scared, but I was tired of hearing her never give him any credit.

I forced my voice to calm a notch. "I will grant you that your birthday present two years ago from him was not well planned, but that was because he had hoped the garden would be finished in time."

"But the garden was your idea. He never put any work into it." Her voice broke, and she was close to dissolving in tears again.

I didn't manage to keep the entire growl out of my voice. "Wrong! That garden was *his* idea. *He* designed it, *he* worked in it, and that pond you like so much was *his* idea as well, and *he* did most of the work for it." My momentum kept me going as I watched a tear run down her cheek. "And those flowers that you had looked everywhere for, *he* went all the way to Darya to find them for you. *You* never gave him a chance."

She turned and ran from the room. Suddenly, I felt like a popped soap bubble. What had I done?

No, it couldn't be true. I had set up the image of Danren in my mind as an unconcerned, heartless, tyrant. He didn't care about me, but Narden rarely became *that* angry. Never before had he become that angry at me. Would he defend Danren like that if I was right? It betrayed everything I knew of Narden to doubt him, but it betrayed everything I thought about Danren to believe him.

I found that I had run to the garden. I came here when I was upset, and my feet must have brought me here out of habit. Before, though, this had been the garden from Narden and everyone else here, except Danren. Now, it was the garden from Danren, and others had helped a little with it. Why had he given me a garden? Had he expected something?

The flowers that he'd given me this year were planted near the pond he'd designed, because it was the area that was the warmest and most humid. What had he thought he would get out of it?

I walked slowly back to my room. My world had crashed down on my head. Lord Drenar and Renard were both dead, Narden was mad at me, and Danren wasn't the awful person I had believed he was. Was there anything that could be counted on to stay the same?

When I reached for the door handle, I realized that I had been running with the book Lord Grath gave me. Pulling the door open with my other hand, I hurried to the little desk to put the book down. I rarely read it except when studying the languages, but tonight, I opened it in the middle and just started to read.

I found in the morning that I had fallen asleep on the desk. When I looked in the mirror, I also found that I had several sets of lines running the length of my face that strongly resembled the edge of the book. I closed it up and began to rummage through the desk. I didn't spend much time in these rooms other than to sleep or bathe, so the things in the desk belonged to Danren or were general writing instruments, which I was looking for.

I had come to the conclusion that I should apologize to both Narden and Danren, but I had trouble believing that I would say such things to Danren when I saw him. My conclusion was that I should write a letter. If it sounded good enough, and I could memorize it in time, I could just recite it to him. Otherwise, I could just seal up the letter nicely. Perhaps I could find a gift that he would like too.

What did Danren like anyway? I could not think of a single thing that he would enjoy. I knew it wasn't because he didn't have interests. I bit my lip as I realized, it was because I really didn't know anything about him. Maybe he would like some of the flowers from my garden. The orchids were blooming beautifully, and since . . . I swallowed hard at the thought . . . he had given them to me, it might be a nice gesture to have some of those with the letter.

Where in this desk did he keep paper? I had searched three of the five drawers and found quills, inks, and stacks of official-looking already-written pages, but where did he keep blank paper?

Finally, in the last drawer I found a stack of blank paper. I pulled out the stack in frustration and then dropped it on the floor in surprise. Why was Narden's book in here?

I pulled it out and flipped through some of the pages to be certain. It was the same nondescript print with the same unmarked pages. What was it doing here?

I hurried out of the room, this new concern throwing all else out of my mind. I saw Narden across the courtyard, probably discussing troop arrangements on the walls with Ishmerai. Glancing around and up, I found Ishmerai's counterpart, Hafiz, circling the skies above.

When they were through, I hurried to meet him. He wasn't paying attention when I came up, only noticing me when I was a few steps away. He started becoming a bit pale.

"Are you all right?" he asked. Before I could answer, he continued, "I didn't mean to get that angry last night, and I never should have yelled at you like that."

"It's all right," I told him, "you were probably right anyway."

It was nice to know that she wasn't too upset, but I wondered how she really was handling everything. She hadn't changed out of the dress she was wearing yesterday, so she probably was up all night.

Suddenly, she held my book up in front of me. What was she doing with that?

"Where did you get that?" It was supposed to be in the desk.

"I was looking for some paper and found it underneath a stack in Danren's desk," she told me. "What is he doing with it?"

I had to think fast for that one. "He keeps it for me, since it's hard for me to read it consistently by myself."

The "drop, read, pick up, drop, read" method was a pain since the next place was usually not where it had been, so context was hard to follow.

"Typically, he leaves it somewhere that I can find it, but he's a little distracted currently."

"Why didn't he just tell me so I could bring it to you?" she asked looking over the worn cover.

I didn't mean to, it was just reflex, but I realized I gave her a "is that a legitimate question?" look complete with cocked eyebrow.

She laughed slightly and turned the book over in her hands.

At that moment, Besnik came running up.

"Lady Ari'an," he panted, "Galen would like your help if you're not busy."

I knew what that actually meant. They did this to Danren all the time. What he was actually saying was, "Come quick! It's an emergency!"

I told her I would deal with the book if she wanted to go, which she did. It was barely sun up, and already there were emergencies. This was not going to be a pleasant day.

Night finally came, along with a loll in the frantic pace. I was searching to find Narden, when Armel told me that he had left to find Danren because an important letter had come.

I turned, wondering when he would be back and stopped short. I felt the blood drain from my face. I'd never cleaned up the desk this morning. I had been in such a hurry to figure out what was going on with Narden's book that I had left everything where it had fallen. I had planned on getting back to pick everything up before breakfast, but I had barely had time to snag a peeled boiled egg for that meal. Had anything gone right today? I ran through the halls, hoping that Danren wasn't back yet.

What on Arnbjorg had happened here? I knew she'd found Narden's book, but had she thrown a fit to find it in my possession? Had she thought I'd stolen it? At least the open inkwell on the desk wasn't spilled. It would have completely ruined Ari'an's book if it had tipped.

I had never known Ari'an to go through this desk before. As I picked up the scattered papers, I made a mental note to go through everything in the desk myself to make sure there wasn't anything else that might upset her. Not tonight though. Tonight I was too tired to even light a fire in the hearth and read a little as I usually did. I still needed to figure out how I was supposed to tell Ari'an that we needed to leave for Calanthe by the end of the week.

King Viskhard had decided to hold a funeral for Drenar. Of course, His Majesty was too busy to actually attend, but several of his "close" advisers would be holding the event.

Event it would be too. Very few of the people who actually went would be at all concerned that my brother was dead, or that they'd made his grieving family travel all the way to Calanthe for a funeral that would turn out to be another one of the gala events of the season.

We were having a border crisis, and they wanted to throw a party. My whole family would have to attend, or the king would take it as a personal insult even though he wouldn't be in attendance himself.

How on Arnbjorg was I supposed to tell Ari'an?

The door behind me slammed against the wall, and I jumped to my feet. I barely managed to keep from scattering all the paper over the floor again. Spinning around, I saw Ari'an, pale as a clean sheep, standing in the doorway trying to catch her breath.

"What's wrong?" was my automatic response.

Had Hramn lit the horse stable on fire *again*? This would be three times in two weeks. I turned to glance out the open balcony. The stable looked fine. It must be something far worse . . .

"Is it Adenern?" Certainly only something such as him being maimed or . . . worse . . . would send her racing up here looking for me.

He wasn't supposed to be here. There wasn't a glow under the door from the hearth. Danren always lit a fire at night if he was the first one in the room. I knew, because I would find somewhere else to sleep when there was such a glow.

I had to come up with something fast. "No, I didn't think you were here." *That* sounded original!

It took me a moment to gather my thoughts. There wasn't anything wrong. No one important was mauled or killed. She hadn't been looking for me. It took longer than usual to come to the end of the trail of thoughts. I really needed to sleep.

If she hadn't been looking for me, why had she burst in here like that? This was just great. Maybe it was because I was tired, maybe it was because I couldn't think of another time when I would see her, or maybe I was just too overwhelmed with everything that was going on that I told her about the funeral then.

"Ambassador Agung and Honorary Court Bohurnir are holding a funeral for Drenar in King Viskhard's name in fourteen days, and we have to be there." I waved at the letter on the table.

She looked like she was still recovering from the shock of finding me there, so I added, "Anyway, goodnight. I hope you sleep well."

She never wanted to talk to me anyway, so I might as well leave. She'd recover faster if I wasn't around.

He dropped the stack of papers he'd picked up off the floor in the drawer, pushed it closed, and walked into his room, closing the door behind him. He left the lamp on the desk.

Slowly, I walked toward the letter he had waved at. He was upset to find his desk in that condition. For once I couldn't blame him. There wasn't anything left in me to hate him with. I was too worn-out. I felt a sob stick in my throat.

I stopped at the table and looked down at the letter. The all-important letter that had demanded he return was an invitation to a party! There was no doubt in my mind that it would be anything less than a drunken mess. I knew both Agung's and Bohurnir's reputations. They used any excuse to throw an extravaganza, but that they would consider doing such a thing with all the problems that Rem'Maren and Maren were having was ludicrous.

I didn't want to admit it, but Danren was needed here, not at some carousing revelry. I was needed here too, but there was the king's seal broken on the table. It wasn't an invitation. It was a demand that we drop everything and go . . . Go *what*? Celebrate that someone dear to us was dead? These people were disgusting!

I clinched the letter in my fist. I wanted to throw it into the fire, but there wasn't one. The thought of starting one up was too much for me, and I crumpled into the chair next to the table, crying.

I pulled my boots off and collapsed on the bed. I didn't care that I hadn't changed my clothes. I was very close to not caring about anything anymore, when I heard a faint sob from the other room.

I felt everything inside me wrench at the sound. She was hurting, and I couldn't do anything to help her. I couldn't walk out there and try to comfort her. She hated me. I couldn't get Narden for her. I couldn't do anything.

Pulling myself from the bed, I walked to the door, sat down against it, and prayed. Maybe the Mighty One would help her. The low crying slowly faded.

In the morning, I awoke there, stiff, sore, and with my legs entirely asleep.

CHAPTER 35

TRYING TO
START OVER

The hectic pace doubled as we prepared to leave. Somehow, maybe he had already been working on something, Faber pulled together two extra dresses for me before we left. I barely saw Danren, much less had a chance to talk to him. I still wanted to apologize, but I didn't know what to say. Maybe it was better this way, because he looked exhausted every time I did see him. I never noticed before how much he actually did around the fortress.

The end of the week came too soon, and I had barely packed a few things. That morning we were hurried to Einheim and Jair who were waiting to take us. Hafiz and Besnik flew surveillance.

Two others joined us as well, Hramn who was new this year and only thirteen. He had caught on to flying as if he had done it all his life. Bikendi was the other. The two of them carried trunks strapped to the sides of their saddles.

I had hoped that Narden would be able to take us, but he couldn't be spared either. He wasn't there when we left. I wanted to tell him goodbye, but much like the other little things at Caer Corisan, it would be one more thing pushed aside, because of everything else that was more important.

We traded the dragons in for horses and a carriage at a way station. I felt as though I was losing everything familiar as I watched them take to the skies as we drove off. They followed the caravan to Elea at least, but the next day, as we left, I couldn't find them again.

I was even lonelier since I rode in the carriage by myself. Danren was on horseback, as well as the escort that Dreanen had sent to accompany us through his territory. I knew two of the ten riders and had never seen the coachman before. I wished again and again that I would have brought something to do. I had not done any needlework for at least six months, and that would have been fun. I should have at least brought a book to read, but I hadn't even thought of that.

Instead, I stared at the countryside as it changed from forest to pastureland to farmland.

I knew that Ari'an wouldn't want my company on the trip, so I'd asked for an extra horse. It might not have been the safest arrangement, but I could use my sword just as well as any of the escorts, especially since Armel had taken it into his head to spar with me every day he had a chance. I didn't mind the practice, but it was annoying to be beaten so thoroughly by him every time.

The trip was thankfully uneventful. We arrived without as much as a nail falling out of a horse's shoe. I had been on edge the entire trip, because of everything that had occurred on the borders. Apparently, there wasn't a threat in the main lands of Faruq. Someone even asked why we traveled with so many guards. I thought there weren't enough.

As evening loomed closer, the first of the castle spires came into view. Torion Castle was designed to sprawl across the landscape. Caer Corisan was built so thickly that a dozen dragons could hit the walls at the same time without dislodging a stone. This castle climbed toward the sky in thin towers. As we approached, I wondered how many of the towers a dragon could knock down in a single dive. This was a showpiece. It withstood the weather, but it probably cost a fortune to heat in the winter . . . not that I had ever heard of Lord Bohurnir ever holding a . . . a . . . whatever these were to him, in the winter.

We were shown to our rooms, located in one of the towers of course, and I was relieved to find that my request for a second room with another bed had been heeded. It was set up as a servant's quarters, but I was too tired to really care. The room was next to the main sleeping room. Both opened into a parlor area. At least, there was a table for eating and a couch in front of a grandiose fireplace. I wondered if a fire was lit in that, how long it would even burn, with a chimney that thin.

I noticed that Ari'an looked pale and asked if she was all right. I hoped she wasn't getting sick. It was bad enough that we even had to be here. She shook her head, but the color didn't come back. There wasn't exactly anything I could do for her, and she would probably feel better if I wasn't around, so I just pulled my trunks into the little room and closed the door.

Immediately when we walked in, I noticed that unlike Caer Corisan, there was only one main sleeping room. I felt my blood turn cold at the thought. There was a little room for a servant to sleep in, but only the one main sleeping room. Danren asked me if I was all right, but I refused to tell him my concern. He would probably laugh.

To my shock, he took hold of one of his two trunks and dragged it into the servant's room. A moment later, he pulled the other one in, bid me good night, and closed the door.

Thankfully, there was a chair next to me. Quickly, I sat down and stared at the closed door for several moments. Certainly, he wasn't going to sleep in a servant's room! I sat stunned for a long time, but the door never opened.

When I finally regained the use of my jellied legs and convinced myself that he wasn't coming back out of the room that night, I attempted to pull one of the trunks into the large sleeping room. The carpet wouldn't release it, so I pulled out a sleeping gown and hurried into the other room.

I had thought that I wouldn't sleep much, but the exhaustion from the past weeks and the stress from the trip took over. I woke a little late in the morning.

Realizing that I had only the dress I had worn the previous day with me, I peeked out the door. I found Danren sitting at the table in the middle of the room with a few mounds of papers scattered about it. Pulling yesterday's dress on, I hurried out of the room, hoping that he would be too busy to notice me. I was wrong.

I glanced up when I heard the door creak and saw Ari'an cringe at the sound. Was that the same outfit she had worn yesterday? Her hair looked rumpled. Had she slept in those clothes too? Was the trip that tiring for her? We should have taken another day for traveling, but Zait had come in with an injury at the first of the week, which set us back a day. That and . . .

"I just need to get—" She motioned at the trunks still in the center of the room.

I was an idiot. Why hadn't I thought to take those in for her last night? Probably I was too exhausted from the trip to think straight, but that wasn't a legitimate excuse.

As I carried the trunks into her room, I realized that I didn't know what to do about breakfast. Earlier, a servant had informed me that breakfast would be brought to the rooms. I hadn't paid him much mind at the time, but certainly, Ari'an wouldn't want to eat breakfast here with me.

She was typically gone by the time I woke. I never asked where she went, since I knew she wouldn't want me asking about her activities. Perhaps Dreanen and Pher'am would be here. Either she would eat with them or I could.

Dreanen was having a harder time than I was though. He and Father were settling affairs from Drenar's estate. Dreanen would be taking it over, a slightly disconcerting concept, but not something that could be avoided, and it was possible that they would be arriving later than we had.

I walked out of her room to find her letting in a servant carrying a tray of delicacies. I asked the servant if my brother had come yet before she left. There had been no word of him.

I bit my lip looking over the tray of interesting tidbits. I was hungry from the trip, but I had never eaten a meal with Danren before. I wasn't sure I should start now. He probably wouldn't expect me to. I could make up some excuse to leave. Certainly, I could think of something.

"You never gave him a chance," Narden *had told me.* It was true I *had* never given him a chance.

"W-w-would," my mind demanded that I stop stammering, "you mind if I joined you for breakfast?"

He didn't respond for what seemed like ages, but I knew it must have been only a moment.

I felt that if it hadn't been attached so securely to my face, my jaw would have made a hole in the floor. It took far too long to recover from the shock, and I was glad that she was looking at the tray instead of me the whole time.

"I-if you would like," I finally managed, "but if you would rather spend the meal with Lord Perparim and Lady Lindita, that would be fine."

"I would rather stay here," she answered and sat down in one of the two chairs at the table.

Of course he didn't know, but I had insulted Lord Perparim's nose as a child, and Nori'en had paid quite a large sum to soothe his pride. Part of that price, I'd found out, would have been some of my bride price. I would have laughed at the thought of spending a meal with him and his wife, if I hadn't been concentrating on not stammering.

I cannot remember another meal where I was as careful as to what I said or what I reached for. I watched her hands constantly, making certain that I never reached for the same thing she did. I tried to find safe topics to talk about and talked about the weather a little, mentioning that I hoped for an early winter this year. She looked slightly surprised by that, and I had to explain that an early winter would lock up the passes. Very few attacks happened in winter.

"Do you think that Narden is all right?" she asked. "He told me that he wouldn't be at Caer Corisan while we were away."

"He will be as safe as we are," I told her, "since he doesn't patrol the borders anymore."

"He doesn't?" she asked. "What does he do when he's not at Caer Corisan?"

I had never asked, but I assumed that he patrolled like the other dragons. I thanked the Mighty One every time he came home, assuming that he had survived another patrol unmarked.

"He," Danren told me after taking a bite, "checks up on the other dragons and does whatever needs to be done, I'm sure."

It was nice to know that Narden was safe. I supposed that much like Armel and Galen, who also did not patrol, that he was too important. I smiled a little at the thought. I was proud of him. I had never thought that he would run Caer Corisan, and he did it well.

It was nice to see her smile, even if it was only at the thoughts in her own mind. She would come back to eating breakfast with me soon enough, and the smile would flee. She turned her head slightly to look at the table where a breeze from the open window was shifting some of the papers around.

"What are you working on?" she asked.

"There have been several attacks around Brahn, which is one of the stops on the winter supply route. I was trying to find a safer way around in case some dragon slayers or assassins decide to stay there through the winter to cause trouble," I told her.

"Have you considered routing through Maris?" she asked still looking at the pile of papers. Her interest surprised me.

"We were thinking of going through there or around Rauha," I told her.

"But that is on the other side of Rem'Maren," she said emphatically.

"Yes, but Maris is a port town and had some incidents a couple of months ago, where as Rauha has been one of the only peaceful places this year," I argued back at her, "but now you see the dilemma."

She stood up from the table and paced to the window. "Not going through Brahn would cause a problem too, because they are used to having the fresh supplies come through there during the winter."

"Yes, so we were planning to make drops there every six weeks or so to compensate for it." I stood and walked over to the desk. "Armel asked me to find a suitable substitute route, but we may just stay with going through Brahn."

"And run the risk of an attack in winter?" she asked turning to look at the desk again.

I pulled the map I brought from one of the drawers, opened it, and brought up Rem'Maren and Maren on it. I noticed Ari'an came a few steps closer at the sight of the map.

"Here are the options I can come up with," I told her. "We could use the old route and hope for the best from Itsaso to Ryuu through Brahn to Kerr and then Caer Corisan, but you know the dangers of that, and if possible, we would like a safer route."

I told the map in el'brenika to switch to green now. The original route and towns were in blue. Then I continued. "Instead we could still use Itsaso and Ryuu but route through Rauha and Blerta instead, but Blerta is almost as unfriendly to dragons as anyone outside of Rem'maren is, so it's almost as dangerous to go there."

The next route I traced in yellow. "Itsaso to Isra to Rauha would still start at the same place, but because of distance, there would be twelve watches flying between the towns, instead of the eight that the other two routes would have."

I stepped back from the desk surprised when she asked the map for purple in el'brenika. When had she picked that up? I couldn't remember ever hearing that she was learning that language. She'd never said anything to Narden about it either.

"H-have." I tried again, "Have you considered starting from Mirna instead and going to Ryuu then Rauha and Nyr?" The route would still have a coast town, but Mirna was not a port like Itsaso was, and it was known to be dragon friendly. Ryuu would still be the same, but the third stop would be Nyr, which was a new village that year so still very small.

He looked at the new route for a moment then said, "We would have to supply Brahn, and Kerr that way." He said it in el'brenika though.

I felt my face flush, but he was looking at the map, not me. Armel had been working with me on the language, but I had never meant for Danren to be the first to know.

"You won't tell Narden, will you?" I replied hoping my accent didn't sound too terrible. "I had wanted to surprise him."

I smiled at the statement, she had a good tone, and the words were clear. "I will leave it to you to tell him. I know he would be surprised when he first finds out."

"Anyway," I continued, "we could also go from Rauha to Kerr instead of to Nyr."

"That would backtrack though," I told him, knowing that Kerr was farther west than Nyr.

"Yes, but it would save the extra trips to Kerr through the winter," he replied asking for orange from the map and having it trace in that alternate route.

A thought ran through my head, and I laughed. Noticing Danren's head shoot up, I quickly stopped.

"I'm sorry," I stammered reverting back to the common tongue. "I just thought that with all the colors, it looks like a rainbow fell on some of these towns," I tried to explain, but it was a childish thought.

She'd laughed. I had really just heard her laugh. I was so shocked that I looked at her directly, something I tried to avoid whenever possible.

I glanced back at the map quickly and smiled. "Would you agree to this route then?" I asked as I ran my finger along the last one we had discussed.

She nodded, and I wiped off the other towns and asked for those four to recall to a command in colors. Clearing those towns as well, I then asked for the route to make sure it worked.

These maps still fascinated me, so I forgot my embarrassment for a moment as I watched the places disappear. Danren said something in el'brenika that I didn't quite understand, and then took the last four towns off.

One more statement that sounded like it included what he had just said brought the four towns back in, only this time they were traced in with thin lines of all the colors in a rainbow. Was he mocking me?

He had a slight smile on his face as he cleared the map entirely and rolled it up. He *was* mocking me.

"Is that all you brought to occupy your time?" I asked.

The cold tone to her voice made me wonder if I had offended her.

"No," I told her, "I need to figure out the supplies we can pick up and distribute with the new route and work out all those details."

"Oh," she stated, "well, I hope you do not miss too much of the memorial."

With that she turned and walked into her room. I stared at the door that had not slammed, per say, but had closed much harder than necessary. I flopped into the chair and leaned my chin on my hand. What had I done to upset her now?

I shuffled through the papers, looking for the supply charts I had. I missed them at least twice, because I couldn't figure out what I had done to offend her. I'd thought the conversation went well. In fact, that was the best conversation I'd had with her since the wedding. She hadn't seemed too nervous, and she didn't have that despising look on her face that was typical whenever she spoke to me. It must have been that I spoke to her in el'brenika, I decided. What else could it have been? I should have known better. I began to look through the papers again and found that I was holding the list I needed in my other hand.

CHAPTER 36

THE FUNERAL

When I finished dressing and fixing my hair, I found that Danren was no longer in the main room. Instead I found a servant waiting to show me to the grand hall for dinner. It was still two watches before midday. I groaned inside realizing how long this meal alone would be.

I was seated at the end of a middle table with my left side facing the walkway, designed to allow the servers to easily pass back and forth among the tables. There were too many guests for a normal U-shaped arrangement. Instead, tables were set up in rows facing an open area for entertainers.

I never would have thought twice about which side was against the aisle, except for the conversation I happened to sit next to. My left upper arm wore the engraved dragon band, which declared me as a member of the House of Rem'Maren by marriage.

Apparently, the lady seated to my right thought it was her duty to share all the horrific things that she heard about the different ladies of the houses. I managed to ignore most of it, wondering when this meal would end. They never touched most of the food set in front of us, and I found later that what was left was not even given to the servants, but sent to the pigs and goats.

"Have you yet seen the Lady of Rem'Maren, the younger one?" one of the ladies next to me asked, probably trying to change the subject.

"I doubt she will be coming," the one next to me said. I glanced over at her for the first time and found that she was born to the House of Almudina from the mark on the back of her neck and married to someone else in the same house by the band on her arm.

Since I had looked at her, she must have considered it her duty to include me in the conversation. With a straight face, she told me, "I heard that she was terribly burned by one of those horrific dragons."

"Lady Pher'am was burned?" This was news to me.

"No, no," she told me in a voice meant to humor a child, "the Lady Ari'an, the youngest daughter of the House of Nori'en."

I never discovered quite what came over me at that point, but I decided to let her continue on this topic for a while. I wanted to know how far she would go.

"Lady Ari'an?" I asked her in a shocked voice.

"Yes, yes," she replied sounding excited, "she was burned from head to foot, I heard it from the wife of the Lord of Suvora herself."

I wished Narden was here so I could tell him about this conversation later. He would find it so hilarious. "From head to foot?"

"Yes, yes," she continued, "that was right after the beast attempted to eat her alive."

Someone else made the shocked exclamation to that statement of "Eat her alive?"

"Yes, yes." She turned to the new speaker. "I heard he did manage to take off her hand."

I saw Danren walking toward me and quickly decided on what to say, interrupting him before he greeted me, "You must hear this story."

As I turned back to the speaker, she emphatically told me, "No, no, it is no story. The wife of the Lord of Suvora assured me that it was perfectly true."

I had never thought of Ari'an as a person who enjoyed gossip. I found that most of what people spread stories about had as much truth in it as a cake has salt. Somewhere back at the beginning of the actual event, something happened like a child jumping over a puddle reflecting the sky, and the story would grow till a town had lost all its foundations and flew around one of the moons.

"She was telling me how Lady Ari'an was burned by a dragon from head to toe," Ari'an continued.

"What?" If I hadn't placed my hand on the table and leaned down slightly when I walked up, I would have taken a step back.

"Yes, yes," Lady Yente of Almudina replied emphatically, "on top of that, her hand was devoured by the foul beast at the same time."

I didn't mean to, but I looked directly at Ari'an wondering what was going on. She looked surprised only for a moment, but then winked. I glanced at the ladies sitting with her at the table and then back at her. She was playing a joke.

He was going to give it all away, and I wasn't through yet. I did the only thing I could think of to give him a hint. I fought the warm sensation in my cheeks when I winked at him. A shocked look came over his face, he glanced at the other ladies, then back at me, and I watched one side of his mouth tilt up slightly.

"This is no laughing matter, I assure you," the talebearer reproached him.

"Oh, I understand that such a thing would be horrific," he told her with a straight face. "Do you know if the dragon chewed her hand or swallowed it whole?"

Such a question! I couldn't look at the ladies' responses in case I gave myself away, but I heard at least three gasp and one body landing hard against the back of her chair. I wanted to throw my head back and laugh.

"Well, I would hope that the beast would have the courteousness to swallow it whole," she exclaimed at him, "but I suppose I should not expect such things from a *dragon*."

"It was my understanding"—how did he manage to keep a straight face?—"that dragons did not eat people."

"Well, this dragon had obviously not received that information, since he tried to eat her alive," she told him sharply.

"Have you met a dragon, my lord?" one of the other ladies asked.

I glanced at Ari'an, who was looking away from the table as if she was going to roll off her chair with mirth. It was a wonderful thing to see her so amused. She nodded ever so slightly and bit her lip while scrunching her face.

"As a matter of fact, I have met quite a few dragons," I told her, was it Lady Eulalia of Sparins or Lady Olalla of Almudina, they were twin sisters.

"Was there something you needed, my lord?" the storyteller asked in a tone that implied that she obviously didn't believe me.

"Why yes," I answered and turned to Ari'an, who had regained enough composure to turn to look at me slightly. "Your sister has arrived."

Her face lit up at that news, and she stood to leave as the storyteller asked, "Which sister?"

Ari'an turned to look at her as a smile spread across her face. "Why I only have one sister, Lady Pher'am."

I never forgot how quickly her face turned as white as a clean sheep. I leaned toward her slightly as she stared at my armband. "You may wish to check your stories next time, even if they are perfectly true."

I turned and walked toward the nearest exit with Danren a few steps behind me. I needed to find a place to laugh before I choked from holding it in. I saw an open lounge room and darted in. It only had enough space for a couch and a lounging chair, but it would do.

"Close the door quickly," I told Danren, since he was still following me.

When I heard the latch click shut, I fell into the chair and threw my head back to laugh.

I chuckled slightly at the situation, but it was so nice to hear her laugh that I just watched her for a few moments, taking a seat on the couch.

As she wiped tears of merriment from her eyes, Ari'an said, "She actually believed it too. She actually believed that a dragon would try to eat me then roast me alive when he didn't succeed."

She laughed again, but then stopped suddenly. Her head snapped forward, and she looked frightened.

Suddenly, I realized that I told Danren to shut me into a room lacking windows and only one door with him alone. What had I done? I looked around frantically for anything that might help me. While casting my eyes around, I noticed Danren's face and gasped silently.

He had his eyes closed and was taking a deep breath, but his face was marked by a deep pain. It passed quickly. He stood up and walked toward the door.

"Lady Pher'am and Dreanen will be waiting for us," he said, opened the door, and walked out.

"You never gave him a chance." Narden's words echoed in my mind again. "He's never hurt you."

He didn't look at me as he waited out in the hallway. I realized that he rarely looked at me. In that respect, he acted much like Drenar had. He would look past me or next to me, but he didn't meet my gaze except on very rare occasions. As I followed silently behind him, I thought back over the time of our marriage. Just as Narden had said, he had never hurt me. He had never even touched me, just as Narden had pointed out.

"Watch your step, my lady," I heard him say, and I stopped suddenly.

Looking down I noticed a slight rise to the floor. It was too short to call a step-up, but this section had obviously been added at some point, and the floor didn't quite line up. For some reason, that warning over such a little thing forced a decision through my mind. I had not written the apology to him before because my pride dictated that I should not sink so low. The man deserved an apology. He deserved to have every nasty thing I said about him erased from time, but I couldn't do that. He never treated me with anything less than respect and courtesy, and he deserved at least the same from me. He deserved more than that, since I had treated him so badly.

"May I speak with you privately for a moment?" I asked pulling my gaze from the rise on the floor to his face.

I met his gaze for only a moment before he diverted his eyes and looked past my head.

"Of course, my lady," he answered. "Would you rather talk after seeing your sister?"

She was slightly pale. The dining hall was crowded, and her performance with Lady Yente was uncharacteristic. I hoped she wasn't becoming ill.

"I-I"—she took a deep breath—"I would like to speak with you now, if that is all right."

"Of course, my lady," I told her, "our rooms are on the next level up, or there should be an empty room nearby."

She paled further. "Our rooms will be fine." She then hurried up the nearest flight of stairs and came very close to running to the room.

I followed slowly behind her, wondering if she was nauseous from all the strange food. She wouldn't want me near her if she was sick.

I cautiously stepped to the doorway to find her standing in the middle of the room. Well, at least she wasn't throwing up.

"Are you all right?" he asked as he closed the door behind him.

I forced myself to turn around and face him. "Sir," I told my hands, realized that I should look at him, and forced myself to look up. Again, I watched him meet my eyes for only a moment then shift his gaze to look past my head.

"Are you feeling ill, my lady?" he sounded . . . deeply concerned.

"I-I"—I took a deep breath—"I am not ill, sir. I wanted to apologize to you."

In my surprise, I looked directly at her. I realized my mistake but noticed that she didn't look away. I wasn't sure why, but I kept my eyes with hers.

"I haven't treated you properly," I continued and saw his face calm from the shocked expression he'd had a moment before. "I have been cruel to you to y-your face and behind your back," I paused to steady my voice. "I never gave you a chance."

He took a step back, and the shocked look returned to his face.

"I-I"—I looked at my hands to steady my voice—"I meant to apologize to you before, but I put it off."

This was an odd time to bring something like this up, considering someone was waiting for us. Why would she suddenly think of doing this now? I watched her as her gaze glanced around a bit.

"Ari'an," I began, "why don't you sit down, and we can sort this out."

I sat down on the nearby couch, gripping my hands together to keep them from shaking. I expected Danren to sit next to me, but he first found a glass and poured some water, setting the glass on the stand next to me. Then he pulled the desk chair over to about ten steps away.

He continued in a soft tone, "You've been hurt, Ari, and I do not want to hurt you anymore."

It surprised me slightly to have him use my nickname.

I nodded again. "You're not like most of the men I've met," I said, just above a whisper.

There was silence for a moment. Glancing up slightly, I found that he was biting back a smile.

"I'm sorry," he told me with a slight chuckle to his voice that he seemed to be trying to suppress. "You have no idea how true that may be."

We left to meet Pher'am and Dreanen once my hands stopped shaking. To his credit, Danren didn't bring up the conversation again.

CHAPTER 37

A MATTER OF HONOR

Three days into the funeral, I awoke to a crash in the main room. Taking the fire poker as silently as I could from its stand next to the little hearth, I crept toward the door. I slowly opened the door, praying that the hinges wouldn't give me away. My hands shook so badly, I was certain they rattled the poker.

I saw two figures in the main room. "I told you to be careful," the one sitting on the desk chair hissed in a whisper.

"It is much easier to be careful when you can see." The second man laughed.

"Dreanen, what are you doing here?" I asked realizing who the second was. Certainly, he was up to some prank.

He stood up, since he had been stooped over the broken pitcher that he had knocked off its stand. "Apparently, waking you, my lady," he told me, "it is such a fine morning that you shouldn't miss it."

"Who's with you?" I asked, watching the shape in the chair.

"Why Danren of course"—he started laughing—"but it is hard to recognize people in the dark."

He lit a lamp on the desk and moved it to the table.

I closed the door wondering what the two of them were up to. I didn't expect anything odd from Danren, but with Dreanen involved, who knew what would happen? I dressed quickly and hurried into the main room.

I stopped instantly, realizing that Danren had a gash across his right arm. Dreanen had ripped off the sleeve of the shirt earlier and was now untying the makeshift bandage, which dripped blood on the carpet.

"What happened?" I asked as I ducked back into my room for my kit.

"Oh, he just had a little run-in with Lord Astucieux," Dreanen called after me.

I came back to find Danren glaring at his brother. Dreanen replied by chuckling as he cleaned out the wound.

"Let me do that," I ordered, wondering how well a man who took few things seriously could actually manage such a task.

"You don't have to," Danren said, suddenly looking up at me. The motion jarred his arm, and he gasped. "We can call Meade in."

"Meade has been drunk by midday for the last three days," I told him. "Do you really want him anywhere near you?"

"Dreanen is doing fine," he told me.

I glanced at Dreanen then back at Danren. I didn't want to tell him that I thought his brother's ability to treat wounds was questionable. It turned out that I wouldn't need to, because Dreanen laughed out loud.

"You might as well give in," Dreanen said. "She has a point."

I wanted to kill him, but couldn't put the effort into it. I had noticed the skeptical look on Ari'an's face when I had suggested it, but I didn't want her to feel that she was the only one able to.

"She has worked with Galen quite a bit, so you won't find anyone better." Dreanen stepped away allowing Ari'an to look over my arm.

I glared at him and mouthed. "I'm going to hurt you."

"On that note"—he chuckled—"I take my leave. I hope to see you at breakfast."

He turned and walked out of the room. I had half a mind to get up and drag him back, but Ari'an had already threaded a needle to begin stitching my arm.

I realized as Dreanen left that I was completely alone and within arm's reach of Danren. I felt my stomach drop to my feet, and I held my breath for a moment. Suddenly, I realized how stupid my fear was. He had every opportunity long before this, and at this moment, he was bleeding and apparently upset with Dreanen. I focused on putting the stitches in his arm and tried to even out my breathing.

"What happened?" I finally managed to ask as I pulled out a couple of bottles and looked at the labels. I finally found the one I wanted and worked on finding a sling.

"I'd rather not talk about it," he told me.

I didn't know how to tell her what had happened, and really didn't want to. I searched frantically for a different subject and only managed, "Did you bring all that from Caer Corisan?"

She held a scale knife in one hand as she looked through the case.

"Well, I certainly didn't find this here." She waved the knife slightly.

"Were you intending to patch up many dragons while you were here?" I asked.

"No." She pulled a sling out of the case. "W-will you see if this fits while I fix you something for the pain."

She set the sling on the desk instead of handing it to me. I looked at it for a moment, realizing again that she would never actually trust me. She mixed a couple of spoonfuls of powder into a glass of water as I fitted the sling.

I stood up and moved toward the table swaying slightly, remembering the bad blow to my head.

"Are you all right?" she asked as I leaned on the table.

"I'll be fine," I answered as I sat back down.

"That's not what I asked," she said sharply. "Drink this." She set the glass in front of me as she went back over to her kit.

I had a good idea what the answer was, but I asked anyway, "What is it?"

"It's willow bark, of course," she answered, pulling out a candle and a focus dome. "It's not that bad, just swallow it all at once and then eat a few grapes."

She must have noticed the face I made at the glass.

"Have you ever tasted the stuff?" I handled the glass gingerly knowing full well that a few grapes would do nothing about the taste.

"Yes, I have," she told me coming back to the table.

As I downed the mixture, I saw her slice an orange and set the quarters in front of me. "Eat those," she ordered. "It should help."

Surprisingly, it did. "When did you find that out?"

"From Majorlaine," she told me lighting the candle and adjusting the dome to reflect the flame.

"Does Galen know?" I asked.

"He probably does," she paused for a moment, "but I think he likes to make people suffer, not die mind you, but suffer just enough so they won't do it again."

I laughed at that. It sounded like something Galen with his gruff exterior and constant complaints about having to patch people up would do.

"Look at me," she ordered, and out of sheer surprise, I did.

The bright light made me instantly shut my eyes though.

"Look at me, not the light," she told me.

Seeing spots, I focused on her face. She watched my eyes closely through the dome. It was an interesting contraption that focused a single candle flame to a single line, which was what blinded me a moment ago. I didn't think about the device for long though.

I had never before been close enough, except for perhaps as a child when I wouldn't have paid any attention, to actually notice her eyes. They were too green to be blue and too blue to be green. It was an intriguing combination. The color flecked. I wondered if Faber took that into account when he made her dresses. He probably did. He had an attention to detail that was baffling. He probably planned things together, just so they would bring out a certain color in her eyes.

She moved the light away, and I blinked. "Well, I don't think you have a concussion," she told me. "Where did you hit your head?"

I motioned to the left side of my head.

"What are you thinking about?" she asked.

I started at the question, causing a jarring pain to run through my arm and my head.

"You probably don't want to know," I told her.

Galen always made it a point to ask the people he was working on what they were thinking about. I thought it was to help them focus on something else. Perhaps, it was just because he was nosy but didn't want to look like he was. Whatever the reason, I had picked up the habit.

I saw the knot on his head. "Come now, I've seen plenty of wounds. Were you thinking about the fight?"

"No." I felt him cringe as I put pressure on the lump.

"Something about Caer Corisan?" I would need to find something cold for him to hold to his head to stop the swelling.

"No, not exactly," he answered.

"About the patrols then, or the supply routes?" I moved to put the supplies back into my kit.

"No, nothing like that." He leaned his head forward and rested it in his hands.

"What then?" I was too curious by that point.

"You don't want to know," he answered from inside his hands.

"Come now," I insisted, blowing out the candle and putting it with the lens back into the kit.

He took in a rugged breath. "I was thinking how pretty your eyes are."

I would find later that I had cracked the lens by dropping it.

It took me a moment to manage, "I-I-I n-need to find a cold p-press for y-your head."

I nearly ran from the room and almost collided with Dreanen in the hall.

"Is he all right?" There wasn't a hint of laughter in his voice.

"Yes, he's fine," I told him and started walking down the hall.

"Is he going to live?" I stopped from surprise at the question.

"Of course he's going to live," I told him. "Lord Astucieux is the most skilled knight in the kingdom, why was he even in such a fight?"

I needed something to take my mind off Danren's last statement.

"Didn't he tell you?" Dreanen didn't sound too surprised, just relieved, probably because his brother wasn't going to die.

"Of course not." I knew I was snapping, and I tried to control my voice better. "He said he didn't want to talk about it." I'd left him alone on that point. Why couldn't I have let the last thing alone too?

"Oh," he lowered his voice, "Lord Astucieux questioned your fidelity, and Danren challenged him."

I froze instantly. Slowly, I managed, "And he lost." There was no possibility that Danren could have won against such a seasoned knight.

"Lord Astucieux?" Dreanen said with a lighter tone to his voice. "Yes, he lost very disgracefully, especially after that swing trying to take Danren's head off."

I borrowed Narden's statement of choice in such situations, "What?"

"You do realize that my brother can hold his own for at least a sixth of a watch with Armel," he told me. "*I* stopped sparring with Armel when I couldn't make it past two swings."

"He's never won though!" I watched some of those matches.

Dreanen threw his head back and laughed. "Find me someone who can beat Armel in a match, and I will fly you to the moons."

When he stopped laughing and noticed my lost expression, he was considerate enough to explain the course of events.

I was entirely certain that I wouldn't see her again until the end of the funeral, and then only because we had to travel back to Caer Corisan together. I'd told her, only because I hated to lie to her. I would pay for it, though, far worse than anything Lord Astucieux could have served me, even if he had managed to take off my head.

"The Lady Ari'an is a whore who opens her legs to any man passing by," the words echoed back through my head, and I gripped the table feeling my temper rise again.

He'd actually made the comment yesterday morning, to a group who merely laughed politely. He knew both myself and Dreanen were listening. How could he not since we were both in his line of sight? He must have assumed we would do nothing about it considering his reputation.

I wasn't considering his reputation when I answered, "Take that back, sir." The "sir" was an afterthought actually.

I remembered now that Dreanen's face went from outrage at the statement, to shock at my reply, and then a sly smile. Only Dreanen could have managed to smile at such a time.

"It would not be a fair fight, my lord." The "my lord" had an edge to it as he replied.

The people around him were staring. Some laughed behind their hands, but I wasn't concerned with them.

"Then if you can keep yourself from being slobberingly drunk tomorrow morning—" I started, but he interrupted me before I could finish the statement.

"You are too young to die, my lord, but if you insist upon tempting the gods, that is up to you." He had a dark look to his eyes and a dangerous tone to his voice. "I will see you on the field before the dawn breaks."

He turned and stormed off in a very dignified manner. At that moment, I began to realize who I had just challenged, the most well-known knight in the king's service. He killed three contenders in last year's tournaments. I knew that honor did not play into his tactics unless it was an infringement of his own. Then no one would scream "foul" louder. I was going to die. With a sick laugh, I'd thought, "Well, at least Ari'an will be happy."

I didn't remember much more from that day and found that I arrived at the field before Lord Astucieux the next morning. I had reconciled myself to my fate as best I could, but if I was going to die today, I would not leave this world lightly. The field was in fact the tiny courtyard of the castle, but it would do. The barrels and crates against the walls could be a problem if I got too near to them. Keep it in the open. I'd last longer.

I waited with Dreanen until the sun began to rise, wondering if I had the right place. Finally, Lord Astucieux came in with an entourage of at least fifteen men.

The group walked right past the crates where Dreanen and I were sitting by the entrance.

"It appears that the boy decided to miss our little rendezvous," I heard him say.

I felt my temper rise again as I stood. "I am afraid, sir, you are late, since our rendezvous was set for before *dawn broke."*

He turned to me with an angry flare to his eyes. "You would have been absent if you had any sense."

It took him another quarter of a watch, at least, to "prepare" for the match. I knew that it was just a show to shake my nerves, but instead I noticed a few winged shapes circling far above the field. I watched them for a moment wondering if they were birds, or why five dragons would be up there. When one of them started a barrel roll, then went into a series of loops, I knew what they were.

"Why are there dragons up there?" I asked Dreanen.

"They probably came to watch," he replied evenly. At times like these, I envied his perpetually amused personality.

I glared at him at that moment though. "Who told them?"

"Well, I did of course," he replied evenly.

"Do you often invite people to watch others die?" I snapped at him.

"You're going to kill him?" For once he sounded genuinely surprised.

"Of course I'm not going to kill him." Why he looked totally baffled was beyond me.

He didn't have a chance to reply though, since Lord Astucieux chose that moment to walk to the center of the field.

I joined him, saluted with my sword, and dodged the first sweep he made halfway through his salute.

I knew that he was stronger than I, so I needed to avoid a locked confrontation. Thankfully, Armel had shown me numerous ways to slide out of a lock. I watched Lord Astucieux's temper rise as I continued that tactic. Apparently, he wasn't accustomed to having someone avoid his assaults.

He threw innumerable insults at me, apparently hoping that I would make a mistake because of them, but I honestly was too busy staying alive to pay attention to what he said.

He locked me to the hilt of his sword. A slight twist to one side then a hard one to the other and I was out of that, but the hard swing at my head was unexpected. Duels weren't supposed to involve head blows. Thankfully, it was the broadside of the sword, or I would have found myself meeting the Mighty One.

I thought I heard Dreanen yelling something, but I really didn't care what it was. I was now slightly dazed and feeling nauseous.

Lord Astucieux yelled in fury as I parried another blow to the left and sprung out of another lock to the right. I swung around expecting a blow to my side and found the sword coming at my head again, only this time with the sharp of the blade. A leap left, and the blade sliced into my arm instead.

Reeling backward, I now had a throbbing head, sweat trying to blind me, and an almost useless left arm. I knew I needed to end this now one way or the other.

I knew a move that Armel had used to disarm me six months ago, but when I'd used it on him, I had found that he knew how to counter the move and actually disarm the attacker. I had not mastered the reply to that countermove and would certainly find myself face-to-face with the Mighty One if Lord Astucieux knew the counter, but it was the best I had.

Fake to the left, duck right under the attacking arm, close in for a sweep to the wrist with the side of my hilt to a pressure point. The sword was out of his hand. A dodge to the right and back, switch my sword to my left hand, and catch his sword. Spin, two steps, and around his back. A hard blow between the shoulder blades with his hilt, and stop the other blade just next to the neck.

Dreanen told me on the way back to the room that he would cherish the deathly pale look on Lord Astucieux for quite some time, but I couldn't see it from my position.

"Stand down," I hissed at him from behind, and he raised his hands in surrender.

I stuck his sword in the dirt behind him and turned to walk away. I saw Dreanen point and yell after a mere moment.

A swift swing around and up, and I sliced cleanly through his wrist. I didn't watch to see where the hand and sword fell. He staggered backward, and I closed in. Slamming the broadside of the blade into his knees, I felt the bone shatter through the vibration of the blade. He collapsed to the ground on his face, blood pooling around his wrist.

"Kill me," I heard him say.

"No," I told him, "I am not you."

"Kill me!" he screamed louder as he rolled onto his back.

I didn't answer, seeing his squire along with a few of his entourage running toward us, some with drawn swords. I was still going to die, lovely. I heard Dreanen come up beside me and draw his sword. Great, now our father would be completely childless.

Suddenly, they froze, and I watched the rest of the entourage bow. The chargers quickly followed suit.

"Royalty's behind us," I told Dreanen shakily.

"Yes, I would think that would be a safe assumption," he replied. Leave it to him to make a snappy remark at a time like this.

"Stand down, my lords," a voice said behind us, "I do not desire to lose more of my army today."

I was reluctant to sheathe my sword, first because I didn't trust this group, and second because there was blood on the blade, but arguing with royalty was out of the question. I took several steps back before following Dreanen's lead and putting the sword away. I turned slowly keeping an eye on the group. I bowed watching the people behind me as much as I could.

"Take him away," he said.

Oh great, now I'm a royal prisoner, I thought rising from the bow.

I heard shuffling behind me and watched the squire and a few others carry Lord Astucieux away. The royal must have been speaking about him instead of me. As they retreated, I finally focused on the man in front of me. If things could get any worse, I wasn't exactly sure how. I should have let him kill me, because it wasn't just any royal standing there. It was in fact the king of Faruq.

"I desire to speak with you when you have cleansed," he told me.

I really wanted to just fall over and never wake up after that next bow. I managed to walk off the field and turn down a hallway before slumping against the wall. Dreanen helped me the rest of the way to my rooms.

Now, to add to all that, Ari'an would still hate me for the rest of her life. I'd been doing so well too. We'd gotten to the point of being cordial and could sometimes call it friendly.

I should go see the king though. I was as cleaned up as I was going to be for a while. He wasn't even supposed to be here. I headed toward my room to change my shirt and heard the main door open.

"I'll be right there, Dreanen," I called, but there was no answer.

After changing, I walked back into the main room, almost running into Ari'an. What was she doing here?

"I brought you something for your head." I followed her gesture to the table.

"A steak?" I honestly couldn't think of anything else to say.

"T-they didn't have any ice that wasn't being used for the meal," she explained stepping away from me.

"I suppose everyone can't live next to a glacier," I said, walking toward the slab of meat.

"Are you sure they can spare this?" Ice was expensive in this area, but a cut of meat like that wouldn't exactly be cheap either.

"They can now," Ari'an sounded miffed. I hoped I hadn't upset her again.

CHAPTER 38

DISCUSSIONS WITH A KING

I knew the kitchen could have shaved a little off the bottom of one of those sculptures, but no, they couldn't damage the decorations. I demanded that steak instead and walked out with it and the plate without waiting to hear them tell me no.

I heard objections behind me, but I really didn't care. My head was reeling from everything that had just happened, and if they wouldn't give me ice from their precious sculptures, I would have something that would work nearly as well.

A knock sounded on the door, as Danren put the steak to his head. It was probably Dreanen, since he had gone to inform Pher'am about the morning's events and said he would return soon.

When I opened the door, I didn't recognize the well-dressed man standing there, or the overdressed short fellow who looked a little full of himself who was stepping away from the door. The first man had an air of authority about him, and glancing at his hands, I did recognize the king's signet ring. He wasn't supposed to be here.

I noticed that Ari'an looked surprise when she opened the door then made a low curtsy. I leaned my head in my hands for a moment. He must have thought I was ignoring his request. That would be one more thing to list against me. I rose and bowed to him as he entered, feeling my head swim a bit from the motion.

"Please, have a seat, Your Majesty," I offered more because I needed to sit down than to be courteous. Etiquette demanded that I remain standing as long as he did.

He entered, waved off whoever came with him, and sat across from me. As I returned the cut of meat to my head, I wondered what the proper procedure was for holding meat to an injury in front of royalty.

"Will you join us, lady?" he asked Ari'an, who still looked rather shocked.

"I came to offer my physician to assist you, but I perceive that Meade has taken care of your injuries," he told me, "I had not known he did such fine work."

I could picture Dreanen falling out of his chair laughing if he had been there, and I was very glad he wasn't.

"No, Your Majesty," I corrected him, "my lady did the work."

He turned to Ari'an, who took a seat at the table and seemed to be recovering from her shock. "I have underestimated the caliber of the nobility of Rem'Maren."

That was a surprising statement, but I was certain that I had received so many shocks today that nothing else would surprise me. I was wrong.

"I understand," he continued to speak to Ari'an, "that you commandeered my dinner for the treatment."

I instantly pulled the steak from my head, looked at it in shock for a moment, then stared at Ari'an, horrified.

"I-I-I did not know that it was for you, Your Majesty," she explained. "They would not give me any of the ice." This was too much. "They acted as though the decorations were more important than the meal, so I took the steak."

"Do you often take such things to treat injuries?" he continued. Was that a twinkle in his eye?

"No, Your Majesty," she answered and, to my surprise, meeting his gaze. "At Caer Corisan, the injured are *given* ice when they need it."

She was pale, and I noticed her hands shaking on her lap. I wanted to do something to take the pressure off her, but with as much trouble as I was in, I couldn't exactly spill water on his lap.

"Tell me, my lady," he continued, "about how many injuries have happened from the border incidents in the last three months?"

I saw the color return to her face as she answered, "Two hundred thirty-six."

"Exactly?" He seemed surprised at the prompt answer.

"There will be more now, but when I left, that was the number since first harvest, Your Majesty." She moved her gaze from his to stare across the table.

"You keep the tally?" he recovered quickly.

"No, Your Majesty, Armel keeps the records." I could remember too many of those injuries, and I didn't want to at that moment.

He turned back to Danren, and I rose to my feet. "If you will excuse me, Majesty, I would like to prepare for dinner."

He nodded that I could go, and I walked as steadily as I could to my room and closed the door behind me. My knees gave out beneath me, and I slid to the floor leaning against the door. I didn't like these memories. I had watched Flamur bleed to death. I had sawn off Pepim's arm to stop the infection from spreading. I had sewn Bikendi's wing back together in five spots. These were memories I fought as hard as I fought any from my years at the temple.

"I intended to meet with your house to discuss the border situation, while I was here," the king told me as Ari'an disappeared. I hoped she would be all right. "Now, that I am here, I find that your father has not come yet, and you are severing the hands off my best knights."

"I did challenge Lord Astucieux, Your Highness," I tried to explain. "He had surrendered and then attacked me."

"I saw what happened, lord," he replied.

I wasn't sure if that was a good thing, depending on what he'd seen and what he decided to recall. I looked back down at the steak in my hand and said nothing.

"The only way to defeat Lord Astucieux was to do what you did. It is why no one has before," he continued. "Lord Astucieux does not surrender. He also does not show mercy."

There was silence for a moment, and I realized he was waiting for a reply. "Yes, I know, Your Highness."

"Yet you challenged him anyway. Had your places been reversed, he would have killed you. Were you so certain you would win?" he asked.

I choked back the sarcastic laugh that wanted to escape and coughed for a moment instead.

"No, Your Majesty," I finally managed, "he insulted my wife."

"Your wife does not have the most spotless of pasts," he told me evenly.

My temper got the best of me. "I, more than most, know quite well what my wife's past does and does not include." I looked up and realized that I had just snapped at the ruling monarch. "Your Majesty," I added in a calmer tone.

To my surprise he leaned back in his chair and smiled. "Are all the lords of Rem'Maren like you?"

I wasn't certain if he was making fun of me or not, but I knew I had disgraced myself well enough today. "No, Your Highness, Lord Drenar could stay calm in any situation, and Lord Dreanen is much more easygoing."

"I have not heard such things of the lords of Rem'Maren," he said thoughtfully.

I thought about what he might have heard and threw caution to the wind. I had already dug my grave anyway, I might as well start filling it in. "I heard someone tell Lady Ari'an not four days ago that a dragon had tried to eat my wife, only managed to bite off her hand, and scorched her out of spite. Now, tell me, Your Highness, what have you heard of the lords of Rem'Maren?"

He laughed. I felt my jaw drop, and quickly forced it closed.

"That one is new to me, lord," he replied, "but I have heard enough things as far from reality as that often enough. Tell me, lord," he continued, "how did your wife come to be in Verd?"

I was startled by the question and glanced at Ari'an's door to ensure it was still closed. "She was taken," I told him returning his gaze.

"She did not run away?" he asked evenly.

I caught myself before scoffing at such a thought. "No, Your Highness, she did not run away."

"How was she taken?"

"She was separated from the riding party during a land tour," I kept my voice as low as I could manage and be sure he heard me. I didn't want Ari'an to know what we were discussing. She had suffered enough from it.

"How was she separated?"

"She had stopped to look at a booth selling dyed kittens and took a wrong turn trying to catch up."

"Certainly, someone in Verd recognized her as Faruq nobility. She is marked as all nobility are, is she not?"

That time I did scoff. "From what I understand, it was a selling point: 'Come spend the night with a lady of Faruq.'"

"Did no one believe her when she told them who she was?"

I thought about how to word that reply. "If you watch Lady Ari'an in a group, you will find that she will say very little. Those of the House of Nori'en are notorious for speaking their minds. As a child, she was forbidden from saying anything to guests at meals because she once questioned the length of Lord Perparim's nose. She learned silence quickly in Verd, as any would, if a word sent a spike through their tongues."

"She could not escape?"

"When my father found her, Your Highness, they shackled her to a bed in a room three stories above the ground because there was a window in the wall."

"You do not consider this a one-time mistake? Verd is a valuable trade partner."

I was holding my temper as best I could considering. "They sell us stone, and we sell them our children. The transaction is not equal."

"You would favor a war with Verd then?"

I set my elbows on the table and leaned forward. "I fight a war with Verd, Your Highness. It just is not called that."

He leaned back in his chair again, deep in thought. After a moment, he asked, "Would you consider a position at court? I would prefer an adviser who speaks his mind as you do."

I was taken back by the offer. I had been waiting every moment for him to call in guards to haul me away, and now, I could join his court? No one in Rem'Maren had ever been made such an offer. Then again, we couldn't exactly accept it.

"No, I am afraid not, Your Majesty," I told him, and he looked quite taken aback by the answer. One did not refuse royalty.

"What are your reasons, lord?" he asked.

I glanced at Ari'an's closed door. "Lady Ari'an is married to me and was not married to Lord Drenar for one primary reason, Your Majesty." Looking back at him, I continued, "Lord Drenar was a public figure. He was required to travel often and without much notice. His wife would have had the same requirements, and Lady Ari'an should not be forced into a public role like that." I looked back at the door again. "She should be allowed to live out the rest of her life in as much peace as possible, but with the current border situation, even that is denied her."

The king studied me for a moment. "You have more love for your wife than most, and I see why you were so quick to challenge Lord Astucieux," he finally replied.

Love? I had never thought of it like that. "Love is a choice, Your Majesty," I told him as he rose.

I followed him to the door to see him out.

"If it does not offend you, Your Majesty, I may need to miss the dinner this evening." The room had begun to spin slightly when I stood up, and I wanted to rest for a very long time.

"Take whatever time you require, Lord Danren," he replied.

I bowed and watched a short pompously dressed man meet him outside my door. Staggering back into the room, I sat on the couch. I slowly lay back, since the room still turned in odd directions, and I didn't want to fall off the couch. I tried to comprehend what had just happened and failed miserably. The nagging question was: why was he even here?

I realized as I sat against the door that Danren knew much more than I ever imagined possible. How did he know? I was shaken by this new revelation long after I heard the king leave. I heard Danren walk through the room, but didn't hear his door shut behind him.

A few moments later, or was it a whole watch, I heard a knock on the outside door. Danren asked who it was in a muffled tone.

I didn't catch the answer, but Danren's reply was much louder. "Get in here, now!"

"Where have you been?" I snapped at Dreanen as he came in.

"Oh, around." He grabbed an apple out of the fruit bowl and began rolling it across his hands occasionally dropping it. "Apparently, His Majesty made a special trip here to meet us."

"Us?" I asked, wondering who that encompassed.

Through a bite of apple, he replied, "The lords of the House of Rem'Maren."

I sat up suddenly at that news and felt my head spin.

"Lie down." He glanced around and then walked toward the table. "Ah, this must be the king's dinner that the servants are in an uproar about."

He held it out to me when he came back, and I stared at it in complete horror. "I can't use that!"

"Whyever not?" Why did he sound so surprised?

"As you said, it's the king's dinner." I glared at him.

"I don't think he wants it now." Why did that statement make me feel worse?

I took the steak and held it to my head.

"You have quite a wife," he told me.

I snorted lightly. "Yes, few people would steal a royal meal."

"Now, I'm sure she didn't know what it was being used for, and from what I gather, the servants were rather uncooperative," he replied lightly as he moved a chair over.

"How do you know all this?" Dreanen was, oddly enough, a good source of information.

"People talk to me for some reason."

There was a moment's silence then. "Ari doesn't seem to like you very much."

"What does that have to do with anything?" I really didn't want to talk about how much Ari'an didn't like me.

"She's never told me why." He was digging for something.

"Of course not," I snapped, "you're rarely around."

"You haven't hurt her, have you?"

"What?" I sat up so fast that the room decided to make a circle before settling into its proper place. "I've never touched her." I held the steak to my head hoping that would help what felt like horses trotting around my skull.

"Never?"

I felt my temper rise, and I glared at him. "What are you getting at?"

"You've been married two years now." He had a keen look in his eyes.

"You're insinuating that I've been less than honorable with her." I heard my teeth grind and felt the sharp pain run along my head.

"Have you?"

"No! Sex is a gift, Dreanen," I growled at him, "not something to be stolen or bartered with! It's not something that should be bought or sold. You know that."

"Yes"—he rose—"but I wanted to make sure you did." He took another bite of apple and actually chewed and swallowed before continuing, "I also wanted to make sure of your motives with that run-in with Lord Astucieux today."

If I hadn't felt so dizzy, I would have chased after him. He had no business prying into such matters.

As he left, a servant entered, presenting me with a royal invitation for Ari'an. I told him to leave it on the table, and we'd deal with it. Not exactly the response he'd expected, but I really didn't care anymore.

Eventually, I pulled myself to my feet and changed into a dress that wasn't bloodstained. I slowly opened the door and found Danren sleeping on the couch. I hoped I hadn't been mistaken about the concussion. I let him sleep and hurried back to the kitchens to make another demand, that his meal be delivered to our rooms.

I found Dreanen as I came back from the kitchens. We chatted a bit about the king. Dreanen mentioned that he looked older than he was, probably because of all the responsibility he inherited ten years ago. I remembered celebrating the coronation, but I hadn't actually been there. The king was only a few years younger than Drenar, but had the worry lines of a sixty-year-old at times. He had his mother's brown hair and eyes, but his father's broad-shouldered stature.

Dreanen left me at my rooms, and I found Danren still sleeping on the couch. A note with the royal seal lay on the table. Opening it as quietly as I could, I found that the king wanted to escort me to dinner. I had hoped to skip the meal, but turning down such an invitation was unheard-of.

I found a servant wandering the halls, and commissioned him with the task of finding paper, quill, and ink. When he returned, I found Danren's seal and quickly wrote my reply. As the servant left, I realized that I couldn't wear this with His Majesty as an escort. I rummaged through my closet for that elaborate dress Faber insisted on sending. I prayed a blessing to him for his foresight as I changed.

There was quite a bit of whispering at dinner, probably about me. I could only imagine what story Lady Yente would come up with to explain why I was escorted by the king. At every table, the story of the duel was elaborated as His Majesty spoke to me throughout the evening. I gave as short and quick of answers as I could, since I was uncomfortable being the center of attention.

The king walked me back to the rooms after the meal. "Would you, lady, be willing to speak to the court about your experiences in Verd when spring comes?"

The dinner questions had all been light conversation. This question stopped me in my tracks. I completely forgot who I was talking to.

"Why?" I asked.

I certainly did not want to talk to anyone about those years, much less the court.

"What currently delays the declaration of war on Verd is that we have no firsthand evidence, lady," he explained. "What we have currently is a trail of tales but no actual accounts."

I didn't really want a war. What I wanted was to forget, but I knew that people disappeared across the border of Verd every day. They weren't nobility, and no elaborate search was made for them. They would just disappear, with only tales told of how it happened.

"If I am able, Your Majesty, I will come to testify," I finally answered.

I entered the dimly lit room to find Danren rummaging through my medical bag. He looked up, holding a bottle in his hand.

"What are you doing?" I asked trying to comprehend the situation.

"I was looking for some Valerian," he told me sounding rather sheepish.

"Were you trying to go back to sleep?" I asked, wondering why he was looking for that.

He looked down at the bag. "No, actually I hoped to do some work, but my head won't stop pounding."

"You wanted Valerian for that?" That didn't make any sense.

"It helps pain, right?" he asked, eying the bottle in his hand skeptically.

"Of sorts, but it mostly helps with sleep." I took a few steps toward him and glanced over the bottles he had on the table.

"Oh," he sat down, looking confused.

I was concerned about his head. "How many fingers am I holding up?"

Why couldn't someone come up with a more creative question than that? I absolutely hated that question.

"Well, that depends on which side of the world you're on."

Ari'an looked taken back by that reply, but recovered quickly. "On this side of the world, if you please, precisely in this room, at this moment, if you would."

It was a quick comeback, and I was impressed. "Well, I can't see your other hand, so I can't tell if you're holding up fingers on that hand and attempting to trick me."

"Are you trying to be difficult, or do you not see my hand clearly?" she replied, sounding slightly ruffled.

"Galen accuses me of trying to be difficult," I replied.

She looked puzzled for a moment, but then asked, "If you were selling fruit to me, and I held up this many fingers to tell you how many pieces of fruit I wanted, how many would I be asking for?"

That was, by far, a more entertaining way of asking, "Two."

"Thank you," she said glancing over the bottles on the table. "How long did you want to stay up?"

"No more than five watches," I replied as she picked up a bottle and pulled a spoon and a measuring cup out of the bag.

She deftly measured some liquid from the bottle into the cup, then went to the stand, poured a glass of water, and stirred the liquid in.

"Here," she said setting a sickly-green-looking concoction in front of me.

"Oh, that looks appetizing," I said eying it warily.

"Wait until you taste it," she said as she cut an orange into sections.

"That's comforting," I replied swishing the liquid around.

"Just drink it." She sounded exasperated as she moved the bottles back into the bag.

I made a face and downed the drink as quickly as possible.

"What did you do with the steak?" she asked.

I stared at her blankly for a moment and then managed, "I'm not certain. Maybe someone came and took it away," I told her between bites of orange. That stuff was nasty!

"I hope they don't serve it to someone," she said, closing the bag back.

"Majorlaine might, but they just seem to throw things away here." I had finally managed to get that taste out of my mouth.

I saw her smile slightly then a concerned look returned to her face. "King Viskhard would like for me to speak to his court in the spring."

I had been dreading such a thing. "He asked you?"

She nodded.

We couldn't exactly refuse him something like that. "Did he tell you when?" Other than spring. I hoped we would have more notice than this funeral.

She shook her head. "No," she whispered.

I noticed she was holding her arms across her stomach to keep them from shaking. "Are you all right?" I asked.

"I-it's been a rough day," she whispered, "and I wish Narden was here."

I tried not to show the sting I felt at that statement. "Why don't you sit down, and I'll get you a glass of water."

Before I could object, he rose and walked to the stand. I pulled the chair out and sat. I cringed again at the thought of how mean I had been to him, and how many nasty things I'd thought about him. He set the glass down in front of me and returned to his chair.

"Are you tired?" he asked.

It was barely evening, and there was still to be a dance tonight. Thankfully, the king hadn't asked to escort me to that. Perhaps he'd heard that I hadn't been to any of the dances yet.

"Not exactly, it's just too many people had wanted to speak with me tonight just because the king was my escort."

I glanced up worried that he'd think that was a silly complaint, but he looked concerned.

"None of them even noticed me before." I glanced back at my hands holding the glass. "I know it's supposed to be an honor to sit with the king, but I would have preferred sitting where I had before."

"Has Lady Yente started telling interesting stories again?" he asked.

I laughed at the memory. "No, actually, they talk about the weather and the food mostly, occasionally about a new fashion, but they avoid talking about specific people now."

She laughed. I had believed she would never even smile in my presence again, and here she laughed.

"Sir," she said after a moment, a concerned tone to her voice, "how did you know?"

"Know what?" I glanced up at her, slightly confused.

"W-when you were talking to His Majesty earlier." She paused to ring her hands.

"You weren't supposed to be listening to that." The words flew out before I could stop them. I did have a policy of letting her have as much blissful ignorance as possible. She knew too much about things she never should have been involved with anyway.

"The walls have ears," she whispered.

I didn't really want to tell her. "Do you honestly want to know?"

She seemed to think about that for a moment then nodded ever so slightly.

"You told Narden," Danren told me.

For a moment I couldn't breathe. Of course Narden had told him.

"Narden trusts you," I finally whispered.

He didn't reply to that. He merely sat there watching his fingers. Finally, he said, "I'm sorry," rose, and walked into his room.

I was alone.

I looked around the room, over the papers piled on the desk, over the half-eaten meal on the table, and finally to the steak that lay half against the arm of the couch and half under a cushion. That steak made me laugh. The whole day had been somewhat absurd, and a steak stuffed into a couch seemed to describe it perfectly. I went over and pulled the thing out and plopped it back on the plate that lay on the floor nearby.

I flagged a servant in the hallway a moment later, handed her the plate, and asked her to dispose of it. She seemed startled for only a moment.

Regaining her composure, she bobbed a curtsy. "Yes, my lady."

CHAPTER 39

ON THE WAY HOME

Two days later the planners of the gala decided to have a "social lunch," which really meant that the drunken brawl between Lord Arkaitz and Lord Garaile the day before had damaged too many of the tables, and they couldn't be repaired in time.

The meal was eaten standing while being "social" with people you didn't know. That wasn't what happened of course. Everyone congealed in their normal groups and only politely greeted each other as they passed.

I watched Ari'an as she made her way—some would say politely, I knew she didn't want to be jostled by the crowds—to the food tables. We hadn't spoken much other than occasional greetings in passing over the past couple of days.

I saw the ambassador from Itzal begin to walk toward the table as well. Itzal was a providence in Verd, and what the man was doing at what was supposed to be my brother's funeral was a mystery I didn't like. I had seen him once or twice, but never near Ari'an before.

I set down my glass on a counter, making my way toward the food table as well. A servant stopped me to hand me a sealed message. The seal was from Caer Corisan. I quickly opened the letter and skimmed it. Mael had been injured looking for Hramn and Bikendi, whose bodies were found near the pass. The letter requested "that we return as soon as we were able," a veiled way of saying get there immediately, if not sooner.

I looked up to see that the ambassador had Ari'an's arm. She was staring at him completely terrified.

I felt someone brush my elbow, so I moved to the side to let them pass.

"My lady," I heard a voice say. The sound made my skin crawl, but he wouldn't be talking to me. After the king left yesterday, everyone had forgotten me again.

"My lady," the voice came again slightly louder this time, and a hand rested on my arm, "may I speak with you."

The voice had an accent I didn't like, and the touch made me want to vomit. I looked up at the speaker and saw the last man I had ever expected to see again.

He bound my hands to the corners of the bed . . . He held my head still so the first priest could ram in the bridle . . . He led in the breeders . . . It was the second priest.

"Let me go," I whispered. I wasn't supposed to speak, but I wasn't in Verd.

"I wish to speak with you," he said with a quaver to his voice.

"Let—" I began again, but I was cut off.

"Let her go." The voice was low, almost a growl next to him; and instantly, he released my arm.

I forced myself to look away from him, and to my complete surprise, I found Danren standing partially behind him. He was whispering something in the priest's ear, but I didn't stay to find out what it was.

"I should kill you," I told him with my dagger point in his back, I turned the blade slightly, debating it. I had seen Ari'an terrified before, but this time there had been added to the terror a tone of utter despair, complete hopelessness.

"I'll let you live, this time, but if I ever find that you so much as thought about coming near her again, your life is mine." I pushed him away and hurried in the direction that Ari'an had gone.

I wondered how I would find her, but when I turned the corner, I nearly ran over her. She was leaning against the wall, her head in her hands and shaking terribly.

"Ari, can you hear me?" I needed to find out if she was still aware of anything.

She nodded in her hands.

"Where are you?" I continued, wondering if any of the nearby rooms would possibly have a fur or at least soft blanket or throw.

"Calanthe of Almudina," she whispered, "but I want to be home."

"We can be there in two days, three at most," I told her.

She snapped her head up and stared at me. "What?"

I waved the note that was still in my hand. "We have to leave. There are problems at Caer Corisan, so we might as well go now."

I looked down at my hands.

"Do you need to pack anything, or would you like to leave now?" he asked.

"Now?" I didn't believe that was an option.

"I'll get a carriage from the stables or at least a couple of horses," he told me. "I know Hafiz and Einheim are nearby, possibly Zait as well. We can flag them once we're a league away." He looked down the hall and then turned back to me. "Would you like to wait in the rooms?"

I nodded. Apparently, he had taken my question as my answer. I looked back toward the dining room. The farther I could get from that man, the better.

It took longer than I wanted to get the horses from the stable. The stable hands made some excuse about the carriage needing repairs, so I demanded they saddle the horses instead.

I didn't like the idea of leaving without an escort, but the captain of the guard gave me some line about not being able to spare anyone. After quite a discussion, I managed to haggle him out of three men to get us to Bora, "but no further," he insisted.

Back at the stable, I found Dreanen in an argument of his own with the stable hands. His argument was far less heated than mine had been, but he had the unique ability to leave the other side turned in circles and agreeing with him when he was finished. Usually, it was entertaining to watch, but currently, I was in far too much of a hurry.

"I need five horses ready within the watch," I told the stable hand.

"Make that six," Dreanen told him, and followed me out. "I'm going with you," he told me as we walked across the yard avoiding the milling groups of people. "There was a raid near Shpresa"—he waved a letter similar to mine—"and I need to get back."

"Is Pher'am coming?" I asked, wondering if we needed another horse.

"No," he answered, "she's staying here to cover my escape." He chuckled slightly. "She's actually quite good at such things."

I looked sharply at him. "Does she know?"

"Of course not," he replied evenly, "I'm under the same oaths you are, but she is a fantastic diplomat." He added softly, "That will come in handy considering my new line of work as the eldest."

He walked with me until his rooms, excused himself to pack a few things, and said he would see us in the stables.

I walked into my rooms to find Ari'an setting down a couple of small bags. She'd changed into a warm riding outfit with a thick cloak.

"I need to change," I told her and ducked into my room.

I sat down in one of the chairs to wait. Most of our things could be sent back to us, but the motion of packing had kept me from thinking, but waiting was hard. I rearranged the fruit in the basket on the table, picked out some to take with us, and bit my nails.

It felt as though Danren took an eternity to pack such few things. Soon, I was following him to the stables though.

"Dreanen is coming with us to the pass," he told me as we walked. That was a bit of a relief. It would be nice to travel with a friend.

"Will there be enough dragons?" I asked remembering that he had only mentioned Hafiz and Einheim.

He stopped for a moment and then looked at me. "I can ride with Dreanen if Zait isn't nearby."

I wasn't certain what to think of that. I hadn't expected Dreanen to be tagging along, and I actually didn't have a second thought about traveling alone with Danren this time. I had been trying not to think about anything. My mind was constantly returning to the temple.

As we continued across the open courtyard to the stable, I noticed Danren pull his knife out and seemed to examine it. It caught the light a few times. Then he put it back away.

"Is something wrong?" I asked as he turned a corner to avoid a group of merrymakers.

"No," he told me, "I would just prefer as few people notice we're leaving as possible."

"No, I mean with your knife," I asked.

He stopped suddenly and glanced around. "No one ever showed you that?" he asked, turning back to me and pulling the knife back out.

"Showed me what?" I asked watching the knife.

"I'll take that as a no." He turned the knife over in his hand. "What I did was signal that we needed transport and how many we needed," he told me. "Do you have a knife?" he asked.

I shook my head, and he unfastened the small sheath from his belt.

Handing the knife to me, he added, "You probably won't need this yet." He held out the sheathed knife to me. "I can show you some of the messages after we're back at Caer Corisan."

She didn't take the knife. Of course she wouldn't take anything from me. I would feel better if she had it, but it could wait.

"Armel can get you a nice one back at Caer Corisan," I said. "He may even want to make you one." I began to put the knife back.

"I don't have a belt," she explained.

"Didn't Faber make you pockets?" The reply was out before I realized that I didn't want to corner her.

She blushed. "Yes, I'm just not thinking straight right now."

She paled a little as she pulled a couple of apples from one of the pockets. Why was she carrying fruit like that? She held the pieces out to me, and I noticed her hand quiver a little.

"You don't have to do this," I told her, "I understand."

I glanced up at him. *"You never gave him a chance,"* I heard *Narden tell me again.*

"I know," I whispered as I continued to hold out the fruit. "Will you put this in that bag." I motioned toward the one closest to the wall.

He didn't move for a moment, then set the bags down. Taking the apples from me carefully, he never touched my hand. He unfastened the knife again and held it out to me. I wondered what he would do if I touched his hand while taking the knife. I could picture him grabbing my wrist and laughing like someone at the temple might have, but the picture didn't seem right.

He opened the bag I'd indicated. He looked surprised for a moment, but then composed his expression. What had I packed in there besides food? I couldn't think of anything.

"What is it?" I asked, hoping I hadn't had him open my clothes bag.

"Nothing," he told me putting the apples inside.

I hurried to the bag and looked inside.

As I took it from him, he said lightly, "Next time, you may want to empty the cup before packing it."

"I thought we'd need water." The contents of the bag were wet from the tipped glass, and a pool had developed in the bottom. I began pulling the contents from the bag and dumped the water out on the floor.

"I hadn't thought to pack food, so you're ahead of me," he said.

I glanced up at him and realized that he wasn't making sport of me. I laughed and then began to cry. It was just too much.

Oh no! I hadn't meant to send her into a fit.

"Did you pack a blanket?" I couldn't think of anything else to say.

She shook her head, so I pulled the cloak off that I was wearing. It wasn't fur, but it was at least soft. Dropping it over her shoulders, I knelt in front of her.

"Ari, I need you to stay with me," I told her.

"I know," she whispered. She gripped the extra cloak in one of her hands and looked at it. "I'll be all right in a moment," she said as I fumbled through my pockets for a handkerchief. After I set it on the bag in front of her, she reached for it and half laughed and half sobbed. "I'm just having a bad day."

"I know," I told her, "we'll be back at Caer Corisan soon, and it will all be over."

She smiled and wiped her eyes. "Why?" I heard her whisper.

I glanced around wondering what exactly she meant by the question. "Why Caer Corisan?" I asked, and then answered, "because it's the safest place I know of for you."

I looked back at her and found her watching me with a studying look. I glanced around again in surprise.

"No," I whispered, looking back at my hands as they rung the handkerchief, "w-why are you being so nice?"

It didn't make sense. I'd rarely treated him with anything but disrespect or disdain, and I was beginning to see that he had never reciprocated.

"Why shouldn't I be?" he asked sounding puzzled.

I fought the answer out, "because of me," I finally managed.

"What?" He sounded quite lost.

"And because you have a temper," I finished.

"Yes," he said, sounding slightly amused, "and you have hands. Would you like to tell me something I don't know?"

"W-what?" I managed to laugh a little.

"Are you two coming, or should I leave without you?" I heard Dreanen call from down the hall.

Danren jumped to his feet. "We're coming. There was just a problem with the proper storage of beverages." He looked back at me as I returned to my feet as well. "Are you all right?"

I wanted to start crying again, but managed to hand him back his cloak and nod instead. Why did he have to sound so concerned?

CHAPTER 40

SECRETS

We rode steadily, arriving at Bora by midday. After dismissing the guards, who seemed less than pleased to have ridden that far that quickly, we waited. We sent the guards with payment for the horses, since they wouldn't be returned. I didn't like paying for something that I wouldn't keep, but haste demanded it.

I hadn't seen either Hafiz or Einheim signal that they could find a place to land yet. After a conference with Dreanen, we decided to head into the countryside. Bora was far too populated to meet up with the dragons near the town. I had qualms about leaving without an escort, but we were still in Almudina.

About two watches later, I saw Hafiz signal that they could land, and we followed them several leagues into some grazing lands. They were carrying saddles, which we soon had on their backs. I relaxed considerably once we were airborne. Dreanen rode behind me on Hafiz while Ari rode on Einheim. We no longer had to follow the main roads or even any of the paths. We could be at Caer Corisan by midday in two days, since both dragons agreed to fly through the nights.

It was a silent trip, mostly because of the necessity of haste. Danren and Dreanen occasionally discussed something or another, but I stayed out of the conversations. I was far from an expert at riding a horse, but I did remember the basics from my childhood. I watched Danren or Dreanen signal a few times, but couldn't understand the message.

Once we were airborne, exhaustion took over. Strapping one of my arms to the saddle, I laid my head in the other one and dozed through the night.

A whistling sound woke me from a sound sleep. Hafiz shouted next to me, and then a horrified yell followed. My stomach raced up my throat as Einheim began to plummet. Einheim's left wing was sliced clean through, with what, I couldn't tell, but he was trying his best to check his fall with his good wing and what was left of the other.

I was going to die. No one was going to recognize even the tiniest fragment of my body after this fall. Einheim might be able to survive, but I was going to die. The terror of the realization froze me.

Suddenly, Einheim's plummet stopped, and we lunged upward. My stomach, which had been firmly lodged in my throat, plunged to my feet, giving me the distinct feeling that I should hurl. I felt a hand grab my free arm and a cold blade slice near the other. I glanced up and found that Dreanen had my free arm while Danren held a sword. He yelled for me to give him my other hand. I managed to pull it loose from the sliced moorings, and felt him grab my wrist.

Another whistling sound, and Dreanen lost his grip. Einheim continued to plummet, occasionally able to catch the wind to check himself. I hoped he would survive the fall. Far below, I made out a band of ten men and a ballista in a clearing and much too much open air in between.

I smashed into Hafiz's side and felt the wind crushed out of my lungs. Blood splattered my face as Hafiz began to spiral.

"Aim for the lake!" I heard Danren yell.

Hafiz continued toward the ground, more controlled than Einheim's fall, but I could feel his labored breathing next to my face. Dreanen regained my other hand, and the two pulled me part of the way up. I still couldn't breathe.

"Hold your breath!" I heard Danren yell, but I shook my head frantically.

I had no breath to hold.

A hand clamped over my mouth and nose. I wanted to scream, but I didn't have the air to. Suddenly, frigid water shocked my body. Trying to gasp, I found the hand pressed too hard against my face to allow it. For a moment, we continued to plunge downward, then another arm wrapped around my waist and pulled me forward as I felt the stirrups kicked loose. My head broke the surface, and the hand over my mouth released. I gasped for air, only to have a shattering pain shoot through my chest. A sword hilt pressing into my stomach didn't help me breathe either. Danren dragged me through the water and onto the shore. A pool of blood rose from the middle of the lake, as the sound of men crashing through the forest undergrowth emanated behind me.

I struggled to pull myself to a sitting position and turned my head to find Danren stumbling to his feet, bringing his sword to a defensive position. A splashing sloshing sound to my left produced Dreanen, who pulled his sword from its sheath and stood next to Danren. Five men crashed into the clear area by the lake. The two defenders would never win. First, they weighed at least fifty pounds more than usual with the soaked clothes, and secondly, Danren was still recovering from the injuries from Lord Astucieux.

I glanced toward the lake, hoping that Hafiz might reappear. Swords clashed behind me, and I heard a demand for surrender in Verdian. The lake showed no signs of giving up its prize. The blood had ceased rising to the surface. What was left now rippled toward the shore.

As my lungs began to accept air again, I heard a body fall. Expecting to see Danren or Dreanen lying dead or fatally wounded in front of me, I was shocked to find one of the attackers staring up at me from dead eyes. I stumbled to my feet as another body fell to the ground.

That attacker wasn't quite dead and rolled toward me reaching for my ankle. I stepped back to avoid the grip. A gurgling sound came from his throat, he choked on his own blood and lay still.

Two dead. Two others were stumbling away, holding wounds that gushed from their sides. The last ran into the forest, fleeing for his life yelling something about men possessed by the demons of dragons.

Perhaps they could win, I thought, until I heard the others breaking through the forest underbrush.

There had been others. I'd seen them. The sounds of the fight must have drawn their attention. The forerunners should have been able to kill the dragon and subdue the passengers, but they obviously hadn't succeeded. The rest were on their way. Had they killed Einheim already, or was he so close to dead that they could leave him unattended? We couldn't win now. I felt my knees give way underneath me, and I sank to the ground. It was hopeless.

I glanced behind when Ari collapsed, believing that the oncoming group had shot her with an arrow. Her face was pale, but I saw no sign of blood.

A searing pain shot through my right arm, forcing me to drop my sword. I should not have let my guard down. My legs flew from underneath me, and I fell face-first into the dirt. My right arm failed to take the weight of my fall and collapsed beneath me.

With brutal efficiency, my arms were wrenched behind me and tied, cutting into the wrists. I heard Dreanen fall beside me and heard the sounds of his arms being tied. We were pulled to our knees and turned to face the water as a ruthless figure walked in front of us toward Ari'an.

"What do we have here?" he sneered pulling Ari'an's head up. "A nickin traveling with a dragon?"

He wrenched her head around, pulling her to her feet. She didn't make a sound, but pain crossed her face.

"Let her go," I growled at the man, but he paid no attention.

In fact, all the captors were focused on her.

"Turn," I told Dreanen in el'brenika.

The man pulled the hair up from Ari'an's neck and released his hold on her face before she had fully gained her feet. She slipped and fell, a handful of hair coming out in the man's grasp.

She whimpered in pain, and the man slammed the back of his hand across her face, turning her sideways with the force of the blow. With another swift move, he ripped the sleeve from the right side of her dress, exposing the brand from the temple on her upper arm.

"We just became as rich as kings." He laughed. "This is the one with a price on her head. Kakios will pay pretty for her."

He took two steps back, laughing, putting him at just the right angle to keep me from hitting Ari.

I looked at the boots of the man. An odd sound was coming from behind him. Almost the sound of a gentle wind creaking through the trees. I glanced up. What I saw behind him made me think that I had finally gone insane. My mind was making up what I wanted to believe.

Dreanen gave a nonchalant shrug, like I had seen him do so often, and then he seemed to concentrate on something. Danren's face had a deep burning anger about it, focused on the man who had held me. It was changing from the tanned skin tone to a blue. For a moment I thought that he must be suffocating, but I vaguely remembered that it was impossible to strangle yourself by holding your breath.

Dreanen's hands snapped free from their bonds and came around in front of him. They were at least three times the size they were supposed to be, a golden color to his elbows, and scaly. A blue color spread over his clothes from his elbows and knees. I glanced back at Danren to find that he was still glaring at the leader, but his face was no longer his own. The same blue color was spreading over his clothes, but the blue was flecked with gold. His arms came around in front of him as his bounds broke as well. He supported himself on his left, because of the injury to his right. Could it even be called an arm anymore? I closed my eyes, trying to force my mind to stop making things up.

"See how she cowers? See the fear?" the leader sneered. "No noble born would cower like that. She's a fraud."

It was impossible. I'd gone insane, that was the only explanation. It might be better in Verd if I was insane though.

I heard the roar of fire, a man's scream, and then a dead thump in front of me.

I torched the man as soon as I could. He would not touch her again. The other six turned around suddenly and stared in horror. I swung around, smashing two with my tail, feeling their ribs then their spines shatter beneath the blow. I lost my footing with the move and lurched to the right barely managing to keep upright. Pain shot through my leg.

I heard Adenern torch another one and saw the man race toward the water only to be thrown into another of the attackers by Adenern's tail. Now, they both burned. Adenern slammed another into a tree with his front leg and took off after the last retreating figure.

"Get on," I told Ari, finally looking at her.

She looked around as if completely dazed. I couldn't exactly blame her, but time wasn't on our side.

"Ari," I told her as she turned her head to look at me. I couldn't meet her gaze. "It'll be explained when we get to Caer Corisan, just, please, get on."

She pulled herself slowly to her feet and began to walk toward me as if expecting to fall or trip at any moment.

I heard a man's scream from the forest, and I turned to yell an order at Adenern, "Find Einheim and get him back to the fortress."

"What about Hafiz?" he called from the trees.

"Yes, find him too," I called back.

I felt a hand on my side and moved my right front leg to help her mount. She didn't weigh much, but even that pressure on my hurt limb made me gasp. Once she was situated, I took off. I knew I'd have to be extra careful since she wasn't in a saddle, but I also knew that she'd ridden bareback on dragons before. I climbed as high in the air as I dared. Height would be an ally in this situation, since the higher a dragon flew, the less likely we were to be noticed, but I couldn't risk having Ari pass out from the thin air.

I noticed that the ropes had cut deeply into my wrists before they broke, and there was blood running from the wounds over my claws. Another stream ran down my right front leg where I had ripped open the stitches during the fight. The cool morning air numbed the pain, and I focused on getting to Caer Corisan as quickly as possible.

I couldn't convince my thoughts to work in any resemblance of a pattern. Continuously, my mind replayed what I had just seen. It was impossible. Those were stories told to scare children. My mind must have invented the scene to make me believe I wasn't on my way back to Verd. I kept trying to convince my mind to go back to what was really happening, but I couldn't. I shouldn't be on a dragon's back heading to Caer Corisan. Narden shouldn't be here. I should be in a dragon hunters' camp or in a wagon heading to Verd. The biting wind felt so cold against my soaked clothes that I almost believed that I really was on a dragon.

Even more absurd than all those thoughts was the idea that I had seen Danren actually change into Narden, and Dreanen had changed into Adenern. Adenern wasn't here now, probably because there was only so much that my mind could make up at one time and still manage some measure of believability. Not that any of this was believable, but my mind was doing an absolutely fantastic job of making it appear so.

I considered letting my mind fall into this imagined world, actually believing this was real. It would be so much easier to be insane and believe in this world than to exist in the real temple. I didn't want to be insane though. That was the only thought that kept me fighting to see what was actually going on. Try as I might, I couldn't. Eventually, the cold seeped into me too deeply. All I thought about was balancing with numb fingers and legs on a dragon that I knew didn't really exist.

Ari didn't say anything during the flight. I didn't blame her. It was a lot to take in. I hadn't spoken to anyone for two days when I'd found out, and I had still been a child then. I wondered what was going through her mind. She'd probably never speak to me again in any form. I eventually became so exhausted from flying at top speed that, had she said anything, I wouldn't have been able to answer anyway.

Late afternoon finally brought the dim outline of Caer Corisan against the distant horizon, or at least Mount Salma, which was in fact Caer Corisan as well. I wanted to fly faster to reach it, but I couldn't. I was having trouble at the speed I was going, and my breath was coming hard. I just resolved to get there.

I never expected to actually see Caer Corisan. I thought that I would just stay on the dragon forever. When it did show on the horizon, I thought that it wouldn't get closer, but it did.

Within half a watch, Narden was circling for a landing. The faces that looked up at the dragon distracted me so much that I didn't pay attention to the landing. The usual nonchalant look to see who it was turned into stares. The faces ranged from concern, to surprise, to complete shock, to horror, and even to anger.

I would have liked to circle a few more times, slowed down more, but exhaustion was taking its toll. I didn't want to collapse before landing. I came in faster than I liked and realized too late that I still couldn't put weight on my right front leg. The leg crumpled beneath me. I smashed into the dirt and careened across the courtyard. Finally, I stopped by colliding with the west wall. More sickening than that, I felt Ari's weight lurch forward with the sudden movement then disappear. I'd thrown her.

I demanded that my legs work so I could stand up and find out how badly I'd injured Ari, but my limbs heard the order and sent back a resolute refusal. I was too tired to do anything but try to breathe, even that seemed like too much of an effort. I heard the bustle around the courtyard, but my head refused to lift or my eyes to see anything. Every breath was ragged, sending pain through my lungs.

I felt the jar of the landing and started to grip the spikes along his neck, but I was too late. Suddenly, Narden lurched to one side, and there was nothing under me but air. I put out my hands to break my fall and was frightened for an instant, before I hit the ground and slid. When I came to rest, I felt the pain in my arm. Looking at it, I wondered why it was hanging at such an odd angle.

Suddenly, a group of people crowded around me. I knew most of the faces, but I couldn't answer any of the questions because of the screaming pain in my arm.

Most wanted to know what had happened, but an authoritarian voice rang behind them, "Get away from her, you clouts!"

Instantly the men backed away. Later, I would remember that they hadn't left entirely. For now, all I noticed was Majorlaine kneeling in front of me. I didn't remember much more from the courtyard other than that my arm was set, splinted, and placed in a sling. I hoped that had been the order, but I was never quite sure since the pain blurred the memories so badly.

As she helped me up, I noticed that Narden hadn't moved from against the wall.

"Is he all right?" I asked Majorlaine.

She told me to watch my step, but didn't answer my question. We went to my rooms, where Majorlaine began cleaning out the cuts I had from the slide in the dirt. My right leg was at least not too torn up, but my skirt had been shredded on that side. My arm hadn't fared as well. On top of being broken, it seemed that Majorlaine picked most of the courtyard's pebbles out of it as well. My forehead had a few scrapes, but my arm had shielded it . . . mostly. The rest of the courtyard seemed to be imbedded in my palms.

Majorlaine jumped when someone knocked on the door. She yelled for them to come in, interrupting a not too coherent story about some butterflies that had either gotten into my garden or her kitchen. I had never seen her this flustered before, even when five dragons had all come in with injuries. I was beginning to collect my thoughts enough to wonder, if I was making all this up in my head, why things didn't seem more normal.

Anuj, one of the boys who currently helped Mintxo in the kitchen, came in.

"Galen needs you," he told Majorlaine.

She seemed as shocked by the statement as I was. Galen and Majorlaine were always at such odds that he never would ask for her help. Perhaps I was insane after all.

"It's that bad?" she asked, as she stood and hurried to the door.

"He broke his lungs, ma'am," he told her.

She was too upset to even tell him not to call her ma'am.

I was left standing in the room, alone, with a broken arm in a sling and a half-bandaged hand. Had it been the hand of my broken arm, I might have been able to finish it, but it wasn't. It was the hand of my good arm, and the other hand had already been wrapped to the point of immobilizing it.

I wasn't sure what to make of everything. I sat in front of the fire for a moment, feeling the warmth. My senses seemed to be telling me that I was still sane. I had felt bitterly cold during the flight, a state that was perfectly in line with the fact that I had been plunged into a lake and then flown at top speed through half of the day. I was still somewhat wet though the fire was helping to change that.

No voices had cut in saying "Get up, wretch" or "Filthy nickin" in any language.

I rose from the chair and walked to the balcony, my arm still throbbing. In the courtyard below, I saw the frantic movements of people. Armel was there blocking people from swarming where Narden still lay against the western wall. He issued orders; and the people, both humans and dragons, would slowly do whatever he said. They continued to glance over their shoulders as they walked away though.

Narden didn't move. I couldn't make out whether he was breathing or not. Galen and Majorlaine were having a discussion, and both looked quite worried.

What had the boy said about Narden? He'd broken his lungs. I knew the term, but couldn't remember what could be done for it. It meant that he'd pushed himself far past exhaustion at too fast a pace. It could be fatal. He could stop breathing.

I was too confused to feel worried or even concerned at the moment. If my mind was playing tricks on me, I should be able to just believe hard enough that Narden was all right, and it would happen. I closed my eyes and tried to believe that the dragon would get up and walk nonchalantly across the courtyard. In a moment, he would call for me to come down to see him. Any moment I would hear his voice. Any moment . . .

The moment never came. Slowly, I opened my eyes and saw that nothing had changed aside from someone was hurrying across the courtyard with a steaming pot.

It didn't prove that I wasn't insane. I could have lost enough control of my mind that I couldn't convince it to do what I wanted. I hadn't been able to get it to show me where we were going before. I had thought getting it to show me something slightly different would be easier, but I was greatly mistaken.

The afternoon passed. Someone came up with a meal on a tray at one point, but left before I could even manage a question. Evening came, and still the dragon lay against the wall, unmoving. The panicked atmosphere had lessened, but I wondered if that was due to everyone growing used to this present emergency.

I had seen it happen often enough. The panic came when an injured dragon arrived or something of that nature; the courtyard would flare with activity, but as the crisis continued, the more level-headed would haul away the gawkers, and life would continue on. It would be more hurried. People would look over at the injury stables, or wherever things were happening whenever they were within sight.

More was often accomplished during those times. An odd thing, but probably because of the heightened tension. I remembered once when Armel had started working on a table. He had worked on it for a month and completed two legs and started on the top. Hafiz, Besnik, and Hramn all came in with injures one day, and he finished the top, the other two legs, and two of the chairs within two days before we announced that the three dragons would be all right.

I wished for something to do, but with a broken arm, and the skin on both hands shredded, I couldn't help with much of anything. I could go to the kitchens, but would probably be sent away, or asked to stir something constantly, and that would accomplish about as much as my pacing.

I hadn't eaten anything from the lunch tray, so I waved the boy off who brought supper. He at least noticed the dangling bandage and finished wrapping my hand, but he didn't have any new information about Narden.

Eventually, I noticed the sun sink below the horizon. I could no longer make out the activity in the courtyard through the darkness. Occasionally, a torch walked across, and there was a torch left near Narden, but not close enough for me to see by.

Soon, I noticed that I had gone through the motions of preparing for bed. I had taken every step out of habit, even with my injuries. I debated going to bed, and realized that time would go faster if I could sleep.

With as many circles and loops that my mind was going through, I was convinced that I wouldn't be able to sleep. I was wrong. Exhaustion claimed me.

I jumped awake from the crow of a rather loud and off-key rooster finding it was morning.

CHAPTER 41

EXPLANATIONS

I went through the motions of getting ready for the day. When I walked to the balcony, I was shocked to find that the dragon was gone. I almost panicked right then, except that an odd knocking sound filled the room.

I heard a muffled voice ask if I was awake.

I had always wanted to call out in answer to that type of question, "No, I'm sleepwalking," but I didn't think of that now.

Instead, I went to the door and opened it.

The last thing I was expecting to see was the bottom of a table with the legs pointed at me, but that was indeed what I saw.

"I was hoping to join you for breakfast," said the voice slightly less muffled now and recognizable as Armel's.

"Of course." I stepped out of the way of the table as he walked in with it. "Do you often bring your own table to breakfast?" I continued as he set it down.

"My lady," Armel replied in mock horror, "I'm hurt!"

I stared at him for a moment, noticing for the first time, the bandage around his head. From the look of his shirt, he had another wrapped around his ribs. Not that it was stopping him from moving furniture! What was he thinking?

He ran his hand along the table lovingly. "I only bring my own table to special breakfasts."

"He's dead," I whispered.

Wouldn't that be the only reason that Armel would make a special trip up for breakfast? He was here to tell me the news.

"Who's dead?" he asked arranging the table.

It was the table from the first time I'd visited, I realized, as he, again, ran his hand across the surface.

I began to say something but realized that I didn't know who to say was dead. My mouth moved, but no sound came. Armel glanced up as I motioned vaguely at the balcony.

He watched me for a moment then laughed.

"Narden's fine"—he moved the table slightly—"or at least he will be. Galen says he'll need to take things easy for several months. He said that meant absolutely no sparring with me." Armel shrugged.

"He's not dead?" I finally managed to ask.

He looked up and studied me. "No, he's not dead." He pulled a chair over from the normal table. "Come sit down, my lady."

"He's not able to talk too well right now, but he mentioned something that has me slightly concerned."

Pulling another chair over, he sat across the table from me. "I am trying to sort out what occurred, my lady. Do you know what happened to Hafiz and Einheim?"

I nodded slowly. "Einheim was shot through the wing, and he fell."

"Who was riding him?" he asked.

"I was," I whispered.

I could see ground rushing toward me and then the wrenching feeling from the sudden stop.

"Who was riding Hafiz?" he asked.

"Danren and Dreanen."

I could see them hanging on to me as Hafiz held Einheim.

"Dreanen was with you?" That surprised him.

I nodded, and he asked, "Do you know where he is now?"

I started to say that he was with Hafiz, but I wasn't sure about that. That was a part that was clear in my memory, but impossible.

"How did you come to be with Narden?" he asked, when I couldn't answer.

I stammered incoherently for a few moments then went silent.

"I see," he said slowly. "Aside from your physical injuries, are you all right, my lady?"

I shook my head slightly. "I've gone insane, sir," I whispered.

I had heard him mumble to the table, and I watched as it colored in and began to write in names. I had wanted to see this table again, but never remembered to ask about it. I noticed that Pher'am and her children's names scripted in as did mine a moment later.

"Why do you say that?" he asked, in response to my previous statement.

"It's impossible," I whispered.

"What's impossible?" he asked.

"They changed," I whispered and glanced up at him. "Things like that don't really happen," I continued. "It's just stories . . ." I trailed off.

He had given the table another command in el'brenika. It meant *turn* because Maren is more than it appears, or something similar. The names remained, but the sky behind the tree was turning dark with dots of white flecked through it.

"What stories?" he asked.

The base of the tree was turning blue as was the top.

"The ones about children turning into dragons because they're naughty," I said, watching as splotches of greens and browns appeared on the two blue spheres.

It almost looked as though clouds colored in over the splotches, making it appear as though they were islands in a marble. The tree trunk changed to an open doorway through which I saw the original scene of the grassy hill with the tree curving into the sky.

When the background stopped changing, I glanced at the names. The bottom names remained the same as did the one that had been on the tree trunk but was now on the doorframe. The women's names all remained the same as well, but the rest of the men's names began to shift, some changing completely, others changing by a few letters, or just rearranging the letters. I looked at the names I knew and watched Lord Grath's alter to Tragh, Drenar's to Renard, Dreanen's to Adenern, and finally Danren's to Narden.

I stared for a while then whispered, "I don't understand."

"If you are in fact insane," he began, and I was even less encouraged by that beginning, "nothing I say will change that. I, however, do not believe you are insane, because that would make many of us here insane as well."

I pulled my gaze from the design on the table and stared blankly at the edge.

"What you are having trouble understanding is probably how and why someone would turn into a dragon." He went silent, watching me.

I wasn't sure what to say to that. If I was in fact insane, nothing would change that, but if I wasn't . . . The question did seem to be why would someone turn into a dragon and how would be nice to know too.

He continued after a moment, "The why has nothing whatsoever to do with whether a person is bad or not. It actually is part of bloodlines."

Another pause, and I heard a slight rustling sound. Then he unrolled one of the blank maps. It was actually the backside of the map.

"Four bloodlines to be specific," he continued, "and you're familiar enough with them."

The four pictures of the five dragons began to color in. I gasped as I began to grasp what he was saying. It wasn't just Narden and Adenern that were human, but their entire family line and the three other lines as well . . . or was it the other way around, and Danren and Dreanen were really dragons . . .

"Now, I'm going to try to explain this the best I can, but I don't fully understand it, so if you don't, I won't be surprised," he continued.

That didn't make me feel too hopeful.

"Far away from here," he continued, sounding as though he was telling a story that he had told many times before, "farther away than crossing the oceans or crossing any of the lands was a group of people who wanted to be immortal. Now, they didn't want to harm themselves to become immortal, so they tried their ideas on others.

"They had slaves, so the masters convinced some of the slaves to try the ideas.

"They used lots of different reasons." He motioned to the red dragon and the golden one. "Raleigh and Otto believed that they would be able to stay young forever and so get . . ." he paused for a moment and glanced away from me. "This was the main reason that most tried the ideas. It was to be able to get involved with many young women." He cleared his throat and continued, "Indigo believed he would become equal if not greater than the masters and overthrow them. Gary believed it would fix his deformities, and Diggory followed his father.

"The ideas had something to do with mixing blood, or some part of animals that had longer lives, or such with the slaves' bodies." He paused again then said, "The ideas failed, and the slaves began to get sick and die."

"What?" I asked, surprised by this turn in the story.

The dragons here were not dying from some sickness.

He smiled slightly and continued, "Gary had some knowledge of the one god and cried out for help, since nothing else could be done. The Mighty One was not thought highly of there, so from what I gather, it was rather a shock when he responded." Armel laughed for a moment then sobered. "He sent people known as Wanderers to help."

He paused thinking about it for a moment. "Not many believed that the Mighty One had sent help, and even fewer wanted to accept that help. In the end, it was only those five who accepted. They were brought here to escape.

"They willingly decided to follow those ideas and mix their blood, so there was a judgment as well. They were asked if they would rather spend all their lives looking like they were half men and half beasts, or half their lives as men and the other half as beasts. They decided on the latter. We are granted our childhoods, but pay for those years through our youths. Since it was only men who were part of the mixing, our daughters do not turn. Oddly, we have longer lives though we are not immortal, but that leads to watching the wives and daughters we love grow old and die before us.

"I don't understand all of it, but I can try to answer any questions you may have," he told me at the end of the story. "We are blessed that Gary is still with us, because he can answer questions that I can't." He chuckled lightly. "Though his answers sometimes make less sense than the questions."

I was trying to understand what he'd said. Men who became dragons not because of something they did, unless it was Gary, but rather because of decisions made by those long dead. It didn't seem fair, but I wondered how many times children paid for a parent's choice.

I thought about the history of the dragons on Arnbjorg. I thought about Narden or Danren or . . . both. I wasn't entirely sure how to consider everything.

"Why wasn't I told sooner?" I finally asked.

Armel sighed and then answered slowly, "There was a time when our wives and children were freely told of . . . well . . . everything, but we found that our wives often left us, a few went to extremes and killed their children, their husbands, or themselves. We eventually decided that we would have all the first turning youths take an oath never to tell anyone who was not one of us, and as far as possible to hold their two identities separate from each other. Occasionally, there was a special case, such as yours, where we considered telling you, but the rule is that the counsel must vote unanimously or nothing is said."

"Edur was concerned that should something happen to Danren, and you married into another family, your loyalties would shift." He trailed off. "Danren"—he chuckled—"or Narden used to hound us every meeting. He stopped since Drenar's death though."

With a sudden shocked sensation, I began to put names together. Renard couldn't have saved Drenar because they were the same person. Armel was Mael. Galen was Cumas. I continued putting names together until I reached Hafiz and Ishmerai. I had seen both of them at the same time, but who was their counterpart?

"What about Hafiz?" I asked.

Armel smiled. "They're identical twins."

433

"Oh," I managed. Well, I supposed that made some sense. "If it's all right with you," I finally managed to continue, "I'd like to think about all of this by myself for a little while."

"Of course, my lady." He rose and bowed to me. "Let me know if you have any questions."

The door closed behind him, and my thoughts suddenly became very mixed up. I stood and walked toward the balcony.

The story made sense, sort of, but I had been raised to understand that such things didn't really happen. They were only made up by peasants to scare their children into behaving. I might have figured it out on my own, I realized, if it hadn't been so completely impossible . . .

I put together some more humans with their dragon counterparts and found that I couldn't match a lot of them with anyone else. Most of them were dragons, and I wondered if there came a time after living the length of several lifetimes that they no longer wanted to change back and forth.

Looking out over the courtyard, I noticed that everything seemed normal. How could anything be normal? I rubbed my arm and wandered over to my medical bag to find something for the pain.

Danren had wanted to tell me up until Renard's death, but then what had happened? I nearly choked at the sudden realization, not breathing for several moments.

I knew what had happened. My knees gave, and I crumpled to the floor. I had told Danren, as Narden, that I wished he was dead instead of his brother.

What had I done?

What was I to do now?

I was unconscious most of my first day back, so I found out later that Armel had explained to Ari what had happened, that Adenern, Hafiz, and Einheim had returned safely, and that I couldn't stand up, shift positions, or even breathe without hurting *a lot*.

I wondered how Ari was taking things. I had never wanted her to find out this way. I had hoped nothing like that would ever happen, but this was Maren. Even if Faruq wasn't at war, we were. We should have been more careful, we should have had a guard, we should have . . . I beat myself up for watches waiting for any news.

Ari hadn't left our rooms since we arrived. That worried me. I could understand her not coming to see me. I had desperately hoped she'd forgive me, and we could work out some sort of arrangement. However, she hadn't gone to help Majorlaine or Galen. Anuj said he'd seen her walk down the stairs, stop at the bottom, turn around, and hurry back to her rooms. Armel, Majorlaine, and several others checked in on her, but she barely said anything to them. As far as they could tell, she hadn't had any incidents, but she sent people away when they visited her.

After a week, she finally began to help Majorlaine again, but she never came to the injury stables. I never even saw her walk by the entrance. She would hate me for the rest of her life, I realized sadly. I couldn't think of a thing to change it. I didn't blame her. She had every right to despise me. I'd lied to her. I'd tricked her. Perhaps it wasn't entirely my fault, but what did that matter.

I would try to make things as easy on her as possible. I could get some things from the rooms and start sleeping somewhere else. I'd avoid her whenever I could so she wouldn't end up in any awkward situations. I wasn't sure if it would be better to give her presents or not.

With a sudden stab, I realized, she would probably want a divorce. Again, I couldn't blame her. The only snag with that was that she might end up remarried to someone who would mistreat her. Perhaps she would be willing to settle for a separation. She could move to Ryuu to live with Pher'am and Dreanen, and never have to see me again . . .

The burning in my lungs was quickly becoming the least of my worries.

I tried for days to gather enough courage to go see Narden. I knew I should, but I couldn't think of what to say. I tried writing a letter, but realized I was ruining too many sheets of paper and had nothing to show for it after a week. I finally decided to go back to my routine, and just run into him one day. I quickly found that I was avoiding the recovery stable.

I finally came across an idea. Maybe I could manage to just go to the stable and offer to read to him. There was a problem though. He no longer kept his book in the desk. I supposed that I could read from my book, but I thought it would be more meaningful if I used his. I hadn't seen it during the funeral, so he'd probably left it here. I would have too, if I'd been him. I would have asked about it, if I'd seen him with it. The book was probably in his room . . . I hoped.

I had never been in his room. I'd avoided going near it. I condemned myself for ever thinking that he might pull me in there. How could I have not seen that he was far more honorable than that?

I slowly opened the door to look in, hoping that the book would be in plain sight. He might have hidden it away somewhere so I wouldn't find it again, but would he think I'd look in here? Apparently, he hadn't, because the book was resting on a stand next to the bed.

Darting in, I grabbed it. Turning around, I noticed that the room was set up rather plainly. A wardrobe was against a wall, the stand next to the bed, and the bed itself were intricately carved to match, Armel's handiwork. A few scrolls and things were with the book on the stand, but there were no other decorations.

I hurried out and closed the door behind me. I took a few moments to calm down, but I knew there was no reason that I should be scared.

I studied the book realizing that the cover was showing wear. I smiled, wondering how many more times Narden could drop it before it fell apart.

I made my way down to the injury stables. As I approached, I found that I walked slower and slower. I was trying to talk myself into and out of going, at the same time. What was he going to think, since we'd been here for a week, and I'd never even sent him a message? What would I have said? I had started several dozen messages and never managed to complete a single one. They were all ashes now. I hadn't wanted anyone to find them.

If I just made it to the stables, I would have to go in. As early as it was, the courtyard was just beginning to come to life, and no one took notice of me.

I stopped next to the doorway, catching my breath. This shouldn't be this hard.

"How are you feeling now?" I heard Galen ask from inside.

His gruff personality might make things easier if I teased him a little, or it might make things harder, if he started in on my not coming sooner. I didn't know whether to continue in or not.

The response made the decision for me, "Like a dragon hit me in the ribs."

It wasn't the statement that froze my blood, but the voice. I realized for the first time that Narden and Danren had slightly different sounds to their voices. It was probably one of the reasons that I hadn't caught on sooner.

"Did you hear something?" Danren asked.

"Probably Anuj throwing buckets around again," Galen replied. "Breathe as deeply as you can."

Looking down, I realized what the sound was. I'd dropped the book, and of all things, the front cover had come off along with a chunk of the first pages.

I grabbed the book and raced from the courtyard. I fled through the halls until I reached my rooms. Once there, I slammed the door behind me and slumped onto the couch. What had I done?

I couldn't keep the tears back. Why ever had the book decided to break at that point? Narden had dropped this book time and again, and nothing ever happened, but I drop it once, and it falls to bits! I held the pieces together as best I could through my blurry vision.

Armel could fix books, I suddenly remembered. I'd have him fix it. Hopefully, he could do it quickly enough that Danren wouldn't notice.

I found a handkerchief and wiped my eyes, washed my face, and started from the room. At the top of the stairs, I froze.

He was looking at the stairs themselves as he walked up, so he didn't see me. I dashed back to the room, thankful for the thick carpet to hide any sounds. Panicking, I hid the book in the first place I could think of, tossing it behind the couch, and ran into my room. I closed the door as silently as I could, lay down, and peered under it. It felt like forever before I heard the knock on the main doors.

Galen wanted me to turn as soon as I could so he could assess the damage this way as well. It didn't hurt to breathe lightly, but some movements still stung, and I, certainly, couldn't breathe deeply. After the quick exam, he sent me on my way.

I wasn't sure if I wanted to meet up with Ari'an yet or not. I hadn't worked out quite what to say to her or how to respond to everything she might say to me. I was certain it was going to turn out badly, and I deserved it.

I sighed at the bottom of the stairs, realized the mistake too late, and cringed. I knew how much that hurt. I made my way up the stairs. Stopping at the door, I wondered why I had never thought of how to enter this room. I'd had a week, but it had never crossed my mind.

I couldn't just stand there, in case she opened the door and walked into me. That wouldn't do at all, and it was about the time that she would go to help Majorlaine with breakfast.

I knocked.

No answer.

I pushed the door open slightly, no sign or sound of movement.

"Hello, anyone in here?" *Could I have thought of something more stupid to say?*

Still no answer. Mighty One be praised. She wasn't there. There was no light coming from her room, but the main fire was still blazing. I sat down in front of it wondering what to do.

Should I go looking for Ari'an or wait until she was ready to talk? I stood back up and began pacing the room. If I went looking for her, would I just end up in the same situation as when we were first married? I stopped and stared across the room. If she didn't want to talk to me, she would just avoid me, and since she now knew every corner in the fortress, I wouldn't find her easily. I'd wait for her then, I decided, and if I ran into her somewhere, I'd figure out what to say.

During this time, a question kept nagging at the back of my mind. Now that I had a decision, it came to the forefront. Why was there paper behind the couch?

I walked over and pulled out a few sheets. They were from the Book, and they looked like they were from my copy, but my copy wouldn't be out here stuffed behind the couch. It was in my room. Ari'an's copy was quite different, so where did these come from? I looked behind the couch and gasped, immediately cringing at the pain. It was my book, and it had been thrown there.

Had I left it in the desk again? Perhaps I had. After fishing the pages and binding from behind the couch, I slumped onto the seat and stared at the broken, torn pieces. She really did hate me to do something like this. What was I going to do?

I decided, if I saw her, I wouldn't mention it. I considered leaving it behind the couch, but couldn't bring myself to. Hopefully, she wouldn't remember throwing it there.

Why on Arnbjorg had I left the book out there? I should have brought it with me, but my first thought was to hide it, and the next was that behind the couch was the closest place to hide it. I cringed when he walked over and pulled out the pages and then the rest of the book.

He sat down on the couch and stared at the book for a long time. He looked devastated. His father had given it to him when he started training, or first turned, or whatever it was supposed to be called.

I probably should have stepped out of my room right then to explain, but I didn't. Instead, I decided to avoid him, as much as possible, until I figured out what to say.

Winter set in, and I still hadn't spoken to him. My arm was completely healed, and I'd barely seen him.

CHAPTER 42

FEVER

Winter came but not the rest we had hoped for. The fever hit hard that year. It was the worst that Galen had seen in a hundred and fifty years. Because of the dragons, Rem'Maren suffered considerably less than the rest of the kingdom. If one of the men who could turn began to feel sick, he could turn and not catch it. The women, children, and men who weren't dragons suffered terribly though.

At Caer Corisan, I put together herb kits that Majorlaine knew would help and mixed liquids that Galen swore by. The short days and long nights were a blur of activity.

No one was allowed to come to the fortress who had the illness. Because of that precaution, Caer Corisan was spared, for the most part, but each day the death toll climbed in the villages, and a new outbreak was reported.

I realized one day, just past the middle of winter, that I had not seen either Danren or Narden for a month and a half. I couldn't even remember hearing him come to the rooms at night. I inquired as nonchalantly as I could of Armel about him, and found out that both he and Dreanen had been doing patrols and supply runs all winter, because the men and dragons who normally did them were trying to take care of their families. I had noticed that when men or dragons were here, they were so worried about their families that they were little help.

Danren was due back at the end of the week, but Dreanen had been too busy to stop unless dropping off supplies. I realized that I missed them. I still hadn't figured out what to say to Danren or Narden, and would probably try to hide somewhere if I did see him. I wished, yet again, that I hadn't damaged his book, but I was too busy to think about that for long.

The week ended, but from what I gathered, Danren stopped only to turn. Narden set out on a supply run the next day. Galen left to take medicines and survey the villages. Majorlaine, against all objections, did the same on the following day. She said she'd had the fever last year, so she wouldn't be affected by it now.

I stayed. I worked long into the cold nights, doing what I could, and feeling fairly useless. I didn't know whether I wanted to go to the villages or just work on the medicines. Either way, I felt helpless, and that made me restless. For the third night in a row, I fell asleep at the table I worked at.

An alarm sounded before dawn. An injured dragon was coming in. I almost felt relieved by the sound, since injuries could be tended. Galen could fix the dragon up. I rose to go to my rooms to dress and arrange my kit so I could assist him. Suddenly, I froze. Galen wasn't here. Neither was Majorlaine. Why had they both gone at the same time? Who would . . .

The running footsteps interrupted my thoughts, as did the frantic call, "Lady Ari'an, come quickly."

The boy stopped at the door panting. "It's Adenern."

Once he began, the words flooded out of him while my blood ran cold. "He was on a patrol through the pass." His words ran over each other. "But the pass is thawing early this year, and he was attacked. Armel doesn't think it's serious, but he'd like you to have a look."

I hurried with the boy to the injury stables, finding Adenern barely harmed. He actually seemed upset to be patched up at all. He tried to make a few jokes, but stopped midthought.

He had a gash from a spear or javelin across his shoulder and a few arrow wounds at the edges of his wings. When Galen came in later that day, he told Adenern that he should still be able to turn and go home in a couple of days. His mood brightened considerably then.

Majorlaine returned the next morning with news that there were far fewer outbreaks than she had expected. The next couple of days brought similar reports, and then Adenern turned.

He began to look pale after about a watch, then passed out entirely. There was a frantic rush of activity, as Galen tried to discover what had happened.

Majorlaine told me about the symptoms, and it was clearly not the fever. I had a terrible feeling that I knew what it was, but I asked to see him, hoping I was wrong. He was delirious when I arrived, he had chills but not a fever, and his skin was clammy.

I heard Galen enter with someone else as he explained the symptoms to the newcomer. He went through a list of illnesses, but said that none of them were right. He explained that Dreanen shouldn't have become sick at all, and certainly not that quickly.

"Unless it was in his blood," I said softly.

After a moment's silence, Galen asked, "What do you mean?"

"Verd has a poison that takes a few days to start working," I began, wishing that I was wrong, but what else could it be? "If any of the weapons had been coated with it, it would have been in his blood already, and when he turned . . ." I trailed off.

"It would take effect," Galen finished. "Are you certain of this?"

I nodded. I knew the symptoms. I'd felt them myself.

"Do you know what this poison is called?"

I shook my head. I'd never been told a name.

"He cannot turn in this state, and even if he could, I don't know what effect this poison would have on him. Is it deadly?"

"It can be if . . ." I was fighting off memories. It was used as a punishment, and I had watched another die from it. It was supposed to be a lesson. It was always terrifying, when I would find they'd put some in the food, because I didn't know if they would let me die or not.

"Is there an antidote?" Galen asked.

I nodded. "The party that attacked him will have it with them. If any of them come in contact with it, they can be treated."

"I can work on an antidote, but without knowing what type of poison, I'll be working blind."

"Are Hafiz and Einheim still here?" The voice shocked me out of my thoughts, and I quickly looked toward the speaker.

Ari'an hadn't looked up when we came into the room. I almost walked back out, but Galen was still describing what had happened. She seemed to be looking for something specific, and I hoped that I would be able to duck out before she noticed me. She was pale, but I wasn't sure if that was because of Dreanen's condition or too much work. At least, the fever had spared her.

Suddenly, she interrupted, but she didn't look up. I didn't like seeing that look on her face. It meant that she was remembering something from the temple. I watched as she fought back those awful memories. I found out that Galen wouldn't be able to easily cure this, but we could possibly get the antidote, if we were quick enough. I spoke before I thought and watched her face turn from shock to horror when she saw me.

"Yes," Galen answered me, "as are Jair, Besnik, and Derxan."

"We'll leave in the morning then," I told him, hurrying from the room.

I paused only after turning a corner.

Danren was gone before I could recover. I glanced at Galen, wanting to know why he was back, but unable to ask.

"He got in last night," Galen said, anticipating my question. "The weather has been fair lately, so the supply run didn't take as long."

My mind whirled. I saw the devastated look he'd quickly hidden. It was like looking at someone who had just been stabbed by a friend. I needed to do something, but Galen was asking what I knew of the antidote. I described what I could remember, but I wasn't sure how much help I would be in recreating it. I knew it by sight and smell and taste, but not by what was actually in it. With a start, I realized that although I would be no help to Galen, I could help the search party. I knew what they were looking for.

I forced my legs to carry me out of the room. Hurrying down the hall before I lost my nerve, I had to find him.

I heard footsteps. Looking up, I expected Galen. To my shock, Ari'an rounded the corner, then froze. I should have gone farther away. Standing up, I said that I was just leaving, but as I turned to go, I heard the last thing I ever expected.

I hadn't thought he'd be just around the corner. I thought I would have a few moments to word what I was going to say. My nerve was fleeing as he turned to leave. I couldn't ignore this though. If I did, Dreanen might die.

"I need to talk to you," I managed to get out, then added, "please?"

He stopped and slowly turned around. I couldn't hold his gaze.

"What?" was my surprised answer.

I hadn't meant to meet her gaze, and when she immediately looked away, I was somewhat relieved.

"I need to go with you," she said, hurrying her words.

"What?" I didn't understand.

"I know what you're looking for," she continued.

"You could tell Einheim." I didn't want her to feel trapped.

"It's complicated, and if you're not sure of what you're looking for, someone may try to trick you," she continued.

"It's too dangerous for you to come," I tried, wondering if anything I said would make a difference.

She took a breath then looked up.

She paused for a moment then said, "It's dangerous for you too."

I accidentally met her gaze. "That's different."

She didn't look away.

I'd surprised him. Of course, I'd surprised myself too. He glanced away quickly.

"It's not safe," he said firmly.

I gathered my nerve. I was going with this expedition, whether he wanted me to or not.

"Sir, do you really want to risk poisoning him worse if someone manages to trick you?"

He cringed and remained silent for a long moment.

She was offering to save Dreanen, but the choice was unthinkable, to risk his life . . . or hers. If it was anyone else, I would have accepted the offer in an instant, but to risk her . . . What if something happened? On the other hand, she knew what no one else did . . .

"Galen will need you here," I told her, hoping to dissuade her.

"I won't be any help here, sir. He knows what he's looking for," she said.

Why was she so determined? I pondered that for a few moments.

It seemed like an eternity before he said anything, and then his answer seemed forced, "As you wish, my lady."

He bowed and walked away. When I could no longer hear his footsteps, I sank against the wall, sliding to the floor. Majorlaine found me there and helped me to pack.

CHAPTER 43

SEARCH FOR A CURE

We left before dawn the next morning. Twelve people were in the party, including Ari'an. Six were dragons, the other six human. We flew quickly to where the attack on Dreanen had taken place then began tracking the raiding party back through the pass. The end of the day came, and we hadn't found them. How much time did we have? The only person who would know was Ari'an, but she hadn't spoken to me since the day before.

I wanted to talk to Danren again, but what could I possibly say? I thought about bringing up Dreanen's condition, telling him that we had at least a week to find the raiding party, or that I'd told Galen everything I could remember about how to keep him alive longer, but he was always busy with something or another.

I had plenty of time to think during the long flight the first day. I had wondered if Danren would turn for the search, but he hadn't, at least not yet. I wanted to talk to someone about what that was like, but I could never quite word the questions with Armel. I realized as I watched Danren that I wanted to ask him . . . well, Narden, but technically they were the same person. I'd had months to get used to it, but I still had trouble. Some days I woke up, still wondering if I was insane.

The day ended, and we made camp in a clearing by a stream. The place was still snow locked, so it was safe from any raiding parties. Watching the dragons clear the snow from the ground was interesting. They had to be precise so they wouldn't catch a nearby tree on fire.

I noticed that I had my own tent as did Danren, but the other four humans shared a tent with one or two dragons. I realized that was why Rem'Maren had such large tents.

I chided myself for not bringing something to do in the evening twilight. I was tired from the ride, but not as exhausted as most days. Finally, I realized that I had been staring at the fire in the middle of my tent for at least a watch. The smoke curled up to the top where it escaped through a netting. Making my way to the cot that sat a few steps from the fire, I glanced around, one last time, at my medical bag and then at the slightly larger bag of belongings that I'd brought. I closed my eyes, and was surprised to find that it was morning when I opened them again.

Hafiz scouted that morning, as we headed farther into the pass. He came back just before noon. He'd sighted a raiding party breaking camp by the Chayyim River. Hopefully, it was the right one. Xander and Snebik turned for the ambush.

The raiders never expected an attack from seven dragons and three humans. I had Einheim keep Ari'an away until the battle was over. Surprisingly, this group of dragon slayers surrendered rather quickly. However, they did spend an extensive amount of time begging the humans not to let the dragons eat them. I considered hitting each one over the head with the flat of my sword every time they said it.

We'd brought the means to transport the six dragon slayers to Ryuu for trial, but I pondered if anyone would wonder if they ended up dead. They had killed Zait, who had been missing for a week. They had planned to turn his wings, which they still had, into a saddle. They had almost killed Dreanen . . . We had a limited time to return to Caer Corisan . . . if it wasn't too late already. I drove that thought from my mind.

They deserved to die, but killing them in cold blood would make us no better than them. They would stand trial.

Ishmerai got one of them to give him the antidote for Dreanen. I didn't like the way the man looked. When Ishmerai asked Ari'an, she confirmed my suspicions. The mixture pointed out would instantly kill anyone who drank it. Ari'an suggested that Ishmerai have the man try it to make sure it was right. I smiled slightly when I heard about that. She did find the right mixture, after the man made five other wrong guesses.

When she pulled the right mixture out of the man's confiscated bag, he became enraged. I heard him begin to curse, and I debated coming over. If he insulted Ari'an . . . Then I saw Ari'an turn white as he broke from Ishmerai's hold and lunged at her. He ripped the container from her hands and hurled it onto the frozen river. It shattered on the ice. I was behind him before he could take another breath.

The man turned his livid gaze at me as he pivoted toward me. The look instantly turned to shock as he looked down at a sword sprouting from his chest.

The sight of his dead body collapsing at my feet almost made me vomit, but I turned quickly to his bag. I had to find an empty vial, pot, anything. The powder that had been in the little pot, now broken on the ice, would disappear into the ice if I didn't get some of it immediately.

I almost caught her as she fainted but realized that she would never forgive me if I touched her. Then I realized that she hadn't fainted but was frantically pulling containers from the dead man's bag. I wanted to ask if she was all right, but it seemed like a stupid question. I tried to find something else to say.

She picked a glass vial out randomly, stood up, and headed toward the river.

"What are you doing?" I exclaimed.

She gingerly put a foot on the frozen river and started toward the center.

"That"—she motioned toward the broken container on the ice—"is all he had."

I watched as she walked carefully toward the spot. I couldn't move my legs. I wanted to run after her and pull her back, but the ice would never hold both of us. Only a few leagues down river, the ice had thawed completely. I glanced around and found that Einheim was watching as well. He was tensed to spring should anything happened. Would waiting for something to happen be too late?

Listening to the ice creak beneath me sent tremors up and down my spine. I was the lightest person of the group, and there wasn't time to debate. That powder dissolved instantly in water, and might dissolve into the ice as well.

I reached the broken pot and found that some of the powder was still there even though some had already pooled into the ice. I scraped up as much as I could and slowly rose.

The ice sounded louder now. I just had to make it back to shore. Corking the little vial, I quickened my pace.

She was walking faster as she returned. I was relieved that she was hurrying, but concerned that her haste might crack the ice. Only a few more yards . . .

Her foot slipped out from under her, and she collapsed on the frozen river. The ice held for a moment, then a sickening crack ripped through the air. She disappeared under the water.

Before I could react, a red streak hurtled past me and into the river. Was it a watch, a moment, or just an instant? Einheim burst back through what was left of the ice down the river. He held a soaked, unmoving figure in his front claws.

He looked panic-stricken as he reached the shore. He could land just fine now on four feet, but he couldn't manage two. He'd crush her. I sprinted to where he was trying to hover and yelled for him to drop her. He looked at me as if I'd lost my mind, then seemed to realize what I meant. He angled the body at me and let go.

She stirred slightly as she fell the ten steps. I saw panic line her face, then I caught her. I knew she'd never forgive me, but nothing else could have been done.

I heard Ishmerai command Einheim to dry off, and then the explanation that he should breathe fire over his scales. I heard running steps as I tried to set Ari'an on her feet. I glanced over my shoulder, ready to pull my sword if necessary. Ishmerai was running toward us, pulling off his cloak as he came.

Her legs didn't seem to be able to hold her up. I couldn't tell if the shaking through her body was the cold, shock, or fear. It might have been all of them. I knew I needed to let go, but I couldn't let her collapse into the snow.

Everything happened too quickly. My foot slipped. I tried to catch myself without breaking the vial, and landed hard on the ice. I glanced at my hand finding the vial intact.

Then I heard the crack. I watched in horror as the ice shattered around me. The shock of the icy water drove the air from my lungs.

An instant later, I felt claws grip me and haul me through the water. I gasped when we left the river, but tried to hold as still as possible. The claws were red, and I knew that Einheim wouldn't be able to maneuver, if I tried to reposition.

The next moment, Danren yelled for him to drop me. I jerked at the statement and began plummeting through the air. Then someone caught me, and immediately tried to get me to stand up.

I wanted to stand up, but my legs didn't agree with me. I couldn't stop shaking. It was so cold. So many things had just happened. I watched Ishmerai pull my soaked cloak off and put a different one on, but it felt no different to me.

"We have to get her dry," Ishmerai said, stating the obvious.

I knew that and cringed, realizing the only tent up yet was mine.

"Get the fire blazing in my tent," I ordered him.

He hurried off, and I turned my attention back to Ari'an. Her legs still weren't holding her weight.

"Ari'an, can you hear me?" I needed to know how far the shock had gone.

She nodded almost imperceptibly.

"Can you walk?"

I tried to take a step, but couldn't. I tried to shake my head, but wasn't sure if I'd even managed that. Then I felt him lift me and begin to jog toward his tent.

I was so cold, or was I warm? I couldn't tell anymore. I wanted to go to sleep, but I knew I couldn't. I fought to stay awake. Suddenly, a wave of heat hit my face making me gasp. Opening my eyes, I watched as Danren tried to get me to stand again. When I didn't, he lowered me to the ground where I at least managed to sit up.

"We have to get her dry," I heard Ishmerai say.

"I know," Danren responded in a tense tone as he lowered me to the floor.

He turned to Ishmerai and ordered him to leave.

Ishmerai hesitated for a moment, then hurried out of the tent, securing the flap behind him. I pulled the thickest blanket I had off my cot and tossed it around Ari'an, taking Ishmerai's now-soaked cloak off her.

She would never forgive me for this, but there was no other option. "Ari'an," I said slowly, "can you still hear me?"

She looked up at me, fear inscribed on her face, and nodded.

"You have to get out of your wet clothes," he told me.

I understood what he was saying. I even knew, better than most, why. I tried to untie the laces on my dress, but my fingers wouldn't cooperate on my hand. The other one continued to clamp around whatever it was holding. I couldn't think what it was, but I knew it was important. I must not let go.

I glanced up at Danren and found that his back was to me as he rummaged through a trunk.

He pulled something out, asking, "Are you finished?"

"I . . . I can't," she stammered out.

I turned back to her. That was the first thing she'd said since she fell.

"What?" I blurted out.

She glanced away from me quickly. I couldn't believe I was doing this too her, but she'd freeze if she didn't get out of those clothes.

I saw a shaking hand reach out from under the blanket. With a start, I realized that she wasn't saying that she wouldn't undress with me there. She was saying that she couldn't.

I felt sick as I pulled my dagger from my belt. Looping the long shirt I'd found across my other arm, I walked to her.

"I'm sorry," I whispered, knowing that it would do no good.

I laid the blunt edge of the dagger against the center of her neck. She began to shudder harder, but sat up straighter. I was never going to forgive myself for this. I pulled the blanket tightly closed over the hand holding the dagger and sliced down.

As he hit each layer of clothing, his hand sawed slightly to cut the hem. I shuddered at the pressure of the knife against my skin, but couldn't feel the cold metal. I clamped my eyes shut. A wave of exhaustion swept over me, but I knew I couldn't sleep. I mustn't sleep.

The knife stopped at my waist and pulled away. I felt cloth brush my face, so I opened my eyes to find Danren maneuvering the long shirt, he'd pulled out, over my head. He somehow managed to get it under the blanket.

Glancing up at him, as my dress fell off my shoulders, I some-how got my arms into the shirt. For the first time, I realized how frightened he was. He pulled me back to my feet, and I managed to step away from my soaked clothes. He cringed and pulled the blanket off. The shirt fell almost to my knees.

I realized as soon as I took hold of that blanket that it was beginning to soak through. As soon as Ari'an was dressed, I pulled it off, threw it aside, and pulled another one off the cot. I wrapped it around her shoulders. She managed to grip it with her shaking fingers.

"Ari'an, can you hear me?" I asked again.

The look that crossed her face, if it hadn't spoke so much of fear, would have been clearly irritated. I almost laughed, but I couldn't.

"You know more about healing than I do," I tried to explain. "What else do you need?"

I tried to think through what I knew about freezing. I needed to get warm, actually warm. I alternately ached all over from the cold and felt warm enough to sleep. I needed to get actually warm, so my body wasn't deceiving me like this.

"Warmth," I stammered out.

I managed to glance up briefly and saw the realization cross Danren's face. He seemed horrified, but quickly pulled off his cloak and the outer layers he was wearing.

"I'm sorry," I heard him whisper, as he pulled the blanket off me and draped it around us both.

I felt him pull me against him and begin vigorously rubbing my back. My mind began to clear as the pain from the cold completely won. I wanted to scream from it but could only whimper.

"I'm sorry," he whispered again, and I heard his voice break. "I won't hurt you," he told me.

I realized again just how honorable he was. He never would intentionally hurt me. He was better than that. The pain from the cold and the situation overwhelmed me. I began to cry.

What had I done? I felt her sob against me and fought to control my own pain. I would never have done anything like this if her life wasn't at stake. She would never believe that though. She probably thought I was taking advantage of the situation.

I couldn't keep my voice under control at anything above a whisper, but I told her anyway that when this was over, she would never have to see me again.

She would certainly want a divorce now. Perhaps Dreanen would be able to convince her to stay with him and Pher'am . . .

Dreanen! I gasped in disbelief. He was going to die. This entire expedition had been for naught. Now, on top of that, Ari'an might die as well. We should have just brought all the hunting party's equipment back with us. Then Ari'an could have stayed at Caer Corisan, and Dreanen might have lived. They would have both been fine. Why hadn't I thought of that before?

The cold was finally fading. I could control my shivering somewhat. I could feel the warmth from the fire on my back and Danren's warmth in front. I had thought that I would never feel warm again, but I did.

Suddenly, I heard him gasp at some realization, then, a few moments later, moan as if he'd just lost everything. I looked up. The expression of hopeless despair written on his face shocked me. I couldn't make myself believe that he was that upset by the offer he'd just made me. I wouldn't accept it. I didn't want to never see him again. Then I heard him painfully whisper his brother's name.

I pushed away from him, and he let me take a step back, trying to compose himself. I looked down at my clamped fist. Did I still have the antidote? My knuckles ached from clenching the vial. I reached for Danren's hand, causing him to jump.

"What are you doing?" he asked in surprise, a broken tone still in his voice.

I gripped his hand and pressed the vial into it. He stared at it blankly for a moment, but then recognition began to change his features.

"Is this . . ." his voice trailed off as he looked from the vial to me. Shocked, he met my gaze. I fought not to glance away.

"It's the antidote," I told him as he stared back down at the vial.

I couldn't believe it. Could things have changed that quickly? Ari'an was standing on her own, not even quivering, and I was holding Dreanen's antidote? Was it real?

I pulled the stopper from the bottle. I felt Ari'an pull at my hand, and I almost dropped the vial. She leaned forward looking into the bottle.

"It's fine," she told me. "It's supposed to be that odd shade of blue."

I looked into the bottle and began to breathe again. I turned to run from the tent. If Hafiz and Einheim left immediately, they could be at Caer Corisan by evening. Dreanen could be recovering today. Was it possible?

"Danren!" The shock in her tone stopped me at the entrance.

I turned back, wondering if she still needed me here.

To my surprise she was pointing at something. I glanced at what and laughed. I had nearly run out of the tent in an undershirt and breeches. I was going to freeze *myself* to death!

The laugh surprised me. I hadn't heard Danren laugh very often, but it sounded so much like how Narden laughed.

He pulled on a couple of layers, threw his cloak around his shoulders, and hurried from the tent. I couldn't help smiling. He looked so thrilled, I marveled. I'd never seen him look like that before. I heard him yell for Hafiz, then issue orders to have him and Einheim leave immediately.

I sat down next to the fire, listening to the excitement outside. I wondered if he would come back. It was his tent, though aside from his bags being different from mine, it was exactly the same. Would he send someone else with my things? When would we leave? I wanted to go home, but would I get another chance to talk to Danren? I needed to talk to him. I knew that. I would rather talk to him when he was in a good mood. I needed to explain so many things. I needed to turn down his offer. I . . . I was surprised by the realization . . . I needed my friend back.

I was so tired though. I stretched out next to the fire. I could feel the warmth seeping into my skin. The last of the chill was subsiding. I coughed. Things would get better now. The fever had nearly passed, there were only a few outbreaks now. I'd talk to Danren when he returned. I'd make sure he returned, because if he sent someone else, I'd just ask them to go find him for me. I began to doze.

I found several things to occupy myself with after seeing Hafiz and Einheim off. I knew I needed to go back to the tent. I couldn't send someone else. I wouldn't subject Ari'an to that. All she was wearing was one of my shirts, and she wouldn't be able to change back into her old things. I'd have to ask her what she wanted and where to find it.

She should have a lady-in-waiting to help her with things like this, I realized, but what young woman would want to work at Caer Corisan? Maybe I could find someone when we got back . . .

What would be the point though? She'd be leaving soon, and I'd never see her again. I glanced at the tent. Was I stalling because the longer we stayed here, the longer she'd be around? I was being selfish. I hurried back toward the tent, but realized that I was creeping along once I was near it. I shook myself. She deserved better than this.

I called before entering. There was no response. I gingerly moved the tent flap back and saw, to my horror, Ari'an collapsed on the floor. I should have never left her!

CHAPTER 44

NURSING ARI'AN

I felt someone lift me to a sitting position and shake me awake.
Finally, I could hear someone yelling my name. I opened my eyes to
find Danren shaking me. What was he doing?

"Y-you shouldn't be sleeping," he stammered. "You need to
wake up."

I looked at him, puzzled for a moment. Why shouldn't I be
sleeping? I glanced around and remembered that I was in his tent.
That must be it; if I slept, I should sleep in my tent, not his.

He was still talking though. After a moment, I realized that he
wanted to know if he should keep me awake. Why were my thoughts
so sluggish? I remembered that I'd come very close to freezing, but
I wasn't even the slightest bit cold right now. In fact, I was rather
warm. I started to shrug off the blanket, but then remembered that
all I had on was one of his shirts.

"I'm hot," I finally managed to say.

I shouldn't be hot. I glanced at Danren's face and saw the same
thought mirrored there.

"Are you all right?" he asked, sounding quite concerned.

I stared at his knees for a moment, forcing my tired, overheated
mind to work. I was not all right. I shouldn't be hot. I shouldn't be
having this much trouble thinking.

"Do I have a fever?" I asked vaguely.

I saw Danren reach for my forehead, then ball his hand into a fist, and quickly pull his hand away.

"Do you have a measurer in your kit?" he asked.

I nodded vaguely. He rose and hurried from the tent again. I stared at the fire. It almost looked as though the flames were making faces at me.

A moment, or at least it seemed like a moment later, I was shaken awake again. Why wouldn't anyone let me sleep? Dazed, I looked into Danren's face. Surprise crossed his features.

"I brought your kit and some clothes," he told me.

I stared at him blankly, why did I need either of those? I glanced down and remembered that I was just wearing his shirt. That explained the clothes, but why the kit? Did he not feel well? Why was I so hot?

"You needed a measurer to see if you have a fever," a panicked edge to his voice.

A fever? That might explain why I was so warm. I reached for the kit, opening it. I stared blankly into it for several moments. What was I looking for? I glanced up at Danren puzzled. Why couldn't I think? Why was Danren here? I glanced around. Why wasn't I in my tent?

I felt Danren pull something from my hands. Why had I needed my kit? Was he hurt? He didn't look hurt. He held out my measurer to me.

"Why do I need that?" I finally asked, staring at it blankly.

"You might have a fever," he told me, slowly, with forced calm.

I took the measurer and put it under my tongue, wondering if Danren was upset with me. Had I done something wrong? I couldn't think of what I'd done. In fact, I couldn't think of much of anything. Danren rose suddenly and left the tent.

I stared at the tent flap for a moment. Why had he left like that? I glanced around. There were some of my clothes on the ground next to me. Was I supposed to get dressed? I picked up a few pieces, realizing that I couldn't put them on over the shirt I had on. I started to take the shirt off, but it caught on something sticking out of my mouth. I pulled what I was holding in my teeth out. Why did I have a measurer in my mouth? The liquid wasn't normal. It was too high. Was this my temperature? Did I have a fever?

With a fearful realization, my thoughts cleared enough for me to think straight for a moment. I might not just have a fever. I might have *the* fever. Unlike Majorlaine, I'd never had it before. The long days of searching and especially the fall into the river, could have triggered it. It usually came on suddenly. The fever itself would rise at an alarming rate within a watch or two.

I glanced at the measurer in my hands. Why was I holding a measurer? NO, I had to think clearly. I needed to do something. I saw the pile of clothes again. I needed to get dressed.

I quickly found Ishmerai and dispatched him to Caer Corisan. I had to get Galen here quickly. I frantically thought over who we had here with medical training. I froze. Ari'an was the person we'd brought for such things. She was almost as good as Galen, and she was supposed to stay away from any fighting. Nothing was supposed to happen to her. Why hadn't I thought she'd get sick? I raged at myself for even letting her come.

I quickly rummaged through our food stores for teas and broths. Anything that Ari'an might be able to drink even in her delirious state.

I hurried back to the tent. I called at the flap. There was no answer. I entered slowly, glancing around. She was crumpled by the fire again. The measurer lay on the floor near her, and she was dressed in her own clothes.

I sat her up and, again, began to shake her gently. Her eyes fluttered open, but barely focused on me. I wasn't certain which would be worse, if she did recognize me and went into one of her fits, or this blank stare.

"Ari," I called to her, "stay with me."

I glanced at the measurer. Was that measure from her, or was that from being too close to the fire? I felt her slump against me.

"Ari!" I shook her again. "You can't go back to sleep yet."

I rummaged through her kit and found willow bark powder. I grabbed one of the broth containers, it was cold, but at least it was something. I poured both into a cup.

"Ari," I told her as her eyes looked at me without recognition, "you have to swallow this."

She took the cup from me and stared at it blankly. I took it back and held it to her lips. She took a few swallows automatically. I hoped she'd swallowed enough. I set the cup down and felt her lean against me. I shook her again. This couldn't be happening!

I was shaken awake, but couldn't understand why. Why couldn't I sleep? I just wanted to sleep. I glanced up at whoever had woke me. Why wouldn't he let me sleep? I swallowed whatever he put against my mouth. Maybe he'd let me sleep now. I leaned forward as the exhaustion took over. I wondered if I would wake back up, but my thoughts wouldn't clear enough to know why that was important . . .

The nightmares were so real. Only later would I be able to distinguish actual memories from the horrific visions that plagued me through the fever. Often I heard a voice calling me out of the terror. It was a voice I knew. I would find out that it was Danren, but through the fever, I could connect the voice only vaguely to Narden. It pulled me out of more nightmares than I could ever count.

Often he would beg me to "swallow a little more" or ask me to "just sit up for a moment." I could never remember, if I did what he asked or not. All too soon I would fall back into the nightmares.

Galen didn't want Ari'an transported from the camp or even moved from my tent when he arrived the next day. He told me that the added stress could be fatal. Fatal . . . This fever had been fatal in far too many cases already. I couldn't lose her like this. At least, if she divorced me or went to live with Pher'am and Dreanen, she'd be alive.

"Mighty One have mercy, not like this," I repeated so many times I lost count.

The days dragged on, and the nights were even longer. Galen came as often as he could. Even he seemed worried. He impatiently explained everything we needed to do for Ari, every precaution we needed to take.

He once snapped, "If Lady Ari'an was well, she'd explain everything."

He instantly realized what he'd said; for the first time in my life, I saw him cringe.

After a week, was it only a week, it seemed like months, he told me, "If the fever breaks . . ." then trailed off.

I waited for him to finish. *If the fever broke* . . . If it didn't . . . NO, no, not like this. Mighty One have mercy, not like this.

"If the fever breaks," he finally continued, "it will mean one of two things." He paused again. Why wouldn't he just say whatever it was? "She'll either start recovering or . . ." He looked at me. "You should turn," he told me.

I wanted to run him through with my sword!

"How long has it been?"

"Going on four weeks," I answered with a forced calm that I didn't feel.

"You'll turn in your sleep if you don't soon. It's already beginning to show."

"I'm not sleeping." I felt an edge come into my voice.

What was the other possibility if the fever broke?

"You can't keep pushing yourself like this," he continued, "not as a human."

"I won't leave her," I almost growled.

He began silently packing up his kit. I almost grabbed his shoulder and ripped him back around.

Instead, I took a ragged breath and said between clenched teeth, "She'll start recovering, or what?"

He took a long breath of his own. "Or she'll never wake up."

I looked at Ari'an lying on what had been my cot. She'd used it far longer than I had now.

"Mighty One have mercy, not like this."

I felt the slight breeze from the second tent flap opening. Galen had left.

We'd put up another tent around my original one, to keep in more of the heat. The fire blazed constantly. It felt like the middle of summer. Ari'an began to toss. The all too familiar look of terror crossed her face, and again, she began to shudder.

I sat down next to the cot, talking to her and praying.

Three more days went by. Nothing changed, except that Ari'an looked even thinner, drawn, far more pale. Then the fever finally broke. *Mighty One have mercy, not like this.*

I felt hungry. It was the first normal feeling that I could remember having in what seemed like forever. Then I felt a hand move behind my shoulder and lift me to a sitting position.

"Just for a moment," a voice explained, "while you get a drink."

It took me a moment to place the voice. It sounded almost like Narden's but not quite right. With a start, I realized it must be Danren.

"It's all right," such a familiar phrase in such a familiar voice.

I relaxed a little, because of the sound.

Feeling a rim pressed to my lips, I tentatively took a sip. It was chicken broth, and it tasted so good. I took a big swallow and reached up to steady the bowl. I heard a gasp, and the bowl quivered slightly. I opened my eyes to look at it.

"Ari?" I heard Danren, as his voice had a strange quiver to it that seemed to match that of the bowl.

I took another drink, as the bowl steadied.

"Not too much," Danren told me, his voice wavering.

"I've been sick." I felt stupid as soon as I spoke.

"Yes," Danren said, "you had the Fever."

I watched the bowl as his hand set it on a little table next to the cot. I recognized several vials of powders and liquids sitting near it. I'd never thought Danren would do healing work. I quickly realized that his arm was behind my shoulders as well. I then noticed . . . Was he blue behind the ears? Was I seeing things?

He turned back to me, and I watched a look of pain cross his face as he saw my shock. I looked away, and he gently set me back against the pillows.

"How long?" I asked, as he stood up.

"You've been sick for a week and a half," he answered. "How do you feel?"

I thought for an instant. "Hungry."

I heard him laugh. It wasn't his normal laugh. It had far too much tension.

"I'll find out what you can eat."

With a start I realized why I was on a cot in a tent.

"Dreanen!" I exclaimed. "What happened to Dreanen?"

There was a moment's pause then a slightly better laugh. "He's fine . . . Thanks to you."

I thought for a moment, then looked up as a slight cold breeze brushed my face. Danren was gone.

I hurried from the tent into what had become a semipermanent camp, but slowed as I took a few steps. She'd woken up. I slumped against a tree. She'd *woken* up. She would be all right now. *She'd woken up.* I wanted to laugh or yell, but the only sound I heard was an odd sob. Realizing it was me, I slid down the tree and set my head against my knees, my hands covering my hair. I laughed and sobbed feeling . . . I couldn't tell what for sure. Completely relieved maybe, but far more than that. I didn't care about the mud or the cold. *She'd woken up.*

"Thank you," I choked out. "Thank you."

I stared at the lean-to that Ferrer was using to upkeep our weapons, and then glanced at the structured mess tent. Those poles were actually three steps into the ground to keep the tent secure. Five other housing tents were here now in addition to the ones we'd originally brought. There were patrols around this area to ensure our safety while we waited for . . . Ari'an to wake up . . . *She woke up!*

Hearing a dragon hurrying toward me, I tried to pull myself together.

"Lord Danren," Einheim sounded frantic, "what's wrong? What happened?"

Loyal, quick, honest Einheim, if he'd been able to turn, I might have left her care to him once in a while, but he was too young. He still had years left before he could be human again.

"Lord Danren?" such concern in his voice. "She isn't . . ."

I laughed, the first real laugh in what seemed like years. "She woke up."

He stared at me for a moment, not comprehending, then his face began to light as the information sunk in. "She woke up?"

I nodded.

He let out an enormous yell and sprang into the sky, yelling the whole time, *"She woke up! She woke up!"*

I watched him loop and spin and yell. Everything that I wanted to do, but I wondered if I'd even be able to stand. What was I supposed to do out here?

Food! I was supposed to get Ari'an something to eat. What was I doing sitting in the mud when she needed something to eat? What had Galen said she could eat, if she woke up? If she woke up . . . *She had woken up!*

Mintxo was toasting some bread and frying eggs when I arrived at the mess tent.

He glanced up and immediately asked, "Is it true?"

I nodded. "She woke up."

He looked as though he wanted to jump and spin and race around like I could still hear Einheim doing outside, but instead he turned back to the makeshift cookstove and began turning everything over that was on it, rather energetically. I watched as he ruined at least three sets of eggs in a few moments. I'd have to remember to tease him later about that, since he always hounded Ekaitz so much whenever he made a mistake.

A moment later, he turned back to me, scowling. "What are you doing here?"

"She said she was hungry," I told him. She woke up, *and she was hungry.*

His face lit up as he moved to the stores. I heard a jar crash, but he didn't notice. Another thing to tease him about later. He came back with a jar, a spoon, and a bowl. He scraped two pieces of toast off the stove, put them on the bowl, then took one back.

"She probably shouldn't eat too much," he said, looking disappointed.

He hurried to the tent flap and opened it for me. "Come back, and I'll have some rice mash ready for her." Turning back to the stores, "Nice warm rice mash."

Three men met me right outside the tent.

"We heard . . ." Ishmerai began, and then looked up at the figure of Einheim.

"Yes," I laughed, "she woke up."

Because the number of people at this camp grew while we waited for Ari'an to . . . wake up . . . *She woke up* . . . I found that I couldn't go more than ten steps without someone stopping me to ask, but I didn't mind telling them again and again, "She woke up. Yes, she woke up."

By the time I reached the tent, Xander was whistling, Ishmerai was tuning his vollin, while sitting under a tree, Hafiz had gotten into a friendly tussle with Besnik, probably to make up for all the unfriendly ones they'd had over the last week and a half, Einheim was still swooping and spinning above the camp, and a large puff of smoke had issued from the mess tent.

I stopped at the entrance to the tent and said it one more time, trying to convince myself, "She woke up."

She was sitting up. *She was sitting up!*

"What is going on?" she asked, sounding concerned.

I glanced behind me wondering what she was talking about, then realized that the clamor from the camp, probably, didn't make any sense to her. "She wo—" I stopped myself. "You woke up."

She looked in disbelief between me and the tent flap.

"What are they doing?" she finally asked, as I set the bowl and the jar on the little table next to the cot.

I fumbled for a moment for the right word, then laughed. "Rejoicing."

She still looked confused.

"We were really worried about you."

We were really worried about you . . . I took the piece of toast he offered me and began to eat it. We . . . He'd been worried too. I felt emotion choke me for a moment. Danren was busy poring what looked like smashed fruit into the bowl he'd brought, so thankfully, he didn't notice. He held it up to his nose for a moment and sniffed it.

I must have looked surprised when he turned back to me, because he immediately began to explain, "Mintxo was so . . . well . . . excited about you waking up that I didn't ask what this was. It seems to just be sauced apples."

The enigmatic look on his face almost made me laugh, but instead I asked, "Were you expecting him to give you something else?"

He chuckled. "I'm not sure what I was expecting." He stirred the fruit. "But in Mintxo's current state, I wasn't sure that I should trust whatever he'd given me."

He held a spoonful out to me. My jaw dropped, not to accept the bite, but at the thought of not being able to feed myself.

Danren guessed that something was wrong.

"I'm sorry," I stammered.

What was I thinking? She didn't want me to help her. It proba-bly scared her terribly to wake up, when I was helping her. She hated me, I reminded myself. That was the main reason I'd dealt with most of her care while she was sick. There was no reason she should hate someone else.

I glanced down at the bowl, slightly at her, then around the tent. She seemed too weak to sit up without some assistance. Currently, she was leaning back on her arms. I could hold her up, but then I'd still be touching her. I could help her to a chair, but that might be worse than just helping her sit up.

"Would you hold the bowl for me?" she asked softly.

I could do that, as long as she only needed one arm to keep her up.

I felt so incompetent, not even being able to feed myself properly, but Danren was gracious. He held the little bowl and never commented on how badly my hand quivered at times. I was so weak. I wasn't even certain that I could stand up.

When I finished, which took far longer than I would have liked, he set the bowl on the table.

Standing up, he said, "Mintxo promised some warm rice mash, if you'd like it."

"That would be nice," I told him, but I wasn't sure how much longer I could stay sitting up.

When he left, I lay back down. I was so tired, and all I'd done was sit up for a little while to eat!

I hurried back to the mess tent, trying desperately to think of something so Ari'an could feed herself without having to rely on my help. I stopped and glanced back at our blacksmith, Ferrer, polishing swords. He was sitting next to a table that was about two hands-breadth taller than the little one next to the cot. It was about two steps longer too. That table could be set over the cot, and Ari could eat from that. She could even lean on it, if she needed to!

"May I have this?" I asked, hurrying toward Ferrer while pointing to the table.

He gave me a puzzled look for a moment, then told me, "The sword you have is far better, my lord. Armel made that one"—he motioned at my scabbard—"himself."

"No," I corrected him, "the table. May I have the table?"

His look only became more confused. "The table, sir?"

"For Lady Ari'an," I began to explain, but he immediately jumped up and began tossing the clean swords on the ground.

"For her ladyship?" he rambled. "Of course, my lord."

I glanced at the mess tent. I would need to move the table first. When I turned back, Ferrer was holding it, looking at me expectantly.

"I'll get it," I told him, taking the table from him.

He looked completely disappointed, but I didn't want Ari'an under any more stress than was necessary, and visitors, even well-intentioned ones, might be too much. Also, if I let one person in, even with the pretense of moving in a table, everyone in the camp would bring by something to put in the tent in order to see her.

I called before entering, and for once heard a soft response. Once again, I realized that she was indeed awake, but the elation was fading. She'd still be leaving as soon as she fully recovered. At least, she was alive though.

She turned her head toward me as I entered, and looked slightly puzzled.

"Maybe you should check before making me eat that," she said. Was she actually joking? "I'm not sure that's rice mash."

I chuckled at the comment. "No, Mintxo isn't that far gone."

I set the table down next to the bed, took a breath, and then hefted it over the cot. Ari'an looked slightly frightened as it swung over the cot, but it was perfect. It left about a hand span between her legs and the base of the table and spanned the cot with two handsbreadth length to spare on either side.

I tried to keep my voice as calm as possible. I'd had tables lofted over beds I'd been in before. The memories weren't ones I wanted to relive at that moment.

"What's that for?" I finally asked.

"For you to eat off of." I caught a note of accomplishment in his voice.

I looked at the table as he left again and saw it for what it was. It was just a table. I glanced at the entrance and realized that he was trying very hard to make this as comfortable for me as possible. The table would allow me to eat without assistance. I choked up for a moment. Why was he always so kind to me? I'd made his life miserable for years, but he was still trying to make me comfortable.

I turned slightly on the pillows. I was so tired.

"Mighty One bless him . . . please . . . somehow," I whispered.

The tent had more furnishings now. There was the chair that Danren sat in while helping me eat. Next to that was a small table with the medicines. As I started to doze, I wondered if he'd been sleeping in my tent, because I was in his.

CHAPTER 45

A DRAGON LORD'S CHANGE

I awoke later feeling far more rested. I still felt weak, but at least I wasn't completely exhausted.

I immediately noticed the smell of food rising from somewhere in front of me. I glanced at the table over the bed and saw steam rising from one of Armel's contraptions. This one was used to store food to keep it warm. It was a pot with a lid, but the pot was about two fingers thick, sort of. It was more two pots, one inside the other with something between the two that stayed warm. I didn't know all the details, but I knew it worked.

I sat up slowly, leaned against the table, and gingerly touched the lid. It wasn't scalding, but it was warm. I took the lid off, laying it next to the container. Inside was the rice mash that Danren was going to bring me. He must have gotten the container after he came back and found that I was asleep.

Wondering where he was, I jumped and almost knocked over the food, when I saw him, sitting next to the head of the bed, slumped slightly forward. I stared at him for a moment, before realizing that he was asleep.

What took me so long to comprehend, though, was the blue. It had spread from just behind his ears to cover his whole ears and part of his face. It seemed to still be spreading too.

I remembered that Armel had told me about this. If one of them didn't turn from human to dragon when they were supposed to, they could hold it off for a while, but not for long. If they didn't turn on their own, they'd start turning when they relaxed, specifically when they slept.

The blue was beginning to take on a scaly look, and his collar was picking up the color too. That was a grace, I'd been told. A special blessing from the One that they couldn't quite explain why or how it worked. Their clothes would turn with them, and when they turned back, they were still dressed. The clothes needed a very thorough washing, I'd been told, but other than that, they were fine.

I remembered seeing both Danren and Dreanen turn months ago at the ambush, but that had happened so quickly, I couldn't believe what I was seeing then. This change was taking place rather slowly. He retained most of his human features, but the blue took over. Then as the scales appeared, they began to be accented with the gold. The brilliant blue taking over the colors of the clothes was amazing to watch.

I jumped when Danren stirred slightly in his sleep. He reached up to scratch his face and accidentally jabbed himself in the eye. His hands had turned slightly, and his nails had taken on a clawlike appearance. He awoke and stared at his hand for a moment before letting out a groan. His hand balled into a fist and landed on the little table lightly, surprisingly lightly.

He shook his head and sighed, leaning forward slightly. The change took over rapidly then, and Narden was standing in the tent. He looked like he was about to do that familiar shake of his scales, when he stopped to glance at me.

I probably looked rather stupid, staring at him wide eyed with my mouth gaping.

His expression changed from the slightly miserable one he'd had when he'd turned, to one of shock.

"I'm sorry," he whispered, and hurried from the tent.

I wouldn't see him again at the camp. I would occasionally hear his voice outside the tent giving orders though.

Galen came that evening to check on me and told me that I could go back to Caer Corisan in a few days.

I hadn't meant to fall asleep. With all the excitement from Ari'an waking up, I thought I'd be fine. I was wrong.

After coming back to the tent, and finding her asleep, I'd retrieved my food warmer and set the bowl inside. That would keep the rice mash warm for several watches. I wondered how long she would sleep or how long she should sleep. I hadn't thought to ask Galen about that. Of course, when I'd had the opportunity to ask him, no one was certain that she'd ever wake up at all, much less need to wake up after waking up . . . I wasn't making much sense to myself . . .

I watched Ari'an sleep for a while. She was sleeping peacefully, no thrashing or cries of pain. It was amazing to see. I hadn't believed I'd ever see her sleep peacefully. Leaning against the back of the chair, I marveled at the sight.

The next thing I noticed was that an innocent scratch of an itch nearly took out my eye. I stared at my hand in disbelief. I'd done the one thing that I wasn't supposed to do. I'd fallen asleep. My hands were too far gone to be able to maneuver much of anything in this state.

I turned. Then I realized that I couldn't hear Ari'an's rhythmic breathing. I glanced at the cot to find her staring at me, horrified. What had I done?

I didn't go back to see her after that. She wouldn't want to see me anyway. I started to organize the breaking of camp. Galen arrived that evening to check on Ari'an. He told us that we should be able to leave within three days. Three days . . . then what?

CHAPTER 46

DECISIONS

I stayed away from Caer Corisan as much as possible that spring. It wasn't too difficult with border raids starting up again. It seemed to me that Ari'an was content to stay as long as I wasn't there. At least, I didn't hear any news that she was leaving. I knew I couldn't stay away forever, but at least for now, she was safe.

I needed to talk to Danren . . . or Narden, either one, I supposed, but neither one would stay at Caer Corisan for more than the briefest amount of time. As spring began to turn to summer, my patience wore thin. I had to apologize to him, and he wouldn't stay around to let me. Finally, I worked out a plan.

Adenern was coming that month for a visit. Danren hadn't been at Caer Corisan for his previous visits. Instead, they'd met up at the caves. I had a message delivered to Dreanen, requesting that he stop by Caer Corisan before visiting his brother. He did not respond, but Adenern did arrive at Caer Corisan within a week.

He seemed cordial enough when I met him in the courtyard, but was slightly on edge, when I asked him to take me to see Danren.

"Danren's patrolling," he told me.

I knew what that meant. I'd been picking up the terminology.

"I need you to take me to see Narden then."

He smiled slightly, then sighed deeply. I'd never seen Adenern look as serious as he did now. Taking over as the heir had settled him substantially. Drenar's death had been hard on all of us.

"You really shouldn't divorce him," he told me.

I watched my hands for a moment, trying to word my response.

"He's done his best to keep you safe," he continued. "He was under oath not to tell anyone. He tried to get the counsel to grant him or someone permission to tell you for years. I know he's upset you, but he's not perfect." After a moment, he continued, "Also, you couldn't exactly get anything out of it. Danren doesn't have a very large official holding, and the bride price was insubstantial, so it really wouldn't be worth the effort."

He paused to clear his throat and looked awkward for a moment. "That and I know Danren never tried anything with you. If you go back home, you might end up married to someone else, and . . . well . . ." he trailed off, looking uncomfortable.

I tried to keep a straight face, but seeing Adenern discussing something serious without making jokes was so different that I almost laughed.

"I wasn't planning to demand a divorce," I told him.

He broke into a broad grin, which quickly turned serious again. "You really shouldn't move in with Pher'am and me either. Not that you wouldn't be welcome," he quickly added. "It's just that, well, you wouldn't be able to talk about"—he motioned vaguely around—"things much. You couldn't even talk about dragons very often."

"Pher'am doesn't like the dragons?" I asked, finally interrupting for a moment.

He leaned his head closer, saying sadly, "Mother visits rather often."

Lord Grath's wife had a deep prejudice against the dragons. The exact details weren't clear, but she blamed the dragons for her sister's, Lord Grath's first wife, death.

I nodded.

"You really do fit well here. I mean, aside from the problems with Danren. He's tried really hard to keep you comfortable. I know it hasn't been easy for you here when he's around, but . . ." his voice trailed off.

"I wasn't planning to move," I told him trying not to laugh, because he looked so awkward.

"You weren't?" The shock on his face was too much, and I finally laughed. He glanced around slightly. "Am I missing something?"

I wanted to tell him, "Probably," but he'd been trying so hard with his speeches that I couldn't bring myself to tease him.

"Why do you want to talk to Danren then?" He looked entirely confused.

I looked at my hands for a moment. "I need to apologize."

"You what?" He sounded completely lost. "Why can't you wait for him to come back?"

"He hasn't been coming back, and if he does, he leaves before I can talk to him," I explained.

He still didn't see what the problem was, but I insisted that he take me to Narden. Finally, he agreed and arranged a bit of an escort for the next day. Ishmerai and Einheim would fly surveillance.

I almost called the whole thing off too many times. I barely slept and packed and repacked the few things I was going to take almost as many times as I decided not to go.

When morning finally came, I found myself on my way to the caves of Gary's line. I was terrified. I wasn't entirely sure how he felt about me. I mean, I had told him, as Narden, that I wished he was dead. That wasn't exactly minor. He'd always acted polite to me, but was that just because he was too nice to treat me poorly. Would he suggest a divorce? Did he want me to leave? His life would be much easier if I wasn't around. I realized that he must feel like he was walking on fresh eggs anytime he was around me.

I should ask Adenern to take me back. This was pointless. He'd never forgive me. I couldn't make myself heard over the wind. I was stuck. *Why* had I gotten myself into this?

Narden wasn't in the front cave when we landed. I quickly removed the saddle Adenern had on.

Then I heard Adenern ask, "What are you doing here?"

I was behind his leg and couldn't tell who he was talking to. I hadn't heard Narden come in.

There was a slight pause, then the wrong voice answered in a slightly irritated tone, "I live here, remember?"

Oh no! It was Danren! Yes, I'd come to apologize to him, but I'd expected Narden. Yes, they were the same person, but I was used to talking to Narden about difficult subjects. What was I going to do now?

What type of greeting was that? He hadn't even asked how I was, not that I was doing well.

"No," he replied slowly, "you live at Caer Corisan."

I laughed ironically at that.

"What have you been doing?" he asked, looking me over.

I knew I looked rather odd, especially considering I was practically covered in mud and had a few holes in my clothes.

"You know that some of the pools haven't been heating right for years," I explained. "I was cleaning some of the pipes out."

"You look it," he told me.

"Thanks," I answered, sarcastically.

I decided to change the subject since he seemed, for some reason, slightly put out by my ruffled appearance.

"What are you doing here this early? Is anything wrong?"

"No," he said casually . . . too casually, but he didn't say anything.

"So why are you here this early?" I prompted.

"Well," he thought for a moment, "to sort of deliver a message, I suppose."

He didn't continue . . . again.

"A message about what?"

"Well," he paused, this was rather irritating, "Ari would like to talk to you."

I choked. It was finally happening. "About what?"

"I think she'd rather tell you that herself," he paused.

"Has she packed already?" I asked.

476

"Well, she packed a few things, but not much," he answered.

The moan I heard in response ripped me open inside. I kicked Adenern in the leg. He shouldn't be doing this.

"I knew this was coming," Danren replied finally.

"I doubt that," Adenern answered.

I kicked him again. He didn't pay any attention.

"Oh, go away," Danren snapped.

"Are you going to talk to her?"

"Eventually."

"When?"

"Go away." There was a forced calm in his voice that worried me.

"A different question then."

I glared at him.

"Aren't you touchy today," he bantered.

"Go away," I was losing patience with him.

"Not until you answer this question." He smiled.

"What question?" I snapped.

"The one you won't let me ask."

"What question?" I couldn't keep the growl out of my voice.

"All right, but I thought you'd want to be calmer when I asked," he told me, continuing immediately. "Do you love her?"

The question caught me off guard. I hadn't expected anything like that.

"Love is a choice," I finally sputtered out.

"So what choice have you made?" he asked casually.

I felt for my sword and realized it wasn't on me. I glanced at the table where I'd left it. From now on, even if I was dredging out pipes, I would carry my sword. I really wanted to hack at him at that moment.

"That's none of your business," I snapped.

Why was I taking this out on him anyway, I wondered, aside from the fact that he was annoying me.

"It doesn't matter anyway," I said softly, not expecting him to hear me.

"It might." Why did dragons have such good ears?

"Go away," I didn't yell it this time.

"Do you not know? Do you not want to admit it?" He paused. "Do you just not want to tell me?"

"Go away."

"This might be easier if you just answered the question."

"Go away."

"All right," he shrugged, "but I warned you."

I watched him walk into the room of pools.

Danren wasn't looking at me . . . yet. This wasn't going at all as I'd planned. I wanted to kill Adenern myself, and I could tell that Danren did too. Well, at least we had something in common. I stopped myself from laughing at that absurd thought.

Danren glared at the entrance to the room of pools for a while, then ran his hand over his face and through his hair. He balled the hand into a fist and glared at the room of pools again. He then looked up at the ceiling and, finally, at the cave entrance, where I was still standing.

I wasn't certain how he was going to react. He stared at me for a moment. I knew I should say something, but I couldn't think of anything.

His voice was calmer than I'd expected when he spoke, and the words were not anything that I thought he would say, "Excuse me for a moment, my lady."

I couldn't think straight for the longest time. Finally, I realized that I had to figure out how much time I had. A week . . . two at most . . . Two weeks to figure out what to say to her when she told me she was leaving. Now the hard part, what to say? I stared at the ceiling then glanced at the entrance . . .

It took me a moment to realize that I wasn't hallucinating. Ari'an was standing there, looking rather out of place, and holding a saddle. *What had he done?* My mind went entirely blank for an instant, then fixated on one thought. I told Ari'an to excuse me and walked out of the room. I was going to kill him.

Adenern turned around when he heard me coming.

He looked slightly puzzled and motioned toward the doorway. "Shouldn't you be in there?"

"You're," I said, in a far more even tone than I thought possible, "dead."

He actually looked nervous for a moment, then calmly told me, "Do you want one of the things she remembers from her time here to be my corpse lying on the floor?"

I reached for my sword and again found it missing. Apparently, I was going to kill him with my bare hands, and then permanently attach my scabbard to my body.

"What were you thinking bringing her here?" I snapped, trying to figure out how I was going to do this.

"It was her idea." His easygoing tone was grating.

"What?" I could turn, but by the time I was finished, he might have fled.

"She insisted that I bring her to speak to you."

"What?" Did I still have my dagger on me?

"She said that you'd been avoiding her, and she needed to talk to you."

"What?" Yes! I did have it! Maybe I could cram it down his throat.

"You're not listening to me, are you?"

"What?" If it did enough damage on the way down, it just might work.

"I'm leaving."

"What?" He turned around and began walking toward his cave.

"Where are you going?" I yelled at his back.

"I already told you," he called.

There was a pause as I watched him walk away. He couldn't leave! He wasn't dead yet!

"You should probably go talk to your wife," he called from his cave.

I stood there staring at his cave. What was I supposed to do now?

Danren left the room. For a moment, I wondered if he would leave me stuck in this mountain. He obviously didn't want to talk to me, but would he go that far?

Then I heard that eerily calm tone again, "You're dead."

Oh no! He was going to attack Adenern! I hurried to the table to set the saddle on one of the chairs. There was a sword on the table. What was a sword doing there? Then I realized, Danren hadn't been wearing his. He couldn't attack Adenern without it . . . unless he turned, then the sword wouldn't be any use to him anyway.

I heard his footsteps coming back. I froze. What should I do? I had the insane urge to flee, but where would I go? Hadn't I come here to talk to him anyway?

CHAPTER 47

COMMUNICATION

I might as well get this over with, I realized. I still couldn't think of what to say when I saw her.

"Mighty One have mercy," I prayed, "please, let something come to me."

I walked back into the cave and looked toward the entrance. I opened my mouth to say something, but first, there was no one there to say anything to, and second, I still didn't know what to say.

I glanced at the curtained side room. It didn't look like it'd been disturbed. Then I looked toward the table. I'd left all the furnishings where they'd been when she was staying here. She was standing by the table, and she'd set the saddle down on one of the chairs.

I felt rather idiotic standing there with my mouth open, so I began to walk toward the table. Maybe I could come up with something in the few steps . . . Since when had the table been that close to the room of pools?

Maybe I could stall. I could take a few moments to put my sword back on . . .

"Where's my sword?" I asked.

If that wasn't the dumbest thing to start the conversation with, but I was, suddenly, focused on that one thing. I'd left it on the table. I glanced at the saddle. Had I left it on the chair? Why would Ari'an put that on the one chair that was occupied?

I lifted the corner of the saddle. No, it wasn't under there. I glanced around the shelves, and then realized that Ari'an was standing on the other side of the table from me with her hands behind her back. She said something that took a moment for me to understand. Why was she hiding my sword behind her back?

"It was my idea," she'd said.

"Do you have my sword?"

She nodded.

I finally realized what she'd said, but the statement didn't make any sense. Her idea to hide my sword?

"Your idea about what?"

"My idea to come here . . ." she said, "to talk to you."

I couldn't believe that. Adenern had probably planned the whole thing. He was good at convincing people of things. I must have shown my disbelief, because she suddenly sounded defensive.

"I sent a message to him to talk to me before he came to see you. I'd already decided to have him bring me here before he even came to Caer Corisan."

I realized that she was completely serious. She'd been that desperate to tell me she was leaving that she'd decided to come here herself. I felt the blood drain from my face. Pulling out the chair nearest to me, I sat down. I wasn't sure that I could take this standing up, but I might as well get it over with.

To my surprise, she didn't continue. Instead, she hurried to the cupboard and pulled out the water pitcher and a stack of glasses. What was she doing? She somehow managed to juggle the sword, the cups, and the pitcher without spilling anything. She set the cups on the table. Poured water into one, and pushed it toward me.

I stared at it for a moment, then motioned at the sword. "May I have that back?"

She glanced at the sword, then at me. "I don't want you to attack anyone. It was my idea."

I suddenly realized that she must think I would come after her.

The soft moan I heard nearly tore me apart. Danren took a deep breath.

"Ari'an," he began softly, "I would never attack you." I stared blankly at his end of the table, while he continued, "I understand your concern, and I know why you've come to this decision. I'll see to it that you get to . . ."

I realized that I didn't have any idea as to where she wanted to go. I stopped myself before saying that. I already sounded like a complete idiot. I probably shouldn't make it worse.

He sighed again. He looked utterly defeated. Maybe I shouldn't have come. Maybe I should go to live with Dreanen and Pher'am. Maybe I should go back to my parents.

I bit my lip. I'd come here for a reason, and he still deserved that much.

I could only manage to whisper the words, though, as I began, "I came to apologize. I'm sorry I . . . I know I never treated you well . . . You were right . . . I never gave you a chance. I didn't handle finding out about . . . turning well either. I'm sorry."

I sat down on the chair nearest to me. What was I supposed to say now?

I'd been listening for a location, Torion Castle, or Ryuu where Dreanen and Pher'am lived, anywhere. I needed to know where she wanted to go, but I didn't catch a place. Had I missed it? I tried to bring back what she'd said.

She'd started out with "I came to . . ." What had she said? "Apologize."

I stared at her blankly. *Apologize?* What did she have to apologize for?

His head suddenly shot up, as he stared at me, shocked. I couldn't exactly blame him. Then the familiar question came. I almost laughed when I heard it.

"What?"

The smile surprised me. I had never expected to see her smile around me again, but here she was looking at her hands with that little bit of a smile on her face. The smile disappeared after a moment, and she looked toward me. Then she looked directly at me. I saw her blush slightly and look down at her hands again. I needed to pull myself together. This certainly wasn't going how I'd thought it would.

"You don't need to apologize," I told her. "You have nothing to apologize for. If anyone should be apologizing, it should be me."

She did look up then, in shock. "What would you possibly have to apologize for?"

I dropped my gaze. I couldn't meet her eyes to explain this. "I lied to you."

There was a pause then her voice quivered, "About what?"

I glanced up. How could she not remember?

"About the whole dragon . . . thing . . ." I trailed off.

"Armel said you took an oath not to tell anyone," regaining some control over her voice again.

"Yes, but . . ." I'd wanted to tell her, but I'd been forbidden time and again.

"Armel told me that you'd asked the counsel for permission several times," she continued.

"Yes, but . . ." I'd asked the counsel every time they'd convened, but Edur had always voted against the idea.

If the counsel wasn't united on things like this, approval was denied.

"Were they upset when you told me?" she asked.

I almost chuckled, but stopped myself. "Only Edur was. He wanted to skin me up one side and down the other."

"Who's Edur?" she asked.

I realized that she'd never met him. That was probably part of his problem. Certainly, if he'd met her, he would have approved, but it was too late for that now. He was rather livid.

"Edur is the eldest member of Indigo's line."

"Oh," she said, trailing off for a moment. "He's upset with you for telling me."

"Upset?" I did chuckle this time. "No. Furious, yes."

"I'm sorry," she said, looking up from her hands. "I didn't mean to cause you so much trouble."

"This isn't trouble," I told her. "It's just Edur. He's always a bit . . . stodgy."

"Like Gary?" she asked.

"No," I laughed at that comparison. "He's nothing like Gary." I thought for a moment. "Both of them have suffered a lot, but Edur is unforgiving and vindictive. Gary is . . . tired."

"What happened to Edur?" she asked.

I sighed. "He told his wife when he was first married about . . . turning, and she . . . didn't take it well."

"Did she leave him?"

"No," I replied slowly, "she tried to kill him, and then . . . killed herself instead."

The gasp didn't surprise me. It wasn't a pleasant story.

"She was with child at the time," I finished.

I glanced up to see Ari'an staring at me with her mouth open.

"W-why?" she stammered.

I stared at her blankly for a moment. "Her husband had told her that he turned into a . . . a dragon . . . in her eyes a monster, slightly more often than every other month."

"I see why he didn't want you to tell me," she finally managed.

"I told him you were different, but he always just scoffed at me and said that he'd thought that too," I replied.

He'd told Edur that I was different. I felt about as tall as an ant at that moment. How could he have ever thought that?

"I'm sorry I disappointed you."

There was silence for a moment, so I glanced up. Danren looked rather perplexed.

"He was probably right about not telling me," I continued, fidgeting with the scabbard across my legs.

"What?" I smiled at the familiar statement, almost laughing.

I had heard Lord Grath correct him and Narden so often about making that one-word comment, but they both, or rather he, still used it whenever he was surprised.

"I haven't made life exactly easy on you," I continued.

"Well, if I'd been allowed to tell you when we were married . . ." his voice trailed off then continued lower, "things might have been different."

I thought about the wedding for a moment. I wondered how I would have taken it if he'd told me then. I couldn't rightly say. I wasn't entirely sure I would have understood at all. It hadn't been an easy time for me. I glanced up and noticed that Danren looked concerned. I must have had a troubled look on my face.

"The wedding was a shock to me," I tried to explain. "You see, my father had told me that I wasn't engaged to anyone, since my original engagement had been called off while I was . . . gone."

He seemed slightly upset for a moment, then asked with a forced calm to his voice, "When did he tell you that you weren't engaged?"

"Just before Pher'am married Dreanen," I answered, his tone made me uneasy.

After a moment, he continued almost to himself, "About a year before . . . You weren't engaged then."

I looked up at him rather puzzled. He seemed to be confused for a moment then asked, "Didn't anyone tell you?"

"Tell me what?" I asked

"Why you were married to me?" he continued, still looking concerned.

I glanced back down at the scabbard. "I always assumed it was because no other house would make an offer."

There was silence at the other end of the table. I finally glanced up and saw Danren staring at me with his mouth open. He caught himself when I looked up. He still looked upset, but his mouth was closed.

"N-no," he slowly said, after another moment, "it wasn't because no other house would make an offer." He paused again, then looked down at the edge of the table. "It was because of what house, or rather who in that house, was going to make an offer and what that offer would have been."

I tried to word the question nagging at me, finally managing the simplest form, "Who?"

He still didn't answer, so I finally gave up. "You don't have to tell me if you don't want to."

"N-no," he sighed, "you should know, but it's just . . ." he trailed off. "Lord Astucieux was going to offer a court seat for you."

My mind reeled for a moment. "Whatever for?" A court seat was one of the highest honors in the kingdom. "Why would anyone offer something like that for someone who wasn't even . . . who had been . . .?"

Suddenly, I realized why someone, Lord Astucieux especially, would offer such a thing for me. I felt the blood drain from my face, and I began to quiver. I looked up at Danren in horror, but he wasn't there anymore. I watched, rather confused, as he trotted into the small side room. Finally taking a breath again, I found myself completely appalled at my thoughts. I managed to stop shaking in the short amount of time it took Danren to return. He still set the old fur blanket on the table in front of me.

Danren continued to speak, but I barely heard what he was saying as he told me that my father had requested Lord Grath make an offer, any offer, for me, and it would be accepted. Lord Grath had made the only offer the House of Rem'Maren could afford at that time, and I'd been married to Danren instead.

I was still staring at the blanket in horror. Not that there was anything wrong with the blanket, but because of the contrast. That blanket was a symbol.

I might have ended up as one of Lord Astucieux's . . . *wives* was too polite a word, even concubines seemed too pleasant, but instead I was now married to Danren. Danren, the man who never touched me except on the very few occasions when my life had been threatened. Danren, who was always polite to me, no matter what I said to him. This man, who at the slightest sign that I might go into one of my shaking fits went to get a blanket to help me.

He was still talking though. "With that being the case . . . you may want to reconsider a . . . a divorce. I don't know if he'd still make the offer, but it might be better if he didn't have the opportunity . . . Dreanen is more than willing to let you live with him and Pher'am . . ."

I reached out and pulled the blanket to me. What had I done? I'd always thought the worst of Danren. I'd always thought that if he had the chance, he'd . . . he'd had plenty of chances, I realized again, and he never took a single one. I felt the tears begin, and I knew I wouldn't be able to stop them.

I pulled the blanket up to my face and began to sob.

"I'm sorry. I'm so sorry," I whispered.

What had I done?

I'd tried to tell her the best way I could think of. I'd thought that it would be best to just tell her as briefly as possible to get it over with. I was wrong. I watched her cry, feeling completely helpless. I wanted to tell her that everything was all right, but it wasn't. I wanted to tell her she was safe, but I was certain that she felt trapped.

She kept saying she was sorry, but I couldn't figure out why.

Finally, I told her, "I'm sorry too. I know this isn't what you wanted. I know you deserve better than this."

Looking up, she tried to compose herself with a reasonable amount of success. She tried to say something, choked on a sob, and bit her lip. She didn't bite hard enough to make her lip bleed. It always horrified me when she used to do that.

She took a shuddering breath and finally managed, "Do you want me to go live with Dreanen and Pher'am, or . . ." she paused for a moment, "or would you rather have the divorce?"

He was staring at his hands rather intently. "It would be safer for you there."

He hadn't exactly answered the question, so I grasped for a thread. "Adenern said that I might not like it there."

Danren let out a breath and shook his head. "Why would he say something like that?"

The question wasn't directed at me, just at the room in general, but I answered anyway, "He said that Pher'am isn't very fond of dragons, because of Lady Margree's influence."

"You'd do just fine then," he said softly, "you probably aren't very fond of them now either."

"What?" the question was out before I caught myself.

His head shot up, and he looked directly at me for a moment.

He reached for the pitcher, to give himself something to do, almost poured more water into his cup, and then realized that the cup was still full. He shook his head, set the pitcher back down, and fidgeted with the cup.

"Danren," I began, I needed to know the answer to this question, "do you want me to leave Caer Corisan?"

Danren didn't respond for a moment. He didn't even move and seemed to not even breathe.

Finally, he said, "It would be safer for you at Ryuu than to go through with a divorce."

I steadied my voice as best I could. "T-that wasn't what I asked."

He shook his head, and then finally said, "It doesn't matter what I want."

I was shocked by that response. Then I wondered why. He'd never been selfish before, so why would he be now.

"I-I'd still like to know," I said softly, chiding myself that I couldn't keep my voice steady.

He sat silently for a moment. "I doubt that."

"Just answer this one question, please," I said. "Do you want me to leave?"

He sighed. "Will the answer affect your decision?"

I wasn't going to lie to him. I couldn't, not after he'd tried to be honest with me. "Yes."

"Then I won't answer it," he said staring at the floor. "The decision is yours. I'll see to it that you arrive wherever you want to go."

I took a deep breath. "I'd like to stay at Caer Corisan, but if you want me to go live with Dreanen and Pher'am, or if you want the divorce, I'll do that."

He looked up with that shocked expression etched across his face. I knew the question was coming before he even said it.

This entire conversation had been nothing like I'd expected.

"What?" The question was out before I could stop it.

She stared at her hands, and I almost believed that I could see that little hint of a smile again. Then I realized what she was saying. She was comfortable at Caer Corisan. The transition would be hard on her. There had been too many major changes in her life. I shouldn't expect her to make one more. I was the one who would have to leave.

"I see," I finally managed, "I can find out if Armel will take over running Caer Corisan again. I'll stay here as often as I can, and I can stay elsewhere when I need to."

She looked up, distressed. "So you do want me to leave."

I mouthed the question, but managed not to say it this time.

Instead, I told her, "No, if you want to stay at Caer Corisan, I can make other arrangements. It would be the safest place for you. I don't have to stay there."

"You don't want to be anywhere near me then." Her voice broke.

"I didn't say that." It came out far harsher than I'd meant to sound. I fought to soften my tone. "If you want to stay, I can work it out."

"You wouldn't want to stay there though." I could see the tears running down her cheeks.

I felt my own voice break slightly. "It doesn't matter what I want."

"Why not?" The intensity of her tone caught me off guard.

"I . . . you . . ." I stammered, "What?"

"What do you want, Danren?" The tone tore me open.

"Why is this so important to you?" I asked, as I stood and took a few steps away.

"I need to know," she answered, her voice sounding slightly more even.

"Why?"

"Because I want . . ." she began to blurt out, but I turned around and interrupted.

"Yes, tell me that first." I took a step back toward the table. "What do *you* want?"

This was the key. I'd see to it that whatever her answer, she'd have it, even if it was something entirely unreasonable like ruling the kingdom. I'd see it done, or die trying.

She steadied herself, then looked up at me. "If I tell you, will you answer the same question?"

This felt like a child's bargain. I'll tell you my secret if you tell me yours. I opened my mouth to say something, then realized there weren't any words there yet.

I took a deep breath. "Are you sure you want to know?"

She nodded.

"All right then."

"I'd like . . ." Her voice faltered slightly, and she took a deep breath. "I'd like to be your friend, again." She paused for a moment. "I miss having someone that I can talk to about . . . anything."

"What?"

I couldn't quite comprehend what she'd just told me. Had I lost my mind . . . or had she? How could she possibly want that?

She smiled slightly. "When you fostered with my parents, I could talk to you even though I was just a little kid and you were going to training within a year or two." She took a short breath. "When you rescued me from the temple, you were always there to help me . . . become human again."

Her eyes were beginning to look glossy. The last thing I wanted was to see her cry again, but I couldn't breathe for a moment. She didn't want to leave Caer Corisan because I was there. I stepped back to the table and sat down.

"But," she continued, "if you want me to leave, I will."

"I don't want you to leave," I whispered. "I want . . ." I trailed off.

I needed to keep my end of the bargain.

Resting my elbows on the table, I leaned into my folded hands. "I want you to be safe. I want you to be happy."

I took a deep breath and almost laughed.

Laying my hands back on the table, I told her, "If you want to stay, that's fine . . . that's wonderful, and . . . I'd be honored to be one of your friends."

I stared at the pitcher for a moment before her movement caught my attention. Before I could stop her or move away, she reached across the little table and took hold of my hand. I almost jerked away, but I didn't want to startle her. I felt like I was watching a tiny bird play within an handsbreadth of me. I realized that I couldn't move, even if I'd wanted to.

She rubbed her fingers across the back of my hand for a moment then lifted it to her face and did the unthinkable. She lightly kissed my fingers and then rested her cheek against my hand.

"Thank you," I barely heard her whisper.

I wanted to jump up and hold her. I wanted to tell her that I'd never let anything happen to her. I wanted to swear my life to her, but if I did anything, I was certain I would terrify her.

CHAPTER 48

TURNING TO
A DRAGON

She let go of my hand after a moment and looked awkwardly around. Staring at her hands, she asked if I wanted to hear about what had been happening at Caer Corisan lately, since I hadn't been there much. I did know most of the goings-on. I'd asked Hafiz to keep me up to date, but I wanted her to keep talking. I wondered if I was going to wake up soon, and she would be gone . . . but I had felt her hand. Dreams didn't feel . . .

We chatted about Galen and Majorlaine's latest arguments, Armel's newest creation, and Ekaitz's latest fiasco. Ari'an laughed occasionally. I had to fight myself to keep from staring at her when she did. It was so good to hear her laugh again, and with me, not Narden. When she did catch me watching her, she'd blush and watch her hands until I frantically came up with something to ask about. She had such a pretty blush.

After a while, she stopped, fidgeting with her cup. I let her alone. She seemed to be wording something.

Finally, she managed to softly begin.

The question Adenern had asked him kept playing through my mind as we talked. The question terrified me, but made me intensely curious to know the answer at the same time. I finally worked up the courage to ask.

"Adenern asked you something that I was wondering about . . ." I glanced around the cave before continuing, "You didn't really give him an answer."

"Today?" he asked.

I nodded.

"Adenern was incredibly irritating today," he replied.

I laughed slightly. "He was trying to help."

"I'm not sure if he did or made things worse." But he smiled as he said it.

"He asked you . . ." I closed my eyes, I didn't want to see his reaction. "He asked you if you loved me."

He didn't answer for a long moment. I wondered how the mountain birds could still sing at a time like this.

"Love is a choice," he finally said.

The words sounded forced. I wasn't sure what to make of them.

"Th-that's not an answer," I finally stammered.

Another long moment passed. "Do you actually want to know the answer?"

It was my turn to pause. "I . . . I'm not sure . . .," I finally managed.

He sighed. "Ask me when you're certain then." He didn't pause long before adding, "Speaking of Adenern, I should have him take you home."

He stood and left the cave before I could object. I didn't want to leave yet.

Danren returned after far longer than I expected.

I managed to ask when I heard him reenter, "Will you return now too?"

He didn't answer, so I looked up. He looked irritated as he turned toward the cave entrance. Looking out, he signaled with his sword. He waited for a moment then hurried back to me.

"What's wrong?" I asked, hoping that my question hadn't upset him that much.

"He's gone," Danren answered through gritted teeth.

I began to ask what he meant when Einheim's form darkened the entrance. If I hadn't been concerned about Danren, I would have laughed at the memories of Adenern and Narden landing just like he did.

He shook himself when he was back on his feet. He did a dragon's bow to Danren and myself. I noticed he looked nervous. That wasn't a good sign.

"Where's Adenern?" I could tell that Danren was struggling to keep his voice under control.

"He . . . h-he . . . he left, sir," Einheim answered.

"When?"

"Shortly after he brought Lady Ari'an."

I felt sorry for him. Einheim was always so nervous around the lords.

"Who did he say would take Lady Ari'an back to Caer Corisan, or did he not think of that?" Danren almost growled.

"He . . . he said . . . he said that you . . . that Narden would take her back." The young dragon watched Danren nervously.

Danren turned around, probably to get his temper under control, and seemed surprised to find me standing near him.

"It's not his fault," Ari'an told me in a low tone. "Don't blame him. He couldn't have stopped Adenern from leaving."

I knew she was right, but it was easy to be mad at him for no reason. I turned my focus to visualizing the different ways I could maim Adenern or Dreanen.

I needed to figure out how to get her back to Caer Corisan. Did I have a saddle anywhere that would fit Einheim? I didn't believe so. He was so slight. The two saddles he did have were both specifically designed for him, and they were both, I was certain, either at Caer Corisan or Mount Arwa, where he roomed, which was even farther away.

I could send him to Caer Corisan tonight, but I didn't like having dragons flying alone, because of all the problems with raiders. I could turn and accompany him, but that would leave Ari'an here alone. Even Gary wasn't here right now. He was meeting with Edur and Mael about my . . . situation. They had been discussing that topic for months.

Her voice cut through my thoughts. "Einheim, will you excuse us for a moment. We will call you back when we're ready."

As Einheim left, I looked at her as if she'd lost her mind. What were we getting ready for?

She paled when she saw my gaze, and I immediately forced a neutral look onto my face. After the amazing afternoon, I didn't want to ruin it by insulting or scaring her. She was now watching her hands fidget with each other.

"Wh-what would you like to do?" she asked.

I quickly explained that she couldn't ride Einheim and that I shouldn't leave her alone while I accompanied him.

"We could spend the night here," I continued. "You could sleep in your old room, and I could sleep in Adenern's quarters, but that would be on the hope that someone else would come tomorrow that could take you back."

"You don't have a saddle here?" she asked softly.

"Well, yes, but it wouldn't fit Einheim," I replied.

"You wouldn't want to take me back yourself," she whispered.

"Ari," I immediately chided myself for the slip, "Ari'an, I wouldn't ask you to do that."

"Wh-what do you mean?" her voice quavered.

I tried to word my thoughts. "At best, it would be awkward for you. At worst, it would be a horrible experience. I wouldn't ask you to do that."

"Wh-why would it be so bad?" she asked.

"It's me," I told her, somewhat surprised that I would need to explain this to her.

"Y-you don't want to take me?" She was fighting not to show that she was hurt.

I took a deep breath, her reaction startled me. "No. No, I wouldn't think you would want me to."

"Why?" The word hung in the air long after she'd whispered it.

"Because it's me, with everything I've put you through, I . . ." I fought to word this and finally managed, "I wouldn't think you'd want to."

She took a step toward me and gathered her strength, met my gaze, and said, "Danren, I would be honored if you would return me to Caer Corisan."

I stared at her blankly, and then stammered, "Wh-what?"

To my shock, she laughed.

I continued to stare at her for a moment, and then found myself chuckling with her. I'd forgotten how contagious her laughter could be. I started toward the little room after a moment.

"Are you going to turn now?" she asked, sounding shy.

"Well, I was going to pull out a saddle first," I told her ducking behind the curtain.

"May I . . ." her voice trailed off, "may I watch?"

My first thought was why would she want to watch me retrieve a saddle, but then I realized that she was asking to watch me turn. I moved back through the curtain.

"What?" he asked, staring at me with a confused yet blank look on his face.

"If you don't mind, and it's not considered rude or . . . anything."

Danren set the saddle down and watched me for a moment.

"Never mind," I said quickly, "it wasn't right to ask. I shouldn't have said . . ."

He was walking toward me, studying me. I shifted under his gaze and watched my shoes.

When he was a few steps away from me, he stopped. "Do you want to see me turn?"

"I didn't mean to upset you," I began to apologize. "I don't know all the proper etiquette . . ." I trailed off. "I'm sorry."

"You didn't answer the question," sounding far too calm for someone I'd just insulted.

I tried to explain, "I just . . . it wasn't polite, I'm sorry."

"Ari'an, I've never been told that it's impolite," he replied.

"I didn't mean to offend you," I whispered.

"You didn't," his tone even.

I slowly looked up at him. He didn't look offended. He didn't look upset. In fact, he looked somewhat amused. He turned his head slightly, running his hand through the hair by his ear. I gasped when I realized that the blue was beginning to show.

"You don't have to do this for me," I blurted out.

He smiled slightly. "It's rather difficult to stop once started."

Was he teasing me? I couldn't tell for certain, and the blue spreading through his face, down his neck, and into his clothes distracted me. This was a slower change than the one I'd seen in the tent.

"You're stalling." I gasped.

He smiled. "You were the one who asked to watch," his voice slightly strained.

"You don't have to do this for me," I tried to sound authoritative.

He turned his head back to look at me. I gasped at what I saw.

"Do you want me to stop?" he sounded concerned.

"No, it wasn't that," I mumbled.

He leaned forward and set himself on his front legs. "I didn't mean to scare you."

I pulled my gaze up his front legs and then up his neck to meet his eyes.

"It wasn't the turning that surprised me," I swallowed hard.

He looked confused for a moment, then his gaze relaxed. I forced myself not to react. This was what had made me gasp. It was how he was looking at me. It was a look that told me that he would do anything I asked. He would do anything to make me happy. The realization that the only thing . . . the only person who ranked higher than I did to him was the Mighty One. He was fighting . . . leading an undeclared war, because I had been hurt. He stayed away from Caer Corisan, because he thought that was what I'd wanted. Now, just now, he turned, because I wanted to watch.

I reached forward and gently laid my hand on his nose. He stopped himself from crossing his eyes, closing them instead.

"You don't have to do this," he said softly.

I stepped forward and hugged his muzzle like I used to. "Thank you," I whispered. "Thank you so much."

I couldn't breathe, not because of where she was but rather because my lungs wouldn't work. I would have asked, "What?" but I couldn't manage even that.

I hadn't expected this reaction. I wasn't sure what I'd expected, but certainly not this. I finally managed to take a ragged breath. She quickly let go and blushed. I glanced away to let her regain her composure.

"I have something to ask you," she said quietly.

I looked back and found her meeting my gaze.

"I was wondering . . ." she began then stopped.

I stood quietly waiting for her to gather her confidence.

"Is there a reason," she continued slowly, "that you don't call me . . . Ari . . . much anymore?"

The question startled me, I hadn't known what to expect, but that wasn't it.

"I didn't think you'd want me to," I told her. "I know I've slipped on occasion, but I tried not to."

"That's the only reason," she asked her hands.

"Yes," I replied.

"You can call me Ari then." She looked up as she spoke. "I don't mind."

"Are you certain?"

She smiled and met my gaze. "Yes."

"You made a promise to me when we were married," she continued in a serious tone.

I laughed to lighten the mood. "I made several promises to you when we were married."

"Yes, but this one I want to release you from," she said.

This didn't sound good. Had she reconsidered?

"You said that you would never touch me unless you had my permission or my life was in danger." She took a ragged breath and then quavered, "You have my permission."

I blurted out, "What?" as I nearly fell over. "Ari, you don't have to do this!"

"I know," she whispered, "but you deserve my trust."

It took me far too long to recuperate. I needed to say something, but what could I possibly say in reply?

I finally managed, "Thank you, Ari. I won't betray you."

"I know," she whispered. Then she smiled. "Now, since that's all over, would you like to head out?"

I threw my head back and laughed, realizing that she was laughing with me.

After getting the saddle on, we exited the cave. Einheim joined us, and we headed to Caer Corisan, arriving just after night fell.

CHAPTER 49

RESTORATION

I shocked Narden quite a few times over the next weeks. He was rather busy catching up on things that he'd neglected while he was avoiding me. I'd find him when I finished my work and help him with whatever tasks I could or just keep him company. It was my presence that surprised him. After years of avoiding Danren and all the misunderstandings, I guess he expected me to stay away.

Meanwhile, the fever had taken its toll on the rest of the country and even on Verd, causing the board skirmishes to calm down considerably. The invitation to the capital never came that year.

It seemed that Rem'Maren had been the least affected by the plague. Things became so calm that Dreanen and Pher'am decided to throw a festival. Something to lift the spirits of the people after Drenar's death and the hard winter. I worked on the travel arrangements so Danren wouldn't have to.

I quickly discovered that Ari was full of questions. She would come searching for me to answer something or another.

The conversation usually began with, "I have a question for you."

She would say it in such a shy tone, that I'd almost laugh.

Then she'd gather her courage and blurt out something like, "How did you feel when you found out about . . . about . . ." then she'd trail off.

I explained to her that it was quite a shock to find out, but then rather exciting.

"Exciting?" she asked sounding shocked, "I would have been terrified. How could you have been excited?"

I did laugh then. "Well, I kept on going over what I knew about dragons and found that the prospect of leaping off cliffs, flying around mountaintops, and breathing fire was exciting."

She looked at me as if I'd lost my mind, then laughed with me. "I suppose that does make sense, men do have a tendency to do outlandish things."

"Well, I tried to keep it under control, but what could you really expect from a youth?" I replied.

"How long did the thrill last?" she asked.

It was an innocent question, but I wasn't certain how she would take the answer. "Until I found out you were missing."

She stared at me for a moment, finally mumbling, "I don't understand."

"It was a bit of a power trip at first," I explained. "Here I was seventeen, learning about flying to heights I'd never dreamed of, discovering that I could turn practically anything into a pile of ash, believing, completely believing that nothing could ever touch me or anyone I—" I had started to say, "cared about," but stopped myself. I wasn't certain how she'd take that. "I'd been friends with," I continued instead. "Then I found out that my friends weren't untouchable. Evil still happened to them."

I paused, she didn't seem upset, just taking it all in.

"I couldn't imagine that you'd run away, so something must have happened to you," I told her. "I'd gotten a thrill out of sneaking away to watch over you, sort of a guardian angel complex." I chuckled. "I found out later that everyone I was sneaking away from knew exactly where I was off to, so much for secrets."

She smiled then, so I continued, "Years of searching for you took the excitement away, leveled me out. Adenern took up teasing me that I'd matured faster than he had."

"W-why do you think . . ." she began shakily, "that had such an effect on you?" She tried to joke, "It didn't level Adenern any."

"I'd been better friends with you than he was," I explained.

She excused herself at that point. I hoped I hadn't made her uncomfortable, but I was being completely honest with her.

I'd realized before that he'd do anything in his power to keep me safe, including laying down his life. Now, I was beginning to see the more intricate pieces. Narden searched for years to find me. He continued to search even after my family declared me dead. I soon discovered that his determination had kept Lord Grath expending resources on the search.

I found that I couldn't stay away. I enjoyed being around him, and after he'd look up in surprise to find me nearby, he'd fall into a mood that said he was thrilled I was there. It was such a little thing, but I could at least do that.

He answered my questions openly and honestly. I soon learned what I'd never been able ask Armel, Lord Grath, or even Adenern.

After a couple weeks had passed, I began to wonder when Narden would turn again. I avoided asking though, because I was more comfortable with him as Narden than I was with Danren. I knew they were the same person, but I'd developed the habit of opening up to Narden. I could lean against his side and talk about anything at all, but how was I supposed to talk to Danren?

The days continued to go by. Spring would bring summer soon, and the festival was planned for the beginning of summer.

My garden came back to life as well, which brought a new question for me to ask Narden.

I found him going over some defensive procedures with Armel, so I waited in the hallway until they finished talking. It took a while. At one point, Armel made a comment that Narden should probably head out soon. I almost gasped, thinking that he might leave.

Then Armel continued, "You know Lord Danren hasn't been here for a while, and there are things he needs to do that you can't accomplish. Perhaps you should find him."

I almost laughed. He was making an allusion that Narden should turn. The dragon didn't reply except with a slight snort, and then the conversation returned to matters of defense. Eventually, Armel left the room, noticed me standing next to the doorway, and bowed politely.

"My apologies for keeping you waiting, my lady," he told me jovially.

I stared at the doorway when Armel greeted Ari'an. How long had she been waiting? Why hadn't she said something to let us know she was there?

She walked into the room, I nodded to her, but then looked at the map on the table. I needed to get that ridiculous grin off my face. Things were going so well between us. I didn't want to ruin it by letting her know how much I enjoyed her visits.

She walked over to the table saying, "I have a question for you."

I had the grin under control by now and looked over at her.

"What's this?" she asked, fingering the map on the table.

I cocked an eyebrow. "I don't think that's what you intended to ask."

She laughed softly. "I'll get to that."

I looked over the map. "I was going over security for the festival with Armel, trying to work it out so as many people can go for at least a few of the days as possible."

Ari looked up at me, glanced around, then whispered, "Some will turn partway through?"

"It's mandatory," I explained, "so that as many families can be with their husbands and fathers at least some of the time."

"Will you"—she glanced around again—"turn partway through?"

"No," I told her slowly, "Danren has to be there the entire time. It's part of being a lord." I glanced back at the map. "I'm not sure whether that's a benefit or not."

She glanced around, then said in a teasing whisper, "So you'd rather be out torching some field or terrorizing an unsuspecting village?"

I was surprised by her tone, so it took me a moment to reply, "That or capturing some innocent princess and waiting for some knight to kill me."

"So maybe it's a good thing you'll be otherwise occupied. I'm not sure I'd actually want you dead," she teased back.

The statement surprised me so much I stared at her for a moment. She seemed to realize what she'd just said, and blushed.

She took a breath, then continued, "I wouldn't want you hurt, and I'm sorry I ever said otherwise."

I searched frantically for something to say to change the subject. I finally realized, "You never did ask your question."

She glanced around, pulling herself together, then looked directly at me with some of that teasing look back on her face. "It's about the garden."

"Is something wrong with it?" I asked.

"No, but"—she took another breath—"it really did come from you, didn't it?"

CHAPTER 50

THE GARDEN

His response shocked me. I watched his temper flare. Immediately, he glanced away and took several ragged breaths.

"No," he finally said with forced calm, "the garden was from Danren."

As he looked back at me, he was trying to hide it, but I could tell that I had hurt him drastically.

"I'm sorry," I tried to explain. "I don't understand what the difference would be."

He took another ragged breath. "I . . . he . . ." He sighed. "There is a difference, but . . ." He glanced around. "I'd rather not explain it like this."

"How would you like to explain?" I asked, trying to speak louder than a whisper.

"I'm not the one to explain," he began to say.

"Oh," I whispered.

He probably didn't want to tell me at all.

"Danren should probably do that." He glanced away as he continued.

I was surprised by that statement. "Do you know when he's coming back?"

He let out a forced chuckle. "He could come back anytime, but . . ." He glanced at me again. "I wasn't certain that you'd want him to."

"Why not?" I blurted out.

"It's just that . . ." he began, trailed off, and then continued, "I wasn't certain that you'd . . . I mean, if you'd like . . ."

He looked so utterly cornered and miserable.

"Well, you tell Danren," I interrupted, "that if he'd like to join me, I will be in the garden he gave me."

She turned around and walked out of the room while I stared after her. It took me a couple moments to realize that my jaw was hanging open. What was that supposed to mean anyway? Did she want me to turn and go explain in the garden, or did she not want to deal with the explanation? What was I supposed to do?

She hadn't seemed upset. If anything, she'd seemed amused by my dilemma. Why couldn't she just say one way or the other if she wanted Danren to come back?

Finally, I decided to take my life in my hands. I turned, wondered if I'd made the right decision while I changed my clothes, and then walked to the garden. I realized just after coming around the final corner of the hallway that I'd been walking perpetually slower the closer I came. I shook myself and hurried to the entrance.

I wondered if Ari had given up and left already. I peeked around the doorway and found that she was sitting in the clover looking out the opening. The growth was more established now. Ari had even planted a fruit tree near the pond. It was several years old now and might even bear its first crop this year. The pond still had the solid stone boundary around it that Armel had helped me design. The stepping stones that made a meandering path were still there. They had moss growing around them though. The place looked like it had always been here.

Slowly, I walked through the doorway. I wondered what I was supposed to do to let her know I was there. Had she noticed already, and was just ignoring me? Had I made the wrong decision, and she didn't actually want me there?

Finally, I settled on just saying, "Greetings." It didn't come out as solidly as I'd hoped it would. In fact, I sounded like a shy kid, trying to find enough nerve to talk to someone.

Ari didn't look back, just responded, "Greetings." At least she didn't sound mortified that I was there.

I took a few more steps. "Do you mind if I join you?"

That sounded slightly better.

"Not at all," she said, patting the clover next to her.

She didn't sound upset, but she still hadn't looked at me. I walked over, sitting down a couple of steps away from her.

I frantically searched for something to say. "I heard you were looking for me."

"No," she said evenly.

"What?" I looked at her before I could stop myself.

She fought to keep from laughing, and she had a ridiculous grin on her face.

"I think you're confused," she replied, very slowly to keep her voice even. "I believe you were looking for me."

"You're enjoying this!" I exclaimed.

That apparently was the last straw. She threw her head back and laughed.

Well, if she was going to torment me just for the fun of it, I could do the same. "Here I was scared to death that you didn't actually want me around, and you're just toying with me."

"You? Scared?" She laughed. "I didn't think dragon lords got scared."

"You're misinformed," I told her, trying to sound authoritative.

"Why don't you enlighten me then?" she replied.

Ari tried to get the laughter under control, but from all appearances, she failed.

"Toadstools," I said evenly.

That answer surprised her into silence for a moment. "Toadstools?"

"Yes, toadstools," I replied and looked out the opening.

"What about toadstools?" I'd piqued her curiosity.

"I don't like to eat mushrooms, because I'm scared that one of them might be a toadstool, and I'll be poisoned," I told her, trying to sound casual.

She stared at me for a moment. I peeked at her out of the corner of my eye.

Finally, she looked out the opening and replied, "Ivy."

"Oh?" I returned.

"I don't like ivy because I'm scared I'll run into the tainted stuff, and end up with a rash," she replied.

"Ivy." I glanced around the garden. "I see."

"I doubt that," she replied.

"Oh?"

"There isn't any here," she said evenly, apparently trying to fight off a grin.

I sat quietly for a few moments, giving her sidelong glances. When she seemed to have her laughter under control, I tried a more serious topic.

"I've noticed something . . ." I paused to find the right word, "interesting about the way you've been treating Narden lately."

She shifted slightly and looked at me. The puzzled look on her face didn't change while she thought. I didn't believe that she would think of what the change was.

"I wasn't being rude," she finally began. "I know I've been around . . . him often, but h-he didn't seem to mind."

"No, he doesn't mind, from what I understand," I told her.

"Did I say something I shouldn't have?" she continued, sounding concerned. "I didn't mean to."

"Not that I know of," I replied.

"Then what did I do wrong?" she asked.

"I never said you did anything wrong, just different," I told her.

I glanced over and found that slightly irritated look that I remembered from my days at Torion Castle creeping over her face.

"All right then," she said, sounding slightly less irritated than she looked, "what have I been doing differently?"

"You're teasing him," I told her.

She mouthed the word, "What?" but managed not to say it.

"You never used to tease Narden," I continued.

"I," she began, "did . . . n't." She appeared slightly shocked by the realization.

"You used to tease me, while I fostered." I attempted an imitation of a little girl's voice, "If you fall off your horse one more time, they're never going to let you ride a dragon."

"I didn't sound like that!" she exclaimed.

"You're right," I told her. "You sounded far more like a girl."

She glared at me. It was like the playful glares she used to give me when we were young. I couldn't help smiling.

"Well, if he doesn't want me teasing him, he can tell me that!" she shot back.

"I didn't say he minded," I replied evenly.

"Then what are you saying?" she asked.

"I'm saying"—what was I saying? Then I knew—"it's nice to have my old friend back."

She stared at me for a moment, then seemed to recover. "So you're saying I'm old!"

I threw my head back and laughed. Soon, she was laughing with me.

"I wanted to have a conversation like this with you for years," I finally managed to tell her.

That statement sobered her more than I'd intended.

"I'm sorry," she began. "I know I was awful."

I reached over and patted her hand. "I'm not mad at you. I was never mad at you." Then I realized what I'd done, and quickly pulled my hand back. "I'm sorry. I didn't mean . . ."

Her smile cut me off. "I don't mind," she told me.

She reached across the grass and lifted my hand to her face.

Leaning her cheek into my palm, she said, "I trust you."

"You don't have to," I fought to keep my voice from sounding as choked as I suddenly felt.

She smiled against my palm. "You deserve it."

I closed my eyes to gather my thoughts, and she released my hand. When I opened them, she was looking back out of the opening.

"I . . ." she began, and I sensed the shy questioning tone returning to her voice, "I have a question for you."

"Oh?" I asked, trying to sound like I didn't know what was coming. I began frantically to try to word the answer.

"H-how . . ." She paused to take a breath. "How is it that this garden was a gift only from you?"

He stared out of the opening for a long time. I wondered if he'd refuse to answer. Glancing around, I realized that I might not want to know the answer.

"You rarely spoke to Narden about gardens," he softly continued, "I . . . I remembered, that as a child, you had loved to play in the gardens at Torion Castle."

He paused for a while again, and I asked, "Is that it then?"

"No," he sighed, "I wanted to give you something . . . something meaningful, that would show you that I wasn't going to harm you."

Glancing around, he continued, "I remembered everything I could about the things you liked from those old gardens and tried to add as many of those memories as I could to this."

I glanced around and began to see those touches.

"I even did quite a bit of the work. Several other people helped, and yes, Narden did some things that I couldn't, but I wanted this to be from me."

He fell silent again, but after a moment, he added, "I wanted to show you that I cared."

It took me so long to find my voice, and even then, it only began as a whisper, "I'm sorry. I didn't understand. I thought that you were taking credit for something he did . . ." Then a new question came to me, "Why didn't you present the garden to me yourself?"

He thought for a moment, a look of concentration on his face. Then I watched as his eyes opened wide, and he cringed.

"You were mad at me at the time," he told his hands.

I frantically searched through my memories for what I had been upset about. I couldn't find it.

"About what?" I asked.

He shifted slightly and glanced out of the opening. "You heard me singing, and it upset you."

I gasped as I suddenly remembered the incident. "You . . . you . . ." I tried to articulate. "You sounded too much like Narden."

His head turned slightly to look at my wringing hands.

"I'd thought that Narden had come back early, but then I found you, and I was angry." I gasped.

"Ari," he said in a calm tone, "it's all right. You don't need to worry about it."

I looked up at him, and he cringed at the horrified look on my face.

Danren closed his eyes and took a deep breath. I felt the tears stinging my own eyes. Why couldn't I see then that he wouldn't hurt me? Why had it taken me years to even notice? How could I have caused him so much anguish, and he never retaliated?

He scrambled for a handkerchief as I felt the tears begin to fall. When he held it out to me, I couldn't take it. I stood up and scrambled a few steps away.

"How could I . . ." I whispered.

"Ari," the broken sound to his voice tore my heart open. "It's all right."

I heard him stand up and take a step toward me. Then he stopped, and I knew he wasn't sure what he should do.

I turned back to him. "I'm not mad at you," I began, but then my voice broke.

"Ari, I didn't mean to upset you." The tone to his voice was forced calm.

"Y-you . . . you didn't," I managed to reply.

I noticed a slight movement, he held the handkerchief out again. For a moment, I stared at it, but then I forced myself to look up. I read a pain there deeper than my own anguish. As Narden, he would have come closer, talked to me, and if possible brought a blanket, but I'd tied his hands as Danren. As Danren, I'd never allowed him to help me. I'd never allowed him near me. I'd never shown anything but terror to him when I needed comforting.

At that realization, I threw myself at his open arm. He stepped back from the impact, but I stayed with him. I had to stay with him.

For a moment, he didn't do anything. I tried to word an apology, but the only sound that escaped from my throat was a sob.

His hands gripped my shoulders, and I felt him try to push me away.

"Ari," his voice broke, "Ari, don't."

"Please . . ." I managed to whisper, "please."

"Y-you'll hate me." He couldn't keep the pain out of his tone.

"No," I managed to whisper, "I need you."

The pressure on my shoulders weakened. "What?"

"I need you," I whispered again, "please."

"Ari," he began, "is this what you want?"

"Yes," I felt my own voice break, "I need you . . . please."

His hands moved from my shoulders around my back, and I felt him hold me gently against his chest. Then I felt a sob. For a moment, I thought it was me, but then I realized that it wasn't. The sound didn't repeat, but I felt moisture seeping into my hair. What had I done?

"Danren, I'm sorry," I blurted out.

"It's all right," he gently whispered into my hair.

"No," I cried, "please, forgive me, please. I've hurt you so much. Please . . ."

I couldn't say any more because of my own sobs.

"It's all right," he whispered, "I never could hold anything against you. I can't forgive you now, because I already had, long ago. There's nothing left to forgive."

Then he told me that he'd rather start over than have us bringing up past transgressions constantly. How could he so easily forgive me? It was one more thing that reminded me of how much he cared.

Convulsive sobs raked through her body. There had to be more I could do, but what? I tightened my grip slightly to keep her from falling. She leaned against me as though I was the only solid thing in the world. I couldn't step away. She'd fall. I longed to stroke her hair, but if I moved, she might go into one of her fits. It had been so long since she'd had one. I would never forgive myself if I caused her another one. I couldn't tell her what I wanted to. I couldn't move my hands, stroke her back or her hair. I balled my hands into fists as I realized that my fingers were twitching.

I forced the familiar words through the pressure in my throat, "It's all right. You're safe."

"I know." She sobbed brokenly.

"I won't hurt you."

"I know." She sobbed again.

"Ari, it's all right." I felt the break in my own voice and fought to master it.

"I know." She managed not to sob out the words this time.

I held her for another moment and realized that she was regaining her composure. Loosening my grip, I felt her begin to pull away.

I mopped at my face with my sleeve, and then offered the still-dry handkerchief to her. After staring at it for a moment, she reached out and took it. She dried her own face, but I realized that she was still watching me. Looking up, I found a slight smile on her face. It looked so out of place with puffy eyes, red nose, and tear streaks.

"What is it?" I asked baffled.

The slight smile turned to a grin as she answered, "You're a mess."

"What?" I shot back, "I'm a mess! You . . ."

She interrupted me by erupting into laughter. I stared at her for a moment, then joined her.

When she finally stopped, she glanced around while I took a few deep breaths.

"Would you like to give me a tour?" she asked.

"What?" I stammered.

"A tour," she repeated and motioned around the garden.

"You know everything here, probably better than I do," I told her, puzzled.

She looked down at her hands, wringing the handkerchief. "I'd like to know what you did," she said shyly.

After a moment, I finally managed to agree. I moved my arm to point out something nearby, but then she stepped up to me and put her hand into my arm. I stared at her hand resting there, for a moment.

"You don't have to do this," I finally managed to tell her.

"I know," she replied softly, "but I'd like a *proper* tour, if it's all the same to you." She said "proper" in the teasing, nose-in-the-air fashion that she used as a child. I laughed.

"Well then, my lady," I began, trying to sound as formal as I could manage, "shall we begin?"

She nodded her assent, and I began to show her around the garden.

CHAPTER 51

DANCING

A few days later, I asked Danren if he ever got tired of eating alone.

He seemed confused for a moment, then grinned, "Would you care to join me for dinner tonight, my lady?"

I felt my cheeks redden as I realized how obvious that had been, but I consented.

Dinner together became a regular occurrence over the next few weeks. I also began looking for him, like I had with Narden.

I found, though, that Danren began to disappear somewhere in the fortress for about a watch each day. No one seemed to know where he was hiding. I asked him a couple of times about it, but he always skirted the question. My curiosity was getting the better of me, and I began to look for him during those times.

It took me about a week, but I finally noticed music coming from one of the unused portions of the fortress. I searched for a couple of days, and again realized just how enormous the fortress was. The boys who came to begin their training here would often explore these tunnels under the fortress. They'd drag up old treasures, which Armel would explain what they used to do.

One day, however, I managed to follow the music to its source. I saw the contraption plunking away its melody through the large open door leading into the hallway. I'd seen Armel fixing these boxes before. They came in so many sizes. This was one of the larger ones that would play an entire song, and could also change songs by swapping out the cylinder.

As I crept closer, I noticed counting coming from the room in Danren's voice. I glanced around the corner of the doorway and almost laughed.

"What are you doing?" I asked.

Danren froze in the dance step he was halfway through.

He stared at me for a moment, then managed to ask, "What are you doing here?"

I debated several responses as I walked toward the musical box. The large room was entirely empty except for the table that the musical box sat on and the crate of cylinders next to it. I glanced over the pile of cylinders on the table. They were all dance music.

I finally decided on, "Spying on you, of course." I paused then realized that I might be ruining something that he'd planned to surprise me with. "Were you doing this for me?"

He started to walk over when he answered, "Of course not."

I nearly dropped the cylinder in my hand, as I spun around to look at him. He'd sounded completely serious when he'd answered, and he looked serious now.

She looked so shocked. I wondered how she could even think of such a thing.

I hurried to explain, "I would never ask you to dance."

The expression on her face changed from shock to confusion. She turned away to look at the cylinders again, but I thought I'd seen the expression change to hurt. I didn't understand. Why would this upset her?

"W-what are you doing then?" she asked, after a moment of staring at the cylinders.

"Practicing," I told her as I stepped closer to the table. I wanted to see her face.

She turned so I still couldn't see her as she asked, "Whatever for?"

"The festival," I replied as I continued around the table.

"Who are you planning on dancing with there?" she asked.
"Pher'am."

Why did her hair have to fall like that? It was at just the angle needed to keep me from seeing her clearly.

I believe her response came out before she intended, "You'd ask to dance with Pher'am but not with me?" She immediately began stammering, "No, don't answer that . . . I didn't mean . . . It's not important."

"I wasn't planning on asking her, but she threatened me at the funeral."

What was going on? If I didn't know better, I would have thought Ari was jealous.

"Threatened you?" She finally looked at me. She was hurt, but at the moment, she was too surprised to cover it.

"She told me that the next time she saw me, I had better dance, and if I wasn't willing to dance with anyone else, it would be her. She made it quite clear that if I wasn't ready, she would be sure to make me look like a fool," I tried to explain while attempting to figure out why this would upset Ari.

"She said *that*?" she replied, looking at me in surprise before catching herself and turning away.

"Not in those words, of course. Pher'am made it sound like she was doing me an impressive favor, and that if I refused, it would sully both her dignity and my honor . . . I still haven't figured out how she manages to do that, but hopefully Dreanen does. It could be a useful talent for him to have." I was still at a loss as to why this was a problem though.

She smiled slightly. Pher'am was known for not only getting people to do whatever she thought was proper, but also to make it appear that it was entirely their idea . . . most of the time, at least.

"So you're just doing this for Pher'am?" She was fidgeting with her hands again.

"Sort of." I took a step to the side to try to have a better view of her face. "I don't exactly want her to make a scene."

"Do you think she would?"

"Not only would she make a scene, she would manage to do it in such a way that I wouldn't stand a chance of making it out with either a shred of dignity left or not dancing with her."

"So you never intended to dance with her?" At least she didn't sound jealous anymore.

"Not on my own accord, at least." I shrugged. "I figured I didn't have any business dancing with anyone."

"Why's that?"

"Well, I know you don't dance anymore, and if I wasn't going to dance with my wife, I shouldn't dance with anyone."

Her head shot up in surprise, and she stared at me for a moment. "Who said I don't dance anymore?"

"What?" I stared at her with my mouth open.

"I can still dance. I'd be out of practice, but I could!" she snapped.

"You had an . . . an . . . episode at Torion Castle when you returned there when you were practicing . . . I . . . I would never demand that you put yourself in that position again . . ." I tried to explain.

"Oh," she whispered so softly that I almost missed it. "You heard about that?"

"You told . . . Narden about it." I wasn't certain that she wanted the answer.

"Oh," she whispered again. Turning around, she began to walk slowly toward the doorway.

Ari paused at the door, and I took the moment to study her. I wasn't quite certain, but I had a suspicion that she wanted to dance. If I was wrong though . . .

"Is Majorlaine going to help you at all?" she asked, glancing over her shoulder.

I couldn't help but laugh slightly. "I'm not sure that I would have the courage to ask her, and even if I did, I'm not certain that she would be the best choice."

"So you don't have anyone to help you?" She still had that whisper to her voice, so I walked toward her to hear better.

She looked up at my approach. "Ari," I began searching for the right thing to say, "what are you asking?"

After glancing around and blushing slightly, she replied softly, "Would you consider letting me try to help you?"

I didn't immediately reply. I hoped she would look at me or at least in my general direction. She did after a moment, and I bowed.

"I would be honored, my lady, if you would favor me with this dance," I told her.

I rose and offered her my hand as she curtsied in response. She had such a wonderful smile on her face as she accepted my hand, and I led her toward what I'd been using as a dance floor.

I felt almost giddy as Danren bowed to me again and left to restart the musical box. He returned, bowed once more, to which I responded with another curtsy.

"It's the Tharaleos," he told me as the music began, "but if you feel at all uncomfortable, let me know. We can stop at any point."

I nodded, but knew that I would fight any such feelings. The Tharaleos was a dance without much contact. It was designed for groups and didn't have intricate movements either. In fact, I couldn't think of a simpler dance to begin with.

"How long have you been practicing?" I asked after a few moments. I'd remembered all the patterns and steps, so I thought that I could begin the other part of dancing etiquette, polite conversation.

"About a week," he replied.

I wasn't certain if he was concentrating more on where his feet were going or where his hands and arms were supposed to be.

"You're only on the Tharaleos?" I asked, teasing him.

He looked up at me, studied me for a moment as we passed, and then smiled. "Actually, I started with the Neurikos, since it was one of my favorites."

"That is a nice one, and it has a pleasant rhythm," I replied. "Why did you choose this one next? That one is far more complicated."

"I didn't choose this one next," he replied. I couldn't quite place the tone in his voice. Was it embarrassment? "I tried the Baymata."

"That one's more complicated than the Tharaleos too. Why progress to this?" I was slightly confused.

"I wouldn't say that I progressed to this one," he replied, not looking at me. "It was more of a regression," he finally continued. "I couldn't manage either of them after a couple of days each."

"You've been working on the Tharaleos for three days?" I asked.

"Four . . . actually." He sighed, sounding . . . was it discouraged? "I thought that if I couldn't master this, I had no business dancing and would just have to tell Pher'am that."

"You seem to be doing fine," I told him, trying to cheer him up.

"It must be my lovely partner, because I wasn't doing this well moments ago," he replied with a bit of a chuckle, but then froze.

I almost ran into him as he stared at me. I'd felt my face pale when he'd said that, but I was trying not to show it.

"I'm sorry," he told me, sounding mortified, "I shouldn't have said that."

I forced a smile onto my face and lifted his hand for the next maneuver.

"I thought polite compliments were proper when dancing," I tried to tease.

He renewed the steps awkwardly. "I didn't mean to offend you." Motioning at the room, he continued, "This hasn't been going well for me."

"I wasn't offended," I managed, "just surprised."

I wondered if he actually thought I was lovely, but then I realized that Danren wasn't one to say such things without . . . It had been a slip of the tongue, but . . . I felt light-headed when the music ended. I forgot to curtsy and walked from the room. After taking several turns through the empty halls, I collapsed against a wall and slid to the floor.

Tightly gripping my hands together, I tried to stop them from quivering. I didn't hear the footsteps before he spoke.

What had I done? I had to find her and apologize. I had to make sure that she was all right. I never should have asked her to dance. Why had I even considered it? Why did I have to ruin everything?

I followed her footsteps until they stopped, and then approached slowly, trying desperately to think of what I should say.

I saw his shoe come into my line of sight, and then a gentle whisper, "Ari . . . I didn't mean to upset you. I'm sorry. I should never have asked you to dance."

"Th-that wasn't it," I stammered. I'd wanted to dance.

"Do you want me to find a blanket?" he asked, and I glanced up to watch him look around puzzled.

I laughed ever so lightly and saw him smile.

"I'm not sure that you would find one down here."

He waved his hand at the abandoned hallways. "I'm sure there's something somewhere."

"It might take you years to find it," I teased.

He took a breath and said softly, "Well, at least then I wouldn't be upsetting you."

"You didn't upset me," I insisted.

He sighed and shook his head. "Would you like my vest then?" he asked.

I saw the fear on her face and closed my eyes. I was just making things worse. Why couldn't I manage to help her?

"Yes, please," she whispered. I nearly fell over.

"What?" I stared directly at her and saw her blush. Looking away, I asked, "Are you certain?"

She answered shakily, "Yes, please."

I pulled my vest off and handed it to her. Was that disappointment I saw as she reached out and took it? Quietly, Ari leaned forward and wrapped it around her shoulders. She ran her hand over the leather for a moment.

"Do you want me to leave?" I asked, wondering if it would be better if I wasn't there.

To my surprise she shook her head. "I'm not upset with you," she said, "honestly, I'm not."

"What?" How could that be?

"You just surprised me, that's all," she continued.

I watched her silently for a moment.

"Did you mean it?" she whispered.

"Did I mean to upset you? No, of course not." I sat down across the hall from her and watched her sigh.

"No," she said shakily, "the . . . the part about your . . . your partner."

I swallowed hard. "You are a fine dance partner." I had an idea as to what she meant, but I didn't want to upset her again.

She sighed. "I haven't danced since before . . ."

"Well, you have me beat," I joked. "I haven't danced since I left Torion Castle."

Ari glanced up at me, surprise on her face. "Why not?"

I chuckled, trying to keep the mood light. "It wasn't exactly high on my list of priorities when I was able to turn back." I glanced around. "I mean, remembering how to handle a sword, ride a horse, bow . . . dancing wasn't on the list, I'm afraid."

"Until now . . ." she finished for me.

I laughed. "Until now."

I watched her smile and felt better. Then that look returned to her face. The one that said she was working up her courage to ask me something.

"Danren," she began, "did you mean it?"

"What?" I didn't want to return to this topic.

"You said, 'It must be my . . .'" Her voice trailed off.

"Ari," I thought I'd sidetracked her, but I was wrong, "you don't have to do this?"

She cringed and ducked her head, opening her eyes to stare at her hands.

"Did you mean it?" she asked again.

"I . . ." I needed to answer her, "I didn't . . ."

The pained cry she made cut me off. She pulled herself to her feet and hurried down the hallway.

"Ari, wait!" I called as I gained my own feet and started after her. "Please, let me finish . . ." then I stopped.

I was only making things worse. I heard her steps falter and halt. Slowly, she pivoted around. Her body was quivering. How could I? I'd done the one thing that I never wanted to do again. She began to slowly walk back.

"Then finish." The words were forced.

"Ari, I'm sorry," I faltered, "I upset you."

"That's what you were going to tell me?" she snapped.

"Ari," his voice broke.

I wasn't sure that I felt sorry for his discomfort. I looked away, disgusted with myself. He'd been nothing but a gentleman to me, and here I was being angry over a slip of the tongue. Why did it matter if he thought I was pretty or not? Why did it hurt that he didn't? He'd always treated me with dignity and respect. Why did I want more?

"Ari," he began, a slight quiver still in his tone, "I don't know if you want me to answer the question still, but please, let me finish." He took a deep breath and glanced around. "I . . . I didn't mean . . . *to* say it." He shook his head and stared at the floor between us. "I've been frustrated for a week with this"—he motioned back down the hall—"but that isn't an excuse. I never would have said something like that to you normally, and I'm sorry."

"You didn't mean to say it," I forced myself to continue, "but you meant what you said?"

He watched me for a moment, then asked, "Do you want to know the answer to that?"

Did I? I thought for a moment, then slowly nodded.

He sighed and looked away. "Yes, Ari, I meant it."

I tried to think for a while, to come up with some type of response. Then suddenly, I realized that I wasn't standing in front of Danren. With a start, I discovered that I'd turned around and walked away from him. I was heading toward a part of the fortress I knew. I glanced around. He wasn't with me. I'd just walked away. I stopped and rested my head against the wall. How could I have been so rude?

Retracing my steps, I went back to the hallway that we'd been talking in, but Danren wasn't there. He wasn't in the room either. I searched for a watch, but finally had to give up. He would come back for supper, I thought, so I could talk to him then.

I waited for several watches in the dining room, but he never came. Even though I didn't feel hungry, I picked at the food out of habit. Finally, I made my way to our rooms. He wasn't there yet, so I sat in front of the fire waiting.

I watched her walk away. Leaning against the wall, I slowly slid to the floor. Certainly, she would hate me now, and with good reason. I had no business saying such things. Hadn't she been through enough without my incompetence adding to it?

She wouldn't want to see me at dinner, and I wasn't the slightest bit interested in food. I worked on things that I could have done later, but Ari wouldn't want me around. The sooner I finished, the sooner I could turn. Then I would head out on a patrol or something.

The lamp began to flicker, and I realized how late it was. I made my way up the stairs, certain that Ari would be asleep. Quietly, opening the door, I began to tiptoe toward my room, but then I saw the figure out of the corner of my eye.

"Ari?" I breathed, realizing that she was sitting in front of the fire.

She didn't look up. She didn't even stir. I wondered if I had offended her that much.

"Ari, I'm sorry." Still no response.

Then I realized that I had been right before I'd entered the room. She was asleep. What was she doing out here? I hurried to my room as quickly as I dared and returned with a blanket. After spreading the cover over her, I watched her for a moment. She was so peaceful, and peace was something that I had tried so hard to give her.

I caught myself reaching forward to brush a strand of hair off her face. She was so lovely . . . Cringing, I pulled back my hand before

I touched her. What was I doing? What was I thinking? How could I? Fleeing toward my room, I realized that the door shut behind me far harder than I intended. I had to leave soon. I couldn't keep doing this to her.

CHAPTER 52

BEING TOGETHER

I woke with a start. Glancing around, I realized how late it was and that Danren had still not come. Then I noticed the blanket. I hadn't seen this one before. It felt a bit dusty, but the fur was still soft. Where had it come from . . . I stared at Danren's room. He hadn't disturbed me, he wouldn't have wanted to, but he'd brought me a blanket. I wasn't certain that I could possibly feel any lower. I needed to talk to him, but there wasn't a light showing under his door. He was probably asleep, and since he'd let me sleep, the least I could do was return the favor. Instead, I stumbled to my room and fell into bed.

The next morning, I found that I slept later than I'd wanted to, and when I knocked on Danren's door, there was no answer. I hurried to help Majorlaine and rushed through everything that I needed to so I could find him.

I never seemed to be able to catch up to him. Someone would direct me to where they'd last seen him or heard that he was, and he wouldn't be there. Then someone else would point me to the next place. Finally, I decided to head down to where he'd been practicing. Danren had been there every day for a week, maybe he would show up today.

If it all went according to plan, I would be able to leave the next morning. Most of the things I should have already done . . . but it had been such a pleasure to just chat with Ari in the afternoons. I'd put things off. Well, those days were over.

I needed to clean up the room where I had been practicing and return the musical box to Armel. I'd just have to tell Pher'am no, and take whatever ridicule she would hand to me.

I waited for what seemed like watches. I had expected Danren to be there already, so I had a nice speech planned . . . but he wasn't there. I waited, playing a few of the cylinders, but then I realized that if Danren heard music, he'd know I was here, and he wouldn't come into the room. So I sat, and waited, and paced, and waited, and finally convinced myself that he wasn't coming.

I headed toward the door, wondering where I could start looking. The door came open far too easily, and I stared up in surprise.

"What are you doing here?" The words were out before I could stop them.

The door practically flew open, and I jumped, staring at Ari.

"What are you doing here?" I asked, and then continued to stare at her.

It took me a moment to realize that she was expecting me to answer the same question. Motioning at the table with the box and the cylinders, I told her, "I came to clean up."

She moved back to let me into the room. Why was she here? I stepped past her and walked toward the table.

"Why?" The question stopped me.

I fought the urge to look at her. "I'm leaving tomorrow, and I need to return everything."

"You're . . . *leaving?*" Shock in her voice. "Why?" She didn't wait for me to answer that question. "It . . . it hasn't even been three weeks yet, and you said you had some extra time." Taking a step back she clapped her hand over her mouth in shock. "It's me, isn't it? It's . . . it's because I upset you yesterday. I didn't mean to. I'm so sorry. You surprised me. I've . . . I've been looking for you to . . . to apologize. I'm sorry."

It took me a moment to realize that she'd stopped, and that I was just standing there with my mouth hanging open. I swallowed, took a breath, and finally managed, "I'm confused." Wasn't that brilliance incarnate! "I thought I was the one that upset you. You walked away . . . not me."

She cringed. "I know. I'm not sure why I did that, but I'm sorry. I didn't know what to make of . . . what you said."

"I shouldn't have said it," I was searching madly for what I was supposed to say *now*.

"No, it was fine. It just . . . I mean . . ." She turned and walked back to the musical box. "People used to tell me before . . ."—she motioned vaguely—"that I would grow up to be a beautiful lady, a gem in the realm . . ." She continued after taking a deep breath, "But no one ever said anything like that after I came back. I can cover the scars, but everyone knows they're still there, I suppose." She toyed with one of the cylinders for a moment. "Do you . . ."—a deep breath—"do you actually think I'm . . . pretty?"

She didn't look up but continued fidgeting with the cylinder. Silently I prayed, "Mighty One have mercy," and took a deep breath. "Ari, I didn't say you were pretty . . ." I saw her cringe and quickly continued, "I said you were lovely. You . . . you're far beyond just pretty."

I glanced away, expecting to look back, and find her walking toward the door, but she was still standing there. In fact, she was staring at me. I saw her shiver slightly, and quickly glanced around.

What was I supposed to say now? I had hoped he'd say "Yes" or perhaps "Quite," but I hadn't expected that.

Finally, I managed to whisper, "Thank you." After another a moment, I managed, "Do you really have to leave?"

Glancing up, I saw him clamp his mouth shut and swallow.

Finally, he said, "No."

"If you want to leave, that's fine," I babbled, feeling so dumb.

I heard him start walking toward me. "Ari, do you want me to stay?"

"Well, you weren't done practicing, and you said you still had a lot to catch up on." Why couldn't I stop babbling?

"Do you want me to stay?"

I finally managed to keep from saying anything and just nodded. Glancing up, I watched a wonderful smile spread across his face.

I felt my cheeks warm and glanced away. "We should probably start then."

"Ari," he said softly, "you don't have to do this."

I fought to manage, "I know."

He began walking toward me again. "Are you certain this is what you want?"

I bit my lip and nodded.

I felt like I was flying. I honestly don't remember if I bowed or asked her to dance, or did anything that was proper. I finally managed to get my concentration back after stepping on her toes a couple times. I can't say that the dance went well, but I enjoyed it, and she seemed to as well. When the music stopped, I bowed, and then couldn't help but laugh at all our mistakes. Ari stared at me for a moment, but then laughed along with me . . . and so the days continued.

Over the next couple of weeks, I often found Ari waiting for me by the musical box. She typically was looking over the cylinders, picking out whatever song she wanted to dance to that day.

I decided early on to let her pick the music. If I ever wondered about a song, I would make sure that she wanted to dance to that one. She always did.

As the dances became more complicated, they began to have more contact as well, intimacy almost. I brushed it aside, thinking that more complicated dances were like that.

I realized after the first few days of dancing with Danren that I wanted . . . something else . . . more perhaps. I felt excitement race through me when his hand would brush mine. I would feel slightly light-headed as he would lead me to the center of the room, my hand resting on his arm. The next dance I picked, I made sure that he would have to hold my hand for one of the maneuvers.

Try as I might, I couldn't drive the thought that it would be nice to have him hold me against him, like he had in the garden. A few days later, I found a dance where he would have to set me in the crook of his arm against his shoulder. It would only be for a moment, but I hoped that would be enough for me.

For days I had been wondering if the garden somehow vented to this room. I'd noticed a scent in the air that I had noticed in the garden. I would catch it only briefly, and then it would disappear again. It reminded me of flowers and herbs, but it was unique. I considered asking Ari if she knew what flower had such a scent, but I kept forgetting.

I came to the dancing room that day, and greeted Ari formally, asking her to dance. She graciously accepted, set the box to playing, and laid her hand on my arm. I vaguely remembered this dance and went through the motions as best as I could. Ari seemed to be in more of a hurry than usual.

I treasured these moments that I had with her. Watching her gracefully move to the music, I wondered how much better she would have been at this if . . . If only . . . I so often plagued myself with if only.

She sighed in frustration when I missed several steps, and we had to back the cylinder up yet again.

As Ari turned back from the box, I told her, "If you don't want to do this today, or if I'm keeping you from anything, we don't have to continue."

I watched her eyes widen. "No . . . no, there's nothing else. I have everything done."

"Well, maybe we should pick a different dance," I suggested. "This one seems to be frustrating you. I know I'm not that good yet."

"No, that's not it," she began then stopped. Glancing at the musical box, she asked, "Do you not want to do this one?"

"It's fine," I told her. "You just seem to be on edge. Is something wrong?"

"No," she shook her head.

Something was going on, and I couldn't figure out what. Ari walked back over to me and made the next steps in the sequence. I caught up to her, trying terribly hard not to make any more mistakes, which, probably, doomed me to stepping on Ari's toes three more times in the next few moments. Then there was that smell! Where was that coming from?

I tried not to act like anything else went wrong. I didn't want Danren to suggest another dance again, attempting to focus on the moment helped a little. If I paid attention to Danren's hand gently holding mine through a turn, or keeping my feet out from under his, things seemed to flow a bit better. Then I realized that it was next! I hoped neither one of us would make a mistake again.

I stepped out to the end of his arm, holding his fingers lightly, then turned, wrapping his arm around my waist, and pausing for the moment with the back of my head against his shoulder. It would just be for a moment, an instant . . . but the moment continued.

I felt Danren pause, his face pressed into my hair. I couldn't breathe. What was he doing?

"It's you!" The exclamation caused me to jump.

He moved away to arm's length and turned me to face him. Then he stepped toward me and pressed his face into my hair again. I didn't know what to do. I hadn't expected this. What was he doing? I knew I shouldn't feel scared, I knew I could trust him, but a shiver ran through me anyway.

I felt his muscles tense, and he quickly stepped away.

"Ari, I'm sorry." He looked completely mortified. "I didn't mean . . ."

"Wh-what were you doing?" I managed to ask.

Hadn't I wanted him to hold me? I just hadn't expected that.

"I've . . . I just . . . I'm sorry, Ari, I never meant to scare you," he told me.

"What were you doing?" I asked again, managing to keep my voice even, but hiding my hands behind my back so he wouldn't see them shaking.

"I . . ." he glanced away looking awkward, "I've noticed a scent recently . . ."

Danren didn't continue after a moment, so I prompted, "What kind of scent?"

Why couldn't I get the trembling under control? I felt my arms quivering now.

"I thought it was coming from the garden." He still looked awkward.

I wondered what this had to do with anything.

"I noticed a scent . . . a smell like lilies, but more . . . with . . . I don't know how to describe it, but I thought it was coming from the garden . . . but it's not." He glanced around.

If I hadn't been fighting so hard to keep myself in check, I would have laughed at how sheepish he looked.

"I didn't mean to scare you, or do . . . that." He motioned to where we'd been only a few moments before.

"It-it's f-fine," I said, trying to keep my voice even and failing miserably.

"Ari . . ." I heard his voice break again. He turned and hurried over to the table. "We shouldn't be doing this."

He pulled the cylinder from the box and set it back into its case.

"No!" I snapped, realizing that my voice was far from controlled.

He didn't turn around, but leaned over the table. "Ari . . . I don't want to hurt you."

I hurried over to him and grabbed his arm before he could put the music box back in its case too. I pulled him around and looked up at him. He looked . . . he looked . . . heartbroken.

"I-I w-want to d-dance with you." I couldn't stop shaking.

"Ari," his voice broke again, "I'm hurting you!"

I threw myself against his chest. I wanted him to hold me, to comfort me. I couldn't stand seeing that look on his face.

"Ari"—he set his hands against my shoulders—"don't do this for me."

I couldn't keep the quiver out of my tone. "I'm not. Please, don't leave me."

I felt his grip tighten slightly on my shoulders. I wrapped my arms around him, praying that he wouldn't push me away. His grip loosened, and his hands slid to the middle of my back.

"Is this what you want?" he asked softly.

I nodded into his shoulder.

With his face pressed into my hair, he told me, "I don't want to hurt you."

"You won't," I whispered.

Looking up at the ceiling, he let out a deep breath. "How can you be so certain?"

"You said you wouldn't," I whispered, "and you're a man of your word." I laughed ever so slightly. "You'll keep your promises even if it costs you everything."

"Ari . . ." his voice broke again, and again I felt moisture begin to seep into my hair.

I wanted to say so many things, but I was convinced that I shouldn't. I didn't understand why, after I'd terrified her by smelling her hair, she was letting me hold her like this. Why she would even want me near her at all.

Fighting to gain some semblance of control, I managed to get my own feelings restrained.

"It's all right," I told her.

"I know," she whispered.

"Then why are you still shaking?" I asked.

She tried to laugh. "Because the rest of me hasn't realized that yet."

I chuckled lightly and took a deep breath, catching the smell of her hair as I did. Reflexively, I put my nose to her hair and breathed in again.

Realizing what I'd done, I stammered, "I'm sorry . . . I didn't mean . . ."

Ari laughed. She actually laughed. "It's fine," she told me. "I don't mind. You just surprised me . . . earlier. I was expecting . . . something else."

She'd calmed down, so I asked, "What were you expecting?"

Her body shivered slightly, and I chastened myself for asking.

"The next motion . . .," she finally answered. "I was expecting to turn against your shoulder, turn out, have my toes stepped on, step on yours, and finish the dance."

"You didn't have to pick one that made you uncomfortable. If I don't know some dance or another, I could just tell Pher'am to pick a different one," I told her.

"And have her embarrass you?" Was she teasing me?

"Ari, you don't have to do this for me," I told her evenly.

"I want to dance with you," she whispered, "it's . . . it's nice."

"You shouldn't pick ones that make you uncomfortable then," I reasoned.

"I wanted this one," she whispered.

"What?" Had she lost her mind? "Did you remember all the steps?"

She nodded into my chest. "I thought it would be . . . nice."

"Ari, I don't understand," I told her, hoping that she would explain.

I listened to her breathing for several moments. Then she finally whispered, "Neither do I . . ."

Her breathing was normal though, and she'd stopped shaking. As much as I wanted to, I knew I couldn't hold her there forever. I gently pushed her a step away, leaving my hands on her shoulders. I saw the effort it took, but she looked up to meet my gaze.

After a moment, I asked, "How are you feeling? Are you all right?"

She smiled and nodded.

"Do you mind if we finish for the day?" I asked.

Shaking her head, she glanced at the musical box. "Will you let me come back tomorrow?"

"If that is what you'd like," I told her taking my hands off her shoulders. Then I smiled and bowed. "My lady."

I had wanted her to laugh, and she did.

I was fairly certain that Danren would stop me if I tried to play that dance again right away, so for the next few days, we worked on ones that needed a bit of improvement. I didn't understand why, but I felt both completely safe and somewhat terrified when I was close to him. I knew I could trust him, but some part of me still didn't seem to believe it. I knew I couldn't live with that fear for the rest of my life, so I made plans to play that dance again.

Danren would have to turn soon, so the day before he was to leave, I decided to try that dance again. He recognized it immediately, but I told him that I was trying to overcome my fears, so he acquiesced.

Perhaps I just imagined it, but I thought that he held me against his shoulder for a moment longer than necessary.

CHAPTER 53

HAUNTED

I thought that I would fill my free watches with tasks while he was away. Narden needed to check on a few dragons and meet with the counsel again. They still hadn't come to a decision about his insubordinate actions. I wasn't sure that I wanted them to come to a decision. I didn't want Danren to be in trouble for saving me.

I had forgotten what time of year it was though. I had forgotten, but my dreams hadn't.

Every year since my rescue, I had been plagued by nightmares at the time of the spring tours. It was the time of year that I'd been taken. For between a week and a month, I would fight off nightmares that were so real that I would wake up silently screaming. I tried not to sleep, but would eventually collapse from exhaustion. I jumped at every sound while I was awake, and awoke to every imagined or real sound when I slept.

I wished that if I had to go through this, that I would have a matching time of pleasant dreams that coincided with when I had been rescued. Maybe I did, and pleasant dreams were just harder to remember . . .

I couldn't focus on almost anything after the first week and a half. Trying to accomplish things was futile, and I ended up pacing the halls of the fortress . . . until I was exhausted. I'd consider going back to my room, but . . . but I wouldn't. Eventually, I would stop walking . . . Then a few watches later, I would scream myself awake, staring at a wall I didn't recognize . . . in a hall that I didn't remember . . .

Throwing myself to my feet, I would run until I found a place I recognized. Sometimes, I would end up back at my room. The familiar place would help. Sometimes I would find myself at the dragon stables, but if anyone was there, I would hurry away. The garden would calm me when I was there, but then I would flee from it. Voices would plague me, telling me that I was nothing. I didn't deserve to be in that beautiful garden.

Sometimes I would come to the room that Danren and I danced in. I would try to organize the cylinders, but eventually, I would just sob. I knew I needed help, but I was too terrified to ask. What would people think? It had been years. Why did these dreams . . . these memories . . . still haunt me? Why couldn't I be like everyone else?

After two weeks of traveling through Rem'Maren checking on tasks, border stability, and the like, I went to see the counsel. After another week of telling the counsel, yet again, why I had turned in front of Ari, why I had ordered Dreanen to turn, and why I risked the safety and security of our people for her, I left. Yet again, there wasn't a resolution. Yet again, I was told that I would be called back.

At least I'd left Ari in high spirits. I'd been concerned about leaving her. She didn't do well around this time of the year, but she was in a fantastic mood when I'd left. I hoped she would be happy to see me.

After turning, I immediately asked about her when I returned to Caer Corisan, but I couldn't get a straight answer from people. Eventually, I came to realize that no one had seen her for several days.

I hurried to our rooms. She wasn't there. After quickly bathing and changing my clothes, I began to search. She wasn't anywhere near the courtyard. There wasn't a sign of her near any of the kitchens. No one at the horse or dragon stables had seen her in a week. She wasn't in the garden, though the clover was trampled in several spots.

I began searching the lower halls. One at a time, looking through each room as I came to it. I hoped she would be in the little dance room, but she wasn't.

Night fell. I had to return to the courtyard for a lamp. I wondered if I'd missed her while I was gone, but I had no way to know. I continued farther into the depths of the fortress.

I turned a corner and froze. There was a shape curled against the wall.

"Mighty One have mercy," I prayed again, not certain whether I wanted the shape to be Ari, or something, anything else.

I didn't want to find her like this.

I'd ran as far as I could. My legs collapsed under me. I could hear their voices. They'd find me soon. I had to get up . . . but I couldn't. I slunk against the wall, hoping that they wouldn't find me. Maybe they wouldn't think to look here . . .

Hearing footsteps, I glanced up. There was a light coming. I could hide in the darkness, but they'd find me with that light. I couldn't run any farther. I could barely lift my head.

"Please . . . Mighty One . . . please . . . have mercy," I whispered, and curled into a ball, hoping desperately that they wouldn't find me.

The footsteps stopped. Maybe there was a corner . . . another hallway . . . maybe they wouldn't see me. Then the steps started again, first one step . . . then two . . . then they were running toward me. The light stopped on the floor in front of me. I turned my eyes to look at whatever priest it was.

I knew the man kneeling beside me. He wasn't a priest. I couldn't place him from the temple . . . but I knew him.

Turning from him, I whispered, "No," and tried to crawl away . . . but I couldn't.

"Ari," I heard my name . . . *my* name . . . no one at the temple called me by my name. He'd said something else. What had he said?

I felt something warm wrapped around my shoulders, but then he lifted me, and I began to quiver. I couldn't stop. I pushed against his chest, but he wouldn't let go. What had he said? What was he saying now?

He'd said, "Ari." He'd said my name . . . what else? "I won't hurt you . . ." he'd said that . . . Somehow, I believed him. I stopped hitting his chest and felt a sob rake through my body. Throwing my head back, I screamed.

Gripping the man's shoulder as hard as I could, I buried my face into his shirt. I screamed again.

"Ari." I knew the voice. I fought to remember. It wasn't from the temple. "It's all right." His voice was calm, but with an edge . . . a pained edge. "I'm taking you back to our rooms," it continued.

Our rooms? I threw my head back and looked around frantically. The stonework was wrong for the temple. This was gray, and the stones fit together intricately. The temple had beige stones that were smaller, more detailed, carved . . . but less . . . safe . . .

"It's all right," he told me again.

"Danren," I whispered. It was Danren. I was safe. They wouldn't find me if I was with him.

It was Ari. I ran to her body crumpled on the floor. She had to be alive. Setting the lamp down, I saw her move. She was alive! Her gaze turned toward me. Complete terror filled her face. Dark circles ringed her eyes, and her lips were cracked.

"Ari," I breathed.

She mouthed, "No," as she turned from me.

She tried to rise on just her hands, but collapsed back onto the floor.

Pulling my jacket off, I wrapped it around her shoulders and turned her onto her back.

"Ari," I said softly, forcing my voice to remain calm even though I wanted to holler.

I wanted to yell for help, but who would hear me down this far into the mountain?

"I won't hurt you," I told her.

Knowing that I had to get her out of there, I picked her up, holding her tightly against my chest.

She tried to push herself out of my arms. I was shocked by how much force she put into the blows when she looked so weak. I fought to keep her still. I couldn't drop her. She threw her head back, and screamed, one of those terrifying silent screams. To my shock, she stopped hitting me. Instead, she clung to my shoulder and sobbed. In a moment, I felt her scream again. Later, I would find a bruise engraved into my skin where she'd held on.

"Ari," I told her softly, "it's all right. I'm taking you back to our rooms."

She could rest there. If needed, I could have Majorlaine look at her, but there would be no help for her here. "It's all right," I repeated as calmly as I could.

I felt her whimper silently, and then whisper, "Danren."

I wasn't certain if it was good or bad that she knew who I was. Slowly, almost imperceptibly she began to stop shaking. As I walked into parts of the fortress that I was at least familiar with, her grip on my shoulder began to lessen. By the time I reached our rooms, by some miracle, she had fallen asleep.

Getting the door open took some maneuvering, but I finally managed. Having figured out the trick, her door wasn't quite so complicated. I debated laying her on the couch in the main room. I'd never been in her private quarters before, and had never intended to be. I decided that she would possibly feel better waking up in her own bed rather than somewhere else.

Returning to the main room, I sat in front of the fireplace. I prayed that she would be all right. I hoped that she wouldn't hate me for leaving her when I did, or for bringing her back up here. How long I sat there, I don't know, but then I realized that if Ari was cold, she'd wake up. After building a fire both in the main room and in her room, I returned to the chair.

What had I done? I'd left her during what I knew was a terrible time of year for her. I'd thought she was all right when I'd left. She'd seemed fine, but I should have known. I should have been here. Of all the people who could have kept her from this, I could have. This was my fault. She shouldn't have to go through this, ever.

I listened as the watches were called through the afternoon and into the evening.

CHAPTER 54

RECOVERY

I opened my eyes as I rolled over. Staring at the curtains, I slowly recognized them as the ones in my room in Caer Corisan. I couldn't remember falling asleep here. Fighting to remember what had happened, I came to my flight into the corridors of the fortress. I couldn't be sure how long I had fled through those hallways. Then I remembered looking up at Danren. He'd found me. He'd come for me, as he always did.

As I pulled myself out of bed, I realized that I was filthy. After quickly changing my clothes, I made my way to the door. Softly opening it, I looked around at the main room. I was amazed to see that it looked normal. There was a fire merrily blazing, and there was a tray of fruit, bread, and cold meats on the table.

Then I saw movement. Horrified, I turned slowly to look at the fireplace again. A man was sitting there. I couldn't tell who because his back was shadowed. The form was hunched forward, his head resting in his hands. Glancing at the main doors, I realized that I wouldn't be able to escape without him noticing. I stood frozen for several moments, barely daring to breath. He didn't move. Maybe he was asleep. I took a tentative step forward.

He moved. He turned his head slightly. I clapped my hands over my mouth to keep from screaming. Holding his fist against his forehead, he barely shook his head. I recognized him as he shifted slightly. I watched him rub his palm over his eyes then return to staring into the fire.

It was Danren. I was still safe.

I'd been sitting there for watches. The sun had set long ago. At one point, I'd realized that if Ari woke up, she might be hungry. I'd debated going for the food myself, but decided not to. I rang for someone to come, waited at the door for them, and told them what I wanted. I had no idea how long Ari would sleep, so I asked for things that would keep a little while.

"Is everything all right, my lord?" the boy had asked. He was one of the newer arrivals. He'd turn for the first time within the year.

"Not exactly," I told him. "If you could also send Galen up to talk with me, that would be appreciated."

Then I closed the door and went back to the chair. It didn't strike me as prudent to discuss Ari's condition with him. I did need to ask Galen about it though. I couldn't tell when I was carrying Ari, if she was physically injured. Realizing rather quickly that if I wasn't waiting for Galen or the food, they would knock on the door. Not knowing how soundly Ari was sleeping, I couldn't risk having the noise wake her.

The food had come, so had Galen. I'd spoken with him about what had happened. He looked irritated, but I wasn't certain about what. He was often irritated about something or another. I'd requested that he not disturb Ari while she was sleeping, and assured him that I would call for him soon after she awoke.

Then I went back to the chair and waited, and here I was. As far as I knew, Ari hadn't woken up yet. Every once in a while, I would glance at her door, but nothing changed. I'd fight breaking down. She never should have been in this situation. This never should have happened. I mashed the tears out of my eyes, and then I heard a slight whimper.

Bolting to my feet, I spun to face Ari's room. There she was. She'd changed her clothes, and the dark circles had faded around her eyes. Either that or I just couldn't tell in the dim light.

"Ari?" I took a step toward her, before catching myself. Stepping back again, I asked, "Are you all right? How do you feel?"

She glanced around the room, still looking frightened.

"Confused," she finally whispered. "I've been here?" she asked looking toward me.

"You were wandering around in the base of the fortress," I told her.

"But I never left here . . . Caer Corisan?" she asked, glancing around again, still looking frightened.

"No . . . You should eat," I told her, "it'll help you feel better."

"You came for me." She followed the motion of my hand toward the food and stared at it.

"I found you, yes." I didn't fully understand her questions.

She took a step toward the table and then froze. That terrified look returned to her face as she slowly turned to look at the balcony curtains. The breeze had just stirred them slightly.

"There's no one there," I told her. "It's just the wind."

She glanced around with that frightened stare, so I walked over to the balcony.

Pulling back the curtains, I told her, "See? It's safe."

I turned around and jumped. I hadn't expected her to be standing right there. She'd followed me to the curtains, and now she looked out on to the balcony. While biting her lip, the terror slowly faded from her face . . . but not completely.

"Would you like me to light some lamps?" I asked her.

When she nodded, I stepped around her and began the task. To my surprise, she followed me.

"You could sit down to eat," I told her once.

She glanced at the food again, but as I began to move to the next lamp, she continued to follow me.

I didn't know what to say, so I worked silently, unnerved by her presence. Finally I managed, "Ari, are you all right?"

Staring at the floor at her feet, she shook her head. "I'm scared."

"I know," Danren said. He sounded broken. I pulled my gaze from my feet to look at him. "Would you like me to turn?" he asked. "We'd . . . have to go to a different room, but if you'd feel better with Narden . . ."

I glanced around the room again. "A different room?" I didn't want to leave.

"Yes, I'm not . . . he's not allowed in here, or on this floor for that matter," he told me.

"Why?" I realized that I'd never seen Narden on this floor, or any dragon for that matter.

Danren tried to laugh. "He might singe the carpet."

I smiled at the thought, and looked up again. Danren's jaw had dropped open, and I felt a grin spread across my face.

He pulled his mouth shut, then asked, "Do you want me to leave?"

I panicked and threw myself at him.

I braced myself for the impact, expecting her to start hitting me again.

"No," she cried out, but instead of hitting me, she held on. She'd wrapped her arms around my back. "No," she whimpered, "please, don't leave me."

"I won't," I told her.

Slowly, I put my arms around her and then lifted her. I felt her whimper silently.

"I won't hurt you," I told her, as I began moving toward the chairs near the table.

"I know," she whispered.

I froze at that statement. "What?"

She didn't say anything more, but I did feel her begin to shake a little. "You should rest . . . and eat." I told her as I started back toward the table.

I set her down on the couch, planning to take the chair next to it, but she didn't let go of my arm. She glanced around the room with that frightened gaze again. I sat next to her on the couch. Reaching for a roll, I pulled it in half, added some meat, and a slab of cheese.

"You should eat," I told her again.

She gingerly took the roll from me and fingered it. Slowly, she began to nibble at it. Gaining momentum, she finished the roll and reached for another. Glancing away, I smiled and wondered if I should call for Galen. I decided against it just yet. After two more rolls, one with meat and the other with cheese, Ari began to slow down. She ate an apple, though, and then drank two cups of juice. She poured a third, but she seemed to be fingering the cup just to have something to hold.

"You had me pretty worried," I said, hoping that I could get her to talk some.

"I'm sorry . . .," she mumbled.

"You have nothing to apologize for," I told her. "I should have been here. Then none of this would have happened."

"But you had to go," she said softly.

"I should have said 'no.'"

"I'm sure the counsel would have loved that," she replied.

"What?" Was she teasing?

She smiled ever so slightly. "They would have had a fit. Can't you imagine?"

"Yes, I can," I replied watching her keenly.

"I wouldn't have wanted you to get into any more trouble because of me," she said.

"I could have gone later, thought of some excuse or another."

"What about the next time? Would you have postponed that one as well?" She was staring at the balcony.

"As long as it wasn't around this time of year, I probably wouldn't need to," I replied.

She slowly faced me, looking scared again. "You remembered."

"Yes," I admitted, "I thought you would be all right because you'd seemed to be in high spirits when I left, but I should have known. I shouldn't have gone."

To my surprise she studied me for a few moments. "You remembered . . . and I forgot."

"What?" I stared at her for an instant before catching myself and glancing away.

"I . . . I didn't remember until the nightmares started," Ari glanced around again, "and then I fled . . . It started with just a watch or two when I woke up, but then I found half a day gone." She stared at her hands. "How long was I down there?"

"I . . . I don't know," I told her. "No one had seen you for a few days, but . . . no one knew for certain when they'd seen you last."

"I thought they'd find me . . ." She frantically glanced around. "The priests . . . I thought they'd find me . . . so I ran."

"You don't have to talk about this if you don't want to," I told her trying to sound calm.

I knew I was anything but calm. These *men*, and I had a difficult time thinking of them as such, still hurt her even though they were nowhere near the fortress. Men I could fight, but how could I fight dreams?

Ari watched me for a moment then, staring at her cup, she whispered, "Thank you."

"What?" What could she possibly be thanking me for?

"You came for me," she whispered.

"I shouldn't have left," I groused.

To my surprise she smiled slightly. "You brought me back, and . . . you stayed." She bit her lip for a moment. "Thank you for caring about me."

I watched her play with her cup for a few moments before I could manage to simply say, "You're welcome."

She took a few sips and glanced around nervously again. By the look on her face, I knew what was coming.

Eventually, she said, "Danren . . . I have a question for you. Why . . ." her voice broke, "why am I so blighted?"

"What?" I replied in shock.

"I fled into . . . I don't even know where I was . . ." she snapped, "to escape people who weren't even here."

"Ari . . ." I wasn't certain what to say, but finally managed, "This isn't your fault."

She turned on me. I was surprised to see her that angry. "Then whose fault is it? I ran away from dreams! I got distracted by silly little kittens and got lost! I got lost! I asked someone for directions! Whose fault could it possibly be?"

I hadn't heard her scream in rage like that since we were kids. I wasn't certain what to make of it, but I knew it wasn't her fault.

"Ari, if you want to blame someone for what happened, now or then, blame me," I told her as I stared at the food tray.

"You?" I think I'd surprised her out of her anger for the moment. "How could this possibly be your fault?"

"I wasn't there," I replied, still unable to look at her. "Either now or when you were taken."

I glanced over and saw her shaking her head. "No, you came for me."

"I wouldn't have needed to come for you if I'd been there to begin with." I fought to keep my voice even.

"I won't blame you for this," she said.

"Then don't blame yourself either," I managed not to snap.

"Then whose fault is it?" she asked, sounding frustrated.

"Any half-decent person would have helped you find your parents," I began. "Anyone with even the slightest notion of decency would have believed you when you told them who you were. Anyone who wasn't as depraved as they could possibly be would have—" I couldn't control my temper anymore. I knew I would begin shouting myself, so I stopped.

It took me a moment to regain enough control to manage, "Ari, I'm sorry."

I glanced over at her to find her shaking. I sighed and began to stand up.

To my surprise, she gripped my arm. I looked at her but quickly looked away. She had a frightened look on her face.

"Ari, I'm scaring you," I told her, hoping she would let go.

"No," she said frantically, "it's not you. Please"—she glanced around the room with those frightened eyes—"don't leave me."

"I should at least get you a blanket . . . or something," I said.

She looked around again then stood. "May I come?"

I stared at her for a moment, and then froze as she lifted her eyes to look into mine.

"Ari," I whispered, "you don't have to do this."

She didn't look away. I sighed and started toward my room. Her hand didn't leave my arm.

CHAPTER 55

HELPING HER THROUGH

I pulled the fur blanket from on top of the wardrobe. It was the one I'd covered her with when she had fallen asleep in front of the fire. Turning to offer it to her, I realized she was looking around the room.

"You haven't been in here before." I glanced around trying to remember if I'd left anything out that I shouldn't have. I typically cleaned up the room before turning, but had I missed something. The sparse furnishings made it simple to look over the room. The wardrobe was closed. The little table that sat next to the bed only had the lamp and my battered book. There was a lounging chair near the window, and the bed itself. Nothing was out of the ordinary, thankfully.

"I-I've been in here before," she said softly taking her hand from my arm.

I stared at her for a moment and fought my jaw closed. "What?"

"I was looking for your book." Her eyes were focused on her fidgeting hands.

I glanced around. "And did you find it?" Why had she wanted my book? I saw her nod. "What did you do with my book?"

"I dropped it," she whispered.

"Is something wrong with your book?" I began to ask, but then I realized *when* she was talking about. "Oh," I finished.

I wanted to explain. I tried to get the words out. Then I looked up at him. Danren wasn't looking at me. He was looking past me, but he seemed to be fighting a hurt look off his face.

"You were angry with me," he finally said.

"N-no," I gasped, and he looked down at me. The hurt still showing on his face. I shook my head and then tried to explain, "I wanted to read to Narden, because . . . because it was something I used to do when I was with him . . . with you at the cave . . . but then I went to the injury stables, but . . . but it wasn't Narden . . . it was you. I wasn't expecting you . . . I thought I could handle talking to Narden . . . reading to him . . . to you as him, b-but I didn't know what to say to you . . . and I dropped the book. It broke. I didn't know what to do, so I ran back up here, and you were coming. I panicked . . . I should have taken the book into my room . . . but I didn't . . . I hid it behind the couch . . . I didn't think you'd find it, but you did . . . and you were so upset . . . I couldn't tell you."

I glanced up at him and saw him mouth the word, "What?" but he didn't say anything for what seemed to be forever.

"I'm sorry. I didn't mean to break it. I didn't. It was an accident," I told him, hoping he would forgive me.

He still stared past me for a moment, but then looked down at me. "You weren't angry with me?"

Shaking my head, I repeated, "I'm sorry."

A smile spread across his face, and then he laughed. The laugh confused me, but I smiled back. What was funny about my breaking his book?

He looked back down at me and sobered instantly.

"Here," he said, handing me the blanket.

I tried to take it, but my hands were shaking too badly. I missed my grip, and it slipped to the floor. Danren immediately picked it up and lifted it around my shoulders. I stepped into his arm, leaning against his chest. To my surprise, he squeezed me to him. Then I felt my feet leave the floor for a moment while he spun me around, laughing.

"You weren't angry with me!" he exclaimed when we stopped.

He moved me to arm's length and stared at me. Then a realization came over him.

He stepped away, looking mortified. "Ari, I'm sorry, I didn't mean . . ."

It was my turn to laugh, a bit nervously, but I laughed. What he'd done was unexpected, but normal. I should expect someone who was excited about something to act a little odd.

He walked to the door in an arc around me. "I'm sorry."

It took me a moment to follow him, but by then he was almost to the main door.

"Danren, wait," I called, hoping he would stop.

He did, but it seemed to take quite an effort. Slowly, he turned back to face me.

"Ari, I didn't mean to do that."

"And I didn't mean to break your book," I replied, as quickly as I could manage.

"That was an accident," he told me.

"Danren," I glanced at the floor, "please, don't leave me."

I watched the battle that raged inside him for a moment, but then he walked over to a chair by the fireplace. I slowly walked over to the couch and sat down.

I searched for something to break the silence, and finally managed, "You're not upset that I broke your book?"

Shaking his head, he told me, "No, the book can be fixed."

There was an awkward silence for a few moments. I managed not to jump when the curtains blew in. Danren glanced around, but quickly returned to staring at his hands.

"I've been thinking . . ." he began, then trailed off for a moment. He sighed and then looked at me. "Would you like a lady-in-waiting?"

I stared at him blankly for a moment, and then finally managed to say, "I don't understand. I haven't had one for this long, why would I need one now?"

"You should have had someone about to help you," he told me. "I apologize for being remiss in this matter."

I wanted to tease him about switching into such a formal tone, but he looked rather miserable at the moment.

Instead, I asked, "Why now, though?"

"I thought about it before," he went on. "Actually, I realized that I should look into it at the funeral, but then . . . everything happened."

"So you haven't had a chance," I added.

He shook his head. "No, I had plenty of chances, but when we returned . . . I thought you would leave, so there wasn't a reason. I realized that I haven't taken the time to ask since finding out that you were staying."

"I don't really need one," I told him. "What would they do anyway? I know it's not *proper* for me to pick out my own clothes and, in some circles even, to dress myself, but I prefer it."

Danren blushed slightly and glanced away. "Perhaps for company then. You should probably have someone else to talk to other than Majorlaine, maybe someone closer to your age."

"I do talk to more people than just Majorlaine," I quipped, "and I thought you were reasonably close to my age. Unless, you don't like talking to me."

"Ari!" His voice was harsher than I expected, so I jumped. He immediately cringed and then took a long breath. "I'm sorry," he continued, "but I meant another woman to talk to."

"What would she do the rest of the day, when she wasn't talking to me?" I asked, trying to point out that I really didn't need anyone.

"There are plenty of things to do around the fortress. You know that," he told me.

"Do you have someone in mind?" I asked. "I would think it would be hard to find someone for such a . . . position."

"I was thinking about one of Majorlaine's daughters, actually," he replied.

I gaped at him. I hadn't even realized that Majorlaine was married, much less had daughters!

"They know . . ." He seemed to stumble to a halt. "Galen told them."

"Why would he tell them?" This was becoming more and more confusing. "What does he have to do with any of this?"

Danren stared at me for a moment. "Don't you know?"

"Know what?" What was he talking about now?

He looked puzzled as he told me, "Galen and Majorlaine are husband and wife."

I gaped at him. "What?"

He smiled slightly, the first time in about a watch, but didn't reply.

"They hate each other!" I exclaimed.

"They don't hate each other," he replied, looking almost like he could laugh. "They just disagree about practically anything medicinal."

"What ever is the difference?" I exclaimed.

"Galen loves Majorlaine dearly. He has some trouble showing it . . . at least in public. Also it's a bit odd to talk about around here, since she was barely twenty when they married."

"Barely twenty?" I asked, still rather lost by what he was telling me. "Twenty is a rather . . . old age for a woman to marry at."

"He was over two hundred," he said softly.

I choked on the sip of juice I'd just taken. "Galen is over two hundred? *Years?*"

"Well, it certainly isn't goose feathers," he quipped back.

I was slightly surprised by the teasing.

"He doesn't look it," I stumbled. "He looks like he's barely thirty, and Majorlaine . . . she's at least fifty now."

"That's part of the reason no one talks about it . . . It's hard to explain . . ." he told me, more subdued.

I thought for a moment, trying to sort through things, and then asked, "How old will you look when I am fifty?"

"That . . . depends," he said, after a moment.

"On what?" I asked.

He forced a smile. "Whether I live that long."

The statement shocked me so severely that it took me a while to respond, "W-whether you live that long? W-what is that supposed to mean?"

He sighed heavily before replying, "Gary's line is short."

Suddenly, things that I had applied only to the dragons began to fit into place.

"My father is part of the counsel, because he is the eldest of Gary's descendants, but he is almost three centuries younger than any other member." He stood and paced toward the balcony for a few moments, but then turned back. "Traditionally, someone from Gary's line was Caer Corisan's regent, but for five generations, Armel held the position, because no one from Gary's line survived through their married years."

"Married years?" The words were out before I had a chance to stop them.

The conversation was a strain on him, he looked agitated, but not angry as he paced back toward the balcony.

"Nobility marries shortly after being able to turn back, partly because the line is short, and partly . . . because we're nobility. Anyone else can marry or not whenever they choose, but nobility marries early. Typically, there are twenty . . . or thirty years at most of marriage . . . then if the wife hasn't died . . . our deaths are often faked . . ."

I sat silently for a moment before I could manage to ask, "What of you then?"

Danren smiled slightly. "I have you to thank for making me an exception." He glanced at me before continuing, "I became coregent of Caer Corisan while still married. The fortress has its first lady and its youngest regent all at the same time."

"Do you plan to . . . to fake your death in fifteen years?" I asked shakily.

"That would depend on you," he replied softly.

"On me?" I asked. "Why on me?"

"You may be uncomfortable here with a . . . a husband who looks almost as he does now when you . . . don't," he finally managed to say.

"You offered to let me leave now," I began. I saw him suddenly look directly at me, but I couldn't manage to pull my eyes from my hands, "and I refused. I doubt that I will change my mind as time passes."

I glanced up to see him smile. He seemed to be fighting not to laugh.

Looking away, he finally managed to say, "Thank you, Ari."

She smiled in return.

We talked for several watches about different things. I brought up the matter of the lady-in-waiting again. Ari finally agreed to consider meeting with Majorlaine's daughters to see if she might get along with any of them. It wasn't an outright acceptance of the idea, but it was a step.

I needed to have someone with Ari for several reasons. If I'd had a lady-in-waiting for her already, she would never have gone that far recently. Someone would have, if not stayed with her, at least found her before she was so lost. Ari didn't need a nursemaid, but she did need someone to care.

It couldn't be me though. I cared too much. Desperately, I needed to step away from the situation. I could have terrified her for the rest of her life by swinging her around the way I had earlier. She'd handled it, but it could have been far worse. I didn't want to step away from being with Ari, and I knew that was exactly why I had to. This was becoming far too . . . too . . . intimate.

When dawn was not far away, I finally convinced Ari that she should at least try to sleep. She slowly made her way to her room.

Turning toward me, she whispered, "Thank you."

I wasn't certain what she could possibly have to thank me for, but I nodded in reply and smiled slightly. Turning back to stare at the fire, I let my thoughts wander.

I awoke with a start, realizing first that the last thing I'd been thinking of was the smell of Ari's hair, and secondly that she was kneeling in front of me, stoking the fire.

"Ari," I blurted out.

She jumped to her feet and spun to face me. "I . . . I didn't mean to wake you."

I rubbed a hand across my face, trying to collect my thoughts. "I'm not certain that you did."

"Oh," was the only thing she said.

I glanced at the balcony to find that it was at least midday. "I should be going," I told her hauling myself to my feet.

She fidgeted with her fingers, and I realized that she was shaking a bit.

"Are you all right?" I asked, chiding myself for not noticing sooner.

"I . . . I . . . I only had a bad dream," she said. "It wasn't real."

I wasn't certain if she was trying to convince me or herself.

"Are you all right?" I asked again.

"I'm just a little . . ." She started walking toward the door, but then stopped. "I'm a little scared. That's all. It was just a dream." She watched the door for a moment, and then asked, "Would you ring for some food?"

"Of course, but . . ." I wasn't certain what to say. As I walked over and pulled the cord to the kitchen.

"I just don't . . . I don't want anyone seeing me like this." She turned and hurried back toward the fire.

She looked almost like she would walk straight into me, so I stepped to the side. It startled her. She jumped and looked up at me, and then glanced around as though she wasn't quite certain where she was.

"Ari, I know you don't want anyone to see you like this, but you shouldn't be alone," I told her.

Her eyes ran over me, seemingly without seeing me, but then she pulled her gaze to my face and focused for the moments it took her to say, "You're not anyone . . . not just anyone . . . you're my . . . my friend." She ducked her head to study her hands as her fingers intertwined, then loosen, and then laced again. "I think . . . maybe . . . that's why I hated you . . . I'm sorry . . . I thought that if you knew what your childhood friend . . . how I panic when . . . when nothing's wrong . . . how I can't stop shaking when I'm scared . . . you would . . . you'd despise me."

"I don't, Ari." I wanted to say more, but I knew I shouldn't.

"I know," she seemed to whimper, then she laughed in an ironic tone. "You've seen me worse."

"Ari . . ." I wasn't certain what to say, but I managed, "it's all right. You're safe here."

She looked at me, and whimpered, "I know." Glancing around frantically, she took a step toward me. "I know . . . I just can't get the rest of me to believe it."

I stepped back but bumped into the couch.

"Please . . ." I heard her whisper. She glanced at my face, then at my shoulder, and took another step toward me.

"Please," she whispered again.

I held my ground and opened my arms to her. As she ran into my chest, she knocked the breath out of me for a moment.

"Ari." I couldn't manage more than a whisper myself and fought not to say what I wanted to more than anything else. Instead, I told her again, "It's all right."

"I know," she whispered back.

She had stopped shaking by the time the knock sounded on the door. I was certain that I must have imagined it, but I thought, for an instant, that she seemed reluctant to let go. She did though, and I hurried to the door.

The food smelled wonderful, so I quickly set the tray down on the table. I sat on the couch before realizing what I'd done. Before I could change seats, Ari sat down next to me. She set her hand lightly on my arm, almost as though she needed reassurance that I was indeed there.

I dished up some of the eggs, bacon, and sausage on a plate and handed it to her. After serving myself, I began to eat. It took me a moment to realize that Ari was just pushing her food around.

"You should eat," I told her.

"I know." She smiled ever so slightly. "I'm even a little hungry."

"Then what's stopping you?" I asked.

She swallowed hard. "I don't think . . . I'm not going to be able to . . . to dance with you today. I'm too . . . too shaky."

It took me a moment to put my jaw back and say, "I wouldn't have asked."

"I know," she sounded almost desperate, "but I . . . You never asked unless I insisted anyway, but I . . . I . . . I wanted to." Her voice dropped to a whisper, "I'd been looking forward to it . . . but . . . but I don't think I can . . . not today."

She looked up after a moment and laughed. It took me a moment to realize why. Then I glanced away, rubbed my hand over my beard, and hoped that when I took it away, my jaw wouldn't drop open again.

"I thought you were just doing that as a favor to me," I finally managed to say.

"Well, I was," she told me, "sort of, but I . . . I enjoyed it too."

I tried to wipe the grin off my face.

After taking a bite of eggs, I told her, "Well, if you ever feel up to it again, I would be honored."

She smiled slightly. "Thank you."

Finally, Ari began to eat. She jumped when the breeze picked up the balcony curtains, when a horse neighed from the courtyard, and again when a dragon landed.

"I believe that may have been Ara'ta," I told Ari. "It sounded rather . . . uncoordinated."

She glanced at me and then back at the balcony. "Who? I . . . I don't believe I've met an Ara'ta."

"Do you remember Ataar, the lad with blond hair, green eyes?" I asked. "He came about a month ago."

She nodded, and then a look of recognition spread across her face. Quickly, jumping to her feet, she hurried to the balcony. "He has gold tips like y—Narden, only they stop halfway back. The end of his tail's gold too," she called.

Narden had seen Ara'ta two weeks ago, so I already knew what he looked like. Ari turned to me as I approached.

"He looks so dazed," she said as we watched him stumble slightly crossing the courtyard.

"I would think so." I laughed, pointing. "Look what he hit."

Majorlaine's little food cart lay broken into pieces. As we watched, a chunk of the wagon fell off the wall where it had been smashed.

Ari laughed ever so lightly. "Narden was like that once."

"Actually, I do believe he was worse. He almost smashed the pony too." Instinctively, I began to put my arm around her shoulders.

I caught myself and pulled my hand away, but not before Ari turned around, asking, "You almost killed Majorlaine's pony?"

She froze when she saw my arm returning to my side. I cringed. "Ari, I didn't mean . . ." She turned to look at the broken cart. "I'm sorry," I began, but she stepped back, leaning against my shoulder. "Ari," I couldn't manage more than a whisper, "you don't have to do this."

"I know," she replied softly.

Raising my arm, I held her against my shoulder. I leaned down and took a breath of her hair before I realized it. Jerking my head back up, I felt her laugh lightly.

"You're awfully shy for a dragon lord," she teased.

"I didn't mean . . ." I began, but she interrupted with a laugh.

"Do you know how often you do that?" she asked.

As I glanced up at him, Danren looked puzzled for a moment. "No, I . . . I didn't mean . . ."

I laughed. It felt good to laugh, and it was so nice to laugh with him near.

"You do that every time you . . ." I faltered for a moment, "you hold me." I laughed lightly to try to keep from becoming nervous. "You even do that every time we practice dancing."

I glanced up to see him looking horrified. "Ari, I never meant . . ." he stammered to a halt.

I turned around, and he took a step back.

"Ari, I'm sorry." He looked away from me.

"You know," I told him stepping toward him, "if you like my hair soap that much, I could mix some for you."

"No, it wouldn't be the same." I watched him realize what he'd said and cringe.

Later I would realize how mean I was being, but at that moment, I was enjoying making him squirm far too much. He backed into the balcony door and began to shift around it. I stepped up to him before he could escape. Leaning against his chest, I smiled.

"Ari . . ." He choked.

I saw his arms move to embrace me, but then fall back to his sides. His hands balled into fists. I could hear his heart racing and feel every breath he labored to take. His hands unclenched, and I watched them rise to my shoulders. Expecting to feel his arms wrap around my shoulders, I relaxed into him. To my shock, he gripped my shoulders and pushed me away.

"Ari," he choked, "I'm sorry."

Then he was gone. Before I could stop him, or even say anything, I heard the doors close.

I had to leave. It wasn't fair to Ari to . . . to . . . take advantage of her like that. I knew that I wanted to hold her. To promise her that nothing would ever hurt her again if I could stop it, but I was convinced that it wasn't right.

As quickly as I could, I found a boy to watch the stairs going up to our room. If she began to wander again, I would need to know, but I couldn't be with her at that moment. I needed to find some control. I located Majorlaine next and asked her to check on Ari in a watch if she hadn't left the room. Then I threw myself into planning border patrols, training programs for the newly turned, and anything else I could find.

I stayed late checking supplies by lamplight in the kitchens, stables, and even the armories. Finally, as the middle of the night watch was called, I made my way back to the room. I was certain that Ari would be asleep by then.

Walking into the room, I noticed that the main fire was still burning, though it was working on the last log. I glanced at Ari's

562

room and sighed with relief that there was no light under the door.
Then I caught movement out of the corner of my eye by the fire.

I felt my breath catch, and I stepped back against the door.

CHAPTER 56

TALKING TOGETHER

He looked horrified, and I wondered if I'd done the right thing.

"Danren," I couldn't keep the hurt out of my voice, "I need to talk to you . . . please."

I watched him close his eyes and take a deep breath.

"Are you all right?" he asked.

I wasn't certain.

Her face was shadowed, so I couldn't make out how hurt she looked, but she sounded broken. I wondered if it was because I'd left or if she'd had another nightmare.

She didn't answer when I asked if she was all right. I watched her shadowed hands wring each other, but she didn't say anything for a long time.

"Wh-when," I finally managed to begin. All afternoon, I had rehearsed these questions, so I would be able to ask them, "you promised that you wouldn't touch me, you didn't know who I was?"

He seemed taken back by the question, because his first reply was, "What?" I waited for his actual answer, "No, you were still veiled, and the last person I expected to be married to . . . was you."

I swallowed hard and forced myself to continue, "I released you from that promise . . . I-is . . . i-is it . . . because I'm . . . I'm . . . defiled . . . th-that you still do not want to touch me?"

"What?" he asked again.

I waited, trying to fight the tears that wanted to fall.

How could she possibly think that?

"No," I finally managed to answer, "I don't want to hurt you."

At that moment, I realized that by trying to avoid the one thing I didn't want to do, I had run right into it. I gasped at the shock of that realization, and then realized what I needed to do.

I expected my feet to rebel, but found that they willingly carried me to where she was standing before I was quite ready. She took a step back, but then stopped. Following her through that step, I gently cradled her head to my shoulder. I felt a sob rip through her body before she wrapped her arms around me.

"You don't have to do this," Ari whispered when she could manage to say anything.

The irony struck me, and I laughed slightly. "I'm the one who's supposed to say that."

I felt her give a half laugh, half sob. She continued to cry as I worked out what I was about to say. I knew I had to tread carefully. Taking a deep breath before I began, I realized that I had leaned my face into her hair again. I sighed, wondering if I would ever manage not to do that.

"Ari," I began, "I would like to try to explain why I act the way I do toward you."

I felt a shiver run through her body, but it didn't continue. She nodded slightly.

"While," I glanced around and then lowered my voice slightly, "you were staying at Gary's caves, I realized that I would never be able to view any woman the same way ever again." I shook my head slightly. "Adenern and . . . I used to fly around joking about the wives we would have. We'd tease each other that the other one would end up with someone horrible." I felt Ari shiver again. "Then we rescued you, and everything changed. We stopped even discussing what life would be like when we could turn again."

Pausing a moment, I gathered what I would say, "I still knew that I would marry, very shortly after being able to turn actually, but I couldn't daydream about what type of woman I wanted anymore. Women were precious. Like the finest porcelain dishes or the most expensive silk. They were people to be treated with the utmost respect, dignity, and honor." I fought the choked sensation in my throat for a moment. "I knew that I would treat my wife with as much respect, dignity, and honor as I possibly could. I had everything planned out, including the promise I made you.

"Never did I even imagine that I would marry you." Laughing lightly at the thought, I told her, "I would have thought that I would marry the queen mother before marrying you."

I heard her laugh slightly in return. Leaning back, I looked down at her tearstained face. I snaked a handkerchief out of my pocket and tried to mop away her tears.

I had longed for these little gentle touches, to have him brush my tears away. Slowly, I looked up into his eyes. It appeared that his own heart was breaking because I was crying. I buried my face in his shoulder again, and he returned to gently stroking my hair.

"I made more promises that day than just that one to you," he continued, "but I never told you any of those before." He paused for a moment. "The one I swore to my father was that if it came between your safety and your knowing our *great* secret, you would know. I also promised myself that I would keep you safe, even if it cost me my own life. I swore that I would honor your every wish or whim as long as it didn't cause you or someone, other than myself, harm. I would do everything in my power to make you happy."

He paused for a long time, and I felt him take a breath of my hair. I smiled slightly.

"Then I found that you hated me." He took a deep breath. "I had hoped to that point that things might one day improve between us. That perhaps one day I would know the simple pleasure of escorting you"—he shrugged—"somewhere on my arm, that we could at least be friends. I gave up any hope of that though. I had to. I knew that I still had to do everything in my power to protect you, to see that you were happy, but I knew that the only time you would be comfortable around me was when I was Narden."

It took him a few moments to continue, "Then you found out, and I was certain you would leave. You would hate me entirely now. I tried to imagine life without you, and it was completely bleak. I never hoped that you would forgive me. I never hoped that"—he leaned back again and traced my face, tucking my hair behind my ear—"I'd be here. I never could have."

I swallowed hard as he ran his fingers through my hair again.

"Are you all right?" he asked.

When I nodded, he stepped back, dropping his hand to his side.

"Could we . . . talk . . . for a little while?" I asked.

He nodded. I shivered slightly as I moved back toward the fire. To my surprise, Danren sat on the couch. I watched him for a moment and then sat next to him, leaning against his side. He awkwardly put his arm around my shoulder. I laughed slightly.

"I'm not used to this." His voice sounded slightly muffled since his face was in my hair again.

I laughed again, leaning into him a bit more. I hadn't realized how much I wanted him just to be near me, to gently run his fingers through my hair. I cringed when he hit a tangle though.

He pulled his hand away and mumbled an apology. I leaned forward and laid my head on his knees.

"Ari," his voice was a bit strained, "I don't want to hurt you."

"You won't," I told him.

"Would you mind letting me finish?" I asked, trying not to either laugh or sound miffed.

"Sorry," she mumbled, and then fell silent.

I was having a hard time believing that I was there. I kept expecting to wake up, but I could feel her hair under my fingers.

"I don't know what exactly you want me to do," I continued, "or say most of the time. I'm used to not touching you, or even being anywhere near you when I'm"—I glanced around slightly and lowered my voice—"human." For a moment I paused. "I'll do my best to try to discover what you want, but please, be patient with me."

She didn't answer for a moment. "You've always been patient with me," she finally said, "I hope I can be as patient with you."

I shook my head and chuckled, watching her smile in response was wonderful.

"Would you," Ari began softly, "like to practice dancing tomorrow?"

"Are you ready for that?" I asked.

"I'm not certain," she whispered, "but I'd like to try."

"I don't want to scare you." I hated seeing the slightest bit of fear on her face.

She laughed lightly. "I'm going to be a little scared. This is new for me."

I studied her for a moment. "Well, this is new for me too, so I guess we'll just have to get our knuckles bruised," I told her, quoting one of Armel's favorite sayings when he was training me in swordplay.

She looked up and gave me a quirky smile.

An odd look crossed his face, and he glanced away.

"What's on your mind?" I asked.

I had the vague recollection that I had seen that look on his face before. He shook his head slightly, but didn't answer.

"Oh, tell me," I replied, "please?"

He looked at me almost sadly and moved his hand from caressing my hair.

"You're beautiful," he answered shakily.

I gasped, I may have even jumped slightly, sitting up. That wasn't what I expected, but then I remembered when I had seen that look before. It was after his duel with Lord Astucieux. Danren had complimented my eyes.

Glancing up at him again, I saw the quiet sadness there as he stared at the fire. He expected me to flee as I had before.

Quietly, I set my hand on his chest. "Thank you."

He stared at me. "What?"

I laughed.

CHAPTER 57

GROWING TOGETHER

The days took on a new pattern when I was human. Ari would be up and around the fortress before I awoke just as the years before. I'd see her watching the sunrise on one of the parapets as I munched on breakfast. Mighty One be praised that it had only taken six months after we were married for Mintxo to stop insisting that we eat every meal in the dining hall.

After midday, I would meet Ari to dance for a watch. She was slightly shaky the first few days, but soon she seemed to regain her confidence. She added a few more dances with moments where I could hold her. We would part company afterward, with sore toes and laughter.

A few watches later, I would meet her again, to show her a few sword techniques. Armel found a light but incredibly sturdy sword for her. He told us that it was from when the dragons first came to Maren. The skills that forged that blade had long since passed from our understanding. I showed Ari as many defenses as she could manage with her strength. We also went over a few offensive blows that she would be able to perform reasonably well. I had insisted on these times, because if, Mighty One forbid, something happened where she was caught alone and needed to purchase either some moments for reinforcements to arrive or an escape, she would be capable.

Near sunset, I would meet her for our evening meal. Then as night closed in, I would find her waiting for me by the fire. For another watch, I could gently hold her, stroking her hair, her hands, or occasionally her face.

I wondered when these days would end. Certainly, this couldn't last forever. One day, I might scare her accidentally, and then . . . perhaps, I would be able to beg her forgiveness, but I did not know.

Then one day, I hurried down to the dancing room, hoping that I hadn't kept Ari waiting too long. When I reached the room, she wasn't there. I quickly began to retrace my steps, hoping to find her.

I took the stairs to the next level three at a time and nearly collided with her at the top. She looked nervous, but smiled slightly.

"I didn't mean to keep you waiting," she told me.

"I thought I was the one running late," I quipped.

Ari laughed lightly. "I guess I shouldn't feel so badly then."

She glanced at the cylinder in her hands and didn't notice the arm I'd offered her. I tried not to feel slighted as I followed her down the stairs.

"I thought we could try a . . . a new one," she said as she placed the cylinder on the box.

"If you like," I told her.

She seemed pale, yet when she would glance at me, her face flushed.

"Are you all right?" I asked.

She nodded, but didn't say any more.

"Did you have a bad night?" I tried to get her to talk.

Ari shook her head. "No, I slept fine."

"We don't have to do this today if you don't feel up to it," I told her.

"No!" She spun around. "No, I-I'd like to do this . . . today."

The first few notes were playing, so I tried to place what the steps were. Leading her to the middle of the floor, we began going through the first few motions.

The dance seemed to be going reasonably well, but something was wrong. Ari was avoiding looking at me. I thought of the last few days while also trying to keep track of the next few steps.

Nothing seemed out of the ordinary. Step left, step back, touch hands. Nothing unusual had happened. Lean her on my arm, turn, spin her out. No one had suffered any major injuries. Bring her back to my side, turn, lean again. This dance was more intimate than normal. Spin out, turn, step forward. Was that bothering her? Bring her back to my side, step right, turn. She'd picked the dance, if it was a problem, why pick this one? Turn, lean, pause . . . *kiss her!*

I froze at the turn. Certainly, she hadn't realized that was part of the dance! Could I just move through the motions without . . . No, I'd already stopped, and Ari was staring at me.

"I don't think Pher'am will ask about this one," I told her, hurrying to the box.

I wasn't certain, but I thought I heard her begin to object, but nothing followed the slight sound . . . until I heard her footsteps. At first, I thought that she was coming over to pick a different cylinder, but the sound began to recede. I spun around and saw her walking toward the door.

What had I done?

I followed her, calling, "Ari, wait." She didn't stop. "Please . . ."

She took one more step, but then stopped. Her head was tucked against her chest, and she was shaking slightly.

"Ari, I'm sorry," I told her. "I didn't mean to upset you."

"You . . . you didn't," she said softly.

I took a step toward her, and she cringed, freezing me in my tracks. "Ari, I don't think Pher'am will ask me for that dance," I tried to explain.

"I know." Her voice was still low.

"Then why did you pick it?" I asked, baffled.

She shook her head. "It doesn't matter."

Suddenly my mouth went dry. I realized that she had done something almost exactly like this before.

"Ari," I choked out, "do you remember all the steps to this dance?"

For a moment she didn't move, then she shrugged. "It doesn't matter."

Slowly, I walked toward her. "Ari." I set my hand on her shoulder and tried to get her to face me.

At first she didn't move, but then she turned around. She continued to stare at her shoes, but now I could tell that she was crying.

"Ari," I couldn't get my voice to work properly, "what are you asking?"

Had she actually wanted me to . . .

"It doesn't matter," she whispered, as I watched a tear course down her cheek.

"Please, Ari," he said, as his hand dropped from my shoulder.

I didn't want to admit what I had just tried to do, especially now. I needed to answer him though. Danren deserved an answer. I'd thought I wanted to know, but now I wasn't certain. I'd been daydreaming for months . . .

"Danren," I couldn't manage to keep my voice under control at anything more than slightly above a whisper, "do you love me?"

"What?" he asked.

That was the answer I'd been expecting, at least at first.

"Love is a choice," he told me after a moment.

I knew that answer as well.

"Yes, and love is an action. You've said that already." My voice rose slightly as I felt my face flush with anger.

"What do you want me to say?" he asked, taking a step back.

"The truth . . ." I snapped, "just tell me the truth, so I can move on."

Looking up, I felt my anger disappear like water through a net. I'd seen this look on his face so often. It was far more intense this time though. It was a look of deep pain and sorrow that I wasn't sure that even I could relate to. Turning away, he walked slowly back into the room.

I saw him close his eyes and take a shuddering breath. "I'm sorry, Ari," his tone sounded like I was tearing his heart out, "but, yes, I love you."

Feeling faint, I fought to stay standing. I hadn't expected that answer, not after he'd stopped dancing.

"Because you choose to?" I choked out.

"It's more than that," he whispered. "I chose to when you . . . hated me, but now . . ."

"I know you've always treated me with dignity," I whispered.

Love was an action, and he had always acted with honor.

"I . . ." he was fighting to speak, "I would never have told you. I would never have told anyone."

"Why?" I took a step toward him.

He snorted slightly before answering, "Expectations. I wouldn't ask anything of you. I wouldn't."

"Why not give Adenern a straight answer when he asked?" I wondered out loud.

I couldn't believe she was still there. She should have fled by now.

To answer her question, I took a hard breath. I needed to get it together.

"I didn't need him after me to . . . to woo you." I knew I shouldn't be this upset.

Brushing roughly at my eyes, I knew I was losing her. I'd known this was coming, so why did it feel like someone was running a sword through my chest? I heard her soft footsteps and wondered when I wouldn't hear them again. Turning, I expected to watch her back disappearing down the hall, but instead she was standing right in front of me.

"Ari?" I stared at her for a moment. "What are you still doing here?"

For a moment, she looked puzzled. Then she reached up and brushed my check. I jumped as though I had been shot with a crossbow. She stared at me in confusion.

"Ari, I'm sorry," I whispered.

She looked me directly in the eye, but I couldn't meet her gaze and glanced away. Out of the corner of my eye, I saw her raise her hand. I expected to be slapped, but instead she tilted my head back toward her. I studied her shoulder for a moment and then met her gaze.

"Sorry, for telling me?" she asked.

"That you found out." I couldn't understand the look in her eyes.

"You were expecting me to be angry, or at least scared," she said, softly.

"Aren't you?" How could she not be?

She glanced down for a moment and laughed softly. "Maybe a little scared."

"I'm sorry . . ." I began, but she cut me off.

"I'm going to be a little scared. This is new for me," she whispered.

Then she looked up at me and stepped forward, leaning against my shoulder.

"Ari," I forced out the words, "you don't have to do this."

"I know," she whispered, looking up at me.

"Ari," I choked, "what are you asking?"

She smiled, and a mischievous look crossed her face. "Would you like to kiss me now?"

"What?" I exclaimed, as I tried to step back and only managed to ram my leg into the table. "Ari, you don't . . ." I stopped and glanced past her to where we normally danced. "Is this what you want?" I barely managed the words.

Her smiled answered without the nod that followed.

I was a nervous wreck! What was I supposed to do?

He stared at me blankly for a moment, and I expected to hear the common, "What?" come from him, but I didn't. Instead, he leaned down and, very briefly and awkwardly, kissed me.

I couldn't help myself! I laughed. He stared at me like I'd just slapped him, which only made me laugh more.

"Look!" he snapped, then calmed his voice remarkably well, "It's not as though I've had any practice at this."

"I know"—I giggled—"now."

He glared at me for a moment, then pushed me away and began to walk toward the door.

"No, please . . ." I began, trying to control my laughter, "don't go."

Stopping, he turned at the doorway and looked back at me. I could see the hurt in his face, even as he tried to hide it.

"I didn't mean to upset you." I had my voice under control now as I walked up to him.

He looked down at me, but didn't reply.

"I'm sorry." I ducked my head, feeling completely inept.

"It's all right," he said, slowly.

"Please, come back," I begged. "Could we at least finish one dance?"

He sighed, but then returned to the box on the table. I walked to the table as well and watched as he picked up a cylinder and stared at it for a moment.

"Danren," I began, "I'm sorry. I thought . . ."

He didn't look up, but asked, "What did you think?"

"I thought you'd—" The excitement and laughter had all disappeared. Now, I just felt like crying. "I'm sorry," I whispered.

"Did you think that I went around flirting with other women? Perhaps I sneak off and bed a different woman every month?" His tone was harsh.

"Danren, please," I begged. "I'm sorry."

"Answer the question, Ari'an," he demanded, staring at the cylinder in his hand. "What did you think?"

I felt my voice break, but managed, "I thought . . . that you had at least kissed some other woman before."

"I've always been faithful to you," he said in a low tone.

"You weren't always married to me," I tried to point out.

"Oh, and I was off doing all this, when? While I was a youth?" he snapped.

"No, of course not, but maybe when you turned back . . . before we were married."

I couldn't figure out how to stop this. Every question he asked just sent me deeper into a pit.

"Of course!" He glared at me. "While I was here trying to relearn how to walk on two legs, eat with utensils, sleep in a bed, write the alphabet legibly, fight with a sword, and all the other things that it takes to be human?"

I looked up at him and felt the tears in my eyes. "Danren, please . . ."

Watching his face change from the anger that glinted there to the quiet sadness that I'd grown accustomed to, hurt more than his angry words.

"Ari, I didn't mean to scare you." He set the cylinder down and glanced at the doorway. "I should go."

"No, please," I begged, "I'm sorry. I didn't mean it."

He looked at me with that pained gaze, and I choked on a sob.

"Ari . . ." his voice trailed off, "is that really what you think of me?"

I shook my head. "No, no . . . I thought you might be slipping off to see someone before . . . before I knew, but not now. I know you're not like that. I'm sorry." A sob cut me off before I could say anything else.

"I've always been faithful to you," he told me again.

"I know," I choked out.

"I don't know what you want from me, Ari," he tried to explain. "I don't know how far you want to take this."

"I didn't mean to insult you," I whispered, watching my hands.

He sighed. "I know you didn't, and had I been thinking straight, I wouldn't have been angry." To my surprise, he chuckled slightly. "I know that was a terrible kiss."

"Well, it could have been worse," I quipped through my tears.

"Oh?" He was studying his own fingers too. "How's that?"

"You could have stepped on my foot." I wasn't certain if I was laughing or crying anymore.

"Well, at least I did something right." He glanced at me.

I stepped toward him and laid my head against his shoulder. He took a heavy breath and then wrapped his arms around my back. After a moment, he began stroking my hair with one hand.

I giggled slightly.

"Now, what?" he asked.

"Promise you won't get mad?" I asked.

He sighed, and I glanced up to see a slightly bemused smile on his face. "All right."

"I've never heard of a fairy story where the hero rescues the lady and then can't kiss her." I laughed.

He grinned and tried to sound authoritative, "Well, typically, at least from what I've heard, the lady is rescued from a dragon by a handsome prince . . . I always wondered where all those princes came from anyway."

"Maybe it's the same prince," I said merrily. "He just goes around rescuing all those different ladies."

Danren had quite a mischievous look in his eye as he replied, "Well, that would explain why he always manages to kiss the damsel properly."

"He has too much practice." I laughed up at Danren. Then I leaned against his chest again. "I think I like my story better."

"What?" The shock in his voice made me look up.

"It turns out the dragon is much more loyal than that prince," I told him.

He looked slightly bemused, but then became serious again. "I wish that the dragon had never needed to rescue you."

"I know." I glanced down.

I couldn't keep from laughing at my next thought though.

"Now what?" Danren sounded like he was trying to be stern but failing miserably.

"I guess the moral of the story is that you need practice." I giggled.

"I would hope the moral would be something better than that!" he exclaimed. Then he laughed with me. "It's not likely I'm going to get practice anyway."

"Oh?" I asked, glancing up at him shyly.

I could feel myself blushing. I watched the realization strike him as it had done earlier. He grew pale with his mouth open, glanced at my lips, and then looked into my eyes.

"What are you asking?" he finally managed.

I glanced at the buttons to his vest. "Well, you obviously aren't going to fly around kissing anyone else, so I guess that only leaves you one option."

I watched him swallow hard. "Is that what you want?"

I barely managed to nod.

I felt his hand behind my head, and he leaned closer. "You're not going to laugh this time, are you?"

"I'll try not to." I barely breathed.

He kissed me gently and pulled away quickly.

"How was that?" he finally managed to ask.

"B-better," I stammered.

In the distance, I could hear the watch being called.

"We should probably call it a day," I whispered.

"Are you all right?" It wasn't the answer I'd expected.

I managed to nod slightly.

"Do you want me to walk you to the stairs?" he asked.

I shook my head. "I'd like to just sit for a moment."

"Would you like me to stay?" He sounded so nervous.

Again, I shook my head. "I'd like to be alone for a little while if that's all right."

He watched me for a moment, but then released my shoulders and walked away.

Barely managing to stay standing while he left, I slid to the floor as soon as he turned out of the doorway. What was I doing? It had seemed like such a nice idea at the time. Now, I felt heady. I could barely breathe. What had I gotten myself into? What would Danren expect now?

A simple kiss had been what I wanted, just to answer my question. I wanted to know if Danren saw me just as a friend or if he might . . . I shivered half with fear and half with excitement. He loved me . . . but what was I supposed to do now? What would he expect?

Finally, I realized that the lamp was beginning to flicker out, and if I didn't want to be here alone in the dark, I needed to leave. When I reached the courtyard, I realized that it was almost time for dinner. Danren would be waiting for me. What would he expect?

Slowly, I made my way to our rooms. There was firelight flickering under the door. I froze. I felt terror grip my limbs. My hand wouldn't reach for the doorknob, and to my shock, my feet began running back toward the stairs. Halfway down the stairs, I managed to stop. I held onto the railing as though it was the only thing between me and . . . and what? What was I so afraid of? What Danren might do?

I forced myself to climb the stairs again. Danren wouldn't have kissed me if I hadn't pushed him to. One step. He wouldn't have told me that he loved me if I hadn't asked. Two more steps. He would have left if I hadn't called him back. Five. He had never intentionally hurt me before. Ten. I attempted to stop panting. There were three steps left . . . and the entire hallway.

Danren could be trusted. I reached the top of the stairs and stumbled down the hallway. In a moment, I was standing in front of the door again. With both hands, I grabbed the doorknob and threw it open, stumbling. I saw a grin disappear from Danren's face as he looked up at me.

I jumped to my feet when I saw the terrified look on Ari's face.
"What happened?" I asked as I started toward her.
She cringed against the doorframe. I froze.
"Ari, what's wrong?"
"Nothing." She sobbed.
"What?" If nothing was wrong, why was she so scared?
"I . . ." She glanced around frantically. "It's just me."
"Ari, who hurt you? What happened?" If someone had so much as pointed a menacing finger at her, they would pay.
"No one." She sobbed, and seemed to throw herself into the room.
"What?" I wasn't certain if I should try to stop her or see where she was heading.
"Please . . ." she begged, and her voice trailed off as she came to a halt before running into a chair.
I took a step toward her, and she cringed.
"Ari . . ."

I'd hurt her. I realized. Mighty One have mercy. That had to be it.

"No," she moaned and frantically looked around again. "Please . . ."

She took a step toward me and froze. Her whole body appeared to want to flee in terror.

"Ari . . ." I began, but stopped when she flung herself at me.

I barely managed to catch her and keep us both standing.

"Ari," I began again, "I'm sorry. I'm so sorry. I should have known better. I'll never kiss you again or mention anything that happened today either."

She sobbed, and then moaned, "No."

"Ari, I didn't mean to hurt you . . ."

"You didn't," she sobbed.

"If it wasn't me, who was it?" I asked. It had to be me . . . didn't it?

"It's just me," she whimpered.

"What?"

She wasn't making any sense.

"I'm scared," she whispered.

"Yes, I know," I said as calmly as I could manage, "but why?"

She shook her head.

"Ari." I took a breath. How was I supposed to sort this out? "Did I scare you?"

She shook her head.

"Did someone else scare you?" If it wasn't me, it had to be someone.

She shook her head again.

"Then who scared you?" I fought to keep the frustration out of my voice.

"I did," she wailed.

"What?" I still couldn't get her to make any sense. "Ari, I need you to calm down. Take some deep breaths."

She fought for the first couple of ragged breaths, but then managed them more easily.

I led her to the couch, sat her down, and knelt in front of her. "Ari, I need to know what happened."

"Nothing," she whimpered.

I knew that couldn't be the case, something had upset her.

"Ari, please, I'm trying to understand. I want to help, but I don't know what went wrong."

"Nothing," she choked on a sob.

"What?" I realized that I would have to wait until she calmed down to get an answer.

I moved to sit on the couch next to her and leaned her against my chest. For a moment, she shuddered, but then buried her face in my shoulder and began to sob again.

"It's all right," I told her softly. "Whatever it was, I'll do my best to make certain that it never happens again."

"No," she moaned and began to sob harder.

"It's all right," I repeated.

After half a watch at least, she stopped sobbing, but reverted to the short breathing that happens sometimes after crying too much. Mighty One be praised that did not last long. Fishing out a handkerchief, I helped her mop up her face.

"Are you all right?" I asked.

She glanced around, but at least didn't look terrified anymore.

"I'm sorry," she whispered. "I was just scared."

"Can you tell me what scared you?" I asked.

"It was just me," she whispered.

"What?" Even when she was relatively calm, she wasn't making any sense.

She took a deep breath. "I was scared because I forgot."

"Forgot what?" At least this was something new.

"I forgot that I could trust you," she whispered.

"What?" What did that have to do with anything?

"Please, forgive me," she whispered, "I know you won't hurt me."

Vaguely, I began to see what had upset her, but it didn't make sense. "You thought I would hurt you?"

She sniffed, and for a moment, I thought that she might start crying again. "I wasn't certain what you would expect . . . now."

"What?" I tried to bring my thoughts together. "Expect about what?"

She shivered slightly. "About . . . about . . . kissing me . . . or . . . anything else."

"What?" I couldn't managed to control the exclamation.

"I know it was stupid. I know you wouldn't . . . do anything . . . but I scared myself," she blurted out.

"What?" She'd thought . . . "What?"

"I'm sorry," she whispered.

"Ari, I won't kiss you again if that's what you want. I won't mention it or even hint at it," I told her.

"No!" she exclaimed again.

I gaped at her and mouthed, "What?"

A slight smile crossed her face. "I was wondering when you would finally wear out that word."

"Well, at least someone is enjoying this," I quipped back.

She smiled a bit more.

"You should eat," I told her. Glancing at the tray of food, I grimaced. "But maybe not that."

Ari followed my gaze and laughed ever so lightly. "Well, the bread should still be good, although the drowned fly in the butter is a bit much."

CHAPTER 58

ON THE WAY TO CELEBRATE

The days moved steadily on. The borders remained quiet, both countries still recouping from the losses over the winter. The end of summer approached softly.

I feared and relished my time with Ari, wondering when it would end, and what would bring that end about. She asked me to kiss her occasionally. I wondered which would be the last.

Soon, I watched her excitement over the upcoming festival. The entire countryside had the same excitement. It was wonderful to watch people coming alive with anticipation. Ari seemed to make every step part of a dance. She laughed and teased. Would it end after the festival?

Soon we were packing to leave, and I was assailed with questions that I had never been trained to answer.

"Do you think the blue or the violet looks better?" Ari would ask, twirling around the room holding a dress. "Should I wear ribbons in my hair or clasps . . . or would a comb look best?"

How was I supposed to answer? I still regretted not getting a lady-in-waiting for her. She would have known the answers. Ari always made some excuse or another whenever I brought up the subject.

"I'm rather busy right now, could we discuss this later?" She was always busy when we discussed this.

"It's too nice of a night to talk about this." It could be hailing stones the size of wagon spokes, and it still would be too nice of a night to talk about this.

I loathed making this decision alone. The lady would be to help her. If Ari didn't think she needed help though . . . I still hated leaving her alone when I had to check on the cave residents, or talk to the counsel, or any of the other countless things that seemed to keep me away from the fortress.

I felt almost as though I was a little child waiting for presents. I had been to festivals at Torion Castle, but Danren and everyone else I spoke with assured me that this would be nothing like those. There were two reasons. First, this was a festival to celebrate what the Mighty One had done for all, instead of a staged revelry to appease some god or another. The second reason was less formal. Dreanen was involved with all the planning. I could argue with that easily. Pher'am was also involved with all the planning.

The first reason stood though. I had been around Caer Corisan for years, and never seen any celebration meant to appease the Mighty One. There had been celebrations, each exciting in a dragon sort of way. I had learned early to always carry at least a small bucket of water around, and that if someone yelled, it was best to just duck to the ground. No one was formal at those times. Occasionally, someone got drunk, but they were quickly taken to a room where they wouldn't disturb anyone while they sobered. Entirely different from the almost frightened airs around Torion Castle, when everything must be accomplished exactly right or the god would smite us. It was a relief to not worry about a god's wrath because someone tripped while walking with holy candles.

Faber created an entirely new wardrobe for me for every meal at the festival. He also made three extra dresses in case some ill befell one of the others. He did matching outfits for Danren, although he seemed less appreciative of Faber's fine skills.

When the day came to leave, Hafiz chided me about how heavy the trunks were that he was carrying and that I should have found a lighter wardrobe. I had the unique pleasure of informing him that *those* particular trunks all belonged to Danren. Granted that Danren's wardrobe was not in them, but I neglected to inform him of that. Hafiz did in turn send some unpleasant looks at Narden later, but he didn't seem to notice.

The flight to Llinos was fantastic and wonderfully uneventful. I hadn't been on a long flight since the trip to Narden's cave. I loved feeling the wind, watching the birds scold and duck out of the way, and even saw a few low clouds drift beneath us.

I was riding Narden, which just added to my mood. I put him through his paces, which seemed to surprise him. It also seemed to amuse our entourage. I caught them laughing after many of the dives or loops we did. Eventually, I felt Narden laugh too, as he took me through some maneuvers that I hadn't asked for. It was only fair, but he didn't come out of dives quite as quickly as I would have liked.

Narden and Hafiz both turned when we reached the meeting point. The trunks were reloaded onto a wagon and the top of the carriage. Riding in the carriage, I watched the few leagues to the inn pass. I found myself sore when we reached the inn, but still happy.

The inn was decorated for our brief visit. I discovered why almost immediately. It belonged to Hafiz and his brother, Ishmerai. Their wives pampered me with fancy pastries and bubbling baths. They were so determined to "provide the lady with all the luxuries that she could not enjoy living in that horrible fortress."

With all the effort that they put into every endeavor, I didn't have the heart to tell them that the food I ate at the horrible fortress was prepared by a man who had been preparing delicacies for a century and half. Not to mention that he had learned his trade from his father, who had crafted masterpiece dinners for over five centuries. Explaining the pipe water was entirely out of the question as well. I had almost forgotten what it was like to have boiling hot pails of water poured into a tub in order to bring it to a reasonable temperature.

We traveled the next day by horseback and coach, and I was so tired when we arrived at the next inn that I was asleep before Danren had finished bringing in my travel trunk.

Breakfast the next morning was to be served in the rooms so that we would have as much time to relax before journeying on as possible. I was studying a pot of flowers on the table, wondering if these flowers had been picked especially for me, when the knock sounded on the door. Had the women gone through their beautiful flower beds looking for only the best to grace the room?

"Come in," I called lightly with my back still to the door.

I heard the tray being set down, and then a man's voice asked, "Is there anything else you need?"

I froze, vaguely recognizing the voice.

Then he said the word that I would know from him anywhere, "Lady?"

I spun, accidentally knocking the pot of flowers to the floor with a crash. I heard scuffling in the room next to mine, as I stared at the man.

He glanced away from me at the floor. "It is you."

Suddenly, I saw Danren standing behind him, and the man's face turned as pale as a clean sheep.

I was reaching for my vest when I heard a shattering sound come from Ari's room. I didn't know what had happened, but if Ari broke something, it couldn't be good. My door slammed against the wall as I rushed to her room.

In her doorway stood a slight but tall man with hair almost as red as Einheim's scales. Pulling my knife with my left hand, I also gripped the hilt of my sword with my right. I quickly stepped behind him. He was carrying a tray of food. Perhaps he just startled Ari.

Then I heard him say, "It is you."

He knew her, and from the stunned look on Ari's face, I could guess from where. I pressed the point of my knife against his back and felt him tense.

Sliding my sword out for good measure, I told him, "If you so much as twitch without my permission, I'll kill you." Then I shouted, "Ishmerai, get up here."

I heard his footsteps pound across the floor below and ascend the stairs. I could feel the man begin to shake through the knife, and soon heard the dishes on the tray clattering.

"Don't hurt him!" It was the last thing I would have expected Ari to say.

I looked at her questioningly.

"Please," her voice appealed, "I can explain."

I stared at her for a moment, and then sheathed my sword.

"Take him downstairs," I told Ishmerai.

He gruffly began hauling the man toward the stairs, which tipped a pitcher of milk off the tray and shattered it on the floor. I watched them descend the stairs.

"Are you all right?" I needed time to word my other questions.

She nodded and watched her hands for a moment. "It's not what you think."

I wondered what she meant by that. "What do I think?"

"He wouldn't hurt me." She glanced around the room frantically. "He never would."

"How do you know that?" If Ari knew him from her days at the temple, I was certain that there was no reason to trust him.

"He . . . h-he . . ." She began to shake slightly, and I quickly found her cape hanging from a hook on the wall.

I brought it over to Ari and offered it to her. She stepped forward and leaned against my shoulder. Pulling the cape around her shoulders, I watched her rub the fur lining with her fingers.

"He wouldn't hurt me," she told me again.

"You can't *know* that," I insisted.

"I do!" she insisted right back.

"How?" I couldn't imagine why she'd think that.

"He . . . h-he . . ." she stopped for a moment and then blurted out, "he wouldn't bed me unless the priests stayed."

I choked. There was far too much in that statement that . . . that I didn't want to understand. For a moment, I couldn't breathe.

Ari never said much about her days at that temple, and I never asked. I didn't want her to suffer through the memories. They haunted her enough as it was. Then I realized that Ari was still talking.

"He's like me," she was saying.

"What?" I could barely manage the word.

"His parents lived in Almudina. They were in debt. They couldn't pay." Her voice raced on so that I could hardly catch everything she was saying. "A group of merchants came through and offered to buy him . . . because he had red hair. The merchants sold him to the temple."

I felt my temper flare at parents who would sell their children, at people who would buy them, and finally resting again on a religious establishment that would exploit such a thing. Again, I felt the rage that I'd felt when we rescued Ari. If I could have, I would have found every one of those temples and burned them to the ground.

"Please," Ari whispered, "don't hurt him. He's like me."

I finally found a question I could manage to ask, "How do you know all this?"

"He told me," she whispered.

"I thought you didn't talk at the temple." I tried to put the pieces together.

"I didn't . . . I only said a few words to him after he'd been there several times." Ari began to cry. "I thought it was a trick. He asked me if I could understand him when he first came. I didn't say anything. I didn't. He could tell because my eyes widened. I was so surprised that . . . that one of them spoke. I couldn't help it. He said he wouldn't do anything to me . . . unless the priests came. He barely touched me. He untied my wrists and my ankles and then sat against the door. He told me his story. Please"—she sobbed—"don't hurt him."

"I won't," I told her, another sob raking through her body.

I managed to move her to the chair by the table.

As she sat down, I told her, "It's all right."

She smiled slightly. "I never thought I'd see him again," she whispered. "He told me that if he ever found a way to escape, he'd take me with him." She took a shuddering breath. "I wish I could have returned the favor."

I waited until Ari was calm before I left to speak with the man. Finding Faber guarding a side room to the inn, I opened the door. The man sat at a table with Ishmerai watching him.

"You may go," I told Ishmerai, who promptly looked at me as though I had left my wits at Caer Corisan.

I looked at him to let him know that I was indeed serious, and he told me, "If I hear the faintest hint of trouble, I'm coming back in."

As he left, I turned my attention to the man. He looked like he was about Ari's age, perhaps a few years older. His hands fidgeted like Ari's did. He glanced up, but didn't look at me. Another thing he had in common with Ari.

"If it pleases my lord," his voice was tense, he seemed to have rehearsed this statement while I was upstairs, "I would like to explain." He had the accent of Almudina, but it seemed to be blending into the Rem'Maren dialect.

I motioned for him to continue, and his gaze shifted around the room nervously.

"I . . ." he trailed off. I wondered if he had rehearsed anything else, or if he had assumed that I wouldn't let him talk.

"What were you doing at Lady Ari'an's door?" I prompted.

"I brought up breakfast"—he glanced about again—"my lord."

"Why you?" I inquired. "Why not send someone else?"

He watched his hands for a long moment and then mumbled, "I wanted to know if it was lady, my lord."

A woman's scream from outside the door interrupted the conversation. My sword was drawn before I reached the door. Throwing it open, I saw Faber and Ishmerai both grappling with a black-haired young woman. When she saw me, she somehow managed to break through their holds and throw herself at my feet.

She was shaking violently, and I could barely make out the words that she said through her hysterical sobs.

It sounded like, "No harm. No harm," but I couldn't be certain.

I felt someone grab my sword arm from behind, but I slipped it from the man's grip.

"Don't hurt her, I beg you, my lord," he howled from behind me.

I wanted to turn to look at him, but I couldn't exactly move my legs at the moment.

"Mighty One have mercy," I breathed. "Why would I hurt her?"

"Please, my lord." His anguish was apparent in his voice.

"I'm not going to hurt her," I snapped.

This entire morning was absolutely ludicrous! Ishmerai was trying to break her hold on my ankles, but her grip was like iron.

"Please, let me speak with her, my lord," the man behind me begged.

I finally realized that she was indeed saying, "No harm! No harm!" over and over.

"I have no intention of harming you," I told her, forcing my voice to sound calm.

She looked up, but still appeared terrified.

Pointing at the man behind me, she wailed again, "No harm!"

I glanced at him and then focused on her again. "Unless he attacks someone, I have no intention of harming him either."

"No harm?" It was a question this time.

"No." I shook my head and smiled at her as calmly as I could manage.

Something about her struck me as familiar, but I couldn't place it. I certainly had never seen her before.

The young woman rose to her feet and curtsied quite eloquently. She didn't look up though, but continued staring at my feet.

"Please, my lord," the man behind me pleaded, "she's smart, but she doesn't talk well."

"Well, thankfully, she's not the one I'm trying to talk to." I glowered at him for a moment, but quickly stopped when he took a few cowering steps away from me.

I stepped back into the room, sheathed my sword, and motioned for the man to sit again. I turned to close the door, but the frantic look on the young woman's face made me stop.

"Would you like to join us?" I asked her.

She looked terrified, but glanced past me at the man. He looked at me and then nodded to her. Darting past me into the room, she fled behind his chair.

I told Ishmerai to bring another chair. He walked up with it, looking at me questioningly.

"I'll explain later," I replied.

After closing the door again, I set the chair next to the man's and held it for the young woman. She glanced around terrified. Her eyes would rest on everything but my face. Suddenly, I realized what was familiar about her.

"She's from the temple as well," I said, looking at the man.

He looked startled for a moment, frightened even. She stared at my shoulder in horror. I left the chair and motioned for her to sit. Slowly, she stepped to it and sat down.

"Yes, my lord," he told me. He paused for a moment and watched her. "When they came for me, they bought her too."

"What?" I needed an explanation for quite a few things.

"What do you know of the temples, my lord?" he asked, fidgeting with his hands.

"More than I'd like," I replied harshly.

The woman jumped. I chided myself for scaring her.

"They sell." I was choking trying to find a way to answer.

The man studied me for a moment and then seemed to visibly relax. "My lord," he began, "they will on occasion sell . . . people to individual . . . clients." He glanced at the young woman. "There are those who don't like the practice, and they'll buy . . . them to get them out of the temples."

"Is that how you escaped?" I asked.

He nodded. "I asked them to find lady . . . her ladyship, but they said that they'd heard rumors of a noble escaping when dragons attacked the temple." He paused and studied his hands for a moment. "I asked if they'd get Ileana instead."

I nodded to the young woman and told her, "Ileana, it is a pleasure to meet you."

Her eyes grew wide for a moment; she glanced at the man, who nodded to her. She rose quickly and curtsied again.

"Ileana was born at the temple, my lord," he continued.

I choked on that statement and stared at the young woman for a moment.

"She only knew a few words when I met her," he informed me, and I forced my attention back to him. "She knows more than she'll say now, but she's scared to talk."

"Her hair's black though," I pointed out, "not red."

"We blacked it, my lord," he told me, "with axle grease. It grows in dark now, but it still shows some of the red in the sun."

I nodded, taking in what I could. "I'm afraid I never asked your name," I interrupted.

"I'm called Sotiris now," he said.

"You weren't before?" I needed a little time to comprehend all the implications of what he'd already told me.

His voice turned harsh. "I was named Kakar by my parents, but they sold me." Derision came into his tone. "They were *disappointed* that they couldn't get as much for me as they would have for a girl."

"How did you come here," I directed the subject back, "after leaving the temple?"

"Rem'Maren, my lord," he began and then paused. "It's known to be safe. It's not legal to sell people in the rest of this kingdom, but it still happens, but here it's . . . it's not right." He paused again. "Many come here because of that. It's not legal in Verd to travel out of the country with . . . with those purchased. They risked their lives to get us out. If they were found, they could be executed. The judge considers a fine or worse. We traveled in a wagon, under the floor. Fruit or wheat or whatever on top, and we were between the floors."

"I've seen these wagons," I mumbled remembering them from different patrols.

His eyes widened. "They don't approach the fortress, my lord." He seemed almost frantic to prove that I couldn't have seen them. "They're afraid of the dragons."

"Yet they travel our pass," I pointed out.

"It's the quickest route," he explained.

"Are you still in contact with your rescuers?" I was beginning to form a plan.

He didn't answer for a moment and then stammered, "Y-yes, my lord."

I glanced around the room. "Do they bring others from the temples here?"

Sotiris's eyes flitted around the room, before resting on the table. "Some, my lord."

"What aid do they need?" I asked, and his eyes snapped up.

"My lord?" he asked, and glanced at Ileana.

"I have been attempting to draw the king's attention to this matter for some time now, but have not gained much success," I explained. "Although I do not like the idea of increasing these temples' funds, this is a temporary aid."

"Berjouhi was supposed to be here a few days ago, my lord," he began after studying me for a few moments, "but we haven't heard from her."

"Was she traveling the pass?" I asked.

He nodded.

I left the room and spoke briefly to Ishmerai. He in turn hurried outside to alert Einheim, who was part of the bodyguard. If the woman was still in Rem'maren's mountains, Einheim would find her.

Glancing up, I found Ari slowly walking toward me from the stairs. She glanced around the main room and then looked back at me.

"They're in that little room," I told her, when I'd crossed the room. "Are you all right?"

She nodded, and then asked, "They?"

"Sotiris escaped with a woman named Ileana," I told her.

Ari's eyes widened. "When?"

"I don't know exactly," I told her, "but it was after your rescue."

She looked past me at the door, and I glanced over my shoulder to see it close quickly.

"Did you want to speak with them?" I asked.

After a moment, she shook her head. "I don't think I could. I don't know what to say, and seeing him again scared me."

594

"Can you travel?" I asked. It was close to midday, and we were supposed to have left in the morning.

She nodded.

"Would you mind if I rode with you?" I wanted to make sure that she was all right and explain what I had discovered.

The slight smile she gave me as she nodded reassured me some.

Taking our leave of Sotiris and Ileana, we continued on toward the festival.

After I explained as well as I could, Ari sat silently, staring at her hands for a while.

"I'm glad he got out," Ari finally whispered.

I nodded, and we rode silently on.

CHAPTER 59

FESTIVAL

It was late in the evening when we finally arrived at Dreanen and Pher'am's home. Their two blond children ran out to greet us, before we could even leave the carriage. I had never met them before, but apparently they knew Danren, because he swung their oldest, a little girl, up into the air as soon as she reached him.

He teased her for a moment, "Now, who are you?"

The little girl squealed and told him, "I'm Ti'anha."

"Ti'anha?" he continued. "You could not possibly be Ti'anha. She is not as tall as you."

She giggle and told him, "I am growing."

"Growing? I did not realize little girls grew. I always thought they stayed little forever," he teased.

"Of course not!" She looked mildly irritated. "I am going to be a lady soon."

Setting her down, he told her, "All too soon."

Danren turned his attention to Juna'yad, their two-year-old boy, as Ti'anha looked at me.

She took a few shy steps toward me and curtsied. "Welcome to our home, Lady Ari'an."

I smiled at her and curtsied in return. "It is an honor to be your guest."

A little boy's shriek brought my attention back to Danren. I gasped as I watched him throw the giggling little boy into the air.

My breath didn't continue until he returned the child safely to the ground.

Then I laughed as the boy shrieked, "Again, again."

Because of the delay at the inn, we had not arrived in time to have the quiet dinner with Dreanen and Pher'am that was planned. There was enough light left for us to quickly tour the grounds though. I imagined each of the now empty booths coming alive in the morning as the festival began. Every once in a while, I almost believed I heard the distant laughter of children.

I jumped when Juna'yad came tearing around the little building I was in front of. Then I realized that the children's laughter was real.

"Hide, hide," he shrieked.

He ducked behind me, just as Danren came jogging around the same corner. I stepped back and almost fell over Juna'yad, but Danren quickly caught my arm and steadied me. He glanced over my shoulder with a mischievous look on his face that I hadn't seen since we were children.

"Lady Ari'an," he said with teasing formality, "I do not presume that you have seen a little lord come this way."

I heard a giggle behind me as I asked, "A little lord?"

"Yes, about this tall," holding his hand to his knee.

"Are you certain it was a little lord?" I asked, trying not to laugh myself.

"Yes," he looked around and then whispered, "he was telling me that a dragon was going to find him."

"You may wish to keep looking, my lord," I told him, unable to keep the wide smile off my face.

Danren took a few steps away, and then Juna'yad ran at him, yelling, "here, here."

Spinning around, he caught the little boy in his arms.

"Don't eat me!" he squealed.

"Dragons don't eat people," Danren informed him, "but they might take you for a flight." With that, he lofted the boy on his palm and spun him around his head.

Feeling as though we were being watched, I turned to find Ti'anha peeking around the corner of the booth. I smiled as her shy eyes watched me. Then I knelt and held a hand out to her.

"Which booth is your favorite?" I asked as she approached.

She quietly took my outstretched hand and pointed toward the far end of the grounds with her free hand.

As we walked along, I began to ask her a few questions.

"Do you like having a little brother?" I began.

She nodded shyly.

On impulse, I said, "But you would have rather had a little sister."

Her feet stopped, and she looked up.

"How did you know?" she gasped.

I smiled down at her. "I wanted a little sister when I was young."

"You did?" Her eyes grew wide.

I nodded.

"Did you get one?" she asked.

I shook my head. "No, I never did."

"My apologies." The phrase seemed so odd coming from her, but she said it as though it were perfectly normal.

I smiled, wondering at how hard Pher'am was working on her children to make certain they were proper. I also wondered if Juna'yad being a dragon lord would undo much of this training.

Glancing around at the booths, I wondered what the little boy would look like as a dragon. He had Dreanen's gold hair, but Pher'am's brown eyes. Would he be mostly brown then, with gold highlights or marks, or would it be the other way around?

At that moment, I realized that we had stopped in front of the booth that would house ducks tomorrow.

"Do you like ducks?" I asked the little girl.

She nodded. "They're so soft when they're little."

Retracing our steps, we found Danren looking for us while holding Juna'yad to his shoulder.

"I thought you came this way," he told me, in the fading light.

"You seem to have a tired passenger," I observed.

"Not tired," a groggy voice objected as the little boy rubbed his eyes with the hand he didn't have wrapped around Danren's neck.

We made our way back to the estate to find Pher'am waiting to whisk the children away. Dreanen was also waiting to talk with Danren about final arrangements. After excusing myself, I went to the rooms that they'd shown us earlier.

Glancing around, I couldn't locate our trunks in the main room. I walked to the larger bedroom and jumped when I found Danren's trunks piled with mine. Then I laughed. He hadn't planned this. Dreanen and Pher'am's staff had brought in our belongings. A slight smile touched my face as I imagined Danren stammering over an explanation and then an apology.

He didn't disappoint me. I was sitting in front of the fireplace watching the flames when he arrived. I didn't look up when he walked in, just in case my face betrayed my voice.

"Would you like the large bedroom?" I asked.

"No," he answered, "you can have it." Then I heard him chuckle. "I can't exactly picture the dresses Faber made for you fitting in the little room. Especially if it's anything like the servant's room at the funeral."

"Were you planning to dress in that room then?" I motioned toward the main bedroom.

"Of course not," he sounded slightly flustered, "I'll be fine. I managed to talk Faber out of making my clothes quite as elaborate as he wanted to anyway." There was a slight pause, and then he asked, "Is there something wrong with the main bedroom?"

"Why don't you look?" I asked, forcing my voice to remain even.

He made his way to the room and walked in. I didn't have long to wait before he was out, hurrying toward me.

"Ari, it's not what you think," he began. "I didn't tell them to move everything in there."

I stole a glance at him, and found him flushed.

He racked his hand through his hair and continued, "I don't know why they would have put everything in there."

I glanced away, fighting not to laugh.

"Ari, I'm sorry," he told me, trying to make amends. "I'll move everything out of there."

"Everything?" I barely managed to whisper the word without giggling.

"Well, everything of mine, of course, not your things. I'll leave those. I'm sorry, Ari. I didn't mean for this to happen," he paused finally, probably expecting a response.

"Ari?" He took a few steps toward me.

I didn't manage to turn my head in time.

"Ari!" he sounded so appalled that I couldn't manage to keep it in any longer.

She threw her head back and laughed. It was almost contagious, but I was still annoyed that she'd teased me like that. Had my things ended up in her room at the funeral, she would have probably went into a shaking fit, but now she was laughing! I stormed up to her chair and glared down at her. This only caused her to look up at me and laugh harder.

"I'm this close"—I pinched two fingers almost together—"to doing something."

She giggled and took a breath. "What might you do?"

She barely managed to say that before laughing again.

"I don't know," I thought frantically for something that would make her stop, "kiss you."

She did pause for a moment, but then laughed. "You wouldn't dare."

"Oh really." I pulled her to her feet and did just that.

I felt her gasp against me and then shiver. Quickly, I let her go, and she sank back into the chair. Her face was pale for a moment, and then it flushed as she began giggling again.

"I didn't think you would." She laughed, jumping to her feet.

She started to lean against me, but I held her away.

"You are incorrigible," I told her, storming toward my room, "I'm going to bed."

She howled in laughter as I reached my room, realized my things weren't there, and had to storm back over to her room. In her room, I paused to catch my breath, and then found that I too was chuckling at the situation.

I heard the door open behind me and tried to growl, "I'm not laughing."

She walked around me and then leaned against my chest. I laughed, holding her there. I couldn't help it.

Eventually, I managed to retrieve my things from her room, but I almost dropped two of the trunks on two separate occasions, when Ari spontaneously began to laugh again. It shouldn't have been that funny, but we were far too tired, and it was far too late.

I felt like I would sleep until after midday when I finally collapsed on my bed. Sadly, I was mistaken because with just the first hints of dawn peeking through the curtains, a weight landed on my chest. Opening my eyes to the sensation of having the air forced out of my lungs, I saw Juna'yad merrily bouncing up and down on my chest.

"Get up, get up," he yelled, sliding off me.

His feet hit the floor, and he began tugging me out of the bed by my fingers.

"Go away, you little imp," I groaned, which only made him laugh and pull harder.

"I hope you didn't wake Ari like this," I told him, rolling out of the bed.

"Ti'anha," the little boy squealed. I could only hope that since Ti'anha was so shy, she hadn't scared Ari. I didn't like to imagine what an awakening such as I had would have done to her.

I was surprised to find Ari and Ti'anha sitting in the main room when I emerged. Ari looked like she hadn't been startled awake, and Ti'anha looked like she had been awake for watches.

Glancing at the door, I was slightly relieved to find that it could be locked. I wasn't certain how many mornings like this I could take. I'd discuss locking the door with Ari later, when the children weren't around.

"Why don't you offer him a roll?" Ari asked Ti'anha, who immediately picked one off the breakfast tray and handed it to me.

Ari looked surprised. "I thought she'd be nervous around you too," she whispered as I sat down.

"Ti'anha?" I smiled at the little girl who grinned back. "No, I know her too well."

"Do you come here often?" Ari asked, looking slightly confused.

"I used to come every two or three months, but I haven't been in a while," I told her.

"You never offered to bring me." She sounded hurt.

"I didn't realize you'd want to come," I told her honestly. "Next time, if you're not busy, I'll bring you along."

She smiled.

"You're going to come back?" The little girl looked at Ari wide eyed. I could tell that the two would be inseparable during most of the festival, and I was right.

I realized that after two days of Ti'anha completely absorbing Ari's time, I was jealous. Why I was jealous wasn't entirely clear, but I knew that I wanted to spend time with Ari during these festivities as well.

Ti'anha enjoyed talking to Ari. The little girl asked Ari every question that came to her mind from, "How did the man make the ducks blue?" to "Why do you always carry a sword around? You are not a knight."

I shouldn't have been jealous. Ti'anha spoke freely with so few people. Still, I couldn't shake the feeling.

Pher'am had asked for her dance the first day, so I was surprised when she approached me the third day and told me, "I have a dance for you."

I pulled my gaze away from Ari and Ti'anha, who were several booths away, and looked at the hostess.

"Of course, my lady," I told her and bowed.

She took my arm, and I began to move toward the grassy area set aside for dancing, when she subtlety moved in the opposite direction. I glanced at her and then shrugged. A few moments somewhere else would distract me. To my surprise, however, Pher'am walked us up to Ari and Ti'anha. Ari glanced at me questioningly, but all I could do was look blankly back at her.

602

"Your husband would like to dance with you," Pher'am said smoothly.

Ari paled and glanced at me at the very moment that only one word came to my mind.

"What?" I stared at Pher'am.

Pher'am quite deftly slipped her arm out of mine and placed Ari's there instead.

"You said you wanted to dance," I told her.

"No, my lord"—she blinked at me—"I said that I had a dance for you. I am afraid that I never said with whom."

"You are twisting words." I glared at her.

"You did say that you would dance," she told me, "and I know you keep your word."

I glanced at Ari and was surprised to find a slight smile on her face. Turning back to Pher'am, I found both her and Ti'anha were already a booth away.

"We don't have to do this," I told Ari.

"I know . . . " she paused for a moment, "but the dances lately have been so lively that it wouldn't hurt anything. They're like the ones we first practiced."

"Are you certain?" I asked her.

She nodded, blushing slightly.

I led her to the grassy dance area, and just as we stepped out, the music changed to a couple's dance.

Ari and I glanced at the musicians at the same moment. I knew that she recognized the tune as well as I did. I glared at Pher'am, who was now walking away from the musicians' stand, but she took no notice of me. Then I heard Ari laugh. I glanced down at her, surprised by her amusement.

"I never expected Pher'am to set us up like this." Ari grinned at me.

"We don't have to do this," I told her.

"You told Pher'am that you would dance," she reminded me.

"Yes, but I apparently didn't specify with whom. I could find Ti'anha. No one would think anything of my dancing with her." I began scanning the crowd for the little girl.

"You don't want to dance with me then?" She sounded hurt, but when I glanced down, I recognized the teasing glint in her eyes.

"You know that's not it," I told her with pretend irritation.

She smiled. "What is it, then?"

I waved at the dancers. "This would be the same as a public declaration."

"Declaration of what?" Was she holding her breath?

I glanced around and then leaned closer to her.

Barely whispering, I told her, "That I love you."

I did hear her gasp before she replied, "You don't want people to know?"

"No, I would be honored to set up an announcement, but I doubt you would . . . " I paused, watching her for a moment. "Did you ask Pher'am to do this?"

She shook her head, as a blush colored her face.

"Is this what you want?" I hoped for her answer, but what if . . .

She glanced up from her hands and nodded.

I barely managed to keep from shouting. Instead, I bowed to her and asked, "Will you honor me with your presence for this dance, my lady?"

She curtsied in reply, "Of course, my lord, but perhaps we should wait for the next one since this dance shall end in three steps."

I took her hand and set it lightly on my arm. To Pher'am's credit, she had apparently told the musicians to continue playing couples' dances for a time, because as I led Ari on the grass, another began.

It was a dance that we both knew well. After we had completed a flourish maneuver that had taken quite a bit of practice to master, I happened to glance at Pher'am. I was certain that if she hadn't been quite as proper, her mouth would have hung open. As it was, she didn't manage to keep the shocked look off her face.

"What is it?" Ari asked from my arm.

I grinned at her. "Oh, I don't believe your sister actually expected us to do well at this."

Ari glanced in Pher'am's direction and grinned as well. "Dreanen's with her now."

At the next turn, I was able to catch sight of them again. Pher'am motioned toward us and seemed to be frantically discussing the situation with Dreanen. Well, at least as frantic as Pher'am ever became. Dreanen, meanwhile, seemed quite amused.

We ended the dance with Ari leaning over my arm.

"I wish we could do something to really shock them," she mused quietly, her eyes sparkling with merriment.

"Well, I could kiss you," I teased her.

"Would you?" Her eyes grew wide.

I heard Dreanen erupt in laughter as I listened to Pher'am shrill, "You knew! Didn't you?" I smiled that even she could be less than completely proper if goaded.

I knew it looked like I was still kissing Ari, but I'd felt her go limp against my arm, and I didn't want her to stumble when she stood up.

"Are you all right?" I asked.

Her eyes focused on mine, and she nodded. Carefully, I set her on her feet and led her to the opposite side of the field from Dreanen and Pher'am. It took me a few moments, but I finally found a less-attended part of the festival. Ari leaned against the side of a booth for a few moments, catching her breath. She was still smiling, but hadn't looked at me again since leaving the field.

"Are you all right?" I hoped she didn't have regrets.

"You asked me that already," she teased, and finally looked up at me again.

The smile was still there.

"Can we talk this evening?" I asked.

She looked slightly concerned, but nodded. Soon, she wandered off to find Ti'anha again. I decided to avoid Pher'am and Dreanen and walked toward the estate.

CHAPTER 60

HOW FAR?

I didn't know what exactly Danren wanted to talk about, and I certainly did not know what to expect. Two watches after sunset, I realized that I was avoiding my room. Gathering my nerves, I made my way there.

Danren was already there, staring into the fire. He rose and turned to me when I entered. The look on his face made me want to cry. It seemed as though I were the most precious thing imaginable to him. I hurried to him, and he held me for a moment. Then gently pushing me to arm's length, I let out a slight cry of dismay and looked up at him. I saw his heart break across his face for an instant before he closed his eyes.

"Ari, please," his voice was shattered, "I need to know something."

"All right," I answered softly.

When he looked at me, his eyes were glassy. "How far is this going?"

I must have looked confused, because, after a moment's pause, he continued, "You want me to hold you . . . I've told you that I . . . " his voice hushed as he looked at me, "I love you." He took a moment to collect himself. "I've kissed you . . . I've even announced all this publicly." His grip tightened slightly on my shoulder. "Is this as far as this is going? If it is, that's fine. If not . . . I need to know where the line is. How far do you want this to go?"

I felt terror rise in me. Stepping out of his grasp, I saw pain knife across his face, but he let me go. His hands clinched by his sides.

Was he asking to bed me? No, I couldn't . . . could I? He'd always been kind to me, and I treated him like dirt most of that time. Would this make up for that? Would he stop being kind to me if I refused? Would he not touch me, hold me, dance with me . . . kiss me, if I didn't give him this?

"What are you asking?"

I didn't realize that I'd spoken until Danren took a ragged breath and turned to lean on the hearth. He seemed to be struggling for words.

"Do you want to bed me?" I managed to whisper.

Instantly, he spun around. "What?"

"Is that what you're asking?" I whispered.

"What?" He didn't stop with that exclamation this time. "Of course not!"

"So you don't want to bed me?" I felt strangely confused.

He fumbled incoherently for a moment and then told me, "That can't be answered."

I finally managed to look at him again, feeling even more puzzled.

"Any way I answer that will condemn me," he explained. "If I say no, you'll probably feel safe, but slighted, as though you're not good enough. If I say yes, you'll be terrified that I'll take advantage of you."

I understood what he was saying, but found that at the same time, I both wanted to know which answer was correct, and was terrified of either choice.

"What are you asking then?" I managed to whisper.

I heard him let out a hard sigh. Glancing up, I watched him try to rephrase his question once again.

"Is what we're doing now as far as you want to take our marriage?" he finally managed.

"Doing now?" I sought clarification.

"Holding you . . . "

At those words, I stepped toward him. I found that I wanted him to hold me. I wanted to be safe. He seemed reluctant to draw me to him, but after a moment's hesitation, he did. Slowly, I began to comprehend his question.

"Are you asking if I want to stop what we've been doing? This . . . dancing . . . " I trailed off.

"Partially," he replied. "Do you want to go back? Stop doing what we're doing? Just be cordial to each other? Do you want things to stay the way they are? This is the line, and we won't go any further?"

"Further?" I questioned. "What would be further?"

"I don't know, but if this isn't the line, I need to know where you want to stop," he clarified.

I thought for several moments.

"I don't want to go back," I managed, pressing my face into his shoulder.

Leaning against him, I pondered the other two possibilities. Every step we'd taken, I never would have fathomed before. Now, I couldn't imagine what else we would do. If I said I didn't want to go any further, Danren would honor that. Even if, one day, I found one more step I wanted to take, he'd refuse. He would keep his word. The line would stand.

"I don't know," I whispered.

"What?" I felt him lean back to look at me.

"I don't know where I want this to end," I explained softly.

"So you don't want to draw the line here?" He was searching for clarification.

"I don't know." I couldn't decide either way.

"Where would you want to go from here?" he asked.

"I don't know," was the only reply I had.

Feeling his frustrated sigh made my soul ache.

"So you don't know," he summarized.

Any other time, I probably would have laughed, but all I could manage was a slight nod.

"All right," he told me, "if you ever do find where you want the line, will you let me know?"

I nodded again. "I'm sorry," I whispered.

"It's all right," he told me. "I'm just at a loss trying to sort out everything that's happened."

"Do you want to sit down?" I asked.

He sighed again, but moved toward the couch. When he was situated, I curled up next to him, resting my head on his leg.

After a few moments of quiet, I tried again, "I'm sorry, I couldn't define what you were asking for."

"It's all right," he repeated. After another moment, he sighed and began to stroke my hair. "This has all been rather . . . unexpected."

I did laugh lightly at that comment. "Yes, quite."

He laughed in reply, "You mean to tell me you didn't plan all this?"

"No," I responded smiling. "I did try to plan parts . . . but you kept ruining them."

"What?" he exclaimed, "I didn't know what you were trying to do most of the time! On top of that, with everything you've been through, how was I supposed to even guess that you might want . . ." his voice trailed off, and I glanced up.

He was gazing down at me with that look in his eyes again. As though I were most precious . . . pure . . . undefiled . . . as though nothing in the world was worth more.

"Want what?" I whispered, trying not to let the tears show.

He looked into my eyes and swallowed hard. "Me to love you."

I smiled and moved closer. "Yes, please."

He stared at the fire for a long time, seemly fighting his own emotions. I wanted to stay there forever, but all too soon there was a knock on the door. Stifling a laugh because of Danren's groan, I sat up. He pulled himself up from the couch and walked to the door.

I had expected to find one of Dreanen's servants outside the door, asking if we needed anything. Instead, I found Dreanen himself standing there with that infuriating grin on his face. He didn't wait to be invited, but stepped into the room.

"Do you know how upset you made my wife?" He laughed, slapping me on the back.

"I'm so glad I could help," I told him in a tone that I hoped portrayed that I didn't want him there.

"She's been planning how to get you to actually notice Ari for months. Almost as long as we've been planning this whole thing," he waved an arm around. "In fact, she began working out those plans so early on that you may have ruined her entire concept of this festival."

"Perhaps," I hoped he would get the hint, "she should mind her own affairs."

"Oh, she does," he told me, completely oblivious. "How long have you been wooing Ari anyway?"

"I'm not," I told him flatly.

At that moment, Ari laughed lightly. I quickly turned to the fireplace to find her peeking over the back of the couch. Dreanen glanced at me with a look that said quite obviously, *You're not? I don't believe you.*

I wanted to hit him, but Ari just threw her head back and laughed. I glared at the back of Dreanen's head as he walked toward her.

"Am I interrupting?" he asked.

She smiled lightly. "Yes."

He laughed at her answer. "Then I won't stay long."

"You're wrong though," she told him.

"Excuse me?" he asked, looking puzzled.

"Danren hasn't been wooing me," she said with both a straight face and without a hint of laughter this time.

He looked between the two of us for a moment. "That wasn't an act."

Ari laughed, and I fought a smile. I was beginning to enjoy having the tables turned.

"Are you joking?" he asked Ari, who promptly became serious and shook her head.

"Everyone at Caer Corisan will eat you alive if that was put on," he exclaimed.

"Dragons don't eat people," both Ari and I said at the same time.

She grinned at me, as Dreanen looked between the two of us again.

"What is going on?" He seemed ready to hit *me* now.

I couldn't help but laugh. I knew that Dreanen had come to tease Danren, and he didn't deserve that, especially after I couldn't give him a solid answer. It was pleasant to see him trying to sort everything out, and failing so miserably. I needed to give Dreanen an answer though, because I knew Danren wouldn't.

"Danren treats me with . . . dignity and honor." I hadn't thought this would be quite so hard. "I realized that I . . . never gave him a chance." I took a long breath. "He's never pressured me . . . or even asked for anything for himself that I hadn't already asked for . . . " I trailed off, and finally managed to ask, "Does that make any sense?"

Dreanen had a quirky smile on his face when I looked up at him.

"Yes," he replied evenly, "you're wooing him."

"No!" I exclaimed, "It's not like that!"

He just grinned and slapped Danren on the back as he left. "Congratulations, you've been smitten."

Danren glared at him as he waved and closed the door.

"I didn't mean . . . " I fumbled to explain, "I didn't say . . . "

"He knows what you meant," Danren told me. "He just likes to tease."

He walked over and leaned on the mantle for a moment. Then he began to laugh. Standing up, I walked to him and put my hand on his shoulder. I hoped he was all right. Turning to look at me, I caught a mischievous look in his eyes.

"I'm going to duel with him the next time he's at Caer Corisan," Danren told me, grinning.

"But you're so much better than him!" I exclaimed and then realized Danren's intent. Laughing, I asked, "May I watch?"

He chuckled as he put his arms around me. "I'll make sure you have a choice seat."

Two more days passed, and I was glad to see that Pher'am didn't try any other matching endeavors. Ari did seem to spend more time with me though. Ti'anha tagged along most of the time, but I didn't mind. We did receive some pointed looks a few times from people we knew, but we did our best to ignore them.

The evening of the fifth day, I walked to our rooms alone. I had been looking for Ari, but hadn't found her anywhere among the dwindling crowd on the grounds. Noticing that her door was open slightly, I assumed that she hadn't come back yet. I stretched out on the couch, looking at the fire and wondering where else Ari might be. Perhaps she was with Pher'am or telling Ti'anha or Juna'yad goodnight. I knew I shouldn't miss her this much, but I did enjoy the new depth of our friendship.

A slight movement caught my eye, and I glanced at the nearby chair. I jumped in surprise to find Ari curled up in it, grinning at me. The chair's back was to the door, so I hadn't noticed her when I'd come in.

"Care to join me?" I joked, waving my hand at the other chairs in the area.

Her grin faded, and she watched me for a moment, before standing up and walking to the couch.

As she sat in front of me, I fumbled to explain, "I didn't mean here."

"I know," she said softly.

She took a breath and then lay down with her back against me.

I nearly jumped off the couch, but would have pushed her onto the floor if I had.

"You don't have to do this," I managed.

"I know," she repeated, but didn't move.

"Ari . . ." I fought to figure out what to say, and settled on what I had been saying in these situations, "Are you certain this is what you want?"

After a moment, she nodded slightly.

It seemed like forever before I worked up the nerve to put my arm around her.

"Is this all right?" I asked.

She laughed lightly and nodded.

I sighed, breathing in the scent of her hair and watching the firelight play along her tresses.

Soon, I felt her take that customary breath before saying, "Danren, I have a question for you."

I laughed slightly and replied simply, "Yes?"

"If I hadn't been . . . taken . . . what do you think our lives would have been like?"

I thought for a moment. "I've heard that I was supposed to inherit the western region originally, Maris and the coast to Itsaso."

"No," she told me, "I mean between us."

"Us? There wouldn't have been an us. You would have married Lord Perparim, and I would have married . . . I've not actually heard who, but someone, I'm sure," he replied after a moment.

I sat up slightly and turned to stare at him. For some reason, I hadn't thought of that.

"No," I argued feeling slightly frightened, "I couldn't have married Lord Perparim."

"You would have," Danren replied softly.

Frantically, I tried to work out how I would have still married Danren, but I realized that it never would have happened.

"I would have," I whispered.

"You would have been happy," he told me. "Lord Perparim is a good man."

"But what about you?" I asked.

He glanced away. "I already told you."

I tried to keep the tremor out of my voice. "You mean that we wouldn't be here if I hadn't been taken?"

I could tell that the question upset Danren, because he leaned up and licked his teeth. It was an odd habit, but I'd realized that the dragons did the same thing. "No, I doubt Dreanen would have had this festival without Pher'am. Depending on who he married perhaps, but probably not."

The shock of realizing that Pher'am and Dreanen wouldn't be married left me speechless for a moment. Their wonderful children would never have existed. There were too many things that were good that would never have been.

I stared at Danren for several moments before I finally managed, "I can't picture life . . . like that."

I glanced around feeling almost as though the walls would disappear any moment, and I would be far away, in a life I didn't know.

"I can," Danren whispered.

Twisting, I stared at him. He must have seen the pain and fear in my eyes, because he glanced away.

"You would never have been taken, never hurt . . . violated like that. You would have been safe." His voice held muted wrath as well as pain. "You wouldn't live in fear."

"I wouldn't know you!" I exclaimed sitting up.

This wasn't how I had pictured things when I'd asked the question.

"You'd be happy," he whispered.

"You can't know that!" I argued. Then I gasped. "Would you have rather had that life?"

I couldn't tell if he was wishing things were that way or not.

His voice broke slightly as he spoke, "Ari, I love you, but I would pay any price to have kept that from happening to you."

"No," I choked, beginning to cry.

Danren hesitated for a moment, but then sat up and gathered me to him. I sobbed into his shoulder for several moments before I could manage to speak again.

"I never thought," I choked on a sob, "about it like that."

He gently stroked my hair, waiting for me to continue.

"I thought we'd still be together. We'd still be here." I felt my lip tremble for a moment. "I'd be . . . whole, and we'd be happy . . ."

When I didn't continue, he told me, "I didn't mean to upset you."

"No," I choked, "I didn't think." I looked at him and watched him pale as I said, "You'd be a father. You're wonderful with Pher'am and Dreanen's children."

"Ari," I heard the tension in his voice even though it was barely more than a whisper, "I'll never ask."

I sobbed and hardly managed to say, "I know, but it's your right."

"Ari!" His voice was so sharp that I couldn't bring myself to look at him. "Just because I can do something or even though everyone believes it's *proper* or my right, doesn't mean I should. It doesn't make it correct."

It took me so long to stop crying into his shoulder.

Finally, I managed to say something, even though it was, "I'm ruining your shirt."

He chuckled slightly. "Faber will be happy to know that I need a new one."

That made me laugh as Danren pulled out a handkerchief and began gently wiping my face. He shifted slightly and missed his handhold on the edge of the couch. Falling back he smacked his head on the armrest. I slipped quickly to the floor and knelt in front of him. Carefully, I began examining his head to see if he was hurt.

"Ari," he whispered, and I focused on his eyes, "I would pay anything, but since I can't go back, I'm thankful that I have the honor of caring for you now."

I felt the tears threatening again. His head seemed unhurt to my shaking fingers.

After a moment, I returned to the couch and lay against him again, staring into the fire.

"Do you think," I managed to ask, "that the Mighty One . . . that I was taken . . . so you . . . so we could be together?"

He didn't reply for several moments. "That's a hard question. I'm not certain that I know the answer. I believe that if your years with me are pleasant, the Mighty One is redeeming your time. I also know that there were plenty of people who chose not to do anything when you were taken."

"What do you mean?" I asked.

"There was a tavern maid who saw your conversation with the drunk," he began to explain, "but she didn't tell anyone. There was a merchant who passed the wagon. He even spoke to the man, but he just continued without doing anything. The dealer who bought the horse knew that horse was stolen, but sold it as though it was perfectly legal." I could feel his tension.

"How do you know all this?" I interrupted.

He scoffed before answering, "My father led most of the search, and we were . . . involved with a lot of it as well."

"I'm grateful," I whispered.

I could hear the smile in his voice when he answered, "You're welcome."

There was silence for a while, before he continued, "I believe that there is a balance. The Mighty One can do anything he chooses, but he allows us to make our own choices as well." He paused again before saying softly, "It seems as though we often make the wrong ones."

"I wouldn't say that," I told him. "You do quite well."

"Thanks." I heard him laugh slightly.

"I honestly don't understand why . . . things happen the way they do," he continued. "Certainly, he could have kept you from being taken, but . . . he didn't . . . I just don't know."

Ari didn't ask any more questions. I watched the firelight play in her hair and pondered what she'd said and asked. She deserved better than what had happened to her, but I couldn't change the past. I could only hope to make her future better.

I was startled when I heard the middle night watch called. I hadn't realized how late it was. Ari was relaxing against me, and I didn't want to disturb her. I knew I had to though, so I shifted slightly.

She jumped and glanced around the room for a moment, before leaning against me again. I sighed.

"We should go to sleep," I told her.

"Mmmm." She snuggled into my shoulder.

"You're tired," I tried again.

"Mmmm." She sighed.

I sighed in return, but mine wasn't content, more the slightly exasperated variety. Finally, I managed to get Ari to sit up, but she just leaned against me from that position instead. This wasn't working! She seemed to be almost asleep already. I really should have paid closer attention. After a few more moments, trying to decide what to do, in which Ari seemed to fall asleep completely, I lifted her and walked to her room.

It took some maneuvering, but I managed to pull the blanket back and not drop her on the floor. She would have to sleep in her dress and explain the wrinkles to Faber on her own. I pulled the blanket over her. Resisting the urge to kiss her forehead, I walked toward the door.

"Stay," the word was so light, I was certain that I hadn't really heard it.

Pausing at the doorway, I whispered, "What?"

I was almost ready to step out of the room, when I heard it again, "Stay."

I looked over my shoulder and saw Ari's wide eyes watching me. Glancing over the bed, I fought thoughts of holding her all night . . . waking up with her safe in my arms.

"No," I told her. "We've both had more wine than we probably should have today, and you're tired . . . You'd hate me in the morning."

I walked out of the room, not knowing if I would be able to resist another plea.

I barely managed to get the word out. I didn't know what he would consider it an invitation for, but I didn't want him to leave. It had been so comfortable nestled in his arms.

"What?" he asked, so low that I almost couldn't hear him.

It took me a long moment before I could force the word out of my throat again.

He looked at me and then at the bed. He was considering it. I felt my hands begin to tremble. What if he accepted?

"No, we've both had more wine than we probably should have today." I felt relief, but also disappointment. "And you're tired . . . You'd hate me in the morning."

Then, he was gone. Confused, I turned over. Why had I done that? What was I expecting? What would he have done? I trembled under the blanket, from fear instead of cold. What did I want?

CHAPTER 61

A PLOT

I wasn't certain how long I lay awake thinking, when I heard a crash from the next room. Sitting straight up, I made out a hissed whisper of, "Get out, now!"

Was that a giggle? I reached for my robe, and then remembered that I was still dressed from the day. I'd in fact been lying on my light sword. Hurrying from the room, I wondered, if it came to such a thing, would I be able to fight someone with it?

The scene I walked into was the last thing I expected. A woman, I could not remember ever seeing before, was stretched on the couch while Danren was standing over her. I almost went to the obvious conclusion, when I took half a moment to think about what I was seeing.

Danren looked livid. He grabbed the woman by the wrist and pulled her to her feet. He was trying to propel her to the door, but she wasn't cooperating. In fact, she seemed to be trying to angle him either back toward the couch or toward his bedroom.

"Get out!" I heard him hiss again, slightly louder.

"You do not truly mean that, my lord." The woman giggled and attempted to reach for his shoulder.

He grabbed her hand, and she tried to trip him. Barely keeping his balance, he glanced over his shoulder and froze. He was looking straight at me. I watched the anger drain from his face, replaced only by pale shock.

The woman must have noticed the change because she glanced past him. She ducked from my line of sight and whispered something I couldn't hear. Danren released her when she tried to twist out of his grip, but instead of escaping through the door, she ran to me.

Flinging herself at my feet, she cried, "Please, my lady, help me."

I'd gone to my room, hoping I'd done the right things. The conversation had been rough. I was surprised that Ari was pleased with the life that she had now. I would have thought that she would want something else . . . almost anything else . . . especially since she could have married into a higher family. I wondered if she would think differently if she hadn't been taken. Then, I realized, yet again, how futile that line of thought was. Sighing, I bent to the lamp I'd brought. Then, I heard the door open behind me.

Turning around, I began to ask Ari what was wrong. To my shock, it wasn't Ari quietly shutting the door behind her. In fact, as far as I could recall, I'd never seen this woman before in my life.

"Quiet, my lord," she began. "We wouldn't want to wake anyone."

What was going on? I was far too tired to think straight, but when she took the few steps toward me and ran her hand over my shoulder, I began thinking quite a bit more clearly.

"Mighty One have mercy," I prayed, as I reached to pull her hand away.

"You'll pray more things than that tonight," she breathed, and leaned up.

I pushed her away far more violently than I probably needed to, but my sluggish thoughts were finally falling into place. At first, I wondered if I was asleep, but immediately threw that option away. I wouldn't realize if I was asleep, that I was asleep . . . at least I was fairly certain of that.

"You play rough, my lord." She giggled, stepping toward me again.

"Get out!" I snapped at her.

"I will." She tried to brush my shoulder again, but I grabbed her wrist.

I began pulling her toward the door. In the main room, I tried to drag her to the doors, but she was stronger than she looked.

"You're going to wake my wife!" I hissed at her.

She giggled. "Oh, we wouldn't want that."

Then she pretended to trip over a vase that was sitting next to the couch, causing it to break on the floor. She used this as an excuse to fall on the couch.

I barely caught my balance, and she giggled at me again. "Join me, my lord, this does not have to take long."

I glared at her and glanced at Ari's door. It hadn't opened yet, so maybe she was sleeping so soundly that she hadn't heard the noise.

"Get out, now!" I hissed at her through my teeth.

She drawled out, "You don't really want that," and then giggled.

I grabbed her arm and pulled her to her feet. Before she could gain her balance, I began dragging her toward the door. Halfway to the door, she regained her footing and tried to pull me back.

"Get out!" I wasn't certain how much longer I'd be able to keep my voice down.

"You do not truly want that, my lord," she said in a sickeningly smooth tone, as she tried to touch my shoulder again.

I wasn't stopping, but when she slipped in front of me, I had to brace myself on the table to keep from falling. Hoping that she hadn't woke Ari, I glanced over my shoulder. To my horror, my wife was standing in her doorway.

How much had she seen? What had she heard? What would she believe?

I glanced at the woman in front of me, who sneered almost silently, "This will be much easier."

I pushed her away, expecting her to head toward the door, but instead she ran toward Ari. It took me a moment to realize that she was going in the wrong direction. Then I went after her. She would never attack Ari. I felt my blood begin to boil again. The woman reached Ari before I did.

"Please, my lady, help me," she begged as she flung herself at Ari's feet.

"What?" I was doomed!

Ari would never believe me now! I watched as Ari reached down, pulled the woman to her feet, and then backhanded her . . . The woman seemed as shocked as I was.

Only then did I realize that someone was pounding on the door. Dazed, I walked over to the door and opened it. The man outside seemed surprised to see me. He was dressed as a servant, but I didn't recognize him.

"Get . . . Lord Dreanen," I told him.

He glanced past me and seemed to make an attempt to step around me. I heard running footsteps from down the hall and glanced at those two servants, who I actually did recognize.

"Will one of you get Lord Dreanen?" I probably sounded more abrasive than I should have, but my temper was getting the better of me.

"Who are you?" I shifted to completely block the man from entering the room.

"What's going on in there?" he asked me, trying to get past again.

"You!" I heard one of the servants snap, "You were dismissed yesterday!"

I glared at the man, wondering if I could hit him without making things worse.

"You do not understand!" the woman cried when she recovered from the blow I'd just given her.

"Oh?" I began pulling the sword from its scabbard.

She saw my movement and stared at my hand.

"He approached me!" she lied.

This time, I hit her with the hilt. She staggered backward.

"My lady, please!" she wailed.

"If you expect any mercy from me," I began, suddenly completely convinced that I could use my sword, "you had better tell me the truth."

"Why do you not believe me?" she whimpered.

"Because I know Danren." I realized that I'd just growled at her in the same tone that Danren used when he was angry.

"You do not understand," she whimpered, staring at the sword.

"Oh?" I asked, attempting to sound less livid.

"He will kill me if I tell you." She was still staring at the blade.

"What makes you think I will not?" I asked in an icy tone.

Her gaze finally moved from the weapon to my face, which she stared at in shock. I continued to glare at her, while fingering the hilt.

What sounded like a body hitting a wall, finally drew my attention away from the woman to Danren. I hadn't realized that he'd walked away, until I saw him turn from the door and enter the room with a tired-looking Dreanen.

I didn't pay attention to what they were saying for long, because I saw the woman begin to move away. I smoothly moved the sword tip to the edge of her neck.

"Try me," I whispered furiously.

If possible, her face turned even paler.

Dreanen finally arrived, looking like he'd fallen out of bed, his robe half on.

"What's going on?" he mumbled, looking at the man in front of me. He seemed to wake up a bit more. "You were dismissed."

"I thought your lordship should know that Lord Danren has been seducing the women servants of your house," he told Dreanen.

My last bit of restraint gave way, and I hit him as hard as I could. Dreanen looked from me to him as I turned to walk back into the room.

"Hold him," he told the servants, and then trotted to catch up with me. "Where are you going?" he began, and then quickly added, "What happened?"

"To get my sword," I growled at him.

I had taken it off to sleep but, thankfully, hadn't begun to actually change my clothes.

"All right . . . ," he said slowly. "What happened?"

"Some woman . . . " I motioned toward where Ari and the woman were.

I watched Dreanen glance over. Then he turned and stared.

I followed his gaze to find Ari holding the woman at sword point. My first thought was that she had perfect form. She'd easily be able to take off the woman's nose, ear, or do substantial damage to any part of her face with just a flick of her wrist. It took me a moment to shake that thought loose, and then I almost felt sorry for the woman. She looked terrified. Almost, but I couldn't bring myself all the way to pity. I did, however, completely forget about retrieving my sword, and instead walked toward Ari.

"Explain, now," I heard her growl.

I'd never heard that tone from Ari before. The woman glanced at Dreanen and me, and Ari deftly twisted the sword into her neck.

"You shouldn't be looking anywhere else," Ari told her.

The woman stared back at Ari and began to tremble. "Please, my lady, it was not my idea."

"Whose idea was it then?" Ari replied in a dangerously even tone.

The woman took only half a moment to consider her answer before blurting out, "Lord Astucieux sent me."

"Lord Astucieux?" Dreanen asked, and then paused for a moment. "Sent you to do what?"

She glanced at Dreanen for only an instant and then focused on Ari again.

"The lord asked you a question," Ari told her.

"I was supposed to . . . to . . . seduce Lord Danren." Her voice shook as she spoke.

Dreanen choked. "You were supposed to . . . what?"

Ari moved the sword back slightly, and the woman collapsed to the floor sobbing.

The sounds of a struggle erupted from the hall. I heard a body hit either the opposite wall or the floor, and then running. I glared at the doorway where I could see one of the servants picking himself up. The other wasn't in view. I dashed into my room, pulled my sword from its scabbard, and headed out the door. Dreanen was ahead of me, and in front of him, I could barely make out the other servant.

Before I reached the entrance, I heard the servant shout, "Stop him! Lord Danren . . . "

Then the sounds of another fight reached me. This time the body did hit the wall.

Expecting to find the servant lying against the wall, I was surprised to find the man who'd been fleeing. My surprise disappeared when I realized that Ishmerai stood over him.

"Did you want him alive, my lord?" he asked as calmly as someone might ask, "Did you want toast or eggs this morning?"

His iron calm unnerved me when I first met him, but I'd grown used to it within the second year of being . . . well . . . a dragon.

"Alive if you would," I told him, regaining some calm. I glanced at the man who was holding a now gushing nose. "At least for now."

We dragged the man back inside and threw him into a chair. Dreanen grinned at me from behind the chair, looking for all the world as though he was having the time of his life. I was beginning to feel like hitting him too.

"What were you doing at my room?" I snarled at him.

The man almost sneered at me, but then seemed to think better of it.

"Catching you in the act," he finally said.

"What?" I snapped.

For a moment he seemed to consider what he was about to say. "I was to report that you flirted with the servant women and then took them to your room at night." He shrugged, and then cringed because the movement made his nose bleed more. "I was coming up to catch you in the act tonight." Taking a moment to glare at me, in which I gritted my teeth and took a better grip on my sword. "It shouldn't have been hard. You're married to a nickin after al—"

He passed out as soon as I clubbed him with my sword hilt. I debated taking his head off, but then remembered that Ari was still dealing with the woman.

"Well, that lasted longer than I thought it would," Dreanen said as I stormed down the hall.

I turned to glare at him. He wasn't looking at me though. Instead, he had his head tilted slightly and looked rather bemused at the man.

He glanced up at me and grinned. "Should I have someone treat his nose or just let him bleed?"

I shook my head, still glaring at him, turned around, and left. I wondered quite often how Dreanen could look at life as such a game. Then I'd usually wonder how Pher'am managed to stay sane. Currently, I just wanted to hit him.

I made my way back to the room, where I was surprised to find several servants staring in the door. I was almost amused . . . almost.

"Move!" I ordered, and watched as they scrambled out of my way.

Inside the room, I found what they had been staring at. A terrified-looking woman tied to one of the table chairs with the ripped-off hem of Ari's dress gagging her. It took me a moment to realize that what the woman was tied with were sashes from Ari's other dresses. The problem was that I couldn't see Ari anywhere.

"Ari?" I asked the room.

The woman looked over at me, seeming as though she would go into hysterics if she could scream, but the gag wouldn't allow that.

Then I heard it, "I'm here."

I turned toward the fireplace and realized that Ari must be sitting in the chair that had its back toward the door. I walked toward it to find Ari fingering her sword.

"Please, would you send her away?" she asked softly.

I ordered the servants in the doorway to take the woman away. They quickly did, whispering among themselves. After closing the door behind them, I turned back to Ari.

Her sword clattered to the floor as she stood and walked into my arms. It was a bit awkward, since I was still holding my own sword, and the scabbard was still lying halfway between the doorway and my bedroom. I leaned over and set it on the couch, hoping that I would remember it was there before someone sat on it.

Then Ari sobbed.

"I'm not . . . " I tried to whisper through my tears, "I'm not . . . "

"Shhh," Danren tried to calm me, "it's all right."

"She said that," I tried to explain, "that it should have been simple . . . easy . . . to seduce you because you . . . you are . . . married to a nickin."

I felt his grip tighten around me, even to his hands balling into fists.

It took him a moment to reply, but then he said amazingly gently, "You're right. You're not."

CHAPTER 62

ANOTHER DAY

I wasn't certain that I'd be able to face this last day of the festival, but Ti'anha made things so enjoyable, that by that evening I was laughing with her as she picked out the duckling she'd just won. Two watches later, after helping Pher'am put her and Juna'yad to bed, I made my way back to my rooms. I wondered where Danren had been all day, but wasn't surprised to find him sitting by the fire.

He didn't look up until I'd closed the door behind me, and began walking toward him. I knew from looking at him that he hadn't slept the previous night or that day.

"Would you like to sit?" he asked, sounding as though he were exhausted as he motioned at the chair.

"Are you all right?" I asked, joining him on the couch.

He started slightly when I sat next to him and stared at me for a moment. Finally, he smiled ever so slightly and stared back at the fire.

"I missed you," he finally said.

"I missed you too," I replied and reached for his hand. He squeezed mine in return. "I didn't see you at the festival," I added.

Typically, I'd at least see him in passing; and the last few days, he'd spent almost the whole day with me.

"I was . . . talking to our . . . ," he said sarcastically, "visitors."

I had thought that was where he'd been. It was the only thing that I could think of that would keep him away from the last day of the festival.

"What happened?" I asked in a whisper.

He glanced at me and then stared back at the fire. "What?"

"Today, when you were talking to them . . . what happened?" I clarified.

"You don't want to know," he replied, after a moment.

"Please?" I asked softly.

Danren looked at me with pain in his eyes. "Lord Astucieux apparently sent . . . the woman . . . she's one of his . . . of his . . . "

He glanced at me, and I squeezed his hand slightly. Considering his temper, it probably surprised some people that he was so opposed to insulting others. In this case, he didn't even want to use a shaded term for this woman. I hoped that he understood that he didn't need to tell me she wasn't even one of the concubines of Lord Astucieux.

Seeming to guess my intent, he continued, "The manservant is apparently one of his household servants."

"What will happen to them?" I asked, when he didn't continue.

"We're sending them to trial." He sighed heavily. "Since they're both attached to the house of Lord Astucieux, it will go before one of the king's judges."

"Will you need to go?" I asked, hoping that if he did, I would be able to travel with him.

"I don't know." He sighed again and stared into the fire.

After a few moments, he ran his hand through his hair and then he licked his teeth. I rose and walked behind the couch. He turned to look at me, questioningly.

"It's all right," I told him.

He gave me a rueful smile, but then jumped when I began rubbing his shoulders.

"I'm not going to hurt you," I teased.

He didn't respond for a moment and then said, "You don't have to do this."

I smiled. "I know, but I want to."

Slowly he leaned back again and let me work the tension out. When I'd done all I could, I rested my hands on his shoulders. He glanced up at me. The pained look in his eyes was clearer than it normally was.

"Ari'," he said softly, "I love you." Turning to the fire again, he covered his face with his hands. "Please, believe me."

I walked around the couch and knelt in front of him. He didn't look up.

Rubbing his knee, I asked, "Who are you trying to convince?"

He did look up at that. "What?"

I smiled. "I know. You don't have to convince me."

Closing his eyes, "I'd never . . . "

"I know," I told him softly.

"You've hurt enough," he continued as though he hadn't heard me, "I'd never . . . "

I decided to tease him, hoping to lighten the mood. "So you might if I was someone else?"

He didn't seem to grasp that I was teasing. "There'd be no reas—" he began, but then he seemed to realize what he'd started to say.

I instinctively pulled my hands from his knees. The blood drained from his face, and he shifted as if to back away. The couch wouldn't let him, and he couldn't move to the side without bumping me. I knew he wouldn't touch me. Terror gripped me anyway. I felt my hands begin to shake. Fighting hard, I kept from fleeing. I knew Danren. He was an honorable man. He wouldn't hurt me. He'd had every opportunity, and he never had. There was no reason to believe he would now.

Gripping my hand, I tried to focus on exactly what he'd said . . . what he'd actually meant. If he were married to someone else, he wouldn't have an affair because he could . . . bed his wife. He'd told me that he would have wooed her. He wouldn't have forced her, but he would, especially by now, be able to bed her. I tried to calm myself as I continued to reason. He wouldn't have an affair now, because he wouldn't hurt me like that. Did he mean that he wanted . . .

"Th-that's the answer then," I began, failing to keep the tremor from my voice, "you want to . . . bed me."

I saw the shock on his face. "Ari . . . that's . . . that's an armed question." The pain in his voice was unmistakable.

I fought for control for my voice, but managed only to quaver out, "I-I'd like to know."

He looked away.

"You should have married someone far higher, someone far better," he said.

At first, I thought he was avoiding the question. I almost demanded a yes or no, but then I realized that he wasn't avoiding, he was trying to answer as best as he could.

"You're a beautiful woman. I never meant to hurt you. I would never ask . . . " He paused for a moment. "Sex is a gift," he finally whispered. "It's not something to be demanded, or sold, or bartered, or stolen. It's supposed to be sacred . . . not . . . not cheap. It's supposed to be a . . . a physical act to reflect a marriage commitment, to consummate the joining of a couple for a lifetime."

What he was saying sounded amazing. I wished I'd been able to experience that. I fought off the terrors of my memories as he spoke.

"I'd never ask," he continued. "I know you've been hurt. What happened to you was . . . " he searched for an adequate word, "horrific. I never wanted to hurt you more." After a moment, he whispered, "I'd never ask. Please, believe me."

He fell silent, and even though he hadn't answered specifically, I could tell what his answer was. I watched as the pain in his face intensified. Rising to my feet, I saw him cringe and then glance away. He almost jumped off the couch when I sat next to him. At least, he was looking at me now. Of course, he was staring, and his mouth was hanging open, but he was looking at me. I smiled and realized how shy I felt.

Taking his opposite hand, I whispered, "Thank you."

"What?" he exclaimed.

I laughed. Danren continued to stare at me.

What was she still doing here? I was certain that she would flee from the room while I was still talking . . . but she was still here. Not only was she still here, Ari was now sitting next to me, holding my hand and looking at me as if I'd just said something amusing.

After several moments, I asked the only thing I could think of. "Are you all right?"

She nodded, blushing. I wanted to touch her face, but I knew . . . or was fairly certain that she would bolt if I did. However, she leaned against my shoulder. I shifted so that I could put my arm around her, and leaned back against the couch. Realizing that I'd been holding my breath, I took a gasp of air.

Ari laughed again. What was going on?

"Do you want to move the line?" I finally asked, "Go back some." Certainly she'd want to be less intimate now . . . Wouldn't she?

I felt her shift and glanced down to see her biting her lip. I hated watching her do that, remembering times when she was so frightened by her memories that she would bite her lip until it bled.

She glanced away and whispered, "Would you want to . . . stay . . . tonight?"

"What?" I couldn't think of what she was talking about.

We were already staying at Ryuu tonight. The plan was to leave in the morning. I glanced to where Ari was looking and found her staring at the door to her bedroom. Slowly, I realized what she'd just asked.

"What?" I exclaimed. Certainly, she couldn't mean . . . "What?"

She turned her attention to her fingers. "If someone tried anything tonight," she tried to argue a point, "you wouldn't be alone."

"Ari!" I couldn't keep the shock from my voice, "I wouldn't . . . " What exactly was she asking? "No one's going to . . . to try anything tonight."

Starting from her cheeks, her entire face had flushed. "You don't have . . . Just in case . . . I mean . . . "

I wasn't certain how many sentences she would start. In fact, I wasn't certain of anything anymore.

Finally, I managed to interrupt her, "How much wine did you have today?"

Her face shot up, and she stared at me, wide eyed.

"I didn't have any," she snapped.

"Because of what I said last night?" I asked shakily.

She blushed again and nodded, focusing on her hands.

"Ari," I managed to whisper, "what are you asking?"

Her blush deepened. "I just . . . It's . . . You . . . "

Realizing that I should probably try something different, I asked, "Are you asking . . . for me to bed you?"

She only looked up for an instant, wide eyed. All the color drained from her face. I felt her tremble against me.

"Or just to sleep?"

She relaxed ever so slightly, bit her lip, and nodded.

I realized that I'd just sighed with relief. I'd meant everything that I'd said before, but I hadn't intended to pressure Ari into something I knew would terrify and hurt her. Noticing that she was glancing at me, I realized that she was still waiting for my answer.

What was I supposed to say? I took a moment to sort things out in my head and found that I was just as confused as before, perhaps more so.

"No!" I finally managed, more forcefully than I'd intended. "No," I said softer, "it's been too hectic of a day, and . . . you probably wouldn't ask if it hadn't been such an exciting week."

I couldn't tell if Ari was disappointed or relieved. She looked like she might start several sentences again, but actually didn't say anything. Finally, she stood and walked toward her room. Glancing around, she bit her lip and stopped at her door.

"Ari," I called to her.

She turned, looked at me, and then looked away.

"I'll compromise with you." She watched me for a moment, but seemed confused. "Not tonight, but if you ever ask me again . . . I'll stay."

Her face cleared, and she stared at me for a long moment.

"Thank you," she finally whispered, turned around, and walked into her room.

Closing my door, I slumped to the floor. I heard Danren rise from the couch and walk to his own room, closing the door behind him. I began to cry. I wasn't entirely sure why, but I wept for a long time. Finally, I pulled myself to my feet, changed out of my tearstained clothes, and crawled into bed.

I didn't think I'd sleep very soundly, but the next thing I realized was that someone was calling the dawn watch.

Being uncertain about everything that was happening, I didn't know if I'd done the right thing. I made my way to my room and prayed that Ari would be all right. Pulling my book from the dresser, I tried to read in the lamplight. I couldn't focus and finally tried to sleep. I couldn't manage to do that either. I tossed, paced around the room, redressed, and wandered to the kitchens. Confusing the servants, when I realized that I wasn't actually hungry, I came back to the rooms, paced around the main room, stared out the window, and finally watched the sky begin to lighten after a miserable night.

I looked over in surprise when I heard Ari's door open. Then I chided myself. Of course Ari would be up now. She always watched the sunrise.

Trying to sound as jovial as I could, I bid her a good morning. She didn't reply at first, so I glanced at her.

Danren looked terrible. He showed dark circles under his eyes. His skin had the pale sleepless complexion to it, which I'd seen in Galen when he stayed up for a couple days tending to injuries.

"What happened?" I asked, wondering what could have possibly kept him up for another night.

Ari stared at me for a moment, and then asked a completely incomprehensible question, "What happened?"

"What?" What could she possibly mean?

"You were up all night, why? What happened?" She glanced at the door. "Did someone else come?"

"No," I told her, "I just couldn't sleep."

I was touched by her concern. Again, she watched me for a moment and then asked me to sit down. I wandered over to the couch, as she went back into her room, and came out with her treatment bag.

I laughed slightly. It felt good to laugh.

"Don't you ever go anywhere without that?"

She smiled, walking over to the table, and picked up a cup from the day before.

"Of course not," she teased, "I never know when someone might need something."

"Like their head patched up," I asked, hoping I didn't sound as delirious as I felt.

Ari laughed softly and then walked over with the cup.

Handing it to me, she ordered, "Drink this."

I stared at the smelly mixture. "What is it?"

"Valerium," she said evenly.

I think she knew that I didn't remember what that was.

"It will help," she said, "just drink it quickly."

I wanted to hold my nose, but couldn't manage that and drinking from the cup, so I just gulped it as fast as I could. It was one of the most disgusting things I had ever tasted.

"I know it's awful," Ari said apologetically, but she had a slight smile on her face.

"I am completely convinced that healers enjoy causing discomfort," I told her. "Maybe it's to make sure we don't make the same mistake twice."

"It'd be nice if it worked that way, but you'll probably get into trouble again," she teased. "Just rest," she continued, "I'll take care of things."

"What?" I stared up at her. "We need to leave in two watches, and there's all the packing still to do."

"You're not leaving in two watches," she said evenly, as she walked back over to the table. "That will help you sleep."

"What?" I surged to my feet, and immediately felt dizzy, "I thought you were giving me something to wake me up."

"You need sleep, not a hard day of travel," she told me.

"I'm going to have to turn in three days!" I exclaimed.

"Then turn on the trip." She walked toward the door.

I sank back to the couch as I said, "I need to tell everyone."

"Don't worry. I'll take care of it," she told me softly, as she opened the door.

The last thing I remember was staring as the door closed behind her.

I spoke to Dreanen and Pher'am about staying an extra day. Ti'anha and Juna'yad were thrilled, but I explained to them that they might not see much of us, because Danren was so tired.

"We should be able to have a nice dinner together," I told them.

They were disappointed, but almost instantly became excited about dinner. I watched them hurry to the kitchen as fast as they could.

I headed to the stables next and informed Ishmerai that he could stop preparing the horses. He looked at me confused, so I explained that Danren hadn't slept well, causing him to be unfit to travel. He shrugged and began pulling the harness back off one of the carriage horses.

When I made it back to our rooms, I informed the servants outside that we weren't to be disturbed. I didn't want to give Danren any excuse not to sleep.

Walking in, I found Danren passed out in one of the most uncomfortable positions imaginable. He was half on the couch back, slumped against the armrest with his head almost, but not quite, reaching his hand. Gently shaking him, he startled awake.

"What?" He stared at me in shock.

What was Ari doing in here?

"You shouldn't sleep like that," she said evenly. "You'll hurt your neck."

I straightened, realizing that I wasn't in my bed but on the couch. The light told me it was midmorning.

"We should be going," I said groggily.

"No, you should be sleeping," she said. "You'd fall off your horse."

She was right. I leaned against the back of the couch and closed my eyes. Hearing Ari sigh, I barely managed to open them again.

"Here." She sat on the far end of the couch and pulled on my shoulder.

I nearly fell over on her. "What?"

"It's all right," she told me.

I felt her fingers stroking my hair.

He was asleep again in an instant. I probably shouldn't have given him quite so much of that herb, but he needed rest.

Watching him breathe, I wondered if he snored. I almost laughed but didn't want to wake him. How many wives didn't know whether or not their husbands snored after this many years of marriage? Well, I had plenty of time to find out today.

For a while, I admired his hair. A middle golden color, it slid through my fingers softly. I wished my hair was that color. The darker straw color in mine was offset only by the red undertone. I wondered how many people actually thought my hair was straw colored instead of just seeing the red.

Watches past, my leg had long since fallen asleep, and I was quite hungry. I didn't want to wake Danren though. Finally, as the sun sank toward the other horizon, he stirred. He looked entirely confused when his eyes opened.

That fireplace wasn't in my room! What was I doing out here? I glanced up and found Ari smiling down at me. Realizing that I was lying on her leg, I quickly sat up. She grimaced and began to rub her leg.

"I'm sorry, I didn't mean to . . ." I began, but she smiled through her grimace.

"It was my idea," she told me. "You may want to change for dinner. I promised Ti'anha and Juna'yad we'd be there."

"How long . . . " I glanced at the window and felt my jaw fall.

It was evening. I'd slept all day . . . on Ari's lap!

"Long enough," she replied, sounding like she was trying to tease through the pain knifing through her leg. "I'll let you stay up this time."

"I'm sorry . . . " I began, but she quickly interrupted me.

"You will be sorry if you're late for dinner." She motioned toward my room. "Those children will never forgive you."

She didn't seem upset that I'd spent the entire day sleeping on her, so I decided not to bring it up again. "Thank you," I did tell her, as I rose and headed for my room.

CHAPTER 63

ON THE ROAD

We finally managed to leave the next morning. Juna'yad cried, and Ti'anha tried to be proper and not cry, but in the end, she did too. She wanted to know if Ari would come back with me next time I was there. I wasn't certain when that would be or under what circumstances, so I couldn't promise her. Ari did tell her that she would try to come the next time she could, and that quieted the little girl some.

"She's quite fond of you," I told Ari, as I helped her into the carriage. She smiled, and then waved to the two sniffling children in the doorway.

"Did you want to join me?" Ari asked, as she settled into the carriage.

It was tempting. I wanted to talk to her about everything that had happened, but, "No, I need to do . . . something."

I was far too rested to sit in a carriage for watches. I needed to focus on some sort of action, like riding. It didn't help that I was pushing when I needed to turn. Behind my ears itched, which wasn't a good sign.

When we neared the little inn that we'd stayed at before, I was disconcerted to find both Cumas and Einheim lying outside. I set my horse into a gallop as soon as I saw them. They were probably terrifying Sotiris and Ileana with their presence, not to mention everyone else in the area. They looked up at the sound of the approaching horses.

"What happened?" I realized as I asked, that I'd heard that question far too often in the last few days.

"After we swapped again with Besnik and Derxan, we found your missing wagon. It took two more days to backtrack through the pass to find the lady you'd asked about. She had another woman with her, who was fairly torn up. They're inside. Their . . . escort," Cumas said the last word sarcastically but with a pleased look, "wasn't happy to see us, my lord. Two of them escaped on horseback, but the other woman was injured, so we brought them here."

One of the pleasant things about Cumas was that he was always concise. He'd told me practically everything I needed to know, except one thing.

"Why are you still landed?"

"The woman, that you sent us for, asked us to stay until she could come out to speak to us." He smiled.

That was puzzling. I didn't expect anyone from Verd to actually want to talk to a dragon, even if the dragon had just rescued them. I trotted to the inn, dismounted, and handed my reins to the stable hand. Glancing down the road, I found that the carriage was still a little behind. Quickly, I asked Ishmerai, he and Faber had accompanied me, to explain things to Ari. Then, Faber and I entered the inn.

Sotiris was almost to the door when I entered. His eyes widened when he saw me, and then he quickly bowed.

"My lord . . . " he began, but seemed at a loss after that.

"The two women," I began, "how are they?"

"Lady Berjouhi is fine, my lord. They didn't harm her because she's noble, but . . . " he faltered. "I don't know her name, my lord, but they beat her and . . . the lady tried to stop them, but they wouldn't . . . She's in a bad way, my lord."

"Do you have a healer here?" I asked, suspecting the answer.

"No, my lord, the nearest one was sent for, but I don't know where he is, or how long." He trembled slightly, probably afraid that I'd go into a tirade because of the negative answer.

I waved aside his apology and hurried back outside. Ari was listening to Ishmerai explain, and hadn't even gotten out of the carriage yet.

"Do you still have your kit?" I asked.

"It's in my blue trunk," she said, jumping down before I could help her.

I hurried inside, guessed that she was upstairs, and asked where the injured woman was without looking at who I was talking to.

"She's upstairs in the last room, lady," the voice answered.

I froze for a moment and then managed to glance at Sotiris.

"You're a healer, lady?" he asked, staring at me with wide eyes.

"Y-yes," I managed to tell him, "I learned after . . . "

"You better hurry, lady," he said glancing away. "She's in a bad way."

I quickly took the stairs two at a time. I made it to the back room and found another woman in peasant's clothes sitting by the bed. She watched me while I went over to the injured woman, who also watched me but with terror in her eyes.

"I'm here to help," I told her, and then repeated it in Verdian.

She shivered and glanced at the other woman. I quickly, but gently, picked up her hand, checking her life beat. It was fast, but not changing. She'd been beaten, that was clear from the cuts and bruises on her face. Whether her captors had done worse, I didn't know yet.

"It's all right," I told her, and continued to repeat everything I said to her in Verdian. "You're safe now. No one will hurt you here."

There was a knock on the door, and I called for whoever it was to enter. I glanced at Danren as he entered, and hurried over for my kit. Placing it on the little table next to the bed, I pulled out the herb I'd given Danren the day before and asked the other woman to pour a cup of water for me. She did, and then handed it to me.

"This will help you sleep," I told the woman, as I helped her sit up. "That's all it'll do. I know it smells terrible, but I need you to drink it."

Her terrified look told me she would refuse. "It will hurt less if I can treat your wounds while you sleep."

She frantically looked around, and I felt my own hands begin to tremble. I knew how frightened she was. Her gaze eventually fell on the woman next to the bed. The woman nodded, and she finally drank the contents of the cup.

I asked Danren to get some boiling water and clean rags, while I waited for the woman to doze off. Meanwhile, I began setting out what I thought I'd need from my kit. The woman was asleep by the time Danren returned.

I asked him to leave, since I knew that I would need to undress her. Her wounds wouldn't be limited to her face. He hesitated for a moment, and then told me that if I needed anything, he'd be just outside. I smiled that a lady of the realm was healing, and a lord was content to fetch. Rem'Maren was not like any other house in Faruq.

Waiting was agony, but Ishmerai soon came up to ask if I wanted Cumas to turn. I told him that for now, Ari was tending the woman. I wished I knew her name, but the only person that knew was the noblewoman, so I asked him to find the innkeeper for me. Soon, Sotiris came up the stairs, looking nervous.

"Where's Lady Berjouhi?" I asked.

He stared for a moment, and then glanced at the room. "Wasn't she in there, my lord?"

It was my turn to stare.

"Her clothes were torn when she arrived, so she's wearing one of Ileana's dresses," he explained.

I probably should have guessed that, but I'd thought she was just one of the inn's servants. Dismissing him, I went back to praying while I waited. After what seemed like an eternity, Galen walked up the stairs. He almost walked right past me and into the room, but I stopped him.

"If Lady Ari'an needs your assistance, she will ask," I told him.

He didn't seem happy about the situation and glared at me.

"If she needs you, she'll ask," I replied evenly.

He raised his fist and knocked on the door before I could stop him. I fought down the urge to glare at him. Ari quickly cracked the door.

"Diagnosis," he ordered.

Ari looked at him for a moment and then stepped out of the room, closing the door behind her.

"Do you have time to be out here?" I asked, knowing that I would have to talk to Galen about usurping me in this situation.

"I can spare a moment," she told me. "I have all the major wounds treated."

Galen impatiently waited, but I told Ari to take her time. She seemed to almost smile as she stared at the floor, and her eyes traveled from my boots to Galen's shoes.

"There are no broken bones," she finally began. "They beat her, but didn't break any bones." She wiped her hand over her face. "She had an infected gash"—Ari measured out about a forearm between her hands and then about a finger's width—"on her back. I cleaned it out. Nothing else is infected. I'm working on the minor cuts and the bruises now." She glanced back at the door. "I shouldn't be more than another watch."

"I should examine . . . ," Galen began, taking a step toward the door.

"No!" Ari blocked his path. "You'd terrify her if she wakes up."

He seemed on the verge of arguing, but Ari looked at him harshly.

"Trust me," she told him, "when she wakes up, she'll be frightened. Having you in there could send her into a fit."

He didn't seem happy about the situation, but accepted it and stepped back. Ari smiled wanly at me and walked back into the room.

"I don't typically assist," Galen snapped at me.

"I don't typically accept that tone from people," I replied angrily.

He stared at me for a moment, and then seemed to finally grasp the situation.

Taking a hard breath, he told me, "I'm not used to standing idly by and watching people bleed."

He racked his hand though his hair and then motioned me into another room.

Following him in, he pulled the door almost closed and whispered, "We brought her from the ford to here, and all that time, I didn't know if she was bleeding to death. You arrived just after we had."

"I understand," I told him, "but in Rem'Maren, I'm a lord, and you need to respect that."

He gave me a smirk, bowed, and said loudly, "Of course, my lord."

I glanced out the door and found Sotiris walking up the stairs. He was quietly carrying a tray of food.

"You have good ears," I told Galen, impressed.

"It comes from listening to so many hearts beat, my lord," he replied.

I walked out to meet the innkeeper. He glanced around without actually looking at either of us.

"I brought you some pigeon, my lord," he told me. "I thought you might be hungry."

I noticed that there was enough for several people. The man ducked into the room we'd just exited. He quickly arranged chairs around the table. When he exited, he glanced at the room where Ari was and shuffled his feet without moving.

"We think she will be all right," I told him.

The man glanced at me, and then at the room. "Thank you, my lord."

He quickly made his way back down the stairs, and we soon heard him telling someone else downstairs. I glanced toward the sound and found that it was Ileana.

I hadn't spoken much to the other woman in the room. Occasionally, I asked her to hand me something that lay near my kit, but other than that, silence reigned while I bandaged the young woman. The woman in the chair watched everything I did with a keen interest, but didn't ask any questions. It rattled my nerves when I thought about it, but most often, I was focused on the task at hand. Otherwise, I thought too much about what her captors had done to her.

When I finally finished, I sat on the end of the bed, and tried not to shudder. I wanted to have some control of my tremors before I faced Danren. He never liked it when I trembled. I believe it scared him. Focusing on that caused me to laugh slightly. Of all things, I could scare Danren, the lord who had defeated the great Lord Astucieux in single-handed combat. It was rather amusing. Glancing up, I found the other woman looking at me as though I'd lost my mind.

"I'm sorry," I apologized, "I was trying to distract myself."

"Successfully, I presume," the woman said with a thick Verdian accent.

I motioned at the door. "My husband is probably worried sick by now."

"You are the Lady Ari'an joined to the Lord Danren of the House of Rem'Maren?" she asked.

The formal question caused me to study her before answering, "Yes, and you are?"

She pronounced a title in Verdian, causing me to jump to my feet. I'd been asking a Lady of Verd to assist me while patching up what she would consider a nickin.

"Please, do not be startled," she explained, "I was traveling with Ozgur"—she motioned at the woman on the bed—"when we were ambushed." For a moment she paused and then asked, "Are you the lady that Sotiris speaks of?"

I took a moment to stop my hands from shaking before I could nod.

"You are also a . . . " She seemed to search for a moment and then said the Verdian word for *healer.*

"In a way," I replied, returning to my kit to pack my things.

"Are all the ladies of Faruq as versatile?" she asked.

I studied her for a moment and began to realize something.

"No," I replied, "I am something of an exception."

She seemed disappointed.

I quickly continued with my next question, "How old are you?"

She glanced up at me quickly, and then masked her surprise. "I do not see how that is relevant."

645

"Neither is whether or not I am a healer. We are, in fact, having a conversation," I told her, and then asked again, "How old are you?"

She seemed to debate for a moment, and then looked at me boldly, "Sixteen."

I nodded. That was what I'd thought. She was still rather young. It also explained why she was so bold.

"How long have you been smuggling people out of Verd?" I continued.

She paused again and then asked, "Is it true that you live with dragons?"

I cocked an eyebrow at her, as I finished putting away my equipment. "Yes."

"Do you live in one of their caves?" she continued.

"How long have you been smuggling?" I asked again.

She looked away almost shy and then gave me that challenging look again. "Almost a year."

"It is highly possible that a dragon's cave is nothing like what you imagine," I told her.

Her eyes widened before she caught herself and resumed a more dignified look.

I continued, "I live in a fortress built into a mountain, which is likely nothing that you would imagine it to be either."

Her eyes widened again. "Caer Corisan?"

I had to smile. She was trying so hard to be proper, but failing just as much as I used to when something exciting was mentioned.

"Yes, Caer Corisan."

I asked if she wanted to wait with Ozgur, and she said she did.

"Will you find out if a message could be sent to my husband?" she asked.

I paused at the doorknob, coming to terms with that revelation. "Who is your husband?"

She told me a title in Verdian and where his residence was. She also informed me that he helped with the smuggling.

A moment later, I went out to talk to Danren and Galen. Danren sent Hafiz and Einheim immediately. Since she'd been arrested, it was likely that her husband would be imprisoned or even executed as soon as word reached the other rulers in the area.

I asked for a tray of food for Berjouhi and Ozgur, which was quickly brought up, while Danren discussed what could be done for the two women. The inn was apparently a stop between the temple and establishment at a permanent location. Sotiris and Ileana could help Ozgur cope with the changes from the temple to a normal life, but what about Berjouhi? She couldn't return to Verd, and the inn wasn't suitable for a noble, even if she was in exile.

"Could she come to Caer Corisan?" I finally asked.

Danren stopped in midsentence, and Galen stared at me for a moment.

"What?" I'd been expecting that question.

"You've been asking me to consider having a lady-in-waiting, and that's a position acceptable for a young noble," I explained.

He stared at me for a moment, considering the idea.

"You barely know her," he argued.

"I don't know any of Majorlaine's daughters," I pointed out.

"She could be a spy," he tried again.

I could tell he wasn't putting a lot of effort into dissuading me.

"Do you think she would have been caught smuggling Ozgur out of her country if she was?" I pointed out.

He paused for a moment and finally asked, "Do you think you could be friends with her?"

I smiled remembering the excitement she'd often showed even in the few moments I'd spoken to her. "She reminds me of myself when I was young."

Danren watched me for a moment. "Would her being from Verd affect you?"

I fidgeted for a moment. "She was trying to help people who are in those temples. I don't think her nationality would bother me." I smiled. "Einheim's from Verd as well, and I'm friends with him."

Danren watched me again, and then finally smiled and nodded. "I might get into trouble for this, but I'll make it work for you, if I can."

"The counsel's just a bunch of old coots anyway," Galen cut in.

I stared at him questioningly. He was on the counsel.

Looking gruff, he stared right at me and said, "I would know, wouldn't I?"

I laughed.

Ari told Lady Berjouhi about our plan when she came down the stairs later.

For a moment, she gaped at Ari, and then seemed to regain some of her composure. "You live at Caer Corisan."

Ari nodded.

"With dragons." The excitement in her voice reminded me of what Ari had said.

The tall young woman looked older than her sixteen years.

Ari nodded again.

She clapped her hands together before she could catch herself. Quickly regaining some measure of control, she curtsied delicately and accepted Ari's offer.

CHAPTER 64

LADY-IN-WAITING

It was amazing to me how lively things became at Caer Corisan with the addition of Lady Berjouhi. I remembered how everyone had behaved when Ari was visiting or when she first came to live here.

Surprisingly, the counsel was not nearly as upset as I thought they would be. Yes, they went through the motions of being angry about my not consulting them, but they didn't demand several hearings about whether or not Lady Berjouhi would be allowed to stay. They did reiterate that I was not to tell her, but said they would discuss the matter of informing her after it became evident that she was capable of the secret. While I was having such semifavorable results, I broached the subject of letting any of Majorlaine's daughters come to live at Caer Corisan who wanted to, and was told they would discuss it. Well, at least that wasn't a no.

Meanwhile, Hafiz and Einheim executed a rather impressive rescue mission for Lady Berjouhi's husband.

When they arrived at the manor where the couple lived, Ishmerai was informed that the lord had been arrested and scheduled for execution because of his treasonous acts. He was to be transported to Sela, the capital, for a public display. Oddly, the transport entered the forest that lay between the manor and the capital, and was never seen again. There was a forest fire around that time, so it was assumed that the entire party was caught in the blaze and perished . . .

Lord Athanaric arrived the next week, appearing as shaken as anyone possibly could. He didn't seem thrilled with having to discuss his situation with a dragon. In fact, and not surprisingly, he didn't seem even slightly comfortable around even Einheim, who'd been traveling with him for several days.

An excited yell echoed around the courtyard, and the man spun away from me to find the sound. I watched his face change from surprise to relief as Lady Berjouhi came racing out of the main hall. She threw herself into his arms. I excused myself, backing away as he began a litany of questions involving everything from her health to how she'd gotten here. His eyes shone, and he began to relax for what must have been the first time in over a week.

I glanced around and found Ari watching the reunion from the entrance. Making my way toward her, I glared at a few gawking people around the courtyard.

"I'm glad he's all right," Ari told me.

"I wouldn't say 'all right.' His entire world collapsed in less than a month, but he is safe," I replied.

She smiled and told me, "She's been so worried."

"I can imagine." I motioned into the hall, and she walked in.

As I followed her, she told me, "Berjouhi's been trying to both decorate her rooms for both of them, and just her in case the worst had happened."

"Berjouhi? We're on a single-name basis now," I teased.

She smiled and replied, "Yes, as a matter of fact." Then she added, "Well, I don't in fact know about you, but she did say that Danren could call her Berjouhi." She looked almost shy for a moment as she continued, "He's coming back in a week and a half?"

I had to smile. "He'd come back sooner, but he's making up for the festival."

Footsteps behind drew our attention. As we both turned around, we found Berjouhi leading her husband into the hall. He was beginning to look nervous again.

"Your dragonship," she began curtsying to me.

For some reason she'd taken to calling me that. It was the oddest title I'd ever heard, but there weren't in fact leadership titles for any of the dragons.

"My lady"—she continued with a curtsy to Ari—"this is my husband, Lord Athanaric of Illtyd," she paused and then added almost awkwardly, "or formally a lord of Illtyd." Turning back to her husband, she introduced Ari and then informed him that he'd already met me. "Lord Danren is out on business"

"He is not here?" the young lord asked, before he could hide the shock in his voice or on his face.

"No," Berjouhi shook her head, "he had matters to attend to immediately after he returned from Rem'maren's—" She paused for a moment and looked horrified. Every once in a while she did this. She couldn't think of our word for something.

"Festival," I supplied for her and nodded to the lord.

He looked embarrassed for a moment and then said, "I am under the impression that you and Lord Danren arranged my rescue." He glanced at me, but I waited for him to continue. "I would like to thank you." He glanced at his wife for a moment. "We always knew the risks, but when I heard that she had been captured, I could not dare hope that something might save either of us."

"And now we're both here and safe," Berjouhi cut in. "Isn't it wonderful?"

Wonderful did not appear to be what he thought of the entire situation, but he smiled at his wife anyway.

Turning back to me, he continued, "I am not familiar with dragons . . . " He paused, glanced at his wife, and awkwardly added, "your dragonship. I know the stories which are circulated through my land, but those appear to be mistaken."

I was proud of the young man. It took a lot of courage for him to say all that.

"You are welcome, your lordship," I replied.

"Your dragonship," Berjouhi began. I needed to tell them not to call me that, but I wasn't going to interrupt her. "I know that you have done much for us . . ." She paused for a moment and then glanced at Ari. "I was hoping to ask another favor," she continued.

It was Lord Athanaric's turn to look confused, but before he could interrupt, she continued, "I request that you speak to Lord Danren about considering Athanaric as his armor bearer."

I should have told her that the dragon lords didn't typically wear armor, but only managed, "What?"

Out of the corner of my eye, I saw Ari stifle a laugh, but the shock on Athanaric's face was more distracting.

He stared at his wife for an instant, before politely asking us to excuse them. Their whispered conversation only carried a few statements to us. I caught that she was explaining that she was now Ari's lady-in-waiting, and that it would be a perfect position for him. He interrupted that he knew practically nothing about swordplay or armor. She tried to explain that Danren was a good lord and that it would be an honor to accompany him. There was a question about not knowing him for very long, and the explanation that Ari had told her a lot.

I glanced at Ari, who smiled and said, "You should consider it."

"What?" I caught myself and continued, "Danren can't take an armor bearer, squire, gentleman-at-arms, or whatever else you would like to call it anywhere when he turns."

"I know," she replied, "but he could have someone around when he's . . . available."

"Exactly how would the other half of the time be explained?" I hissed.

She smiled sweetly.

Trying to change the subject, I asked, "Exactly what have you been telling her about Danren?"

I was surprised to see her blush slightly. "I'd rather tell him."

At that moment, I heard the conversation end behind me and the couple start back toward us. Turning to acknowledge them, I found Athanaric looking nervous.

"Please, excuse my wife's overt request, but if the lord considers me for any position within his court, I would be grateful," the young man told me.

"You should ask him yourself when he returns," Ari told him.

I shot a pointed look at her, which she ignored.

"Would you like to join me for dinner?" she continued, motioning toward the dining hall.

Mintxo had been fussing over Ari and Berjouhi all week, insisting that they eat formally. I hoped it wouldn't have to continue when Danren returned, because . . . well . . . I enjoyed the quiet dinners alone with Ari.

Lord Athanaric had objected that he didn't have anything suitable to wear, when Berjouhi laughed and informed him that shouldn't be a problem. Faber would be thrilled to have another person to outfit. Berjouhi had expressed her awe multiple times at his ability to provide her with a suitable wardrobe so quickly.

I excused myself and left Ari to entertain the couple. She'd become fast friends with Berjouhi, and the new arrival would probably feel far more comfortable without a dragon around.

It took Athanaric longer to settle into life at Caer Corisan than it did Berjouhi. She seemed to find everything an adventure, asking more questions than I had ever thought of. Athanaric was far more reserved, although he did offer to let me call him only by his name after a week.

After watching Narden's polite but confused reactions to the "your dragonship" term, I informed both of them that they could just call him Narden. It took Athanaric the better part of the rest of the week to actually manage to stop.

He tried so hard to act like being around that many dragons was perfectly natural. There were more than usual about, because of everyone attending the festival. They were now making up the time. Athanaric would startle every few moments as yet another dragon landed, just walked by, or started blowing smoke into the air because of an argument. I had to reprimand both Jair and Ara'ta for purposefully getting into a brawl just to frighten the man.

When I handed him a headache remover and sleep aid one day, he looked so tense that he nearly dropped the packet of herbs. He stared at it blankly, before he finally managed to ask what it was. I patiently explained again, but he still looked baffled. I waved

Berjouhi over and told her to steep the herbs for a quarter of a watch, insist that he drink the mixture, and put him to bed. She laughed and merrily led him away.

Narden walked up behind me and asked if he was all right.

"No," I informed him. "Berjouhi told me that she didn't believe that he's slept much for several days."

"I don't doubt it," he replied. "He looks it."

"He'll be out for the rest of the day now." I chuckled. "He will wake up rested, but probably not knowing why he was sleeping."

Narden shook his head. "I wish there was something that I could do for him, but talking to him seems to make him terribly nervous."

"When will Danren be back?" I asked.

Narden grinned. "I would think you missed him with as often as you ask that."

He was teasing me, but I still felt my cheeks warm.

"Tomorrow," he told me.

"He should make it a point to spend some time with Athanaric," I advised.

"I believe he was already planning on it," the dragon informed me.

I was searching for the young man the next day when I almost ran into him as he walked groggily down the stairs from the nobilities' rooms.

He stared at me for a moment in shock, and then blurted out, "Who are you?"

I managed to keep myself from laughing at the question and replied, "Danren of the House of Rem'Maren." I watched his eyes widen, and a horrified look came over his face. "You must be Athanaric, formerly Lord of Illtyd."

He began stumbling through an apology, but I interrupted him, "It's all right. I'm not going to take offense."

He stared at me for a moment in disbelief, but finally managed to say very formally, "How do you fare, your lordship?"

I managed to stop myself before groaning. Somehow he had managed to stop calling Narden "your dragonship," but apparently he hadn't been told not to call me something similar.

"If you do not object," I began, "refrain from calling me 'your lordship.' This is Caer Corisan, the capital of Maren. I am here by leave of the dragons."

Again he stared for a moment. "I thought you were lord of Caer Corisan, your—" He cringed. "My apologies, I—"

I stopped him before he could continue, "I was searching for you."

He turned pale.

"Would you care to join me for breakfast?" I asked.

"I would be honored, your—" He cringed again.

Before he could begin another apology, I started back down the stairs. He followed quietly. The meal was also quiet. I tried to keep the conversation lively, but Athanaric didn't respond much. When he did, he usually tripped over a "your lordship" and wouldn't finish what he was saying. Finally, he glanced around.

"May I be honest with you?" he asked, in almost a whisper.

With as poorly as the conversation had been going, I was tempted to sarcastically tell him, "No! I want you to lie to me!" but didn't. Instead, I calmly told him, "I would prefer that."

He went perfectly still and forced himself to admit, "I am not comfortable here." I watched him quell a "your lordship" before he continued. "I realize that everything that I ever knew about . . . dragons is erroneous. I am trying to adjust to the change, but"—he glanced around nervously—"I do not know what to do." He looked at me, begging for help with the expression on his face. "What should I do? How can I keep from having one of them eat me?"

He almost began another series of questions, but I interrupted, "Dragons don't eat people."

He stared at me as though my head had just grown another set of ears.

"They do not?" he finally managed to ask.

I sighed. This was going to be a long conversation after all. I made up my mind to sit through it, even though there were so many things that I was behind on.

"No," I told him, "they don't."

"I was always told—" then he stopped. "I suppose that is the error. I was always told and never found out the truth."

I spent the next two watches explaining what I could about the alliance between Rem'Maren and Maren, what dragons did and did not do, and countless other things about dragons—from how to patch up a wound to how best to awaken a sleeping dragon. Athanaric sat enthralled through the whole thing. I knew that if any of his manners masters could see him at those moments, they would have been appalled. His eyes widened until I didn't think they could get any bigger, and then they did. It was rather impressive to see. Then his mouth slowly began to open. By the time I finished, he was gaping at me.

It took him a few moments to realize that I was finished. Finally, he closed his mouth and swallowed.

"I," he began, "I did not know."

"I would never have expected you to," I replied lightly.

He glanced around again and then leaned toward me. "If you will pardon the question," he began, "how did you manage to adjust to this?"

I smiled. I had probably had a harder time adjusting to the information that I was given than he ever would to merely being around dragons.

"I had twelve years to adjust," I shrugged.

"The training of Rem'maren's army is done in Maren then?" he asked. "You do not in fact go to be trained as knights?"

I shook my head. "No, we will never be knights."

He glanced around. "Where are all the youths then?"

I almost faltered on the question, but caught myself. I worded my answer carefully. "Basically, each youth lives as a dragon for those years. You won't see them at Caer Corisan."

He didn't reply for a moment, so I rose.

"If you will excuse me," I told him.

He stood as I did. "I have kept you from your duties. I am remiss. My utmost apologies."

I waved off his statement. "You needed the time. Don't worry about it."

I could feel him watching me leave the room and wondered how he would cope with the new information.

After working on too many things that I needed to accomplish, I found that it was already evening. Time had fled from me during the day, so I hadn't even been able to greet Ari yet. I'd seen her across the courtyard or at the end of a hall, but someone would appear demanding my attention before I could catch up to her.

CHAPTER 65

DINNER

As I made my way to the dining hall, my frustration mounted. I didn't want to have a polite conversation with Ari while dining with Athanaric and Berjouhi. I wanted to have a private conversation so I could find out how she was doing. So many things had changed during the festival and since. I needed to be certain that she was all right. She'd been friendly whenever Narden spoke with her, but it was impossible to have a completely private conversation with her as a dragon, especially, with extra dragons around.

As I gripped the door handle to the dining hall, I realized that my palms were moist. Opening the door, I found only Athanaric and Berjouhi. When Athanaric saw me, he instantly released Berjouhi's hand and appeared as though he'd been caught. Berjouhi laughed.

From what we had gathered, Ari and I knew that Athanaric's family had been smuggling people out of the temples for a generation. When he married Berjouhi and moved to a separate estate, he'd stopped working with his family for several months. Then Berjouhi discovered everything, and to his shock, she'd insisted they begin again. Berjouhi was so enthusiastic that his parents had wondered how they'd ever managed without her.

That didn't explain why Ari was late though. I couldn't think of any reason. There weren't any serious injuries. As far as I knew, Majorlaine didn't need her help this late in the evening. Typically, Ari was waiting for me. Had she lost track of time somewhere? That thought stung. I'd thought that she would be as excited to see me as I was to see her. Perhaps she was upset that I hadn't met her during the day.

Berjouhi watched me too keenly while I approached the table. Finally, I glanced at the table itself and found it was only set for them. They'd even begun eating.

"What's going on?" I asked skeptically.

Berjouhi laughed before answering. "I would consider it obvious that you should be with your wife."

I glanced around the room. "I was expecting her to be here."

Another laugh. "I believe she is waiting for you in your chambers."

"Why would she be waiting there?" I couldn't imagine that Mintxo would agree to a simple dinner like we used to have, especially since it was my first night back.

"I believe she is expecting to dine with you," was the smiling reply.

Turning around slowly, I made my way back through the doors while Berjouhi's laugh followed my confusion out. I could not fathom how anyone would be able to convince Mintxo to send a simple meal to our rooms, especially since it was my first day dining with Athanaric and Berjouhi.

When I reached our rooms, I realized that however much I wanted to speak to Ari privately, I was not prepared for this encounter. With my hand on the door handle, I attempted to gather my courage. What if, instead of just not meeting up with each other through the day, Ari had been avoiding me? What if her pleasant demeanor with Narden had just been a polite front? What if it was all over? I tried to prepare for the loss if it came, realizing that it would have been far better to lose her back when I'd believed she would divorce me. For her sake, I would cope, but . . .

Suddenly, the door swung open, and Ari almost walking into me.

I'd waited almost an entire watch. Where could he be? I thought that I'd soon be able to see the carpet worn through from my pacing.

Finally, I decided to find Danren. I knew that he was incredibly busy, but I also knew that I could convince him to come have dinner with me. I had to.

Flinging the door open in frustration, I almost walked into him.

"Where have you been?" The words were out before I could stop them.

"What?" I knew that would be the response.

Then I realized that he was planted in front of the door. "How long have you been here?"

He seemed to collect himself enough to answer, "A little while." Studying me, he asked, "Are you all right?"

The question surprised me. Why wouldn't I be?

I nodded slowly. "Is something wrong?"

I hadn't heard any alarms, but perhaps it was something that wouldn't be announced.

"No." He was still studying me as though he expected me to flee.

I felt my cheeks warm under his scrutiny.

"I missed you," I whispered, hoping to break the tension.

His eyes widened, and then a grin spread across his face.

I smiled back and asked, "Did you want to come in?"

He followed me in asking, "How did you manage to convince Mintxo that we should eat up here?"

"I didn't." I turned to see his reaction and found that he was only watching me.

"What?" he asked, looking down at me.

"Berjouhi arranged everything," I explained, trying to contain both my excitement and frustration.

"Berjouhi?" He was looking over my outfit.

"It was her idea, and once she explained her plan to Mintxo, he couldn't be talked out of it," I continued.

He still looked confused, but said, "You look beautiful," and then asked, "but why are you dressed formally?"

I felt like yelling, "Will you look around!" but managed instead, "It seemed appropriate."

"What?" He stared at me. "Why would you dress formally for a simple din—" Finally he looked past me.

I thought that his eyes might come out of his head if he kept staring like that. Berjouhi had completely redecorated the room with satin curtains and silk tapestries. She'd found everything buried in the storage rooms of the fortress. There were even intricately woven rugs on the floor. The furniture had been taken out and replaced with a long table and two places set at the far end. The table was far from empty though. The feast that Mintxo prepared would have fed us for a week, but I knew that the leftovers would be eaten. Berjouhi had found a beautiful couch to place in front of the fireplace as well.

Finally, Danren managed the one word that I knew was coming, "What?"

I laughed and took his arm.

"How . . ." he began and then changed to, "This was Berjouhi's idea."

"Mostly," I replied, managing to get him seated.

A grin spread across his face then. "Remind me not to worry next time."

I glanced up questioningly, as I set a cylinder into the box at the other end of the table. The music filtered through the room.

"I keep thinking that you might change your mind," he explained, as I returned to the chairs.

I looked at him, still puzzled as he rose and held my chair.

"I suppose you aren't having second thoughts about what happened at the festival then?" he asked, as he returned to his chair.

"Why would I?" I asked, as he poured my drink.

"It's something I worry about," he told me. "I keep thinking that you might get scared and . . ."

I smiled watching his nervous response. I knew I shouldn't be pleased that I could unnerve a dragon lord, but I couldn't help laughing a little.

He smiled at me and asked if I wanted lamb, soup, or salad to begin with.

I watched Ari carefully throughout the meal, but she seemed pleased with the event. Early on, I realized that I was quite under-dressed for the occasion, but I couldn't pull myself away to change.

When the meal ended, I decided that anything that I planned to do that evening could wait until tomorrow. Rising, I asked Ari if she would like to dance. Her face answered before she curtsied and took my arm.

Later, she asked to sit and watch the fire. When she settled against my chest, I couldn't think of anywhere I'd have rather been.

After several quiet moments, I asked the question that had been eating at me since I'd spoken to Athanaric that morning. "What have you been telling them about me?"

Ari glanced up at me and laughed. I couldn't help but laugh with her.

"Well," she began, settling against me again, "at first Berjouhi broiled me over what exactly you expected from me."

"What?"

"She seemed to be concerned that you were . . . well, I don't need to tell you, but don't worry, I convinced her that you were completely honorable," Ari continued.

"Honorable?" I could think of plenty times when I had failed Ari, so honorable shouldn't have been my description.

She just nodded though. "I explained how I had originally judged you, and . . . how wrong I was. I also told her how careful and concerned you are about me."

I ran my tongue over my teeth before replying, "I hope I can live up to your good opinion."

She smiled up at me and then shifted to lay her head on my lap. "You do."

I refused to let her start dozing as she had at the festival, so after about a watch, I sent her to bed.

She looked up at me expectantly when we stood, so I asked, "May I kiss you?"

I'd never seen her face light up quite like that before.

A watch later, after I had let Mintxo and Berjouhi carry away all the food that was left, and had thanked them for their thoughtfulness, I settled into my own room.

I was just beginning to doze off when I thought I heard a knock. I sat up and stared at my door, groggily wondering who would want my attention at that watch. I watched my door begin to open slowly and woke up substantially more.

"Danren," I heard Ari whisper.

"What's wrong?" I tossed my covers off and began to rise.

"N-nothing," she said softly, glancing everywhere but at me.

I watched her for a moment unable to think of why she would be standing there if nothing was wrong.

Her voice shook as she spoke again, "M-may I stay?"

"What?"

I'd made sure that I wouldn't be in this situation with her again. I'd sent her to bed early. I'd stayed up until everything was carted away.

"Please," she whispered.

I'd promised her that if she asked again . . . "You just want to sleep?"

I saw her nod and bite her lip.

"Are you certain . . . about this?" I had to concentrate to keep my voice steady.

She nodded again.

What was I supposed to do? I moved over to make room for her, and she quickly lay down.

Watching her shiver for a moment, I told her, "You don't have to do this."

"I know," she whispered and then shifted against me.

With her back to me, I couldn't see her face.

"Ari," I asked as calmly as I could, "are you certain this is what you want?"

I saw her nod.

After several moments, I asked, "Do you want me to hold you?"

She didn't respond immediately. I knew she was far too tense to be asleep already though. Then she nodded again.

He ever so gently placed his arm on my side as his hand rested against my stomach. I wanted to be here, I had to tell myself time and again. I wanted to be with him. Every breath seemed to be a struggle to keep from whimpering. Every instant, I fought to keep the shaking limited to my hands. I wanted to be here. He wasn't going to hurt me.

Painfully slowly, I began to breathe in something other than short gasps. Danren didn't move. He didn't do anything, but rest his hand against my stomach as I'd asked him to. I knew he wouldn't, but some part of me was still terrified.

Two watches were called before I managed to relax completely. Finally, I unclasped my hands and found that they weren't trembling any longer.

I knew that Danren had tried to stay awake with me, but he'd had a long day. I both heard and felt his breathing slow through that first watch. While he slept, he didn't stir.

When I woke the next morning, I found Ari sleeping against me. I still had my arm over her side, but during the night, I'd shifted a leg on top of hers. I tried to move my leg slowly so I wouldn't wake her.

Suddenly, she stiffened. A frightened cry escaped from her, and she bolted. She was out of the door before I could even think. I quickly rose and changed from my night shirt and sleeping breeches into clothes for the day. Then I hurried into the main room.

I could hear Ari crying softly in her room. Making my way over to the door, I made out a second voice.

"Did he hurt you?" Berjouhi asked.

Ari didn't give a verbal response that I could hear. I knew I needed to talk to her though. When I knocked on the door, Berjouhi flung it open and glared at me.

She began yelling at me in Verdian, but she was speaking so quickly that I couldn't make out what she was saying. I caught something about taking advantage, another bit about a ruining a nice plan, and I think a statement about swine's feet . . . but I wasn't certain about that. I watched her for a moment and then turned my attention to Ari.

"Are you all right?" I asked in a calmer voice than I felt.

"Of course she is not all right!" Berjouhi stormed at me. "What would you expect after what you did to her!"

"What?" I asked in surprise. Had Ari said that I'd . . .

Ari pulled herself to her feet. Her face was marked by tears, and she was shaking. "No," I saw her lips move, but no sound came.

Berjouhi began to rage at me in Verdian again. I wanted to push past her, but I couldn't bring myself to. What if Ari didn't want me around her? I tried to study the ranting young woman instead.

"What did she tell you?" I tried to sound calm, but it was hard with the young woman yelling.

"She did not need to tell me." She jabbed her finger into my chest. "I know what you did to her."

I saw Ari behind her and was shocked to see her try to pull the furious woman away. Her hands were shaking too much to manage a grip.

"Please," she whispered. "No."

The woman glanced at Ari and then glared at me. Ari was becoming more frantic.

I decided to remove at least one thing that was upsetting her.

"Get a fur blanket," I ordered Berjouhi, and then I did the hardest thing I'd ever done.

I walked away.

The morning was hard. I didn't eat. I decided to work on several monotonous things that I needed to accomplish. I knew that I wouldn't be able to focus on anything complicated. That didn't make any other task easier though.

The monotony gave me time to think. My thoughts kept traveling the same cycle. I'd promised Ari. She'd asked. Except for when she was lost in the tunnels, this was the worst episode that I had seen in years. She'd recovered so quickly when I'd found her lost in the tunnels. Would she recover this time? What had I done?

A noise behind me broke my thoughts. I turned to find Berjouhi standing there. She looked both nervous and confident at the same time. It was an odd combination.

"I need to speak with you," she began immediately.

At least she sounded calm. I didn't feel like going through another tirade. I nodded for her to begin.

"What happened?" She didn't look accusatory, but I wasn't certain that I wanted to tell her.

She was Ari's lady-in-waiting though.

"I'm not certain," I began.

"What happened last night?" she prodded.

I fought the urge to tell her to mind her own business. She probably needed to know to help Ari.

"We ate dinner," I summarized, "danced a little, and then talked."

"You danced?" she pried. "Was that your idea?"

Swallowing my temper, I replied, "I asked if she would like to. Ari knows she can refuse."

"Does she?" Berjouhi asked pointedly.

I couldn't keep the glare completely out of my eyes. "Dancing together was not my idea originally. Ari insisted."

"Did she?" the woman asked.

I knew that I couldn't keep my temper out of my reply, so I remained silent.

"Did you insist that she sleep with you?" She looked directly at me.

"What?" I gained control after a moment and a few breaths.

All she'd probably seen was Ari fleeing from my room that morning. If Ari had been too upset to explain, of course Berjouhi would jump to that conclusion.

"No," I finally managed as evenly as possible, "she asked." Before she could ask anything else, I held up my hand to stop her. "Look, if I intended to harm her, would you be here?"

Her puzzled expression told me enough.

I began to explain, "I have asked Ari for months to accept a lady-in-waiting. I wanted her to have someone to help her, especially when I'm away. If I were going to harm her . . . force her, as you seem to be implying, you wouldn't be here."

The woman was silent for a few moments, watching me intently with something between a vicious glare and acceptance on her face. I wondered how she managed such contradictory expressions at the same time.

"That is what Ari'an informed me," she finally said.

"What?" I stared for a moment, and then snapped, "If she already told you that, why were you interrogating me?"

"I desired to hear your explanation," she said evenly, turned on her heel, and walked away.

When I realized that she was gone, I slumped against the wall. No wonder Athanaric always looked so confused! His wife was an enigma!

I needed to find Danren. Every time I considered leaving my room, fear took over. Try as I might, I couldn't determine exactly what the fear was from. I shouldn't be afraid to talk to Danren. Somehow, I knew that it wasn't facing Danren that scared me. I knew Danren. It was more general than that. I found myself asking for the Mighty One's mercy, and so much more. By evening, I knew what I needed to do in order to defeat my fear. What I didn't know was if Danren would agree. I refused to live like this though.

I was concerned about Berjouhi's reaction as well. I had tried to explain, but I knew I didn't make any sense for a while. Finally, I'd convinced her that Danren hadn't hurt me. Then she'd left. A watch later, she'd returned with a tray for the midday meal. I didn't eat much. When I asked her to arrange for Danren to eat with me that evening, she looked as though she had never heard such a horror before. I insisted, and she finally gave in.

It was difficult to believe Berjouhi when she found me just before the evening meal. Ari wanted to eat with me. After what had happened, I never expected such a request. Berjouhi saw my confusion, but didn't comment on it.

I was slightly annoyed when she insisted on escorting me to my rooms. She probably wanted to be certain that I didn't hurt Ari. The distrust stung, but I could understand it. When she opened the door and I stepped through, I immediately found Ari staring at me from the fireplace. She looked haggard.

"Ari." I wasn't certain if he actually said my name or only mouthed it.

I could tell that he was upset. His concern was written across his face. Once I took the first step toward him, I found that I could finally cross the room. In a moment, I found that I'd thrown myself into his arms. I felt him take a breath of my hair.

"Are you all right?" he asked.

He tried to push me away, but I couldn't let go, not yet.

I tried to nod, but found that a sob escaped instead. A moment later, I jumped in surprise when I heard the door close. Glancing up, I found him staring at the door. I looked at the door myself, wondering what could possibly be so interesting about it. It looked the same to me as it always had.

"What?" Danren asked.

For once the question didn't tell me anything. Typically, I had some idea as to what he was confused about. I felt my mouth work, but couldn't manage any words.

"She left." He sounded puzzled. Before I could manage to ask why he would think Berjouhi would stay, Danren explained, "After the . . . talk we had earlier, I didn't expect her to leave."

He fished a handkerchief out and began to gently brush away my tears. I just stared at him, hoping that she hadn't yelled at him.

"Do you want to talk?" he asked when he finished.

I nodded. He led me to the long table that was still set up from yesterday. Berjouhi had cleared away the dishes, but had refused to allow anyone to take the furniture. I smiled slightly at the memory and glanced up to find Danren looking slightly relieved. I explained how that young woman had stared down Mintxo when he'd come for the leftover trappings.

Danren smiled, but didn't laugh.

"What is it?" I asked, wondering why he wouldn't find that humorous.

"Having been on the other side of one of those encounters, I probably can sympathize with Mintxo too much," he explained.

"You've only been back two days?" I couldn't imagine that he could have offended Berjouhi. Then I remembered his previous comment. "What did she say to you?"

He shrugged.

"What did she say to you?" I insisted.

"She only asked a few questions," he summarized.

"What questions?" I realized later that I had managed, at least for these few moments, to forget my own fears and problems.

He studied me for a moment and then sighed. "It was just some questions about my role in last night." My puzzled looked caused him to continue, "Ari," he paused for a moment, "I never expected you to ask again. Berjouhi was . . . concerned that I had demanded that you sleep with me."

"What?" I exclaimed before realizing that I'd only said Danren's phrase. He didn't seem to notice, and I continued as quickly as I could manage, "I told her what happened."

"She said that," he replied. "I think she just wanted to . . . confirm the story."

"Should we send her away?" I asked.

I liked Berjouhi, but if she was going to accuse Danren, I wasn't certain that she should stay.

"What?" At a different time, I might have laughed at his shocked look. "Send her away because she was concerned about you?"

I hadn't thought about it like that.

"She shouldn't have thought that you would . . ."

That he would what? A few years ago, I would have thought the same possibilities about Danren, but not anymore.

"She doesn't know me," he replied evenly. "Yes, being interrogated by . . . that young woman"—he watched for me to smile, and I did—"was . . . uncomfortable, but if she hadn't shown any concern, I would have wanted her to leave."

"How did you get to be so . . ." I searched for the word and had to settle for, "good?"

He smiled. "I'm only trying to follow my god. I don't always succeed."

I smiled back at him and set my hand on his.

He started to pull his hand away. "I don't want to hurt you."

"You won't," I replied.

He stared at me for a moment. "How can you say that after . . ."

From the way his face suddenly paled, I could tell he hadn't meant to say that.

"I was scared," I explained as best as I could. "It wasn't your fault. I was just scared."

He studied me for a moment, and then said softly, "Ari, I'm sorry."

"I don't blame you," I insisted.

He smiled slightly. "Thank you."

CHAPTER 66

TO NOT LIVE IN FEAR

It took me a couple of days to carry out my plan. The main room was refurnished. Berjouhi wanted to rearrange things completely, but I wasn't certain that I could handle anything more yet.

I did manage to tell her what I was planning. When I looked up, I found her staring at me as though I had misplaced my senses.

"You cannot possibly mean to!" she exclaimed.

"Why not?" I asked.

I'd expected some sort of surprised response, but her horrified expression was a bit much.

"You were terrified last time," she insisted.

"I don't want to live in fear," I told her.

"Do not repeat what frightened you then," she told me.

"No," I realized that I was fidgeting with my fingers. "I don't want to be scared of this."

It took me most of a watch to convince her of my determination.

"I have never seen any who has been so long from the temples," she finally told me. "I do not know what to say."

"I'll be all right," I insisted, "Danren won't hurt me."

She studied me for a long moment and then nodded slightly. "I will believe you."

It took me another day to take hold of my courage enough. I waited until Danren's light went out, before crossing the main room. Slowly, I pushed open the door. I saw Danren immediately sit up.

"Who's there?" he demanded as he reached for his sword.

"It's me," I managed.

"Ari?" His surprise stopped him before he was fully out of the bed. "What's wrong?"

"Nothing," I managed just above a whisper, and then forced myself to take a step forward. "Please, may I stay?"

The silence extended for a while, and then the question I was expecting, "What?"

I couldn't manage an explanation at that moment.

All I could whisper was, "Please?"

The last thing I ever expected was to be in this situation again. I had begun sleeping with my sword on the table next to the bed back at the festival. Continuing that practice didn't seem like a bad idea, since Lord Astucieux wanted my reputation destroyed. I wasn't certain that he wouldn't make another attempt. This way I was prepared wherever I was.

I wasn't prepared for this.

"Ari . . ." What was I supposed to say? "Why?"

When her voice finally answered, it was broken, "I don't want to live in fear."

That still didn't help me decide what to say.

Finally, I managed, "You want to sleep with me to defeat your fear?"

There was another silence before she whispered, "Partly."

"What?" This still wasn't making sense.

"Please," she whispered.

"Why?" I barely managed. I couldn't make out her face. I couldn't even tell if she was playing with her fingers because she was nervous.

She finally answered, "I want to."

"What?" I couldn't have heard that.

When her voice broke again as she answered, I crossed the room and was holding her before I could catch myself.

"I know I'm safe with you," she told me.

Her body was shaking slightly, but as she leaned against me, she began to relax.

"It was so nice to fall asleep in your arms. When I woke up, I panicked. I shouldn't have been scared, but I was." After a moment, she whispered, "Please, let me stay."

"Mighty One have mercy," I breathed. It took me several moments to manage, "Are you certain this is what you want?"

I felt her nod and heard her whisper, "Yes."

Before dawn the next morning, I woke. Again, I found that I'd shifted my leg over hers while we were sleeping. As carefully as I could, I moved, turning away slightly. Immediately, I felt Ari tense. Again, before I could even think, she bolted for the door. Sitting upright, I covered my face with my hands and groaned. Not again.

The door didn't open. I looked up just in time to catch Ari as she threw herself at me. I wasn't certain if she would try to attack me or just wanted to be held.

"It's all right," I told her as calmly as I could manage.

Her body was tense and shaking.

"I'm sorry," she managed. "I—" A sob broke from her, interrupting whatever she was going to say.

"Mighty One have mercy," I prayed.

She cowered in my arms for at least half a watch. Occasionally, she would glance around with a terrified look on her face. Then her head would duck back against my shoulder. Slowly, she stopped sobbing, then she stopped crying, and eventually, she stopped shaking.

I was upset with myself for being so scared. I knew Danren wouldn't hurt me. Stopping before I opened the door, I turned and saw Danren's devastated look. I ran back to him. I had to hold on to what I knew about his character.

I cried, upset that I'd questioned his integrity again, upset that I couldn't control my fear, and just because I was so scared.

When I was finally able to speak coherently, I howled, "I shouldn't be like this."

I felt him take a deep breath, but he didn't reply.

"I'm sorry," I whispered.

I could only imagine how upsetting this was for Danren.

"It's all right," he whispered. "I didn't mean to scare you."

"You didn't," I blurted, and then clarified, "It's not your fault. I shouldn't be like this. I should be able to . . ."

He took a deep breath again and told me, "You don't have to do this."

"I want to," I felt my voice break slightly. "I know I'm safe with you," I tried to explain. "It's so nice to be in your arms."

"You're going to come back tonight, aren't you?" he asked softly. "You don't . . ." his voice broke, and he took another breath, "have to."

"I know," I whispered, "but I want to."

I wasn't certain what to say next. It wasn't wrong for her to want that. I hoped that I wasn't giving into her requests just because I wanted her near me.

"May I get something?" I finally managed to ask.

Ari looked up at me and then leaned away, relaxing her grip on my arms. I quickly rose and opened my closet. From the top shelf, I pulled down the fur blanket that I kept there. Returning to the bed, I tossed it around Ari's shoulders. She watched me as she pulled the blanket around herself. She looked like she might begin crying again.

"May I grab a couple handkerchiefs?" I asked.

Her lip quivered as she nodded, and I saw a tear begin trailing down her face. I quickly pulled open the dresser drawer and snatched a handful of handkerchiefs. Again, I returned to the bed. Sitting next to her, I began mopping her face. A few more tears escaped her eyes, but she didn't start sobbing again.

Hearing the dawn watch called, I asked, "Would you like to watch the sunrise?"

She glanced at me, and then at the window, before nodding.

I quickly rose and pulled back the curtains. The window was glassed clearly, one of the marvels of Caer Corisan. Many of the windows had this type of glass. No one knew anymore how they had been made so large, perfectly clear, and able to rise into the wall to allow air in.

I returned to Ari. I sat and leaned against the headboard, staring at the increasing light of the mountains. The rustle next to me drew my attention, and I soon watched Ari lean against my chest.

"I love you," I whispered, before I could catch myself.

She looked up at me and smiled. After trying to say something for a moment, and not managing whatever it was, she turned back to the window.

Her face cleared as the sun appeared. I'd seen her across the courtyard watching the sunrise before. It was amazing seeing the rays pick-up the color of her hair, almost like watching a controlled fire. The hues ever changing. It was magnificent.

When the sun had fully appeared above the mountainous horizon, I looked up at Danren. He smiled at me with an unusual almost hazy gaze.

"It was beautiful," I told him, glad that my voice had finally settled, and I didn't feel like crying.

"Mmm," he mumbled, smiling more broadly, and taking a breath of my hair.

He'd done that several times while the sun crested the horizon.

"Did you even watch the sunrise?" I asked, beginning to feel like teasing him.

"What?" His gaze finally cleared.

He looked up at the window and stared for a moment.

Glancing back at me, he looked embarrassed and finally answered, "Partly."

"What were you watching?" I quipped.

He reached up and ran his fingers through my hair. Then he seemed to realize what he was doing and pulled his hand away.

Danren swallowed hard before answering, "I guess I was watching the sunrise in your hair."

I pulled a handful around to look at it. My hair was mostly tangled from sleeping. I should have braided it, but I had such a weak grip on my courage that I hadn't wanted to wait once I knew that I was coming to Danren.

I felt him take another breath of my hair and then pull back.

"It was like watching a fire," he said nervously.

"It's red." I felt the tears begin to build again.

I hated the red in my hair. I tried so hard to hide it.

"It's . . ." he took a strand and fingered it loosely, before softly saying, "beautiful."

The statement stopped my tears. I stared up at him shocked.

"How can you say that?" I yelped.

He looked at me for a moment.

Mighty One have mercy, I prayed silently. It took me an instant to understand why Ari would object to my compliment.

Carefully choosing my words, I told her, "Just because your hair is a little red doesn't mean you are worthless."

She gasped and then ducked her head.

"You are a beautiful woman, Ari, and that includes your hair," I continued. "They're wrong."

At that statement, she looked up again, but didn't reply.

"You were created by the Mighty One, and he doesn't make mistakes. Any who believe that just because someone has red hair is inferior are wrong." I took a breath. "They can make it seem like their belief is valid, but it will never be true. The truth doesn't change because of someone believing or not believing it."

I watched her swallow and look back down at the handful of her hair that she held.

"Thank you," she whispered.

I smiled. "Are you feeling up to starting your day now?"

She looked up and smiled back. "I already started my day, but if you want to lounge around the rest of the morning, I'll leave you to it." She continued teasing, "*I* have work to do."

I laughed and watched her walk toward the door. As she turned the knob, she looked back at me.

"Thank you," she whispered.

I swallowed hard and replied, "I love you."

Her smile made her face light up, and then she left.

I left Danren's room and looked up to find Berjouhi hurrying toward me. She looked like she'd been pacing.

Immediately, she began plying me with questions, "Are you well? Did he hurt you?" and any number of others that asked the same thing.

"I'm all right," I replied.

"What happened?" She pulled me toward my own room, opened my door, and hurried me in.

I explained briefly that I'd slept with Danren, again become scared, but managed to stay.

Feeling a smile warm my face, I added, "And we watched the sunrise."

Looking up, I saw that Berjouhi was staring in disbelief at me.

"He did not force you?" she finally asked.

"Of course not!" I snapped defensively.

Then I remembered that she didn't know Danren.

"He would never force me," I added more calmly.

She still continued to stare. "How could he not?"

It was my turn to look confused, and then I began to explain that Danren kept his word. Even to his own hurt, he would not break his promises. We both followed the Mighty One and desired to honor him. Part of that was Danren's unwillingness to break his word. He would on very rare occasions, but that usually involved saving someone's life. I explained how he'd helped me, when I'd fallen into the river on the search for Dreanen's antidote. Also, I explained how he'd believed that I would either divorce him or at least leave because of such occurrences.

When I finished, Berjouhi continued to stare at me. She quickly recovered her voice though, and began plying me with questions about both Danren and the Mighty One. The questions ranged from comparisons of the gods she knew to the Mighty One to why Danren would touch me now if he'd promised not to.

I explained as best as I could about the Mighty One, noting the difference between the festival that was to thank Him and the traditions I grew up with to appease the gods of my family.

Danren was easier to explain, but I did have to take a few moments to tell her that I had released Danren from some of his promises to me.

"Will you release him from his promise not to bed you?" she finally asked.

I felt my cheeks warm at the question. Part of me screamed, "NO!" and insisted that I would never be safe if I did. Another part gently reminded me of Danren's character. I knew that even if I did release him from that promise, he would not take advantage.

"I don't know," I finally told her.

At that moment, the next watch was called, and I realized how much of the morning was gone.

"Will you come with me?" I asked, as I jumped up to change out of my sleeping garments. "I will be more than willing to answer your other questions while we work."

CHAPTER 67

CHANGES AT
THE FORTRESS

It had taken Berjouhi several days when she'd arrived to come to terms with all the tasks that I did around Caer Corisan. She'd asked if all the ladies of Rem'Maren worked like servants. I'd laughed. I didn't mind the work, and it didn't feel like servants' work to me.

Explaining that Caer Corisan was different from anywhere else wasn't difficult. It was in fact rather obvious. She'd had trouble comprehending that there were only a handful of permanent residents while everyone else was passing through on their way somewhere. Once she'd watched the comings and goings for a few days, she'd understood though.

As we worked that day, I discreetly examined Berjouhi. I had wondered about something during the time she had resided here, but I wanted to be certain before I brought up the subject. As I watched her, I decided to ask.

Pulling her aside at a free moment, I told her, "I have something to ask you."

She smiled warmly, waiting for the question.

"Are you with child?"

Her face paled for a moment, and then she glanced around, asking, "How long have you known?"

"I've thought it was possible since the first week you were here," I explained.

She looked shy and abundantly happy at the same time. "I wanted to tell you, but Athanaric was not convinced that I should, because of our status."

She grabbed my hands and danced around me in a circle. "I will tell him that you know. He will have to let you tell others."

Before I could stop her, she raced off to find her husband. I laughed at her joy and wondered if that was how women normally felt about having a child.

I continued on to the injury stables to help Einheim with a cut wing. Before long, I heard footsteps. I knew whom those steps belonged to. I had realized that I knew the sound back at the festival. The hilt of his sword would click against his belt, and one stride was ever so slightly shorter than the other.

I hurried into the walkway between the stalls. Feeling the smile that I couldn't help spread across my face, I felt my cheeks warm slightly.

I was slightly nervous about finding Ari. She was supposed to be in here. At least this was the last place anyone had seen her. I waved to Einheim as he left a stall and walked out of the door. I considered asking him if Ari was still here, but glanced down the walkway before I could say anything. Her face glowed as she hurried toward me. I felt my pace quicken slightly and couldn't wipe the grin off my face to save my life.

I stopped about four paces from her, but she took the next steps. It was wonderful to have her in my arms. I took a deep breath of her hair, felt her shift closer against my shoulder, and decided to kiss her hair. I felt her laugh and almost forgot that I'd come to ask her something instead of just to find her. Ari took a step back and looked up at me.

I glanced around and then softly asked, "May I kiss you?"

Her smile answered before her nod.

After a moment, I found her standing at arm's length again. It was amazing to see that smile on her face, especially knowing that it was directed toward me.

"I need to know something," I told her eventually. "I heard something about Berjouhi."

The look on her face changed to one of concern. "What did you hear?"

"I wanted to find out if you knew anything about it, but I was also looking for her to find out for certain," I explained.

"What did you hear?" she asked again, shaking my arms slightly.

"Do you know if she's with child?"

Ari's face paled, and her voice didn't sound convincing when she asked, "Where did you hear that?"

"Did she tell you, or is it just a rumor?" I prodded.

"Who told you?" She looked slightly frantic.

"You don't want to know how many people told me," I explained. "I got lost after hearing from Galen that Mintxo told him."

"They rarely even speak to each other," Ari exclaimed.

"My point exactly," I replied. "I need to know if it's true or not. Caer Corisan is good about not prying into secrets, but news does travel fast. I need to find out if Berjouhi or Athanaric said something or if one of the boys just started a rumor." I paused. "If it's not true, I need to put a stop to it before anyone leaves on patrols."

"I'm not supposed to say," Ari told me, ducking her head.

I smiled. It was fairly clear what the answer was, but if they didn't want anyone to know, I would honor that.

"Do you know where Athanaric or Berjouhi are?"

Ari shook her head and then leaned it against my chest and shoulder. It was amazing to be able to hold her, and for a few moments, I enjoyed her presence.

A voice behind me interrupted too soon. "What would become of Athanaric and Berjouhi, if Berjouhi indeed was with child?"

I quickly pushed Ari away and turned to face the young woman. I was a bit too dazed to properly handle another confrontation with her. Studying her for a moment, I realized again that she had a unique way of portraying several things at once. Currently, she looked excited, nervous, and pleased. Perhaps there was a slight hint of realizing a suspicion. At least, she didn't look angry.

"I would have to discuss how that would affect their status," I replied.

"Danren!" Ari exclaimed behind me. "We can't send them away."

I turned back to Ari. "I'm a coregent here."

She smiled mischievously. "I doubt Narden would have an objection, if you don't."

"I'd also like to discuss this with Armel. I respect his advice." I tried to hint that there was more to this.

"Armel turned Caer Corisan over to both of you, in its entirety, last year." She smiled. "It was his decision then, and who stays or goes is your decision now."

"Do you believe that raising a child here would be unsafe?" Berjouhi asked.

I turned back to face her. "No, it would be safe. Possibly safer than most places." I couldn't help but smile. "The place would probably liven up the way it did when"—I glanced at Ari, now standing next to me—"you came."

"Which time?" she asked.

"Both," I replied evenly.

It was wonderful to hear her laugh.

"You are not concerned that the dragons would injure a young child?" Berjouhi asked.

"What?" I quickly phrased a different statement, "The dragons would not pose a threat to any child." I quickly clarified, "I would expect you to ensure that your child didn't wander into the injure stables or training areas."

"Then they can stay?" Ari asked.

I stared blankly at her for a moment before I realized what that statement must have sounded like. "I still need to discuss this with Armel . . . and Narden."

"You knew they were married when you agreed to let them live here. Children were bound to come eventually," Ari pointed out.

The argument was valid, but I quickly explained why I'd never considered it. "I try not to think about children."

I suddenly felt terrible. Of course Danren didn't think about children. It probably hurt him too much to consider them. He excused himself to find Armel and left before I could say anything in reply.

"The two of you are married?" Berjouhi's question shook me.

I looked at her puzzled and tried to word a reply. My mouth worked, but the words didn't come.

"You are legally wed," she reworded her question, "it is not just said to protect you?"

I stared at her for a moment. "Yes, we're married."

"He has never demanded children of you, even one heir?" Her words stung even though they were in a normal tone.

This young woman was far too perceptive.

"No," I hugged my arms, trying to keep the trembling in my hands from showing. "H-he has the right to, but . . . h-he told me once that even though he has the right, that doesn't make it correct for him to demand . . ." I bit my lip, fighting tears.

I heard Berjouhi step up to me, and then she hugged me. I laughed through my tears. Danren had been right. It was nice to have someone to talk to.

"I am afraid that I misjudged your husband," she told me. "I now believe he is the honorable man you told me he was."

I smiled slightly. "Perhaps you should tell him that."

After a moment, she agreed that she would. I glanced up and found that her expressive face looked embarrassed.

She looked around, growing excited again. "Athanaric is concerned that the dragons might hurt our baby."

My shocked look must have caused her to clarify. "Not intentionally, only they might step on one so little. They would not know that a baby would not move. Perhaps burn him by accident."

"Are you hoping for a boy?" I asked, needing a moment to stop feeling defensive.

Her excited expression changed slightly to add a note of apprehension. "I had, but I do not know now." Before we were desirous of an heir, but now . . ." her voice trailed off before she continued, "There is nothing to inherit."

I spontaneously hugged the young woman. "Even if you leave Caer Corisan," I assured her, "Danren will see to it that you have a comfortable place."

Her one-word answer surprised me, because she was normally so verbose. "Why?"

I caught myself before replying with Danren's one-word answer, "What do you mean?"

"I heard that your Danren hated everything and person of Verd," she explained, her face reflecting her honesty. "Why would he be concerned about our welfare?"

"No," I explained as best as I could, "Danren doesn't hate the people . . . well, he probably would at least threaten or possibly kill any of the priests on sight." I remembered how he'd reacted at the funeral to the priest who'd spoken to me, and he hadn't even known who the man was.

"So would I," Berjouhi mumbled.

I looked up surprised and then laughed. "I don't think Danren could hate you considering what the two of you did."

Her excited face took on a hint of worry. "Did you know that we received a letter from Athanaric's parents?"

I nodded.

She added surprised to her expression. "You did not ask."

"If you wanted to tell me," I replied, "you would. Otherwise, your business is your own."

The surprise deepened. "Caer Corisan is like no place I have ever been." She continued as an excited smile brightened her eyes. "I have the feeling that several people knew that I was with child before you asked."

I smiled. "I wouldn't be surprised. Caer Corisan is good at keeping secrets."

Berjouhi had a quizzical look on her face but didn't reply.

"Have you seen Galen yet?" I asked. "He'll want to make sure that you're both well."

"No," she replied, "I was considering asking Majorlaine some questions."

"Either one would be fine, but either one will breathe fire if you don't see them first," I teased.

Whichever one was first would gloat for the next week. The other would fume. It was going to be an interesting week.

"Could you not?" she asked, bringing me out of my thoughts in time to catch an odd look on her face.

"Me?" I fought off memories of being roughly examined. "N-no, it would be better if either Galen or Majorlaine saw you."

"Would you come with me?" she asked nervously.

I glanced up. It surprised me that this confident young woman could be nervous. This was her first child though. She had every reason to be a little scared.

"Of course," I told her.

As we left the stable, Berjouhi suddenly clapped her hands and did a little hop. "I know! We will ask both!"

I laughed in agreement, wondering all the while if she would still be able to make such sudden movements in a few months.

I found Armel looking over some of the water pipes around the kitchen. We'd had a little trouble with one of the large lines not running clear.

"I've been expecting you." He glanced up and then continued working.

"Of course," I replied. "Then you know why I'm here."

"Tell me anyway," he responded, while pulling one of the pipes off.

I was concerned that water would spray out, but realized when it didn't that Armel would have stopped the flow before doing such a thing.

"Berjouhi is with child," I began, "and I'm not sure whether they should stay here with a baby."

"Galen is fully capable of delivering a baby, and if Berjouhi is uncomfortable with him, Majorlaine can also," was the reply.

"I know it would be safe for Berjouhi to deliver here," I informed him. "I even know that everyone would be as careful as possible around a little one. No one has ever even singed Ari, and I know we'd be even more cautious with a baby."

"Do they want to stay?" Armel asked, sounding odd because of his head stuck into the pipe.

"I'm not certain. Berjouhi seems to, but I haven't spoken to Athanaric yet. I have a feeling that he's concerned about the child's safety, but I don't know if he has other worries as well," I told the pipe.

"Caer Corisan was built to support families," Armel's voice told me, and then echoed through the other end of the fixture.

It took me a moment to grasp that. I'd never seen more than ten permanent residents at Caer Corisan. The place could be run with very few people, because there were rarely more than fifteen dragons coming or going on any given day. The structure wasn't set up for that though, I realized. The corridors that led into the mountain continued for leagues. There were any number of places that could open into the air like Ari's garden did. For several moments, I took in the information that this was designed to be a thriving city, not a tiny stop between here and there.

"Your actual concern is the counsel," Armel's voice said, in the pipe with his legs sticking out.

"Well, yes," I replied. "I'm already in their disfavor, because of the incident with Ari."

"Someone is always in the counsel's disfavor. If it wasn't you, it would be someone else. Also, not all the counsel was against your decision," the pipe told me.

"Yes, and I appreciate the support," I replied.

"Did I ever tell you about what I did to infuriate the counsel when I took over?" The ankles wiggled.

Surprised that there was a story that I hadn't heard from Armel, I said, "No, I don't remember that."

The pipe laughed. "We used to cart water from the falls."

"What?" That was absurd. "The falls are on the other side of the mountain."

"Indeed," he continued. "I had marveled at the ingenuity of the cave homes set into the mountains. Each with simple access to water, and wondered why this place would be designed without such a convenience."

The pipe banged for a few moments before continuing, "I started exploring and found that not only was this place to have an easy water source, the system was ingenious."

More banging occurred before he continued, "The counsel was livid that I would set such a system back up. 'We were fine before,' was the basis of their argument. 'We don't need to change.' Not a one of them complains now. They have trouble even thinking about Caer Corisan not having such a luxury."

"So you're saying that I should ignore the counsel?" That didn't sound right to me.

"No"—the ankles wiggled for a little while—"but you should examine motives. If the reasoning is just because it's tradition without any solid backing, there's no real reason to keep it. Also, if there are no qualms from the people actually involved, there isn't necessarily a problem. Finally, you were given charge of Caer Corisan to rule as you see fit. You've got a good mind and a solid faith, use them."

I laughed. "I really don't have a problem with them staying," I told him as I rose to leave, "but I'll pray and think about it a bit more."

"Before you leave," the voice asked, "would you give my legs a yank?"

I stared at the pipe for a moment and then laughed again. "I guess you're glad I came along," I told him as I helped him out.

After a couple more days, and a discussion with Athanaric about his concerns, we decided that the expectant couple could stay as long as they wanted.

A few days after that, I received the summons to see the counsel. They were occupied with several matters currently and would not be able to schedule my visit for a couple months. That told me two things. There were those on the counsel who didn't approve, but most of them didn't see a problem with my decision. In a slightly odd way, that was encouraging.

CHAPTER 68

OLD DRESSES

As fall faded into winter, I decided to clear out my closet. Faber might be able to find another use for some of my fancier dresses, or perhaps he could rework them so that I could use them again for something.

Berjouhi helped sometimes, mostly insisting that I try this dress or that one on so she could see how it looked. She often cooed over the designs, complimenting Faber's work so much that, I knew if he ever heard, he would turn bright red from embarrassment. He did enjoy having his work admired, but he blushed easily. I always found that surprising. I thought he would have more control after two centuries, but apparently, he didn't.

It took us a couple months to accomplish this closet cleaning, since Berjouhi and I both did any number of other things around the fortress. I had decided to finish one night after she retired. It wasn't late, but Berjouhi fatigued early in the evenings now. I only had a few dresses left to sort anyway.

When I pulled out the last one, I froze. I hadn't seen this dress in half a decade. The simple beauty of it was still apparent. I could almost feel the terror again from the last time I'd worn it. Fighting my fear away, I looked over the dress. There was no reason this dress should make me afraid.

It was beautiful in its simplicity. The lavender fabric gleamed even in the lamp light. The two pieces didn't seem damaged in the least from my neglect. Wondering if it would still fit, I tried it on. It was actually a bit loose in places. Probably because I was far more active here than I had been at Torion Castle.

I heard movement in the main room. Wondering if Berjouhi had returned for some reason, I walked out. It was Danren, but the look on his face made it worthwhile.

He stared at me for a moment, and then managed to close his mouth.

Slowly walking toward me, he asked, sounding quite concerned, "Have I missed an occasion?"

I shook my head and smiled, watching his eyes admire the dress. He wouldn't notice that it didn't fit perfectly.

"This was the last dress in my closet," I explained.

His eyes grew wide for a moment, and then he said in a tone that told me he was trying to remember. "I've seen this before."

I nodded and spun around letting the skirt flare out a little. He stepped up to me when I stopped and gently fingered the tiny golden chain around the collar.

"It wasn't at the funeral. It's too celebratory for that," he told me, concentrating, "and it certainly wasn't at the festival."

"I could have worn it at the festival," I teased.

"You didn't," he told me, walking around me in a slow circle.

"You know that for a fact," I teased again.

He glanced up at my face, and I saw him blush slightly even in the low light. I gasped, realizing that he remembered every dress I'd worn at the festival.

"It's beautiful," he told me, looking into my eyes and placing his hand against my cheek.

"You don't remember where you saw it," I returned to teasing.

He looked so embarrassed as he shook his head. "Where else have we dressed formally?"

I laughed. "Perhaps early on in our marriage," I hinted, "*very* early on."

He concentrated for a moment, and then recognition dawned on his face. "You . . ." he stopped and gaped at me. "You're all right wearing this?" he finally managed.

I nodded. "I was a bit frightened when I found it, but I'm fine now."

He returned to fingering the tiny chain; deep concentration on his face.

"What is it?" I asked wondering what could possibly make him focus like that.

"I remember not liking the chains," he told me. "I thought they made my new wife look like a prisoner. I didn't like that idea. Marriage shouldn't be a prison."

"Do you know the story behind this dress?" I asked.

"What?" he replied.

I laughingly explained how my original dress was ruined in a mishap, and how Faber created this dress in only three days.

"The chains were easy to place," I explained. "We didn't have time to create lace or anything like that."

"You're having some of these dresses redone?" he asked.

I nodded.

"Are you going to have him rework this one?" he continued.

I smiled. "Perhaps. Would you like to have the chains replaced?"

His mouth worked for a moment, and he finally managed to softly ask, "Do you feel like a prisoner?"

"No," I quickly told him. Realizing that I needed to reassure him, I continued, "I feel loved."

He stared at me for a moment, and then a broad smile crossed his face. "I do love you, Ari." He caressed my face for a moment and then asked, "May I?"

I smiled up at him and nodded. It was wonderful to have him kiss me while I was wearing this dress.

His hand caressed my back under my hair, traveled down to my waist, and then began to return. I know he didn't intend to. The two pieces of the dress fit so perfectly together that no one would guess they weren't one. Returning, his hand slid under the top piece of the dress and touched my skin.

Danren froze, and then I felt him begin to pull away after an instant. I didn't want him to leave yet, so I kissed him back. After a moment, he relaxed slightly, returning my affection. I felt his fingers move against my side, and then slide up ever so slightly.

I didn't know what might happen. Fear and excitement battled inside me. Before I could stop the sound, I whimpered.

Immediately, Danren tore away.

Mighty One have mercy! What had I done? How could I? Backing away, I ran into the desk and heard everything tumble across the surface. I stared in horror at Ari for a moment.

"I'm sorry," I finally managed. "I didn't mean to hurt you."

Turning, I fled to my room. When the door closed behind me, I sank to the floor. What had I done? After a moment, I heard what might have been a sob. How could I do that to her?

"You didn't," I managed to whisper to the closed door.

I stumbled to the desk chair before my knees wouldn't support me. I fought the tears and lost. Hearing the broken sob come from my throat, I forced myself back to my feet. Again, I stumbled forward until I reached my room and closed the door behind me.

My garments were strewn everywhere. There wasn't a place to even sit anymore. I wasn't certain that I had ever intended to use this room again except to dress, while Danren was here.

My tears were angry now, not frightened. I wasn't angry at Danren. I knew that. For a long time, I struggled to comprehend what I was feeling and why. I wasn't upset that Danren had touched my side. That was an accident. I wasn't upset that he'd left his hand there, or had caressed my skin, or even that he'd begun to move his hand.

I'd been scared, but not terrified. I wasn't certain what would happen. We'd never been in that situation before. I knew that Danren could stop. He'd proved to me time and again that contrary to anything that the temples in Verd taught, men could control themselves.

One watch passed, and then another. I changed out of my dress and then stared at it. I ran my fingers over the fabric and cried again.

I prayed through another watch as I slowly calmed, sitting against my door with my head on my knees. I wanted Danren to come looking for me. I wanted to have him hold me and comfort me, but I knew that he was just as upset as I was. Why, though, was I upset? He hadn't done anything wrong! He deserved to do more, especially with everything that I'd put him through.

Suddenly, I discovered why I was upset. I stared at the dress for a long time as I accepted the realization. I wasn't upset that he'd touched me. I was upset that he'd stopped. Feeling the emotions flood through me, I knew that I'd wanted him to continue.

CHAPTER 69

REDEEMER

It took me at least half of another watch to come to terms with that. The rest I spent trying to decide what to do. I was scared. That was understandable though. To actually realize that I wanted a man to bed me was terrifying.

This wasn't just any man though. This was Danren . . . my husband. A man who was so entirely committed to my welfare that he questioned every time I wanted to do anything more intimate. He loved me so deeply that he never would ask to bed me even though he had admitted that he wanted to. In those moments, I realized that his desires were defined by his loving commitment to me as well. He would never consider approaching another woman for favors because he loved me so deeply.

I cried again. Trying to come to terms with what I wanted. I knew I loved Danren. I'd known that probably since I'd demanded that Adenern take me to see him. I was terrified to admit it. If he knew, he might try something had been my reasoning. I was a fool. Danren would have been honored to know, but he would never have taken advantage of that information.

I wanted to trust him. I knew I could, but it was the difference between the knowledge and the action that trapped me. My fear was as much of a bond as anything the priests used to tie me with. I'd done many things to get past those fears, but I needed to do this as well.

Hurrying from the room, I went to the kitchens to prepare a tray of food. There I left a note that no one needed to bring food later. Next, I left a note for Majorlaine that I wouldn't be able to help her the next morning. There were few people, whether humans or dragons, in transit right now, so she wouldn't need my help anyway.

I wrote up another note and hurried to tack it to Armel's door so he wouldn't come looking for Danren. Returning to the kitchens, I grabbed the tray.

Then I made my way back up stairs. It was two watches before dawn, and I didn't like the idea of waking Berjouhi. I knew it was necessary though. I would have to explain to her so that she wouldn't attack Danren later on. She would also be able to keep anyone from disturbing us.

After placing the tray on the table, I made my way to her and Athanaric's rooms. I knocked on their main door, but no one answered. That wasn't surprising, they should be sleeping. I quietly opened the door and walked to their bedroom. Knocking again, I called out for Berjouhi. After another try, I heard movement in the room.

She soon emerged looking sleepy. "What is amiss?" she asked, adding concerned to her expression.

"Nothing," I reassured her. "I just needed to tell you not to disturb us until someone comes for you, and if you would make sure that no one else disturbs us as well, that would be nice."

Skepticism clouded her expression. "Ari'an, would you explain what you intend to do?"

"I intend," I tried to sound sure of myself, "to convince Danren to bed me."

For a moment, she was speechless, and then she said several not quite coherent statements. I wondered if I should be impressed that I'd managed to strike her wordless. As best as I could, I explained that I was in fact sane, I wasn't ill, and I wasn't drugged. It took me a bit longer to explain that I wanted this.

When I finally convinced her, I went back to my bedroom to dress. I decided to wear my wedding dress. It seemed appropriate to me. After taking a little time to brush and pin my hair nicely, I found that there was nothing left for me to do but wait. I walked into the main room, paced, and prayed.

I couldn't find answers to my questions. Praying didn't seem to help. I should apologize to Ari. After passing through several watches, I walked into the main room. Ari's room was dark. Perhaps she'd been able to sleep.

I paced around my room and then heard movement in the main room. When I peered out, I saw the doors close. A tray of food lay on the table in the middle of the room now. Why had someone been up that early in the kitchens? Glancing at Ari's room, I found it was still dark. I turned back into my room and sank onto the bed, praying again.

I was startled awake by the calling of the dawn watch. Rising, I held the curtains back to look across the courtyard. Ari wasn't on the far parapet. She wasn't watching the sunrise. I needed to find her. Pausing at my door, I wondered if it would be better if Berjouhi found her. Ari might not want to see me. Pulling the door open, I walked out, heading for the hallway.

"Danren." The voice froze me in my steps.

Turning, I found Ari, standing near the balcony, the dawn light catching her hair. She looked beautiful . . . I shouldn't think that!

"Ari." I took a few steps toward her before stopping. "I'm so sorry. I never meant to hurt you. I . . ."

She laughed. I stared at her for a moment as she walked toward me.

"You didn't hurt me," she told me.

"What?" I stumbled on my thoughts for a moment before managing, "I did scare you, and I didn't mean to. I should have . . ."

Again she interrupted, "You didn't do anything wrong."

"What?" How could she believe that?

I couldn't convince my mind to say anything as I stared at Ari.

"You never changed out of your dress," I finally managed.

It wasn't what I wanted to say, but at least it was something.

She glanced down and smiled. "Actually, I did."

"What?" That didn't make any sense.

"I decided to put it back on." She looked back up at me.

"What?" This time I at least managed another question as well. "Why?"

She blushed and bit her lip before saying, "I thought you might like to continue."

"What?" I stared dumbly at her as she picked up my hand and placed it on her side, against her skin, and under the dress.

As quickly as I could, I pulled away and stepped back. "Ari are you all right?"

She nodded, smiled, and stepped toward me. I backed up a few more steps and ran into the desk again. I turned to catch whatever was rolling off, missed the inkwell, and watched it land on the floor. At least it was capped.

Turning back, I found Ari right there. She was so close that I could smell the fragrance from her hair. Reflexively, I backed into the desk again and cringed.

"You know I just spent the last half a watch picking that all up and putting it back," Ari told me.

"I'm sorry," I quickly replied, trying to take a step away from the desk, only to find her right there.

She smiled almost teasingly.

Taking a deep breath, I tried to steady my thoughts. Even through the scent of her hair and the feel of her presence less than a hand's breadth from me, I forced some measure of composure.

"A-Ari, why are you doing this?" I didn't like the shaky sound of my voice, but at least it was a complete, legitimate question.

"I told you." Her tone had that playfully teasing sound to it.

I didn't want to ask this, but I needed to get her to back away. "Are you trying to see how far you can push me before I break?"

She stared at me for a moment, but didn't move away.

"I've been torturing you," she finally said. Before I could answer, she continued, "Every time I've asked for something more, it's been torture for you. You've had to change all the rules you lived by with me, and all the time, you wanted more."

"Ari," my voice broke on her name, but I tried to continue anyway, "I never asked for more. I didn't mean to touch you like that yesterday. I'd . . ."

"Never ask," she finished for me, "but you admitted that you wanted more."

"Ari," I began again, but she didn't let me finish.

"You're not asking now." She swallowed quickly before continuing, "It's a gift. It's not something to be demanded, or sold, or bartered, or stolen. It's supposed to be sacred, not cheap. It's supposed to be a physical act to reflect a marriage commitment, to consummate the joining of a couple for a lifetime."

I stared at her, realizing that she'd just repeated what I'd told her months ago at the festival. It wasn't just a statement now. She was offering, and I was having trouble breathing.

"Ari," I finally managed to whisper, "why?"

She watched me for a moment and then said softly, "I want to be your wife, Danren, completely."

When she leaned against my chest, it took every bit of strength I had not to put my arms around her.

"Ari," I began, but she interrupted with just one whispered word.

"Please."

Reflexively, I then put my arms around her.

I almost pulled back, but paused to ask the one question that I had to know the answer to, "Are you certain this is what you want?"

Turning her face up to me with a smile, she nodded and then softly answered, "Yes."

"If you're scared, we don't have to," I tried to qualify.

"I'm going to be a little scared," she replied, finally taking a step away from me, her hand still laced in mine.

"I don't want to hurt you," I continued.

"You won't," was her reply.

How could she be so certain?

"If you want to stop, just tell me."

I realized then that I was following her toward my room.

She smiled back at me. "I won't."

"I mean it." I stopped her just before walking through the door. "If you want to stop at any time, I will."

Her eyes misted for a moment. "I know," she told me and then tugged me the few steps into the room.

"Should we tell someone . . . something so we're not interrupted?" I didn't exactly want to explain, but I certainly didn't want Berjouhi or anyone else walking into even the main room.

"Don't worry, I took care of all of that." She smiled, momentarily looking nervous and biting her lip.

"We don't have to do this," I told her. "I'm supposed to leave this morning."

Ari glanced down. "I know." She laughed ever so lightly. "I knew I had to work this out now, because I won't see you for almost a month."

"If you want to wait," I began, but she interrupted.

Her smile was teasing again. "Wait? Then you'd have any number of arguments lined up."

I smiled back down at her and tried to run my fingers through her hair. Almost immediately, a little comb snagged my hand, causing her to cringe.

"I'm sorry. I didn't mean. . . . I didn't think that . . ." I stumbled over the apology.

Ari laughed.

I gently removed the little comb from her hair and then stared at it in surprise. Turning her head with the tip of my finger, I found the matching one on the other side.

Removing that one as well, I finally managed to say, "I gave you these."

She nodded. "For our second anniversary." She fidgeted with her fingers as she continued, "I'm sorry that I didn't get you anything that year."

"Do you actually like them?" I asked. The design had struck me as something she would like since they were made as matching butterflies resting on roses. "I've never seen you wear them before."

"They're beautiful," she replied softly. "I never wore them then because they came from you. I just found them again while I was cleaning."

The thought of those years was painful. We'd come so far. I glanced down at Ari feeling my mouth go dry. I desperately wanted to do this right, which was going to be difficult, because I'd tried never to think about any situation like this.

After fingering her hair for a few moments, I finally managed to ask, "Would you mind if we prayed?" When she just looked confused, I added, "Just quickly."

Ari laughed.

"That's a wonderful idea," she said as she stepped into my embrace.

I don't remember most of what I actually said. Most likely I asked for guidance. I begged for it in my heart. When I finished, I heard Ari thank the Mighty One that I'd accepted this gift.

When she looked up, laughing, she asked, "Are you finished stalling?"

I decided to tease her back. There was no reason that I couldn't enjoy these moments to their fullest.

"No," I told her. "I'm just getting started."

Her eyes went wide, and I wondered if I'd scared her, but she quickly recovered and teased, "Well then, take your time."

After placing the combs on my dressing stand, I returned and spent as long as I wanted just caressing her hair. She leaned her head against my chest and seemed to enjoy the attention.

When I moved to tracing her face with my fingers, I tried to remember every line, every time she smiled, and every time her eyes widened.

I came to a standstill after caressing her neck. That little delicate chain laced up the front of her dress, and I couldn't see a tie anywhere. I was about to ask when Ari laughed. Glancing at her face, I saw a look of recognition there.

"Here," she told me and placed my hand at the bottom of the lacing where the chain connected to the skirt. "There are two little clasps."

I continued to stare in confusion for a moment before seeing what she was talking about. It took me longer than I wanted to finally get the chain loose. After unthreading it, Ari shrugged the piece to the floor.

Focusing on her eyes, I set my hand on her shoulder and gently began to turn her. Confusion marked her eyes for a few steps, and then they took on a look of fear and pain. I stopped.

"If you don't want to . . ." I began, but before I could finish, she turned the rest of the way.

I saw her bite her lip, and still look at me over her shoulder with a fearful gaze in her eyes.

"You don't have to do this," I told her.

"I know," she replied. "I trust you," she continued. "You won't hurt me." She gave me a shaky smile. "I already told you that I was going to be a little scared."

I continued to watch her face as she fought her fear.

After a few moments, she smiled again and told me, "It's all right."

I laughed as the tension broke. Wasn't I supposed to tell her that?

Slowly, I studied her back. I had hoped that the scars would have faded more than this. They were less obvious than when I'd last seen them, but they were still clearly there. When she'd first arrived at my cave, some of these had still been fresh. Most were short, from quick blows. A few stretched across her back. One in particular ran from her shoulder across her back to disappear under her skirt's waist.

I released a ragged breath and grimaced. I was having a difficult time keeping my temper. At that moment, I felt again that I should go to that temple and tear every stone and beam apart.

Finally, I managed to look back at Ari's face. To my surprise, she no longer looked scared. Now, she looked concerned.

"It's all right," she told me.

I didn't mean to snap, especially not at her, but my tone was harsh as I demanded, "How can you say that? After all they did to you?"

She took a breath and turned to lean against me. "Because, my love, the Mighty One is a redeemer."

I stared at her coming to terms with her words.

"What they did will never be right, but the Mighty One brought good from it. Almost all of Faruq is now aware of what happens in those temples. You are helping to rescue others from those places with the connections that Athanaric and Berjouhi have. My sister is married to a good man."

"What about you?" I managed to ask.

"I'm married to a man who loves me so deeply that he would hurt himself for years to keep his word to me. You taught me that I could still love, and I do love you, Danren." I saw tears begin to course from her eyes, and I quickly brushed my thumb across her cheek. "You helped me heal." She ended ever so softly. "I wouldn't have you if it hadn't happened."

"That doesn't make it right." My temper had left me as I watched her cry.

Now, I felt helpless.

"No," she repeated, "but the Mighty One is a redeemer."

I sat in the main room, staring out the open balcony. Danren had left in quite a hurry only a little while ago. I laughed to myself at the memory.

He'd been so gentle with me. That's what had surprised me the most. I'd expected him to be rough, possibly to accidentally tear my dress or grab me too hard. That was what I had always experienced before. With him though, every touch, every kiss, every caress had been gentle.

I could feel the tension and excitement in him both through my own touches and his. The control he showed was amazing. So many times he stopped and told me that we didn't have to continue, that we could stop, or asked if I was certain. Even though I had to fight my fear at every new touch, I didn't want him to stop. I wanted to finally consummate the marriage we'd had for this many years.

How slowly he moved to something else was wonderful. I could tell that he was trying to memorize every part of my body. The time he took blessed me too. I could control when I was scared, and by the time he moved to something else, I was enjoying his attentions.

When he finished, he held me so close to him. I'd heard him talking, but couldn't quite make out the words at first. Then I'd realized that he was praying. I felt tears in my eyes yet again, as I heard him thank the Mighty One for the gift that I'd just given him.

His words had slurred after a short while, and then faded completely. To my shock, I found that he'd fallen asleep. A jolt of terror ran through me. Sometimes the men at the temple would fall asleep when they were finished with me. It was a task completed, and then they moved on to the next important thing.

I shook those thoughts loose as I remembered how haggard Danren had looked when he left his room that morning. I knew then that he hadn't slept much that night. I should have gone to him sooner, but I couldn't change that anymore. It was no wonder that he'd fallen asleep. He must have been completely exhausted.

I'd watched him sleep for a little while, and then nestled against his chest. I could hear his heart beat and feel his breath in my hair. I added my own silent thank-you prayer to the Mighty One as I tried to sort what I felt.

I realized that I'd dozed off myself, when I heard Danren exclaim in horror, "I fell asleep!"

I jumped at the sound and looked into his face.

"Ari, I'm so sorry," he told me looking frantic. "Are you all right? Did I hurt you? Are you scared? How do you feel?" The questions came so quickly that I had to wait until he stopped before I could answer.

I laughed, and he looked at me as if I'd lost my mind. He seemed to calm slightly after a moment.

I replied, "I'm all right. You didn't hurt me. No, I'm not scared."

"How do you feel?" he repeated.

I'd been trying to figure that out, and as I looked into his concerned face, I finally knew. "I feel whole."

He gaped at me. For a moment his mouth worked, but he couldn't seem to actually say anything.

Then he held me tightly against his chest and whispered, "Thank you."

A few moments later, the second watch of the afternoon was called. I felt Danren sit up partially at the sound.

I looked up at him and found him staring at the closed curtains in horror.

He looked back at me and choked out, "I have to go."

"I know," I told him.

I had never intended for this to take so long, but once Danren fell asleep, I knew that I wouldn't wake him.

"Will you be all right?" he frantically asked me.

I nodded.

"If you get upset, you'll find someone, right?" he continued.

"I will," I told him, though at that moment, I couldn't imagine ever being upset again.

"Maybe I can get back in a week," he'd told me.

I laughed and informed him that if the counsel let him go in a week, he still had everything else to accomplish along the border.

"Two then, I might be able to make two," he informed me.

I laughed again.

He looked distraught. I knew he didn't want to leave me.

"Three tops, I should be able to get everything done in three weeks at most."

"I know," I told him.

When we'd left our rooms a little while later, we'd found Berjouhi sitting in the hall working on some embroidery. I'd felt a blush creep up my cheeks under her scrutiny, but she'd only nodded when Danren asked her to check on me after he left.

When we'd found Armel, he almost began to say something, but instead just looked the two of us over. I almost felt vindicated when Danren flushed under the questioning gaze. After Danren turned, I waved as they took off for their meeting with the counsel.

Now, I sat staring out the balcony. Danren would probably be gone all three weeks. On top of the meeting with the counsel, he wanted to check the passes before they closed up completely, and make a thorough check of the mountain borders. Things had been quiet all summer, but there had been a few attacks in the autumn.

Berjouhi came to speak with me later in the afternoon. It didn't take as long as I'd thought to reassure her that I was all right.

I asked her to go after a little while, wanting to be alone with my thoughts and feelings. When she returned to call me to dinner, I requested a few things brought up. Her concern was evident, but she soon returned with a small tray.

Again, she studied me, and again I seemed to meet her approval. At first, I was a bit offended, but then I realized that she was concerned. Her actions were those of a friend.

When I walked into my room that night, I suddenly remembered that I had done nothing about the clothes piled all over my bed. It took me a moment to decide that Danren wouldn't be upset if I slept in his room. He might even consider it a compliment. The familiar atmosphere helped put me to sleep.

In the middle of the night, I woke from a nightmare. I fought the terror, upset that a wonderful day could be ruined by an imagined danger. Curling into Danren's blankets, I caught his familiar scent. I calmed as quickly as I could, wishing he was there. Finally, I dozed off again.

The next morning, after watching the sunrise, I went to find Berjouhi. I'd promised Danren that I would, and though I was all right now, I wanted to keep my word.

CHAPTER 70

WHEN PLANS CHANGE

The next week and a half passed without any other incidents. Then one morning when I approached the stairs to the courtyard, I had a sudden surge of terror coupled with the desire to throw myself down those steps. I froze, trying desperately to place the thought. I'd done that a few times at the temple. By doing that, I'd caused myself to lose one of the . . .

No, that was impossible! I couldn't be . . . Things like that didn't happen after only once . . . I realized that I wouldn't know. I'd never before had the option of only once.

Hurrying back to my room, I collapsed into the chair by the fireplace. I needed to cope with all the emotions raging through me. Terror tried to dominate, but occasionally, I'd feel excited, worried, or confused.

Eventually, I managed to consider the possibility with a little more reason. I counted days in my head, thinking back over the last month. I quickly realized that I'd know for sure by the time that Danren returned.

The meeting with the counsel was uneventfully eventful. Even though no specific decision was reached, it was noted that since I was in charge of Caer Corisan, I did have the authority to decide who lived there on a permanent basis. I was informed that I was still to keep my oath about the turning.

The issue about Ari knowing had disappeared a while back. It was accepted as a fact, even though they couldn't agree whether or not it was the right decision.

Einheim and I checked the passes before the snow began to fall. We were stranded for a few days because of the storm. Checking borders when we couldn't see just wouldn't work.

Although it was still cloudy, we headed out when the snow stopped. We'd at least be able to check several leagues of terrain before it started up again.

I heard the shout just before I saw the glint against the snow. Hollering a warning to Einheim, I dove to the side. The ballista bolt skimmed past my shoulder and tore through my right wing.

Angling away from where the bolt launched from, I crashed through trees, ripping scales off as I checked my fall. A sickening crunch sounded as I collided with a thick trunk. Pain tore through my right shoulder, and the world was suddenly black.

When I woke, the night sounds surrounding me said that I was at least still alive. Opening my eyes, I glanced around, and saw nothing. Slowly, I raised my head and felt pain knife through my right front leg, shoulder, and wing. The snow fell away from my face at least, and I found that I was alone. I forced my concentration to focus and could make out muffled dragon prints in the snow around me. There were no human ones as far as I could tell. I didn't know what had happened to Einheim, but at least there were no attackers to deal with.

I needed to put distance between myself and where they might be. I knew that I'd landed at least a league away from their camp. The river was farther on. I couldn't hear any search, but the thickly falling snow could be muffling the sounds. That could work in my favor as well. It was currently obvious where I had landed, but if I made it to the river, I could drift downstream without leaving a trail. If the snow kept up, it could cover my tracks but wouldn't change the downed trees.

Traveling would make a search difficult for either side though. I couldn't risk being found by the hunters, so I started toward the river. My progress was slower than I liked because on top of being unable to fly, I couldn't put weight on that leg. It was the middle of the next day before I made it to the river.

When I arrived, the only thing I wanted to do was collapse and sleep. I compromised and collapsed into the river. The current took me leagues downriver before I could make it back to the shore.

I tried to stay awake, but failed. Soon I found that I was in a pattern. I would wake, feeling like my body was on fire. Stumbling to the river, I would lay half in and half out, trying to cool off. Later, I would wake again, feeling half frozen. Then I would stumble to a covered embankment nearby and pass into oblivion.

I began to hallucinate. The fever that I suffered from bending events around me to its own purposes. Occasionally, I thought I heard Ari's voice. Other times, I heard Galen or Armel. The fever turned each voice from a memory into a nightmare.

The three weeks passed, and I knew. I managed to calm my terror to a mild thought. Excitement, however, kept trying to take over. I was adept at hiding my condition. I'd learned that at the temple. Whether that was good or bad, I couldn't quite tell, but I knew that I wanted to tell Danren first.

When the three weeks were almost past, Einheim returned alone. His side was torn up, but the damage was mostly superficial. Narden, he told us, had been shot down. Einheim had been able to remove the attackers, but hadn't been able to rouse Narden when he'd found him in the forest.

Einheim had flown for a day and a half to reach us this quickly. Immediately, Armel sent out search parties. Soon messages came back informing us that Narden wasn't at the attack site. Another snowstorm hit, grounding the search for days.

As the weather warmed enough to melt the snow a little, they continued looking for Narden.

I was sick with worry. I knew I had to eat, but forcing down the food was hard. What if he never came back?

I prayed for his safe return, and watched the skies.

A week and most of the next passed without a sighting. Hope was fading faster than the days. He'd been alive when Einheim had left him, but each day that passed . . . What would happen if he didn't return?

One night, a loud knock woke me from my light sleep. Hurrying to the door, I discovered Ishmerai standing there.

"They found him," he told me, "but he's in bad shape. His wing's torn through and his shoulder's dislocated."

I could tell there was more. "What is it?" I quickly asked.

"An infection's set in, and he's delirious with a fever because of it," he told me after a moment's pause.

"Where is he?" I asked, hurrying toward my room.

"Galen requested that he stay in a room downstairs," he told me.

I waved him away and ducked into my room to change. Then I made my way to the empty rooms below.

Galen's request made sense. A delirious dragon had a tendency to light things on fire. The stables, even though they were stone, contained a lot of items that would burn.

The roar of pain led me directly to where they were. I peeked in the door to find Cumas standing over Narden. He was moving Narden's front right leg gingerly. The roar must have been from when Cumas set the shoulder.

Narden was pale. He was unconscious now with his head lulled back against the window. He was barely breathing.

I began to enter the room, but Cumas looked up and demanded that I stay out. I didn't want to believe that Narden might injure me, but there was no guarantee that he would even realize who I was.

"Get some broth going," Cumas ordered from the room.

I quickly went to the kitchen to set up a large pot of chicken broth. It was unlikely that Narden had eaten while he was missing. At least he was a dragon currently. He could make it considerably longer without food, water, or sleep in that state.

When the broth was hot, I pulled over a wheeled table, set the pot on it, and made my way back to the room.

After adding some medication to the liquid that Cumas requested, I pushed the wheeled table next to Narden and hurried back to the doorway. I watched as Cumas managed to get most of the broth down Narden's throat. Narden swallowed, but didn't seem to know what was happening.

Another week passed before we had the infection under control. There was talk for a while about amputating the wing, but that was a last-chance suggestion.

When the swelling finally began to recede, it was still three more days before the fever broke.

After the first week, Narden had not even breathed smoke, so I'd insisted that I be allowed to help more closely.

Whenever I'd managed to doze off, I'd been next to him. I read to him from his book, but couldn't tell if he heard me. Even if his eyes were open, there was a haze to them, as though he couldn't tell what was actually around him.

He'd finally fallen into a normal sleep the night before. The fever was no longer tormenting him with nightmares. I leaned against his side and let myself doze a little.

I felt cool stone beneath me, which made no sense at all. Shouldn't I feel either nearly freezing water and mud or frosted ground? Pulling my eyes open, I found myself staring out a window. What was a stone wall and a window doing in the middle of a forest?

Hearing familiar voices outside, I focused on the scene. Galen and Majorlaine were arguing about something or another. Exactly what, I couldn't make out. Slowly, I realized that I was looking across the courtyard of Caer Corisan. The exact angle I was watching from was unfamiliar though.

I turned my head to look around the room and found Ari staring at me from my side. At that moment, she was leaning against me, but she quickly rose and stepped toward my head.

"Do you know me?" she asked, touching my nose.

"What?" A moment passed before I realized that I'd probably been unconscious and possibly delirious for a while. "Ari . . ." I was going to apologize, but she flung herself on my face, wrapping her arms around my nose like she used to.

She pulled away after only a moment, and I could see tears shining in her eyes.

"You're going to be all right now," she told me.

I laughed, but the sound didn't come out right, and I ended up choking. Ari quickly ran to fetch a bucket that was on a wheeled table.

"Here," she told me, "drink this."

The bucket had water in it. I began to take long swallows as she went back to the table for a large pot. She set the pot down next to the bucket.

"I'll get more water and have Majorlaine make some actual soup," she told me.

Hurrying to the door, she glanced back at me and told me, "I won't be long. I'll find Galen too. He'll want to see you."

I didn't want her to leave, but I knew she'd be back soon. As I glanced out the window again, I realized that I had no idea what day it was.

I ran into Galen first. I saw him coming in from the court-yard and quickly told him that Narden was awake. He immediately headed for the room, while I continued on to the kitchens.

Majorlaine wasn't in the kitchen when I arrived, but she walked in while I was filling several buckets with water and setting them on another wheeled table. I'd left the one I had been using in the room. It was surprising that I could think clearly enough to fill the buckets.

Narden was awake. Galen had said that if he woke up, there would be a far greater chance that he would recover. If it wasn't for the heavy buckets of water, I might have danced or skipped.

After asking Majorlaine to make some soup, I went back to the room. When I neared the door, I heard Narden's common exclamation.

"What?" I paused for a moment as he continued in a growl, "How long?"

The growl sounded weak. It would take him a while to get his strength back.

I entered the room with the table, and both of them looked at me before continuing their discussion in lowered tones. After closing the door, I pushed the table near Narden and began to pull off one of the buckets.

"That depends on how quickly the wing heals. If you turn now, you will not be able to fly again," Galen continued.

"You're certain?" Narden asked.

When Galen nodded, Narden sighed heavily. "How long?"

"I will check it again in a few days," he replied. "If you rest, you might recover quicker."

Galen nodded to me on his way out, and I found myself alone with Narden. He looked irritated by the news, but I could understand that.

"Are you all right?" I asked laying my hand on his side.

I looked at her, trying to determine how she felt. I knew that she had been terribly worried while I was unconscious, but what about before that? Did she have any regrets? Had she been all right during my planned absence?

"I'm a little upset," I replied honestly. "I had wanted to turn . . . so we could talk"—I glanced out the window—"more privately."

"I would have liked that too," she replied, sounding almost . . . wistful.

"Are you all right?" I lowered my voice to ask.

She looked up at me, began to say something, stopped, and then looked slightly confused.

"I've been worried about you," she finally said.

I wasn't certain if she didn't want to discuss anything other than recent events or if that was all that was on her mind currently.

"Thank you," I told her, and occupied myself with a long drink of water.

When I finished my drink, Majorlaine was coming in with another pot of soup. Later, I would awake and realize that I had barely finished the soup before dozing off again.

I wanted to tell Danren about the baby. Even though I knew that he and Narden were the same person, I wanted the privacy of our rooms to tell him. I'd had a wonderful dinner planned for when he returned, and I didn't want to give up the idea, so I waited for his wing to heal.

That week passed and then the next. The wing was slowly healing back over the gaping hole. As the third week came to a close, I was trying to decide again whether I should wait for him to turn. I was showing now, but since it was winter, I could hide under layers of clothes. No one had mentioned or asked anything, but I wondered if anyone suspected.

I was pushing another wheeled table, trying to decide what to do when I arrived at Narden's room. His voice sounded wrong as he spoke to Galen. I knew the voice, but lost in my thoughts, I didn't place it.

"So I can stay?" he asked.

"As long as you're careful with that shoulder. If you tear it open, you'll have to turn back," Galen replied, as I pushed open the door and froze.

Danren was standing there with his tattered shirt lying on the wheeled table. Galen appeared to have just finished looking over Danren's back and helping him into a sling for his arm.

They both looked up at me. Galen smiled, excused himself, and left the room, while Danren looked sheepish and concerned.

"I wanted to surprise you," he told me softly.

Suddenly, my feet decided to move again. I ran across the room, throwing myself at him. He barely managed to catch me with his one good arm and stay standing. When he let out a slight moan, I quickly pulled away.

"I'm sorry," I told him. "I didn't mean to hurt you."

Quickly, I circled around him to look at his back. The stitches across the gash still held, but for the first time, I noticed something else. Danren had scars on his back. For a moment I didn't understand, and then I began to place them. One long gash was from the attack years ago when I'd first come to Caer Corisan. There was the mark across his arm from his duel with Lord Astucieux. There were other scars as well from different ambushes or accidents.

I didn't like the idea that Danren had been hurt so much. I knew it happened, but the scars didn't show through the scales, so I'd forgotten that they were there. In an odd way, though, it was comforting. Perhaps Danren hadn't rejected me because of my scars, partly because he had so many of his own.

Suddenly, I realized that I had a lot to do before tonight. I'd planned out a nice dinner for when he returned, but now, I had less than a day to complete all the preparations.

"I'll see you at dinner," I quickly told him, and hurried out the door.

I was so excited.

I was entirely confused as I watched the door close behind Ari. One moment, she'd been in my arms. The next she was looking at my injuries. Then she had gently touched some of the scars on my back. I was going to ask her what she was thinking, when she excused herself and was gone.

What was going on? She'd seemed all right while I was Narden, but then again, as Narden, would she consider me safer to be around? I wanted to talk to her.

After making my way as quickly as I could to my room, I changed my clothes. Coming back out, I surprised Ari. At least, it had been easy to find her.

I was about to ask if she was all right and if we could talk when she blurted out, "What are you doing here?"

"What?" I began and then managed, "I was changing my clothes."

"Oh." She seemed to be confused by that reply. "Are you done?"

"Yes." I glanced down at my clothes, thinking they looked fine.

"Did you need anything else in here?" Ari continued.

"I was considering taking a bath." What was going on?

"Oh." She seemed disappointed for a moment, but then added, "Would you mind going somewhere else for that?"

"What? Ari, are you all right?" She'd never before demanded that I stay out of these rooms.

"Of course," she quickly said, but she looked flushed. "Why wouldn't I be?"

"Can we talk?" I wanted to sort things out, make it right, if I could.

"Later," she told me, "over dinner. I'm not ready yet."

"What?" Why couldn't we talk now?

Before I could ask, though, Ari was pushing me out the door.

"Don't come in here until then," she ordered, and then the door closed in my face.

I stared at it for several long moments. What was going on? Why couldn't we talk now? We needed to talk. I wanted to make sure that she was all right. Now, I was standing on the wrong side of the door from her.

Pushing the door back open, I didn't find her in the main room. Calling her name, I walked over to her room.

"What are you doing in here?" she exclaimed from behind me.

I turned to see her duck back into my room, and come back out with her cloak on.

"What were you doing in there?" I asked, walking toward her.

"I . . ." she began, glanced over her shoulder. "It's . . ." She looked up at me as I reached to put my hand on her shoulder. Stepping back and then skirting under my arm, she finished, "Nothing. Don't worry about it."

"Ari, we need to talk," I told her.

This was getting out of hand.

Looking back at Danren, I saw the pain in his eyes. He must think that I was upset with him. I quickly walked back over to him. I'd shed some of my layers and hoped he wouldn't notice anything different just yet. I knew I needed to reassure him though.

He watched me, with that hurt expression until I placed my palm against his cheek. Then he looked confused.

"Ari," he began softly, "I'm sorry that I hurt you. I never meant—"

"You didn't hurt me," I quickly interrupted, beginning to understand how this must look to him.

"What?" He stared at me for a moment, but before he could continue, I interrupted again.

"Please," I told him, "we can talk over dinner. I promise. I'm just really busy right now. I'm not upset with you. You haven't hurt me. Please."

I saw the conflict in his eyes. He was worried about me, and I could understand why.

"You're all right?" he asked.

I nodded reassuringly.

"Could we eat in here so we can talk privately?" he continued.

How perfect! I nearly hugged him in my excitement. Now, he'd think that eating here was his idea and wouldn't suspect anything!

"Yes, of course," I managed, hoping that I didn't sound too unusual.

After a moment of studying me, he walked toward the door. Finally, he left, closing the door behind him. I nearly danced around the room!

If I wasn't mistaken, Ari sounded excited. That was a far cry better than upset or hurt, but just as confusing.

I went to find Berjouhi and asked her about how Ari fared while I was away. I had to briefly explain about my injuries, that Narden wasn't here anymore, and when I'd arrived. Then she finally decided to answer my questions.

Ari had been terribly worried when I didn't return, but when Narden came, she'd thrown all her energy into caring for him. Apparently, before that, she'd been perfectly fine, and even a little giddy. I supposed that was good news, but it still didn't explain her current behavior. After asking her to check on Ari for me and attempting to explain that she'd banned me from our own rooms until dinner, I went to find Armel. Perhaps I could catch up on a few things while I waited to talk to Ari.

Berjouhi opened the door and walked in, without even knocking! I'd never had a problem with that except in the last couple of weeks. Every time I looked in a mirror or glanced down at the floor, I was convinced that someone else would soon notice. Of all the people who might notice, I was also convinced that Berjouhi would be the first.

She was due to deliver in a couple of months. Since her experience was so recent, I was certain that any day she would ask me. I just had to get through this evening, and then I would tell her and anyone else. Right now, however, I tried to nonchalantly step behind the chair by the fire.

"Are you well?" she asked, walking over.

"Of course," I said, probably too energetically, because she looked concerned.

She placed her hand on my forehead, informing me. "You seem warm."

Of course I seemed warm, I was standing next to a blazing fire, and had been hurrying about for a watch! I managed not to tell her any of this, and tried for a reassuring smile instead.

"I feel fine," I told her. "I'm just excited that Danren is back."

She glanced around the room and smiled at my preparations. "I see I assisted in beginning a tradition."

I breathed a sigh of relief. As long as she thought that, she wouldn't guess that I was hiding something.

She chatted for a little while with me, and then informed me that she needed to go reassure Danren.

Teasingly she added, "You should not worry him so much."

When the door closed behind her, I breathed a sigh of relief and collapsed into the chair. After a moment, I hurried to the door and locked it. I didn't want to risk having anyone else randomly walk in.

CHAPTER 71

SURPRISES

I wondered if I was too early, as I made my way toward our rooms. I wasn't certain if I should just walk in and decided to knock. After a moment, I heard the lock turn and found that just walking in would have been difficult.

Ari peeked her head out the door, and I saw her eyes light up with the smile that played across her face. That smile helped lighten my mood considerably. I doubted that she would look quite so happy to see me, if she was upset.

"I would like to change my clothes," she told me. "Would you wait here for just a little longer?"

I nodded and found that I was smiling stupidly at the door after it closed. I paced the hall and still couldn't wipe the grin off my face. I studied several of the tapestries and paced again. How long did it take to change into a different set of clothes?

I was so excited that I could barely manage to tie my laces. I glanced down and wondered if the dress made me appear with child. After debating changing for a moment, I realized that I was, hopefully, just imagining how obvious I looked.

I hurried back to the door and opened it for Danren. To my surprise he wasn't standing there. I glanced down the hall and found him hurrying toward me. He looked as happy as I felt.

When he reached me, he gathered me into his arms and took a breath of my hair. Quickly pulling away, I told him that the food was getting cold, hoping that he hadn't been able to feel the increase of my stomach.

Just a few moments ago, she'd looked thrilled to see me. Now, she nearly ran away from me and moved a chair from the table so that, as she leaned her hands on the back, it stood between us. I swallowed hard and entered the room. Perhaps things weren't all right after all.

"Mighty One have mercy," I prayed silently and sat across from Ari at the table.

"Ari," I repeated, "we need to talk."

"Aren't you hungry?" she asked, sounding happy enough.

She pulled a platter of roasted meat from the stand next to us and served pieces to both of us.

As she went for another dish, I started to reach for her hand, but stopped. If she didn't want me hugging her, she probably didn't want me holding her hand. She paused, glanced at me, and then reached over for my hand herself. I stared at our interlaced fingers for a moment.

"What's going on, Ari?" I asked finally, looking up at her face.

"What do you mean?" she asked, sounding too nonchalant.

"Are you upset with me?" I continued.

"Of course not!" she exclaimed too quickly.

"Ari," I caught myself sounding tense, took a breath, and managed, "Please."

She looked around for a moment, a blush spreading across her face. "I wasn't going to discuss anything weighty until after we'd eaten."

"I don't feel much like eating right now," I replied.

She glanced at the food and then said, "I have a question for you."

The statement was so typical that I almost laughed. She sounded slightly nervous, but almost excited too.

"All right," I replied.

Ari seemed to start her question several times before actually managing to say, "You were wonderful with Dreanen and Pher'am's children."

I raised an eyebrow. That hadn't been a question. I wasn't certain how to respond.

"They have raised them well," I finally told her.

"You'd make a wonderful father," I told him.

I'd put so much thought into the dinner, but hadn't thought much about how exactly I would word things.

"Ari," he replied after a moment, "we've been over this. I'm not going to ask you for a child." I was taken aback for a moment, while he continued, "You gave me a wonderful gift before I left, but I won't ask you again. It wouldn't be fair to you."

Staring at him, I tried to understand. He didn't know. He couldn't know, but what he was telling me disclosed that he didn't want this child. I quickly rose and hurried toward his room. It was habit, but when I realized where I was going, I stopped. I shouldn't be escaping to his room, but to my own. Turning around, I found Danren behind me.

"Please, Ari," he pleaded, "talk to me. What's going on? I thought we discussed all this before."

I wanted to curl into his arms, but knew that I needed to say something.

"I didn't think that would be the only time . . ." I started, but felt my eyes tear up.

"What?" I almost laughed at his response, but couldn't manage anything but a sob.

"I wasn't certain then . . . I thought that we'd want . . . Athanaric and Berjouhi are so happy and excited . . ." I tried, but couldn't manage to keep my thoughts coherent.

"It wouldn't be wise to make such a decision based on how someone else feels," he told me.

She tried to step past me, so I placed my hand on her arm. "Please, Ari, can't we talk about this reasonably?"

For a moment, she stared at me, and then buried her face into my shoulder. At least she hadn't ran away, but she didn't seem to be able to stop crying.

"I didn't mean to upset you," I tried to explain.

I held her at arm's length for a moment, but she wouldn't meet my gaze. Holding her against me again, I tried to sort things out. From what I'd heard from Berjouhi, Ari'd been excited about my return. That wouldn't make sense if she'd been upset by what we'd done. She'd just told me that she'd plan to let me bed her again. I glanced at the table. Had she been planning this evening the entire time, and I'd just ruined it?

"Ari," I tried again, "I thought that having children would hurt you. It would be a reminder every day of what we'd done. I didn't think you'd want that, but if you don't feel that way, we can discuss it."

She glanced up, but quickly glanced down and then away.

"It doesn't matter," she mumbled.

It was the glance down that caught my attention. It seemed as though she looked away so she wouldn't be caught watching something. I looked over her dress, but there didn't seem to be anything unusual about it.

"You look beautiful," I told her, trying to reassure her.

She smiled wanly, but didn't look up.

"Ari, what are you not telling me?" There was something that I was missing.

She looked at me for a moment. Studying me, it seemed, and then she glanced down and away again, as if trying not to look at something, but not quite able.

I'd thought he'd be happy. I'd thought that he'd want a child, this child, but he was still talking in abstracts. Thinking over what I knew about Danren, I tried to come to terms with his thoughts. Of course, he wouldn't assume that I was with child now. This wasn't how I'd wanted things to go. Danren was worried, and I couldn't blame him, especially with the way I was acting.

Taking a deep breath, I looked up at him, surprised to find him studying me intently. He seemed to be puzzling things out. I gasped as he slowly turned me in a circle. What if he guessed?

When I was facing him again, I tried to smile, but he asked, "What is it, Ari?"

I caught myself glancing at my stomach again. I couldn't tell if I was showing or not. When I looked up, I watched realization dawn on Danren's face. He stared at my face for a moment as the blood drained from his own. Then, his gaze dropped to my stomach. Ever so gently he put his hands on either side of my waist and pulled the dress tight. The increase in my stomach wasn't necessarily noticeable with the dress loose, but I could certainly tell that my stomach was larger with the dress tight. Could he though? Danren released one side of my waist and carefully put his hand on my stomach.

"Ari . . ." he started to say, but took a ragged breath before continuing, "this is what you were trying to tell me."

I nodded feeling tears in my eyes.

"I'm sorry," I whispered.

"What?" His voice was shaky.

"I thought you'd be happy," I told him while staring at the floor. "I thought you'd want a child."

"It's not that I don't want a child," he told me slowly. "It's that I thought . . . I didn't think much about it. I never considered it a possibility."

I looked up at him and saw excitement and concern battling for dominance in his expression.

"Are you all right?" he asked.

"I was," I told him.

"Are you all right with this?" he asked, pressing his hand lightly against my stomach.

"I was," I repeated.

"When you thought I'd be happy about this?" he asked.

I nodded.

"You weren't angry that I did this to you or upset at all about what we did?" He seemed to be searching for clarification.

I shook my head and bit my lip slightly. I didn't want to cry, but I felt tears begin to course down my cheeks. He took me into his arms and let me bury my head in his shoulder.

"What if I told you," he began, sounding slightly broken himself, "that I am happy about this?"

I leaned back and looked at him, completely confused. He didn't sound like he was happy about anything.

He gave me a watery smile and told me, "I gathered from Berjouhi that you were excited most of the time I was gone, and then you were concerned about my well-being." He gently brushed my hair away from my face. "Those aren't the attitudes or actions of someone who's angry."

I glanced down. "I thought you'd be happy about . . ."

"Ari," he began, and I looked up at him again, "I am happy about this. I'm just in a bit of shock. Please, understand that this was never going to be a possibility for me. I'd made it a point never to think about such things."

I swallowed and studied his face. The excitement seemed to be winning over the concern. I smiled slightly.

He cut short a laugh, asking, "Why didn't you tell me sooner?"

"I was planning to," I began, and since the mood seemed to be lightening, I decided to tease him a little, "but then you tried to get yourself killed and ruined my plans."

He did laugh this time and hugged me against him. "Why didn't you tell me when I got back?"

"I wanted to tell you as a human." I buried my face in his shoulder feeling my cheeks warm. "Maybe it was silly, but I thought that I should."

"It wasn't silly," he told me. "I just wish I hadn't said all the wrong things."

"It's understandable," I told him, as I stepped back and wiped my eyes. "We should probably eat."

He had a confused look for a moment and then glanced at the tables set with food, as though he just remembered that we were supposed to be having dinner. After laughing again, he led me to the table, pulled out my chair, and asked me if I needed anything.

During the entire meal, he kept glancing at me almost shyly, and every time I reached for another dish, he'd get it for me and serve it. I realized that Athanaric acted the same way around Berjouhi, and wondered if I'd have to get used to Danren fawning over me during the next months.

"Have you talked to Galen?" he asked, interrupting my thoughts.

"Not yet," I replied, "I wanted you to be the first to know."

The grin that spread across his face warmed me from my hair to my toes. He really was happy about this.

"Thank you," he finally choked out. "Will you talk to Galen tomorrow though?"

I nodded and watched him grin at his food as though he didn't know that he was supposed to eat it.

I paced outside the door where Galen and Majorlaine were talking to Ari the next morning. Not being certain if I should be inside the room or out, I'd decided on out. Next time, I was going to be inside.

When she walked out, I hurried up to her and asked if she was all right. She merely beamed up at me and told me that I shouldn't expect Galen or Majorlaine to eat her, even though Galen might threaten on some days. I hugged her and then started interrogating Galen.

I had no idea what to expect and wanted to know. Ari listened to the questions for a little while, laughed lightly, and walked away with Majorlaine.

Galen and I watched them leave, and then he said one thing that turned my world over, "She must have been paying attention to everything we told Berjouhi, because it's almost as though she's already had a baby."

He shook his head and walked away leaving me staring at the hall that Majorlaine and Ari had just left down.

Already had a baby . . . I'd never asked if she'd ever carried a child. I'd never even considered it. Of course she could have, but had she?

I quickly found her in the dragon's kitchen with Majorlaine and asked to speak to her privately. While taking her to our rooms, I glanced at her, only to find her smiling to herself. How could she be smiling, how could she be happy when she'd . . . Maybe I was wrong.

"Mighty One have mercy," I prayed silently.

When we were inside, I turned her to face me. That smile unnerved me, and I wasn't certain how to begin.

Finally, I managed, "Ari, I need to ask you something."

She merely smiled.

I swallowed hard, trying to word things, finally managing, "This isn't the first child you've born, is it?"

Her face paled, and she glanced around. "I thought you knew," she whispered.

"You never told me," I tried to explain. "I know I don't ask you about what happened at the temple. The things would hurt to remember. I guess I should have known, but I just never thought about it."

The excitement had died from her face, and I could see tears forming. "I don't know what happened to them . . . those children. They took them away before I ever even saw them. I don't even know if they were boys or girls or one of each."

She'd borne two children then, in that horrific place.

"I lost three," she continued as I realized that once she'd started, she couldn't stop. "After I bore the first one, I didn't know what else to do. The thought of them having a baby that I didn't know what they would do with was too much. I threw myself down a flight of stairs when they took me out of my room."

She stared up at me, terror at the memories in her eyes.

"I couldn't do that again. I knew that I'd killed a baby. I felt the pain when I lost him," she continued, now burying her face in my shoulder. "When I was with child again, I tripped and fell. It was an accident, but they thought it was purposeful." Her voice dropped to a whisper, "They beat me until I started having pains."

"I carried the next one completely, but they still took that one away. The last one I lost because one of the . . . of the . . . men who came . . . hit me in the stomach with his hilt. He was angry at my performance." Her body was shaking now.

I couldn't say anything adequate, and barely managed, "I'm sorry," as I held her.

Slowly she calmed, but she was nervous for the next few days. I thought about what she'd said, about what had been taken from her. It was more than just those four years that she'd lost. Her life had been irreparably altered. I'd known that before, but this was one more proof.

One night, at least a week later, as we sat watching the fire blaze in our main room, an idea dawned on me. I laughed, and Ari looked up at me.

"I know something that I'm going to do for you," I told her, proud of myself.

"Oh?" She smiled, with a teasing laughter mirrored in her eyes.

"I'm going to woo you," I told her.

She looked at me as though I'd lost my mind. "Whatever for? You already know that I love you."

"Yes, but you should have some good memories, ones that you can treasure," I explained.

The conviction that I was insane left her face, and a tender look replaced it. Her mouth moved to say something, but she didn't manage anything for a moment.

Finally when she buried her face in my shoulder, she whispered, "Thank you."

CHAPTER 72

HONEYMOON

If the excitement over both Berjouhi and my pregnancies hadn't been enough, now Danren was planning an outing. He would grin at me when he saw me. Occasionally, he'd kiss me gently or hug me. His excitement was catching. I had never seen Caer Corisan so lively. The air seemed to declare the events that were upcoming.

When Danren told me the days that he planned for our outing, I informed him that if Berjouhi hadn't delivered by then, we weren't going anywhere. He seemed slightly disappointed at first, but understood.

The Mighty One must have been listening to Danren's prayers, because Berjouhi delivered a week before our planned trip. She presented her frantically worried husband with a beautiful baby girl.

I wondered if I would still have to cancel the trip, because of everyone who wanted to see the baby. Majorlaine, however, quickly stepped in to run interference, after holding the baby herself of course. She kept the visitors orderly and limited, which served to start a few fights in the courtyard between someone who had seen the baby and was gloating, and someone who hadn't. It also served to take the attention off our planned trip.

Galen did find time to give Danren a lecture on what he should and shouldn't allow me to do during our trip.

As I thoroughly bundled up for the cold flight, I wondered where Danren was. I hadn't seen him for about a watch. Making my way to the courtyard, I looked for him, but still couldn't find him.

When I reached the dragons' stable, I found our planned escort, and Narden waiting for me.

Ari's eyes widened when she saw me. Then she hurried up to me and asked, "What are you doing?"

"I wanted to escort you myself," I told her softly.

She looked at me in a puzzled manner, whispering, "Do you have the time?"

I smiled slightly. "I have some saved up from when I was injured."

Her hesitancy disappeared, leaving a warm smile.

"Thank you," she whispered and climbed into the saddle.

The flight brought back memories of the days back at my cave when we used to go flying together. We should do this more often, I realized, as I made a dive that Ari'd requested.

Hafiz and Einheim circled our progress, keeping a watch on the ground while giving Ari and I room to converse privately. It had been decided that I shouldn't travel with less than two guards after the recent incident. I'd agreed, even though I hated pulling extra people away from other patrols.

Hearing Ari laugh through a barrel roll was musical. She asked how my wing felt as I finished the maneuver, and I again reassured her that I was fine.

I was thankful for the clear weather three days later as we crested the mountains before the coast. I heard Ari gasp at the sight. Glancing back, I saw the amazed look on her face. She'd never seen any of the seas before. I'd wanted to take her, but either lacked time, opportunity or the reason to ask her to take such a trip. Perhaps we should just take time each year to make a trip like this.

We came to the huts where we would spend that night. They were a bit drafty, but the fireplaces were large enough to fight the cold. Ari ducked inside, and I glanced around. Hafiz nodded to me, and I quickly turned, pulling my cloak tight against the chill.

Stepping inside, I found Ari starting the fire. I watched her deftly get the wood burning brightly and then stand. Apparently, she hadn't heard me enter, because her eyes widened when she saw me, and she ran into my arms.

I held her tightly for a few moments, amazed that even a few days' travel could make me miss holding her that much. Then I pulled her away from the door and window, and kissed her. I breathed in the scent of her hair when I finished and let her lie against my shoulder for as long as she wanted.

Too soon, she pulled away.

Her eyes glistened with excitement as she asked, "Is this where we're staying?"

"For tonight," I told her, relishing the surprises I had in store for her. "In the morning, we'll head to where we'll spend the week."

She looked at me in surprise. "A week, a whole week?"

"I hope you don't get too tired of having me all to yourself for that long," I teased.

It was wonderful to watch her surprise as I pulled out the ingredients for one of her favorite dishes. It was the simplest one, and housing ingredients in these huts was difficult. She'd have better fare once we reached the island. I smiled at the thought.

As the evening progressed, I realized that Ari was expecting me to bed her tonight. When I realized that, I explained that I wouldn't that night. The hut was too open, and it would be far too cold.

Instead of disappointed, she seemed confused for a moment, and then her eyes teared up. She quickly hugged me. Now, I was confused.

"Thank you," she whispered.

Danren almost burned dinner, but then he'd never done much cooking except as a dragon, and pasta was more complicated than roasting meat until it was black.

He wrapped us up in a blanket and rubbed my back after dinner, occasionally kissing my neck. His attentions brought tears to my eyes three more times at least. He wasn't doing all this to seduce me. He was showing me that he loved me, that he was committed to me.

I woke each time during the night that he rose to stoke the fire. He'd positioned me closest to the embers while he was on the outside. His concern being to keep me warm. He would notice first as it grew colder. I hoped that wherever we went the next day, he would be able to sleep better.

He didn't look haggard when we rose the next morning. In fact, he looked excited. After making sure that I was thoroughly bundled up, he led me to the ledge looking out over the water. I realized that the huts were built into a cliff where it would be difficult to reach without a dragon or a flying horse. The cliff sheltered the buildings on three sides. I hadn't been able to see any of this when we'd arrived the night before.

Now, we stood watching the sunrise over the ocean. It was amazing watching the water change colors to match the sky. I'd never seen anything so beautiful. When I glanced up, I found that Danren was watching me. How could he miss this? Then I realized that he thought I was more beautiful than any sunrise.

When the sun was completely above the horizon, he pointed out into the waves. "Do you see that misty area way out there?" he asked, and I strained to see what he was pointing at.

"I think so," I replied.

"That's where we're going," he told me.

I gasped and stared at him. We were going to fly over the sea! He grinned and then kissed me.

Half of the day passed before we reached the island that he had pointed to. There were others we passed as well. It was amazing watching each one form out of the waves as we approached. Each one was a mountain rising from the depths.

Narden landed, and after Hafiz and Einheim surveyed the island, he turned. Danren and I stretched our legs on the beach for a while. I noticed that it was warmer here and began shedding some of my layers. When we passed a grove of trees that I had never seen before, I saw a bridge crossing a small stream. A path led to a set of stone buildings carved from the mountain.

I gasped at the sight and took everything in for a moment. Then Danren began pulling me forward at a slight run. He kept up the pace till we were almost to the first building, and then he suddenly stopped. Turning to me, he studied my face and then backed slowly toward the door, leading me by the hand. At the door, he fumbled with the handle and had to turn around to unlatch it. I laughed at his irritated expression. Once the door was opening, he turned back to me and led me inside.

The glow in her eyes spread over her face as she took in the sight. The windows depicted scenes from the dragon lords' trip from wherever they'd originally come from to Rem'Maren. Gary was even in some of them. The most amazing part was the color. Armel didn't even know how to portray such images in colored glass without a single seam.

Ari slowly walked toward one of the windows, gingerly touching the glass with the tips of her fingers. As she traveled around this first room, I could hear her gasp in awe. When she finished walking around all the pictures, she returned to me, looking over the walls as though they might disappear any moment.

"How . . ." she began, but didn't continue.

"I don't know," I told her.

I could see that she was beginning to warm. These buildings were heated like the mountain caves, making the temperature in here considerably warmer than outside. Helping her out of her layers, we traveled through the rest of this building. It specifically told the story of Gary's line with all the tragedies and all the triumphs. Here each color was framed and not as detailed. The pictures were more crude, but it was the best that we could do anymore.

When we reached the room that I'd set up as a bedroom, she let out another gasp. I had hoped for that. This room had my story. This room spoke of us. She threw herself into my arms again, and I had to steady myself quickly so we didn't end up sprawled on the ground. She laughed with tears showing in her eyes. She looked beautiful.

After she admired this room, I led her down stairs to the pools. She gasped over those as well. The room was similar in concept to the room of pools in the cave, but the design was entirely different. Whereas the cave's pools were set up to look as natural as possible, this room was designed to show order.

"Galen warned that you shouldn't go into any of the hot pools because of the baby, but you can swim in the large one if you like," I told her.

She smiled up at me and teased, "I can most certainly soak my legs in the hot pools."

"As long as you know that it's all right." I laughed.

We spent the week exploring. The other islands were wonderful to walk around, but most of the time, we spent exploring each other. Occasionally, my fears would plague me for a little while, but with Danren, I was able to soothe them away. It was a magnificent week. When we left, I cherished a promise that we would come back whenever we could.

CHAPTER 73

DISCOVERED

Back at Caer Corisan, I was surprised to find how much Ceren, Athanaric and Berjouhi's baby, had grown in the short time we were gone. It was hard to believe.

Cooing over her with Berjouhi, I told her what I could about the trip.

"Next time," she informed me, "we should all go."

I froze for a moment before managing, "I don't think that would be a good idea."

"Pray tell, why ever not?" she asked.

"I don't think that the counsel would approve," I told her.

"Whatever does the counsel have to do with whether or not we all travel to your islands?" she continued.

"They're Rem'maren's islands," I replied feeling terrible. "The counsel can decide who goes."

"Why would they concern themselves with such things?" Her questions were legitimate.

"They wouldn't like it," I hedged.

"Why?" she asked simply.

"It wouldn't be a good idea," I tried. "It's a private retreat. They might not like having you looking around."

A wry smile crossed her face, as she took her baby and cooed at her. "Perhaps there are secrets there that they do not wish for me to discover."

I tried for a puzzled look, but was too surprised that she'd hit on the mark.

She grinned at me over her baby's head. "Perhaps secrets such as the fact that the dragons are truly men."

My response came out before I could catch myself. "What?"

I quickly managed to wipe the stunned look off my face, but not quickly enough.

"I have watched you, Ari'an, and your husband," she told me looking both mischievous and pleased. "You were worried when he did not return when he was supposed to months ago, but when the dragon Narden returned, your attentions turned entirely to him. Your worries over your husband's disappearance were forgotten."

She studied me for a moment before continuing, "When the dragon Narden, although not fully recovered, left, your husband returned with similar injuries that had been well tended, although not tended here."

"Recently"—she smiled, as though this were the final evidence—"Danren had elaborately planned your trip. However, when you departed, he did not accompany you, although the dragon Narden did. You did not seem disturbed in the least by this turn of events."

I managed to stumble to my feet and tell her, "I need to go."

"I am certain that you do." She smiled wryly. "I will look forward to discussing this further with you."

Seeing Ari scan the courtyard, notice me, and start hurrying over lifted my spirits. That was until I could see the look on her face.

"What's wrong?" I asked, as soon as she was close enough to hear.

She immediately increased her pace and in a moment was in front of me.

"I have to talk to you privately," she whispered to me.

"Is something wrong with the baby?" I hurried with her toward the main hall.

"No," she sounded panicked, "it's Berjouhi."

"Something's wrong with Berjouhi?" I stopped to signal for Majorlaine, but Ari grabbed my arm.

"No," she frantically pulled me along, "not exactly."

"What exactly is wrong then?" I was beginning to panic myself.

"I'm trying to tell you"—she looked as though she couldn't decide whether to cry or scream—"but I need to talk to you privately about it."

As soon as we were in one of the ground floor rooms with the door closed, I asked again, "What's wrong?"

"She knows," Ari exclaimed and crumpled onto the couch in the room.

"Knows what?" I was still stuck on the idea of a physical malady, but couldn't figure out what knowing anything had to do with being injured or sick.

"About the dragons." Ari's voice caught as tears began to pool in her eyes.

"What about the dra—" I froze, realizing what she was saying. "What? You told her?"

"No," Ari stared at me, seemingly begging me to believe her, "she figured it out on her own."

"What?" I began. "How?"

"It was how we acted," she explained. "More how I acted than you. I'm sorry. I never thought . . ."

"Ari"—I moved the hair away from her face—"just tell me, slowly, what happened."

She explained briefly what Berjouhi had said. It was obvious that the young woman knew.

"Did she mention if Athanaric knows?" I asked.

Ari paused, still looking distraught. "No, but she would have told him what she thought." After a moment, she continued, "I'm sorry. I never thought they'd figure it out. I never did. Why would they?"

"You probably would have, if you'd thought about it," I told her. "You never considered connecting Narden to me because you saw two different people."

"What should we do?" She was still on the verge of tears, but holding them back for now.

"I want to talk to Armel first. He'll probably have some sort of advice. He's lived through several types of these discoveries," I tried to reassure her.

Talking to Armel didn't give us any new information. I already knew that the counsel would be unhappy with me . . . again. That wasn't anything new. Armel didn't seem to be upset though. In fact, he told me that it was easier to cope with everything around Caer Corisan when everyone could be open about things. He said that he would deal with the counsel so that I wouldn't have to worry about it too much. That was at least one consolation.

As Ari and I made our way toward Athanaric and Berjouhi's rooms, we discussed things a little more rationally.

"Armel mentioned that Caer Corisan was built to house a city's worth of people," I mused. "It would be nice if there were other people here who knew everything. Perhaps it wouldn't be so lonely."

I glanced at Ari as she replied, "More people means more risk. You could be betrayed easier."

"Wouldn't the company be nice though?" I continued. "I've wondered about the caves and the islands too."

She looked at me, puzzled, but didn't reply.

"The caves seem to be set up to house families. Not just dragon members, but whole families to tend mountain herds and things like that. The islands are set up in such a way that they could easily provide fish and rich farming areas." I sighed. "No one can use them with all the secrecy though."

"It would be nice," she replied. "Maybe you could start with a small group of people. Perhaps with Galen and Majorlaine's daughters, if they married dragon lords. They already know about turning."

By then we were at Athanaric and Berjouhi's rooms. "Perhaps."

I lifted my hand and knocked on the door. Athanaric almost immediately answered. His face paled when he saw us.

"Lord Danren," he began.

He was obviously disturbed. He only used my honorific when he was tense.

"May we come in," I began. "There are things we need to discuss."

"Of course, my lord." He motioned us into the room. "If this is about the discussion which Berjouhi began with my lady"—he nodded at Ari—"you should not concern yourself with it."

"It is my concern," I told him evenly.

Berjouhi came out of their little one's room at that moment, and we exchanged greetings with her. Then we sat across from them in the couches that they had situated in the center of the room. The young woman looked excited, nervous, and concerned. Athanaric looked haggard.

"I understand that Berjouhi is looking forward to a continuation of the discussion that she began with Ari'an earlier," I began, not entirely sure what to say.

Her eyes lit up, and she moved forward on the couch they were sharing.

"There are other explanations," Athanaric began before anyone else could. "Berjouhi has a vivid imagination."

"What explanations would you offer?" I asked.

"Well," he began. "When La . . . when Ari'an became concerned about the injured dragon, it could have been that event created a distraction so that she could focus on something other than your disappearance."

"The injuries they both suffered were almost the same," Berjouhi countered.

"Yes, but they were not exactly the same. Those events could just be coincidence," he told his wife.

She didn't seem satisfied with that, but held her tongue.

"You could have had some emergency come up, so you were not able to depart with your wife," he continued.

"We never saw him depart at all," Berjouhi inserted.

"Perhaps we merely did not observe your departure," he countered.

"Is that what you believe?" I asked, wondering who he was trying to convince.

"I . . ." He glanced at Berjouhi. "I consider it an honor to be allowed to reside here."

"That's not an answer," I told him. "What do you believe?"

"I . . ." Again he glanced at Berjouhi, then very quietly and slowly said, "I believe that my wife is, in this matter, correct."

The young woman looked thrilled, but then glanced at me, and again added concerned, "Will you send us away because of our knowledge?"

"No," I replied.

"It is true?" Athanaric seemed surprised to admit it.

I smiled slightly. "It is."

Berjouhi sprang up and hugged Ari. It was amazing that she could look entirely dignified while exuding so much energy. I would have to introduce her to Pher'am. It would be interesting to watch their interactions.

"What will be done with us?" Athanaric asked, sounding shaken.

"What?" I caught myself and continued. "What do you mean?"

"If you will not be exiling us, what will you . . ." he seemed unable to continue.

"What do you have in mind?" I asked, wondering what he thought I'd do to them.

Berjouhi seemed to calm suddenly, turned slightly pale, and returned to her seat. The concern had been replaced by full-blown worry. It almost appeared to be dread.

"Will we be executed, my lord?" he asked, in that quiet slow tone.

"What?" It took me a moment to fully comprehend what he'd just asked.

"Of course not!" Ari exclaimed next to me. "Why would we execute you?"

He stared at Ari for a moment, before managing, "It is apparent that we were not intended to discover this."

"We do not typically execute people because they discovered something," I told him.

It appalled me that he would think that about Maren or Rem'Maren for a moment, but then I remembered that he was from Verd, and that was common practice there. It was in fact common in many of the houses in Faruq.

"Well, those are indeed pleasant tidings," Berjouhi managed to reply before her husband. She even continued before Athanaric had fully recovered, "What sorcery is involved?"

"What?" That thought appalled me.

"There isn't any sorcery," Ari replied. "It's in their bloodlines. It's passed down."

Athanaric had just managed to recover, but seemed to be in shock again.

Berjouhi, however, was not. "Inherited?" She did stare for half a moment though. "Why then are there no female dragons."

"It only passes to their sons," Ari explained.

"How is that possible?" Athanaric finally managed a question of his own.

"I don't entirely understand"—Ari glanced at me—"but their daughters won't pass on the bloodline either."

The next few watches were spent discussing questions and the history of the dragon lords. It was interesting to hear their questions, many of which I had to tell them that they would need to ask Armel. He seemed to grasp the history and be able to explain it better. Then again, he had been explaining these things for a few centuries.

CHAPTER 74

AT THE CAPITAL

Two things happened over the next couple of months. First the counsel, to Danren's amazement, only fussed a little about Athanaric's and Berjouhi's new knowledge. Apparently, they had already been discussing the possibility and were becoming accustomed to Danren causing such things.

The second was the request from King Viskhard. My presence was finally requested at the beginning of autumn to present my case. The request could not have had worse timing. I was due to deliver within a month of the date on the request.

Danren sent several petitions throughout the summer requesting a different date, but each was returned with a polite, enigmatic reply that informed us the date was not changed.

Finally, with every single one of our friends voicing their disapproval for every reason from health concerns, to not being safe to fly, to the slight possibility of an early snow, we accepted the invitation. We would end up countering each objection with the simple fact that we were not able to deny the king's request in this matter.

Dreanen pointed out that Danren had denied the king's request once before about not becoming an adviser. It was a right that the dragon lords had, more of a necessity actually, that had been worked into the agreements to allow the dragon lords into the kingdom.

Danren pointed out that refusing the adviser's position was because he couldn't perform the task. Turning every few weeks negated being able to stay at the capital. The current request could be performed, although it might be dangerous.

He did ask me if I thought that he should refuse, but I assured him that we were making the right decision. I had been through far worse at the temple while carrying a child than the discomfort that traveling would bring.

Berjouhi was livid that she would not be able to come herself. Her baby was so young still that everyone, but her, considered it too much of a risk. She argued with me that if I could take the risk in my condition, certainly, she could in hers.

The answer was still no though. We left without her or Athanaric.

With all the fretting that everyone had done about the flying part of our journey, that turned out to be the most comfortable. There were not rutted roads that needed repairs or mudholes to pry the carriage out of while we flew.

After the first day of travel by road, we actually decided to let the carriage travel on empty, and we would fly to the woods near the capital. There we would meet up with the carriage again and travel the half a day on those roads.

We arrived without any celebration, which was fine by both Ari and myself. The trip had been exhausting enough without adding forced cheerfulness to end it.

Conditions didn't improve when we were shown to our room. The room was done in a recent style. It was the size of all our separate rooms and then some, but everything was in the one room. The bed was in a section accompanied by a wardrobe. Another section contained a desk and a harp. Still another section seemed to be designed for entertaining. Another was for dining, and lastly a bathing area.

I didn't like the lack of privacy, and I doubted that Ari would either. Turning to her, I found that she wasn't looking at the furnishings all over the room, but was staring at the lamps set into the walls. Her face was white as a clean sheep.

"What is it?" I asked. "Is it the baby?"

She slowly pulled her gaze away from the lamps to stare at me. "N-no," she finally stammered.

Now, she began taking in the room and to shake.

"What is it?" I asked again. As I stepped to her, she buried her face into my shoulder.

"Th-the rooms at the temple were like this," she finally whispered into my shoulder.

"What?" I couldn't manage anything else.

I'd only seen one of those rooms, and that was through the dust and debris from tearing through the wall. The interior design of the place was never something I'd considered.

Danren never left me, but he did spend the next seven watches trying to get us moved to a different room. He first had to convince the room servant that it was not the state of the room that was the problem. The furnishings were beautiful. It was the room itself.

The servant finally went to fetch the steward of the area for us. Danren had to explain again why we wanted a different room. He was discreet about what he told anyone, but the steward was unable or unwilling to comprehend why we were not satisfied. He offered another room in the wing, but Danren discovered, before we moved, that it was designed the same.

Arguments ensued about our status, which Danren insisted didn't matter as long as we could get a different type of room. Others followed about not being able to relocate us on such short notice. If they could move us to another room in this wing, why not to another wing, Danren pointed out. The steward didn't seem to comprehend that argument. He finally went to fetch his overseer.

Then we began again, but still accomplished nothing. We finally reached a compromise of sorts. They extinguished all the lamps, decided that no one would enter our room without knocking, and that a bar would be placed on the inside of our door to ensure our privacy.

With the lamps out, I finally managed to calm down a little. The lamps were always on at the temple. They could be filled from the other side of the wall. Even when one lamp was cleaned, all the others remained burning.

The darkness was a comfort. I leaned against Danren and tried to relax. I was exhausted, but couldn't sleep. Finally, after we lay awake for three watches, Danren rose and moved a couch in front of the fireplace. There we watched the flames dance.

I wished for the thousandth time that day that Berjouhi had been able to come with us. I knew that she would have been able to get a different room for us. Her tenacity wouldn't have been defeated by such logistics. I would have been able to stay with Ari while Berjouhi traveled all over the castle to arrange things. That way, Ari wouldn't have been subjected to all the arguments. In the end, I'd failed completely.

Ari wasn't able to sleep, which didn't surprise me. Finally, I gave up as well and moved a couch to the fireplace. Perhaps this atmosphere would help her calm down.

She rested silently against me for so long that I thought that she'd finally fallen asleep.

Instead, I was surprised when she asked, "Are you hoping for a son or a daughter?"

"What?"

"I thought we could use a distraction," Ari informed me. "I realized that we'd never actually talked about it, and I thought it would be pleasant."

"We could use a pleasant distraction." I sarcastically chuckled.

She sighed seeming disappointed.

"It's a good idea," I told her.

After a few moments, she asked, "Well?"

"Well, what?" I was in my own irritation.

"Are you hoping for a son or a daughter?" she repeated.

I felt like a goose but managed to reply, "A daughter of course."

"What?" Ari turned and stared at me in the dim light, surprised by my answer.

"Don't you want a daughter?" I asked, returning her puzzled look.

743

"I thought you would want a son, an heir," she told me.

"I don't need an heir," I replied.

She still looked shocked, so I continued, "I've spent years knowing that I wouldn't have an heir."

"Certainly, when you thought about it, you wanted a son," she told me.

"I tried not to think about it, and succeeded up until almost a year ago," I replied.

"Why wouldn't you want a son?" she asked.

This seemed to be upsetting her more than I would have imagined.

I lowered my voice and whispered into her ear, "I am concerned about what any son of mine will have to go through. It's been hard for me to adjust to everything, I do not look forward to passing such things on."

She stared at me looking hurt. "You never want a son?"

"Ari," I began and then sighed, "I do not believe that I have any way of determining such things. Our child will be either a son or a daughter. That has already been decided even though we do not know."

She stared at me for a moment before saying, "If it's a son, will you be pleased?"

I swallowed hard at the thought. It was still hard to believe that I would be a father.

"Yes," I told her, "I will be completely pleased with either."

"Would you love a son?" she asked hesitantly.

"Of course!" I was surprised that she would even ask such a thing. "Would you love a daughter?" I replied, knowing that she would.

She stared at me for a moment before looking away. "I was hoping for a son."

"What?" I quickly continued, "Because you wanted me to have an heir?"

"Partly," she told me, "but also because a daughter might have my hair, and that would be dangerous for her."

"A son might have your hair as well," I informed her.

She let out a little cry of surprise. "I always thought that he would look like you."

"And I always thought that she would look as beautiful as her mother," I replied.

"You *wanted* a daughter who looked like me?" She seemed more shocked now.

"Why not?" I asked not quite understanding her dismay. "You are beautiful, and I am honored to have you as my wife."

"But what if something happened?" Ari exclaimed.

"I can promise you that whether we have a son or a daughter"—I gently pressed my hand against her stomach—"if anyone tries to harm her . . . or him, they will have quite a fight on their hands."

Ari stared at me, not comprehending.

"Do you believe that any child of ours will go anywhere without a dragon escort?" I asked.

Comprehension dawned on her face, a smile began to form, and then turned into a grin.

"I suppose not." She laughed and then leaned back against me.

In less than a watch, I could tell that Ari had finally fallen asleep. Exhaustion won, which was a relief. She slept the next two watches, but at dawn, the door to our room tried to open.

I glared at it, since the sound had awoken Ari. However, I was glad that I'd insisted, and won, the debate over the bar. Whoever was out there had not, by any means, knocked.

It took me a while to regain feeling in my arm and leg where Ari had slept. She walked to the door, opened it as much as the bar would allow, and peeked out. There was a brief discussion that I couldn't hear, and then Ari began to pull the bar out.

"Wait," I called, almost falling as I tried to stand on my pain-laced leg.

"It's a servant with breakfast," she told me.

"You shouldn't be pulling that out," I informed her, limping toward the door.

I gave Danren an exasperated look. Everyone was treating me like a cripple. I was with child, not without arms! I sighed though, realizing that I'd treated Berjouhi in much the same way.

Danren actually struggled a little with the bar, but that seemed to be because of his arm and leg not working properly. I felt sorry for the servant in the hallway. He was holding a tray and couldn't do anything but balance the heavy thing.

When the bar was out of the door, and the servant walked across the room, I told Danren to stay where he was. He looked at me oddly. After the servant left, I informed him that I didn't want him limping across the room with someone watching. He laughed, replaced the bar, and did, indeed, limp across the room. I thought he was exaggerating the movement though.

Not long after breakfast, I was called to speak to the king. We were told that I was to come alone, which sent Danren into a temper. He did escort me all the way to the throne room though. They didn't forbid him from doing that at least.

He prayed with me before I walked into the throne room, which raised some confused stares from the people around us, but made me feel better. The Mighty One was my god, why should I be afraid of anyone on the other side of the door.

I was still nervous though. I dreaded telling so many people about my time at the temple. I managed to focus on the king, approached to the appropriate distance for my rank, and curtsied to the proper level. Pher'am would have been so proud.

"Lady Ari'an by birth of the House of Nori'en by marriage of the House of Rem'Maren, welcome to my court," King Viskhard told me.

"Your Royal Majesty," I replied, again pleased that I could remember the proper words, "it is an honor to represent my lineage before you."

After a few more formal lines, he finally reached why I was there. "I am afraid that your presence here is under unpleasant circumstances. Will you please inform us of the events surrounding your years between when you were of the age of fourteen and eighteen."

I began my story. I paused too often to gather my thoughts or my courage. The Mighty One was with me, because not once did I begin to quiver or stammer. I thanked him later that Danren was praying for me the entire time I was before the king.

During one pause, I heard someone step from the crowd behind me.

"Your Excellent Majesty," the voice began and immediately froze me to my place.

I knew that voice. It haunted my nightmares. I couldn't move, and I could barely breathe. This was the voice of the first priest.

King Viskhard recognized him, and for the first time in my life, I heard the man's name. It was Kakios Itzal of Aintzane. The king asked if his interruption could not wait until the end of my discourse. The priest insisted that it could not.

"If it pleases Your Majesty," the smooth voice continued, "this . . . lady has no proof of the events that she describes. What evidence can she produce to support her fantastical tale? Who can she produce as a witness to collaborate these circumstances?"

I couldn't answer. My mind was entirely blank. I was terrified by this man's presence. How could they let him be here while I spoke? I tried merely to breathe.

"She offers none," the priest said after . . . I couldn't imagine how long it had been.

Another voice answered from behind me that caused me to stop breathing entirely.

"If it pleases Your Majesty," the second priest said, "I will offer my testimony to that of Lady Ari'an's."

In Verdian I heard the first priest hiss, "What are you doing?"

The second priest did not answer him but said, "Your Majesty, I will not only collaborate her ladyship's account, but also describe other events from the temple where she was imprisoned."

"I command you to stand back," the first priest hissed, again in his own language.

"I would also request sanctuary, Your Majesty," the second priest continued, "because the retelling of these events will doubtlessly label my person as a traitor to my own realm."

"Will you accept the testimony of Bakar Kemen of Aintzane to accompany your own?" the king asked.

It took me a moment to realize that he was speaking to me. "I do not know what he will say." I don't know how I managed to get the words out. "I do not wish to hear what he will say."

"If you wish then, Lady Ari'an," the king told me. "You may return to your quarters while we hear the testimony of Bakar Kemen of Aintzane."

I barely remember leaving. I clearly remember collapsing against Danren. I don't remember going back to our room.

After calming down for a watch, Ari finally told me that two of the priests from the temple were here. Two distinct options tore at me. I could either, against everyone's, including Ari's, insistence, hunt them down and kill them both or I could stay with Ari. The Mighty One kept some sense in me, because if I killed two dignitaries from a different country in cold blood, I would end up executed. What would happen to Ari or our child then?

I couldn't challenge the two men as I had Lord Astucieux because their "rules of conduct" were different than ours.

I hollered at a minimum of ten different servants over the next week. No one would tell us what was going on. They insisted that we stay in our own room. Meals were brought, but those servants either didn't know or weren't saying anything.

When Ari would finally fall asleep, I spent the time pacing until exhaustion claimed me as well. I kept my sword within reach at all times and the door barred. That raised confused looks from the servants, but they were more than happy to leave after I yelled at them for a few moments.

CHAPTER 75

THE KING'S
QUESTIONS

One morning, when I was fully prepared to inform whoever dared come that we would be leaving tomorrow, a knock sounded on the door. The knock surprised me. As often as the servants were informed that they would not be admitted before identifying themselves, they always tried to open the door first.

I walked to the door and called out, "Who is it?"

"I present His Royal Majesty King Viskhard," a herald called.

I wasn't certain whether to be outraged that he had finally decided to "grace us with his presence" or relieved that this was finally someone who would be able to answer our questions.

I quickly pulled the bar loose from the door and opened it with a bow.

The king entered, acknowledged my presence, and informed me, "I require to speak with your wife privately."

If he hadn't been the ruler of all the Houses, I would have challenged him right then. We had been as much as prisoners in his dominion for a week, and he dared request to talk to Ari alone.

I opened my mouth to tell him that any further things that needed to be discussed with my wife would be done in front of me, when I felt a hand rest on my arm. I glanced at Ari to see her as composed as possible.

"It will be all right," she told me softly.

Before I knew what had happened, I was standing on the wrong side of the door with the herald who had announced the king. I sat down on a bench, pulled a whetstone out of my pocket, and began sharpening my sword. Whenever I glanced up, I was pleased to see that the herald looked increasingly nervous.

The king walked to one of the chairs in what was supposed to be an entertaining area and sat. He motioned for me to join him. I walked over, folded my skirt under me, and carefully sat.

"I thank you for your continued patience in these proceedings," he began.

I nodded, but couldn't quite manage to say anything that wouldn't have sounded rude. Watching Danren curb his temper, as much as he did over the last week, had worn my nerves. I had come to the realization that I had a temper of my own.

King Viskhard looked around the room and asked, "Why are none of your lamps lit? They would increase the light and are a marvel to behold."

I supposed that was his attempt at simple talk. In other circumstances, it might have been a reasonable attempt, but considering everything, it was not.

"Your Majesty," I began trying to keep the sarcasm from my voice as much as possible, "this room does not suit me. This knowledge to you, it is designed as the rooms where I was held in the temple were designed."

The king looked surprised and then disturbed. "Why did you not request different quarters?"

"We did, Your Highness, but every request we made from the cleaning servants to the steward himself was met with the basic answer that we were not to move," I informed him.

He frowned. "I had commanded that you be given treatment of the highest honor."

"Does that include being told not to leave this room over the last week?" I caught myself after a moment, "Your Majesty?"

He did not answer for a moment and then informed me, "I will have this matter looked into immediately."

I smiled ever so slightly. I was tired. I was due to be delivered within three weeks. I was not happy. I was trying very hard to be as polite as possible and realizing that I was not succeeding.

"Do you wish to move to different quarters at this time?" he asked.

"Your Majesty," I, at least, managed to begin with the proper address, "we are departing tomorrow. I do not see how moving to different quarters now would be pertinent."

"I have not been informed of such arrangements," he told me.

"My husband was going to tell one of the servants today," I told him, entirely forgetting any honorific. "I wish to be delivered in my own home."

"Had we known of your condition, we would not have asked for your presence here until the spring," he told me.

"You are mistaken, Your Majesty," I told him, trying not to sound cold. "We sent messages every week until we had to depart, informing your court of my condition. We were told each time that we were required to attend."

He looked surprised, then angry for a moment before composing himself.

"Another matter to be sought after," he told me.

I managed to hold my tongue, but did not hold on to any hope about receiving the answers. He was not a lord from a low House. Therefore, he would not need to bother with informing either Danren or myself about what he would or would not discover.

"I doubt you insisted on speaking to me privately to discuss such arrangements, Your Highness," I managed to say in an almost conversational tone.

He sighed. That surprised me.

Then he told me, "I have heard more about the practices of our neighboring country than I would have ever desired to know. I have only a few questions to ask you."

I nodded actually feeling a little pity for him.

He tried to word a question, looked at me, and sighed again, finally asking, "Since your time at the temple in Verd, have you encountered any such activities in this realm?"

"I know of some from this realm who were sold to the Verdian temples," I replied.

"You have not been approached for such . . ." he seemed at a loss for words.

"From what I understand about my husband's duel with Lord Astucieux, it has been suggested, but no one has approached me specifically," I told him. "Rem'Maren does not allow such sales," I clarified. "It would be severely punished if any even suggest such a thing within that House."

It was a long moment before he asked, "Your child is your husband's then?"

"What?" The word was out before I could catch myself.

Why, of all the habits to pick up from Danren, had it been this one?

The king looked at me in surprise and then seemed to consider how to reword his question. I was appalled. How could he possibly think that I would . . .

"Your Majesty," I felt my tone take on a harsh sound, "I was trapped at that temple. What I did there was not of my choice. I do not . . ."

He held up his hand before I could continue, "You misunderstand me. I am asking if anyone has forced you to provide such services since your return."

I was still upset as I told him darkly, "If anyone had even hinted at such a thing, they would be either dead or at least maimed, Your Majesty."

The king watched me for a few moments, then spoke in a musing tone, "How do you develop such loyalty from others?"

The question surprised me enough that I calmed slightly as I thought about it.

"I would assume that it develops from our belief in the Mighty One. Also, it would partly be because of Rem'maren's relationship with the dragons," I answered as best as I could, remembering belatedly to add, "Your Majesty."

He smiled slightly. "I would like to behold some of your dragons. What I have heard does not suit what I know of the agreements between Rem'Maren and the creatures."

I didn't like the use of the word *creatures*, but it was far more polite than *beasts*. "They are as much people as you or I, Your Majesty," I told him.

He rose and began to walk toward the door. I pulled myself to my feet and walked with him.

When he opened the door, I saw Danren sitting across the hall. He slipped something into his pocket, rose, and then slid his sword back into his scabbard. I wondered about why his sword was out, but the king asked a question before I could ponder further.

I had probably enjoyed watching the steward shuffle nervously. He nearly leapt out of his own skin when the door to my room opened. I calmly slipped my whetstone into my pocket, rose, and sheathed my sword. While bowing to the king, I noticed the steward fumble his own sword that he'd begun to draw and attempt to bow. He succeeded at hitting himself squarely in the stomach. His gasp of pain caused the king to look at him disapprovingly.

"Lord Danren," the king returned his attention to me, "I would like to request that you arrange for my visit to your Caer Corisan in the spring."

My own ill-gotten pleasure at the steward's discomfort disappeared. It was replaced by a nauseous feeling. It was never a good idea to deny a royal request. I'd had to once before when he'd asked me to be an adviser. I had hoped that would be the only time.

"I am afraid, Your Majesty," I told him, "that would most likely be impossible."

The steward gasped and stared at me. The king looked at me in a manner that resembled the disapproval that he'd shown to the steward earlier. This was more intense though.

I attempted to explain, "I doubt that Your Majesty would feel comfortable with the dragons that come and go daily from Caer Corisan."

"To meet your dragons is the reason that I wish to visit your domicile," I was told.

I floundered for a moment, glanced at Ari, who looked as shocked as I felt, and finally found the main reason that I could use.

"Your Majesty," I began, "Maren belongs to the dragons and is a separate kingdom from your own. I rule Caer Corisan as a boon, not as an inheritance. To facilitate a visit, I would need to discuss the matter with the dragons' counsel. I can make no guarantees that they will accept your presence since relations between themselves and Faruq have often been unpleasant."

Mighty One be praised that I'd sounded like I was talking to a king. I felt like a complete fool, but at least I didn't sound like one.

The king studied me for a moment, and then finally said, "I will send you with a message for your counsel."

Then he turned and walked away.

It took the herald a moment to recover, but he was soon trotting after the king. I slumped against the wall, trying to regain some semblance of composure.

I finally looked at Ari, who was still standing in the doorway.

"Can we pack, please?" Her tone sounded almost desperate. "I want to go home."

CHAPTER 76

DELIVERED

We had no further delays leaving the capital. I now sat in Einheim's saddle with Danren behind me. As soon as we'd been able, we'd left the carriage, the escort, and all those holes and bumps in the road for the smooth dragon flight. We were now only a day away from home.

I was so glad to be going back to Caer Corisan that I kept shifting in the saddle. I felt edgy and wished we were already there. Our course would take us over several of the dragon's mountains, and I was still trying to decide if I wanted to ask to visit Narden's cave or go straight home. It wasn't far out of the way. Perhaps we should spend the night there and then make the rest of the trip in the morning. I wanted to be home too though. I wanted to watch Berjouhi's exuberance and hold her baby. I wanted to watch Athanaric try to have a conversation with Zait or Besnik, who seemed to have made it their specific desire to scare the poor man to death.

Suddenly, the choice was made for me. We had to land somewhere safe as soon as possible, and Narden's cave was watches closer than Caer Corisan.

"Ari," I told her for the hundredth time that day, "if you keep moving, I'll have us land, and I'll travel with Einheim by myself."

She laughed at me. I was enjoying traveling like this, and didn't exactly want to move, but it would be safer. Currently, I had my arms around her resting a hand on her stomach. I'd felt the baby move several times during the trip and didn't want to lose the experience.

Suddenly, I jumped and almost fell out of the saddle myself. Warm water was coursing down my knees toward my shoes.

"Ari!" I exclaimed not entirely grasping what had happened.

She looked back at me with horror on her face.

"The baby," she managed to whisper.

"What's wrong?" I could feel my own terror mounting.

"The baby's coming," she told me.

I managed only one word, "What?"

She kicked Einheim, who glanced back and then yelled at him, "We have to go to Narden's cave!"

He looked confused for a moment and then altered course slightly.

"Hurry!" Ari shouted through the air.

He glanced back again and must have seen the panic on both of our faces because he immediately sped up.

"Can't you wait?" I asked.

She looked at me as though I'd lost my mind.

"Babies don't wait," she informed me.

Over the next two watches, Hafiz struggled to keep up. Ari would grip my legs like she was trying to remove them from my body for a few moments and then relax again for a while. My mountain never seemed farther away.

Finally, we arrived at the cave. Danren slid out of the saddle and helped me down. I stumbled slightly, but he kept me from falling. I made my way to the little room while he told the dragons to go to Caer Corisan as quickly as possible.

I heard Hafiz begin to argue, but Danren cut him off and sent them away. I slumped against the doorway grasping the curtain as another pain started. Danren was almost instantly at my side.

"I hope Galen or Majorlaine get here in time," I said when the pain subsided.

"How long . . ." Danren stumbled over his words as I collapsed onto the bed, "does this usually take?"

I looked up at him feeling a stab of terror run through me; fighting it down, I told him, "I'm not sure. It always seemed like forever to me, but the priests once said I was quick."

I saw anger flare across his face, but he took a breath and swallowed hard.

"You'll want to boil some water so it's clean," I told him.

He nodded and headed out into the main area.

I tried to keep him busy as we waited. I thought it might help him. We still ended up sitting and waiting for what seemed like forever. My pains continued to come closer together. I went over what I now knew about births with him.

He grew pale a few times and once in a while squeaked out, "What?" as I explained something or another.

Later, I would remember how adorable he was at that moment, but currently, I was frightened. I knew that the baby wasn't going to wait any longer.

"What?" I managed to choke out when Ari informed me the baby was coming now.

"Please," she gasped in pain as she clenched my hand, "you have to catch the baby."

I don't clearly remember anything else until I was holding a child and frantically telling Ari, "I don't think he's breathing."

"Hang him by his feet and slap his back," she panted.

"What?" How would that help?

"NOW!" she yelled, and I immediately obeyed.

"Harder!" she snapped and then moaned and gripped the bedding again.

I hit the baby's back harder and nearly dropped him when he started to scream. As quickly as I could, I stopped dangling the child by his feet and held him to my chest. Staring frantically at Ari, I couldn't remember a single thing that she'd told me should be done after the baby was born.

As she turned her head to look at me, I saw that she was exhausted and scared.

"Is he really a boy?" she finally asked with tears in her eyes.

I nodded and managed to ask, "Now what?"

She almost smiled. "You need to clean him off and wrap him in something warm."

I went to the hot water basin and dipped in a cloth. I almost dropped the baby again when I burned myself with the water.

"It's too hot," I told her.

"Wait for the cloth to cool a bit," she panted.

When I could comfortably pick up the cloth, I wiped him off as best as I could and then wrapped him in a shirt we'd found for this purpose. It was the softest one that was here.

I walked over to Ari and looked at her.

At that moment, I loved her more than at any other time before, but all I could tell her was, "We should probably get you cleaned up too."

She looked up at me with tears in her eyes and asked, "Please, may I hold him, just for a moment."

I felt like a fool. I quickly lowered him into her arms. She pulled him close and whimpered for a moment. Then she finally got him to stop howling by nursing him.

Watching her as I sat on the edge of the bed brought tears to my own eyes. Mighty One be praised. This was a miracle!

I kept looking beneath the blanket that I was nursing him under. It was hard for me to believe that I was holding him. I'd never held any of the other children I'd bore. I didn't know if they were alive or dead now. I didn't even know if it would be better if they were dead.

He fell asleep soon after he finished nursing. I saw Danren dash tears off his cheeks and grin at me.

"We did it," I told him.

He laughed nervously and then built it into a full sound. I laughed with him and looked down at the baby I was holding.

"Do you have a name picked out?" he asked, when we calmed down slightly.

"Is there a name that you wanted?" I asked.

"It's traditional that the mother names the children." He beamed at me.

I had hoped he would say that.

"Armus," I told him.

He looked puzzled for a moment and then said, "That doesn't sound like a name that comes from your line."

"It's not, but I found it in the word book that goes with the Mighty One's book. It's not actually a name in the Mighty One's book though." I continued after a moment, "It means 'beloved.'"

"Beloved," Danren whispered, gently brushing his finger over the baby's head.

"We can use some more traditional names for the rest," I told him as he returned my grin.

After a few more moments, we managed to get me out of the bed. I still held Armus against me to keep him warm even though I was now sitting out by the fire that Danren had started watches ago.

I heard the mattress that he pulled off the bed fall into the main room. Danren then walked over to me, beamed down at us for a few moments, and then finally seemed to remember that he was replacing that mattress with the one from Adenern's cave.

He managed to return and place the mattress in the room before coming to beam at us again.

"I should probably hold him while you change," he told me.

"Are there any blankets on the bed?" I asked.

His completely puzzled look confirmed my suspicion.

"It might be best if there was some bedding on that mattress for me to sleep on," I told him.

"What?" he asked, and then he seemed to comprehend what I was telling him and walked back into the little room.

I had wanted to hold Armus for a little longer.

Danren returned looking slightly more together. I made my way back to the room and changed. Then I collapsed on the bed. I nestled under the covers and rolled onto my back. Danren lifted the covers and placed Armus on my chest. I sighed beginning to feel my exhaustion overwhelm me. The last thing I remember is Danren lying down next to me and putting his hand on our son's back.

I must have dozed off as well because I jumped slightly when I heard wings outside. Managing not to wake Ari or Armus, I groggily headed out into the main room.

Einheim had just landed and had both Galen and Majorlaine with him. They both tried to jump out of the saddle at the same time, which would have been disastrous. Galen stopped himself and glared at the back of Majorlaine's head as she slid down.

"How far along is she?" Majorlaine barreled over to me.

"What?" I didn't understand what she was talking about.

"How far apart are her pains?" She glared at me.

Why was she glaring at me? "What pains?"

Majorlaine stormed past me and began to hurry toward the room.

I caught her arm and told her, "Don't go in there. They're sleeping."

"Her pains are still far apart then . . ." Majorlaine froze and stared at me as my words seemed to sink in. "They?"

I heard Galen stop pulling things out of the saddlebags.

"Who delivered her?" He was staring at me.

"What?" I wasn't certain how obvious things were.

Galen sighed heavily and then nodded to Majorlaine. "One of us should look them over."

"Of course I will," she barked, and entered the room.

I hadn't had time to object again. Ari was so tired. Couldn't they let her rest?

I stayed at Narden's cave for a week to recuperate. It was pleasant to have Danren fawning over me most of the time. He had to turn at the end of the week, but until then, he made certain that any whim of mine was fulfilled, at least within reason. I did test how far his attentions would go when I requested a flight on the second day there. He looked like he was going to have a fit. After letting him fret for a moment, I told him that I was teasing. He glared at me, and then hugged me.

After that, he beamed at Armus, who was sleeping. He often ended up looking at either me or Armus or both of us with that glow to his face. Even though he had said he didn't need an heir, he was incredibly proud of his son.

When Ari finally arrived home, I was relieved. I didn't like the idea of both of them traveling so soon, but it was necessary. She didn't want to stay at my cave all winter, and once the snows started, it would be too cold to travel with the baby.

Berjouhi was incredibly angry, knowing that Ari had been allowed to travel with a baby younger than her own. Again and again, she told us that if she'd been at the capital, they would have given us a proper room. If she had been traveling back with us, Ari wouldn't have been in such straits. If she had been . . . If she had been . . .

I didn't argue with her. In fact I agreed with her.

When I told her that, she was silent for a moment and then told me, "I am well pleased that you realize your mistake."

Then she stormed off.

CHAPTER 77

A KING'S VISIT

Winter set in with a vengeance shortly after we returned. I was thankful that we'd returned before Ari and Armus were trapped at my cave. It's not that they would have been uncomfortable, but it would have been difficult to get either Galen or Majorlaine to them if something went wrong. Also, I didn't like the idea of having to spend weeks at a time at Caer Corisan without her. There were always things that I needed to be accomplish here, and I couldn't have neglected them all winter.

A mobilization message came from the capital just before the passes were completely snowed in. Forces were to gather for the next spring. The country was finally taking up the war with Verd. The number of men and dragons requested from Rem'Maren was actually less than what we had been expending defending the borders. We would actually have something of a rest.

I should have been thrilled. Everything was finally working out after all these years. One statement from the message slaughtered any relief I might have felt.

Bakar of Aintzane, one of the priests who had violated Ari, was given sanctuary because of his testimony regarding the services rendered at the temples and his new allegiance to Faruq.

I didn't bear that news well. It upset Ari too, but I was livid. I wanted the man dead. Executed for his crimes against her and all the others whom he had done such things to.

It took me a few days to stop lashing out at anyone who mentioned the good news. In a way it was good news. Perhaps there
would be some form of justice in the end. At least Verd, Mighty One
willing, would finally pay.

Athanaric sent messages to his family, informing them that if
they wanted to avoid the war, we could remove them from their
country. Some accepted the offer, but most refused to accept the help
of dragons.

The counsel, meanwhile, was debating the possibility of the
king's visit. Like most other times, they were divided. They argued
back and forth. Rem'Maren did not need to accept visits from dignitaries. However, most of the younger men, those less than a hundred, still had a dual allegiance to both the dragons and the king, so
offending him would not be good.

Finally, they reached a compromise of sorts. The king would be
allowed to visit Caer Corisan if he visited the fortress alone. He would
not be allowed to bring a company of retainers or even a guard. No
one expected him to accept those terms. I was disappointed. I had
hoped that the counsel would be more reasonable than that.

To everyone's shock, and the consternation of half of the counsel, the king agreed. He would come just before the official war
began. Caer Corisan began an almost forced time of preparation.
The difference between the hum of activity for this visit and that of
Ari's was striking.

When the Lady Ari'an had first visited Caer Corisan, everyone wanted to be there. Now that the king of the realm was coming, I kept hearing excuses for why people wouldn't be here. Some
requested to be patrolling, others pleaded that they needed time to
prepare their families for their departures.

I finally realized that it was an issue of power. Ari hadn't represented a threat. Actually, she was a bit of a wonder. A lady of the
realm visiting Caer Corisan. Such a thing had never happened before.

No king had ever visited Caer Corisan either, but he represented
an authority. If the visit went poorly, he could possibly cut some
trade from Maren or even declare war on Rem'Maren. Our position
was terribly precarious.

In the end, many of us did the only thing that could possibly keep everything from going wrong. We prayed.

When the day finally came that the king would arrive, Athanaric and Berjouhi were almost frantic. It was amazing seeing them so worked up. They were frightened that King Viskhard might revoke their status as sanctuaried guests. Berjouhi mingled this with an incredible amount of excitement at the prospect of meeting an actual royal.

We stood watching the skies for the winged horse and dragon escort that would signal the king's arrival. To our shock, only the dragons appeared. I wondered if something had gone wrong. Then I realized that the king was riding one of the dragons. My stomach plummeted. Had there been something wrong with the horse?

Once the king landed, he attempted to dismount and almost fell on the ground. I groaned softly, wondering how many other things would go wrong during this visit.

To my surprise, as Athanaric, Berjouhi, and I went to greet him, I could hear him thanking the dragon for transporting him to the fortress. I glanced at Danren, who was dismounting Einheim. He looked just as surprised.

"You're welcome, sir," Hafiz replied with a dragon's bow.

The king looked thoughtful as he turned to us. I quickly curtsied, and then introduced Athanaric and Berjouhi.

He greeted them politely and asked about their time here. Danren came to join me as they talked. Berjouhi's excitement began to get the better of her, and Danren quickly suggested a tour.

As we walked through Caer Corisan, the king asked questions about the design of the fortress, why it wasn't used to house more residents, and if the place had ever been attacked. Danren answered what he could and, eventually, in the course of the tour, introduced him to Armel.

After the formal introductions, the king mentioned that he was surprised that someone so young would step down from such a position. To Danren and my own horror, Armel laughed and informed King Viskhard that he was plenty old enough to enjoy some relaxing activities.

Mighty One be praised that the king only looked puzzled instead of offended.

At that point, I tried to excuse myself to look in on Armus. He was with Majorlaine at that moment, but I was still nursing him. Again to our shock, Armel suggested that he continue the tour with the king and that the four of us should look to other affairs.

Danren looked like he was going to choke. The king, for a fleeting moment, looked nervous, but then he graciously accepted.

"What are you doing?" Danren mouthed at Armel, but the man only smiled and led the king away.

When we saw them again, it was just before dinner. Danren was beginning to pace, and I could tell he was wondering if Armel would forget that there was supposed to be a formal dinner.

Armel arrived at a perfect moment, just before Mintxo flung open the doors to the kitchen and began presenting the food. To our relief and to Mintxo's great pleasure, King Viskhard formally complimented the meal to him.

He then turned to Danren and informed him, "I may consider requesting him as my own chef."

Danren swallowed hard before saying, "I am afraid that would be unlikely."

The king again looked shocked for a moment, but before he could interrupt, Danren continued, "Mintxo is a resident of Caer Corisan and Rem'Maren. It would be unlikely that he would accept the position."

King Viskhard fingered his glass for a moment and then informed Danren, "It is unusual for people to decline my requests, but I have been refused more times today than I may have been through the rest of my reign."

He eyed Danren, who I could tell was nervous, but evenly returned the king's gaze.

"It is oddly refreshing to find those with such courage." He smiled. "I assume that if I requested your presence as an adviser of my court once more that you would again refuse."

"It is a necessity, Your Majesty," Danren replied.

The king was only going to stay through the next day and then depart the following morning. Now, I wondered if that arrangement was too long.

When King Viskhard finally retired, I nearly collapsed into the chair that I had just risen from. We had spent the last four watches in Ari and my main room answering questions about Rem'Maren, the dragons, how we lived, and any number of other things. I was beginning to catch on to when he was expecting me to decline to answer. There was a certain lift to an eyebrow and an added intensity to his gaze. I wondered if he was baiting me, trying to catch me off guard, but I had lived all my adult life guarded. I hoped I was up to the challenge.

"I don't know if this is going terribly or not," I confided to Ari.

She rested her hand on my arm and nestled next to me. "I don't know either, but I'm trusting that the Mighty One will work it out."

I smiled at her. "That's all any of us can do," I informed her and then added after a moment, "I don't know what I'd do without you."

Her answering smile warmed my frayed nerves.

The next day, the king presented us with a collection of documents. These were the treaty arrangements established between Faruq and Rem'Maren. He had brought them to discuss revising some of the details. I quickly requested that Armel be present for these discussions. The king eyed me keenly, but agreed.

Armel was a great help, but he seemed to banter in too friendly a manner with King Viskhard. The discussions unnerved me. Far too often, Armel had to refuse a request. We couldn't send men from Maren to train as knights. We couldn't make extended trips to the capital under most conditions. We couldn't supply a standing part of the arm unless it was dragon based.

At one point the king seemed to become frustrated after a line of refusals. Armel diffused the situation by suggesting that if Rem'Maren and Maren jointly appointed the adviser that the king was requesting that it might be possible to provide one. He thought about that for a while and then informed Armel that the king would have the power to refuse or remove that adviser.

Tensions rose and fell throughout the discussion. In the end, most of the things that the king requested could not be done, while the rest had to be presented to the counsel.

As he rose to retire that night, he informed me of one last request. "I desire to make a presentation before I depart. Will you assemble your population for the ceremony?"

I caught myself before saying, "What?" Instead, I managed to tell him, "Everyone available should be in attendance."

He smiled and bid us a formal goodnight.

"Decent fellow," Armel said, after the king had left, "pity he's so young."

I stared at him for a moment and then managed to laugh a little. "Not everyone is blessed with your advanced years."

Armel eyed me and informed me, "Watch yourself, you young pup."

I managed to laugh completely at that.

The tension rolling off Danren the next morning was almost tangible. None of us had the slightest notion of what King Viskhard was going to say to everyone. We also didn't know how everyone would react to whatever it was he did say.

When the king stood to address the assembled collection of a few men, a few dragons, a few adolescent boys who hadn't turned yet, and us three women, we all held your breath.

He thanked everyone for their hospitality in allowing him to visit.

Turning to us, the nobles who were standing with him, he continued, "It is my privilege to present to your Lord Danren of the House of Rem'maren the lands between the river Chayyim and the border of your mountains."

Danren didn't catch himself in time. He'd been doing so well, but this was too much.

"What?"

The king looked at him oddly for a fleeting moment and then continued, "According to recent enlightenments, the former Lord Astucieux of Sparins has been removed as a lord of the realm. His holdings have hereby passed to you."

I watched as Danren barely managed to choke back his repetition. He swallowed hard and turned to me.

"Accept," I mouthed.

"I can't oversee another whole realm," he whispered to me.

"These holdings are yours to dispense with as you see fit," I heard the king say.

Danren still looked shaken, but managed to stand and politely accept the gift. The courtyard, in return, erupted in cheering, applause, and flames shooting into the air. The king took a step back at that, but managed to keep most of the color in his face.

Danren quickly distracted him by touching his arm. I knew what he was asking. What had happened to Lord Astucieux?

I finally saw Danren mouth the words, "I see."

It was impossible to hear any of the conversation over the excited clamor around me. I wouldn't find out any of the information until after Danren and I escorted King Viskhard back to his awaiting party. We traveled with them to Sotiris's inn and stayed the night there as well.

CHAPTER 78

THE COST OF
FORGIVENESS

That night, Danren returned to our room after a lengthy discussion with the king. He was grinning.

After he hugged me and spun me around for a moment, he told me, "I know what to do with the new holdings!"

That had not been my first concern, but I was willing to wait.

"Oh," I asked, "and what would that be?"

"I'm going to give them to Athanaric and Berjouhi," he told me.

I stared at him for a moment and then informed him, "That's brilliant!" I wanted to know something else too. "What happened to Lord Astucieux?"

Danren looked pleased for a moment, and then slightly ashamed, "Apparently, he was behind the ill treatment we received at Almudina and also why none of our messages reached the king."

I stared, and then managed, "Oh."

It was good news, sort of. Ultimately, it would have been better if the man had learned from his duel with Danren. I wondered if he would make any more trouble now.

Danren had a slight smile on his face when I looked back up at him.

"What are you so happy about?" I asked.

"I was just remembering that the king's entourage was about to launch a rescue attempt for King Viskhard when we arrived," he told me.

I just stared at him in confusion.

"Apparently, they thought that all the flames coming from the fortress meant that there was a major battle going on." He grinned.

I laughed. It had been rather ridiculous.

Sitting at the little table the next morning, I waited for Danren to return to our room. The excitement of the past few days had kept me from being very hungry, but that state hadn't lasted through the night. I was hungry now, and also impatient for Danren to return, so we could continue talking.

Glancing down, I cooed at Armus, who was playing on my lap with the little wooden rattle that Armel'd made for him. Then I returned to reading in my book, which lay open on the table.

A slight knock sounded on the door.

I smiled, calling, "Come in."

I heard the door open. Turning in my chair, I expected to find Sotiris or perhaps Ileana. Jumping to my feet, I heard the chair tip over and hit the floor. The second priest stood in the doorway.

I nearly tripped over the fallen chair, trying to back away. My voice caught in my throat. I couldn't speak, much less scream.

He took two steps toward me saying, "I wish to speak with you, Lady Ari'an."

I could feel my hands beginning to shake, but I still managed to clutch my son to my chest.

"Mighty One help me," I managed to pray silently, but I couldn't get a sound out of my throat.

"I told you never to approach her again." I nearly collapsed at the sound of Danren's voice.

The priest lowered himself to his knees, and I could see Danren standing with his drawn sword at the priest's neck.

"I apologize, Lady Ari'an, for the blood this will expose you to," the priest said, and then he closed his eyes.

I caught the movement of Danren raising his sword to sever the man's head at the same moment that I saw an outline under the loose cuff of the priest's sleeve.

"Wait!" I finally managed to yell.

Danren paused, his sword still raised.

The priest opened his eyes and looked at me, seemly confused.

"Pull up your sleeves," I told him.

He continued to stare at me.

"Ari?" I heard Danren question.

I took a shaky step toward the priest and then managed another calmer one. I laid Armus down in his little bed.

By the time that I reached him, I was amazingly calm. I could tell that the Mighty One was helping me, because I couldn't have reached down and pulled up his sleeve if he hadn't been.

Danren was watching very closely with his sword again at the back of the man's neck.

Scarred into his arm were symbols. Symbols that I knew. One of them was the one that had been branded on my arm at the temple. This man had watched while I was branded with that symbol. The others I didn't know as well, but I knew that they were also designations from the temple.

The scars on his arm weren't from brands though. These had been carved into his flesh by a knife. Some of them were recent, but others were older. I knew he hadn't possessed them while I'd been at the temple. The robes the priests wore there had sleeves that only came down to their elbows.

"Who did this to you?" I managed to ask.

I couldn't tell if it was actual compassion for this man that prompted the question, or if just the thought of anyone carving such things into someone's skin horrified me.

"I did," he told me. "It was not enough," he continued. "Now, let your husband finish."

The man wanted to die . . . why? I stared at his arm for a moment and then realized what he was trying to do.

"No," I told him.

"What?" I'd expected Danren's reply.

The priest stared at me and then seemed to grow angry. "I deserve to die."

"You serve the wrong god," I told him, an odd sense of calm enveloping me as I stood just a hand's breadth away from the man.

"Ari?" Danren asked.

"Let me talk to him." I looked at Danren, and he lowered his sword only slightly.

"Let him kill me," the priest growled.

"No!" I told him. "You need to hear this." I took a breath and managed to begin. "You've served a god that is cruel all your life. You don't have to. There is a god who is greater, one who isn't cruel. I serve a god who is both just and merciful. Right now, I choose to show you his mercy. You can be forgiven."

His face contorted for a moment and then he told me, "I do not deserve to be forgiven."

"None of us deserve to be forgiven," I replied. "The Mighty One, my god, forgives because he chooses to, not because he has to."

"I deserve to die," he repeated.

"We all deserve to die," I countered.

"No one will forgive me," he growled.

In those next moments, I did the most terrifying thing that I had ever done.

I knelt down in front of him, against Danren's protests, put my hand over the symbol on his arm, which matched mine, and said, "I forgive you."

I knew that I was in a dangerous position. He could easily grab me. He didn't. All he did was stare at me. I rose and walked over to the book that I'd left on the table. Armus laughed and held his arms out to me.

"Not right now," I told him, kissing the top of his head. Then I set the little rattle into his hands. He merrily shook it and then began chewing on it, completely oblivious to the tension in the room.

I returned to the priest, who was still staring at me. I pressed the book into his hands.

"This will teach you about my god," I told him. "Now, go in his grace."

The priest continued to stare at me. Then he looked back at Danren. I motioned for him to lower the sword. He looked at me, questioningly, for a moment, and then pointed toward the hall with his blade.

"Get out," he told the priest.

The priest rose to his feet, staring between Danren and myself and then left the room.

I wasn't certain what had just happened. One moment, I was going to behead one of the men who had tortured Ari, and now, I was watching him walk away. I did manage to step to the door, once he'd walked through it, shut it and lock it.

"Ari?" I glanced at her and then back at the closed door.

She'd returned to the table and was now holding our son to her. Stepping toward her, I quickly sheathed my sword and held her, realizing that she'd begun to cry.

"Why did you do that?" I finally managed to ask. "We would have been entirely justified in killing him."

"I know," she replied, leaning into my shoulder. After a moment, she leaned back and looked down at the baby between us. "I had to."

"What?" I couldn't imagine why she would think that.

"The Mighty One is better than that," she told me. "He forgave us for everything we've done wrong."

"That man is far worse than us," I told her.

She looked up at me. "So he needs the Mighty One even more."

I stared at her for a long time and then managed to tell her, "The Mighty One's better than I am."

She smiled shakily. "Isn't that a good thing?"

I managed to return her smile.

The next morning, we found that priest, Bakar, being escorted in chains toward a carriage. I quickly asked what was going on.

It took me a few moments to get anyone to actually answer. Finally, I found the king himself and asked him.

He frowned at me and then informed me that the man had requested to be in the company, claiming that it would safer for him, considering his status, not to be left alone at the capital. The conditions had been that he stay with the animals and not make himself known to Ari or myself. Somehow, they had discovered that our altercation had occurred. I quickly found that, although they knew that he'd approached us in our own room, they did not know any of the details.

I glanced at the carriage where the man was now a captive. I could leave it. I wanted to leave it. The man deserved to die. Ari had forgiven him though. Also, knowing that the Mighty One was merciful and how often I called upon that mercy left me without a choice. Justice would not be served, but mercy would.

"Will you release him, Your Majesty?" I asked.

The king stared at me, surprise resting on his face. He managed to cover it after a moment.

"Are you certain of your request?" he finally asked.

"Yes," I told him, "my wife forgave him."

I watched as the man was taken back out of the carriage. He looked up and saw me. Immediately, he turned pale, but remained standing. Then he looked at the man unlocking the chains. The guard must have told him that he was free, because he again looked up at me. This time, shock was etched into his face.

I couldn't manage to watch any longer. Turning back toward the inn, I walked inside.

CHAPTER 79

WAR

When we returned to Caer Corisan, we needed something to lift the solemn air that had descended upon our group once the full story about our encounter with the former priest, Bakar, was known. Most thought that we were insane. I wondered about that myself on occasion.

Thankfully, Berjouhi was at Caer Corisan to lighten the mood. She leapt for joy when we informed them of our idea about my new holdings. Athanaric seemed more concerned.

"I am not certain that I would be capable of overseeing an entire House's property," he told us.

He was greatly mistaken. As it turned out, politics was his forte. Berjouhi loved entertaining visitors in their new abode. Athanaric, within only a few years, even managed to endear himself to King Viskhard.

They first settled into their new residence just as the country began the war. It would last ten years. I was not involved with most of it, because of my status as a lord of the realm.

As Verd's borders contracted, Rem'Maren had less and less of a problem with dragon-slaying hunters. Refugees fled through our pass, but few harassed them.

At first, a few of the dragons, then more as the years wore on, began looking out for these groups. They would drop a deer near a group that seemed to have only a few scraps of food in their possession. Faber processed skins into simple shoes. Some of the wives sent blankets that they no longer needed to be dropped in winter. We would wrap bundles of firewood in those blankets. After the first year, the dragons began chasing lost members back to their groups.

Eventually, we began hearing the stories that these refugees told. Night visits of dark beasts who left only good.

It was hard to convince some of the dragons not to harm these people though. We never did convince all of them, but the attacks on these bands were quite rare. We finally came to a compromise. Those who didn't agree would do nothing to harm them, and we would not ask their help for these people.

Early on in the war, I sent a message to the king. It was a request. I understood that I should not be involved in most of the conflict, but there was one place that I wanted to be directly involved in. I wanted to see the temple that had held Ari fall.

The king granted my request, with a stipulation of sorts. Bakar, that former priest, had volunteered to be part of the force that besieged this temple. He knew its weaknesses.

I ground my teeth and accepted. The siege was laid in the third year of the war. Two months after Ari had born our second child. A daughter named Alba, after the beauty of sunrises. A brief joy-filled event in the ravages of this war.

The siege lasted only a month. A short time for the war we were in, but since I was commanding with Armel advising me, we were able to use the dragons to their full effect.

My guilt raged at me every time I saw that priest skitter away from one of the dragons in fear. For a week, they tormented him, and I did nothing. Then I realized my error. He was a person after all. Should we not be better than those, like him, who had tortured Ari, or even those who assumed the dragons were evil incarnate? We knew better. We should act on that knowledge.

I issued the order to stop harassing the priest. It took the second week to fully break the habit. During that time, Bakar sought me out. I'd rarely spoken to the man, limiting our conversations to brief discussions about what defenses the temple had.

He found me in front of my tent, scouring the map I had of the temple. We had already destroyed their towers. It was now only a matter of waiting until the next wave of our reinforcements arrived, and keeping supplies out of the place. When I glanced up to find Bakar standing there, I felt the shock on my face.

"Lord Danren," he began sounding . . . was it nervous or actually frightened? "I wished to thank you for restraining your . . ." he faltered on the proper word, and I felt a scowl cross my face.

"People," he finally managed.

I had not expected him to say that and felt my temper abate slightly.

"Your order is not necessary though," he continued. "I deserve far worse treatment."

I leaned back in my chair studying the man.

Fighting for control over my temper, I managed to ask, "Have you read the book that Lady Ari'an gave you?"

He met my gaze for a moment, and then his eyes skittered away from mine. I felt a jarring familiarity between that movement and the way that Ari had avoided looking at people for years.

"I have, Lord Danren." He actually pulled the book from the satchel that he carried with him. "Does the Lady Ari'an request its return?" He held it out to me.

I did not take it. For a moment, he looked puzzled, and then he set the book on the table. His face was of self-condemnation, as though he suspected that I would never take anything directly from him.

I was tempted to agree, but my god was better than that.

"Mighty One have mercy," I prayed silently.

I knew what I had to do.

Picking up the book, I held it back out to him.

"No," I told him. "It was a gift."

He stared at me for a moment and then slowly took the book back.

"I asked only, because if you had read it, you know that we all deserve far worse than we receive," I told him.

He fingered the book's cover for a few moments and then softly asked, "Lord Danren, is what this book says about your god true?"

He looked up at me with a look of hope that turned to despair on his face. The look to my great surprise was honest. That, I would never have expected from this man.

After a moment's hesitation, I told him simply, "Yes."

He turned and began to walk away looking deep in thought. After only a few steps, he quickly pivoted and returned to my table.

Hope evident on his face, he began, "Your god . . ." then he paused, and the despair returned to consume his expression, "he would not accept one like me."

Again, he turned and began walking away. I wanted to just let him walk away, but I knew that wasn't right.

"Wait," I called.

He turned back to me, looking confused.

Returning he asked, "Did you have a question, Lord Danren?"

He glanced at the map spread in front of me.

"No," I told him, "an answer."

I reached for the book he held. He drew back for a moment, and then handed it to me. His eyes stayed on the book, the look on his face seemed frightened, as though I now planned to take it from him.

Flipping through the pages, I prayed a blessing on whoever had thought to number them and the sentences.

Finding what I was looking for, I began pointing out different stories of kings or prophets who had fallen away from the Mighty One, or those who had never followed him and then came to him.

After a few of these, Bakar interrupted, "None of these were priests."

I thought hard and could not remember any that dealt with a priest, but I did remember one that would fit. Before I turned to it, I realized that Bakar had been standing this entire time. Quickly, I stood, handed him my chair, and went into my tent for another one. When I returned, he was still staring at the chair.

"Sit," I told him.

He stared at me in surprise for a moment and then slowly lowered himself onto the chair.

I flipped the book to the last forth or so and pointed out a story.

"This one isn't about a priest specifically, but this man was completely convinced that he was serving the Mighty One. He worked for the priests. The Mighty One had to physically appear to him and blind him to get his attention." I glanced up, flipping the rest of the pages. "He went on to write most of the rest of this book."

The priest stared at the book for moment, then asked quietly, "Why are you doing this?"

I stared at the book for a moment, and then flipped back to the beginning of the man's story. There I pointed out another man.

"He was crushed to death with stones and asked the Mighty One to forgive the people who were killing him." I couldn't manage to look up at the former priest as I finished, "His prayer was granted."

There was silence for several long moments. I closed the book and set it near Bakar's hands. He seemed to instinctively reach for it. As he hesitated just for an instant, I glanced up. He snatched the book back and stared at me. For now, the hope was clearly visible.

After looking each other in the eyes for a while, the former priest managed to tell me, "I will not kill you, Lord Danren."

"What?" Realization hit me.

He was comparing me to the man who'd been executed in the story!

He looked down at the book in his hands. "You have prayed to your . . . your Mighty One for me."

It was statement, not a question. I had to answer anyway.

"No," I told him. "I couldn't bring myself to before."

He looked up at me, despair again etching across his face. Quickly, he began to rise.

"I will now," I finished.

He paused halfway out of the chair.

"Because it is your duty to your god," he said.

"It was the right thing to do before," I replied. "That hasn't changed, but my wife forgave you. I've let you live any number of times now. I should pray the Mighty One's mercy to you as well." I looked up at him. "I'm not as good as my god. If I was, I wouldn't need him. Part of me still hates you. Part of me wants my god to grant you mercy. A very small part of me. I will pray for you because it is duty. I will pray for me, because I should be better."

The former priest lowered himself back into the chair. He was staring at me in confusion.

Finally, he ran a hand through his hair and told me, "I have met few honest men in my life. That you are one of them is . . . unimaginable."

I almost snorted. I managed to just make a surprised sound. The priest stared at me.

"I promised to kill you," I explained, "if you ever approached my wife again. You're still alive. How honest can I be?"

"Perhaps the mercy of your Mighty One has affected you as well," he told me, looking at the book in his hands.

After a moment, he asked softly, "If you would, Lord Danren, pray that I can come to your god."

"I could," I told him. "I already know that prayer is granted though."

He looked up at me. "How?"

"You have to pray," I told him.

He swallowed hard. "I have never approached a god without a sacrifice."

I reached for the book in his hands, and he hesitantly gave it to me again.

Flipping to one of the places where this story was told, I replied, "This sacrifice was provided for you by the Mighty One himself."

He stared at the pages for a few moments, and then told me, "I have never prayed like your god requests."

"Just act like you're talking to me, only direct it at him," I replied.

The man pushed back his chair and knelt. Then he hurriedly returned to the chair and stared at me for a moment. After that he looked around awkwardly and then fingered the book in front of him.

"Lord Mighty One," he finally began.

I fought the smile off my face. First, the additional title was awkward, but I could understand. Second, I felt a ridiculous sense of joy. I should be horrified that this man dared approach my god.

Third, when he looked up at me after he seemed to finish praying, he asked, "Is that all?"

I barely kept from laughing.

"No," I told him, "now, you have to live the rest of your life meaning what you just prayed."

He paled slightly. "I will fail!"

"Yes," I told him, "so have I. It's a very good thing that the Mighty One is merciful."

For the first time, I saw the man smile. It was an actual smile that expressed the joy in his heart.

CHAPTER 80

SIEGE END

The siege ended with a last attempt by those left in the temple to break through our lines. Most of them died in the attempt although a few were taken alive. Then we stormed the temple.

To our horror, we found no one alive. The prisoners in the temple had been slaughtered by the priests. We stumbled through room after room, finding the bodies.

"This wasn't supposed to happen," I heard someone whisper and realized it was me.

"I did not know they would do this," I heard a voice behind me.

Turning, I found Bakar standing there. He looked as horrified as I felt.

"If I had known this, I would have told you," he continued.

He looked at the woman's body lying in front of me with her eyes gaping and her chest ripped open.

"I did not know," he whispered.

I didn't know how to respond to that. Pushing past him, I stepped into the hall. The human soldiers were removing the bodies. The least we could do was give them some sort of funeral. It would be a mass cremation, but they would have at least that.

Suddenly, I froze. Was that . . .

"Did you hear that?" I asked Bakar.

He stared at me confused. Probably, he hadn't heard the sound. I was a dragon lord, and a bit past due to turn so my hearing was slightly better than normal.

I began running toward where I'd thought I'd heard the sound. Bakar followed close behind me. I stopped where the hall branched off. I couldn't hear anything now. Continuing straight, I began trotting, listening for the sound. Bakar didn't follow.

"Lord Danren," he called, sounding frantic.

I stopped and turned to look at him. He was staring down the other hall.

"The private altar," he said. Turning to me, he continued, "Someone is going to sacrifice on the private altar. It is a last attempt to be heard. They are using a . . ."

I raced past him, knowing already what whoever was there was using. The sound I'd heard was a baby's cry.

We raced through a burned doorway. This part of the temple had been cleared from the air. The roof was missing now, and the scorch marks were evident.

I slid to a halt at the edge of what used to be a balcony overlooking a small open area with a stone altar in the center. Moving any farther, I would have fallen over the edge. Directly in front of me, there used to be a stairway leading down, but all that was left of it was a few charred steps at the bottom.

"Kakios," I heard Bakar gasp, as he came up behind me.

"What?" I was searching for a way down, not seeing one.

"That is Kakios. He is the high priest here. The one that I traveled with to Almudina," he told me.

I followed where he was pointing. Under the part of the ceiling that still remained, I could make out the figure of a man. In front of him was an altar. A knife glinted in his hand as he raised it. I was out of time.

Throwing myself off what was left of the balcony, I turned as I fell. The air caught in my wings, and I hit the ground running. The priest at the altar pivoted at the sound and froze. One leap took me across the area. I slid to a stop, slamming the man aside with my front leg. He flew through the air for fifteen steps before hitting the wall with a sickening crack.

I stalked toward him, but he didn't rise.

Turning toward the balcony, I yelled, "Bakar, get down here."

I didn't hear any motion.

"Now!" I snapped.

Finally, I heard scrambling footsteps. They faded, and I wondered if he was running away. I wouldn't have blamed him, but I did need to talk to him, and I certainly couldn't pick up the baby that was still wailing on the altar.

I breathed a sigh of relief when I heard the footsteps returning from a different direction. I turned toward the sound and found the former priest running toward me. When he saw me looking at him, he froze.

"I need to know if he's still alive," I told him, nodding toward the high priest.

Even from this distance, I could tell that it took all his will to walk toward me and then past me. He kept glancing at me as he cautiously checked the man.

"He is dead . . . Lord Danren." He turned shakily toward me.

"Don't call me that in this form," I told him. "I'm Narden."

He stared at me and slowly nodded.

"For now, don't tell anyone about what you saw," I told him.

He swallowed and nodded again.

"I'll explain things when I have time, but I need you to check on the baby right now," I continued.

He managed to walk past me again and pick up the infant.

"She is not hurt, Lord . . . Narden," he told me as he pulled off his cloak and wrapped her in it.

"You'll have to find someone to nurse her," I told him.

He looked at me with pain and fear in his eyes. "No one will."

"What?" That couldn't be right.

"If I ask some woman from a village near here, they will refuse," he told me. "They will guess that she came from this temple."

"What?" Why would anyone refuse?

"She is a nickin," he told me.

"What?" There was an edge to my voice, and I felt a growl coming.

"They will think that, Lord Narden," he fumbled.

I fought my temper down, trying to remind myself that this was what he'd come from. Of course, he'd refer to this baby like that.

I also had to try to think of some way to save her. She'd need to eat. No one around here would nurse her. She appeared too young to survive on cow or goat milk.

"Ari." I breathed, and Bakar looked up. "Find someone to get Einheim," I ordered.

Caer Corisan was half to three quarters of a day's flight away at full speed. Einheim was fast. He could make it in the half if not sooner.

Bakar quickly returned with two other soldiers, who looked confused to see me for a moment. They soon found Einheim. I sent Ishmerai with the baby and the dragon. They took off immediately.

"Mighty One have mercy," I prayed, as I watched them until they were out of sight.

We watched the skies constantly for any news, so when Einheim appeared with a rider, it was not surprising. Often Danren would send messages to me along with orders for some supply or another. I often wondered if he asked for the supplies just so he could send a note to me.

The siege was going well from everything I'd heard. I wondered about that. What would happen when the temple fell? Would our forces harm the slaves from the temple, or would they be able to tell the difference? Would the priests try to disguise themselves as slaves?

I'd learned that the temple was expected to fall any day, and I wondered as I watched Einheim's approach if he brought that news.

He was flying faster than normal. An alarm sounded. This might mean trouble. Had something happened to Danren?

He landed fast, but Ishmerai managed to stay in the saddle.

"Get Lady Ari'an!" he yelled to the first person who approached.

I ran down the stairs and across the courtyard. When I reached him, he thrust a cloak into my arms. I stared at him until I felt the cloak move ever so slightly.

Almost dropping the bundle, I heard Ishmerai say, "Danren thought you would be willing to nurse her. She's the only one we found alive."

I unwrapped some of the cloak and found a tiny leg. Pulling the other end open, I stared into the child's face. She began to wail, but the sound was weak.

"None of the women in the villages would help her," Ishmerai explained.

I hurried into the main hall and quickly found a room. Unwrapping the baby completely, I tossed the cloak over my shoulder, wondering who it had belonged to.

After what seemed like an eternity, I finally managed to get her to latch on and start nursing. She was weak and very young. I was surprised that she'd survived the trip. I wondered if she would live through the night.

"Mighty One have mercy," I prayed over her.

She didn't deserve to die like this.

Majorlaine brought swaddling and a dress that my daughter had already outgrown. When the baby fell asleep, I changed her current swaddling and dressed her gently.

If she lived through the night . . . If she lived through the night, she might make it.

"Mighty One have mercy," I prayed. "She doesn't deserve this."

Turning back to Bakar, I found him staring at me. He quickly turned away.

"I have some explaining to do," I told him. "We need to find somewhere that we can talk privately."

He led me back into the now empty temple. After a few tries, he found a room that was somewhat secluded and that I could fit into. I didn't want to know what the room had been used for before, but it was currently unfurnished.

"Lord Narden," the priest began before I could, "I will not disclose your secret."

He sounded quite shaken.

"I have two options with you right now," I replied. "I can trust you, or I can kill you."

He swallowed hard staring at the floor. "You have every right to kill me, Lord Narden."

"I've invested too much time in you for that," I continued.

His head shot up, and he managed to look at me for a moment before diverting his eyes.

"What would you like to know?" I asked.

He looked around and then said, "You have been here before."

"What?" That statement was unexpected.

"I saw the dragon that came for your Lady Ari'an," he continued, staring at the wall. "I have noticed that your dragons all look different. I have watched for ones that looked like the dragons that attacked that day. I was planning to avoid them, because if they knew who I was, I would not . . . I did not believe that I would be safe." He paused for a moment and then managed, "You were one of those."

"I was," I told him.

"Your social order is understandable now," he continued, finding a new spot to stare at on a different wall. "You are citizens of your house, so you treat the dragons as citizens." He paused still seeming to think. "This would also explain why you took such involved interest in the fall of my country. When you are dragons, you are hated and hunted. Although you consider yourselves to be citizens, others do not. When you heard of what . . . we did in these temples, you fought to destroy this evil, even though your Lady Ari'an was no longer here."

The man must have taken time to think through all this, while I'd arranged for the baby's transport. He'd apparently figured much of it out on his own.

"I have some questions for you then," I told him.

He glanced up, looking confused but nodded.

"First, the temple had fallen, why would anyone consider making a sacrifice of any type much less of a baby?" I began.

He took a deep breath and told me, "It was believed that a freshly born's blood would protect all who touched it if the freshly born was offered properly."

I felt like throwing up. "What?"

He looked up again. "Many things like that are believed. I . . ." he trailed off.

I managed to nod and moved on to my next question. "Second, will you still serve my god knowing what I am?"

I hated the thought that he would turn away because of this. That feeling surprised me, but it was true.

The former priest actually looked up at me. "Lord Narden, had I known, I would have followed your god sooner."

"What?" I couldn't imagine why that would be.

The man looked embarrassed for a moment. "Forgive me, Lord Narden. I did not mean the disrespect that statement implied."

"What?"

"I could not imagine that your god would accept one who had committed my crimes." He paused for a long moment. "I knew of dragons only from what I had heard. The firsthand knowledge has explained much that I could not understand." He seemed to be stalling. Finally, he looked up at me again. "Your god accepts you. I do not know the terms of that acceptance, but if . . ."

I finally followed what he was saying and almost laughed.

My words came out in more of a growl because of fighting back the mirth. "If my god would accept dragons, he would certainly accept criminals."

"I know more now," Bakar fumbled to explain. "I understand that your kind are just like men."

"We are men," I told him evenly. "Also, the Mighty One accepted me and any who wish to follow him on the same terms that he accepted you."

The former priest fidgeted for a moment, before managing to say, "I do not know the nature of your transformation."

It took a while to answer his questions even though he never seemed to ask one directly.

Einheim and Ishmerai returned late that night. The baby had reached Ari alive, but there was a concern that the tiny girl still wouldn't live. I wanted to go back to Caer Corisan. The thought that Ari would have to cope with the child's death alone shook me. I should have gone, but I was supposed to be leading a siege.

I wondered if I should have led this at all. What if I'd been home, would they have found the child? Could they have saved her? Would it even matter now? Was the tiny girl just going to die anyway? If someone else had saved her, would someone have found a suitable nurse? Would someone have sent her to us?

What if . . . What if . . . the thoughts robbed me of my sleep? The next morning, I worked out details for cleanup. I also sent word to the siege at the next temple. They needed to know that the priests might slaughter the prisoners. Perhaps there was a way of rescuing those kept there.

I also turned command over to Armel. He was currently human and could handle the authority. Cleaning up shouldn't be too difficult.

Bakar approached me before I took off. I realized as he walked up that I'd ignored the complication that I had caused by revealing the turning to him. Sighing, I knew that yet again, I would be in trouble with the counsel. This man was quite dangerous.

"You will have to come with me," I informed him when he came to a stop.

He opened his mouth, about to say something, and then stopped. He seemed puzzled for a moment but then smiled ever so slightly.

"I was intending to ask that boon of you, Lord Narden," he told me.

I studied him for a moment before he continued.

"Without your presence here, I am not certain of my own safety," he explained.

"I don't like the idea of having you anywhere near my wife," I told him, realizing that I had a slight growl in my words.

He stepped back for a moment and then replied, "I understand. I will attempt to avoid her presence whenever possible."

"Because you are under the authority of Faruq, there may be complications with your knowledge, but currently you are under my command," I told him.

"I understand, Lord Narden," he replied. After a pause, he asked, "Will there be horses accompanying you?"

"No," I told him, wondering what he was getting at, "they have to be specially trained to fly comfortably with dragons." I glanced over at where the flying horses were tethered. "I don't want to pull any of them from here yet."

The former priest shifted nervously. I studied him for a moment and then realized his concern.

"You will fly with me," I told him.

He looked up, shocked for a moment before his features calmed.

"Thank you, Lord Narden," he told me.

I smiled at the situation the two of us were in as he walked away. It was interesting that he would find himself again at my mercy. A shift while in flight, and I could easily remove him with or without the saddle.

That would solve the problem with the counsel. If the man was dead, he couldn't cause any trouble with his newfound knowledge. I could find someway to explain the accident to the king.

What was I thinking? I may not like the man, but killing him over something like this was wrong!

I shook myself clearing my thoughts and went to find where one of my saddles was kept. We needed to leave as soon as possible. I still wanted to find out about the baby. If she'd lived, I wanted to explain the situation to Ari. If she hadn't, I wanted to be there to help Ari cope if she took it hard.

I heard the dragons land in the courtyard and wondered who it might be. News would travel to me while I watched over the baby in my rooms. She'd lived through the night, but she was still so weak. I could barely hear her when she cried, so I tried to stay close.

Currently, I held her, having just finished nursing her. She was drifting into sleep when I heard a familiar voice call for me. Narden was here!

I quickly found shoes and hurried as fast as I could down to the courtyard. There I found Narden. He was watching the balcony, apparently expecting me to appear there. I trotted toward him, trying not to disturb the sleeping infant.

He turned his head slightly at the sound, glanced back up at the balcony, and then seemed to realize that I wasn't there. He quickly stepped toward me, which resulted in a protest from Ishmerai, who was pulling off the saddle. The saddle landed unceremoniously in the dirt while Ishmerai glared after Narden.

I laughed. Narden stared down at me looking concerned and slightly confused. Then he seemed to realize who I was holding.

"She's alive," he whispered.

I glanced at the sleeping form. "For now."

He studied me for an explanation.

"She's so weak," I told him. "If she keeps fighting, she'll probably make it, but if she gives up . . ." I let my words trail off.

I glanced at the group that was scattering and felt the blood leave my face. The second priest stood there, confused as to where to go, but not approaching.

Narden followed my gaze and then called to Ishmerai, who was hauling his saddle away, "Find Bakar a room, and see that he's comfortable."

Bakar followed Ishmerai, who was irritated as he set the saddle down.

"What is he doing here?" I asked Narden.

I had hoped to never see that man again.

"He knows," Narden told me in a hushed tone.

It took a moment for the words to sink in. "What?"

"I'll explain," he told me. "It's complicated."

Once we were in one of the rooms, Narden related his tale. I never imagined that man would actually renounce his gods to follow the Mighty One. I supposed that was why I'd given him my book, but I never actually thought that he would.

His part in the baby's rescue and why she was here was also a shock. I wanted to believe that he was trustworthy, but everything inside of me seemed to rebel at the thought. I voiced my concerns to Narden, finding that he had the same ones.

At the end of the tale, Narden and I prayed. We prayed for the tiny child I was still holding. We prayed that Bakar was actually serious about following the Mighty One and that he wouldn't betray us.

The counsel convened almost immediately. That was a surprise, but Armel could not stay for long, making it a necessity. After a long debate, they lectured me on my unconcern for others' safety, but they seemed to merely be covering for the fact that there was nothing anyone could do about the dangerous knowledge that Bakar possessed.

EPILOGUE

AT THIS END

The years of the war finally ended. Hedy was almost eleven years of age when the fighting ceased. She'd fought to live through those first few days, and we'd named her Hedy because of that struggle.

She and Alba were close. They would have their arguments occasionally, but always made up.

We never considered Hedy anything less than a daughter to us.

Armus was preparing to turn for the first time when the war ended. His design would match my own, but I told Ari that his coloring came completely from her. He was primarily green with scales that began at his face as red tipped but faded completely to gold tips by his hind legs.

He spent the decade that it took for the politics to settle as a dragon. I would joke with him on occasion that he had it easy through that time. Politics were never my strong point, and I would have preferred to spend those years as a dragon, instead of assisting in the governmental intrigues.

Politics, however, did interest Armus, and he was always begging me for the details of each visit that I made to the capital. I wondered if he got that interest from Armel, who'd decided to leave Caer Corisan completely in my hands halfway through the war. He was the first adviser that Maren and Rem'Maren would send to the royal court. The tradition would last for the rest of my life.

Armus would become one of those advisers two centuries after his first wife died. We arranged that marriage with Athanaric and Berjouhi for their first daughter. The two were quite a match. They were both so lively, though Armus watched and laughed while Ceren jumped right into things.

He would marry again after becoming a court adviser. I, however, buried my only beloved wife in her seventy-ninth year. Ari's place would never be filled by another, and I never attempted to create a place for any other in my soul.

The former Verdian priest, Bakar, died two decades before Ari's passing, seemingly carrying our secret to his grave. I never did see him again after he left Caer Corisan. He helped with the rebuilding and establishing the new houses of what used to be the country of Verd. He raised places of worship to the Mighty One everywhere he went, so perhaps he did keep our confidence.

LIST OF NAMES AND PLACES

Aedelflaed – A lady of Faruq.

Aedelred – One of Diggory's sons and Gary's grandson.

Adelwin – One of Diggory's sons and Gary's grandson.

Adenern – One of Narden's older brothers, son of Tragh.

Agung – Ambassador who hosted Drenar's funeral.

Aintzane – A territory in Verd.

Alba – Danren and Ari'an's daughter.

Almudina, House of – The ruling house in Faruq.

Anuj – A kitchen servant of Caer Corisan.

Ara'ta – A young dragon of Maren.

Ari'an – Youngest daughter of the House of Nori'en.

Arkaitz – A lord attending Drenar's funeral.

Armel – Master craftsman of Caer Corisan, turns over leadership of Caer Corisan to Danren.

Armus – Danren and Ari'an's son.

Arnbjorg – Name of the world that Faruq and Verd are countries of.

Arwa – A mountain of Maren.

Astucieux, Lord – The ruler of the House of Suvora.

Ataar – A youth of Rem'maren who came to Caer Corisan for training.

Athanaric – A lord of Verd, Berjouhi's husband.

Bakar Kemen of Aintzane – A priest that held Ari'an captive.

Bashkim – A lord of the House of Almudina.

Batel – Lord Drenar's daughter.

Baymata – A dance of Faruq.

Berjouhi – Lady of Verd, also Ari'an's lady-in-waiting.

Besnik – Dragon assistant to Grath at Caer Corisan.

Bikendi – A dragon of Maren.

Blerta – Town in Rem'maren.

Bohurnir – Official who hosted Drenar's funeral.

Bora – A town of Almudina.

Brahn – Town of Rem'maren.

Brin/Brindriny – Stableboy at Torion Castle.

Caer Corisan – The fortress of Maren.

Caer Dathen – Main fortress of the House of Rem'maren.

Calanthe – City where Drenar's funeral was held.

Ceren – Athanaric and Berjouhi's daughter.

Chayyim River – The main river of Faruq, starts in Maren's mountains and traverses the country.

Cristeros – Ari'an's father, lord of the House of Nori'en.

Cumas – Dragon physician at Caer Corisan.

Darya, House of – One of the Houses of Faruq.

Derxan – A dragon of Maren.

Diggory – Gary's son.

Dreanen – Middle son of Lord Grath, one of Danren's older brothers.

Drenar – Eldest son of Lord Grath, one of Danren's older brothers.

Edur – Dragon on the counsel.

Einheim – Young dragon at Caer Corisan, born in Verd.

Ekaitz – Kitchen help at Caer Corisan.

Elea – Town on the border of the House of Nori'en and the House of Rem'maren.

Eulalia – A lady of Sparins.

Faber – Master tailor at Caer Corisan.

Faruq – Danren and Ari'an's country.

Ferrer – Blacksmith of Caer Corisan.

Flamur – A dragon of Maren.

Flutura – A cousin of Ari'an.

Frid – A small river in Rem'maren.

Frodi – Master of the library at Caer Corisan.

Galen – Master physician at Caer Corisan.

Garaile – A lord attending Drenar's funeral.

Gary – Founder of one of the lines of Maren.

Grath – Ruling lord of the House of Rem'maren; father of Drenar, Dreanen, and Danren.

Gwaredd – Lord Grath's twin brother.

Hafiz – Largest dragon at Caer Corisan.

Hana – Renard's wife.

Hedy – Adopted daughter of Danren and Ari'an.

Hin'merien – Pher'am and Ari'an's mother, wife of Lord Cristeros.

Hramn – Dragon at Caer Corisan.

Ileana – A woman rescued from the same temple Ari'an was held at.

Illtyd – A territory in Verd.

Indigo – One of the founders of the four dragon lines.

Ishmerai – Mason and guard at Caer Corisan.

Isra – Town in Rem'maren.

Itsaso – Town in Rem'maren.

Itzal – A providence of Verd.

Jair – One of the young servants at Caer Corisan.

Je'hona – Lady Hin'merien's sister.

Juna'yad – Dreanen and Pher'am's son.

Kakar – Birth name of Sotiris.

Kakios Itzal of Aintzane – High priest of the temple where Ari'an was held captive.

Kerr – Town in Rem'maren.

Kohinoor – The pass from Rem'maren through Maren to Verd.

Lindita – Lady who married Lord Perparim.

Llinos – A small village in Rem'maren.

Mael – Dragon counterpart of Armel, coregent of Caer Corisan before turning leadership over to Danren and Narden.

Majorlaine – Healer and dragon chief at Caer Corisan.

Maren – The country of the dragons.

Margree – Lord Grath's wife and mother of Dreanen and Danren.

Maris – Town in Rem'maren.

Matej – One of Indigo's descendents.

Mattan – Lord Grath's grandfather.

Megara – Lord Grath's first wife, mother of Drenar.

Mintxo – Master chief at Caer Corisan.

Mirna – Town in Rem'maren.

Narden – Youngest son of Tragh, brother of Adenern and Renard.

Neurikos – A dance of Faruq.

Nori'en, House of – One of the Houses of Faruq, Ari'an's native House.

Nor'quitarn – Town that Ari'an was taken from.

Nyr – Town in Rem'maren.

Olalla – A lady of Almudina.

Otto – One of the founders of the four dragon lines.

Ozgur – Woman rescued from a Verd temple.

Parda – Lady who officiates for women at their weddings.

Pepim – A soldier of Rem'maren.

Perparim – A lord in the House of Darya.

Pher'am – Older sister of Ari'an.

Raab – A town with a temple in Verd.

Rauha – Town in Rem'maren.

Raleigh – One of the founders of the four dragon lines.

Regiten – Father of Lord Grath.

Rem'maren, House of – One of the Houses of Faruq, Danren's native house.

Renard – Eldest son of Tragh, eldest brother of Narden.

Ryuu – Capital of the House of Rem'maren.

Salma – The mountain where Caer Corisan was built.

Sela – Capital of Verd.

Seraiah – Lord Grath's father.

Shpresa – A town in Rem'maren.

Snebik – A dragon of Maren.

Sotiris – Innkeeper who knew Ari'an at the temple.

Sparins, House of – One of the Houses of Faruq.

Suvora, House of – One of the Houses of Faruq, borders Verd.

Tam – A young servant at Caer Corisan.

Tharaleos – A simple group dance.

Ti'anha – Dreanen and Pher'am's daughter.

Terigen – Tragh's father.

Torion Castle – The childhood home of Ari'an.

Tragh – Father of Renard, Adenern, and Narden, successor of Gary's line.

Trin'geren – Father of Lord Cristeros.

Verd – Neighboring country to the north of Faruq.

Viskhard – King of Faruq.
Xander – Servant at Caer Corisan.
Yacob – Descendent of Otto.
Yente – A lady of Almudina.
Zait – A dragon of Maren.

ABOUT THE AUTHOR

Once there was a princess who lived in a beautiful castle far away . . . Heidi M. Grant is not that princess. She lives in Maryland with her husband and son. Heidi graduated from Cornell College in the distant time of 2004. She loves God, her family, fantasy, sci-fi, and many other things, but hates housework. Follow her blog at healingwingsheidigrant.wordpress.com and find out more about the characters from *Healing Wings*!

CPSIA information can be obtained
at www.ICGtesting.com
Printed in the USA
JSHW020945280522
26340JS00001B/1